Merry Chris[illegible]
To Ruth [illegible]
from Pris & Jim

TRACIE PETERSON

Alaskan Quest

TRACIE PETERSON

Alaskan Quest

BETHANYHOUSE
Minneapolis, Minnesota

The Alaskan Quest

Previously published in three separate volumes:
Summer of the Midnight Sun Copyright © 2006
Under the Northern Lights Copyright © 2006
Whispers of Winter Copyright © 2006

Cover design by Eric Walljasper

Scripture quotations are from the King James Version of the Bible.

Published by Bethany House Publishers
11400 Hampshire Avenue South
Bloomington, Minnesota 55438

Bethany House Publishers is a division of
Baker Publishing Group, Grand Rapids, Michigan.

Printed in the United States of America

ISBN 978-0-7642-0735-8

Tracie Peterson is the author of over seventy novels, both historical and contemporary. Her avid research resonates in her stories, as seen in her bestselling HEIRS OF MONTANA and ALASKAN QUEST series. Tracie and her family make their home in Montana.

Visit Tracie's Web site at *www.traciepeterson.com.*

Books by Tracie Peterson

www.traciepeterson.com

A Slender Thread • *What She Left For Me*
Where My Heart Belongs

SONG OF ALASKA
Dawn's Prelude

ALASKAN QUEST
Summer of the Midnight Sun
Under the Northern Lights • *Whispers of Winter*
Alaskan Quest (3 in 1)

BRIDES OF GALLATIN COUNTY
A Promise to Believe In • *A Love to Last Forever*
A Dream to Call My Own

THE BROADMOOR LEGACY*
A Daughter's Inheritance • *An Unexpected Love*
A Surrendered Heart

BELLS OF LOWELL*
Daughter of the Loom • *A Fragile Design* • *These Tangled Threads*
Bells of Lowell (3 in 1)

LIGHTS OF LOWELL*
A Tapestry of Hope • *A Love Woven True* • *The Pattern of Her Heart*

DESERT ROSES
Shadows of the Canyon • *Across the Years* • *Beneath a Harvest Sky*

HEIRS OF MONTANA
Land of My Heart • *The Coming Storm*
To Dream Anew • *The Hope Within*

LADIES OF LIBERTY
A Lady of High Regard • *A Lady of Hidden Intent*
A Lady of Secret Devotion

RIBBONS OF STEEL**
Distant Dreams • *A Hope Beyond*

WESTWARD CHRONICLES
A Shelter of Hope • *Hidden in a Whisper* • *A Veiled Reflection*

YUKON QUEST
Treasures of the North • *Ashes and Ice* • *Rivers of Gold*

*with Judith Miller **with Judith Pella

ALASKAN QUEST

Summer of the Midnight Sun

To Jayce

You inspired the name of
my character and have shown
the light of Christ in your
heart and actions. I'm
proud to call you friend.
May God ever direct
your steps.

Chapter One

Last Chance Creek, Alaska Territory

May 1915

"Where is he?" Leah Barringer whispered, scanning the horizon for a glimpse of her brother and his dogsled team. He should have been home weeks earlier, and yet there was no sign of him.

A cold May wind nipped at her face, but it was the hard glint of sun against snow that made Leah put her hand to her brow. They had suffered through weeks of storms, so the sunshine was most welcome, but it was also intense and blinding.

"Jacob, where are you?" Her heart ached with fear of what might have happened. The Alaskan wilderness was not a place to be toyed with, and though Jacob was well versed in the ways of this land, Leah feared for him nevertheless.

Jacob had left nearly two months earlier for Nome. Hunting had been poor in the area and many families were going hungry. He had made the decision to travel to Nome for basic supplies and to replenish the store of goods he and Leah sold from their makeshift trading post. A master with dogs, Jacob figured he could hike out by sled and be back before the spring thaw made that mode of travel too difficult. It was a trip that should have taken two to three weeks at the most.

Storms had made it impossible to send someone out to check on Jacob, and hunger made it unwise. There was nothing to be gained by risking more lives. *Besides,* she reassured herself, *Jacob is as capable as any native Alaskan.* He had the best dogs in all of Alaska too. Leah tried not to worry, but Jacob was all she had. Since their mother died when they were children, they had clung to each other for comfort and support. Their father, a grand dreamer, had dragged them to Alaska during the Yukon gold rush some seventeen years earlier. After his death, Jacob and Leah had made a pact to always take care of each other.

Not that she didn't want more.

Leah was facing the harsh reality that she was nearly thirty years old, and the idea of reaching that milestone was more than she could bear. She longed for a husband and children, but here in the frozen north of the Seward Peninsula, there were few prospects. The natives had little interest in white women. The whites were perceived with skepticism at best and animosity at worst. Most of the natives she and Jacob befriended accepted them well enough, but none had shown an interest in marrying either Leah or her brother.

Leah wasn't sure she could be happy marrying a native anyway. She was not completely comfortable with their lifestyle and interests. Many were steeped in superstitions that she and Jacob could never be a part of. She had shared her Christian faith with anyone who would listen, but traditions and fears were strong motivators compared to white man's stories of a Savior and the need to put aside sinful ways.

And though Nome sported more white men than other areas, most were aging and grizzled, and not at all what Leah perceived as husband material, furthering her matrimonial woes. Added to this, many were just as steeped in their traditions and superstitions as the natives. Most had come up for the gold rush in Nome—hoping against the odds to make their fortune. Few had actually succeeded, and many had lost hope long ago, giving their lives to a bottle or to some other form of destruction.

Ten years ago Jacob and Leah discussed their desires to marry and start families of their own. They agreed if either one found true love, they wouldn't feel obligated to forsake this for the needs of their sibling. Leah had thought they would both find mates and settle down to raise families, but this hadn't happened.

Her guardian after her father's death, Karen Ivankov, understood Leah's distress. The same thing had happened to Karen in her youth. Love and romance had eluded her until she was in her thirties and alone in the wilderness of the Yukon.

Sometimes Karen's long wait to find love and marriage encouraged Leah. Karen often said that when the time was right, God would send a husband to Leah. Leah prayed Karen was right. She prayed for a husband, even as she prayed for Jacob to find a wife. Because, despite their pact from so long ago, Leah knew she would want Jacob to be happily settled as well. But so far God had only sent one person that Leah felt certain she could love.

Ten years ago she had been almost twenty, and Jayce Kincaid had been all she'd ever wanted in a husband. Strong and handsome, brave and trustworthy. At least she'd believed he'd been trustworthy. But what had she known of men at the tender age of twenty? Karen had taught her not to judge men by outward appearances, but rather to test their hearts. Leah had given Jayce her heart, but he hadn't wanted it. He'd actually laughed when she'd declared her love.

"Jayce, I have to tell you something," Leah had told him after arranging to meet him privately.

"What is it, Leah?" he'd asked. "You seem so all-fired serious. Is something wrong?"

"No . . . at least not to my way of thinking."

He had been so handsome in his flannel shirt and black wool trousers. His dark brown hair needed a good cut, but Leah found the wildness rather appealing.

"So what was so important that you dragged me away from the warmth of the house?"

Leah swallowed hard. "I think . . . that is . . . well . . ." She stammered over the words she'd practiced at length. Drawing a deep breath, she blurted it out. "I think I've fallen in love with you."

Jayce laughed out loud, the sound cutting through her heart. "Leah, it's best you don't do any thinking, if that's what you're coming to conclude."

Leah shook her head, her cheeks feeling hotter by the minute. "Why would you say that? Have you no feelings for me?"

"Well, sure I have feelings for you. You're a sweet girl, but you're way too young to know what love is all about."

"I'm nearly twenty years old!" she protested.

"My point exactly. You aren't even of legal majority. How can you trust yourself to know what the truth of your heart might be?" He picked up a rock and tossed it into the creek that ran behind the Ivankov home. "You're just Jacob's kid sister."

"And you were cruel," Leah whispered, her thoughts coming back to the present. She wiped a tear from the edge of her eye. How long would it hurt? Surely there was someone she might come to love as much as she had loved Jayce Kincaid. But it was always Jayce's face she saw—his voice she heard.

Maybe I'm too picky, she thought as she made her way back into her *inne*. It wasn't a true inne, but it served nearly as well. Instead of being mostly underground, like the native homes, the Barringer inne was a bit more above ground than usual—but not by much; it would have been foolish to have it too exposed to the elements. But to live too far underground would have made Leah feel buried, and Jacob, ever thoughtful of her feelings, had struck this compromise. The log and sod creation also lacked the long tunnel that most innes had. Leah preferred the manner in which they'd built their house but would still navigate the entrances to the homes of her friends. The tunnels were the worst of it, she would say, enduring the two-foot-wide crawling space with her eyes closed most of the time. She just didn't like the feeling of being closed in.

The Barringer house also acted as the trading post, so accessibility was critical. Natives were always coming to trade smoked meats, furs, or finished products. In turn, Jacob would take these things to Nome, where he could trade for supplies that they were unable to glean from the land. With this in mind, Jacob had designed the cabin to be partially underground in order to be insulated from the severe cold of winter, yet simple and quick to get in and out of. He had also managed to put in one window to let light into the room they used for eating and cooking during the long winter months. Of course, in the winter there was no light, so they closed the window off to keep the heat from escaping.

Leah entered her home and made her way down several steps to the first room. She and Jacob had set aside this room for the trading of goods. They carried provisions like salt and spices, sugar, canned milk, coffee, and tools. Of course the natives would have made their way in life without these luxuries, but Leah found that, as word spread, the natives seemed more than content to trade furs for white man's goods. And by operating their trading post, they saved the people from having to travel all the way to Nome.

She looked around the small room. The shelves were pretty much cleaned out—she hadn't even had to worry about keeping shop. There were an unusually high number of tools, however, since people had, as a last resort, traded equipment for food. For the first time, Leah wondered if the village could even survive much longer. Hunger was a constant companion, and although everyone was sharing as much as they could, there had already been deaths. Only the strong survived an Arctic winter.

Leah moved to the right and pushed back the heavy furs that sealed another doorway. Inside was a small room her older native friend, Ayoona, insisted they build when Leah and Jacob had first come to the village nearly ten years ago. They called this the stormy day cookroom, and it held a fire pit and had an opening in the ceiling that allowed the smoke to dissipate. The door was covered with heavy furs to keep out the cold, and when they were cooking here, it was a pleasantly warm room that beckoned them to stay—so much so that Jacob had put in a table and chairs when Leah had complained of being tired of sitting on the floor. It made a nice place to eat their winter meals.

The Barringers also had something that most natives had never concerned themselves with, and that was a stove. Leah liked the stove for cooking and baking. She had learned to do her kitchen tasks in native style over the fire pit, but the stove was a luxury she praised God for on a daily basis.

She checked the stove, making sure there was enough heat to keep the kettle of water and small pot of soup hot. She wanted there to be food ready for Jacob when he returned. If he returned. Again she felt a sinking in her heart.

"He must come back," she murmured, stirring the thin soup. Soon, even this food would be gone. Leah would have no choice but to eat what she had when the time came and hope that Jacob would bring more.

Seeing that everything was as it should be, Leah made her way back to the main living quarters of the inne. Here they had their small table and chairs, their beds, and some chests for storage. It wasn't much, but it had been home for a good portion of Leah's adult life.

"Lay-Ya!"

Leah smiled. It was Ayoona. The old Inupiat woman always called her with emphasis on the "ya."

"I'm here in the back," Leah replied, popping out from behind the hanging fur doorway.

"I brought you food," Ayoona said proudly. "My son was blessed today. He caught a seal. The village is celebrating."

"A seal! How wonderful!" Leah nearly squealed in delight. Seals and walruses had been so scarce she actually feared that something bad had happened to the bulk of the animal population.

Ayoona held a pot out to Leah. "This is for our good friend Leah and her brother, Jacob."

Leah took the offering. "Oh, you have our gratitude and thanks. I know Jacob will be home any day now."

The stocky little woman smiled, revealing several missing teeth. "He will come. I have prayed for him."

Leah nodded. "I have prayed for him too. I spend most all my time praying."

"You should come hunt with my family. I am too old, but you are young and strong. You shoot a bow well—you could hunt for geese with my daughters. When the spring is truly come, they will hunt for squirrel, and you can make Jacob a new undershirt."

"I would have to be a very good hunter to get enough squirrels for a shirt."

Ayoona grunted. "Maybe forty—no more. Jacob is not big man."

Leah smiled. "He's big enough. He eats like he's three men."

"He work like he's three men," Ayoona countered, her grin taking years off her wrinkled face. "I go now. We celebrate."

Leah nodded. "Thank you again. I'll get right to work on cooking this."

"Don't cook too much. You whites always cook too much. Takes flavor out."

Leah laughed and gave Ayoona a wave as the old woman offered her a smile once again. Ayoona had become a dear friend over the last ten years. The old woman had learned English as a child in one of the missions, but she'd never been comfortable with it. She often spoke English in a broken manner, shifting more easily into her once-forbidden Eskimo tongue.

Ayoona had been less suspicious of Leah and Jacob than some—although she had perhaps more reason to fear them because of the misery caused her by other white Christians. Still, the old woman had been kind and offered food upon their arrival. Later when Jacob had sat with the village council, Ayoona had defended them to her son—one of the higher-ranking members. Leah would always be grateful for her kindness.

The villagers had been skeptical and wary of Jacob and Leah when they arrived. Whites generally meant trouble in some form. Either they came bringing sickness or they came demanding change.

Jacob and Leah tried to do neither. Jacob actually had taken a job driving the mail from Nome to other villages where mission workers were desperate for news from home. During the winter, it was impossible for ships to venture north for deliveries, but dogsleds were ideal. The mail runs naturally led to bringing in store goods, and before she knew it, Leah had a job of her own, trading goods. She truly enjoyed interacting with the native people.

It wasn't too long after they settled in Last Chance that missionaries showed up to establish a church and school for the area. Leah felt sorry for these kind people of God. They had an uphill battle to fight against the superstitions the shamans had built into their people.

Busying herself with preparing the seal meat, Leah didn't realize how the time had passed. It was deceiving to try to determine the time by the light of the sun. Some months they were in darkness and other months it was light for the entire twenty-four-hour day. The spring Leah had known in Colorado, where she had lived as a child, was nothing like what she experienced in Alaska. The deadliness of the land seemed even more critical when the seasons changed.

Jacob had hiked out when the ice was thick, able to move the dogs out onto the ice for easier passage to Nome. But that wouldn't be safe now. The temperatures and storms had disguised their effects on the land. Sometimes the snow seemed firm, solid, but as the day warmed it would turn to mush. Night would chill it to ice—but not always in a firm manner. Instead thin crusts would form and give false promises of security to the untrained eye.

"But Jacob's not untrained," she reminded herself, checking the stew she'd made. It was little more than the seal meat and a little salt and flour, but the smell was quite inviting.

"He's capable and he knows the route. Something else must have happened." And that worried Leah even more. Jacob might have encountered a bear or gotten hurt separating fighting dogs. The sled dogs were not always in the best of moods.

"Jacob's back!"

At first Leah wasn't sure she'd really heard the call. She put aside the spoon she'd been using and ran for the door. The native who'd brought the news was one of Ayoona's grandsons. He quickly exited the house after seeing that Leah would follow.

But Leah didn't go far. It dawned on her that Jacob would rather come home to a warm house and food waiting than to have her rushing to him in tears. She would have plenty of time to talk to him, and the natives would see to unpacking the sled. She watched the activity for a moment, then turned back to the house to set the table.

Rushing to the stove, Leah threw in more chopped driftwood, then quickly went to the cupboard and pulled out a large bowl. How she wished she might offer her brother bread or even crackers with the meal. *Maybe he will have brought some of each from Nome,* she mused in anticipation.

Soon the door opened, and the fear that had gripped her for the past weeks evaporated. "Jacob!" she gasped and ran to embrace her brother. "I thought you were gone forever. You really worried me this time." She couldn't see his face for the deep parka hood that he still wore, but his strong embrace let her know he had missed her as well.

"Come over to the stove. I'll help you get out of those wet clothes." She led him across the room. "Don't worry about your boots," Leah said, noticing they were dripping bits of snow and ice, and that they were new—not the mukluks he'd left in.

"There hasn't been too much excitement while you were gone. Just starvation, but of course you already knew about that. Nutchuk cut his hand badly while skinning a seal. I stitched him back up, however, and he seems to be doing fine." She thought of the young native man and how scared he'd been. His mother had told him he would lose the hand for sure unless he allowed the shaman to create a charm, but Nutchuk had just become a Christian earlier in the winter, and he no longer believed such things held power. Leah had been proud of his conviction. "You should have seen him, Jacob. He refused to deal with the shamans because he honestly believed Jesus would heal him. It was a real testimony to the rest of his family."

She stood behind Jacob to help him pull the thick fur parka from over his shoulders. "Oh, and Qavlunaq had her baby two weeks ago. It was an easy birth, and her mother-in-law and grandmother delivered him. It was a boy and his father is quite proud."

The coat finally gave way and Leah hung it on a peg, leaving Jacob to finish disrobing. "I've got your supper on the stove. Are you hungry?" She turned for his answer but stopped in shock when she saw the man before her was not her brother.

"Jayce," she whispered almost reverently. The past had finally caught up with her.

Chapter Two

I thank you for the warm welcome," he said, grinning roguishly. "I must say you're a sight for sore eyes. And my eyes are definitely sore. The sun against the snow was most blinding—even with our little slitted masks, the sun still made me miserable."

Words refused to form in Leah's mouth. She could only continue to stare at the man before her. How good he looked—strong and capable. Handsome too. She felt all of her girlish dreams and emotions rush to the surface.

Jayce rubbed his eyes. "It was sure my good fortune to meet up with Jacob. Your family in Ketchikan told me you were out here on the Bering Sea, but I really wasn't sure I could locate you. I can't imagine what Jacob was thinking settling out here, but I'm glad he did."

Still Leah simply watched as Jayce stepped forward to warm his hands at the stove. "Smells good, Leah. I recall you were a good cook, even as a kid."

"As a kid." The words stuck in her brain.

"Hmmm, something smells great," Jacob called as he came through the door. He'd already pulled off his parka, so this time Leah was certain it was her brother. "Kimik told me John caught a seal."

Leah finally found her voice. "Yes. Did Kimik also tell you that his wife gave birth to their son a couple of weeks ago?" She decided that, for the moment, ignoring Jayce was the only way she'd be able to compose her frayed nerves.

"Yeah, he seemed mighty proud," Jacob said, hanging his coat near Jayce's. His sandy brown hair fell across his forehead, and he pushed it back. "So I guess you can see my surprise for yourself. Jayce was in Nome looking for good sled dogs, so I thought I'd bring him home with me and show off some of ours."

"Actually, I went there looking for Jacob's dogs. Adrik told me they were the best to be had."

Leah wasn't ready to deal with Jayce just yet. "Jacob, where have you been? What happened? You should have been home weeks ago. We were all terrified, and the people were on the brink of starving."

Jacob frowned. "I know, and I'm sorry. I couldn't help it; I caught the measles and the doctor wouldn't let me leave Nome. I was pretty sick—not to mention quarantined."

"Measles?" Leah questioned.

"Yes, and then the weather turned bad—you probably experienced it yourself. I couldn't even get word to you. I'm sorry if you worried."

"Besides, Jacob's able to take care of himself," Jayce threw in. "You should have known he'd be all right."

Leah felt her anger rise, and she turned abruptly to stare Jayce in the eye. Those lovely dark blue eyes. "I figured Jacob would be fine . . . it was the people here who weren't faring as well." She tilted her chin upward in a defiant pose, just daring Jayce to condemn her thinking. "Jacob is a very considerate man, and he knew the people were suffering. I knew he wouldn't have left them to die and figured something must have happened to him."

"Well, we're here now," Jacob said before Jayce could comment. "And by bringing Jayce back with me, I was able to split the team, borrow an extra sled, and carry twice as many supplies."

"Which reminds me," Jayce said. "I left some things in the sled. I'd better go retrieve them before they wind up on the store shelves." He laughed and bounded across the room.

"I know the people will be grateful for what you did, Jacob." But Leah wouldn't be among them. She felt the fire leave her and again knew a weakness in her knees that threatened to sink her to the floor. "There's food on the stove. I'll be in the other room putting the things away."

She exited quickly, grateful that Jayce had left the house. She prayed God would help her overcome her shock. She forgot to pray, however, that Jacob wouldn't follow her.

"What's wrong with you? You aren't at all yourself. Did something else happen while I was gone?"

Leah leaned back against the wall and shook her head. "Why did you bring him here?" she whispered.

"Jayce? I already told you."

"Jacob, you know what he did to me. You know how much he hurt me." She looked at her brother as though he'd lost his mind. How could he have betrayed her this way?

"What are you talking about? That was ten years ago. You were just kids then."

"I wasn't a kid. I was nearly twenty years old. In some areas of our country that would be considered almost too old for getting married. Twenty wasn't a child's age, nor was I childish in giving my heart to Jayce. I might have been foolish, but I wasn't childish."

"Whoa!" Jacob said, holding up his hands. "You're really upset about this, aren't you?"

Leah shook her head and hoped her look expressed her confusion. "You really don't understand, do you? It never crossed your mind that his coming here would be a problem for me."

"Well, I guess I figured that everyone would be so happy for the extra supplies, you included, that it wouldn't matter. Look, you aren't the same woman you were back then, and he's certainly not the same man. He even found the Lord, Leah. Isn't that great?"

Leah knew she couldn't protest that bit of news. Jayce's inability to see eye to eye with her on issues of faith had been his one shortcoming. It had also been the one thing she knew would have kept them from marriage, even if he had felt the same way she did.

"I'm glad he's found peace for his soul," Leah said, gazing at the floor, hoping some sort of peace would overcome her anxieties. "But I can't help the way I feel." She sighed. "I can't believe he's here, after all these years."

Jacob came and reached out to touch her arm. "I'm sorry that he still bothers you. I'll ask him to sleep elsewhere if you want me to."

Leah shook her head. "No, I can go stay with Ayoona. But . . ." She lifted her face and saw the compassion in her brother's eyes. He really didn't understand, but he cared that she was hurt. "Jacob, how long will he be here?"

It was Jacob's turn to look away. "I'm not entirely sure. That is to say . . . well . . . he's here to get some dogs. That much you know."

"But what don't I know?" she asked. "What is it that has you upset enough to look away from me?"

Jacob stood and glanced over his shoulder at the sound of Jayce's return. "He's part of a polar exploration group. They want me to join them on a trip north. They want me to handle the dogs."

Before Leah could reply, Jayce shouted from the next room. "Jacob! Where are you? I'm starving."

Jacob looked at Leah and shrugged. "We can talk about it later. I'll go see to feeding him."

Leah watched as her brother started to leave. There was something in his manner—in his tone—that suggested he might really be considering Jayce's proposal. "Wait. You aren't seriously thinking about doing this, are you?"

Jacob stopped midstep but refused to turn. It was enough to let Leah know exactly how he felt. "You are considering it. You're thinking about leaving me to explore the north with Jayce Kincaid." The words were delivered in stunned amazement.

"I'm praying on it, Leah. That's as far as I've gotten. You oughta pray about it too."

He left with those final words still ringing in the air. Leah sat down hard, but she missed the chair. Her backside stung from the impact, but she gave it no mind. Jayce was threatening her security once again.

How can he be here? How could God let this happen? Leah's mind swirled with a million questions. All of which involved Jayce Kincaid.

Her stomach growled in hunger, but she wasn't about to join the men. She doubted she could even choke down food while sitting across from Jayce.

"Hello! I bring the boxes."

Leah recognized Kimik's voice. "I'm coming," she called. "Just put them on the counter."

She got to her feet and dusted off the seat of her pants. There was work to be done. Somehow, someway she was going to have to get a grip on her emotions. But how? How could she exist in the same village, much less under the same roof, with Jayce? If nothing else, his appearance here had taught her one thing.

She wasn't over him. Not by any means.

"Leah okay?" Jayce asked. "I know I'm imposing."

Jacob looked at his friend. "She's fine. She's happiest when she's setting the store straight. With all these supplies, she'll be busy for a time. That will help."

"She acted like she was mad at me," Jayce said, helping himself to the coffee Jacob had made.

Jacob shook his head. "I don't know what she's thinking half the time. Women are a mystery." He ladled another portion of the seal meat for Jayce and then for himself, being sure to leave a portion for Leah. Even though he didn't always understand his sister, he was sure she hadn't yet eaten.

"Did I tell you that we're going to have a couple of women along on the trip north?" Jayce said, seemingly unaffected by Jacob's comment.

"Women on a polar exploration team?" Jacob asked. "That seems a bit strange. What prompted this?"

"Actually it's becoming more typical. Anyway, given that we're only going to do map work on the Canadian islands, it's not deemed quite as dangerous. Of course, you know there are some explorers who claim that there's nothing to surviving the Arctic. Natives do it all the time, after all. So the captain is allowing his wife to join him, as well as some female cartographer. Well, at least she'll be the assistant. Guess she's somebody important from Washington, D.C., and they couldn't get out of it. Even though this is a shared effort, it's mostly a Canadian team. They are, however, trying to earn the respect and interest of the Americans. They want our financial support, you know."

"I'm sure," Jacob said, trying not to think about what Leah's reaction to this trip would be.

"These expeditions are very expensive. I know the team has worked long hours to raise enough money for supplies. We'd have the added expense of a ship, as well, if the captain hadn't volunteered his own. He's an American who's fully sold on the importance of exploring the North. Thinks, along with others, that Alaska and the Arctic hold promise for many reasons. Military wants to consider strategic placement in the North, and I'm sure you've read about the air flights being made. They want to eventually put runways up here and fly people back and forth."

"For what purpose?"

"Well, national security for one. Some of the more innovative men in the governments of America and Canada see benefit in the speed and convenience of flight. Imagine being able to get supplies to Nome and all points north during the winter. Better still, imagine being able to get the sick out to doctors in a timely manner—winter or summer. It'll just be a matter of convincing the old codgers who still want to cling to their horse and buggies."

"But I'm not sure flight will even work up here, especially in winter. How are you going to keep the planes moving when everything is frozen solid?"

Jayce shrugged. "That would come under somebody else's department. I'm just in it for the adventure. You know me."

"Well, I used to. Ten years is a long time. Long enough to change a man or woman from the inside out. You said so yourself."

Jayce nodded. "Seems to have changed your sister. I remember her as a much happier person. Full of laughter and smiles. She seems real serious now."

Jacob drew a deep breath and sighed. "I have a feeling she's only going to get more serious as the days grow longer."

Leah finished her inventory, then immediately sent Kimik out with word that the store was open and that they would allow the people to purchase on credit. It was only a matter of minutes before people flooded the place with their requests and demands. Hunger made people feel angry, and no one had any way of knowing when the hunting or the weather would improve enough to see the bellies of the village filled and satisfied.

"It won't be long before the tomcod will be back. Squirrels and goose too," Ayoona said as she arranged her own small pile of supplies. "I dry you many fish, Lay-Ya."

"I know you will," Leah said, putting down the figures in her book. "You and your family have always been very generous with Jacob and me."

"You good people." She leaned closer. "How good is that new man?"

Leah's mouth dropped open. "I . . . what . . . ? You mean Jayce Kincaid?"

"Jacob's new man. The white man."

Leah tried hard not to seem upset. "We knew Jayce when we lived in Ketchikan with our guardians, Karen and Adrik Ivankov. Jayce was a friend to Jacob."

"So he is good man," Ayoona said nodding. "If he long friend of Jacob, he be good."

"I suppose so." Leah put her book under the counter. "I'm closing up now, Ayoona. I wondered if I could ask a favor."

"Sure you ask." The old woman gathered her things in a basket.

"Since Jayce is here, I wondered if I might stay with you for a few days—maybe until he leaves for his trip north."

"You can stay, Lay-Ya." She moved toward the door. "You come before the storm."

"Is there a storm moving in?" Leah realized she'd been inside for several hours without having a clue what was happening outside.

"Yeah, bad storm. You come soon."

Leah nodded. "I've got to take care of a few things; then I'll be there."

Ayoona pressed through the furs just as Jayce came through. "Where will you be, Leah?" he asked as Ayoona left.

Leah tried to ignore him. She figured if she pretended not to hear, maybe Jayce would leave her to her work.

"Are you purposefully ignoring me, or are you just caught up in your duties?" Jayce came and leaned against the counter.

Leah knew there would be no way to avoid speaking to him. "I'm very busy." Leah began to rearrange several items. "What do you want?"

"I asked where you were going. You told that old woman you'd be there. I just wondered where there might be."

Leah shrugged. "Ayoona's inne. I'm going to stay with her for a few days. This place isn't big enough for all three of us."

"Nonsense. You have families in this village who live eight and ten to an inne. You don't need to leave."

She made the mistake of looking into his face. How many times had she seen this same image in her dreams—wished she might once again be reunited with this lost love? She hadn't fully realized until that moment that she was still in love with Jayce Kincaid.

He grinned as if reading her mind. "You don't really want to go, do you? I mean"—his voice dropped low—"we'd miss you."

"You would?" Leah was barely able to form the words.

Jayce's smile broadened. "Nobody cooks as well as you do—especially not Jacob. I've lived with his cooking all this last week, and if you go, I'll be stuck with it again."

The words sobered Leah instantly. "You want me to stay so that I can cook for you? Maybe wash your clothes too?" She fought her anger. "Is that what this is about? I don't see or hear anything from you in ten years and you want me to stay so I can cook?"

"Has it really been ten years?" Jayce asked. He didn't seem to realize how he affected Leah at all.

"No, it's actually been a lifetime," Leah said, heading for the door. She forced herself to move past him and not give him another glance. If she stopped, she knew it would be her undoing.

Chapter Three

Helaina Beecham stared out the office window. The sight of Washington, D.C., in spring was breathtaking. She loved this city of history and wonder, but it was the abundance of flowers that caught her attention at the moment. Washington was beautiful in bloom. Even the newly planted Japanese cherry trees were doing their best to add beauty to the city, although their blossoms were nearly all gone.

"Sorry to keep you waiting so long, Helaina," said her brother, Stanley Curtis, as he hobbled into the room.

He manages his crutches rather well, she thought as she swept across the room, mindless of the narrow cut of her skirt, to offer her assistance.

"I'm sorry I couldn't have come sooner. I just arrived home this morning and found your telegram waiting for me." Helaina helped him to a large leather chair before adding, "I came straightaway."

"How was England?" he asked, his voice sounding rather strained.

It was easy to see her brother was in a great deal of pain. And why not? Being thrown from a train had resulted in a broken leg, three fractured ribs, and multiple lacerations and pulled muscles. The doctors all agreed Stanley was lucky to be alive.

"Angry. People are so enraged over the Lusitania being sunk by the Germans that they hardly speak of anything else."

"It's no doubt worse here. A great many Americans lost their lives on that ship. I was terrified to think of you traveling the Atlantic at such great risk."

"Well, it is an unspeakable and inhumane crime to target passenger ships," Helaina said, remembering with great sorrow the stories of anguish and heartbreak she'd heard. "And I was more than a little nervous."

"There is a madness that has overtaken the world," Stanley murmured.

"Let us hope America has the good sense to stay out of it," Helaina said, pushing aside her memories. She detested talk of war and the sorrow it brought.

"England was also beneficial to say the least. I have a feeling you're going to be quite interested in the news I have to share." She watched him struggle to prop his leg on the ottoman, not entirely sure if she should help or let him handle it. When he finally accomplished the deed, she breathed a sigh of relief. Stan could be so independent, and she didn't want to make him feel less of a man just because he was injured.

"So I imagine the news pertains to our Mr. Kincaid."

"Indeed it does. It seems he was involved with a team of experts working at the British Museum in London. While there, he apparently walked away with several prized pieces, including a most valuable gold crucifix, several ornate gold boxes, a half dozen or so odd pieces of jewelry, and a wooden box containing an assortment of gemstones that had yet to be catalogued and valued."

Stanley shook his head and gave a whistle of disbelief. "The British Museum lost all of that to Jayce Kincaid?"

"They aren't proud of the fact, but the man is above average in intelligence and quite cunning. I told them not to feel too bad about it." Helaina offered her brother a smile. "After all, plenty of museums in America have fallen victim to him as well."

"He must have pulled off his thievery there last winter and come straight here to Washington," Stanley deduced. "The agency was on his trail from the start. It was just our good fortune to have a man spot him at a party."

"Too bad he couldn't have been on the Lusitania," Helaina murmured. "It would have saved us all a great deal of trouble."

"If Jayce Kincaid had been there, the ship probably wouldn't have been sunk at all—he probably would have stolen it before the Germans could do the deed," Stanley answered, the sarcasm thick in his voice.

Helaina smoothed the straight lines of her no-nonsense gabardine suit. "He's a master. I'm truly surprised the Pinkertons haven't found a way to secure him, however."

"We've tried. I'm the result of that effort going amiss," Stanley said, waving his arm and wincing. "I thought I had Kincaid for sure. I had no idea he would be able to pick those cuffs." He shook his head.

The look of regret on Stanley's face nearly broke Helaina's heart. Her brother prided himself on his career with the Pinkerton Agency. She gazed beyond him to the company placard behind his desk. *Pinkerton's National Detective Agency* framed the ever-famous watchful eye. Below the eye was emblazoned with their equally famous motto: *We Never Sleep.*

Helaina looked back to her brother. "We can't sit around feeling sorry for ourselves all day. You lost your man and nearly got yourself killed. It's done. If you sit here wallowing in regret, you'll never accomplish anything." She got to her feet as if dismissing any further comment. "England wants him as badly as America, so I suggested we work together. Word has it that Kincaid has attached himself to a joint Canadian-American Arctic exploration team."

"I already know all about that," Stanley said, seeming surprised that his sister had any idea of this.

Helaina gave him a coy smile. "I have my sources too. After all, that's why you keep hiring me to help you."

While the Pinkerton Agency had used women in its services since before the Civil War, Helaina wasn't truly a Pinkerton at all. Rather she operated more as an assistant—an independent agent helping her brother. When she found her man, or woman as was often the case, there were always regular agents there to make the arrest. But the beauty of Helaina's involvement was that no one expected this twenty-six-year-old woman of social refinement to be working as a bounty hunter of sorts.

Of course, even Helaina hadn't considered such a duty until three years earlier, when a failed kidnapping attempt in New York had left not only her mother and father dead, but her beloved Robert with a bullet in his head. He'd died before she could return from Europe, where she was visiting friends. She'd never forgiven herself for not being at her husband's side—to die along with him that cold February day.

Stanley had been her only comfort, as had the idea of putting criminals behind bars. Helaina had taken her desire for justice to her Pinkerton Agent brother and begged for a job. In the long run, the agency had found her more useful in a non-official role, and for Helaina, that worked just fine.

"So what are you proposing, Helaina?"

Stanley's voice disrupted her reflective thought. She walked again to the window and looked out on the beautiful spring day. "Probably the same thing you've already come up with, but I'll let you tell me."

"We've arranged for you to join the expedition. Hopefully you can catch up with the team in Seattle before they leave. That is where the American team is gathering. From there they go to Vancouver where the ship *Homestead* is waiting for them. You'll have to leave immediately, of course."

"That's why I have my luggage downstairs," she said, turning. She shrugged. "Although if I'm to go all the way to the Arctic, I'll have to acquire something warmer than gabardine to wear."

Stanley watched her for a moment, then frowned. "I'd rather not send you at all. Jayce Kincaid is not a simple crook or bank robber. He's a killer. He's murdered two of my best agents."

Helaina came back to her chair. "I know." Her tone was rather resigned. "I'll be careful."

"If you get hurt, I'll never forgive myself."

"Look," she said as gently as she could, "I'm a grown woman and am no longer your responsibility. I chose to help. Remember?"

"Don't give me that speech. I've heard it all before, sister dear. You are my only living relative, and whether the law or any other person alive says I have no responsibility to you, I feel I do. I know I do."

He grimaced as he shifted his weight and his train of thought. "The plan is for you to approach him in Seattle," Stanley continued as if trying to set aside his fears. "You'll meet the team and purchase supplies and such. While there, it will be your job to isolate Jayce from the group."

"Do you have a photograph?"

"No. He's never allowed himself to be photographed. However, I helped the agency to put together a sketch. It's over on my desk. I wouldn't count on him to look like this, however. He's a master of disguises. He's even posed as an old man before."

Helaina crossed the room and immediately picked up the drawing and held it at arm's length. She carefully studied the attempt at capturing Jayce Kincaid. He had a lean, healthy look. His hair fell in a rather wild, unruly manner, and his eyes were dark and set in such a way that made him quite handsome. In a roguish way.

"What color is his hair and mustache?"

"Dark brown. He doesn't always have the mustache, but given the nature of the expedition, I would imagine he does. It's also possible that he now sports a beard."

"And the eyes?"

"Dark blue. Very dark—almost appearing black at times."

She never took her gaze from the picture. In her mind the colors came to life. "And his general complexion? Shallow? Pasty? Ruddy?"

"When last I saw him it was a ruddy to tan complexion. He darkens in the summer. I've seen this firsthand. He can look dark—take on an almost Mexican or Indian look."

She could well imagine that. This man could easily fit in different age groups and ancestries. He had a sort of ordinary quality about him, despite his handsome appearance.

"May I have this—take it with me?" she asked, coming back to her chair. She took her seat and only then did she move her gaze from the drawing and return it to Stanley.

"Of course. I had it prepared for you. I also have tickets, cash, and some other things you'll probably need—case file information and background. My secretary has them for you downstairs."

"Good. What is the contingency if this expedition team sets out before I arrive in Seattle?"

Stanley sighed. "I know that the team plans to make its way to Vancouver to pick up the ship they will use. I believe they are boarding a commercial steamer for this purpose. After Vancouver, we have been told the expedition will make its way to Nome, where sled dogs, sleds, and native assistance will be purchased."

"All right, then. I have my first chance in Seattle, the second one in Vancouver, and the last in Nome."

"I hope it won't come to that. I don't know how much help you'll have if the arrest takes place in Vancouver or Nome."

She waved off his protest. "But we have to be prepared. It would be wise if I were to acquire a bank account in Seattle. There's always the possibility I will need more supplies than the cash I carry will allow me to purchase. I'll see to that before I leave Washington. What time is my train?"

"Five o'clock."

She looked at the clock on the wall. "Hmmm, well, that gives me two hours to get to the station. I have a few things to see to." She got to her feet. "Don't bother to get up, Stanley," she said as he began to struggle with his injured leg. Helaina walked to her brother, planted a kiss on his forehead, and smiled. "And don't worry. I always get my man."

"But Jayce Kincaid isn't just any man. Helaina, I'm really worried about you this time."

She could see the concern in his eyes. "Don't bother yourself about it." She tried to sound lighthearted. "Just because he bested you doesn't mean he'll stand a chance with me. I'll turn on my womanly charm and have him eating out of my hand."

Stanley reached out and clasped her wrist. "This man is deadly. It isn't a game. If you suspect that he's discovered who you are, you must get out—and get back here as quickly as possible."

Helaina knew it was futile to argue. "I'll do it. You know I never take chances."

Stanley held her a moment longer, then released her. "Yes, I know exactly how you operate." He gave her a halfhearted smile. "I'll see you soon."

"Hopefully in days," Helaina said, heading for the door. "Shall I bring you anything from Seattle?"

"A new leg," he replied.

"But of course. I hear they sell them wholesale on the docks." She laughed lightly and pulled the door closed behind her before pausing to take another look at the sketch in her hand.

"I'll not be bested, Mr. Kincaid. You've caused harm to my loved one, you've pillaged and robbed, committed murder, and now you're on the run. But you won't outrun me. I always find a way to get my man." She folded the paper and put it into her skirt pocket.

Determination for justice had always driven Helaina Beecham—more so after her family had been murdered, but even as a child Helaina had demanded justice and responsibility from those around her. Her mother had even warned her that she lacked mercy and compassion when it came to forgiving wrongs, but Helaina couldn't help it. If people were going to break the law—do wrong—then there were prices to be paid.

Stanley had once accused her of seeking revenge for the death of Robert and their parents. He had warned her that no amount of service to the agency or anyone else would ever ease that misery, but Helaina knew that doing something was better than doing nothing at all. With each case she told herself the world was just that much safer . . . that other families might never have to know the horror and pain she had endured.

She made her way downstairs, pulling up her skirt ever so slightly. The new war fashions from Europe sported fuller and shorter skirts, but Helaina hadn't yet adapted her wardrobe. In London she had purchased a few older designs by her favorite couturier, Paul Poiret, but most were eveningwear that had been brought into the country prior to the start of the war.

She tried not to even think of the things she'd heard about the war. Cousin fighting cousin, entire countries devoted to the annihilation of another government and people. The labor unions were thriving on the conflict, while the women's suffrage movement in London had lessened their focus on obtaining the vote in order to support the men they loved. They would still be a force to be reckoned with, Helaina believed, but perhaps the day of women voting would be just a little more distant than she'd originally believed.

"Hello, Mrs. Beecham," a young man said, getting to his feet.

"Henry, my brother said you had a packet of goods for me."

"Yes, ma'am. Right here." He handed her a large envelope. "Tickets, cash, and all the information we could get you on Kincaid. We actually have some fingerprint evidence this time. It's not in here, but we'll have it when the time comes for Kincaid's trial."

"I have seen it used," Helaina admitted. "Truly fascinating."

"No two prints are ever alike. Kind of God's way of making sure we were all special, eh?"

She nodded. "Henry, would you be so kind as to arrange for my luggage? I have several stops to make before I head to the station."

"Of course. For you, anything." The tone of his voice and look on his face told Helaina he was still quite smitten with her. Poor boy. He was barely twenty-two, but he'd been more than attentive to her needs since coming on board as Stanley's secretary.

"Thank you, Henry. You're a treasure." She watched him blush and stammer for some sort of reply.

Outside, Helaina hailed a cab. She took a horse-drawn carriage rather than wait for one of the louder, smelly automobiles. Sometimes the contrast still amazed her. The carriages traveled in traffic along with the motorized cars, electric lights had replaced gas for the most part, and there was even talk that soon airplanes would dominate travel and put trains out of business for long-distance journeys.

It was a wonderful time to be alive, Helaina thought. But the shadow of war hung over them. There was no way to tell whether President Wilson would continue to keep them neutral or succumb to the pressures of the so-called civilized world. Helaina wasn't at all sure she wanted America to remain uninvolved. After all, responsible human beings couldn't just turn a blind eye when tragedy and inhumane actions struck another part of the world.

Still, her real concern was Jayce Kincaid. He would now be the focus of her every waking moment—likely some of her sleeping moments as well, for Helaina knew that once she immersed herself in the file on Kincaid, she would even dream about him. Oftentimes ideas would come to her in those dreams, ideas that helped her catch her prey. Her housekeeper in New York would tell her it was God's doing—His way of furthering justice—but Helaina thought such things nonsense and often told Mrs. Hayworth exactly that. The woman was unmoved, however, because of her strong Christian beliefs—beliefs Helaina did not share. After all, if God were really all that Christians held Him up to be, He would have the power to stop injustice and evil. Yet He stood by and did nothing. That didn't sound like the kind of God Helaina wanted to trust in.

Helaina had learned early on that a person had to trust themselves. Trust in their own abilities. That's why she continued to strive toward improving those abilities. She was intelligent, well-read, could shoot, ride, and even play the piano proficiently. Besides English, she spoke several languages fluently, including French, Russian, Spanish, Swedish, and Italian. The latter two were thanks to housemaids who had worked for her family since Helaina was small.

These were talents Helaina had worked to understand and improve. Her abilities weren't God-given, as Mrs. Hayworth would insist; they came instead after hours of hard work. Education was the key, Helaina decided early in life. She was college-educated and widely traveled, and she'd come to realize there was really nothing she couldn't understand or learn if she took the time to do so.

She was a sensible woman, however, and knew the truth of what her brother had said. Jayce would not be easily fooled or manipulated. It was more than a matter of turning to a textbook or relying on the education she'd collected over the years. Helaina would have to be particularly cunning—even devious. But it was, after all, in the line of duty. Stanley had once told her it all was fair in the service of catching criminals. Lies and manipulation were simply tools they used. Tools that Helaina Beecham used quite skillfully.

Chapter Four

The intensity of the storm took everyone in Last Chance by surprise. By the time Leah finished making preparations for Jayce and Jacob, she had no hope of making it to Ayoona's inne without risking her life. With a sigh, she realized there was no choice but to stick out the storm with Jayce and Jacob. After all, it would probably last only a few hours.

But the hours dragged by, and it became apparent that the storm had no intention of letting up. The wind blew in gale force, driving the dry powdery snow and ice like daggers through the air. Leah tried not to let the walls close in around her, but just thinking about Jayce being in the next room was more than she could bear.

I should have left with Ayoona.

It served no purpose to chide herself on the matter, however. There was nothing to be gained by it. With the wind howling outside, Leah tried to keep her mind on things other than Jayce Kincaid.

At first she tried to focus on some sewing. Leah loved to sew and had learned to work with the many furs and skins that constituted the bulk of their clothes. When sewing failed to keep her mind occupied, however, Leah directed her thoughts to some much overdue correspondence. For several minutes she jotted a quick note to Miranda Davenport. News had come last fall, just before the ships stopped delivering mail, that Miranda's mother had passed away after succumbing to pneumonia.

Miranda had been a good friend to Leah while they were in the Yukon. Sister to the man who had married Karen's good friend Grace, Miranda was as gentle and sweet a woman as Leah had ever known. Miranda had married an Englishman named Thomas Edward, but everyone called him Teddy.

After writing to encourage Miranda and Teddy to visit and explore the vegetation that Teddy so loved to study, Leah picked up another piece of paper. She owed Karen a letter and began to share details of the lean spring and Jacob's long absence. It was hard being away from her surrogate mother. Leah had decided that this would be the year she would journey home to Ketchikan for a long visit, and she wanted to let Karen know well in advance. But before she realized it, Leah was writing of all that was on her heart.

I don't know why he's here now, after all this time. What must God be thinking to bring this man back into my life? I'd like to say that Jayce Kincaid has no effect on me whatsoever, but it isn't true. Every time I look up to find him watching me, my heart nearly skips a beat. I have to admit I still have feelings for him.

She stared at the paper, doing her best to deny the words she'd just written. *But I do have feelings for him.* Feelings that ran the gamut. Leah hadn't expected so many emotions to emerge. If she was honest, a part of her was actually terrified of having Jayce here. She wanted to put him behind her—to forget about him—but he seemed to want things to go on as they had before her declaration of love. He seemed to want—no, to demand—her friendship . . . and Leah wasn't sure she could give that anymore. It was one thing to forgive him, but she couldn't bear to set her heart up for the same kind of misery and pain.

Leah sighed and put down her pen. She couldn't just ignore the way he made her feel. She couldn't deny the thrill that rushed through her when she saw it was Jayce she had embraced and welcomed. Why was he here now—now, after ten years of struggling to lay him to rest in her heart? More important, how could she ever trust him again?

"You're sure quiet," Jayce declared. Leah looked up to find him with two mugs. "I thought you might like some coffee. It'll warm you up—unless you prefer another bear hug like when I first got here." He grinned mischievously and extended the mug. "I know I wouldn't mind."

"Thank you, the coffee is fine." She took the cup and pretended to refocus on the letter, although her hands were shaking.

"Looks like I got here just in time. You're so cold you're shaking."

Leah kept her head down to keep him from seeing the embarrassed expression she was sure to be wearing.

Jayce sat down opposite her, much to her consternation. "You certainly are more serious than I remember. Seems to me you were a more jovial kid when last we met."

"I wasn't a kid then," she said without looking up, "nor am I now."

He laughed and practically slammed the mug on the table. "You weren't much more than a little girl."

She looked up, barely containing her anger. "I haven't been a little girl since my father died in the Palm Sunday Avalanche seventeen years ago. I was a child of nearly thirteen when it happened—a girl by all accounts—but

I grew up that day." The coffee cup shook even more. "I don't know why you insist on remembering me as a child, but I'd appreciate it if you'd stop."

He looked at her blankly, as if stunned by her outburst. "I didn't mean to offend you, Leah. It's just . . . back then you didn't seem to have the weight of the world on your shoulders. You were happier."

"Yes, maybe I was." She realized she'd sloshed coffee all over the letter and quickly picked it up to dry. Ink ran in a blur with the dark liquid. "Oh, bother." She crumpled the paper into a tight ball with one hand, while still holding the coffee in the other. "What do you want, Jayce?"

The bluntness of the question took them both by surprise. He shrugged. "I just wondered what happened to you."

Leah wanted to scream, *"You happened to me, Jayce Kincaid."* But instead she drew a deep breath, then took a long draw from the mug. The hot coffee felt good against the growing lump in her throat.

"I grew up," she finally said rather sarcastically. "If you insist on remembering me as a child ten years ago, then that's what happened. I grew up and saw the world for what it was."

"And what was that?"

"Cruel. Harsh. Deliberate." She had no trouble listing her complaints against life.

"Surely it's more than that. Jacob said you like it here."

"I love Alaska," Leah said without thought. "I love the people. I'm less impressed with other elements of life, none of which I intend to discuss with you. Why is it you're here and not somewhere else? Why come to Last Chance when Nome surely offers you more opportunity for . . . for . . . whatever."

"Like I said, I needed dogs for the expedition and Jacob has some of the best, or so I'd heard."

"His dogs are excellent, but how did you know he was even here?"

Jayce smiled, lighting up his entire face. Leah swallowed hard and pretended to sip at the coffee. "I went to see your folks in Ketchikan. Adrik was up Sitka way, but Karen told me you and Jacob had moved west. When I caught up with Adrik in Sitka, he told me that Jacob had some of the best dogs in the world. When I mentioned the exploration to the Arctic, he told me that other groups had acquired hunting dogs from your brother. I figured I might as well do the same. All those folks couldn't be wrong, after all." He paused and looked at his cup for a moment. "I had to admit I was stunned at the length of time between visits. I didn't realize nearly ten years had passed since I'd seen you last."

"Time has a way of doing that up here," Leah admitted. Hadn't it taken her by surprise as well?

"Well, I found out where you were and started trekking up this way. It took some doing to get to Nome, but I managed it. When I got there, I was quite excited to learn Jacob was in town. I was prepared to hike out here all on my own."

"You'd never have made it," Leah said, shaking her head.

"You certainly don't have much faith in me."

She looked him dead in the eye. "No. No, I don't."

Jayce appeared taken aback, his dark, blue-black eyes piercing her with their intense stare. It was then that Leah realized how much he'd aged. Despite the fact that he was still handsome, lines of age were clearly visible around his eyes and mouth. *He's only thirty-two,* she thought. *Only two years older than me. Do I look aged to him?* She touched her cheek absent-mindedly.

Jayce opened his mouth to reply, then closed it again. For a moment he simply seemed to consider her words. It was a good opportunity, Leah thought, to escape.

"I need to go. I have things to tend to in the store before bed. I didn't finish my inventory." She got to her feet.

"Sorry I dozed off," Jacob said as he entered the room. "Sometimes the wind just wears me down. The cookroom was plenty warm too." He looked at Leah first, then Jayce. "So what have you two been up to?"

"I tried to write a letter to Karen," Leah said, glancing back at the table. "But I drenched it in coffee. Guess I'll start over later. Right now I'm going to finish my inventory. Then I'll start some supper."

"And I thought I might read," Jayce announced. "Seems like the perfect time for it. Unless, of course, the wind puts me to sleep."

"It's good for little else. There will be plenty of work after the storm. I'm anxious to show you the dogs and see what you think might work for the expedition. And we'll need to build a couple of sleds and make certain we have the harnesses in good order. It was smart of you to buy that gear in Seattle."

"Well, this expedition has been light on funds, and it seemed the wise thing to do. Although I have to admit, I'm not sure I could even hitch a team these days. But the expedition needs me."

"What exactly is this expedition hoping to accomplish?" Leah asked, wanting to know more.

"Mapping, mostly," Jayce replied. "You know there's a war on in Europe." He frowned. "Or maybe you didn't know. Anyway, you should know about it—after all, it will likely involve us as well."

"We didn't know much," Jacob admitted. "News travels slowly up here—especially in making its way to Last Chance Creek. I brought home some newspapers, Leah. I knew you'd enjoy them."

"Thanks," she murmured. Against her will she turned back to Jayce. "So why should the war concern us if it's in Europe? You don't mean to suggest there will be fighting on American soil, do you?"

Jayce shook his head and toyed with the coffee mug. "I don't believe there will be fighting here, but I do believe we will have to join the fighting if the warring factions don't back down."

Leah came back to the table. "But I don't understand any of this. What does an archduke in Austria-Hungary getting shot have to do with America entering a war?"

"Because whenever there are people who think they are better than others, and willing to shed innocent blood to prove it, bullies will appear to oppress less powerful folk. I've seen the rise of nationalism in Europe. It's fine to be proud that you're French or German, but when you believe yourself to be better than everyone else, it leads to problems."

Leah still didn't see this as a reason to go to war. "But that's their problem—not ours. We're an ocean away."

"Are we?" He raised a brow in challenge. "In case you didn't realize it, Austria-Hungary declared war on Serbia. That brought in the Germans to help the Austrians. Of course, in order to help them, the Germans feel they need to attack France, which in turn brings in Russia, who has an agreement with France. One by one, like dominoes, the countries start falling. Of course, Great Britain cannot stand idly by."

Leah crossed her arms. "That's still Europe and not America. Not even North America."

"But Russia is only a matter of a short distance by ship. Canada is next door. If Great Britain suffers, Canada will come to her aid. Do you not see how intricately we are all connected?"

"I thought it to be one big family feud," Jacob threw in. "Didn't I read that most of the heads of state involved are somehow related to each other? Maybe Leah's right and they should just settle it amongst themselves."

"But it would be no different than if your friends Karen and Adrik began warring with their children. The more intense the fight, the more damage done. Wouldn't you want to help them put an end to their conflict?"

"I suppose, but it's still seems a long way off," Jacob answered, not sounding in the least bit upset by the matter. "By the time it comes to that, the war will be over."

"I wouldn't count on it, Jacob. Some issues—some people—will refuse to just back down and leave well enough alone. I wouldn't count on this being simple. I believe we'll see people fight to the last man if they are allowed to do so."

Leah didn't care for the sounds of such things. "But it would have to take something big to involve America," she said, trying to sound as though she believed it herself. Inside her heart, however, Leah feared Jayce's comments more than she wanted to admit.

"Well, that's part of the reason for the expedition as I mentioned. They are looking to whether we might make more detailed maps of the coast and the islands in the Arctic. We're also to check for the feasibility of creating airstrips."

"That seems out of place up here," Jacob said, shaking his head. "I can't believe it will ever happen. You'll never see planes in this territory; it's too cold. They'd never be able to endure the harsh elements."

"That's hardly what the rest of the world believes, Jacob." Jayce leaned back in his chair. Leah thought he looked rather smug. "Of course, the world also said that flight was impossible—that man was intended to keep his feet on the ground. You'll see, my friend. Air travel will soon be upon us, and Alaska will be no exception. Flight will eventually take over as the main mode of transportation."

"I can only imagine how that would connect us to the rest of America," Jacob said, shaking his head. "Still, I find it impossible to imagine in a place that relies more on boats and dogsleds that airplanes would take over as the main means of travel, but I can tell by your enthusiasm that you don't consider this lightly."

"Indeed not. I'm rarely wrong, Jacob." He laughed and added, "Maybe I should have said I'm never wrong. You'd do well to believe me."

Leah had heard enough. As far as she was concerned, Jayce Kincaid was a visionary with no hindsight or understanding of the past.

You were wrong about me, Jayce. You were wrong about me.

Jayce watched Leah walk away. The long tunic she wore, like a parka made out of cloth, kept her sealskin pants from seeming indecent. Most of the native women wore them, and Leah had apparently adopted the fashion. Jayce thought it marvelous. He'd seen missionary wives along the coast who still wore the cumbersome fashions of American housewives, but they were hardly appropriate for Alaskan winters or summers.

"There are some books on the shelf if you've a mind to read. I brought that stack of newspapers, too, but I think you've already read them all," Jacob said as he settled into a chair with the Bible.

"Do you enjoy it out here—here at the end of the world?" Jayce questioned.

Jacob looked up. "It's never seemed like the end of the world to me. It's isolated, but the people are good. And it's not as though we can't move about if need be. I've even hiked out across the interior in an emergency. There's always a way to get where you need to be—if you have the Alaskan spirit driving you."

"I never figured you'd stay. In Ketchikan you seemed so miserable."

"I guess I was. I wasn't my own man—I couldn't figure out what I wanted to do with my life. I was growing up faster than the ideas would come."

Jayce laughed and slapped his hand on the table. "And I had ideas faster than the growing up would allow for. We are a pair to be sure." He smiled at his friend. "Have you given any more thought to my proposition?"

"Not much. I haven't had a real chance to pray on it or to discuss it with Leah. I wouldn't want to just up and leave her here—not without giving her some say in it. And I'm not sure it would be safe for her to stay alone."

"So send her back to Karen and Adrik. I know she loves them—probably misses them too."

Jacob nodded. "That she does. We've talked every year about her going for a visit. I think this year might be the best chance."

"See, it would work perfectly. Put her on a ship for Ketchikan and head north with me. It wouldn't take much persuading—I'm sure of it."

Jacob shook his head and put his focus back on the Bible. "I wouldn't bet on it. You think for some reason that you know my sister pretty well—but I've lived with her all of these years and I still can't figure her out."

Jayce said nothing to this. He really couldn't answer without giving away the awkward feeling inside his gut. Seeing Leah had done something to him. He wasn't exactly sure what, but he kept feeling an uneasiness that wasn't entirely unpleasant. In fact, in the back of his mind he wondered whether there might be a chance to rekindle the feelings Leah had claimed to have for him so long ago.

"Has Leah never married?" he questioned, realizing too late that he'd spoken aloud.

"No."

Jacob offered nothing more, and Jayce knew better than to press it further. Instead, he picked up his coffee mug and stood. "You want any coffee?"

"No, I'm fine. Thanks."

Jayce nodded, then spied the ball of paper and mug Leah had left behind. Hoping to be helpful, he grabbed up both and headed to the kitchen. He set both mugs on the counter and started to throw the paper into the stove. He paused, thinking of how Leah had been so absorbed in her writing. *Perhaps some of the letter can be salvaged,* he thought, knowing good paper could sometimes be scarce.

Jayce unfolded the balled-up letter and spread it against the hard surface of the wooden table. The words, for the most part, were blurred. The latter half of the letter, in fact, ran together so badly that it was impossible to really figure out the wording. He began to crumple the paper again until his own name leapt from the page.

. . . Jayce Kincaid has no effect on me . . .

The very presence of his name drove Jayce to better understand. A section of words were mangled in black ink and coffee. It made them impossible to read.

Every time . . . find him . . .

More blurring and run-together swirls before the letter ended with a somewhat promising statement.

I . . . feelings . . . him.

He struggled to make reason of the cryptic message. Did she care or didn't she? Was she telling Karen that she had feelings for him or that she didn't? And why should it matter to him? He held the letter up against the lamp, hoping against all odds that it would reveal the answer to his questions. It didn't.

Jayce glanced up, fearing Leah might walk in at any moment and realize what he'd done. He quickly crumpled the paper and stuffed it into his pocket. Leaning back, he tried to reason what it all might mean.

"You're a mystery to me, Leah Barringer," he whispered, "but I intend to solve this before I leave." He smiled and raised his mug. "In fact, I believe I'll rather enjoy unraveling this intrigue."

Chapter Five

Seattle

Helaina looked at the documents in her hand. "Isn't there a ship heading to Nome sooner?"

"Lady, you're lucky to be on that one. Travel north ain't as easy as it is here," a grumpy old man said from behind his ticket counter. "Ice is breakin' up, but the storms are still a powerful threat. Especially in the Bering. It ain't the kind of place for a lady—if you get my meanin'."

Helaina paid him little attention. She was used to men taking one look at her refined appearance and concluding that she was insignificant or too delicate to handle real-world affairs. "Where might I purchase some supplies?"

The man looked her over with a smirk. "I wondered if you were going to try to make it wearing those fancy city doodads. You'll freeze your backside off, pardon my sayin' so, in that." He sneered down his long nose at the sight of her best traveling suit.

"Well, it's a good thing you aren't responsible for me, then, isn't it?" She gave him a look that froze him in place. "Good day."

She left without getting directions to any reputable mercantile. She knew it would be best to move away from the dock area, but at the same time she felt confident the best supplies for the rugged Alaskan travel would be found here.

Walking to the north, Helaina couldn't set aside her disappointment upon learning that the expedition team had headed to Vancouver the week before. Further investigation informed her that they were already on their way to Nome and would await her there. There was no other word or suggestion as to how she was supposed to get to Nome; rather she was left to figure out everything, including needed supplies, on her own.

Well, it wasn't the first time she'd had only herself to rely upon. The smell of fish and rotting guts mingled with salty air and wet wood assailed her nose, but Helaina refused to react. Her mother had always taught her that a lady of quality might have to endure many hardships. The key to doing it well, however, was in controlling one's reaction. A true lady would keep everyone guessing. And that was something Helaina felt she did quite well.

Helaina spied a sign in a waterfront store that read, *There's still gold to be found in Alaska!* The advertisement further suggested that everything a prospector needed for the frozen north could be purchased inside. She decided the claim merited her attention and pushed open the door.

"Hello, ma'am," a young sales clerk said, seeming quite surprised to see a woman. "Can . . . can I help"—his voice cracked and raised an octave before settling back down—"help you? You . . . lost?"

Helaina surmised the teenager was unused to dealing with women. "I'm not lost. I need to purchase goods for a trip I'm making to Nome in the Alaska Territory."

"You're going north?" He seemed rather stunned.

"Yes. I'm to meet my employer in Nome. I'm a part of an Arctic exploration team. I'll need to have gear that will endure the harsh elements."

The boy studied her a moment, then shrugged. "Most of our inventory is for men. I don't know if we have anything . . . small . . . well, that is . . ."

"Oh, go in the back, Daniel, and let me help this poor woman," a man said as he came from somewhere at the back of the store. The teen blushed furiously and made his exit without another word.

"Ma'am, I'm J. T. Brown. This is my store." He extended a beefy fist in greeting.

Helaina liked his no-nonsense approach. "I'm Mrs. Beecham. I need to purchase whatever might be beneficial to me for a trip to Nome and beyond."

"I heard you tellin' the boy you were bound for the Arctic. It's not an easy place. I've been there myself. Went whaling once." He surveyed her stature. "I think I have some boy's sizes that will fit you, but once you're in Nome, you really should try to get some native-made clothes. See if you can't locate a few of the Eskimo women and get them to sell you some fur pants and such."

"I'll make a note of it. Thank you."

He seemed relieved that Helaina wasn't offended. But why should she be? He was only offering wisdom borne out of experience. He wasn't being condescending in his attitude, nor was he smirking at her as though she had no idea what she was talking about.

The man left quickly and reappeared with a stack of clothes in his arms. He placed these on the counter and went back out of the room once again. Helaina began to search the store for other items that she thought might be useful. She located a sturdy pair of boots that looked to be about the right size.

"You'll want to waterproof them," the man said, holding up a tin. "This stuff seems to work the best."

"Then be sure to include it with my other things," she said, leaving the boots on the counter with the clothes. "I'm also going to need a sturdy bag for packing. Do you have something canvas or leather?"

"I do indeed. I have a pack the sailors like to use. I think it will suit you well." He went to the back shelves of the store and pulled down a large black bag. "This one seems to hold a great deal and endure travel. It's guaranteed to be waterproof—they've put some sort of rubber coating on it. Don't know much else about it."

Helaina nodded her approval upon inspection. "It seems quite sound."

The man nodded. "I'd like to suggest something else. It may sound quite forward, but I've heard good things from the men who've gone north, regarding these." He went behind the counter and pulled out yet another piece of clothing.

"What is it?" Helaina asked.

It was the only time she'd seen Mr. Brown the least bit embarrassed. "Well, ma'am, they are . . ." He looked around quickly and lowered his voice, "Men's theatrical tights."

Helaina wanted to laugh at his whispered words. "Are they woolen?"

"Yes, ma'am. I've been told when worn under your other clothing, they help to keep the chill off better than anything else."

"I can't imagine men being too comfortable wearing these," Helaina said with a hint of amusement.

"They get plenty comfortable when faced with the alternative: freezing. Some even wear more than one pair at a time."

Helaina nodded. "I'll take them. In fact, give me three pair."

Mr. Brown appeared quite pleased with himself. They discussed other items, finally settling the selections and the bill, with J. T. Brown's promise to deliver everything to Helaina's hotel by nightfall.

With this arrangement made, Helaina requested Brown secure her a cab. He was only too happy to help her. After all, she'd made it worth his while to have opened shop that day.

Once she was back at the hotel, Helaina pulled off her kid gloves and tossed them aside. Her hat quickly followed suit. She felt a little hungry but decided against lunch. There was simply too much to plan. While contemplating her schedule for capturing Jayce Kincaid, she disrobed and settled into a dressing gown before spreading out all of her information. The sketch of Kincaid was front and center. She found it helpful to study a man's photograph while in pursuit of him. She wished there had been photos of Jayce Kincaid, but even the English hadn't been of help in this area.

She looked hard at the man's face. The eyes were penetrating—almost hypnotic. This was the face of a killer, she told herself.

Helaina tried hard to imagine what thoughts the man might have—what reasoning he might use to justify his deeds. She'd always wondered what thoughts and planning had gone into the events that had taken the lives of her own loved ones, for surely the men involved had contemplated their actions at length. Kidnapping was not something one did without a plan for victims. Even if that plan was death. She couldn't fathom the mind that perceived such deeds as acceptable.

She thought of her husband and how he might have reacted to the attack. Robert Beecham was no man's fool. Wealth had not been handed to him—he had made every cent by using his brain and brawn. Likewise, her father had also made his fortune. There were no silver spoons to be placed in the mouths of the Curtis children. She and Stanley, and another sibling who had died shortly after birth, had all been born into poverty. But her father refused to be kept down. He created a profitable freighting business, then sold it and bought into an equally beneficial manufacturing company. Little by little, step by step, he had increased their fortunes and had pulled the family from their impoverished circumstances.

Robert had come upon the scene as her father began to seek out investment advice. Robert's ability with figures and reading the market had merited him much success. He had made his first hundred thousand before he'd turned twenty-five and was quite confident in his future. It was one of the things that had attracted Helaina to him.

Of late, however, Robert's image had begun to fade from her memory, and his voice no longer haunted her dreams. She knew she'd not only survived widowhood, but had actually overcome it. Loneliness was no longer an issue. She had systematically driven this, as well as sorrow, away with her focus on righting the wrongs of the world. It was her only defense against drowning in miseries that would never bring her husband or parents back to life.

It was times like this that she could only wonder what the future might hold. She was only twenty-six, soon to be twenty-seven in August. She knew she never wanted to marry again. She didn't want children; the world was much too dangerous to contemplate bringing babies into its threat. But what eluded her was what she did want to do with her life. There were entire volumes of things she didn't want, but coming to an understanding of what was important to have, to hold . . . now, that was difficult.

She looked again at Kincaid. He seemed a perfectly normal man, but she knew he wasn't. His past told a completely different story. He'd killed at least two men—Pinkerton agents who were working to retrieve articles Kincaid had stolen—and he'd nearly killed Stanley. She shook her head.

What caused you to become the man you are? Why did you choose to live a life of evil instead of good?

Stanley had once told her that he was convinced men did not choose such things for themselves, rather those things occurred at random. Rather like a blanket thrown down from the mythological gods of Olympus. It fell on whom it would fall, and from that point on their life would be forever changed.

Mrs. Hayworth had a different view, one taken from her Christian beliefs. *"God has a specific plan for each person's life,"* the woman had said. *"Some men will give in to the devil's prompting. God weeps for them."*

God weeps for them, maybe, but He certainly didn't stop them.

When Robert died, Helaina had been bitter at the platitudes murmured and spoken by all those around her. Even his eulogy spoke of God's infinite wisdom and plan for each man's soul. Helaina had decided then and there that, if this, in fact, was the manner and heart of God, she wanted no part of Him. He was cruel to her way of thinking. A robber of loved ones—unfairly stealing away the very heart of those He called children.

Helaina had rejected any thought of God or His comfort after that. Not that she'd really given Him much thought prior to Robert's and her parents' deaths; but now it seemed it was to be war between her and God. A war that she could only win by altering God's plan—by capturing the evil that He allowed to run free in her world.

"I'll find you, Jayce Kincaid. Like all the others before you. I'll hunt you down and see you pay for the things you've done." She held the sketch with trembling hands. "The law will win out and justice will be done. You will hang for the sins you've committed because whether God will punish you or not—we will. We lowly, puny humans will see it done."

Leah felt a deep sense of gratitude when she awoke to silence. The storm had ceased, and the sound of children's laughter could be heard from outside. The missionary school year was completed for the season and the native children, along with the missionaries' kids, were enjoying their freedom.

Throwing back her covers, Leah stretched and yawned. The aroma of coffee and griddlecakes filled the air. She'd overslept, but apparently Jacob had gotten along well enough without her. It was only then that the memory of Jayce Kincaid came back to haunt her.

She grabbed her robe and held it close against her body. Jayce was here. He was staying with them. She found the idea as ludicrous now as when it had first been presented. Jacob had set Jayce up with a pallet in the storeroom. He had teased their visitor that it would be colder than the rest of the house, but that if Jayce was going to explore the Arctic, he might as well get used to it. Then with this arrangement made, Jacob told Leah there was no reason for her to stay with Ayoona.

No reason?

Leah couldn't believe her brother's ignorance. How could he not see or understand the effect Jayce had on her? And how could Jayce be so completely blind to it? As far as either of them were concerned, ten years was long enough to have put the past to rest. Leah sighed. It should have been.

You should just tell him how you feel. The words came from somewhere deep inside. *How can I tell him? It will only serve to embarrass and further hurt me.* But in truth, Leah was already in so much discomfort that talking to Jayce, a man who planned to leave in a matter of days, couldn't be much more painful.

Leah argued with herself for several minutes, but then her gaze fell to the calendar. Jacob had encouraged her to keep meticulous track of the days. With no sun in the winter and no night in the summer, it was easy to lose track of the days unless she kept a ledger.

The day Leah had been dreading had arrived—a taunting reminder of all she had failed to accomplish. May 18, 1915. It was her thirtieth birthday.

Leah stared at the calendar as if to will it to declare a different day entirely. But the truth would win out. She was thirty years old, unmarried, childless. Worse still, there were no prospects of changing any of it.

She went about her duties in a daze. She had dreaded turning thirty. Somehow she could tell herself she wasn't quite so hopeless or destitute while still in her twenties. But this mile marker seemed to make all the difference.

"Well, good morning," Jacob said as Leah came into the kitchen. "I let you sleep on account of your birthday."

Leah looked around frantically. "You didn't tell Jayce it was my birthday, did you?"

Jacob looked at her oddly. "Of course. Why?"

She sighed. "No reason. Where is he?"

Jacob dished up several flapjacks. "Out with the dogs. Here. I fixed you breakfast and I have a surprise." He pulled a small bottle from his coat pocket. "It's maple syrup. I know you love it and haven't had it for a while."

She couldn't help but smile. "That was really kind of you. Thank you."

"I have another gift for you as well." He left the room and returned with a brown paper-wrapped bundle. "I thought you might enjoy this."

Inside was a new traveling case. "It's wonderful," Leah said, not completely understanding the purpose. "But am I going somewhere?"

Jacob nodded and poured her a mug of coffee. "You and I have talked several times about you going to see Karen and Adrik. I think this year would be perfect."

"And what will you do while I'm gone?"

Jacob looked away. Leah could see he was uneasy with her question, and then it dawned on her that he meant to take Jayce up on the exploration offer. "You're going to go with Jayce, aren't you?"

"I think so. I've been praying on it, and . . . well . . . I think it might be exactly what God wants for me." His expression was one of hopefulness—rather like a little boy asking if he might keep a stray dog.

"I see," Leah said, wanting to be supportive. "I suppose to be honest, I was considering it myself—at least going to see the family. I know Karen would love it."

"Look, just think about it. I need to get out there with the dogs. Jayce wants me to show him the best and help him to train with a couple of teams. I'll be busy all day." He headed to the door. "Happy birthday, Leah."

The words rang in the air long after he'd gone. Leah sat down to the celebratory breakfast but found she wasn't at all hungry.

He's made up his mind to go away with Jayce. The thought left her feeling rather empty. It wasn't that Jacob wasn't entitled to his own life. Goodness, but they'd talked about this on many occasions. Leah had always maintained that she'd go back to Ketchikan if Jacob wanted to set out on his own. They'd only stayed together because neither one had anyone else—at least that's what they told each other.

Leah picked at the cakes, each piece drenched in the precious maple syrup. But even this sweet treat couldn't make the meal more palatable. *He's leaving me. He's leaving and going far away.* But it wasn't Jacob's leaving that held her thoughts captive.

"Knock, knock!" a female voice called out.

Leah immediately recognized Emma Kjellmann's Swedish accent. "I'm in the kitchen."

The blond-haired woman immediately pushed back the fur and stepped inside. "Happy birthday."

Leah smiled. Emma was the only other white woman in the village. She and her husband had come to the Seward Peninsula to bring the Word of God to the natives. While there, she'd given birth to three children, the oldest of whom shared his birthday with Leah.

"Thank you. Are we still planning to celebrate this evening?"

"Oh ja," Emma said with a grin. "Bryce has talked of nothing else."

"Well, turning four is a big event. Would you like some coffee?" Leah asked, getting to her feet. "I'm afraid I'm behind this morning. Jacob let me sleep late."

"Good for him," Emma replied, her accent thick. "It's good for you too, ja?"

Leah laughed. "I don't know about that, but I do feel very rested." She held up the pot, but Emma shook her head.

"I've had plenty. I just wanted to let you know that we'd expect you and Jacob at six. Oh, and bring your visitor too. We'll have plenty of food, thanks to Jacob's trip."

The mention of Jayce caused Leah to consider sharing her woes, for if anyone could advise Leah, it would be Emma.

"Do you have a minute, Emma?"

"Ja. Bjorn is seeing to the children, and the baby is sleeping, so he won't have it that hard. What's troubling you?"

Leah came back to the table and sat down. Emma took the seat opposite her. "It's about our visitor."

"You knew him from before, Jacob said."

"Yes." Leah struggled for words. Emma was such a dear friend, but it was still hard to speak aloud what she'd only dared to admit in her heart.

Emma put her hand over Leah's. "You have feelings for this man, ja?"

Leah looked at the woman in surprise. "How could you know that?"

Emma shrugged. "Why else would you be sitting here instead of helping Jacob with the dogs?"

It was true, Leah thought. She was always outside working with the dogs when there weren't people wanting to purchase something from the store. "I was in love with him once—nearly ten years ago. He spurned me, saying I was too young to know my heart. I was quite devastated."

Emma nodded. "And seeing him now is very hard."

"Harder than I thought it would be." Leah met the woman's compassionate gaze. "I thought I'd put this in the past—dealt with the pain. But seeing him again has brought it all back. I just don't understand why."

"Because you are still in love with him," Emma said matter-of-factly.

The words struck Leah in the gut, but she chose to ignore them. "Why would God do this to me? Why would He allow this man to come back into my life to hurt me?"

"Who can know the mind of God?" Emma declared. "You know that God has plans we cannot understand."

"I feel so distant from God. I feel so lost. Does that shock you?"

Emma laughed, surprising Leah. "We have all felt that way from time to time. The very nature of God often makes us believe Him to be unreachable. He is, after all, God of the universe—the King of Kings and Lord of Lords. How could He possibly care about the day-to-day issues of our lives?"

Leah nodded. "Yes, I suppose that's how I feel right now. He mustn't care about those details because this has happened. Yet I know that He cares." She bowed her head. "I feel guilty for even questioning Him, but I cannot understand why Jayce is here."

"Perhaps he's here because the time is right to make things new," Emma said softly. She squeezed Leah's hand. "God wants your heart to be whole, Leah. He wants your trust. You mustn't fear. You are poor in spirit right now. You feel depleted of hope and understanding, but God richly offers both. You'll see. Your love for this man has lasted for ten years. Surely God has a plan for that love."

"Maybe that's what scares me the most," Leah replied, looking up hesitantly. "Maybe His plan won't be what I want it to be."

"Who can know? But I know whom I have believed in." Emma got to her feet and smiled, adding, "And so do you."

Chapter Six

Jayce washed up for the birthday party. He felt they'd accomplished a great deal, and for that he was satisfied. Jacob had helped him to pick out about twenty good dogs, and given the fact that the exploration team would soon be joining them, Jayce knew he needed to work hard to learn their handling. He also needed to help Jacob finish building two sleds.

Maybe that was why he didn't feel right about quitting early to attend a birthday party. Even if that party was for Leah Barringer—although he seriously doubted that she wanted him at her party. Leah's attitude was a complete mystery to him. At times she seemed congenial, civilized . . . but most of the time she was almost hostile. But why?

Jayce wished he could understand the woman. She was more beautiful than ever—her dark brown hair beckoned his touch and her blue eyes were the color of a summer sky. But it was more than her appearance that seemed to draw him. There was something about Leah that he had never been able to forget.

He had to admit that he'd decided to find Jacob and his dogs mostly because he knew Leah would be here. He'd long ago heard of another man near Nome whose dogs were excellent and very reasonably priced, but Jayce had put that notion aside. He had convinced the expedition leaders that his old friend Jacob Barringer would give them a much better deal and perhaps even consider coming along to handle the animals. Given the fact that the expedition was already facing financial problems, it didn't take much persuasion. And while Jayce knew Jacob would supply only the best animals, his decision was driven by a need to see Leah again.

She'd been on his mind so much over the years. When he'd left Ketchikan ten years ago, Jayce immediately found that he missed Leah. Missed her so much in fact, that he'd temporarily left Alaska in order to forget her. But it hadn't worked, and Jayce had come back to the land he loved . . . but not to the woman who captured his thoughts. In fact, he'd done his best to avoid her. Now the expedition had brought them back together. . . . No, he'd brought them back together.

But why? Why did I come? So much has changed. So many years have passed by. She can't possibly care for me after all this time. But in his heart, Jayce hoped that she did. He hoped that somehow he might be able to get to know her again. The time he'd spend here working with the dogs would allow him to see her every day and that in turn would hopefully show him if he'd ruined his chances ten years ago.

Glancing up from the pan of water Jacob had provided, Jayce squinted against the sun. There were several men down by the water's edge. An *umiak*—a small boat made from animal skins—sat nearby. The men seemed to be asking about something. One man in particular held Jayce's attention.

"It can't be him," Jayce muttered.

He watched the man, being careful to keep out of sight. *Why is he here? Is he looking for me?* It would have taken careful investigation for him to find Jayce. Or was it pure coincidence?

This ghost from Jayce's past life rose up to disturb him like nothing else in the world. This man could ruin everything Jayce had worked for.

Jayce eased around the corner of the inne and fought to settle his nerves. He continued watching as best he could and felt only moderate relief when the man and his companions got back in the umiak and pushed out into the water. As the boat disappeared around the bend, Jayce let out a heavy sigh.

"You coming?" Jayce startled to see Jacob watching him. "What's wrong?" Jacob asked. "You look like you've seen a ghost."

Jayce wasn't about to let Jacob know the truth of it. If it was who he thought it was, Jayce could very well be in big trouble.

"I've just got a lot on my mind. The *Homestead* should be arriving soon, and I need to know my way around handling those teams."

"Well, maybe it won't be as bad as you think. I've decided to come with you."

Jayce forgot about the man and looked at Jacob with a grin. "That's wonderful news, Jacob. I can't tell you how excited I am to have you join us. You won't regret it. The pay's not great, but the adventure more than makes up for it."

"I don't think Leah took the news well, but I did mention having her go see Karen and Adrik. I think she consoled herself with that."

"She's not in charge of you, Jacob. A man can't live his life attached to his sister's apron strings."

"That's not the way it is between us," Jacob snapped.

Jayce waved his arms. "Whoa, now, I didn't mean anything by it. I'm sure you two stick together because you have no one else."

"We also happen to appreciate each other's company. We've been looking out for each other since we were kids, and I don't intend to stop until Leah is properly married to a husband who can take up the job."

"I understand perfectly," Jayce replied, feeling an odd sensation run through him at the mention of Leah marrying.

Jacob leaned in, his tawny brown hair blowing back in the gentle breeze. "I care about what she thinks. You should too."

"I do. Honestly, Jacob. I'm sorry."

Jayce wasn't sure why his friend had become so angry, but he wanted to make things right. "I need to go back to the house and get my gift for your sister. Point me in the right direction for the party."

"It's over there."

Jayce glanced across the way to see a reasonably sized wood house. He could only imagine that it must have cost a small fortune to bring in lumber for such a project. The natives and even the Barringers had houses put together with driftwood, whalebone, and sod. It was rumored that many of the missionaries would not come north without better housing, however. Jayce had read an entire report given by one of Dr. Sheldon Jackson's missionaries that told of the unbearable cold when living in less than a reasonable American house. Jayce had laughed at the situation then, knowing that he would probably live in nothing more substantial than a tent once they were on shore mapping and taking geological samplings in the Arctic.

Still, he couldn't begrudge a worker of God good housing. "I'll be right there."

"Well, hurry it up. We're already late."

Jayce tried not to think about the earlier encounter or of the man from his past. He told himself the sun had caused the man only to look like his old adversary. *He wasn't here. I'm safe.*

He hurried to the Kjellmann's house and knocked lightly before opening the door. Surely they were expecting him, and he knew that no one stood on ceremony north of the fiftieth parallel.

The first sight that greeted him took Jayce's breath away. Leah was standing to the right of the door, her expression one of sheer delight. In her arms she held a baby girl. The child was quite captivated by Leah's attention, and Jayce couldn't help but stare. Leah's face fairly glowed. She seemed so clearly at ease with the baby—so happy.

"She'll make a good mama, ja?"

He looked to find Emma Kjellmann at his side. "I think you're right," he said, shaking off the thought. "Sorry I'm late. I had to go back for her present."

"Not to worry. We do things as they come," Emma said. "Although my son Bryce would rather this party come quickly. Are you hungry?"

"To be sure. Jacob worked me hard today." He couldn't help but say this a little louder than need be, as Jacob approached.

"Oh, quit your complaining. I don't know how such a *cheechako* is ever going to make it up north."

"Don't call me a cheechako. I'm hardly a newcomer. I just need a lot of help," he said, laughing. "That's why I'm taking you with me. Somebody has to look out for me."

Emma chuckled. "Well, there's none better. Our Jacob might as well be native. But what's this about you going away?" she asked, turning to Jacob.

"I've been asked to join Jayce's expedition team to the North."

"Why would any sane man want to go farther north?" Emma asked quite seriously. "I may be Swedish, but this is cold enough for me."

"Me too," a man said, thrusting out his hand. "I'm Emma's husband, Bjorn."

"Jayce Kincaid. I'm glad to meet you and equally glad to be invited to the party. Jacob tells me there is actually to be a birthday cake."

"Can't celebrate a boy's birthday without cake," Bjorn replied.

"Can we eat now?" a young boy asked.

Jayce presumed it was Emma and Bjorn's son. Jacob had already told him the boy shared Leah's birthday.

"Ja. We'll eat now, but you promised to say the blessing in Swedish," Emma reminded her son.

Bryce lit up at this. "I know it all. I can do it." He fairly danced to the table.

Jayce smiled in amusement as the boy took his place and called to everyone else. "Come on. We're going to pray."

Leah looked up to find Jayce watching her. She blushed and clutched the baby close as if to shelter the child from harm. Jayce couldn't help but wonder, however, if Leah meant to protect the baby . . . or herself.

"On the occasion of Bryce Kjellmann's fourth birthday," Emma announced, "he is going to offer a traditional Swedish blessing."

They bowed their heads and Bryce began. "*Gud, som haver barnen kär se till mig som liten är.*" He paused for a moment, then added in English, "Bless the food, amen."

"Amen," several people said in unison.

"What did he say in Swedish?" Jayce asked Emma.

She grinned. "Bryce will tell you."

Bryce nodded and smiled. "God, who loves all the children, look on me so small."

"Wonderful job, Bryce." Leah handed the baby to Emma and went to hug the boy. He eagerly climbed into her arms and hugged her tightly about the neck.

He whispered loud enough for the entire room to hear, "I'm glad it's our birthday."

"I am too," Leah replied, giving him a quick kiss on the cheek.

Several of the natives who'd come to the party circled round the two and offered their greetings, blessings, and gifts. It was easy for Jacob to see that Leah was greatly loved. But why not? She was kind and gentle with everyone. Well, maybe everyone but him. For some reason she seemed perfectly content to make him miserable.

After a dinner of seal, tomcod, and some things unrecognizable to Jayce, Emma produced a birthday cake. He knew Jacob had brought some ingredients with him from Nome, but the cake still amazed everyone. It didn't take long for the dessert, heavier than most of the cakes Jayce had known in the States, to disappear.

Then it was time for gifts. There were many hand-carved trinkets for Bryce, as well as several articles of clothing. Leah received new mittens, a traveling pouch, a fur-lined hat, and a small ivory carving. Jayce felt his book of poetry paled in comparison to the other gifts, but she thanked him for it and seemed pleased.

When they concluded the party at nine o'clock, it was still as light as noonday outside. Jayce loved the long days. He felt they afforded him more working time. He motioned to Jacob as they left the Kjellmanns' house.

"I'm going to work more with the dogs. Would you come and help me?"

"It's nearly time to turn in," Jacob protested, his arms full of Leah's gifts.

"We still have plenty of light."

"We'll have plenty tomorrow, too. Besides, I have to take these home for Leah. I promised I wouldn't get sidetracked."

"I can help you," Jayce offered, "and then we can get back to work."

Jacob stared at him in disbelief for a moment. "I'm tired. I'm going home to clean up and go to bed. You do as you like."

Jayce realized he wasn't going to win the argument. "All right. I suppose it will wait until tomorrow."

"I heard from Ayoona's son John that there has been a lot of fog and storms to the south. Your ship will probably be delayed, so there's no hurry."

"It's your ship too," Jayce reminded him.

Jacob frowned. "I know. I just wish I could help Leah to understand why I think it's so important to do this."

"Let me talk to her," Jayce offered.

"No. You've done entirely enough," Jacob countered and headed for the house. "Just leave her be."

Jayce stood frozen in place. What did he mean by that? What had he done? "Wait up!" he called out. "What are you trying to say?"

Jacob waited, but only for a moment. "I said what I meant to say. Leave her alone. It's that simple." His calm was more unnerving to Jayce.

"But why?"

Jacob shifted the items and shook his head. "You really don't understand, do you?"

"I don't know what it is I'm supposed to understand. I thought we were all friends here."

"You rejected Leah—why should she listen to you? She was in love with you, and you hurt her badly."

Nothing could have surprised Jayce more than this declaration. "That's what this is all about? She was just a girl."

"Doesn't really matter what her age might have been," Jacob replied. "It still hurt."

"So that's why she's treating me like she is—all fire and spit?"

"What do you expect? You throw her feelings back in her face, disappear for ten years, then reappear as though nothing had ever happened."

"But ten years is a long, long time."

"Not where the heart is concerned." Jacob turned and began walking again.

Jayce followed but waited until they were at the inne to say anything more. "I never meant to hurt her, Jacob. You know that. I never lead her to believe I cared more than I did. I wanted to explore the territory and travel. I wanted to live a life of adventure."

"And that couldn't have included Leah?"

"I . . . I didn't figure she'd stay. I really didn't figure either one of you would."

"Well, you were wrong. We both love this territory. And if you would have bothered to give Leah a chance, you might have learned that for yourself. You might not have had to spend all this time alone."

"What about you? You're alone."

Jacob shook his head. "Not by choice. If I'd had a woman that loved me as much as Leah loved you, I would have married her on the spot. Anyway, just leave her be—I don't want anything to mess up our friendship, but I won't see her hurt. Besides, we'll soon be leaving, and then you won't have to concern yourself with her."

"What if I want to concern myself with her?"

Jacob eyed him warily. "What do you mean?"

"I mean . . . well, I've been thinking about Leah since I first left Ketchikan. I guess I'd like to know if we couldn't find a way to put the past behind us—if she might feel the same for me now that she felt then."

"Are you serious?"

Jayce ran his fingers through his hair. "I think about her all the time."

"Jayce, you'd better think hard before you say a word to her." He took a step closer, as if to reinforce his next statement. "I'll deal with you myself if you hurt her again."

"I promise you, I have only the best of intentions. I don't want to hurt anyone, especially Leah."

This answer seemed to satisfy Jacob, who then dismissed the conversation as though it were nothing more important than detailing the weather. "A bunch of us are going hunting tomorrow. Want to come along?"

"Ah . . . sure . . . I guess so," Jayce replied, his voice sounding distant even in his own ears.

"I'll get you up at three and we'll head out. After we get back we can work the dogs."

"Three in the morning?"

Jacob grinned as though the entire evening had been nothing but carefree. "That's why I'm going to bed now."

Jayce let Jacob go with that. He was still so surprised by the turn of the conversation—surprised, too, by the warning Jacob had given. Walking away from the settlement, Jayce tried to reason through the things his friend had said. He honestly hadn't given any credence to Leah's feelings ten years ago. He had figured her to be a love-struck child—nothing more.

His heart back then had been focused on Alaska, the land being his only focus. Leah had been fun and good to spend time with. Her quick wit and intelligence had helped to pass the time. Her love of God and strength of spirit, however, had been intimidating to the free-spirited Jayce. He hadn't yet come to understand the importance of a life lived trying to please God.

Leah had tried to help him see the truth of it, but Jayce hadn't cared for the truth. He preferred living for the moment—for himself. But things were different now. He had come to accept Christ after spending a long, lonely week in an isolated camp in Canada. Nothing had gone right in his life for months. In fact, he'd gone to Canada after a trip to New York where he'd run into several unsavory characters. Including the man he'd thought he'd seen earlier in the day.

That trip had been a waste of time and energy. He'd hoped to put some things to rest—to mend some fences and see his family's miseries put in the past once and for all. Instead, he'd nearly gotten himself arrested, and all because of . . . him.

He blew out a breath and stared across the vast, open field. The snow was patchy and melting under the intensity of the sun. Would that it could melt the ice around Leah's heart.

He looked back to the house where Leah was now departing with several of her friends. She was laughing and obviously enjoying their company. She didn't see him, and Jayce was glad to be ignored.

"I can't change the past, Leah," he whispered. "I can't right the wrongs of yesterday, but maybe I can make the tomorrows better." But then again, such a thing would require her giving him a second chance, and that might be impossible. Jayce was set to leave for a summer's worth of exploration. Not only that, but he was taking her brother too. She might not see that as an extension of the olive branch.

"There has to be a way," he declared, shoving his cold hands deep into his pockets. "There has to be a way to make this right."

Chapter Seven

Helaina stood on the deck of the *Ally Mae,* grateful to finally be heading to Nome. Her trip had met with nothing but delays: first the train travel west had been slowed by floods and other complications, then there had been problems with her ship passage. No doubt the *Homestead* was already in Nome awaiting her arrival. But would they wait long enough?

Her anxious nature was only heightened by unanswered questions like that. Her worst fears were that the *Homestead* would move north without her, and along with it her chance to catch Jayce Kincaid. She sighed and looked out at the choppy seas. The night had been unbearable with a squall blowing up to send them tossing and twisting on the water. Helaina thought she might very well be thrown from her berth. But at least here she didn't need to worry about the Germans sinking them.

The captain promised them they would dock in Nome in two days if the weather held. But so far rain and fog had complicated the journey and Helaina figured to count on arriving in Nome only after her feet were safely on the shores of that town.

"Ma'am?"

Helaina turned to find an older man of maybe sixty or so. He looked rough, rather worn from life. "Yes?" she asked in her reserved manner. She lifted her chin slightly and eyed him in an almost grave manner.

"Are you married, ma'am?"

Helaina had already suffered the proposals of a half dozen men headed to Nome. "I am a widow."

The man's face lit up. "Well, I'd like to change that for you. I'm looking for a wife."

"But I, sir, am not looking for a husband," she replied flatly.

"But I'm a good dancer—good kisser too." He grinned and leaned forward. "I could show ya."

Helaina felt sorry for the old man, but at the same time detested his forward actions. "Sir, I thank you for your offer, but I have no desire to marry again." *Or kiss a grizzled old man,* she thought but said nothing more.

She turned her attention back to the water. The old man cleared his throat as if to make further comment, then seemed to think better of it. He sauntered away without another word, for which Helaina was very grateful. She could imagine Robert laughing at the scene. She had always been what he called a "handsome woman," and had known her fair share of attention. In fact, she often used her looks to her advantage. She only hoped that Jayce Kincaid could be swayed by such a simple thing.

The boat heaved right as the waves seemed to increase in size. Once they moved away from the Aleutian Islands, the water and weather were both supposed to have calmed, but so far that hadn't proven true. She'd never traveled to this part of the world, and so far she wasn't that impressed. The cold and isolation weren't at all to her liking.

Once when she and Robert had been courting he had mentioned that he cherished time alone, left to himself in the wilds of the woods in New Hampshire. "I like the solitude, Helaina. There's something refreshing about the silence."

"Maybe for you, but that holds no appeal for me," Helaina had told her husband. "I find being alone like that to be a bore."

He had laughed and hugged her close. "Then you just haven't been alone with the right person in such settings."

The memory made her smile. Despite the grief she'd known in Robert's passing, she wouldn't have traded her marriage in order to have avoided the pain. Sharing the short time they had together was better than no time at all. She had watched other people become consumed by their grief and sorrow. They were unable to be productive—to find a usefulness in life. *Well, not me,* Helaina thought. *I won't be like them.*

A quick glance at her watch confirmed it was well past time to turn in. The lighted skies were deceptive, and Helaina wondered if she'd ever get used to the odd days and nights. Making her way to her cabin, she calculated that, if all went well, she might be able to find Jayce Kincaid and head home within the week. That would be ideal, as far as she was concerned, because already she had been gone from civilization longer than she liked. Even Seattle had paled compared to her homes in New York City and Washington, D.C. Home had always been important to her, even though she traveled many days out of the year away from their comfort. In New York there was always something to do—someone to see—and Mrs. Hayworth to fuss over her. In Washington, D.C., she had Stanley—her last link to family.

For the first time in a long time, Helaina felt homesick. There was a longing deep inside that refused to go away. The only problem was, she was pretty certain it wasn't a place that she longed for. And if not a place . . . then might it be a person?

"What a ridiculous thought. I'm not about to lose my heart—my life—to another person again. I don't want to lose another man as I lost Robert." She looked around, startled to realize she'd spoken the words aloud. No sense in people thinking her daft. Still, the aching persisted. She didn't belong here.

The truth was, she didn't belong anywhere. Maybe it *was* a place she was longing for. A place where she might belong and feel a sense of security and peace.

Two days later, with the storms behind them and calmer waters prevailing, Helaina found herself and her things deposited in Nome. It wasn't much to look at. The dirt streets were narrow, no more than twenty feet wide. Dilapidated buildings lined the thoroughfare—sad reminders of better days gone by. Why, at the turn of the century this city was in its heyday. Gold was found nearby and everyone wanted to be in Nome. Twenty thousand people had called this place home. Helaina remembered hearing stories about it from her father. He'd thought every single gold-fevered ninny to be ignorant, ill-advised, and insane.

Now looking at the sad little town, Helaina could only wonder if he hadn't been right. A strong sensation of loneliness washed over her. This was a town of defeat and desolation. It seemed appropriate that she should come here to nab Jayce Kincaid.

"Ma'am, can I carry your bag? Where are you staying?" It was the grizzled old man again. Already he was reaching to take hold of Helaina's large black bag.

"I'm not entirely sure," Helaina said, glancing up the street. She allowed the man to make himself useful.

"Well, I know a place not far from here. Just up the way. Couple of native women have rooms. There's also a couple of hotels, but they ain't much better."

"Thank you, I believe I would prefer a hotel." She had no prejudice against the natives; however, she'd learned anonymity was easier to maintain in a crowd. Surely the exploration team would also have rooms at the hotel, making it easier for her to blend in.

The man shrugged and headed toward the town. "How long will you be up here?"

Helaina tried not to be annoyed. After all, the man had been kind enough to carry her things. "I'm to join the ship *Homestead*. Are you familiar with it?"

"No, ma'am. Where's it bound?"

"North. It's an expedition to map the Arctic islands and coastline."

"Seems out of place for a woman like you, if you don't mind my saying so."

"Whether you say so or not, that's where I'm bound," Helaina replied.

The sourdough had been correct in his analysis, Helaina thought as they approached a well-worn building. The hotel wasn't much to boast about. The paint was peeling and the two-story frame seemed to sag as if tired. Still, she wouldn't have to sleep on the streets, and hopefully she'd meet up with her companions.

"Now if they don't have rooms, I'll take you on down to my friends."

"I'm certain to be fine. Thank you." Helaina reached out for her bag. The old man seemed reluctant to hand it over, but he finally let it go.

"You remember, too, my marriage proposal still holds good."

Helaina nodded. "I'll remember."

Inside the dark hotel, a heavy smell of cigar and cigarette smoke nearly choked Helaina. A foursome of men hunkered down in the corner over cards. The smoke was as intense as the expressions on their faces. They didn't even notice her.

Helaina glanced around. There was no one else in sight; even the front desk was unattended. Moving closer to the desk, however, she spied an open door to the left.

"Hello in back?" she called, presuming there might be an attendant hiding out.

A large man appeared, cigar in hand, frowned, and then glanced around the room. "You here alone?"

Helaina nodded. "I would like a room."

He approached the desk, still acting as though he didn't believe he was really seeing her. "Well, I got a nice one—best in the place. What brings you to Nome? You lookin' for some disappeared husband?"

Helaina smiled. "Hardly that. I've come here to join an expeditionary group. Perhaps you could tell me if the *Homestead* has come in?"

"Come and gone." He looked at her skeptically. "You say you were to join them?"

She felt as though she'd been punched in the stomach. "Yes. I'm to assist the map maker."

He rubbed his jaw and shook his head. "Well, they've gone on without you. Left a few days ago."

Leah gently turned the book of poems over in her hand and thought of Jayce. Why had he given her this volume? Most of the poetry within dealt with romantic notions and love. She felt confident it wasn't his intent to imply a feeling of love for her, so why had he chosen this particular book?

Jayce's continued presence troubled Leah more than she could say. Even more bothersome was that he was taking her brother away. And with their departure looming, the idea of Jacob risking his life chilled her to the bone. She knew Jacob would only tell her that life in general was a risk—that living in this harsh territory was a greater threat than most folks would ever know—but it didn't comfort her. Many men had lost their lives going north to explore the Arctic. That part of the world was unforgiving.

She put the book aside and made her way to Ayoona's inne. The old woman had invited Leah to come and help her cut up seal meat. The hunts over the past few days had been successful. Seal, walrus, and a variety of fish and birds had made themselves available, ensuring that the famine of the winter was behind them.

Leah got down to crawl through the long narrow entrance into Ayoona's traditional inne. The tunnel gave her a sense of being trapped, but Leah pushed through, peeking out as she entered the house. "Hello!" she called.

"Lay-ya, come in and help me," Ayoona called. Her daughter-in-law Oopick was working to boil some seal flippers. They jokingly called them seal's bare feet once they were cooked and ready for eating.

Leah took up an *ulu,* a popular knife with the women. Its curved blade and wooden handle made it easy to use in cutting thick flesh. Ayoona was already hard at work on the blubber.

"I thought you would be working outside today, but then I fought against the wind on my way over here. I hope it won't blow up a storm."

"It won't be bad," Ayoona promised. "But I get too old to fight the wind. Figured it not too hot to work in here."

"How's the baby doing?" Leah asked Oopick, knowing how proud she was of her first grandson.

"He grows strong," she answered, looking back over her shoulder and grinning. "He'll chew the blubber soon."

"No doubt. I saw him yesterday. He looks very strong," Leah said, trying to keep the yearning from her voice.

"You seem much too sad, Lay-ya," Ayoona said. "The days of sun are with us. We can make much work together. The hunts are good again and there is plenty of food. Why are you sad?"

Leah hesitated only a moment before the words tumbled from her lips. "It's about Jayce Kincaid."

"The man who buys your brother's dogs?"

Leah nodded. "We knew him from long ago. . . . I think I already told you that." She toyed with the ulu, forgetting the seal meat momentarily. "I thought he was the most wonderful man in the world. I gave him my heart, but he said I was just a child and that I needed to forget about him."

"But you didn't forget."

"No," Leah said softly. "I didn't forget."

"How do you feel about him now?" Oopick asked.

"I . . . I still care for him. I thought I'd buried all my feelings long ago, but now I realize I care just as much as I did then . . . if not more."

"Then you tell him this," Ayoona stated. Her weathered old face showed no sign of emotion.

"But he hurt me, and I don't wish to be hurt again."

Ayoona shook her head and went back to work. "You cannot hold the man's foolishness against him. Doesn't the Bible say so?"

"I forgave him for what he did."

"How could you and still hold it in your heart?"

Leah swallowed hard. Was Ayoona right? Had she really not forgiven Jayce? "I don't know what to say," she finally admitted. "I thought I'd forgiven him."

"You need to talk to him. See if he still rejects you."

Leah wanted to know the truth, but she didn't think she could bear another rejection from Jayce. Now that she was thirty, and life with a husband and children was becoming more unlikely, Leah felt it difficult to even broach the subject.

"If he say no to you, then you go back to your family in Ketchikan and find a husband. Bring him back here. You let this man go if he say no."

But Leah wondered if it would ever be possible to let go of Jayce Kincaid. He seemed to be imprinted in her heart, and she doubted it could ever be rubbed away and forgotten.

A cry for help sounded from outside. Someone was calling Leah's name. She jumped to her feet, nearly toppling the table. Certain it must be a medical emergency, Leah scurried down the tunnel to the door.

"I'll be back later, Ayoona," she called over her shoulder.

"Leah! Hurry. Hurry fast!" Niki, a young native boy, called. "Jacob needs you!"

Chapter Eight

Leah was directed to her brother's dog kennel. She felt a momentary sense of panic. What had happened to Jacob? Was he all right? The boy sounded very upset, and the dogs were barking and putting up such a ruckus that she feared the worst. Had a bear surprised Jacob? Was he hurt?

She rounded the corner, seeing a man lying on the ground. The man, however, wasn't her brother. It was Jayce.

"What happened?" she asked Jacob as he worked to secure one of the dogs.

"He was in the middle of a brawl. The dogs got a little crazy with each other, and Jayce foolishly tried to pull them apart. They don't know him well enough yet, and they attacked him."

Leah knelt down and looked quickly at the nasty wound on Jayce's right leg. The blood loss was significant. "Give me your belt, Jacob."

He left the now tied-up dog and quickly came to where his sister worked. He handed her the belt without comment.

"Lift his leg for me," she ordered.

Jayce cried out in pain, his face contorting. Leah quickly slipped the belt up under his thigh and cinched it tightly. "Jacob, make a notch for me to secure the belt."

Jacob worked well at her side, for he had helped her on many occasions. With the belt secured, Leah ordered Niki to run to Ayoona for bandages. She needed to get the bleeding stopped and assess the situation quickly. Leah glanced up to find Jayce watching her. His upper lip was beaded in sweat, even though the temperatures were not that warm.

She assessed his color, noting he was pale. "Try to relax. I know it pains you, but if you fight against it—get your heart rate up—it will cause you to bleed more."

"I feel light-headed," he said in a mumble. "Cold too."

"Jacob, he's going into shock. We need to get his head lower than his heart."

Jacob rushed inside a small shed and came out with an old worn cot. Quickly he positioned it at an angle with the legs at one end collapsed.

"You see to his leg," Jacob told Leah. "I'll take care of the rest."

He lifted Jayce easily, ignoring the man's moans of pain. Leah held fast to Jayce's wounded leg. The movement caused more bleeding, which she knew was bad. Just as they positioned Jayce on the slanted cot, Niki reappeared with Oopick. She carried hot water, while Niki had the bandages. More natives followed after them, eager to know the situation.

Leah and Oopick worked to clean the leg. It was imperative to find if the artery was cut. Assessing the wound, Leah felt confident that, while the lacerations were deep and ragged, the artery was intact. This was very good for Jayce. It would mean the difference between life and death.

Leah's heartbeat pounded in her ears. *He still might die. He might die if you don't do the right things to save him*. Her hands shook fiercely as she wiped bits of cloth away from the skin. Oopick rinsed the wound as Leah directed.

"Let's pack the wound and get him back to the house," she told Jacob. "He'll rest better there."

Jacob called to several men while Leah did her best to secure Jayce's leg with bandages. When she'd completed her task, she stood back. "I'll go ahead and get things ready. Oopick, you come with me."

The native woman was at her side in a moment. They made their way to the inne as Jacob instructed the men to take their places around the cot. Leah left Oopick to hold open the door while she went into their stormy day cookroom. Leah felt this would be the best place to work on Jayce. They wouldn't need it for cooking, and the days were warming up nicely. She stoked the fire in the stove, even as she heard the men making their way down the stairs.

"Just put him in the corner," she instructed the men. "Leave him on the cot."

She could see his color was still bad, and Leah fought to stave off the emotion that was threatening to spill into her voice. "Jayce, you need to lie still. I want to examine the wound and see about stitching it up."

"I'll lie still. I promise," he whispered.

"I'm going to have Oopick put together some herbs. They'll help you relax—maybe sleep. We can also make a salve that will ease the pain."

Jayce barely nodded. Leah was afraid he might lose consciousness, then wondered if it wouldn't be easier for him. At least that way he wouldn't have to endure every poke and prod of her examination.

Jacob leaned in close. "How's he doing? It's pretty bad, isn't it?"

"It's bad enough . . . but not as tragic as it could have been," Leah added, seeing Jayce frown. "I think the artery is fine. If it had been severed, I couldn't have saved him. I'm not sure how much I can really help him as it is. This is a massive wound, and it really needs a surgeon's touch."

"The closest surgeon is going to be in Nome," Jacob offered. "The hospital's good, but I know a doctor who keeps a small infirmary. He's the same man who fixed me up when I was sick with the measles. He could help us, and Jayce could get more personalized attention."

"That's a good idea. I'm thinking we should stabilize him—get the bleeding stopped—then get him to Nome as soon as possible."

Jacob rubbed his stubbled chin. "Most of the snow is gone or melting at least. It won't be good for the dogs. We'd better go by umiak."

"The waters have been so rough lately and the wind is blowing something up," Leah murmured, thinking of the boats made of skins. "Still, I don't see that we have too many other choices."

"I'll get some of the men to come with us, and we can get more supplies. Anamiaq and his family are back, and they have a great many furs to trade, as well as a long list of desired supplies. We'll see what the weather is going to do and then set out. We can stay close to the coast."

"That would probably be a good idea," Leah murmured, hating to see her brother go away again but also fearing what Jayce's fate would be. She felt overwhelmed by the myriad of emotions within her but knew she was his only chance. If she didn't remain calm, she'd be no good to him at all.

"I want you to come too," Jacob said.

Leah eased the tourniquet pressure enough to see how bad the bleeding might be. Jayce moaned and closed his eyes. The wound only oozed and Leah sighed in relief. Hopefully the bleeding would stop completely.

"Did you hear me?" Jacob asked.

Leah eased away from Jayce. "Oopick, please make a paste with the stinkweed. I have some in the cupboard." The older woman nodded and went to work immediately. Meanwhile Leah motioned Jacob to follow her outside.

"What's wrong?" Jacob asked.

"I'll come with you, but you have to know this situation is grave. The bleeding may start up again. I hate to sew on him and risk the possibility of messing it up. The worst of it will be the bleeding and possibility of infection. Animal wounds are always bad."

"Do what you can for him. I'll have everything ready to go within the hour," Jacob said, then reached out to gently touch Leah's arm. "Look, I know this is hard on you. I know you care about what happens to him."

Leah drew a deep breath and met her brother's compassionate gaze. "I do care, and that's why this is so difficult. I . . . well . . . I feel guilty. I thought I wanted Jayce to know the kind of pain he'd caused me, yet at the same time I wouldn't have wanted him or anyone else to know that kind of hurt. Now he's wounded . . . maybe dying . . ."

"This isn't your fault, Leah. You didn't will it to happen, if that's what you think."

"I know," she said, still trying to convince her heart. "I know I didn't cause it, but I haven't been very nice to him. I could have been a better person—a better Christian."

"Then be one," Jacob said, smiling. "We all make mistakes, take the wrong path—but it's more important that we get turned around and go the right way once we discover the truth."

She nodded. "I'll get my things packed. You see to Jayce's things. He may need to ship back to the States after this. I can't imagine him being able to continue with the expedition."

"No, I can't either." Jacob's voice sounded distant. "But I wonder if I should go ahead. They'll still need dogs and a handler."

"I wish you would reconsider. I'm not excited for you to go under any circumstances, but at least Jayce was familiar with such trips."

Jacob dropped his hold. "You think I'm incapable?"

"No, it's not that. But I hate to see you head out there on your own, not knowing anyone. You aren't familiar with the territory, and at least if Jayce were on the team, you'd have a friend."

"I can always make new friends, Leah. Look, I know you worry about me, but honestly, we have to go our separate ways at times. You aren't my mother or my wife—you're my sister. You have a life to live as well." Silence surrounded them for a moment. "I'd better go get things ready or we might as well not go."

Leah let him leave, knowing he was irritated with her. She vowed to herself that she'd not bring up the matter again, but in her heart she knew it would be a difficult promise to keep.

Jacob was relieved to know that John and Kimik were both willing to put boats together and follow him to Nome. It was always better to travel in groups.

"I'll hunt while we travel," John said. He helped Jacob load the last of the furs on a wheeled sled for hauling to the water. "We might get lucky and find more walrus—even a beluga."

"I'm grateful, John. I don't know how long we'll be in Nome. We'll see what the doctor says, and if we need to stay there, you and Kimik can head back after we get the supplies loaded."

Reaching the shore, Jacob looked out across the sea. To his surprise a large ship sat in the harbor. It wasn't one of the usual ships that came north with mail or passengers. Squinting to catch the name on the stern, Jacob realized it was the *Homestead*—Jayce's ship. Already a small launch was headed their way with half a dozen men on board.

Jacob wondered what the captain would say when he heard the news about Jayce. Surely this would cause problems for the team. The dogs were imperative to the project, and the sleds he and Jayce built were desperately needed for travel over the Arctic snows and ice.

Working to pack the furs—some in John's boat and others in his own, Jacob figured to wait for the men to come ashore. He would have to bear the bad news to the captain, then perhaps escort the man to his home so that he could talk with Jayce. If Jayce was still conscious.

"Hello, *Homestead*," Jacob said, leaving his umiak as the men approached.

"Greetings. I see you're heading out. I might warn you there's some rough water out there," a stocky, bearded man announced. He came forward and extended his hand. "I'm Captain Latimore."

"Jacob Barringer." They shared a firm shake before the captain turned to the two nearest men. "This is Cliff Cleary and Andrew Johnsson, two of my men."

Jacob shook hands, while the remaining *Homestead* party secured the launch. "I'm good friends with Jayce Kincaid. He asked me to join your expedition as dog handler."

"Splendid," the captain replied.

"Well, not quite so splendid. There's been an accident, and Jayce is badly hurt. We are just preparing to get him to Nome."

"What kind of accident?" Latimore asked.

"Dogs. I'm afraid they were riled by the scent of something and started fighting. Jayce stepped in, and because they aren't yet that familiar with him, it didn't end well. I'm afraid he'll need to see a surgeon for his leg. I'm doubtful that he'll be able to continue with you this year."

"Now that is a pity. Johnsson here is one of two geologists I was to have on the trip. Kincaid was the other."

"I am sorry. Perhaps you would like to see Jayce for yourself."

Latimore nodded. "Perhaps afterwards you can show me your dogs. We'll still need a couple of teams in order to accomplish all that we have planned."

"I'd be glad to," Jacob said, nodding at the man.

"You other men, stay here. We'll be back shortly."

The team nodded in agreement at this arrangement, taking more interest in Jacob's umiak. "Do you have any more of these skin boats? We'd like very much to purchase at least one more," Cleary called.

Jacob shook his head. "Most of the men are using them to hunt. Winter comes around fast up here and there was a famine last season. We need to lay in a better supply of meat, so I have my doubts anyone will be trading their boats, even at inflated prices."

"Which our expedition cannot afford," Latimore called out as they walked away.

They made their way to the house, where Leah greeted Jacob. "Are we ready?"

"Very nearly. But first, this is Captain Latimore. He's heading up the expedition that Jayce was to have been a part of."

"I see. Jayce is just in here," she said, holding back the fur that covered the stormy day kitchen. "He's quite groggy from the medicine we've given him. He needs to remain calm or the bleeding will start up again."

"Thank you, I quite understand and will give him no cause for alarm." The captain moved past Jacob and slipped into the room.

"Were you expecting him today?" Leah asked.

"No, we weren't exactly sure when he would come. I told him the situation but thought he might want to have a few words with Jayce. How is he?"

"Actually, he looks much better. The shock is wearing off and he's taken some broth Oopick made him. It has some healing properties and will help with the pain. It will also help him to feel relaxed for the trip."

"I'm glad he's doing better. That's an awful wound."

Leah glanced at the fur covering and lowered her voice. "I'm still not sure he won't lose the leg. I'm really very frightened for him."

Jacob frowned. "We will do what we can, Leah. The rest is in God's hands."

"I know, but I can't help but wish I could do more for him."

"You're doing more than most of us even know how. Your nursing abilities have benefited so many here, you just need to have confidence that you'll know what to do—and if you don't, that God will show you."

Jacob felt sorry for his sister, knowing how personally involved she got—and with Jayce involved, it was bound to be ten times worse. "He has the best of care in you," Jacob added, putting his hand on Leah's shoulder. "I know he'd say the same."

Just then the captain came from the room. "He's looking much better than I expected. Very groggy, but the pain seems minimal. He seems to think if he can get proper medical attention, he might be up to joining us in another week or two. I've told him that we'll be in Kotzebue after we leave here. Maybe as long as two weeks. We weren't able to get the native help we wanted in Nome, but one of the men we picked up has relations in Kotzebue, although he calls it Qikiqtagruk." Jacob nodded, recognizing the native name for the town. The captain continued. "He believes he can get us some additional men. Say, you don't have any natives here who would like to come north—maybe help you handle those dogs?"

"I don't know of any, but you could certainly ask around. However, I need to tell you also that I cannot join you at this time. You may purchase the dogs, but I need to help get Jayce to Nome." He looked to Leah and saw her nod of approval.

The captain frowned. "My men won't be knowledgeable with the dogs. We must have them and the sleds, however. Are you certain you can't join us?"

"I have no idea what kind of medical needs Jayce might have. I have to stay in Nome long enough to see him through. Then if he needs to go south to Seattle, one of us may have to go part or all of the way with him." Leah looked rather surprised by this announcement, but it was something Jacob had already considered as a possibility. If they couldn't help Jayce in Nome, he wouldn't just leave him there to die.

"Is there someone who could train my men in your absence?"

Jacob thought about it for a moment. Most of the natives were skeptical of dealing with the whites. "There is a man here in the village who works with me. I'll see if he can help you. If you come with me, we can discuss the payment and the dogs." He looked to Leah and added, "I'll go talk to Anamiaq and send John to help you get Jayce loaded."

"All right."

"Thank you, Mr. Barringer," the captain announced. "This expedition cannot function without the dogs. It is my hope that we can find someone to assist us even yet."

"Most of the natives here are reliable men who know the importance of providing for their family. They won't be easily tempted to venture into the unknown lands with strangers, but you are welcome to try."

Leah directed John and the other men as to how to carry Jayce. They were exceedingly careful to follow her instruction. Most of the men were very respectful, almost in awe of Leah. One of the group had even asked for her hand in marriage, although for the most part the natives married their own people. They were fiercely proud of their lineage and saw no good purpose in tainting the line with what they considered a weaker blood. The man in question had been quite desperate, however, finding himself the father of twins after the death of his wife. Leah had rejected his proposal of marriage, but had agreed to work with the other women in the village to see the babies cared for. One of the twins died despite their best efforts. It had been a bittersweet victory to see the other thrive and grow to be a sweet young boy.

Jayce fought to stay awake, but Leah had given him a heavy dose of stinkweed. She'd boiled the leaves to make a strong concoction that would help with the pain and keep Jayce sedated. Nevertheless, he seemed almost restless to speak—to say something to her. He kept trying to speak the entire time the men were carrying him to the water.

"Leah."

"You need to rest, Jayce. Just be quiet now."

"Leah, I need . . . to . . . need to tell you . . . something."

"It can wait until you're feeling better." Leah put her bag on the rocky shore and moved to the umiak to direct the placement of her patient. "Put him there on the blanket. Yes, that's good," she said as they positioned him perfectly.

Once Jayce was secured in the boat, Leah packed blankets and a down-filled bag around him. She made sure that everything could easily break free in case of capsizing.

As the men walked away, Jayce reached out and took hold of Leah's hand. "I'm sorry, Leah."

"You couldn't help it," she reassured. "Accidents happen, and the dogs are bad about getting excited."

"No," he said, shaking his head slowly from side to side. "Sorry for the past." He closed his eyes. "I didn't know . . ."

She waited for a moment. "Didn't know what?" She wanted very much to hear what he might say, while at the same time she knew he needed rest.

"Didn't know that I hurt you that bad. Didn't know you really loved me."

She bristled but fought to keep her voice calm. "Had I ever given you reason to doubt my word? Why should you have thought my words less than true?"

Jayce opened his eyes. "I . . . I . . . thought you were too young. Didn't think you knew your . . . mind. I thought . . ." His words trailed off.

The old anger stirred, but she forced it down. "I don't imagine you thought much at all about any of it." She tried to leave, but he held her fast.

"Forgive me, Leah. Please."

She looked at him for a moment, his eyes pleading. She bit her lip and pulled her hand away from him. "I do forgive you, Jayce. I already forgave you long ago." She got up and walked away before he could see the tears that came to her eyes.

"I just can't seem to forget you," she whispered against the Arctic wind.

Chapter Nine

They'd ridden the swells of the Bering Sea less than an hour when heavy clouds formed on the horizon. Leah knew the look of danger. Around these parts bad weather blew up quickly and often lasted for days. And if not storms, then heavy fog could also blind their way. It wasn't a good time to be on the open water.

"We'll have to make for shore," Jacob told her. "I wish we could make it to one of the villages, but I doubt we'll have time. I'll send John ahead to make the best choice."

Leah knew Jacob was right. "I'm sure it will pass quickly," she said in encouragement. Glancing at Jayce, she saw that he slept, despite the situation.

"John!" Jacob called across the water. "Find us a place to make camp. We'll wait out whatever is blowing in."

"Sure. I can do that." The native pushed his men into action.

Leah was amazed at how quickly the umiak pulled away from Jacob and Kimik's boats. John and his men were quite strong, definitely used to battling the sea. In their boat, Jacob had the help of four other men. Leah was grateful for this, because she knew she would never be strong enough to fight the rough water. The men were good friends, but Leah knew they would head quickly back to their village as soon as things were arranged in Nome. As much as they admired and respected Jacob, their own families came first, and this was no time to be slack in hunting and laying up food.

Before long, John directed them to shore. There wasn't a lot in the way of shelter, but Leah knew her brother and the other men would find ways to wait out the storm and keep dry.

"Stay with Jayce," her brother told her as the men pulled the wounded man from their boat. "We'll put together a safe place for you both." He left the two dogs he'd brought to stand guard.

Leah reached out to pet the two animals she'd helped to raise. Leo and Addy were strong Huskies who took the northern furies in stride. "You're good dogs," she said, stroking the silky fur. The animals seemed to thrive on her attention.

Jayce moaned as he tried to get up. "Are we in Nome?"

Leah left the dogs and knelt down beside her patient. "No, there's a storm blowing up. We'll have to wait it out."

"I'm sorry, Leah," he whispered, still struggling to try to sit up.

"Stay still. I need to look at your leg," she said, desperate for something to do other than converse with this man.

Jayce fell back against the blanket. "Don't let 'im find me."

The statement confused Leah. "Don't let who find you?"

Jayce shook his head. "Can't find me."

The medicine was obviously making it hard for him to think clearly. Leah knew Oopick's stinkweed solution would further the man's confusion, but Jayce needed to rest as much as possible to keep from moving his leg. Leah opened the jar and poured a small portion for Jayce. She thought about the delay with the incoming storm and prayed it would be enough to keep Jayce from misery.

"Jayce, you need to drink this," she said, putting her arm under his neck.

He opened his eyes for only a moment and then closed them again. Leah managed to get the medicine down him—at least most of it. She lowered him back to the ground. She wasn't used to this vibrant, strong, and self-sufficient man being so weak.

She pushed back a bit of Jayce's brown hair. It had a coarse, wild texture to it, but she liked it very much. How often she had wanted nothing more than to run her fingers through the thick mass. She realized she was stroking his head and pulled away.

Don't let yourself be vulnerable. Don't care too much. The internal warning seemed to fall on deaf ears—or at least a deaf heart. The Bible spoke of the eyes of the heart—did the heart also have ears? If so, Leah knew hers weren't listening.

Leah peeled back the bandages and studied the wound. It seemed about the same. An oozing of blood continued to wet the bandages, but Leah knew this was better than keeping a tight tourniquet on the leg. She had been told by a doctor once that such restriction of the blood flow could actually cause the limb to die.

Please, God, she prayed, *help me do the right thing—don't let him die or lose his leg because of my ignorance.*

"How . . . is it?" Jayce murmured.

Leah was surprised to hear him sound so coherent. "Looks like you've been chewed on by a grizzly," she said, trying to sound lighthearted. "I'm sure you'll have quite a scar."

"One more to . . . go . . . with the others," he said, then seemed to drop off to sleep.

Leah rewrapped the leg and pulled a blanket over Jayce. She glanced up behind them and saw that farther inland the men were making good headway in a small cluster of bushy willows. They had taken the umiaks and positioned them in such a way that, when bound together with rope and tarps, they made a shelter. Jacob had tightly bundled the furs and wrapped them in a protective covering of oiled duck canvas. They would make a soft bed for Jayce, Leah thought.

The men came back to shore and motioned Leah away. They picked up the four corners of the blanket on which Jayce slept and carried him to the shelter. Leah followed, bringing her bag of herbs and medicine. Leo and Addy trotted behind her as if tethered. Kimik was the last to join them, bringing their food supply with him. It was a danger to have it inside their camp, but there were no tall trees in which to hang the bag and no time to build a cache. They would simply have to take their chances.

"Maybe a bear will come out in the storm and smell our food," John said, laughing. "He will say, 'Let me come for dinner.' We will let him come—then shoot him. Then we will eat Mr. Bear." They all laughed at this.

One of the other men got a fire going, and only then did Leah see that they had laid in a generous supply of dry driftwood for their fuel. She felt warm and secure—safe with these men and her brother. The only real worry was whether or not Jayce could withstand the delay.

"I'll make supper," John announced. He unwrapped a pack and pulled out dried seal meat. "There. Supper is ready." The men chuckled again. John always kept everyone in a good mood, and even Jacob couldn't help but join in.

"I'll do the dishes afterward," he said with a quick wink at Leah.

"You are a good man," John said, slapping Jacob on the back.

The storm increased in intensity with a fierce wind that threatened to tear down their little shelter. Kimik sang for them, telling Leah he could make much better noise than the wind. She felt a small amount of comfort in the good nature of her companions. Leo and Addy curled up beside her as if offering her their warmth. Leah gave them each a few affirming strokes before settling down beside them. Before long Leah's eyelids grew heavy, and she no longer heard the wind but rather was mesmerized by her own rhythmic breathing.

In her dreams, Leah was a young woman again. She was taken back in time to Ketchikan and her home in the woods with Karen and Adrik. She had been happy there with Jacob and the rest of her family. Karen had given her husband three beautiful children: Ashlie, a lovely girl who looked a lot like her mother; Oliver, who definitely took after his father; and Christopher, who seemed a happy blend of both.

Leah loved these children as if they were her siblings. She missed them all so much. Ashlie was now fifteen, nearly a grown woman. She'd been almost five when Leah had left home to help Jacob, and though she'd seen the family several times over the long years, it wasn't the same. Little Christopher hadn't even been born when Leah had left Ketchikan, but Oliver had been a comfort to her. When Jayce had rejected her, Leah had spent a lot time helping care for Oliver. Karen seemed to understand.

"He loves you unconditionally. Babies are like that—men are not," Karen had told Leah. She told her this again now, in her dream.

Leah sat at Karen's table and sighed. "It isn't fair that I should love someone so much only to have him reject me. What's wrong with me? Why am I not good enough for him to love in return?"

"I doubt it has anything to do with you," Karen had told her quite seriously. "Jayce obviously has other things on his mind."

"But I want him to have me on his mind," Leah had protested.

She heard the baby cry and started to get up from the table. It was strange, but her legs wouldn't work. Karen only smiled and then faded from view, while the baby continued to cry.

When Leah awoke with a start, she realized it wasn't a baby crying at all, but a combination of the wind and Jayce. She sat up and reached out to touch Jayce's forehead. He was feverish. Leah's chest tightened. The wound was infected—there could be no other explanation.

The heavy overcast skies stole the sun's light, but the small fire allowed her just enough light to see the contents of her bag. Oopick had thoughtfully planned for such a problem. There was willow bark and several other herbal remedies that Leah could use in case of emergency. She pulled a tin cup from the bag and poured water into it before setting it in the coals at the side of the fire. She carefully portioned out some of the willow bark into the water to make a strong tea to fight the fever.

"What's wrong?" Jacob asked, yawning as he sat up.

"He's feverish. I think the wound is infected."

"Can you help him?"

Leah felt her hands shake as she tried to stir the water. "I hope so."

Helaina wondered for several days what she should do regarding her situation. No one in Nome knew anything about the *Homestead* except that it had been in harbor, then had left again.

Nothing made sense or offered her insight—no matter how she analyzed the situation. She tried talking to the chief of police, but he had no solution for her. She had posed the possibility of some natives taking her by boat to catch up with the *Homestead*. The man had only laughed at her and told her how ridiculous her proposal truly was, given the fact that the ship could be all the way past the Arctic Circle by now.

Helaina had finally come to the conclusion that perhaps her only hope was to return home and try another time. Maybe she and the Pinkertons could plan ahead and be ready for *Homestead*'s return to Seattle.

Sleep was hard to come by. Her mind was constantly battling to find a better answer to her problems, while the daylight followed them well into what should have been darkness, and totally ruined her routine cycle of day and night. It seemed this foreign and very strange land would offer her no ease.

She had made one friend. When fierce headaches would not leave her, Helaina made her way to a doctor. Dr. Cox seemed happy to meet a woman of social quality and knowledge. He had treated her headaches for free on the condition she share dinner with him that night. It was the first of many dinners, all of which Helaina had enjoyed. The isolation and boredom would have otherwise proved unbearable. At least Cox offered her lively stories and sometimes important bits of information. Tonight's date proved to be no different.

"There was a tidal storm here two years ago. Most of the damage was to the east of us. It fairly destroyed villages along the coast, both east and west."

"How awful. Were many lives lost?"

"Oh yes. It could have been much worse, however. The natives seemed to realize the dangers in some areas. They moved inland and then went to high ground. Of course, the promise of gold in this land has caused white men to come and settle. But they generally are incapable of dealing with the problems and complications of life in the North."

"Did you come for the gold, Doctor?"

He laughed. "In a sense. I knew there would be a need for a doctor, so I came to offer my services. Which I've done. I haven't regretted my choice, but I am thinking of returning south—to my home state of Colorado."

"I'm sure you'll be needed wherever you go," Helaina offered.

"I'm still surprised that you should want to travel into the vast unknown," Dr. Cox said, pouring himself a large glass of port. "Are you certain you won't have any?"

Helaina shook her head. She knew she needed to keep her wits about her at all times. "Thank you, no. As for the travel, what can I say? I have a streak of adventure in me. My husband always told me I was much too wild to tame." It was true, Helaina thought. Although not in the sense of travel, but rather in her craving of big-city life. There was to be no bucolic farms for this woman.

"It has been good to share your company. My own dear wife of twenty years died only last year. But of course I told you that already."

Helaina nodded. The man was twice her age, but she knew he eyed her with matrimonial contemplation. "It is hard to lose those we love, but I find that putting my attention on the life around me has helped me to overcome such loss."

"To be certain, but one cannot discount the possibility of remarriage."

Helaina toyed with her food. "Well, for myself, I do just that. I have no desire to remarry."

"But you are a young woman—only twenty-six. Even the Bible speaks that young widows should remarry."

Helaina bristled at this comment. People always used Bible references as the definitive beginning and end to any solution. "I care not what the Bible says, Dr. Cox. I have not given myself over to worldly religion and spiritualism."

"Nor should you. The Christian faith is neither one."

"I don't particularly care to move forward with this topic of conversation. I have made up my mind that I have little choice left but to return to Seattle and start anew with my endeavors to go north."

"I wish you would stay. At least until I could accompany you south. Your company over supper has given me something to look forward to," the doctor protested.

Helaina shook her head. "I will go tomorrow and book passage on the next ship. I have wasted entirely too much time."

"I'm sorry you consider it a waste," the older man said, looking genuinely hurt.

Helaina had no desire to devastate the poor man. "Doctor, I do not consider our shared meals to be wasted effort or time. I do appreciate the companionship you've offered and am sorry that I cannot remain and share a friendship with you."

"I would like you to consider sharing more than friendship—"

Helaina put her hand up to silence him. "I know what you would have me consider, but I cannot. Please understand; it isn't that you wouldn't make any woman a fine husband, but I will not remarry. I have no heart for it."

"Love would come in time—don't you think?"

Helaina remembered a shadowy vision of her husband lying dead in a pool of blood. She'd not actually seen the scene except in blurry photographs, but many times she had imagined it in detail. "No. Because I would not allow it to. I'm sorry." She got up from the table, most of the food still on her plate. "If you'll excuse me, I must retire."

Helaina sat in her hotel room for hours after that. She thought of the strange land outside her windows. A harsh, unsympathetic land where the men were so very lonely. People here often had both a deep loneliness and an eternal desire for the land around them. It seemed a curse and a blessing.

"I could never love this land—this harsh land of extremes." Conversation with the doctor told her of long winters with darkness. The silence and isolation drove many people insane. She would not be one of them.

Getting up, she made her way to the window and pulled the heavy drapes into place. There were two sets—both designed to block out the summer light. This world seemed so foreign. She honestly wondered how anyone could stand living here for more than a few weeks at a time. Perhaps it was good that she'd missed catching up with Jayce Kincaid.

She was about to change her clothes and retire when a knock sounded at her door. Apprehensive, she went to the nightstand by the bed and pulled out her derringer. "Who is it?"

"Dr. Cox," the man called out.

She frowned. What did he want with her? Had he thought to come here hoping to change her mind regarding marriage?

"What do you want?" she asked, still refusing to open the door.

"I . . . well, that is . . . after you left, a thought came to me. A way to get you to your ship."

Helaina tucked the gun in her pocket and opened the door. Dr. Cox stood there, hat in hand. "What are you talking about?"

"There's a ship that heads north regularly to deliver the mail. It should be making its way in the next couple of days. At least that's the schedule it's supposed to follow. I checked it out."

"Go on." Helaina wasn't entirely sure this would be her answer, but she had no other leads.

"I thought you might catch a ride with them. They could take you along as they make their rounds. You might catch up to your ship and be able to join them."

Helaina considered his proposal for a moment. "It might work."

"There's something else. I heard from someone this evening that the *Homestead* planned to stop for a time in Kotzebue. One of the natives from Nome hopes to enlist the help of his relatives and get them to join the expedition to help with hauling and such things. The mail ship will go to Kotzebue."

This time Helaina smiled. "Dr. Cox, you have given me renewed hope. Thank you for your kindness."

"Perhaps while you are north, you will rethink your position on marriage," he said, his expression hopeful.

Helaina didn't want to encourage the man falsely, but neither did she want to further his pain. "Obviously this is a land of possibilities. One can never tell what Alaska might convince me to reconsider."

He grinned and bobbed his head up and down at least ten times. "Exactly. One can never tell. Why, just look at this town. One day there was nothing here but a small village—then gold was discovered and the place swelled with people and things. It's like that in Alaska. One minute things seem hopeless and without any chance of working, the next they are teeming with possibilities."

"I can see that you are right, Doctor. Tomorrow I shall go in search of information on catching passage on the mail ship."

He looked at the floor. "Well, good night, then."

"Good night, and thank you." She closed the door quickly, unwilling to give him a chance to speak another word.

Leaning back, she sighed. This was better than she could have hoped for. A ride north and the *Homestead*'s delay in Kotzebue just might be her salvation.

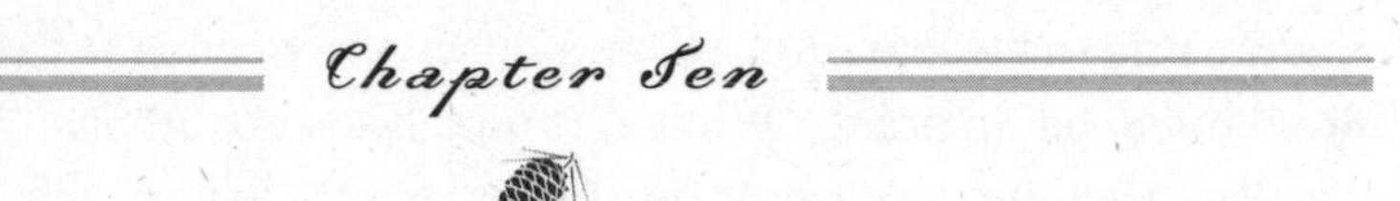

Chapter Ten

The storm eventually passed, but a thick fog persisted, keeping the party land bound. It would be much too dangerous to try to navigate the waters in such conditions, but their supplies were running low and Jayce was growing progressively worse. The leg was swelling and had turned red around the wound. Leah feared blood poisoning or worse, knowing gangrene was a threat in an injury like this. Leah knew it would cost Jayce his leg if the infection went unchecked.

During this time, the men often trekked out into the fog to hunt, leaving Leah alone with Jayce. There was nothing anyone could do for him, so it seemed foolish that everyone should sit idle while the camp grew hungry. Leah found that as she sat beside him, the memories poured in.

In Ketchikan, Jayce had been boyish in charm and nature. He had once climbed a spruce just to impress Leah with his ability. She remembered them sitting together talking about the vegetation and nature of this area of Alaska. It was such a contrast to many other areas.

"The Yukon was beautiful," Leah had told Jayce, "but not this lush and green."

"It's all the rain. This area gets so much more moisture through the year. You would think the snow levels would make up for it elsewhere, but it doesn't. It has to snow a great deal, inches and inches, to even equal a single inch of rain."

Leah enjoyed having him tell of places in the interior. "Some people think Alaska Territory, and all they can imagine is snow and ice. But I've seen places where the natives grow vegetables larger than any I've seen in the States. I've spent winters in parts of the territory that were far milder than those I experienced in New York. It's amazing how we convince ourselves that things should be a certain way—when in fact we have nothing on which to base our assumptions."

Like now, Leah thought as she touched Jayce's forehead. *I know in my heart how things should be, but they are not that way at all.*

Jayce's fever raged on, and Leah knew without looking at the wound again that it was festering. She had thought about poking around to dig into the wound for any debris they had missed, but she couldn't bear the thought of causing Jayce more pain. Especially when it might not be that at all. It could just be a poisoning effect on his system from the saliva of the dogs. So as she prayed, Leah made a poultice using the herbs she'd brought along. She could only hope that it would make a difference and draw out the infection.

As the weather settled on the third day and the heavy clouds moved off to the east, Leah happily relished the sun's warmth and light. Jacob studied the seas with less enthusiasm. "The water is still very rough. It won't be easy going, but I don't know what else we can do. Jayce is getting worse," he told John and the others.

"The water isn't that bad," John said. "We need to get him to Nome, so we go."

"It's the right thing to do," Kimik agreed with his father. "If we stay, your friend might die."

Jacob looked to Leah. She felt he needed her approval somehow. "I'm not afraid of rough waters. Jayce needs a doctor and medicine that I do not have."

"Then we'll go," Jacob said, his gaze back on the waters. "But it won't be easy."

"We will pray," John said, coming to put his hand on Jacob's shoulder. "You always say, prayer changes bad times."

Jacob chuckled. "I always say it when it's someone else's bad time. Of course you're right. We need to pray and trust God to bring us safely to Nome."

Although the trip was arduous, they reached Nome without further difficulty. John called it answered prayer, and Jacob and Leah agreed. It seemed that God had created a corridor of protection just for them. He hadn't exactly calmed the seas, but He'd given strength to the men that they might overcome their obstacles.

Leah was relieved to finally have Jayce in the hands of a good doctor—at least she hoped Dr. Cox was a skilled man. She waited impatiently in the front room of the doctor's establishment and paced back and forth several times, often putting her ear to the door of the doctor's examination room.

"I'm sure he'll come talk to us when he knows something definite," Jacob told his sister. "He took great care of me."

She looked to where he sat slouched in his chair, arms crossed and looking for all the world as if he might doze off at any moment. How could he be so relaxed?

"I'm worried that I missed something," she said, looking back to the door. Already it had been an hour. What was taking so long?

"Are you still in love with him?"

The question took her by surprise. Leah thought to quickly dismiss her brother's words, then shrugged. "I care about him. I have to admit that much. I cannot say that it's love." But even as she spoke she knew it was a lie. "All right, maybe I can say it's love. But I don't want it to be."

Jacob narrowed his gaze. It reminded Leah of when he'd assess prey before shooting on a hunt. It made her feel uncomfortable. "Why don't you want it to be love?"

How could her brother be so dense? "Because he doesn't love me in return. I've loved him for over ten years. Ten years when I found it impossible to think of anyone else. Ten years of longing for the one thing I could never have."

"But what if that's changed? Seems to me Jayce was far more worried about whether you would love Alaska as he did and stay in the North. When I talked to him—"

"You talked to him? When?" she demanded.

Just then the door opened, and Dr. Cox's short Eskimo nurse emerged. "You can go in."

Leah forgot her question and rushed past the woman. The doctor stood over an unconscious Jayce, listening to his heart. "How is he?" Leah asked quietly.

The doctor stepped back and pulled the stethoscope from his ears. "I think he'll rest easier now. The leg . . . well . . . only time will tell. It's infected, but there was a broken dog tooth imbedded deep. I'm thinking it might be the cause of all of this."

Jacob came in at this point. The doctor looked to him first and then to Leah. "Any chance those dogs were rabid?"

"No sir," Jacob said, shaking his head. "No signs of that at all. They were just riled up and didn't know Jayce well enough. He tried to separate them and got himself chewed up."

"Well, I've done what I can. The next few days should tell us a great deal. You did a remarkable job of caring for him," he said, turning to Leah. "Did you train in nursing?"

"Not exactly. I have trained with some missionaries, and when I lived in Ketchikan there was a doctor who let me read some of his medical books. And, of course, the natives have taught me a great deal."

"I see. Well, you probably saved his life. Especially with the onset of the fever. The native willow bark tea is excellent, but I also have some medicine here from the States. I will use it to see which helps him more."

"When will you know if the leg is saved?" Leah asked hesitantly.

"Should see definite signs of healing in the next forty-eight hours. I'd suggest you get a room and get some rest."

Leah nodded, but it was Jacob who spoke. "Keep track of what I owe you. If it's more than this, let me know." He handed the doctor several bills.

"We will settle up when your friend is recovered," the doctor said, taking the money. "I'll put this on his account. Say, how are you feeling these days? Fully recovered from the measles?"

Jacob nodded. "Fit as a man can be. The light bothered my eyes for a time, but I did as you suggested and wore the dark glasses. It helped a great deal."

"Good. Glad to hear it. Our epidemic was short-lived. So many have already had measles and some of the other diseases, but you always deal with those who haven't. Especially the children."

"Will you be with him tonight? I could stay," Leah interrupted, concerned that Jayce should not be alone.

"No, my nurse, Mary, will come and be with him. I've sent her home to let her family know she'll be here through the night. She'll be back shortly. If anything happens, she'll know what to do. I live in the rooms just in back, so she can wake me easily if Mr. Kincaid should have difficulty."

"May I sit with him for a while—just until she gets back?"

The doctor smiled. "Of course you may."

"I'll go over to the hotel and see if there are any rooms," Jacob suggested. "I'll come back for you in a short time."

"Thank you, Jacob." She met his gaze and knew he understood her heart.

Jacob walked the short distance to the hotel. The temperatures were warming up nicely, and he no longer felt the chill he'd known on his journey from the village. He glanced to the skies before entering the Gold Nugget, and as a result walked soundly into another person.

"Why don't you watch where you're going instead of gawking elsewhere?"

He looked at the refined woman and shook his head. "Excuse me, ma'am." He started to walk around her, but she wasn't finished.

"I knew this to be an uncivilized territory, but the rudeness in Alaska rivals any I've ever known."

Jacob stopped and looked at her hard for a moment. "Didn't seem that bad until you got here—maybe you brought it with you."

She reddened. "You, sir, are an ill-mannered oaf."

"And you seem to be a spoiled, insulting ninny," he said, pretending to tip a hat he didn't wear.

The woman's mouth dropped open and her arm shot up to slap him. Jacob merely sidestepped her shot, however. "If you want to be good at that, you'll have to learn not to telegraph your punch."

He walked away feeling rather amused by the stunned expression on her face. No doubt she was some fancy woman from the States, come to Alaska following a gold-sick husband or brother. He'd seen it before, but really didn't care to see it again. He could never really understand why people had to get so riled about little things. He'd meant the woman no harm, yet she acted as though he'd singled her out for an assault.

Mary returned shortly and helped the doctor move Jayce to a bed in another room. The infirmary held two other beds besides the one occupied by Jayce. It was a small but sufficient space that seemed much more personal than the hospital. Still, Leah worried that the hospital might have been better equipped to deal with the situation. She prayed they'd made the right decision in coming to Dr. Cox.

Leah remained at Jayce's side while Mary cleaned the surgical area where the doctor had worked on Jayce only moments before. She hummed a tune that Leah didn't recognize, and that, along with her clanking and clunking around, unnerved Leah. Here, poor Jayce was on his sickbed, possibly dying, and somehow it seemed unfair that life would just go on without worry or concern as to whether or not he made it.

She reached for Jayce's hand, then quickly tucked it back under the covers. If someone came in and found her holding his hand, they might think it odd. And if Jayce woke up to such a thing, he would definitely find it strange.

Leah heard the doctor speak to Mary in a hushed manner. No doubt he was giving instructions to her before retiring. Leah then heard commotion in the other room and knew that Jacob had probably returned. She sighed. It was time to go. At least for now.

"How's he doing?" Jacob asked as he joined her. The doctor was right behind him.

"He's breathing evenly and seems to be at rest. I suppose only time will tell the full story. I only pray we might have a happy ending."

"Prayer is a good way to see that through," Dr. Cox said, smiling.

She held his gaze for a moment before getting to her feet. "I'll see you in the morning, then."

He seemed to sense Leah's reluctance to leave. "I assure you he'll sleep through the night. I gave him a heavy dose of medication."

"Come on, Leah. I'm starved. Let's get some supper."

They left the doctor to his business and headed to a restaurant they'd eaten at on several other occasions. The place had been called Lady Luck in the gold rush heyday, but now it seemed the lady had lost her fortune. The structure cried out for restoration and attention, while inside there appeared to be a moderate number of people willing to overlook her dilapidation.

Once they were seated for dinner and had placed their orders, Leah took the conversation back to when the nurse had interrupted them when she opened the examination-room door. She'd been unable to think of little else. "You said you talked to Jayce. I want to know about this."

Jacob's attention was fixed on a caribou steak. Unfortunately for him it was on the plate of the man at the next table. "I don't remember every word, Leah. I talked to him and asked him to leave you alone—not hurt you again."

"What did he say about that?"

Jacob shrugged. "He didn't understand. He thought you were being unreasonable—after all, it had been ten years."

"Time shouldn't matter."

"I told him as much. He said something about how young you were then and how he loved Alaska and intended to stay and explore and he figured we'd both be gone before long."

"I gave him no reason to believe that," Leah said, her anger mounting. No one made her feel more confused than Jayce Kincaid.

"And he figured he gave you no reason to believe there could be anything more than there was between the two of you."

"Of all the nerve. He made me think he cared," Leah said, crossing her arms. That familiar white-hot flame burned somewhere deep in her heart. "He knew how I felt. He had to have known."

"Maybe not," Jacob said, shaking his head. "He really seemed to be genuinely puzzled by your anger toward him."

"So now you're taking his side?" Leah questioned.

"I didn't know we needed to pick sides," Jacob countered. "Look, I came here to eat—not fight. Besides, I think Jayce—"

Leah got up from the table and threw down her napkin. "I have lost my appetite."

She stormed from the room, knowing even as she did so that her actions were childish. Jacob didn't deserve her wrath. Frankly, no one did. It was her fault entirely that she couldn't seem to put the past to rest.

"I don't understand," she muttered. "I don't know why this can't just pass from my heart and leave me alone."

The front door flew open easily as Leah fled the restaurant, ploughing headlong into a woman. "Oh, bother," Leah said, reaching out to keep the woman from toppling backward. "I'm so sorry."

"People here seem to make a habit of running others over," the woman replied in a refined tone. "But I suppose there's no harm done."

It was then that Leah noticed the woman was white. The revelation seemed to hit the other woman at the same time.

The woman's attitude immediately changed. "You're white. How wonderful to see another white woman."

Leah steadied her emotions. "There are a few of us here in the territory."

"I wasn't entirely sure that was true." She extended her hand. "I'm Helaina Beecham."

"Leah Barringer." Leah was beginning to remember her reason for the rapid departure from the restaurant. She felt rather embarrassed by her escapade. "If you'll excuse me."

"Wait, please. Would you mind telling me . . . do you live here?" Helaina questioned.

"No. Actually I live in a village northeast of Nome. Up on the Bering Sea. We had to bring a wounded man to the doctor. What about you? You sound as though you're new to Nome."

"Indeed I am. I wasn't to be here at all, in fact. I was to join an exploration group in Seattle, but I missed my boat. Then when I tried to catch up with them here, I was once again too late."

Leah frowned. "An exploration group?"

Helaina nodded and put a hand to her hat. "Goodness, is it on straight now?" she asked, pushing it toward the center of her head.

"Yes," Leah said nodding. "Are you by any chance part of the *Homestead* group?"

Helaina halted her adjustment and looked hard at Leah. It seemed her entire demeanor had changed. "Are you familiar with them?"

"Yes. Some. I know they are heading north to map out Arctic islands and study the geological findings. My brother was asked to join the group because he raises and handles dogs."

"I see." Helaina seemed to relax just a bit, but Leah could tell the woman was still rather stirred up about this news. "I wonder if I know your brother. Why isn't he with the *Homestead* now?"

"Jacob Barringer is his name. He's just inside if you'd like to meet him. We brought an injured man here to Nome. We were having dinner when I . . . well . . . it isn't important. I can introduce you to Jacob if you like."

"That would be wonderful," Helaina said, smiling. She smoothed her beautiful dress.

Leah couldn't take her eyes from the creation. "That's a lovely gown. I haven't seen anything like it in a long, long time, but I can't imagine it lasting long up here."

"Have you lived here long?"

"Yes. We've been up here for what seems forever. We came north during the Yukon gold rush. Our father had gold fever."

"How did you come to be in this part of the world if you were in the Yukon?"

"There were several things. Jacob took a job with the postal service, then later he went into business for himself. We run a small store in Last Chance, a small village on a creek by the same name. My brother also raises sled dogs and makes sleds."

"Seems like there wouldn't be too much demand for that kind of thing."

"Oh, but there is," Leah argued. "He's always selling dogs or trading them to the natives. People come from miles around—sometimes hundreds of miles, to buy his dogs. Then there are the exploration teams like yours. The folks from the *Karluk* came to us a few years back."

"That was a tragedy," Helaina said, showing some knowledge of the event. "I certainly hope *Homestead* does better. Surely this captain knows more about his surroundings and won't get his ship stuck in ice."

"Change happens fast up here. Storms, temperatures, animals—they all can come upon you without warning. I'm sure the captain of the *Karluk* did his best to keep his men safe."

"Well, if I recall correctly, the captain wasn't even with them at the end. He'd gone off to get help. Seems unusual to say the least."

"Sometimes we hear stories that don't line up with the truth. No matter what the captain's actions were, we cannot possibly understand all the details that led to that decision."

They seemed to have reached an impasse, but Helaina was unfazed. "So you mentioned coming north with your father. Is he here as well?"

Leah shook her head. "He died trying to reach the gold, but he had already found someone to care for us before heading up over the Chilkoot Pass. We were well cared for after his death. We eventually left the goldfields to settle in Ketchikan. My guardian's husband was part Tlingit, so he wanted to be around his people."

"I see," Helaina replied as though she were trying to put all the pieces together. "Well, I'm quite delighted to have run into you, Leah Barringer."

Leah smiled. "Well, I was the one doing the running, but no matter. Come on inside. I'll introduce you to Jacob. If you like, you can share dinner with us."

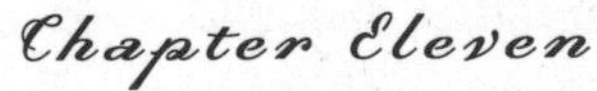

Chapter Eleven

Helaina had eaten at the Lucky Lady on many other occasions. She motioned to the waitress and ordered a small caribou steak dinner and hot coffee before following Leah to the table. The man seated opposite where she stood seemed the brooding sort. His tawny brown hair fell lazily across his forehead and from the look of his jaw, he hadn't seen a razor in at least a week. There was something familiar about him. When he raised his face, she knew exactly what it was.

"Helaina Beecham, my brother, Jacob Barringer," Leah introduced.

"We ran into each other earlier. Much as our encounter," Helaina said, offering her gloved hand. But Leah's brother was less than receptive. The steak on his plate seemed far more interesting at the moment.

"What's this about?" He looked to his sister rather than Helaina.

Leah took the chair she'd obviously occupied earlier, where Helaina noted that another plate of food awaited. With no other choice, she sat down between the brother and sister and waited for Leah to smooth the waters. She knew her earlier introduction to Jacob Barringer had been an abysmal failure, but given his standing and relationship to her manhunt, Helaina figured she should mend some fences.

"I apologize, Mr. Barringer, for my earlier behavior. I'm afraid the bad news I'd received regarding my ship took away my good manners."

"Helaina was asking about the *Homestead*."

"To what purpose?" Jacob asked, finally looking Helaina in the eye.

She saw in his expression that he wouldn't be easily impressed. The men in Nome had been falling all over themselves for her attention, but apparently not this man. "I'm to assist the cartographer," she told him flatly. "I was unable to catch up with the team in Seattle, and they advised me to come to Nome."

"Well, we just left that ship in Last Chance," Jacob said, turning his attention to a thick crusty loaf of bread. "They're heading to Kotzebue next."

"I wonder if there is any chance of you helping me in that matter."

Jacob shook his head. "None whatsoever."

"Jacob! I honestly don't know what's gotten into him. He doesn't usually act this way."

Leah's tone held admonishment, and Helaina couldn't help but wonder at the pair. Brother and sister they said, but it seemed odd that Leah Barringer should be unmarried and traveling with her brother. Then it dawned on her that they might be two of Jayce's cohorts.

The woman she'd spoken to earlier appeared with a platter of food and a steaming cup of black coffee. She put the plate in front of Helaina and then, still holding the cup, looked to Jacob. "Jacob, do you need anything else?" She smiled sweetly, revealing two missing bottom teeth.

"No, Sally, I'm fine," he said. "Good coffee."

Helaina looked to the woman. "Is that cup for me?"

The woman seemed startled to find the mug still in her hand. "Oh, sure, miss. Sorry about that." Helaina only faintly smiled and took the offered drink. Seeing that perhaps a change of subject was in order, Helaina waited for Sally to leave, then ventured a question.

"Leah, are you married?"

"No," the dark-haired woman said. "You?"

Helaina frowned. This wasn't going as easily as she had hoped. "I was. My husband died three years ago."

Leah winced. "I'm sorry."

Had Helaina not seen Leah with her dander up just moments ago, she might have thought her quite temperate, even quiet. But there was something that spoke of a hard, fighting side to this woman. Helaina had learned to read people well over the years, and she could see for herself that Leah Barringer was a woman with a wounded spirit. It was Jacob, however, who proved the real mystery. Usually she could charm her way out of any situation, but not this time.

"Widowhood has not been easy by any means," Helaina said, hoping to enlist Jacob's sympathy. "The days and nights are so different—so strange after sharing such close companionship." She lowered her head and pretended to dab at her eyes. "Robert was a wonderful man, and a murderer cut him down in the prime of his life. Killed my parents too."

"How awful," Leah said, pausing her fork in midair. "I'm so sorry."

Helaina straightened. "I have found the strength to go on. I've decided to use my education to make Robert proud. That's part of the reason I came here—in honor of Robert."

"Well, people come here for a great many things, Mrs. Beecham. I am sorry for your loss," Jacob said, his tone softer.

Helaina studied him carefully. "What of you, Mr. Barringer? Have you a wife and children?"

"No. I have neither." He cut into the steak again.

"So what brought you to Nome? Leah mentioned you came north during the Yukon gold rush. How did you get from there to here?"

Jacob put down his fork. "Mostly by boat," he answered dryly and grinned.

Helaina didn't care for his amusement at her expense, but she, too, smiled. "I suppose that would be only fitting since there is a great deal of water between here and there."

Leah chuckled. "Jacob, what has gotten into you?" She turned to Helaina. "He's probably worried about our friend."

"The man you brought to the doctor?" Helaina questioned.

Leah nodded and picked at her food. "He was also to have been on your expedition to the Arctic."

"Truly? And for what purpose?" Helaina leaned toward Jacob, hoping to gain his favor with her attention.

Jacob looked at her oddly for a moment. Helaina knew he was trying to guess her game.

"I can't really say what his job entailed. He asked me to come along and help with the dogs. I raise dogs—sled dogs. I was asked to join the expedition as their handler. I've lived on the Seward Peninsula for the last ten years, and I'm well suited to Arctic winters. I seriously doubt you can say the same. Even your manner of dress would suggest you have no knowledge of what it takes to be here in Alaska."

Helaina eased back in her chair. Her initial assessment of the man was correct—he was positively rude. "Well, I believe I do have what it takes. I've trained and studied the territory. I possess mapping skills and feel my company is generally well received."

"Be that as it may, you aren't going far in a flimsy gown like that," he said, pointing to her outfit.

Helaina stiffened. "I didn't expect to find a fashion expert in Nome."

Jacob laughed. "Hardly that. But I do know what works up here. Take the outfit Leah is wearing. She has on thick mukluks—solid, warm, native-made boots. They'll endure just about any terrain and temperature. Then there's the sealskin pants. They offer good warmth, especially when layered. Of course, it's nearly summer now so that's not quite so critical here, but it will be up north. The Arctic is cold, even in June." He munched a piece of bread and pointed at Leah's top. "That's called a *kuspuk*. It's also native-made. It's put together like the heavy fur parkas, only it's made of cloth for summer."

"Jacob does have a point, even if he presents it in a rather hostile manner," Leah said, looking at Helaina. "If you don't have warmer clothes, I'm afraid you won't be able to endure the desperately low temperatures. Especially if you stay through the winter, as I was told some of the party plans to do."

"Well, I'm not one of them, but I do thank you . . . both." She looked first to Leah, then settled her gaze on Jacob. "I already have an Eskimo woman putting together an odd assortment of travel clothes for me. Although I did come north with boy's jeans and sturdy boots, as well as woolen shirts and heavy undergarments." She smiled, hoping her expression would mask the lie she'd just told regarding the seamstress.

"That will help a great deal. Especially when the seasons change again," Leah said.

"As I said," Helaina began, "I don't intend to stay on through the winter." She really wanted to talk about the injured man and the *Homestead* crew, and a sudden thought sent her in the right direction. "Unless, of course, the injured man—your friend—is the team cartographer. Then I might very well need to stay on and take his place."

"Jayce isn't a cartographer," Leah offered. "He's a geologist."

"Jayce Kincaid?" Helaina thought her heart might stop. "He's here in Nome?"

Leah nodded. "He was working with the dogs, along with Jacob. They got out of control and he suffered a bad wound. It's infected now, and the doctor is fighting to save his leg—and his life. Do you know him?"

Helaina pondered the news for a moment. "Yes." She realized she had momentarily forgot herself. "Well, that is, I know *of* him. I've been told about him."

"You know of him?" Leah asked.

Helaina didn't want to make them suspicious. "Yes, through the exploration association. I've not met him personally, you understand."

This seemed to satisfy the woman. "He's very passionate about Alaska and learning more of what she has to offer," Leah replied. "He's been up here for many years."

"But he's ill now? Maybe even dying?" Helaina hoped her tone betrayed a reasonable amount of worry.

"He's strong as an ox. I'm sure he'll pull through," Jacob replied in a rather clipped tone. "Besides, Dr. Cox knows his medicine well enough. If he can't do the job, I'm sure he'll send Jayce to the hospital or even to Seattle."

The situation was sounding better all the time. Helaina made a pretense at eating but found she was no longer hungry. Jayce Kincaid was right under her nose—and with very little coaxing, she could no doubt convince Dr. Cox to send him to Seattle. Her journey of woes had finally come to an end.

Leah watched the beautiful woman as she ate and wondered at the relationship she shared with Jayce. It almost seemed that she might be lying about knowing him—like maybe she didn't want Leah to know how well acquainted they truly were. She'd stammered over her answer, after all. But Leah tried to push away such thoughts. She didn't want to feel this way. She cared deeply about Jayce, and if someone else cared about his well-being, then she shouldn't be jealous. Especially now that Jayce was so desperately ill.

Leah couldn't put the matter from her mind, however. Helaina Beecham was a beautiful woman, and no doubt she'd treat Jayce with great kindness and a gentle spirit. *Unlike me,* Leah thought.

She considered the way she'd treated Jayce—how she'd done nothing to be kind or friendly toward him. *Why did I act that way? Why didn't I just put the past behind us and start fresh?* She picked at her food, not really tasting any of it.

All through the dinner—in fact, ever since setting out for Nome—Leah had been dealing with a bevy of emotions. Guilt was right there at the top of the list, but now Helaina Beecham had stirred up one more: jealousy. What if there was something more between her and Jayce, but Helaina wanted to keep it a secret? Leah pondered that idea for several minutes.

"When will Jayce be up to having visitors?"

Leah swallowed the bread in her mouth and felt it stick in her throat. Was this woman somehow romantically linked with Jayce? Surely not, for she'd just talked of her departed husband.

Jacob shrugged and pushed his empty plate back. "I guess you'll have to ask the doctor tomorrow. I doubt he'll want Jayce having too much company right away."

"I'm sure you're right, Mr. Barringer," Helaina smiled at Jacob. "I'm equally convinced, however, that people heal faster when they know there are others around who care. Besides, if Jayce isn't improving—if he needs more attention than what he can get here in Nome—I, for one, would be happy to see him through to Seattle. We don't want him to die."

Leah felt her food become an uncomfortable lump in her stomach. "You are a very kind woman, Mrs. Beecham." She followed her brother's example and pushed back her plate. She could see that Jacob was anxious to leave, and frankly, she was feeling more and more driven to check on Jayce—maybe even talk to him and beg his forgiveness for the way she'd acted.

Leah extended her hand. "It was nice to meet you, Mrs. Beecham, but I'm afraid we need to be going. It's been a long day and we're both quite tired." Leah and Jacob stood. Jacob fished out a five-dollar bill and tossed it on the table.

Helaina surprised Leah by getting to her feet. "Are you staying at the hotel?" She opened her small purse and left money by her coffee cup to pay for her meal.

"Yes," Leah answered. "I think so." She looked to her brother.

"Yes, we're staying there. But just tonight. Why?"

Helaina seemed surprised. "Are you heading back so soon? What of Jayce?"

"We aren't heading back just yet," Jacob said, heading for the door. "Hotels are for the rich. We'll camp down by the boats with our friends after tonight. We're just sticking close for now, in case . . . well, you know."

Leah cringed at the thought that Jayce might die without her making peace. She longed to tell him that she was sorry for the anger—sorry for the bitter way in which she'd acted. What if Jayce died and the last thing he could remember about her was how poorly she had treated him?

Ayoona thought Leah should just tell Jayce how she felt, but now she wondered if she'd ever get the chance. *I've been a fool, acting like a spoiled child. Why didn't I just let the past go and smooth things over with Jayce? I'm a grown woman, I should have known better.*

"I find that I'm quite exhausted. If you don't mind, I'd like to walk back to the hotel with you. I realize it's just a short distance," Helaina said, smiling, "but one can never be too careful." She headed for the door without waiting for them.

Leah leaned toward her brother and whispered. "Jacob, why don't you go ahead and walk Mrs. Beecham to the hotel. I'm going to go check on Jayce."

"But it's late," Jacob said, looking at the clock near the door. "It's nearly nine."

"The doctor said they'd be sitting with him throughout the night. I'll just slip in and check on him. You can come for me after you walk Mrs. Beecham to the hotel. I'll sleep better once I know things are going well."

Jacob nodded, his expression softening. "You did a good job, Leah. You can't berate yourself for lack of skills you've never been trained in. If Jayce doesn't make it, it won't be your fault."

Leah nodded very slowly. "I know . . . at least I keep telling myself that very thing."

Jacob and Leah walked out of the restaurant and joined Helaina. "I won't be long," Leah said, and then turned to Helaina. "Jacob will see you to the hotel. I'm going to check on Jayce."

"Well . . . I could come too," Helaina said, seeming suddenly quite excited.

"No, that's all right. You said you were exhausted, and I wouldn't want to cause Jayce too much excitement—in case he's awake."

Helaina opened her mouth to protest, but Jacob took hold of her elbow. "Come along, Mrs. Beecham. I want to get to bed sometime tonight."

Leah thought Helaina seemed quite upset by this turn of events. *No doubt she has some secret interest in him,* Leah thought. *She probably knows him much better than she's conveying.* A million unkind thoughts coursed through Leah's mind.

"She's young and beautiful," Leah muttered. "She's refined and obviously wealthy, given the tip she left Sally just now."

Leah looked to the sky. *Lord, why does this have to be so hard?* With the sun still lighting her way, Leah couldn't even shed a few secret tears. *Help me, Father. Help me to give this all to you.*

Mary greeted Leah at the door. "Come in. He does well."

"Is the fever down?" Leah asked.

"Not so much, but he rest good."

"Can I see him for just a moment?"

"Sure. He won't hear you, though. Dr. Cox give him more medicine. He say the sleep good for him."

Leah nodded. "I know it will be for the best. And I don't need for him to hear me."

Mary led her into the small room where Jayce slept. "You stay as long as you like. I be right here." She pointed back the way they'd come in.

Leah knelt down beside the low bed. She put her hand to Jayce's brow and smiled. The fever was less—she was sure of it. Reaching for his hand, she held it to her cheek.

"Jayce, you must get well. You must."

His rough fingers against her face gave Leah a sense of well-being. "I'm sorry for the way I've behaved. Just when I think I can let go of the past and control my heart, something happens and I act in a way I regret. I don't mean to hurt you with my bitter heart, but I've suffered so long in silence."

She looked at his pale face. Dark circles seemed to engulf his eyes. *Such lovely eyes too,* she thought. "I once loved you with all of my heart, Jayce. And I love you still . . . but I know it's not to be. I'm thirty years old, and I'll never love anyone as I've loved you." She pressed a kiss against his fingers, then gently placed his hand back at his side.

"I know it's too late for us. Your heart is somewhere else—with someone else. But I just needed to tell you that I am sorry." Sadness washed over her, for the moment seemed so final. She was saying good-bye to a dream. A dream she'd held on to for over a decade.

Jacob was waiting outside for her when Leah exited the doctor's place. He immediately saw tears on her face and asked, "He isn't . . . he didn't . . ."

"No, he's not dead. Actually, he's better. I was just . . . well . . . letting go of him."

Jacob looked at her oddly. "Women are strange creatures."

"You call me strange?" she questioned. "You were nothing but odd this evening. You were downright rude to Mrs. Beecham when she asked for help. What was that all about?"

"I had an encounter with her earlier—at the hotel. She was obnoxious and uppity. Yet at the table tonight she seemed all roses and sunshine. I think she's up to something. There's something about her that just doesn't set well with me."

"What if you're wrong? She seemed nice enough, and she's only trying to get to the job she pledged to do." Leah tried hard not to accuse Helaina of anything out of line.

"If she cares so much about that job," Jacob said, shaking his head, "then why was she so eager to volunteer her time to take Jayce to Seattle?"

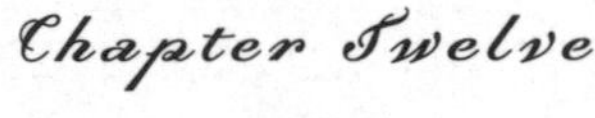

Chapter Twelve

Helaina hardly slept a wink that night. After tossing and turning for hours, she gave up on any real sleep and got up to rethink her strategy. Although she'd nearly blown her cover by succumbing to anger, Helaina felt confident her mission was safe. The Barringer man didn't like her or trust her, and she feared he wouldn't be persuaded by good works or good looks. She had known men like that, and they were always a difficult thing to factor into any investigation. She would have to be cautious with him.

Leah, on the other hand, obviously cared too much about Jayce Kincaid. In fact, Helaina was certain that Leah was in love with him. The woman went from weepy one moment to dreamy-eyed the next. Helaina had seen that kind of nonsense as well—especially with weak-minded women. Leah probably had no idea who she was dealing with, Helaina surmised. Men like Kincaid were powerful manipulators with the right women. Helaina could probably use Leah's attraction to her advantage, however. Women in love enjoyed talking about the object of their affections. Perhaps Leah could lend information that might tie Kincaid to other crimes.

But whether Leah cooperated or not, it didn't matter. Jayce would soon be back in custody and headed to the gallows. *Let her love him, but let her stay out of my way.*

Helaina paced the room and tried to imagine a scenario where she could get Jayce back to Seattle with the least amount of resistance. She wondered if her best choice wasn't to bribe the good doctor. At least that way she could arrange to have the Pinkerton men ready to arrest him, and then her job would be done.

"Dr. Cox would do anything I ask. I'm sure of it."

She went to her wrinkled traveling clothes to assess their condition. They were hopeless, but so was the dress she'd worn the night before. She would have to ask Dr. Cox if there was a laundress in town. She considered the storekeeper's admonition to get a native woman to make new clothes. *If I'd had to go all the way to the Arctic to find Kincaid, I would have done just that. But now that the Barringers have brought him to Nome, I won't need anything more than a ticket back to Seattle.* She smiled at the thought.

The thought of Jacob Barringer, however, made her uneasy. The man acted as though he knew who she was and what she was about. She also worried that he would go rushing to Jayce Kincaid and warn him of the strange woman from Washington, D.C.

Taking off her robe, Helaina quickly slipped into her blouse and skirt. *Perhaps Jacob Barringer is also a criminal.* The thought came amidst a dozen other suggestions. *If he's a criminal and suspects that I might be trouble to him, there's no telling what might happen.* But there was no easy way to find out if Jacob was a criminal. To use any kind of communications with Washington would surely give away her position.

So she turned her thoughts away from the Barringers and considered how she might see to Jayce's transfer to Seattle.

"I can tell Dr. Cox that I've received word from the exploration association," she murmured. "I can tell him that they want to personally oversee and pay for Jayce Kincaid's recovery and that I'm to accompany him to Seattle. That's still my best choice. It's the most beneficial for all concerned."

She continued doing up her buttons, wondering just how she might best approach Dr. Cox. It was always possible that he would say no to moving his patient—especially if that man's injuries were too grave for travel. Perhaps she could suggest he accompany them to Seattle. She could tell him that it was her hope they might get to know each other better, in more favorable surroundings. Maybe she could ask him to give her a couple of weeks in order to get to know him, as she reconsidered his proposal.

Thinking of the funny little doctor, Helaina sighed. He had shown her nothing but kindness. It would be cruel to give pretense to feelings that didn't exist. Helaina sat down and shook her head. She'd never worried about such things prior to this moment.

"What's happening to me? I don't even feel like myself anymore. I used to be competent and capable, but since leaving Washington, D.C., nothing has gone right. I can't even think clearly. But why?"

Her state of mind reminded Helaina of the days just after she'd lost her parents and Robert. Nothing had made sense. She had been incapable of making decisions and choices, and all because of the shock she'd experienced. She knew at times like this her housekeeper would tell her to turn to God, but Helaina had no time or interest in that. What would God do about it? If He cared so much about goodness and mercy, then why wasn't Jayce Kincaid swinging from a gallows?

Jayce opened his eyes and stared blankly at the ceiling overhead. *Where am I?* He fought against the thick cloud of confusion in his head. *Why do I feel so lousy?*

He tried to turn and only then did the red-hot pain in his leg remind him of what had happened. There had been a problem with the dogs. He could barely remember it, as if it had happened in his childhood instead of only . . . when? How long had he been ill?

"I see you're awake," a man said, coming to stand beside Jayce's bed.

"Where am I?"

"Nome. Your friends brought you here, and just in time, I'd say. I believe you'll recover well, but your wounds were quite deep."

Jayce tried to sit up, and the doctor quickly reached out to stop him. "I'd rather you lie flat. It will help the circulation of blood. That leg needs ample blood to stay healthy. I'd hate for you to lose it."

"Lose my leg?" Jayce asked, his eyes widening. "What's going on?"

"Apparently you were in the middle of a group of ill-tempered dogs. They mangled your right thigh. Had it not been for your friends, especially the woman, you probably would have died."

"Leah," Jayce breathed her name. He'd been dreaming about her. She had come to him in the night . . .

"Yes, that's right. Leah Barringer. She was here to check on you last night and again this morning. She's been quite worried."

So she has been here. Jayce remembered her touch—at least he thought he did. Had he honestly known her presence, or had it all been a dream?

"So how am I doing, Doc?" he finally asked, pushing aside the memories of Leah.

"It's really too early to tell. The infection needs to clear and healing begin before I can be sure of where we go from here. These things take time."

"How much time? I was supposed to go north with a team of scientists. We were going to map islands in the Arctic."

"Yes, I heard all about your quest. I even met another member of your team. A Mrs. Beecham. She's trying desperately to make her way north—missed her boat, you know."

"Mrs. Beecham." Jayce tried the name. He'd been told there was to be a woman to assist the cartographer. This must be her.

"Are you in much pain?" the doctor asked as he pushed back the covers.

"If I move the leg, it feels like it's on fire," Jayce admitted.

"That's to be expected. I can give you something for the pain, but it will make you sleep."

Jayce shook his head. "I'd rather clear my mind and stay awake. If it gets too bad, I'll let you know. By the way, where are my friends?"

"They should be here soon. They were already here, but I sent them on to breakfast. I'll bring them back to see you as soon as they arrive. Meanwhile, are you hungry?"

"I could stand something in my stomach," Jayce admitted. He couldn't remember the last time he'd eaten.

"Good. I'll have Mary make you something." He walked quickly from the room, not even bothering to examine Jayce more thoroughly. He paused at the door, however. "I hate to be the bearer of bad news, but I think you must put aside any thought of going north. You will need the next few months to recover, and travel to such a remote and harsh climate would only irritate your condition. Should you get north and have the leg fail you or the blood poisoning return, you'd be sentencing yourself to death." With that he left.

Jayce sighed. Nothing was working out like he'd planned. He wouldn't have another chance to be a part of an exploration team until next year—at least if he followed the doctor's orders. He'd had high hopes of what this expedition might accomplish, and now he wouldn't be there. He balled his hands into fists and smacked them against the mattress, causing pain to shoot down his leg. He winced and gritted his teeth to keep from crying out in pain.

A woman's voice sounded from somewhere in the doctor's house. Jayce strained to listen, and when he heard the woman mention his name, Jayce figured it must be Leah; there was no other woman who knew about him being here. He continued to listen and heard something mentioned about Seattle.

Dr. Cox's voice carried much better. "There's no need to rush the man to Seattle. If I move him now it would be detrimental."

The woman spoke again, but Jayce could only pick up that this was what someone wanted—that they were concerned with Jayce's welfare. But who was she talking about?

He felt helpless to figure it all out and waited, thinking they would come to the room and the woman would reveal herself. By now he was convinced it wasn't Leah Barringer.

But the woman didn't come. Instead, he heard her tell the doctor in a rather agitated tone that he should reconsider what was in his own best interests. It almost sounded like a threat, but that didn't make any sense.

"Why should it make sense?" Jayce murmured. "Nothing else does." He thought about how God was in control, yet with all his plans in disarray, he felt overwhelmed with questions.

Lord, he prayed, *I don't understand any of this. Why would you bring me this far, only to let me be incapacitated? I had a job to do—a job I wanted very much to do—and now that isn't going to happen. I don't understand why things have fallen apart.*

And then without warning a thought came to mind. If he couldn't go north to the Arctic, it might behoove him to go north to Last Chance Creek. There with Leah and Jacob he could spend time learning how to handle the dogs more skillfully. He could also learn more about Leah—maybe even learn enough to tell whether the things he heard her say in his dreams were, in fact, the truth of her heart.

He smiled for the first time. Maybe God had orchestrated all of this in order to give him a chance to make things right with Leah.

Jacob was not pleased to look up and find Helaina Beecham entering the restaurant. Only moments ago he'd left Leah with Jayce; she claimed she wasn't hungry and planned to stay and help Jayce in any way she could. Meanwhile, Jacob had hoped for some quiet time with his Bible, but now it didn't look like that was going to happen.

"Hello, Mr. Barringer," Helaina said in a silky tone.

Jacob felt his defenses immediately go into place. She rubbed him wrong—even in her tone of voice. "Mrs. Beecham."

"I wonder if I might join you?"

"I'd rather you didn't. I'd like some time alone."

She frowned and nodded toward the open Bible. "To read that?"

He heard the disdain in her voice. "Yes. Do you have a problem with that?"

"I just find that intelligent men need not lean on superstitions and traditions in order to make their way through life."

"Then we finally agree on something," Jacob replied. He looked at her hard, challenging her to say something more.

"I was wondering how Mr. Kincaid was doing this morning."

"He's doing better. You could go to the doctor's office just a couple of doors down and find out all the details for yourself. For now, however, you'll need to excuse me."

He turned his attention back to the Bible, aware she had not turned to go. What was it with this woman, anyway? Why didn't she just leave him alone? Slowly, he lifted his head to find her watching him. "What is it now?"

"I just wondered what you could possibly find so fascinating about that book. I mean, most of the people I've known who've relied upon the Christian religion were generally weak-willed and rather on the dim-witted side. You strike me as neither one."

"Well, thank you. I think that's the nicest thing you've said to me."

"I haven't intentionally said anything that wasn't nice," Helaina argued. "I'm sorry if you believed otherwise."

Jacob put his elbow on the table and leaned against it. "What do you want? I mean, I've asked you to leave me alone. I've showed you clearly that I'm not interested in conversation. Is it just that I'm not acting like the rest of the men in this town—falling all over myself to get your attention? Is that what makes me so appealing?"

"I assure you, Mr. Barringer, you are far from appealing to me."

"Good. So leave me alone." He refocused his attention on the Bible.

"I thought Christians were commanded to share their faith."

He sighed and looked up again. "What would you like for me to share?"

She smiled rather coquettishly. "Everything." She pulled out the chair. "I have nowhere to be."

Jacob wasn't about to play this game. He knew she had no real interest in God's Word or God himself. He closed the Bible and stood. "We're all sinners. The penalty for that is death. Jesus came to take that penalty for us. If we accept Him and turn from our sins, we can have eternal life. If we refuse Him, hell is our eternal destination. Would you like to make your peace with God?"

Helaina seemed rather taken aback by all of this. "No, I'm not interested in that, but . . ."

"I've shared the Gospel with you, Mrs. Beecham. You've rejected it, and now I take my leave."

"But aren't you supposed to try to persuade me?" she asked, regaining her composure. She smiled rather alluringly.

"I'll let that be the job of the Holy Spirit," Jacob said. "He's got a much better chance of breaking through your façades than do I."

He left her with that. She was clearly playing a game with him, and he refused to be a part of whatever it was she was trying to accomplish. He walked slowly back to the doctor's office, all the while trying to figure out what Helaina Beecham was doing in Nome. He knew she was to have been a part of the exploration north, but there didn't seem to be any real concern about getting north—not like there had supposedly been when she'd initially met him and Leah.

Jacob opened the door to the doctor's. Mary was there to greet him. "How you do?" she asked.

"I do fine," Jacob said with a smile. "Is Leah still visiting our patient?"

"She help him shave. He not very happy about staying in bed."

"I can imagine. Would you mind if I sit here and read?" he asked, holding up his Bible.

"You read Bible?"

"I do. I love God's Word."

Her smile nearly doubled in size. "I love God's Word too. Only I not read good."

"You should get someone to teach you," Jacob suggested.

"I not go to school. I too old."

"You're never too old to learn," Jacob countered. "There are probably all sorts of people who could teach you to read better. You should start asking at church."

"I do that," Mary replied. "Now I tell your sister you here."

Jacob nodded and settled himself down with the Bible. He read no more than two verses when Leah appeared. "He's doing much better. The leg is already showing signs of healing. Isn't that amazing?"

"And all because something that wasn't supposed to be there was taken out. Seems there are a lot of times in life where you can benefit by removing the offending bit of debris."

Leah looked at him funny. "You're certainly moody today. What's going on?"

Jacob shrugged. "I can't really say. I will say this, however. I've been trying to read the same passage of Scripture for over half an hour. It would sure be nice to get through it."

"You needn't worry that I'll keep you," Leah said, leaning in to kiss her brother on the cheek. "Jayce needs me and you don't. I'll go where I'm needed."

Jacob nodded and waited until she was gone before trying once again to read his Bible. He had just reread the passage from moments ago when Dr. Cox returned from a house call.

"Well, I'm sure you know your friend is doing much better."

"I did hear that," Jacob replied. "Thanks to your sharp eyes and skilled hands, I'd say our friend has a fighting chance."

"Yes, so long as we keep him here instead of sending him off to Seattle."

"Seattle? Why would we need to send him there?"

The doctor handed Mary his bag and turned to Jacob. "Well, according to Mrs. Beecham, that's what the exploration association wishes for her to do. She received word—a telegram, I believe—to have Jayce moved to a hospital in Seattle. I told her I believed it to be a bad idea, however. I have no intention of moving an injured man—at least not at this point of his recovery."

Jacob wondered why Helaina would suggest such a thing. The exploration association had no reason to move Jayce—they had to know the ship was well to the north. "I'm paying for his care, and so long as he improves, I'd just as soon keep him here," Jacob said, sensing that something just wasn't right about the entire matter.

The doctor nodded. "That was my thought exactly."

He left Jacob to sit and wonder at the situation. Mrs. Beecham was definitely up to something, and he knew this for two reasons: One, she acted like a woman with a secret. And two, there was no way anyone could have gotten word to her in Nome regarding Jayce's situation. There hadn't been any delivery of mail, and he'd learned only that morning that the telegraph had been inoperable for two days.

Chapter Thirteen

Leah was encouraged by Jayce's recovery, despite his frustration. He was still in a great deal of pain anytime he tried to exercise the leg, but the doctor also reminded him that it had only been two and half weeks since the attack.

Leah had also been happy when Jacob made the decision to send the other villagers back to Last Chance Creek with supplies, allowing him and Leah to stay indefinitely. Kimik had promised to get Oopick to run the store in their absence, and that settled the matter. Mail and other supplies could now be had via the revenue cutter that regularly headed as far north as Point Hope. The village wouldn't suffer for the Barringers' delay with that faithful ship on duty.

Remaining in Nome had comforted Leah, and in return for her willingness to help in his office, Dr. Cox had offered a small room to her. Leah jumped at the chance to sleep in a real bed rather than in a tent. Jacob had been a little harder to convince. Still, in the end, he had come around to her way of thinking. When he made himself useful in collecting driftwood and cutting firewood, Dr. Cox told him he could sleep in the same room where Jayce recovered. He would have to vacate, of course, should they need the bed for medical reasons, but so far that hadn't been a problem.

"Leah!"

Leah looked up to find Helaina Beecham heading her way. Helaina crossed the narrow dirt street, dressed in native style, much to Leah's surprise. "You look very proper," she told the woman.

"I should hope it would meet with your brother's critical eye for fashion."

"He only said what he did because he worried you'd die up north," Leah said frankly. "The Arctic is not forgiving. Which reminds me, we hadn't seen you in some time and figured you'd found a way to reach your ship."

Helaina shook her head. "I received word from the association that Jayce and I were to head to Seattle. They had hoped for us to be there by now, but the doctor didn't feel Jayce could travel."

"He's doing much better now, but I don't think he knows about the association requesting him to come south." Leah felt a tightening in her chest, noting again Helaina's beauty. Her straight blond hair looked quite lovely in the simple way Helaina had tied it back, and her blue eyes seemed a perfect compliment to her peach-colored complexion.

". . . but of course that depends on how well you know him."

Leah realized she hadn't heard what Helaina had just said. "I'm sorry . . . what did you say?"

Helaina laughed. "I was hoping you might help me persuade Jayce to come with me to Seattle. I was wondering how well you knew him."

Leah tried not to let the question bother her, but it did. "I've known Jayce for over ten years. He stayed with my family for a time in Ketchikan."

"Does he trust you to be honest with him . . . to tell him what would be best for him?"

This question made Leah smile. "No one tells Jayce Kincaid what's best for him—he's a free thinker. He does what he thinks is right and rarely concerns himself with how it will affect anyone else."

"But then most men are that way," Helaina said with a coy smile, "until a woman changes his mind, of course."

Leah said nothing. She'd never had any power over Jayce Kincaid, but it was hard to explain this to the Beecham woman without getting into some of the most embarrassing moments of Leah's life. And she wasn't about to go down that path.

"Well, here's what makes this most critical," Helaina continued. "The exploration association has decided to send a second team north. They believe if they get them in motion immediately, we can be on our way by July. It would mean remaining in the north, but now that I have my Eskimo wardrobe, I don't even mind that idea."

Leah still didn't understand the urgency. "So why can't they pick you up here in Nome? No doubt they will stop for supplies and workers to help on the trip. They could surely pick the two of you up and head out from here. They might even want Jacob and his dogs."

"That would work," Helaina said rather hesitantly, "except for the fact . . . that . . . well, they would like Jayce to hand select the final members of the team. They trust his knowledge of Alaska."

"They should—he knows it better than most people. He's scarcely been out of the territory over the last ten years."

Helaina frowned. "Surely that's not true. I've heard from other sources that he was quite often back east."

Leah shrugged. "He told me he spent some time in Vancouver, but I know nothing about him being back east. In fact, it seems Jacob told me that Jayce had been working at something in the interior of the territory prior to going to Vancouver. He loves this land with such a passion that any person would be hard-pressed to come between him and Alaska."

Helaina was silent, almost appearing to take offense to Leah's words. Perhaps Helaina knew Jayce much better than she'd let on. Maybe she was in love with him and had planned to convince him to leave the land and settle in the States. The aching returned to Leah's heart. *Lord, please keep me strong. Please don't let this hurt me more.*

"I'm headed back to the doctor's office right now. I've been helping out there in exchange for a room. You could come with me and talk to Jayce yourself. Perhaps if you share this good news of how his superiors want him to pick the team, he would be persuaded to come with you."

Helaina nodded. "I have wanted to visit with him. I've held off, however. I wanted him to feel fully recovered before attempting to convince him to leave. I wouldn't want to be the reason for a relapse."

"Then come along. I'm done with my shopping." Leah held up a small canvas bag. "We might as well see how he's feeling."

"But you will try to talk to him—after I'm gone?" Helaina asked. "Try to help him see how needed he is on this project."

"I can try," Leah said half-heartedly, "but I doubt he'll give my words any weight."

Leah and the doctor told Jayce that he was improving with each passing day. His restlessness at being unable to walk long distances caused him to be grumpy, however. The doctor had assured him the stiffness and aching would pass. The wound had been quite deep, after all, and Jayce was fortunate to have a leg to stand on. But even this explanation didn't still the anxiety inside Jayce. He wanted to be back on his own—he wanted to be away from Nome.

"I've brought someone to see you," Leah announced. A woman came in beside her and waited for the introduction. "It's Helaina . . . Helaina Beecham, your teammate."

"My teammate?" Jayce questioned.

"I was to be the assistant cartographer on the *Homestead* expedition," Helaina announced. She moved forward and extended her hand. "Glad to finally meet you. I heard of your injuries when you first arrived but have hesitated to burden you with company."

"I'm grateful for that," Jayce said, giving her hand a brief shake. She looked like a frail thing, much too fragile for life in the north. He doubted if she weighed more than one hundred pounds and surely she wasn't any taller than five foot. And he surmised all of this despite the fact that she wore a loose-fitting native kuspuk and denim pants.

"I heard that your injury was considerable," Helaina continued. "I am sorry for that. Leah tells me that you met your fate while dealing with her brother's sled dogs."

Jayce eyed her warily. Jacob had already warned him about the woman. He was glad to have this advantage, certain that Mrs. Beecham knew nothing of their suspicions. Jacob hadn't even told Leah, for fear that she might let something slip. Jayce watched her for a moment more before finally answering her.

"I was working with the dogs that were to be taken on the expedition. They were spooked, and I, unfortunately, was a stranger in a bad position."

"Well, you appear to have recovered considerably, and that is why I'm here today. The exploration association would like for you to come to Seattle. We are both to travel there."

"For what purpose?" This was exactly the information Jacob had shared. They had both mulled it over for some time, trying to reason what the woman might be about. There was no way she had received word via telegraph at the time she claimed, and there hadn't been time for the mail to reach her from Seattle.

Helaina smiled sweetly and turned to Leah. "Might I have a chair? This will take a little time."

Leah nodded and left to find Helaina something to sit on. When she returned with a wooden chair from the waiting room, Helaina nodded her approval. "Perfect. Now, where was I?" she asked as she took her seat.

"You were about to tell me why I need to go to Seattle."

"Well, here is the wonderful news," Helaina said, looking to Leah as if for confirmation. "There is to be a second expedition. It will leave as soon as the remaining members of the team are handpicked by you."

"By me? Why me?" He looked to Leah. She seemed upset by all of this yet held her tongue, her distress evident in the way she worried the cuff of her sleeve. Had the Beecham woman somehow threatened her or coerced her to remain silent?

"You are the most knowledgeable about the lay of the land. This team will be staying on through the winter," Helaina explained.

Jayce rubbed his stubbled chin. "I have no desire to stay in the Arctic through the winter. I've already promised Jacob to remain with him in Last Chance Creek and practice working with the dogs. We have several important trips already planned."

He could see this news didn't sit well with Helaina, but at the same time he thought a spark of something flared in Leah's eyes. Could it be happiness at this announcement?

"But, Mr. Kincaid, this is a chance of a lifetime. You would be able to handpick the remaining team. The association values your opinion and believes you to be the most capable person to make these decisions."

"I'm sorry, but you must be mistaken," Jayce said, shaking his head. "I have no experience in such matters. They would never ask this of me."

"You're just overly modest, Mr. Kincaid. Your reputation precedes you."

"Truly? And where did you hear of me, Mrs. Beecham?"

Helaina seemed momentarily surprised by this. She quickly recovered, however. "From the association, of course. As well as others. My own brother had heard of you, in fact. He thought you . . . well . . . ingenious."

"I cannot imagine why. I've done nothing to merit such compliments." Jayce made a pretense at struggling to sit up better in the bed. Leah immediately came to his side to assist him. He liked the way she fussed over him and the way her hair smelled of lavender.

"You shouldn't wear yourself out, Jayce. If this is too much, we can go."

"Nonsense. I'm doing quite well. Jacob will be here soon to help me with my walk, in fact." He saw Helaina's mouth tighten at the mention of Leah's brother.

"I am glad that we had this opportunity to chat, Mrs. Beecham. I would be most grateful if you would send my regrets to the association and let them know that I won't be joining them for the second expedition. It might be possible that I could come along next year. But the doctor assures me I would be risking my life to try anything so foolhardy this year."

"I see." Her tone betrayed an obvious displeasure. "I suppose there is nothing I can say to change your mind?"

"Nothing."

"Even if I told you the second expedition would be called off if you refused to join?"

"I find that doubtful, Mrs. Beecham. The men who are funding and overseeing the Arctic exploration are not the type to put all of their eggs in one basket. Certainly not the basket of a lowly geologist. I know them well enough to state quite confidently that if they are planning a second expedition, it will go on without me. Geologists are easy to come by. I met quite a few when I worked in Vancouver for the last year."

"Vancouver?" Helaina asked. "Exactly when were you there?"

"Most of last year. I came north as far as I could get by ship in February, then relied on help from natives to get me to Nome." She frowned only more at this statement. Jayce couldn't quite figure it out. Why should that news upset her?

"You really should tell me sometime how you managed to work your way across Alaska in the dead of winter. I've heard it to be quite impossible."

"For a white woman, it might be, although I'm sure Leah could do it," Jayce replied with a smirk. "I find it hard to believe, for instance, that the exploration team accepted you. You're hardly cut out for living in the north. You're skin and bones. A good Arctic breeze would blow you over."

Helaina's face reddened at this. She clenched her hands together tightly, further amusing Jayce. "I assure you, I am quite strong and capable."

"You've been north before, then?"

She looked to Leah and then back to Jayce. "No, but . . ."

"You have experience in Arctic temperatures of fifty and sixty below zero?"

"No, but . . ."

"Then you probably have firsthand knowledge of winter survival skills?" He arched his brow and stared at her with an unyielding question to his look.

"Mr. Kincaid, I assure you I know very well how to take care of myself in any situation. I am not afraid to listen to the advice of others, but neither do I leave my choices to fate. I am well read on the explorations of other teams who have gone north and failed. I know what is needed and what is expected."

"Ah, but do you know what is unexpected?" He looked to Leah and winked. The action unnerved her completely and thoroughly amused Jayce.

Helaina had clearly had enough. "I will inform the association of your decision, Mr. Kincaid, but I wouldn't plan on being invited to join any future expeditions."

"It's no matter to me," Jayce lied. "I live here year-round. I don't need a sponsorship to study the vast northern wilderness. I make that my life. Unlike some people who must have badgered the association into taking them on this trip, they came to me. They courted and wooed me to join them, much as a man might do when seeking to entice a woman. If they choose not to invite me to another event, I will not be brokenhearted."

Just then Jacob walked through the door. He took one look at Helaina and frowned. "What's she doing here?"

"She came to persuade me to join her in Seattle. It seems there is to be another expedition north. They are putting together a team and want me to handpick the men."

"That's quite an honor, Jayce. You going?" Jacob asked, as if he didn't already know the answer.

Jayce shook his head. "Nah, I couldn't be bothered. This leg is giving me too much trouble anyway. I'm sure heading home with you is the right choice."

Helaina squared her shoulders and lifted her chin ever so slightly. "Well, I should go send word that you will not be joining the team."

"You do that, Mrs. Beecham," Jayce said, moving gingerly to the edge of the bed. Leah reached out to help him once again. He looked up and smiled at her. "Ah, my pretty nurse has come to see me properly cared for."

Leah halted in midstep, almost as if she were afraid to touch him. Jayce thought her hands trembled as she moved forward to assist him. More and more, he was convinced that the past was not behind them, but rather, it had crept quite intricately into the present. And who could tell what that might hold for the future? Especially after he spent the winter living in close proximity to her.

"Come, Jacob. I'm ready for my run," Jayce said, laughing.

Chapter Fourteen

Helaina couldn't put the thought of Jayce Kincaid from her mind. Things he had said caused her grave confusion. First Leah had told her that Jayce had been in Alaska for many years, with no reason to go elsewhere. Then Jayce himself had said that he'd been in Alaska at the very time he had thrown her brother from a train outside of Washington, D.C. And the ease in which he made the statement indicated he was telling the truth. All the things Stanley had taught her to watch for when people were lying were clearly absent: Jayce looked her in the eye and never looked away, and he didn't stammer or hesitate even once when relating his story.

"But he had to be in Washington," she told herself. "Stanley didn't just throw himself from the train. And he knew Kincaid well enough to have his picture sketched out." Helaina took the picture from her purse and unfolded it. It was clearly Jayce Kincaid.

She spread the picture out on her bed, then gathered her other materials. Everything pointed to the fact that Leah and Jayce were lying. She knew Jayce had been in England from summer through Christmas of 1914. This had been confirmed by the men at the British Museum. He had stolen from them, then returned to the United States. But Jayce said he'd been working in Vancouver with the exploration association. That would be easy enough to prove or disprove.

Helaina continued to study her notes. In February, Jayce had nearly been apprehended by two agents. Instead, he had killed the men and left them bleeding in the streets. Then in April, Stanley had caught up with him again. Her brother had nearly met the same fate as his friends.

But Jayce said he had headed to Alaska in February. He had gone by boat for as far as he could, then relied on dog sleds and native guides to get him to Nome. It just didn't make sense. Leah had told her at one point that Jayce had come to their village just prior to the eighteenth of May, but that he'd been in Nome for several weeks before that. It just didn't fit what Helaina knew to be true.

So exactly what was the truth about this situation?

There has to be an answer, Helaina thought. She feared that now it would be difficult, if not impossible, to get Jayce to Seattle. She knew she wouldn't find success in enticing him there, and the time for having Dr. Cox insist on such matters for health reasons was clearly behind them. No, short of drugging him and paying thugs to haul him off to some ship for her, Helaina was out of choices.

The other problem was trying to figure out what Jayce planned to do once his leg was completely healed. Would he stay in Nome or return to Vancouver? Or would he go back into the interior, as Leah suggested? Helaina would have to find out, and quickly, if she was to stay ahead of the mastermind.

She tossed the papers back into her large traveling bag and walked to the window. Looking out she could see part of the street. It was such a hopeless little town. Full of all sorts of unfulfilled pledges and dreams. She longed for home more than ever. New York or Washington—it didn't matter. Although at times like this when she was truly troubled, she always appreciated spending time with Mrs. Hayworth. She'd been a source of comfort and care for many years, and her calming presence seemed to reach deep into Helaina's soul. Still, Helaina was convinced that it couldn't be her faith in God that brought this about as much as familiarity.

Jacob Barringer believed in Christian philosophies, and he was anything but calming. In fact, he was quite an irritant. His smug, pompous attitude was enough to make Helaina want to check out his background for criminal activities. Maybe once she returned to Washington, D.C., she'd do exactly that. But first she had to deal with Jayce Kincaid.

She took up paper and pen and thought of the questions she would pose to the Canadian authorities. She needed to know if Jayce was wanted for other crimes during the past year. She would also need to check with the expedition headquarters and find out the truth of Jayce's employment with them. He claimed to have been there for some time; there was no doubt a record of that. Perhaps she could even learn if Kincaid was given over to long absences—which might explain how he could seemingly be in two places at once.

But even as she jotted down notes to herself, Helaina couldn't keep the image of Jacob Barringer from coming to mind. She would have to contact the Yukon and Alaskan authorities and learn about his past as well. No doubt there were things he would just as soon keep buried and hidden away. She smiled to herself and wrote several questions regarding Jacob.

Duty continued to call her back to her scribbled thoughts on Kincaid. At the top of her list was a question she underlined several times. If she could get an answer for it—she just might solve the puzzle.

How could Jayce Kincaid be two places at one time?

"I think you're right," Leah told Jacob as they finalized the shipping arrangements for a load of rice and coffee.

"Right about what?"

"Going to see Karen and Adrik. Despite your plans falling through, I don't think it should stop my trip to Ketchikan. Do you suppose you could get Oopick to continue running the store for a while? I know there will be a lot of work to do to store food for next winter, but perhaps if I promise to bring extra supplies when I return—maybe bring a few things they wouldn't normally have—it wouldn't be so bad."

"I figure there's nothing wrong with just opening the store once a week," her brother replied. "I mean, it's all well and fine to have it open daily when we're there, but I don't see that needs to be the way it is when we're gone. If Oopick only has to worry about doing business there once a week, then I can't see why it would interfere with her preparations for winter."

"That's true," Leah said, nodding. "I could probably stay a couple of months that way."

Jacob signed a paper offered him by the merchant, then turned to Leah with a big grin. "Now you're talking. You can have a great summer together. My only desire is that you'd be back by September. Would that work? I promised Anamiaq to help him with some trapping come winter."

"Of course. I could even be back sooner."

They walked away from the merchant and headed toward the shipping office. "September will be soon enough. Why don't you make your reservation now? Then you won't have to worry about it."

She grinned. "I wasn't intending to worry about it."

Jacob studied her for a moment and laughed. "Well, I guess given everything else you fret over, I figured you might rest easier if the matter was done and behind you."

Leah considered his words for a moment. "I'm trying hard to understand God's will for my life. I think sometimes I know exactly where He's leading, but other times things seem so obscure. Does that make any sense?"

"Of course it does. I often feel that way myself. I remember back to when we were children—the plans I had then, the dreams. I didn't see myself here, that's for sure. Adventure was something our father craved—not me. Yet here we are."

They began walking again, and Leah couldn't help but ask, "What about Arctic exploration? Are you still thinking you'd like a chance at that?"

Jacob said nothing for several minutes, just enough time to see them to their next destination—the ticket office. "I guess I wouldn't say no to the opportunity. It sure intrigues me, so I guess there's more of our father in me than I care to admit." He grinned at her. "But . . . well . . . I really only said yes this time because I felt the Lord wanted me to be there for Jayce. His faith is just growing—he hasn't really had another man of God in his life. You know, someone to share his faith and discuss Scriptures. With Jayce laid up, we've had some great times of study and prayer. Sometimes the doctor even joins us."

Leah had no idea. "That's wonderful, Jacob."

"I see it all as part of God's plan. Jayce wants more out of life—he needs more. I'm convinced that what he longs for is a closer understanding of who God is and what He wants for his life."

Leah nodded. She knew exactly the meaning of that longing. "I'm glad you've helped him, Jacob."

"I'll tell you something else too." He paused, as if trying to think of the exact words he should say. "I think Jayce is just now coming to realize what he lost when he said no to you ten years ago. I think—and this is just my opinion—that he's sorry for that loss."

Leah thought her heart might skip a beat. She swallowed hard. Could Jacob be implying something more in his words? Could there be a way to reclaim those lost years?

"Why would you say that?" She looked in Jacob's eyes. There was no hint of teasing or exaggeration. His expression, to be honest, was quite encouraging.

"I think he's a smart man—smarter at least than he used to be," Jacob said, looking out at the water. "I know from our talks that he's more compassionate and caring than he was ten years ago. I credit God's touch on his life for that."

Jacob motioned toward the ticket office. "You going to get your ticket or just stand around out here talking?"

Leah wanted to tell him the ticket could wait, but she didn't. Instead, she marched toward the office, contemplating whether Jayce would be upset to find she'd gone. Perhaps her absence would help him to put things in clear perspective. Maybe it would even give him reason to care.

"I can't say I'll be sorry to leave you, Doc," Jayce said, trying to walk without using his cane.

Dr. Cox chuckled. "I'll be sorry to lose you. You're taking the best assistant I've ever had—male or female." He looked to Leah and beamed a smile. "You are a very talented healer, Leah. You should get formal training."

"I'm a little old to be going back to school. Still, I hope the things I've learned here with you help me to help others," Leah replied.

Jayce took several solid steps. "Well, look at me, will you? I'm managing this pretty well, wouldn't you say?"

Leah laughed as Jayce gave a little hop. "You aren't yet up to running behind a sled, but I think once you give yourself a little more time, you'll be fit as the next man. By the time the snows come, you won't even remember this little diversion."

Jayce shook his head. "I'll remember it. I've learned my lesson about wading in to break up fighting dogs."

"So will you leave tomorrow?" the doctor asked.

"Yes. We've been gone long enough," Jacob declared.

"You're welcome in Last Chance anytime you'd like to come visit, Dr. Cox," Leah said, smiling. "I'm sure the people would be glad to welcome a real doctor."

Jacob headed for the door and opened it. "We'll be staying our last night at the hotel just up the street. If you have need of us—you know where to find us."

They parted company and headed to the hotel. Jayce focused on each step, careful not to step into a rut or sinkhole. The leg was much better, but it pained him. Still, he knew he'd probably have nothing more than a stump had it not been for Leah's attentiveness.

He stole a glance at her as she walked just slightly ahead of her brother. She radiated a kind of beauty that other women lacked. He knew confidently that this light came from within her soul. *How could I have been so cruel to her? How could I not have seen the genuineness of her heart?* Once again he regretted the choices he'd made ten years ago.

"I'm so glad to have found you," Helaina Beecham said, greeting the trio at the hotel.

Jayce nearly groaned aloud. What was this woman's attraction to him? She seemed unnaturally intent on keeping track of his health. She constantly asked the doctor about when he might be released and still talked of how she longed for him to join her in Seattle. But he didn't even know this woman.

"What do you need, Mrs. Beecham?" Jacob asked.

"Well, I need your help." She smiled, and Jayce couldn't help but feel that she was yet again up to something underhanded. He and Jacob had talked at length about who she was and why she had attached herself to the party.

Jacob pushed past her and motioned to Leah to go ahead. "I can't imagine that we have anything to offer, but let's go inside so that Jayce can sit, and then you can tell us all about it."

Once they were seated in the lobby, Helaina wasted little time before sharing her needs. "I'd like to come back to your village and learn how to handle the dogs. I've received word that although there will be no second expedition this year"—she looked to Jayce—"there will be another team coming up next year. I volunteered to learn how to handle the dogs and sleds, and the association has granted me several hundred dollars to see to purchases and such."

Jayce noted Jacob's look of annoyance and was surprised when he said, "I suppose we could squeeze in one more person. You will need to bring plenty of winter supplies, however. Once we're up there, I don't intend to be bringing passengers back to Nome."

"I don't mind at all. In fact, I have purchased several pieces from the natives. I have mukluks and sealskin pants, as well as a heavy parka and fur mittens." She seemed quite pleased with herself.

"I'm glad you're finally being reasonable," Jacob said.

"When do we leave?" Helaina asked.

"Tomorrow—midday," Jacob said. "You can sleep late. It'll probably be your last chance for a while."

"That sounds lovely. I'll cherish it." She got up to take her leave. "I'll see you all in the morning."

Leah had refrained from speaking until Helaina was gone. "I thought you wanted to be rid of her. Why did you say yes?"

Jacob and Jayce both leaned toward her at this point. "That woman is dangerous. She's clearly up to something—no good, if you ask me," Jacob said. "I figure it might be wise to keep an eye on her. If you have to have a bear in the house, you might as well determine where he sleeps. Or where she sleeps, in this case. Mrs. Beecham has an unnatural interest in our party—especially in Jayce. We need to know why. Otherwise she could prove to be more dangerous than any of us suspect."

"Well, you are full of surprises," Leah said, shaking her head.

Jayce laughed and eased back into his chair feeling quite satisfied. "You don't know the half of it."

Chapter Fifteen

Leah suppressed a yawn as she prepared to leave Nome. She felt a sense of regret and sadness over leaving Jayce. Yet at the same time, she needed to leave him. She needed time to clear her head and think about the future.

"Are you ready?" Jacob asked.

"I am. I'm tired, so I hope to just go to my cabin and rest. Are you sure you'll be all right with Mrs. Beecham?" She grinned at her brother but just then caught sight of Jayce. "What's he doing here?"

"It's a surprise of sorts," Jacob said. "I hope you won't be mad."

"Mad about what?" Her heart pounded in her ears. Jayce carried a small bag in one hand while balancing his cane with the other.

"He's coming with you."

She looked at Jacob as if he'd lost his mind. "What are you saying?"

"Look, I can't explain it all just now, but we have some reasons to be concerned about Mrs. Beecham's motives for wanting to go north with us. She's lied about several things, including the possibility of a second expedition this summer. She's tried over and over to get Jayce to accompany her to Seattle, but we don't know why."

"I know that much is true," Leah said, remembering Helaina's request that she encourage Jayce to go south. "But I presumed she was merely attracted to him. Why is this going to help?"

Jayce had joined them by now. "Morning, all."

"I was just trying to explain to Leah why you're here," Jacob said. He turned back to Leah. "Helaina has imposed herself on our trip back to Last Chance. Jayce and I are convinced it has to do with him, but we don't know why. If he instead goes with you to Ketchikan, leaving now before she knows what's going on, then she'll be forced to show her hand or come with me."

"But what will that prove?" Leah questioned. She was still unnerved by the idea of Jayce accompanying her on the ship.

"I'm hoping it might prove what she's really up to. Look, I know you didn't plan for company, but it is dangerous to travel alone. I figure Jayce can look after you, and I'll rest a whole lot easier. Please don't be angry with us."

Leah glanced from her brother's pleading expression to Jayce's face. He appeared delighted with the entire matter. "I'm not angry. Just confused."

"If there had been another way, I would have tried it. This seems the only choice other than just calling her a liar."

"And I truly do have business to tend to," Jayce declared. "There are some matters for me to address in Juneau. I can just get transportation from Ketchikan and rejoin you when you're ready to return to Nome."

Leah tried to relax. Jayce wasn't coming to Ketchikan for her company. That much was easy to see. Especially given his last statement. "All right. I suppose the matter is already settled. We'd best be on our way or we'll miss the ship." She leaned over and gave Jacob a peck on the cheek. "Please be careful. She may be dangerous."

Jacob laughed. "More to herself than to me. I plan to put her through the most arduous of trainings. By the time you two get back, she'll be able to run a dog team almost as good as you can."

Leah watched Jacob and Jayce shake hands. "Take care of her," Jacob told Jayce.

"I will. I promise."

The words caused Leah to wince. She turned away. *You'll take care of me for Jacob,* she thought, *but not because you want to. I'm an obligation—nothing more. I have to remember that.*

Jacob was glad to see Kimik and some of the other village men. "I wasn't sure if you'd get word or not." He shook Kimik's hand and gave him a hearty pat on the back.

"Icharaq's brother came just in time. We were headed out to hunt. Are these all the supplies?" he asked, looking at the stacks around them.

"Yes. I sent some other things north on the *Bear*. These were small enough I figured we could handle them."

"Where's Leah?"

"She's taken a ship to Ketchikan to see our family. She'll be back in September—maybe earlier."

Kimik nodded, then called to his companions. "We load now and get home sooner."

"We'll have one passenger. A lady who intends to come north and learn how to handle a dogsled team," Jacob told Kimik.

"A lady? Who is she?"

"Her name is Mrs. Beecham. Ah, there she is now." Jacob saw Helaina walking toward the docks, a young man behind her loaded down with two bags.

When they reached Jacob and the others, Helaina instructed the boy to put her things on the boat. "Just show them which one you want these on," she told Jacob.

Jacob pointed to the nearest umiak. "That one is fine."

The boy deposited the bags and returned to Helaina for pay. She quickly parted with a few coins and dismissed him. "So where are the others?" She looked around, obviously expecting to see Leah and Jayce.

"What others?" Jacob asked, playing dumb.

She looked at him with an expression of great annoyance. "Your sister and Mr. Kincaid, of course."

"Oh." Jacob picked up a piece of rope. "They've already gone." He headed to the umiak, anxious to see what Helaina's reaction would be.

Helaina followed after him, rather breathless. "Why didn't they wait for us?"

Jacob let the matter drag on as long as possible. "Why are you concerned? I'll get you safely to Last Chance."

This momentarily silenced Helaina. Jacob could almost hear wheels turning in her head as she contemplated her next question. He then looked over the remaining boxes, picked up one, and headed to the boat. Before he could return for any more, Helaina was there beside him.

"Good," Jacob said, pointing to the boat. "You can get in and sit there by your bags. We need to balance everything out just right."

"I don't understand why you're being so unpleasant," Helaina said, demanding his attention. "I simply wanted to know where your sister and Mr. Kincaid had gone. You don't have to be meanspirited about it."

"I didn't think I was being meanspirited," Jacob replied. "I just didn't understand why their location was of any concern to you." He looked at her hard, daring her to explain.

"I suppose after these last weeks, I've come to care about their well-being," Helaina said sweetly. "They are good people—your sister, especially. I've enjoyed getting to know her and will be happy to know her better."

Jacob decided he'd played around long enough. "Well, you'll have to wait until September to do that. But meanwhile, you'll get the best dog training available. You'll be able to drive a team like a native once I'm through with you."

"I don't understand. Why will I have to wait until September to better know your sister?" Helaina didn't even bother with further pretense.

"Because she's not coming with us. She and Jayce left early this morning on a ship bound for Ketchikan. Leah's visiting family and Jayce is traveling on from there to handle business."

For a moment, Jacob actually thought Helaina might faint. The color drained quickly from her face as her eyes widened. Then just as quickly as she paled, Helaina's face flushed red in fury. "Why was I not told they were leaving?"

Jacob crossed his arms and looked at her strangely. "Mrs. Beecham, I fail to understand why any of this is your concern. My sister has a life that has nothing to do with yours. Jayce too. You have made yourself a supreme annoyance, as far as I'm concerned, but I'm willing to help you out, given the importance of the situation."

"What would you know of its importance?"

He thought for a moment she might cry. This woman was so strange. She began to pace in front of him even before he answered her. "I know that you said it was critical that you learn how to handle a dog team. You said you were quite happy to spend the winter with us and endure the sub-zero temperatures so that you could better prepare yourself for the exploration planned next year. I've kindly tried to accommodate you on that issue, but now you seem far more interested in something else. What might that be, I wonder?"

Helaina seemed to compose herself. "I simply thought I was to have female companionship, for one. It hardly seems appropriate for me to head north without at least one other woman to accompany us."

"Yet you were prepared to do just that with the Arctic exploration team."

She looked rather stunned at this. It was clear to Jacob that she was caught and had no way in which to escape. He had taken a chance that she didn't know about the captain's wife accompanying her husband. At least he had been right on that account.

"So are you coming with us or not, Mrs. Beecham? I'm going to finish loading the supplies, and then I need your answer." He stalked off, smiling to himself. Let her chew on that fat for a while.

Helaina wanted to throw something at the back of Jacob Barringer's head. She wanted, in fact, to throw him to the ground and beat the smug look off of his face. All of her plans were ruined, and she didn't have the simplest idea of how to resolve the situation. The justice system in this part of the world was so frustrating. Had she felt that the police in Nome would have assisted her properly, she might have engaged them, but her observations had given her little encouragement.

If I tell him that I won't go, it will only make him more suspicious, she thought. Helaina quickly assessed her choices. She could refuse to go to Last Chance, telling Jacob that she'd wait for his sister's return. But she surmised that if she did this, Jacob would probably reject any thought of her coming to Last Chance in the future.

There was a slim possibility that she could catch up to Jayce and Leah in Ketchikan, but she could never hope to maintain her cover under that circumstance. There would be no reason for her to be there, and Jayce Kincaid was not a stupid man. He would easily figure out by eliminating all other possibilities that she was there for him.

If I go with Mr. Barringer, at least I know his sister will return in September. But what of Kincaid? He might not. She had to follow him and not Leah Barringer. There seemed no guarantee that Jayce was coming back to Last Chance Creek.

"So what's it to be?" Jacob asked.

Helaina jumped, not realizing he was standing there watching her. "I must say it's a difficult matter. I suppose I must come with you if I'm to learn about the dogs. I had hoped to further my discussion with Mr. Kincaid about the Arctic as well, but he's not returning until September, I suppose?"

"That's the plan."

She nodded. Since she had no real idea of where Jayce's business would take him, she felt her only choice was to go with Jacob Barringer. "Very well. I suppose my discussions of the Arctic can wait. I'll come with you and learn what I can about the dogs."

Jacob looked at her oddly for a moment. "Are you sure? You're going to be stuck up there for a while. You might be able to get passage on the mail ship, but otherwise—"

"I've made up my mind. This will be fine. I'm sure the experience will be interesting and the time will pass quickly."

Jacob laughed. "I'm sure it will be interesting, but I don't know about the time. If you don't mind, I need you to take your place in the umiak."

She nodded and made her way unassisted into the boat. Her mind reeled from the discovery that Jayce Kincaid was gone. Her brother had been right about one thing: this man's capture was proving more difficult than anyone she'd ever known.

Thoughts of Stanley brought to mind the letter she'd just posted to him. She had told him that plans were delayed but moving along well and she was certain to soon have Jayce in custody. Now she had no idea of how long it might be.

They would have to return to pick up Jayce and Leah and transport them to Last Chance Creek, she surmised. That would at least get her back to Nome. Perhaps she could send a letter to Stanley to have the Pinkerton men transported to Nome to await her arrival. While there, she could work something out to take Jayce into custody.

She relaxed a bit. Surely this would be the answer. Until now there had been no time to get anyone else in place to assist her. But two and a half months was enough time for Stanley to work out the details to send a dozen men to her aid.

Jacob and his men pushed off and climbed into the boat. Helaina was unprepared for the rocking motion as they made their way out toward the Bering Sea. The men's long powerful strokes took them quickly away from the shore and into the deeper waters. She gripped the side of the skin boat and held on tightly. What if they were to capsize? The boats hardly seemed a match for the long journey ahead of them.

"Are you certain we're quite safe?" she asked Jacob.

He grunted as he pulled the oar through the water. "As safe as anyone ever is out here. This is God's country, and He alone holds the future." He smiled for a moment, and then an expression crossed his face that suggested he just remembered something important. "But you don't believe in God—do you, Mrs. Beecham?" He shrugged. "So I'm not sure what or who you think holds your future."

He turned his attention back to the water, leaving Helaina once again infuriated with his snide mannerisms. The boat heaved hard to the right, causing Helaina to retighten her grip. Her gaze fell to the inside of the boat. It was nothing more than a wooden frame with skins lashed around it. She felt her stomach churn and knew without a doubt that she was going to be sick.

"You're turning green, Mrs. Beecham. Are you given over to seasickness?" Jacob called.

Helaina's only answer was to lose her lunch over the side of the boat. She dampened her handkerchief in the sea and wiped her mouth before glancing up. Jacob's look of concern surprised her.

"Are you feeling any better?" He seemed to genuinely care.

"I had no idea it would be this rough," she said honestly. The fight had been taken completely out of her. The boat seemed to settle a bit but not enough. She fought back a wave of nausea.

"You might actually feel better if you lie down. Adjust things as you need," he said, then turned his attention back to the job at hand.

Helaina wasn't in the mood for an argument. She pulled her bag close and used it for a pillow. Lying down did help a bit. She closed her eyes and pulled her arm up over her face to shield the intense sun. This was going to cost the Pinkertons more than usual, she decided then and there.

Jacob watched Helaina as she struggled to get comfortable. He felt sorry for her. He had never figured the spitfire woman would fall victim to the rolling waves. Lying there as she was now, she looked almost childlike—innocent and harmless.

What are you after? Why are you here?

The questions haunted him over and over. Jayce swore he didn't know her from the past. He had no idea of where she'd come from, but he planned to find out. He would send telegrams once in Ketchikan and see if he might get information from some of his friends. Meanwhile, Jacob planned to keep her too busy to be trouble to any of them. If she wanted an Alaskan adventure—he'd give her one she'd not soon forget.

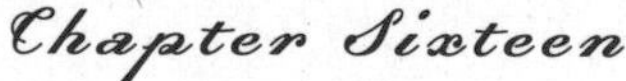

Chapter Sixteen

"What do you call this?" Helaina asked, wrinkling her nose at the food in front of her.

"We call it supper," Jacob replied. "It's actually pretty good—you should try it before turning it down."

"What is it?" She picked at the chunks of meat.

"It's seal meat in its own oil."

She frowned and pushed it away. "Don't we have anything else? Something fresh, perhaps?"

"I got some fish," Kimik said proudly. "You want a piece?"

She nodded enthusiastically. "Yes, I'd like that very much."

Kimik pulled out a newly caught fish and held up his knife. "How big you want?"

Helaina looked at the fish and then at Jacob. "Isn't he going to cook it?"

"I doubt it."

"You mean he plans to eat it raw?"

Jacob nodded and rubbed his chin. "Since he doesn't plan to cook it, that would be my guess."

She gave him a look of complete disgust. "I can't eat raw fish."

"You could cook yourself a piece over the fire," Jacob suggested. "Shouldn't take too long."

"And how would I do that? I don't see any pans or utensils."

Jacob held up a willow branch. "You could use this. Spear it through and hold it over the fire."

"But that stick isn't sanitary. I have no idea what's been on it." She crinkled her nose, as if imagining all the possibilities.

"Suit yourself, Mrs. Beecham."

"This is impossible," she said, picking up her plate. "What about the supplies you're taking with us? Aren't there some kind of canned goods we could open?"

"You gonna buy them?"

"I'll happily pay for a decent meal." She tossed the tin pan in Jacob's direction. "What do you have?"

"I have some canned milk, sugar, flour, beans, canned and dried, and—"

"Open some beans. At least that way I can heat them here by the fire."

Jacob shrugged and got to his feet. "Shall I run you a tab or will you pay in cash?"

She quickly found her bag and fished around until she came up with several bills. "Start my account with this," she said rather snidely.

Jacob noted she'd given him a considerable amount of money. He tried not to react with too much interest and went to find her can of beans. She was already proving to be difficult; the episode of seasickness had only been the start. After that she'd complained about needing to stop for a chance to relieve herself, then wondered if there wasn't some way to apply shade to her section of the boat, and finally questioned Jacob as to whether they'd travel all night. And now she was turning her nose up at the food. It wasn't a good way to get started.

He returned with the beans and tossed the can to her. She looked at it for a moment, then put her hand on her hip. "Do you have something with which to open this?"

He rolled his eyes, hoping to show her just how deep his exasperation ran. "Give it here." He rummaged in his bag and produced a can opener. He made short work of the lid and bent it back without severing it completely from the rest of the can.

"Anything else?" he asked, handing her the beans.

She put the can next to the fire. "A spoon would be nice."

He looked into her blue eyes and crossed his arms. "I'm sure a spoon would be very nice, but I don't have one. I only have the can opener because Leah told me we needed one for the house. Sorry."

"Very well."

She squared her shoulders and assessed the situation without another word. After a few minutes she took up her handkerchief and pulled the can back from the fire. Gingerly touching the metal, she found it to be sufficiently cool, then worked to bend the can lid back as far as possible. To Jacob's surprise, she then lifted the beans to her lips as if drinking from a glass. She'd need to be careful, Jacob thought, or she'd cut her lips for sure.

The men had chosen to sit away from Jacob and Helaina. They seemed to understand that they'd not have the same camaraderie with this new white woman that they'd shared over the years with Leah. Jacob figured it was just as well. Helaina's caustic nature was not something he would have wished on his enemy, much less his friends.

"Don't you ever miss civilization?" Helaina asked without warning.

Jacob thought about her question for a moment. He remembered a time when Denver had been his home. The city had seemed overwhelming, even terrifying. He hated the noise most of all, not to mention the rudeness of people who seemed always to be in a big hurry.

"If you mean big cities full of people and racket, then no," he said softly, "I don't miss it."

"But what about the innovations—the changes? The world is not as you left it when you came to hide away up here."

He looked at her oddly. She had such a strange way of looking at life. Her words were always something of an accusation. "What do you mean 'hide away up here'? I didn't come here to hide. I first came to the Yukon with my father. I stayed up north because I love it. There's something about this country that reaches deep inside a man. I honestly never thought it would happen to me. There was a time, in fact, that I planned to leave as soon as I had the means."

"But what about automobiles and aeroplanes?"

"What about wars and financial failures?"

She cocked her head to one side and studied him for a moment. "Is that really all you think of when you think of America and the wonders of our time?"

"I don't know. I understand that there are great inventions coming to light every day. I realize doctors are learning new ways to help people, and that travel is improving in speed and quality. Still, I know that there are problems."

"Such as?" She dropped the sarcastic overtone to her voice to add, "I'd really like to know how you see it."

Jacob leaned back on his elbows and stretched his legs out beside the fire. "Sometimes I get the newspapers from Seattle or elsewhere. The ship captains bring them or the missionaries carry them back from their trips. I see the complications of life in big cities within the pages. There seems to be a great deal of crime and hunger, yet no one really knows anyone well enough to care. Vast populations of strangers are content to wander through life with no concern or compassion for anyone but themselves."

Helaina frowned and toyed with the can. "The crime is bad, certainly, but the legal authorities are doing what they can to right the wrongs of the world."

"But isn't there something more than just righting wrongs? What about changing hearts? What about turning people from wrong and teaching them to care for one another?"

"And how would you propose to do that?"

Jacob sat up again. "With God, of course. The hearts and minds of people can only be changed when they understand that there is something—someone—to change for. It's the hopelessness that causes them to break the law. It's that which also kills them."

"Or they get killed by other people," Helaina admitted. "Like my family."

"Your situation is a good example. I can't comprehend why your folks and husband were murdered, but I can guess that there was a hopelessness deep inside the man or men who took their lives. There always is. Even when something else motivates the actions."

"Like what?"

"Greed. I once found myself accused of a murder because of someone else's greed."

Helaina perked up at this. Jacob saw that he held her interest completely as she asked, "Tell me about it?"

Jacob shrugged and put a piece of driftwood on the fire. "I had a good friend, Gump Lindquist, who was looking for gold. He'd found some too. He'd also found trouble in the form of a man who came looking for something that didn't belong to him. It's a long story, but the man was someone I'd known from before. He killed the old man as a way of getting to me—threatening me so that I'd help him. But when the ruckus caught the attention of other people—witnesses—the man fled and I was accused of murder."

"But you didn't do it?" she asked.

"No, I didn't do it," Jacob replied, remembering those horrible days. He'd honestly thought they'd hang him, and all because of what Cec Blackabee had done.

"How did you prove it? Was there a trial?"

"Like I said, it's a long story. My guardians were faithful to believe me and to not give up on exposing the truth. The authorities caught the man, even as he confessed what he'd done. Of course, he didn't know the law was standing outside the door listening in. My point is the man who killed my friend was consumed in his own hopelessness. He was overcome with greed and desired gold more than he valued human life."

"And you think God could have changed this hopelessness?"

"He changed it for me. Sitting in that jail, not even seventeen years old, I was sure they were going to hang me. I thought God didn't care. Here I'd trusted Him and He'd let this happen to me . . . let my friend die."

Helaina's face contorted, as if the comment caused her pain. She quickly lowered her focus to the can of beans. "And didn't He?" she murmured.

"No. God didn't just let Gump die, and He certainly didn't desert me. Sometimes the desperation of the moment causes us to feel as though God is far away—that He doesn't care. That's the hopelessness of the world creeping in."

"I really find all of this to be nonsense," Helaina declared, seeming to compose herself once again. It was as if a mask of steel fell into place. "People make choices and do as they will. They are driven by certain motives, I will allow you that. But their choices have consequences and bad choices must be punished. You were fortunate that your friends were able to uncover the truth. But had they not, the law would have had no choice but to hang you."

"That's a rather calloused, coldhearted way of looking at things, isn't it?"

"Not at all. Justice is often mistaken for being cruel, but it's only fair that people pay for their wrongdoings."

The words seemed to come from deep in Helaina's heart. This surprised Jacob. He'd never heard a woman talk with quite so much conviction for punishment. "What of mercy?" he asked.

"Mercy? Mercy has no place in the law. The law is the law. It is written and easily interpreted in order to keep our societies from falling into disorder," she said emphatically.

"I think you're wrong, Mrs. Beecham. I think mercy plays an important role in the law and its interpretation. I think that you can't just see our world in hues of black or white. We are all individual and very human in nature."

"Meaning what?"

"Meaning that we fail. We make mistakes. Sometimes we trust the wrong person and sometimes we're just in the wrong place at the wrong time. If there were no mercy for situations like that, what would happen to people who are innocently accused? Could you really live with the idea of our legal system putting people to death simply because they appeared to be guilty? Does your heart not cry out for mercy and truth?"

"My heart cries out for justice, Mr. Barringer. Only that. Justice is the key to our society maintaining order. Therefore, justice is more important than your mercy."

"There they are!" Leah declared, pointing down the dock to where Karen and Adrik Ivankov stood. Karen, still tall and slender, looked very much as she had the last time Leah had seen her. She smiled and waved enthusiastically at Leah. Adrik, a man who had always seemed larger than life to Leah, did likewise. "Hurry, Jayce." She left him to carry the bags and ran to where the couple awaited her.

Leah fell into Karen's arms and hugged her close. Karen was the only mother Leah had known for nearly twenty years. It was so good to be with her again. Leah wondered now why she'd delayed so long in coming.

"I can't believe you're really here," Karen whispered against Leah's ear. "I've missed you so much."

"I know. I've missed you too. It's been so long."

"And you've brought Mr. Kincaid back with you, I see." Karen and Leah looked to where Adrik and Jayce were in conversation several feet away.

"I really had no choice. He showed up on the shore when I was ready to leave, and Jacob announced that he would accompany me."

Karen turned her focus back on Leah. "What's wrong with that?"

Leah smiled. Karen's once-vibrant red hair was laced now with gray, but her eyes were as keen as ever. There would be no hiding the story from Karen, not that Leah really wanted to. "It's complicated, to say the least," she began. "You remember how I felt about Jayce back when I still lived here with you?"

"Yes," Karen said, nodding. "And how you still feel about him."

Leah nodded and sobered. "Yes."

"But he still doesn't feel that way about you?"

"I think not," Leah said with a heavy sigh. "Yet he's everywhere. He's in my thoughts and in my heart, and now he's here . . . at least for now. He tells me he has business elsewhere. So I don't imagine he'll stay here long."

"Would it matter if he did?"

Leah looked at Karen. "I'm not sure. Sometimes I get the feeling he would like a second chance. I know that sounds crazy, because just as soon as I think that way, he does something or says something that proves to me he can't possibly want that. So while on one hand I wish he would stay and allow us to start over in our friendship, on the other I just wish he would go."

"I've just invited Jayce to stay with us for a while," Adrik announced as they joined the women. "He said yes."

Leah looked to Karen and shrugged. "See what I mean?"

Karen grinned. "I do indeed. But unlike you, I think it matters a great deal more than you'll admit. I think once you let it all settle in, you'll be glad he's staying."

Jayce was glad for the invitation to remain with the Ivankovs. Ketchikan was a beautiful city set against impressive hills—mountains, some might say, although he'd seen much bigger. The Ivankov home was nestled deep in the forest, secluded from the harbor and the worries of town life. Here a man could lose himself by traveling days and days into the deep, dark woods. He liked that idea. He loved the solitude.

Standing in the seclusion of heady pine and fir, the light fading ever so slightly overhead, Jayce found the canopy of tall trees to be a welcoming comfort. They seemed almost to hide him away—shelter him from harm.

"I thought I saw you out here," Adrik said as he stalked up the path.

Adrik was a big bear of a man. Part Russian and part Tlingit Indian, he immediately dwarfed any other person around him. The only person who had never shown him fear, at least as far as Jayce had witnessed, was Karen. Even now Jayce felt rather unnerved by the man.

"I love the quiet. The stillness of the forest is almost too much to bear," Jayce admitted, trying to forget his uneasiness. "It's such a contrast to other places in this territory. So rich and green here, compared to the barren scrub and brush willows of the Arctic."

"It's all that rain and rich soil," Adrik told him. He looked at Jayce and smiled. "Has it changed much in ten years?"

"It's hard to believe I've been gone that long, but, no, it hasn't changed all that much. There are some things I noticed at the docks, but here . . . it seems almost eternally the same."

"Some things don't show the wear of time as much. People do, but not everything does."

The comment made Jayce a bit uneasy, and he quickly thought of what he might say to change the subject. "I've heard that we have approval for a railroad to be built from Seward to Fairbanks," he finally said.

"Yes. There's been a lot of controversy over it. Some people want to develop the land and others don't."

"Where do you stand?"

Adrik looked heavenward for a moment. "I see good on both sides. I hate to think of the land being spoiled—abused. I'm not sure the things that the government hopes to accomplish can ever be realized for this area, and it worries me to wonder how far they will go to be right."

"Right about what?"

"Right about their vision for the territory. You know they are already talking about pushing for statehood next year."

"I had heard that," Jayce admitted.

"Well, a lot of folks in the government think Alaska is the answer to troubles in the States. They think once we get statehood, they can promote moving people here and lessening the population of large cities. I don't think people will be inclined to move here, however, without more incentive than a railroad and thirty-seven cents a day to labor on its creation."

"You may be right. Still, I see exploration and innovation to be beneficial. I love this territory and think it would serve us well to develop some of the cities and areas between them, but I wouldn't want to see it spoiled, and like you I do have my fears."

"Some people just don't see a good thing when they have it."

They stood in silence for several minutes. Jayce felt there was something Adrik wanted to say, but he wasn't at all certain what that might be. He felt a bit uncomfortable waiting for the older man to address him but held his tongue.

Finally Adrik did speak. He turned toward Jayce and the serious expression he held immediately set the stage. "You know you're welcome here. You're a good man, and I'm pleased to hear you've set your life right with the Lord."

"But?"

Adrik smiled. "You're a man who likes to get right to the heart of things, I see."

"Might as well. I figure you have something to say, and I've no reason to keep you from it."

Adrik nodded. "I'd like to know what your plans are."

"My plans?"

Adrik nodded again. "For Leah."

Chapter Seventeen

Jacob looked at the ledger and then to Helaina. They had been back in Last Chance for nearly three weeks, and she still couldn't comprehend the way Leah kept books.

"I don't understand how to figure out what the furs or trade items are worth," Helaina admitted. "I don't know if a new pair of mukluks are worth two cases of milk, a bag of sugar, and a coil of rope. How would I know that?"

"You don't have to know it. Leah can figure it all up later and then reconcile it with the villagers. Don't turn people away just because you don't understand the system. Qavlunaq said you yelled at her. It upset her and she came to me in confusion."

"They all hate me," Helaina retorted. "They are meanspirited and vicious. I don't see why you even bother to help them."

Jacob frowned. He considered what to say to her for several moments while Helaina paced back and forth in a huff. "They don't hate you. . . . They just don't understand you. You have to see it through their eyes."

"Why can't they try to see it through my eyes?"

"Because you're in *their* territory, living off the fat of *their* land."

"Literally. Who in the world ever decided that eating whale blubber and seal fat was a good thing to do?"

Jacob shook his head. She was by far and away the most difficult person he'd ever known. "It's what's available to them, Helaina." He'd long since dropped calling her Mrs. Beecham, even though calling her by her first name seemed somehow unwise. He couldn't really say why. Up here, everyone went by their first name, but using hers seemed to imply an intimacy that did not exist.

She stopped and looked at him hard. "Can you honestly say you prefer this life to something else you might have in a real town—in a civilized state?"

Jacob closed the ledger book. "Are you trying to convince me to leave? Is that your plan?"

She composed herself and pushed back an errant strand of blond hair. "I have no plan. I simply asked you a question. You seem quite content here in this isolated, remote village, yet so many things are missing."

"Such as?"

"Real bathrooms. Electricity. Telephones." She plopped herself down on a stool behind the counter. "There's a whole different world out there. A world that's developed and changed while this place just stays the same. It's probably always been like this—and probably always will be."

"But what's wrong with that? Why must everything evolve into something else?"

She looked at him in complete exasperation. "For the betterment of mankind. Can you not see that?"

"I see problems in the south, just like we have problems in the north. There is good with the bad in both places. I don't see that we have to be a replica of the States just because we're a territory."

She sighed and gazed, unblinking, at the wall behind him. "I didn't expect you to comprehend my thoughts. I don't even understand it myself . . . not completely. It's just this place—the isolation and the negative way the people see me—well, it's all so hard. I don't even feel like myself anymore. Nothing here is familiar or right."

It was the first time Jacob felt truly sorry for her. "Look, I know this must be hard, but better you figure it out like this than to have found yourself stuck at the top of the world. It's even more foreign there."

She shook her head. "I would have survived. You don't know me. I would have gotten by. I can't help that I miss my life. I miss the food and the comfort."

"What? You haven't found comfort in our luxurious home?" he asked, grinning.

Helaina actually smiled at this. "The bathing facilities leave much to be desired."

"A bowl of lukewarm water has always served me well enough," Jacob teased.

"Look," she began, "I'm sorry to be so frustrated and ill-tempered. This hasn't really turned out the way I'd hoped. I'm lousy with the dogs and can't seem to make sense of the store."

"And you're used to being a woman who easily picks up her duties and does them well—aren't you?"

She glared at Jacob, and for a moment he thought she might get angry. Then just as quickly her expression softened. "I am."

"So you're completely out of place in this situation, but that doesn't have to be a bad thing. You're learning new ways, and you are getting better at all of it. Even the dogs. You just have to show them who's boss, and frankly, you've never appeared to have any trouble with that in the past." He smiled again, hoping she wouldn't take offense.

"So where do we go from here?"

"Well, I think it would benefit us both if I go clean up and you get supper ready. I really do appreciate having you prepare the meals. That leaves me free for other tasks."

"It seems the least I can do, given the fact that you've had to leave your home on my account."

"It wouldn't be proper for me to share the place with you," Jacob countered. "Taking up residence together up here constitutes marriage. We don't want to give anyone the wrong impression. Besides, the weather has been fine and the dog shed is comfortable enough."

"It still seems unfair, but I am grateful for what you've done. Ayoona showed me how to make a stew with squirrel earlier in the day. It's been simmering since this afternoon."

"That sounds wonderful. I hope she gave you some of those wild potatoes."

"She did. There are some other things in there that I'm not entirely familiar with, but when she had me brave a taste, I had to admit it was quite good."

"I'm sure it is." He headed for the door. "Just put the ledger away for now. We'll talk about it later and see if we can work out an easier system. For now, I'm going to clean up. I'm starved. Oh, will there be biscuits?"

She laughed. "Aren't there always? I've never met a man who liked biscuits as much as you do."

"Doughnuts." He said the word firmly as if it should mean something to Helaina. At her look of confusion, he added, "That's one thing I really miss from civilization, as you call it. My mother used to make the best doughnuts."

"Maybe I can find a recipe," Helaina offered.

"That would be really nice."

He left her there and headed off to clean up. He thought it very kind of her to offer to make doughnuts, but still he wondered whether or not she'd ever adjust to life in Alaska. He was glad for her sake that she'd not made the trip north with the team on the *Homestead*. She would never have made it. It only made him wonder again—why? Why had she signed up for such a project? *She hates the north—hates the isolation and the cold. So why did she want to be on the* Homestead?

Her lies in Nome came back to haunt him. She was clearly here to bide her time. But why? What was her interest in Jayce? What could compel a woman of her social caliber to follow him to the wilds of Alaska—for that was what she had done. Jayce had told him that Helaina was a last-minute addition to the team—one that had been frowned upon by everyone. Even the captain seemed unhappy about it, but he would say nothing on the matter.

Now she was here, and Jacob knew she was miserable. She didn't fit in with the natives, and she resented the Kjellmanns and their beliefs. At least she managed to put that aside and join them on Sundays for church, however. He thought she did this more out of desperation for some semblance of normalcy than for any desire to learn about God's Word. Still, she had shown interest in his devotions at night. They had even settled into a strange sort of ritual where he would take up the Bible as the meal concluded each evening. He would always read from the Scriptures and sometimes they would discuss what the meaning was and why it should matter to them in this day and age.

Jacob had to give her credit. Helaina had been open to the interpretations and understandings that he shared. She sometimes argued what she saw to be foolishness, but just as often she would ponder passages and ask him questions the following day. This had caused him to start praying for her. Whereas before he could see no reason why he should be saddled with this strange, angry woman, now he wondered if the Lord hadn't brought her into his life for the purpose of sharing Jesus.

After cleaning up, Jacob grabbed his Bible and headed back to the house. He could almost taste the squirrel stew. A smile crossed his face. He'd have to reward Ayoona for her help with Helaina.

They ate in relative silence that evening. Jacob could tell Helaina had a great deal on her mind, and for once he found that he'd really like to know what it was that troubled her. He was on his second bowl of stew, still contemplating how he might approach the matter, when he heard her heave a heavy sigh.

Jacob just decided to wade into the conversation, come what may. "You seem to be carrying the weight of the world. You aren't still worried about those ledgers, are you?"

"No," she said, pushing back her bowl. She stared at the table and said nothing more.

Jacob pushed ahead. "Can you not talk about what's bothering you?"

She looked up. "Do you honestly care?"

Her question took Jacob by surprise. His answer startled him even more. "Yes. Yes, I care. I wouldn't have asked you if I didn't."

"Do you remember our trip here from Nome?"

Jacob laughed. "How could I not?"

She smiled. "I know I was a burden. But do you remember our conversation about hopelessness and mercy?"

"Of course, I remember. It's only been a few weeks."

She leaned forward and folded her hands together atop the table. "I've thought about some of the things you said. Then last night you read from Matthew, and I've been troubled by it ever since."

"Why?" He took up his Bible and opened to the eighteenth chapter of Matthew. "Tell me and we can discuss it."

"Can we read it again?"

"Sure." He drew his finger down the chapter until he came to the twenty-third verse. " 'Therefore is the kingdom of heaven likened unto a certain king, which would take account of his servants. And when he had begun to reckon, one was brought unto him, which owed him ten thousand talents. But forasmuch as he had not to pay, his lord commanded him to be sold and his wife, and children, and all that he had, and payment to be made.' "

"That was the law then, correct?" Helaina asked.

Jacob looked up. "I suppose it must have been."

"So the king did nothing wrong in seeking justice. The man owed him and couldn't pay him. The king had a right to receive his due pay."

"I can agree with that. The man owed a debt." He looked back to the Bible. "Should I go on?"

"Yes. Please."

He found his place. " 'The servant therefore fell down, and worshipped him, saying, "Lord, have patience with me, and I will pay thee all." Then the lord of that servant was moved with compassion, and loosed him, and forgave him the debt.' "

"But he wasn't obligated to do so," Helaina said, stopping Jacob from going further. "The law said that he should pay his debt."

"Correct. The king showed mercy. The servant begged for more time. The king was moved by his circumstance and let him go."

"But the law clearly was on the side of the king. A debt was owed."

"And the king forgave that debt."

"Please read on," she said, her brows knitting together.

" 'But the same servant went out, and found one of his fellowservants, which owed him an hundred pence: and he laid hands on him, and took him by the throat, saying, "Pay me that thou owest." And his fellowservant fell down at his feet and besought him, saying, "Have patience with me, and I will pay thee all." And he would not: but went and cast him into prison, till he should pay the debt.' "

"He did nothing wrong," Helaina said, her tone quite troubled. "The man was entitled to be paid back. Just because the king forgave his debt, that shouldn't imply that the man is obligated to forgive someone else's debt. If you owed me twenty dollars and John owed you twenty dollars, and I told you to forget about paying me back, it shouldn't obligate you to forgive John's debt. The situation in this verse is confusing to me. It was a legal loan—a binding agreement."

"But the man was in the same position as his fellow servant," Jacob replied. "He didn't have the money to pay him at that time. The man never came to him and said, 'I won't pay you.' He simply asked for more time. Who knows what the agreement might have been between the two men. Maybe it was such that the man had lent the money saying, 'Pay me back when you can.' "

Helaina considered these words for a moment. "But it was the servant's right to put the man in prison. Just as it was the king's right to put the servant in prison. The law is the law."

"But mercy is greater than the law."

"That cannot be!" she snapped, and for the first time there seemed to be real anger in her voice. "Nothing is above the law."

Jacob looked at her for a moment. "Do you not see this story for what it is really about? Let me finish the chapter." He found his place quickly and continued. " 'So when his fellowservants saw what was done, they were very sorry, and came and told unto their lord all that was done. Then his lord, after that he had called him, said unto him, O thou wicked servant, I forgave thee all that debt, because thou desiredst me: Shouldest not thou also have had compassion on thy fellowservant, even as I had pity on thee? And his lord was wroth, and delivered him to the tormentors, till he should pay all that was due unto him. So likewise shall my heavenly Father do also unto you, if ye from your hearts forgive not every one his brother their trespasses.' "

"That isn't right," Helaina said, leaning back and crossing her arms. "It's not just."

Jacob shook his head. "How is it not just?"

"The man was under no obligation to forgive the debt owed him just because the king had forgiven him. That makes no sense to me. The man owed a debt and was responsible to pay back that debt. Why should the servant be obligated—forced to break a contract with another—just because his contract had been cancelled out?"

"He should have desired to do it. Mercy had been given him. Do you know what that's like? Because I do. Remember I told you about being in jail—accused of a murder I didn't commit? When I was let go, I knew what true mercy was for the first time in my life. I didn't get to go free because of anything I'd done. I had no say in the matter. My friends went out and found a way to prove the truth—that was the only reason I was set free."

"But you weren't guilty. You owed no debt. This man owed a debt, and I do not understand why, just because one person forgives, another is forced to also do likewise. God makes no sense to me in this—especially when that chapter concludes to say that I must forgive everyone—no matter the guilt or the crime."

Jacob closed the Bible and tried to think of a way in which he might convince her. Sometimes the Bible offered difficult truths. Obviously this was one of those times for Helaina. At least she hadn't walked away from it or put it aside. She had mulled over this Scripture for over a day. There must be a reason.

"You're not a very forgiving person, are you, Helaina?" He wanted to take the words back the minute they were out of his mouth. He couldn't believe he'd actually spoken them aloud.

"I forgive those who deserve to be forgiven," she said.

A thought came to mind. "And who really deserves to be forgiven?"

She seemed to consider this for a moment. "Well, I suppose no one. If they break the law—they must pay the penalty. They don't deserve to get out of whatever punishment is given."

"So do you believe forgiveness should be based on merit?"

"I don't know that I would find that to be true either," she admitted.

He nodded, feeling certain she would say something like this. "Who then merits forgiveness? Is it the person who is truly sorry? Is it the person who made a mistake? Is it the person who simply didn't realize the crime?"

"Ignorance of the law is no excuse," she replied, sounding more like her old self.

"So if it is left up to you, no one deserves to be forgiven." He paused for a moment, then smiled. "Which I happen to agree with. No one deserves it. No one really earns it or merits it."

"Then what of this passage?" She was back to being confused.

"This passage is not just about forgiveness," Jacob said. He gazed deep into her blue eyes, hoping to somehow understand the pain that he saw there. "It's about mercy—compassion. Neither man deserved forgiveness. The law was clearly in favor of the man to whom the money was owed. God wants us to understand that the law is clearly in His favor. We do not deserve forgiveness because of anything we've done to merit it. But God in His compassion shows mercy on us . . . and . . . He forgives. He's asked for us to do the same."

"Threatened us to do the same, you mean." Her words were laced with bitterness.

"But, Helaina, if the love of God is in you—if you know that blessed wonder of being shown mercy—believe me, you'll desire to show mercy in return. You'll want to forgive . . . because in doing so, you'll know God's heart just that much better. You'll feel His presence in that very action of forgiveness."

"I've never needed anyone's forgiveness. I keep the law," she said firmly and added, "I don't compromise it."

"The Lord doesn't compromise the law or do away with it. He found a way to satisfy it through Christ. He loves the law because the law reflects His holiness—His perfection. He doesn't want you to forsake the law, but rather to understand the need for mercy . . . because you're wrong, Helaina. You *have* needed someone's forgiveness—you need *His* forgiveness. Because without it you will face an eternity separated from Him."

She held his gaze but said nothing. He could see that she still felt confused, but the time had come for him to let her make her choice. He prayed for her silently as he gathered his things. "The stew was perfect. Thank you for a wonderful dinner." He started to leave, then remembered something.

"I nearly forgot to tell you. I'll be leaving for Nook tomorrow."

"Nook? Where is that?"

"It's a town up north. Nook is the native name; they call it Teller now. I'm delivering some young dogs. I should only be a few days, but you can never tell how things will go. We're taking the pups by water, and they don't always appreciate that mode of transportation. John will look after the dogs while I'm gone, so you won't have to worry about that—although it would be good practice for you."

"Couldn't I go with you? You know I'm not much use around here," Helaina said, her voice sounding almost desperate.

"No, there won't be room for even one more person. Besides, I won't be gone that long. You'll do fine. Keep the store going and keep track of what people bring in to trade. We'll figure it up later. For the most part, they know what things are worth. They are honest and good people. You won't have any trouble from them."

Helaina spent a restless night contemplating the Bible verses she'd discussed with Jacob and facing the uncertain discomfort of his departure. She finally gave up trying to sleep about the time she heard the dogs start to bark and yip. This was a sure sign that Jacob was up. No doubt, as he gathered the dogs he would take to Nook, the other animals would be miserable—whining and howling their displeasure.

She felt like whining and howling her own displeasure. "How can he just leave me here? No one here cares whether I live or die."

Helaina got up and dressed quickly. She wondered if she should make Jacob breakfast or if he'd take off before she would even have a chance to make anything decent. Looking around the room in complete dejection, she realized that she would miss Jacob. She hadn't thought about Robert in days—maybe weeks. Truth be told, she hadn't even thought about Stanley or Jayce or the job she'd come north to accomplish.

"What's wrong with me?"

And then it came to her. Her interest in Jacob had taken a new form . . . and the thought terrified her. *This can't be. I cannot let myself care about him—nor let him care about me.*

"It's wrong," she murmured. "It's all gone very wrong."

Chapter Eighteen

Helaina heard that the revenue cutter *Bear* was in the harbor and that they were offloading mail and other supplies for the village. Jacob had been expecting a supply of goods for the store, but Helaina had no idea if she would need to pay for it or arrange for the things to be brought to the store. Much to her relief, however, John appeared with a couple of envelopes and the announcement that he and some of the other men would be delivering several boxes for the store. His dark eyes seemed to watch her intently—almost as if he expected her to do something wrong. She felt they all watched her this way, and she hated it.

"Thank you, John," she told him in a clipped tone.

He nodded and handed the envelopes over. "I'll be back."

Helaina looked at the mail and realized one of the letters was for her. The other was marked *Urgent* and addressed to Jacob. The return address suggested it had come from the captain of the *Homestead*. This seemed very strange, given the man was supposed to be somewhere in the Arctic, where Helaina knew there would be no mail service.

She opened her own letter and read the contents. The expedition association in Vancouver had written her to acknowledge that Jayce Kincaid had indeed been with them for a considerable time in 1914 and into very early 1915. He was not a man given to long periods away from the job; in fact, he was just the opposite, often working over the weekend and well past the hours others put in. They further added that his service had been invaluable to them, and they hoped that he would be available to join them again soon.

Closing the letter, Helaina tried to digest the information and make sense of it. She knew for a fact that Jayce had been in England working at the British Museum in 1914. At least a man calling himself Jayce Kincaid had been there. She thought it might be important to write to Stanley and let him know of this news. Maybe her brother could lend some kind of insight to the situation.

Since John had still not returned, Helaina looked at the other letter in her hand. The word *urgent* caused her to contemplate whether she should just open the letter. What if someone were in trouble and needed Jacob's immediate attention? Obviously it was important, or the captain would never have sent it. She decided to open it and risk Jacob's ire.

Dear Mr. Barringer,

Our expedition has run into trouble, as you may have already heard. There has been sickness and problems with the ship, and we found it necessary to return home to make repairs and reconsider our next move. It is a great disappointment to us all.

The urgency of this letter is to let you know that we want to secure your help immediately for our next journey. We are already making plans and would like to have your pledge for next year, along with your help in the planning. Your friend Mr. Kincaid has been an invaluable help with the dogs, and we are grateful that he managed to catch up with the crew.

Helaina stopped and reread this portion of the letter several times. What in the world was the captain talking about? Jayce hadn't caught up with the crew. He was with Leah Barringer. Or was he? Had Jacob lied to her? When Leah went to Ketchikan, had Jayce made his way on the revenue cutter north to rendezvous with the *Homestead*?

Her anger rose with each suggested thought. *I've been duped somehow. Jayce probably realized who I was. I don't know how he could have, but he must have figured it out. Then, instead of making a scene or trying to do me in, he headed out—back to the expedition—knowing I wouldn't be able to join him.*

The sound of the men coming down the stairs drew her attention back to the moment. She quickly folded the letter and stuffed it back in the envelope. She'd have to figure out later what to do.

John and the others brought in a dozen boxes and stacked them in the front room. "Thank you for your help," she told them as they made their way to the door.

"You are welcome," John replied.

She thought about her situation and called after him, "John, is anyone making their way to Nome?"

He paused and turned. "Nome? No. We hunt whale tomorrow. Most of the village will move up the coast. The women are picking berries and other things, and they will trap squirrels and rabbits."

"Then I'll be here alone?" Helaina asked, terrified by the thought.

"The Kjellmanns will be here. A few others."

Helaina nodded, and John must have taken this for her approval because he quickly left without another word. Jacob had said nothing to her about the village taking a nomadic trek north. Who would care for the dogs? Jacob had said that John would be responsible.

She ran up the stairs and outside, hoping to stop John in time to question him. He was nowhere to be found, however. Looking around her, Helaina felt a deep sense of loneliness. *I am at the top of the world and all alone. Stanley is safe and comfortable in his office in Washington, and I am here being made a fool of by a dangerous fugitive.*

In her heart, she wished Jacob were there. *If he were here,* she thought, *I could question him about the letter and Jayce.* But even as the thought came, Helaina knew such a thing would be difficult. How could she question Jacob without giving away her interest in Jayce? And if he saw that interest, would he understand? Would he be on the side of the law?

"He's a Christian," she whispered. "He knows the honorable and right thing is to obey the law and do good. He would surely understand that my desire is only to aid in the capture of a dangerous criminal."

But Jayce was his friend. And friendships tended to make people look at matters differently. She really had few choices. When Jacob returned she would give him the letter and apologize for opening it, then maybe make some side comment about thinking that Jayce was with Leah in Ketchikan.

She smiled to herself. That wouldn't seem so strange. After all, Jacob had told her they were together. It shouldn't seem out of place for her to ask about something like that. It was just a matter of curiosity.

Jayce worked at sharpening his knife in the quiet of the day. Leah had gone with Adrik and the children into Ketchikan, while Jayce had opted to remain behind and tend to other things. Karen, too, had stayed. She had told him that she intended to bake bread and that the first loaf would be ready around lunchtime. The invitation was then extended to join her for the noon meal. Jayce could hardly say no to that.

He rhythmically ran the knife's blade against the sharpening stone. There was something comfortable, almost soothing, in the familiarity of this action. It was something he'd known since childhood, even though he'd been raised in the city with plenty of wealth and servants who could sharpen the knives.

His father had been an outdoorsman who loved hunting, often taking his sons with him. Jayce had found great pleasure in the wilderness lands of upstate New York and Canada, and as the years went by, often it was just him and his father. Those were special times. Times in which Jayce learned to be a man.

His father often told Jayce that God could be found in all of creation. *"When a man looks at a snowcapped mountain or a frothing, wild ocean, he should remember that the Creator of the universe masterminded all of this and more."* Jayce remembered the words as if it were only yesterday that he heard them. He'd had very little appreciation of them as a young man.

His father had often talked of Seward's Folly—the Alaskan Territory—especially after gold was found. He and Jayce had even planned a trip; not for the gold, but for the opportunity of seeing such a place. When his father died Jayce set aside the plans, but after his mother died, he headed west.

Seeing that it was nearly noon, Jayce pushed aside thoughts of the past and decided to check and see if lunch was ready. Already he could smell the heavenly scent of fresh bread. It was a treat he didn't often get. He put away his knife and walked to the log house. Karen smiled broadly at him as he came through the door.

"I thought perhaps I'd have to call you, but then I opened one of the kitchen windows and let the aroma of the bread do the job."

"It did the job well," Jayce admitted. "I must say this is a real treat."

"Come sit here," she said, pulling out a chair. "I have everything ready."

Jayce did as he was instructed as Karen brought a bowl of chicken and dumplings to the table. "Adrik was able to get some chickens last week. We've been enjoying them ever since, although Christopher believes we should keep them as pets."

"Sounds like a typical kid," Jayce said.

Karen turned to retrieve a pot of coffee. "He's not yet ten, but he thinks he's twenty. He has picked up a hefty portion of adventurous nature from both Adrik and myself." She poured Jayce a cup of the steaming liquid, then did likewise for herself.

"I remember being that age. I was just thinking about it, in fact. My father used to take me hunting. I think it taught me a passion for the wilderness. I'll be sorry when we populate the world so much that there aren't any more areas of wilderness."

"That would be sad indeed," Karen said, taking a seat across from Jayce. "Would you say grace?"

Jayce nodded and offered a simple prayer of thanks. "This smells heavenly. I haven't had a meal like this in some time."

Karen brought a plate of freshly sliced bread to the table. "Here, it's still warm."

Jayce took a piece and popped a bite of it in his mouth. The taste was incredible. "Mmmm," he said as he chewed.

"I seem to remember that your father and mother are both passed on. Is that right?"

Jayce nodded. "Yes. My mother had died right before I came north the first time. My father passed away several years before her. It was hard. My entire family seemed to disintegrate the day my father was buried."

Karen's expression was compassionate. "What happened?"

"My siblings were not wise with what my father left behind. They went through the money as if it were a never-ending supply. After they went through what he'd left them, they began to tap into what was endowed to my mother. Before I knew it—long before she'd confide in me as to what had happened—it was necessary to sell her house."

"How sad."

"It truly was. My mother and father had once been esteemed in the neighborhood. By the time my mother died, however, her society friends had long since fallen away."

"Then they weren't really friends at all," Karen said quite matter-of-factly.

"True enough, but that only caused it to hurt all the more."

"So, Jayce . . . will you be with us long?" Karen asked, the tone of her voice adding weight to the seemingly simple question.

Jayce could not help but think of Leah and of Adrik asking him what his plans were for her. Though he had sought her attention, so far Leah had gone out of her way to make sure they had no time alone. He wondered if she was afraid of him—afraid of what he might say. Just as he feared the words he felt compelled to share with Karen.

"I don't know where to start," he said softly. His heart was in great turmoil. "Adrik has asked me what my plans are—what my plans for Leah might be. I told him honestly that I didn't know. I wasn't sure how she felt anymore, and I wasn't sure what to do with the feelings I had."

"And what are those feelings, Jayce?"

He drew a deep breath. "I would . . . that is . . . I . . . well, I care deeply for her. I could now see taking her for a wife—even though I couldn't see it back then."

"Do you love her?"

"I think I do." He shook his head. "No. I know I love her."

Karen's smile broadened. "And have you prayed for direction?"

"I have to admit, I pray and then I tend to find myself caught up in other thoughts. I hurt her so much; I know that well. I was shocked to find her still so bitter about the past. I figured she'd long forgotten me. I had seen her as a child and that her feelings were those of a child."

Karen crossed her arms and leaned back in the chair. "But now you see it differently?"

"Yes. I realize she knew her heart and mind quite well, even then. I suppose because I knew myself to be so unsettled at that age, I couldn't believe anyone else would have the necessary maturity in order to make important decisions."

"This territory is unlike the settled cities of the United States," Karen said thoughtfully. "There are few second chances here. People grow up fast under the midnight sun."

"I know that to be true now. I just need to know if second chances ever happen."

Karen drew a deep breath. "They are rare. But they do happen."

"Mama!"

Karen's attention was immediately drawn away. "That would be Christopher. He always outruns his father in getting home." She got to her feet. "Pray about it, Jayce. Second chances are always possible when God is in the middle of the matter. He is a God of second chances."

Jayce took Karen's advice to heart. He began to pray fervently for direction where Leah was concerned. At the same time, he watched Leah interact with her family. She seemed so happy to be a part of something bigger than herself. For the first time, he knew without a doubt that he wanted a wife and children. He could only hope that it wasn't too late to have such a future with Leah Barringer.

"Are you wanting to be alone?" he asked, coming upon Leah as she sat by the creek that ran behind the cabin.

"No. You're welcome to join me."

He took a seat on the ground beside her. "I remember how much I enjoyed this place. It holds a lot of pleasant memories."

"Yes," she barely breathed the word.

"Leah," he said, pausing to think of how he wanted to word his next thought, "what do you want . . . what are your plans for the future?"

She looked at him oddly, then returned her gaze to the creek. "I don't know. I'd like to have a husband and family, but apparently God hasn't seen that in His plans for me." She grew quiet, as if embarrassed. "I'm sorry," she said, shaking her head. "I shouldn't have said that."

"Why? Can't you be honest with me?"

"Given our past, Jayce, I don't know that I can . . . well . . . it isn't a matter of honesty, but I just don't feel like discussing it with you."

"I wish you would."

A gentle breeze brought with it the scent of rain. Leah shifted to her knees, as if to get up. Instead, she remained for the moment. "I've talked to Karen about going to Seattle."

"Seattle? But why?"

She sighed as though the thought was almost too much to bear. "She has family there. I might be able to stay with them."

"For what purpose?" Jayce asked. He couldn't begin to understand why she would want to do such a thing.

"Because I want a husband and children," she said firmly and looked at him squarely for the first time. "There are more possibilities for me to find such things . . . in Seattle."

She got to her feet then. "Like I said, I shouldn't be talking to you about any of this."

She walked away, heading past the cabin. Jayce thought about going after her, but it almost felt that an unseen hand held him in place.

Seattle? She'd really leave for Seattle?

His thoughts jumbled and twisted in his mind. He thought she loved Alaska. He needed for her to love Alaska, because if he were to marry her . . . The thought trailed off, and Jayce realized he was practically holding his breath.

He had to convince her to stay. He had to prove to her that the things she said to him ten years ago weren't in vain. He loved her. He knew that now . . . now that he faced losing her again.

Chapter Nineteen

"What do you mean you opened my letter?" Jacob asked, looking at the torn envelope. "This wasn't yours."

"I know," Helaina said, sounding somewhat put off. "I thought it was important."

"Important to mettle in my affairs?" Jacob barely contained his anger. "You above all people should know better."

"Why do you say that? I was just trying to help, and you make it sound like I've committed some sort of crime."

"You have." He looked at her hard. "You're the one who's such a stickler for the letter of the law. You broke the law. You took something that didn't belong to you."

"I didn't take it," she protested. "I only opened it. I didn't try to keep it from you or use it to my own advantage." She looked away at this point, and Jacob couldn't help but wonder what she had thought to gain by reading his mail.

"You shouldn't have done it."

She turned quickly. Jacob was surprised to find that her face was quite flushed. She seemed genuinely embarrassed, but her actions gave him cause for consideration. He had long wondered how he might convince her that her hard attitude—her unyielding, unmerciful heart—was wrong.

"I suppose you want to hear that I'm sorry," she finally said.

"It doesn't matter if you are sorry. A thief is always sorry when he or she is caught."

"I'm not a thief!" She began to pace, as was often her way when upset. "I saw that the letter was marked urgent and that it was from the captain of the *Homestead*. I thought perhaps in your absence, I could help."

"It doesn't matter. You broke the law. My mail was a private matter between me and the captain."

She exhaled loudly, paused for a moment, then continued to pace. "I don't understand why you're so upset about this. It's not like I tried to hide the letter or keep it from you. You've read it for yourself. You have all the information you now need."

"Yes. That much is true. But since you are a woman of the law, you should face some penalty for breaking the law."

In exasperation she came at him. "This is complete nonsense."

"No. No, it's not. If we went to Nome and I presented my case to the authorities there, told them of how you tampered with my mail, there would be consequences."

Helaina looked more upset than ever. He wondered for a moment if the authorities in Nome could somehow expose her real purpose for being in Alaska.

Helaina crossed her arms and lifted her jaw ever so slightly. "Why are you being so hard about this?"

"Why are you hard about the law?"

Jacob could see her expression change. She seemed to finally understand where he was coming from. "This is such a small offense," she argued. Her tone suggested a sense of defeat.

"So the penalty will probably be fairly small," he countered. "Unless of course the judge wishes to make an example out of you. They do that, you know. I once saw a situation where a woman stole meat for her child. The boy was dying and without food would surely not last another day. The times were hard and she did wrong."

"She should have gone to someone and begged if necessary," Helaina said, seeming to gather her strength. "There is always another way to deal with a difficult situation."

"The judge apparently thought so too. He sentenced her to three months of labor in the jail. She had no one to watch her son, so he took the boy from her and put him in the orphanage. The child died there a week later. He refused to eat because he wanted his mother."

Helaina grimaced. "It wasn't the judge's fault. The mother did wrong."

"And so have you," Jacob said, trying to sound as stern as possible. "I want you to pack your things. I'm taking you to Nome—to the authorities there."

"What? This is ridiculous!" She came to him and took hold of his arm. "I can't believe you would do this."

"But the law is the law, and I am entitled to justice."

Helaina's expression contorted. It was almost as if Jacob could see every confused emotion as it played itself in her mind. "Can't we work this out?" she asked.

She dropped her hold, and Jacob crossed his arms and stared at her with what he hoped was a fierce scowl. "But you deserve to go before the law."

"I do," she said with a sigh. "I know what I did was wrong. I shouldn't have opened your letter, but it . . ." She fell silent and drew a deep breath. "I am without excuse. I did wrong."

"And you deserve to face your consequences."

She met Jacob's gaze. Suddenly he thought she seemed much younger—so frightened and unsure of herself. "I know what I deserve."

"Then there really isn't a question of what should be done. Is there?" He didn't wait for an answer but turned instead to take up his coat. "I can't trust you."

He pulled on his jacket and looked at her for a moment. She stood before him, speechless. He could see that she'd reached the end of her understanding for the situation. She didn't understand the need to seek forgiveness, because in her mind she'd never done anything bad enough to need forgiving.

"Enough of this," he said, feeling rather sad for her. "I won't make you go to Nome. I forgive you. And though the law is the law, and I have every right to seek satisfaction against you—I waive that right. Let's not speak of the letter again."

He saw her shoulders slump forward in relief, yet still she had no words. "This, Helaina, this is mercy. Remember how it feels . . . because chances are better than not that someone, someday, will need mercy from you."

Helaina stared at the ceiling long after she'd gone to bed. Her earlier encounter with Jacob had left her emotions raw and her heart uncertain. He had terrified her . . . made her realize that he held her life—her secret—in his hands. He could have forced her to Nome, where she would have had to take at least the judge into her confidence. Who knew if that would have allowed her to get off—to go unpunished for her actions.

She rolled over and pulled the pillow to her chest. Hugging it close, she realized that Jacob had helped her to see something startling about herself. It scared her—and made her more uneasy than she'd been in a long, long time.

Unable to sleep, she got to her feet and lit the lamp. "I can't understand any of this. God demands justice himself. I've heard enough sermons to know that."

She went to where Jacob had left his Bible and picked it up, contemplating the well-worn book for several minutes. With a deep breath, she took it to the table and sat down, then drew the lamp closer and opened it. The page read *Micah* at the top. She had never heard of this person, or perhaps it was a place. Scanning down, however, her gaze rested on the eighth verse of the sixth chapter.

"He hath shewed thee, O man, what is good; and what doth the Lord require of thee, but to do justly, and to love mercy, and to walk humbly with thy God."

Helaina trembled at the words. She read them again. Do justly . . . love mercy. God seemed to suggest the two walked hand in hand. But how? She pondered the words, desperate to understand. How could one seek to do justly and love mercy at the same time? It made no sense to her. Surely one would cancel out the other. You could hardly hold people justly responsible for their actions and show mercy. Could you?

"But Jacob just did that with me," she whispered. "He held me responsible—he made me account for my wrongdoing. Then he showed me mercy. I deserved much worse."

She closed the Bible and leaned back. Could it really be that there were times when the law was not to be the focus as much as leniency . . . mercy . . . forgiveness?

She had never felt the need to seek forgiveness from anyone. Not in all of her life—not in the way Jacob suggested that all of mankind needed. Yet Jacob had made her feel a sense of desperation—a sense of need that she couldn't even begin to understand. And not only that; she wanted Jacob to no longer be angry with her. She cared about what he felt—what he thought. She very much wanted his mercy . . . even though she didn't deserve it.

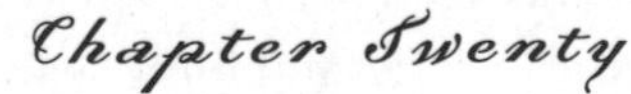

Chapter Twenty

SEPTEMBER 1915

The summer had passed quickly for Leah. She longed for her home in Last Chance, but at the same time she knew she'd miss her family here in Ketchikan. Jayce had been in and out of her world. For a time he had been there with them, then he'd taken off for parts unknown. Leah couldn't help but wonder what he was doing, but she tried not to care too much. She knew something had changed, but she couldn't put her finger on what flickered between them . . . at least not without rekindling a hope that Leah had long tried hard to suppress.

Letters from Jacob told of the frustrations and difficulties he'd had with Helaina Beecham. The woman had at first seemed so angry regarding any mention of God and the Bible. But over the weeks and given the isolation, Helaina had attended church services and appeared to be quite interested in some of the topics. Jacob himself was surprised by her poignant and educated questions. He thought in time her heart might actually be changed to see God as a loving Creator, rather than a stern, unyielding judge.

Jacob also wrote of the village. The hunts had been excellent; fishing had been so good that they had been able to dry a huge supply for winter. Some of the people liked to bury the fish and dig it up for later use. Leah had never been able to get used to this type of eating. To her, the salmon or cod was rotten, whereas the Eskimo people saw it as a delicacy.

But always Leah's thoughts returned to Jayce. He had promised to return in time to head back to Nome with her. He'd also indicated that he'd like to talk to her about something important but that he would wait until they left for home.

"I can't believe you're already leaving," Karen said, holding Leah's clean blouses. "I pressed these, but no doubt after you travel with them, they'll have to be pressed again."

"We're heading into winter at home. The temperatures will be dropping, and before long the snows and ice will seal us in our village," Leah said, smiling. "I'll be wearing so many layers by then that no one will ever see these blouses." The hand-me-downs from Karen were appreciated but were not the most practical for life in Last Chance Creek.

Leah took the clothes and packed them in a small trunk Adrik had given her. There were many other things to take as well. Books were a real treasure, and Karen had given her several to wile away the hours through the long winter months. Adrik had included some items Jacob had requested, and another crate was packed with all kinds of canned goods from Karen and Leah's efforts. It would be a real treat in the village, and Leah already knew she would share generously.

"I hope you won't wait as long to come visit us next time," Karen began. "I know the Lord has put you in that place for a reason, but I miss you and our long talks."

"I do too. Writing you takes some of that longing away, but it isn't the same."

"Who knows? Maybe they'll run us a telephone line from Last Chance to Ketchikan someday," Karen teased. "Wouldn't that be something?"

"Well, if they can run a train line from Seward to Fairbanks, I would think a phone line across the interior won't be far behind."

"Maybe they'll put a train line in as well. Then you could just hop on board and be here in a couple of days."

Leah tried to imagine for a moment what that might be like. "Do you suppose they'll actually ever accomplish something like that?"

"It's impossible to say. Adrik tells me that there are all sorts of plans in the works. They're already pushing for statehood, you know. They plan to propose it to the Congress as soon as possible."

"It doesn't seem very likely that anyone would care if we became a state or not. Most people think we're nothing but ice up here. I heard that from Jayce."

"What else has he said?" Karen asked. The look on her face suggested an anticipated answer.

"Why? What have you heard?"

Karen shook her head. "Oh no you don't. I asked first."

Leah closed the lid on her case and tried to act as though she hadn't thought every day about Jayce and what he might say to her once they were alone on the ship home. "He says he wants to talk to me—when we're alone."

"About what?"

"He didn't say. He said it was important, but that he didn't want to interfere with my time visiting family. Then he's kept himself kind of busy and out of the way."

"I wasn't going to say anything . . ." Karen began. "Oh, I really shouldn't say anything at all." She turned and walked to the window. Lifting back the curtain, she continued. "I guess what I will say is that Jayce has come a long way. He knows the truth of who God is—that He's real and not just some figurehead out there. Jayce cares about this land—almost as much as Adrik." She let the curtain fall back into place and crossed her arms as she met Leah's gaze.

"I think Jayce regrets the past. I hope you'll both put aside what happened back then and start anew."

"But how does someone just put the past away like that? Especially when the past has been your constant companion for so many years?" Leah questioned.

"I would start with God," Karen said frankly. "He's the only one who can help you let go of your regret and bitterness. He's the only one who will help you make sense of this."

Leah thought about Karen's words for days, and even as she boarded the steamer, *Orion's Belt,* Leah contemplated what her former guardian meant by all that she'd said.

"You seem awfully quiet," Jayce said, frowning. "I suppose this is very hard for you."

Leah felt almost startled by his words. She didn't know quite what to say. "I'll miss them—but I miss my home in Last Chance too."

"So you've decided to stay in Alaska?"

"How could I not? There's just something about this place." She smiled and waved to her family on shore. "Everywhere I go it's different; the land is so vast and so unpredictable. I'd actually like to see every inch of this territory." She looked at him and laughed at the stunned look on his face. "Does that shock you so much?"

"Shock me?" He shook his head. "No, not really shock. It's more like a pleasant surprise."

"But why should it be a surprise? I've made no secret about loving Alaska."

"But what of going husband hunting in Seattle? I heard they could be bought on the docks, just like many other things," he teased.

Leah forced herself to rest in God's peace rather than focus on how nice Jayce looked—his dark hair, a little longer than usual, blowing in the gentle breeze. "I'm trying hard to let the Lord lead me," she finally admitted. "But I've never been good at that kind of thing. I'm much too impatient."

"You? I find that hard to believe. You're the most patient person I've ever met. Look at the way you took such good care of me when I had the leg injury. Even now, when my leg pains me, you slow down your pace and walk at my speed. Don't think I haven't noticed."

She smiled and leaned against the railing, pleased that he'd been aware of this act of kindness. Karen had long ago suggested that Leah display only a gentle and loving spirit when dealing with Jayce. In changing her heart in this way, Leah had to admit she felt better about herself and about Jayce. It hadn't been easy, but over the weeks in Ketchikan, Leah had tried her best to just be friends with Jayce and enjoy his company. She had no idea of what might happen in the future, but she wanted to remember the summer of 1915 as one of peace and joy.

That night after supper, Leah thought perhaps Jayce could talk to her about whatever it was he wanted to say. But instead they passed a quiet evening reading in the salon before heading to their individual cabins.

After weaving in and out of a dozen or so islands, they finally docked in Sitka. Leah thought Jayce might talk to her here as they enjoyed a short time on shore, but he never did. Leah sensed he was nervous, and that only served to make her edgy. She thought maybe he wanted to ensure that she wouldn't resort to her old self—dealing with him in a vile, ill-tempered manner, since he planned to live in Last Chance Creek for the winter.

The ship departed Sitka that evening and pushed out into the ocean. It wouldn't dock again until Seward, where the ship would deliver workers for the railroad project.

"Leah?"

It was Jayce. He'd found her at the rail, shivering as she watched the endless waters of the Pacific. "It's getting late. I wasn't sure where you were. You know it's not all that safe to venture around on your own."

"You forget, Jayce, that I'm used to taking care of myself. Jacob is often gone, and I've learned to be independent and capable." She tried not to sound challenging or smug, but she could tell by the way Jayce shrugged that she'd probably said the wrong thing.

"I'm ready to go in," she added with a smile. "It's getting colder."

"There's also quite a squall line on the horizon. Captain thinks we're in for stormy weather."

"Then we should probably get below. I wouldn't want to be responsible for keeping you out and losing you overboard," she teased.

He grinned and took hold of her elbow. "I maintain that you do not have much confidence in me or my abilities."

Leah started to give him a sassy retort, then paused. She looked up at him and realized he was watching her quite intently. Their faces were only inches away, so it seemed only natural that he should close the distance and kiss her.

It felt like something from one of her dreams, and Leah closed her eyes and prayed that she might never awaken. This was her first and only real kiss, and she wanted to memorize every moment of it. She didn't even realize that she'd put her arms around Jayce's neck until he pulled back and whispered, "I wasn't expecting that kind of reception."

She felt her face grow hot, and she quickly jumped back. "I'm . . . I didn't . . . oh . . ." The words died in her throat. What had she done?

He chuckled. "I didn't mind that kind of reception, if that's what has you worried."

She licked her bottom lip, then chewed on it nervously. *What should I say? What can I do? I don't want to appear wanton. Oh, what must he think of me? If he calls me a child or tells me I'm too young . . .*

"Leah?"

She looked up and met his sweet, gentle face. His dark eyes seemed to pierce her through to the heart. "What?" She barely breathed the word.

"I'm not sorry for kissing you. I hope you're not sorry either."

He said nothing more, and Leah, in her state of shock, couldn't make words form in her mouth. Instead, she allowed Jayce to lead her below. Once he was assured she was safely inside with the door locked, he called good-night and left her there.

For several minutes, all Leah could do was stare dumbly at the door. What had just happened? Better still, when might it happen again?

Leah awoke to a horrible pitching of the boat. She sat up in bed, nearly being dumped from her mattress as she struggled to balance herself.

The storm!

Jayce had said there was a storm headed their way. She had an inside cabin, so there was no window from which to observe the situation. She pulled the blanket up around her neck and wondered if they were in any danger. She hoped the weather might pass them quickly and the rocking abate.

For hours she felt the ship fight the waves. Nausea washed over her, but Leah had never been one given to seasickness and refused to succumb to the situation. For a moment, she thought of going to find Jayce. He would be able to tell her if they were in any real danger. Would he be angry? she wondered. Surely it was nothing more than a simple storm, and soon it would pass and all would be well again.

The room seemed to close in, however, as Leah waited in the darkness. *What should I do?* The ship heaved hard to the right, tossing Leah from the mattress. She landed on the floor with a thud, her hip stinging from the fall. She tried to pull herself up, but then the ship slammed down recklessly to the left. Without hope of control, Leah fell hard against the frame of the bed, this time hitting her head.

A knock sounded at her door, but Leah felt unable to rise to answer it. To her surprise the door opened and Jayce entered the room. "Are you okay?" he asked, rushing to her side.

"I think so. I hit my head, but I'm not seeing stars or anything." She let him help her up. They could barely balance against the pitching of the ship. "What's happening? Why are you here?" She felt her breath quicken as she realized he was holding her quite close.

"Listen, Leah, the truth is, we're in trouble. The ship's captain has called for help from every able-bodied man. We're taking on water."

She swallowed hard. "We're sinking?"

"Not if I can help it." He leaned down and kissed her hard. "Leah, I love you."

The words refused to register. She looked at him, dumbfounded. She longed to say something, but, what if his words were simply borne of fear? Perhaps he was just responding to the threat of the storm.

"Don't look at me that way," he said with a laugh. "You look absolutely disgusted with me. I know I've made a lot of mistakes, Leah, but this could be the last chance I have to tell you how I feel."

"I'm not disgusted," she managed to say. "I . . . I don't know what I am. But I'm sure it has nothing to do with disgust."

He kissed her again, then guided her hand to the metal frame of the bed. "Hold tight." She wrapped her fingers around the piece and did as he told her.

"I have to go, but I didn't want to leave without letting you know how I feel. I've been a fool, Leah. I know that now. I wish I'd known it ten years ago."

She felt her senses regroup. "I knew it ten years ago," she said, trying hard not to sound frightened.

He smiled. "But that's because you're smarter than me." The ship seemed to groan beneath them. "Look, I have to go. Stay here unless they call to abandon the ship."

"Do you think they will?"

"I don't know how bad the damage is. I know we're in trouble, but I'm hoping we can turn it around. Get dressed and make sure your things are ready in case we have to leave quickly. And, Leah?"

"What?" She felt her knees begin to shake violently.

"Pray."

With that he crossed the room and left, leaving her door open to the passageway. Mindless of the exposure, Leah fought against the motion to pull on her sealskin pants over woolen tights. They would keep her warm against the ocean air, should they have to seek shelter in a lifeboat.

"Father, please stop the storm. Send it away from us and calm the seas. Oh, help us, Father," she prayed as she began layering her clothes. She had already been wearing a long woolen undershirt that Karen had made for her. She added a blouse over this and a kuspuk to top the blouse. She had no heavy parka, for Jacob had promised to bring that to Nome when he met her there. She couldn't help but wonder if she would be warm enough should they have to leave the ship.

To her surprise, Leah began to realize that the pitching had lessened. She breathed a sigh of relief. The storm was passing. That had to be good. Perhaps the danger had passed. "Thank you, God," she whispered.

Most of her things had been packed into crates and stored in the hold, but what little remained in the cabin she quickly packed in her small bag. As a last thought, she took up the box of matches on the nightstand and stuck them in her mukluks as she pulled the heavy boots on over her wool socks. They might have need of them later, and Jacob had taught her there was never such a thing as a useless item in the Alaskan Territory.

But just as Leah felt that things were improving, people began to run amuck in the passageway. She heard their shouts and their frightened cries.

"I have to get my children!"

"Where's my key? I have to get my things from the cabin!"

"No, sir! Leave everything. There won't be room in the lifeboats."

Lifeboats? Leah felt her feet freeze in place. It was impossible to tell, but she thought she heard a man crying, "Abandon ship! Abandon ship!"

She moved to the door and tried to step out, only to be pushed back inside by a heavyset man who appeared to have the cabin across from hers.

"What's happening?" she asked.

"Didn't you hear? We're sinking. We're to abandon ship now!" the man said before disappearing into his room.

Leah went back to the bed where she'd left her bag. If the man had been correct, she would need to leave her things. She quickly took off the kuspuk and opened her bag. She took out another blouse and pulled it on over the first one. Replacing the kuspuk, she then took up three pairs of heavy wool socks and stuffed them into the top of her pants. The rest could be left behind—along with all the wonderful things she had in the hold.

She felt a sort of listing to the right as she hurried to the hall. People were frantic, nearly throwing each other to the floor as they fought to get topside. Leah avoided them as best she could but found herself slammed against the wall more than once.

"We must get to the lifeboats," a woman sobbed as she pushed past Leah. "We have to or we'll die." She looked Leah in the eyes just long enough to reflect the terror in her heart.

"We cannot panic," Leah said, trying to help the woman to the stairs. "We must be brave."

The woman seemed to absorb this for a moment and finally nodded. "We must be brave." She continued to murmur this over and over as they made their way along the passage.

Leah focused on each step as they fell into line behind the other people making their way to the top. In her mind, Leah cared only about one thing. Where was Jayce? Had he already abandoned ship?

"No, he would have come for me," she murmured.

"Where will we go?" another passenger questioned from behind her. "We're in the middle of the ocean. Who will find us here?"

Other people began to comment on this—each one more terrified than the one before. She prayed for them silently. *Please, Lord, calm their spirits.*

A strong beefy-armed man reached out to pull her up the last two steps. "Come on, miss. Make your way to the port side. We don't want another *Titanic* on our hands. Come on, folks, there's plenty of lifeboats for everybody. Make your way down."

Leah thought of the luxury liner that had sunk only three years earlier after hitting an iceberg. The tragic loss of life had been overwhelming. When she and Jacob had finally heard about the horrific ordeal, it was already old news. Now she might very well live through another Titanic situation.

"Get on down there, lady. There are boats waiting to be lowered."

She searched the decks for any sign of Jayce. He had to be there! He had to be somewhere! She broke away from the pressing stream of people who were rushing to reach safety.

"Jayce!" she called over and over. Her façade of calm fell away. "Jayce, where are you?"

But with everyone else screaming and calling the names of their loved ones, Leah knew it was hopeless. She might never see him again. The thought chilled her to the bone and frightened her more than the idea of setting into the ocean in nothing but a small lifeboat.

She might lose him again. Only this time—it would be forever.

Chapter Twenty-One

Jayce searched the deck for Leah and could find no sign of her. A few of the men were loading into boats where women sat in numb silence, while down in the water, lifeboats were splaying out on the still-choppy waters. Jayce felt bad for the passengers. They were terrified, and with good reason. He hurried to help two of the crew who struggled with the winch to lower one of the boats. The people in the boat were screaming as the mechanism lowered them in a lopsided manner. If the crewmen continued, they'd spill them all into the Pacific.

"Let me help," Jayce said, pushing one of the young men out of his way.

"It's stuck," the sailor said.

Jayce gave the handle a good kick, then pushed with all his might. The winch gave way, and the boat lowered in an even manner.

Jayce glanced up and caught a fleeting sight of a woman. He craned his neck to see around the sailor. It was Leah! He called to her and she stopped in midstep. As she turned, he could see the abject terror in her expression. Hurrying through the remaining men, he reached her and glanced at his watch. "Three minutes."

"What?" she asked, embracing him. "I couldn't find you."

"Well, you have now. Only we have to hurry. The boiler is going to blow this ship sky-high. We need to get to a boat." He glanced left and saw a boat being lowered with only two women. "Come on, hurry."

They ran for the side, and Jayce quickly called to the sailors. "Stop! Two more." The men seemed nervously irritated but waited for Jayce and Leah to board. "Hurry!" Jayce said, motioning to the men. "Then join us. We'll wait for you."

The men lowered them in record speed. They hit the water hard, nearly spilling the old woman at the far side of the boat. She cried out, but held fast to the side with one hand, while gripping what appeared to be a native-made bowl with the other. Jayce could do nothing to help her, and Leah was already trying to comfort the other woman, who was grabbing at her chest and moaning.

"We have to put on life jackets," Jayce called. "They're in the storage box."

Leah went to work to retrieve them. They were wrapped in a canvas-type tarp and looked fairly new. Jayce breathed a sigh of relief at this. He'd heard stories of life jackets that were no good to anyone because of their age and poor craftsmanship.

Leah helped the sick woman, whom they'd learned was named Bethel, into her jacket, but the old woman flatly refused to put hers on. "It's too confining. I know how to swim."

Jayce didn't have the heart to tell her that the cold temperatures of the water would be more likely to claim her life than the water itself.

Jayce looked at his watch. They were nearly out of time—the boiler would blow soon. He pulled on his own life jacket as Leah secured hers, and then he took up oars. "Leah, get the other oars—we have to get out of here." She did as he told her as he looked back up to the men who'd helped them. "Jump for it. We'll pick you up."

There were two other lifeboats nearby. The men on these encouraged the crew as well. "Jump! Jump! We're right here. We have blankets. Jump!"

Jayce watched as several sailors did just that. They hit the icy waters and disappeared into the darkness. Jayce watched for them to reappear. One by one, like bobbers on a fishing line, they came up—fighting and thrashing against the icy cold. Two of the men were quickly picked up by one of the other boats, but none of the sailors were close enough for Jayce to reach.

"Leah, let's row in this direction." He pointed the way, then began to put his back into it. Leah did likewise. They had moved out maybe twenty yards when the first explosion nearly capsized them.

"Keep rowing, Leah. Keep rowing. We have to get away from the ship."

They did their best, but Jayce knew it wouldn't be easy to escape harm. When the second, more deadly explosion came only seconds later, they were pummeled with fiery debris. Jayce kept rowing. He felt something bite into his neck and arms while pieces of the ship came down like rain.

The fire lit up the night, and around them Jayce could see boats fighting to get away from the doomed ship. They were in the midst of utter chaos. No one was paying attention to anyone else; they were only thinking of survival.

Jayce saw a man floating in the water face down. He stopped rowing and motioned for Leah to help him. They reached over the side together and tried to pull the man to safety. Then Jayce's worst fears were confirmed as they rolled the man over. "He's dead, Leah," he said. "Let him go."

"Oh," Bethel moaned behind Leah. "I'm dying."

Jayce looked at the woman. She seemed to be gasping for breath, while beyond her the other old lady had apparently succumbed to her fears and fainted. The cherished bowl lay at her feet, surprisingly in one piece.

The fire was dying away as the ship continued to sink. Here and there fiery debris floated on the water, temporarily lighting their way. It would only be a matter of minutes until they were in darkness once again. Jayce felt the hopelessness of their situation settle on his shoulders. What were they to do now?

Leah turned to help Bethel. "Just rest. The worst is over now. Don't worry your heart anymore."

The woman's tear-stained face haunted Jayce. "I have a daughter in Nome. If I don't make it . . ."

"Shh, you'll make it," Leah encouraged.

"But if I don't, please let her know what happened to me. Her name is Caroline Rivers."

Jayce watched Leah comfort the woman. Her tenderness to this stranger caused Jayce to only love Leah more. Dr. Cox in Nome had said she was a great healer, and Jayce could understand why. Leah had a natural heart for making others feel better.

"Jayce, I think the other passenger is dead."

He shook off his thoughts. "What?"

Leah's expression was stricken. "She's taken a blow to her head. The piece is still there. She's dead."

Bethel began to sob. "We're all doomed. God have mercy on us."

"Come on, Leah. We need to row and catch up with the others," Jayce said, still not certain what should be done.

Leah grabbed up the oar and positioned herself to row. It was the only thing they could do, Jayce reasoned. There were no other options.

Jacob awoke with a start. He didn't know why, but he immediately thought of Leah. He sat up and listened. He had been helping Anamiaq cut thick bricks of tundra sod. The man was adding an addition onto his small house since they were to have another baby.

"Leah?" Jacob said aloud. He could have sworn he'd heard her call him. His uneasiness grew. Something was wrong.

He lit a lantern and checked his watch. It was three in the morning. He yawned and tried to figure out what was wrong. Leah was traveling back by ship. Jacob had planned to leave for Nome the next day. Had something happened? Was she all right?

He tried to lie back down and sleep, but it was impossible. He got up and left the tent, checking on the few dogs he'd brought with him. He and Anamiaq had planned to get the sod cut, then wait to transport it until they could bring out the dogsled teams. It wouldn't be long, given the recent weather. The dogs seemed fine, but they, too, were restless.

"Something wrong?" Anamiaq called out from the tent.

"I don't know. I have a bad feeling about Leah, and I can't seem to shake it. I don't know why, but I just feel like she's in trouble."

The heavy cloud coverage and fog obscured the sun and kept Jayce wondering where they were. They had lost track of the other lifeboats sometime in the night, and now they were on their own. Jayce constantly consulted his compass, hoping to get them back to the closest shore, but he figured them to be quite a ways out. He tried to calculate just how many miles out from Sitka they might have been, but the storm had wreaked havoc with any accurate measurements. They were tossed about all over the ocean; they could be closer or they might be farther away. It was impossible to tell without some sort of landmark.

"I wish we had something I could give to Bethel," Leah said as the woman slept. "I'm afraid for her."

"I know. Look, there's another problem here," Jayce said, glancing at the dead woman at the opposite end. "We'll have to . . . well . . . you know . . . let her go," he said hesitantly. "I don't know where we are or how long it will be before we find help. It's not good for us to carry her body around."

"We don't even know who she is. Bethel doesn't know her. She has nothing on her that identifies where she's from or who she is," Leah protested.

"I know, and I'm sorry." He knew she understood, but he also knew how difficult this situation had become. It could be days before they were rescued.

"It's starting to rain again," Leah said, looking heavenward. "Give me the tarp. I'll see if we can't save some of the water to drink. It won't taste pleasant, but it will keep us alive."

Jayce helped her to accomplish setting up a kind of protection for them, while positioning the tarp to allow for water to run into the dead woman's bowl. This was their only hope for fresh water.

The rain poured steadily for over an hour and showed no signs of letting up. While Bethel slept, Jayce carefully made his way to the dead woman. With Leah's help, they lifted her body over the side and released her to a watery grave. Jayce felt they should say something. "We should pray," he told Leah as the body disappeared in the waves.

"That would be good," she replied, tears in her eyes. "At least God knows who she is."

Jayce bowed his head. "Lord, you know each of us here, just as Leah mentioned that you know this woman. Receive her into your kingdom, Lord. Give her family peace of mind when they hear of her passing." He paused and tried to think of what else he might say in this small, impromptu funeral. "Please guide our way home . . . show us what to do to survive. Keep us from fear, Lord. Draw us near to you. Amen."

"Amen," Leah murmured. "Come on, get back under the tarp or we'll be completely drenched." They huddled together, clutching the edges of the canvas as they sought refuge beneath its canopy.

"We need to keep pushing east," Jayce finally said. "We know we'll find land either east or north, but east is our better bet. We weren't that far out—not so far that we can't catch the current and make it back with a little work."

Leah nodded. "I trust you to know what's best."

He smiled. "Since when?"

She raised a brow and studied him for a moment. "Since you told me you loved me. That caused me to realize you were finally making sense."

"I do love you, you know—that wasn't just spoken out of the horror of the moment."

Leah looked away and shrugged. "I had thought of that."

He turned her back to face him. "Then don't. Because it isn't true. I love you. I knew it back in Ketchikan. No, I knew it the moment I saw you in Last Chance—when you welcomed me home."

"I thought you were Jacob." She frowned. "Poor Jacob. He'll be frantic when news of this reaches him."

Jayce hadn't really thought of how this might affect anyone else. "Your family in Ketchikan will hear of it too."

"They'll all be sick with worry." She shook her head. "I can only pray God gives them peace of mind. They know us. They know our strength. Surely they will have some hope that we will keep each other alive."

Jayce nodded. "I would think so. Especially since they know your determination."

Hours later, as the night came upon them, Leah wasn't at all sure her determination was worth much. She hated to admit her fears to Jayce, but the truth was, this was the scariest thing she'd ever endured. She felt comforted only by her continued prayers and the fact that Jayce seemed so self-assured and confident of getting them to land.

Bethel wasn't doing well at all, and all three of them were suffering from exposure, thirst, and hunger. As the seas calmed, Leah huddled in close to Bethel and tried to keep the woman warm. The tarp offered very little protection, but it was better than nothing. Jayce was tired, and Leah knew it would do none of them any good if he grew ill from lack of sleep. At the same time, she knew they couldn't just drift aimlessly all night. They might lose any chance for finding their way if they didn't stay alert and watchful.

"You need rest," Leah told Jayce as she sat up. "I can row awhile."

"Go ahead and sleep. I'll need your help soon enough."

"You've been at this all day."

"I've rested off and on. Look, I think we're getting closer. You rest, and then you can take over in a few hours."

She nodded and repositioned herself beside Bethel. The woman stirred and asked, "Have we arrived?"

Leah patted her arm. "Not yet, Bethel. Just sleep."

Leah dozed off to the rhythmic movement of the boat. She dreamed of being a young girl and of listening to a Sunday school lesson about Jesus walking on the water. Even in her dream she wished she might have that same ability. *Then,* she thought, *I could walk to land.*

Chapter Twenty-Two

From the moment they set foot in Nome, Jacob knew the truth. *Orion's Belt* had been scheduled into Nome in three days time, but word had already come that the ship had met with problems in the Pacific. No one had heard from *Orion's Belt* since she left Sitka Sound.

"The passengers are probably safe," Helaina tried to encourage. "There have been a great many changes in the rules and laws surrounding safety on ships. Ever since the *Titanic* . . ."

Jacob scowled at her. "This is Alaska, not the civilized world, as you so often like to point out. Rules are often overlooked up here."

"But those ships travel south as well," Helaina protested. "They would have to follow regulations or risk extremely high fines. When the *Titanic* went down—"

"I don't want to hear about this! I have to figure out what to do now." Jacob paced the dock for a moment. "I'm going to Sitka," he finally said. "I'm taking the first available ship. If there are any still coming into Nome." He knew this would be the most difficult thing. There were fewer and fewer ships willing to risk getting stuck in the frozen north.

"I'll come with you."

He turned and found Helaina looking at him quite earnestly. That she would join him on this search for Leah and Jayce touched him deeply. "You don't need to do that," he said softly, "but you are kind to offer."

She shook her head, bits of blond hair pulling away from the haphazard bun she'd secured only minutes before they'd come into town. "You shouldn't go alone. This is a difficult enough situation when you have someone at your side to help bear the load. I won't let you do this by yourself."

Jacob saw her determination. He wouldn't try to stop her. He still didn't know who she really was or why she'd come north, but there was no doubt she felt sympathy for his situation. She might even feel some sense of responsibility, given she'd stepped into Leah's shoes for the past few months.

"All right. We'll go together. I don't know how long we'll be gone, though. If you need to make your way back to the expedition headquarters, I'll understand. If we haven't found Leah and Jayce, however, I'll have to say no to helping Captain Latimore until I figure out what's happened."

"I'm sure he'll understand that, Jacob. Your family should come first."

Helaina waited impatiently for Jacob to return with their tickets to Sitka. She was angry with herself for pretending to care about Jacob's situation, while at the same time she knew it wasn't entirely a façade. She didn't want him to face the possibility of his sister's death by himself, yet she was really more interested in knowing the fate of Jayce Kincaid. Jacob had already told her that Leah's letter mentioned she and Jayce would return together on the ship *Orion's Belt* out of Ketchikan. This had intrigued Helaina, who was still trying to figure out how it was that Jayce could have been north with Captain Latimore, while also being in Ketchikan with Leah. She had just about convinced herself that there were two men—both using the name

Jayce Kincaid. But which was the real one—who was the criminal that she sought? She had wanted to ask Jacob about the matter, but she feared bringing up the fact that she'd opened and read his letter. And besides, she couldn't be sure what side he might take if he knew the truth of why she'd come to Alaska.

Helaina sighed. She would just have to ponder the matter alone.

Kincaid had never been photographed, but the man who had tried to kill her brother was the spitting image of the man she'd known as Jayce Kincaid. She'd even written to Stanley on the subject. His reply was simply *Bring him back.*

"We can't leave until the day after tomorrow," Jacob said in frustration. "I tried everything, but there's nothing. We're lucky to get this one—it's a freighter headed to Seattle. We can get off partway and try to get a ship headed to Sitka after that.

"There aren't as many ships coming north—pretty soon there won't be any. The weather has been much worse than usual, and everyone thinks it's going to be a real danger to keep sending ships up here. The days are slipping away fast, and before you know it the ice will keep captains from risking their livelihood."

"I heard ships often come here and dock out in the unfrozen portions of sea. Then people are sledded across the frozen water to Nome," Helaina said, looking out across the gray waters.

"True enough, but nothing is ever predictable. Sometimes the ships can make it through and sometimes they can't. Eventually the risk is too great and they wait for spring. So many elements are in play. But it doesn't matter. We'll leave when we can. If there isn't a ship home, John and Oopick will see to our things and the dogs. Nothing is as important as knowing whether Leah and Jayce are safe."

"But, Jacob," she said, hesitant to bring up the subject, "what if . . . well . . . what if you don't find them? Ships go down all the time and lives are lost and never accounted for." Helaina had already been struggling with this thought. If they had no account of Jayce's death, she would always wonder if he hadn't just slipped away again.

Jacob looked at her for a moment, and the anger shone clear in his eyes. "You always have to look on the bad side of everything, don't you? If you would just stop trying to be God in your own life, you might realize He has the ability to bring things around right."

Jacob stalked off down the street, leaving Helaina to watch after him in frustrated silence. She wanted to call after him or even run after him and tell him how wrong he was. She wanted to declare for all around that she didn't always think the worst. But instead, Jacob's words about God troubled her more than her desire to have the last word.

He'd accused her of trying to be God in her own life. How ridiculous, she thought. How silly to imagine that anyone would attempt to take on a job like that. But in refusing God's direction in her life, she supposed there was a certain element of truth in what Jacob said. And for reasons beyond her ability to understand just yet, that bothered her more than she could explain.

Leah awoke to stillness. Absolute stillness. There was no wind—no rocking motion. Startled, she sat up to find they had actually beached on land. She thought for a moment that she might be dreaming.

Heavy clouds overhead began to sprinkle down rain. Leah looked for Jayce, but couldn't find him anywhere. More startling was the fact that Bethel was missing. Had she passed on during the night? Had Jayce simply slipped her body into the sea to keep from causing Leah to endure another funeral?

A sort of panic welled up in her. "Jayce!"

She got to her feet and realized that the boat was empty of their few supplies, including the tarp. "Jayce!"

Then she saw him. He came bounding out of the woods, waving his arms. "I'm here. It's all right. I'm here."

She ran to him as rain began to fall in earnest. "I thought I'd lost you," she cried against his neck. "Oh, where were you?"

"Putting the finishing touches on our shelter. I just got Bethel secured and was coming back for you. Come on, we're getting wet."

Leah let him lead her into the forest of spruce and alder. "Bethel's all right, then?"

"She's resting again. I think she's just suffered such a shock that it's been hard on her heart. Watch your step here." He helped her over some fallen trees.

"Yes, I thought that too. Perhaps I can find some plants here to help her." Leah looked around the shore. "Where are we, by the way?"

"I'm not sure, but I'm thinking it might be Baranof Island."

"Then we'd not be far from Sitka," she said, looking as far down the shore as her eyes could see.

"If it is Baranof, we're probably well away from Sitka. Probably the south end of the island. I was here for a time eight or so years ago. It looks somewhat familiar to me, but I can't be sure."

"Well, at least it's land," Leah said. "That's fine with me. I know how to survive here. Out there," she said, motioning back toward the water, "is another story."

They came upon the small camp. He'd done well, Leah thought. He'd placed them in a protected area where large rocks created a natural wall and willows made it easy to implement the tarp to make a shelter. She shed her life jacket and tossed it inside.

"Bethel, how are you feeling?" Leah asked as she crawled under the canvas.

"I'm better, but so very weary. I feel as though I haven't eaten in months."

"We plan to rectify that situation soon," Leah said. "I can make a trap and set it out to catch us something to eat. Plus there are all sorts of berries on this island. They are probably very picked over by the wildlife and natives, but we'll find food. You'll see."

Jayce smiled at her. "I knew we were in good hands," he said teasingly.

Bethel eased back on her bed of spruce boughs, using her life jacket for a pillow. "I can rest now, knowing that we're all safe."

The rain poured down but there was no wind, and for this Leah was very grateful. She looked around the little camp and found Jayce had tried to secure what few things they had. The water pot was there, half full with rainwater, and Jayce had shed his coat to let it dry over another stack of boughs.

"So how are we set for supplies? I see you must have a knife, because you've cut down the branches," she said, meeting his gaze.

"I have a knife, a compass, a comb, some money, and a belt. And, of course, my clothes," Jayce said. "Not really much to speak of."

"At least we have a knife. That means a lot," Leah said, reaching into her mukluks. "And we have these." She took out the matches and held them up.

"You brilliant girl," Jayce said, a grin spreading across his face. "Now we can keep warm."

"And cook food," Leah added. "If we catch some."

"We'll find something. I'll see to that."

"One thing we can get relatively soon is fish," Leah said. "If you make a circle of rocks on the tide floor, stack them high, but not so high as to be out of the water when the tide is in, we can trap fish. When the tide comes in, the fish will collect in the trap, and when the tide goes back out, they will be unable to swim over the rocks."

He got up and took his coat. "I can get to work on that right now. The tide is out and the rain isn't so bad as to keep me from accomplishing the job. Can you build a fire?"

"Yes. I can do that. Bethel will be resting anyway," Leah said, noting that the old woman was already snoring.

They each went to their separate tasks. Leah knew how to dig out dried kindling from beneath the heavy forest ground covering. Here she also found logs, dried and brittle from years of hidden neglect. Before long, she had a fire blazing between an opening in the canvas and the rocky outcropping. The smoke climbed the wall of stone and was smothered in the rain.

Jayce returned just as Bethel was awaking. Leah couldn't help but giggle at the sight of him with his rolled up wool trousers. He carried his boots and socks in hand. "I hope that works. I'm soaked to the bone, and my feet and legs are frozen. If we don't get any fish, it won't be for lack of effort."

"Could I have a drink?" Bethel asked.

"Certainly. Here, let me help you sit up," Leah offered. Jayce took up the little pottery bowl and handed it to Leah. "We all have to share one vessel, I'm sorry to say. But after what we've all come through, I'm sure this is the least of our worries."

Bethel drank her fill, then let Leah help her reposition in order to sit up for a while. Leaning back against the rock, Bethel offered them both a smile. "I have lived through worse, but not much."

"Where are you from, Bethel?" Jayce asked, settling down to warm himself by the fire.

"I was actually born and raised in California. Then I married a man of God who desired to come north to preach the gospel to the natives of this new territory. We lived most of our life near Prince of Wales and Kotzebue."

"I know that area well," Leah replied. "I live in Last Chance Creek, not far from Cape Woolley. My brother and I often go to that area to trade and collect furs."

"Why, we were practically neighbors," Bethel said with a nod.

"Is your husband still living?" Jayce asked.

"I'm sorry to say I lost him last year. We had just celebrated our fiftieth wedding anniversary not but the day before." Tears came to the old woman's eyes. "I'm afraid it is still difficult to talk about. I miss him a great deal."

Leah patted the woman's arm. "You needn't cause yourself pain on our account. Tell us instead about your life as a missionary. How fascinating that must have been. When did you go north?"

Bethel composed herself a bit and then spoke. "We married in 1864. The Civil War was going on, and people were fighting bitterly in the east. In California, gold fever and other problems consumed the minds of men. My husband suggested we get involved with ministering to the poor souls who came to pan for gold only to lose everything, including the shirt off their backs. We spent a time in California and Nevada, but it was never what my husband really wanted. One day in the late 1870s he came in to me. He had heard about a man who was setting up schools and missions in Alaska. Have you heard of Sheldon Jackson?"

"Of course," Leah said. The man had been responsible for starting many missions and schools in her area as well. There had also been an interesting experiment with introducing reindeer stations that had caused quite a stir among the natives.

"Dr. Jackson encouraged us to come to Sitka first, and then he persuaded us to go west to Teller and the other places I mentioned."

"So you've been in Alaska all these years," Leah said, shaking her head. "You've seen the gold rushes come and go but have remained to outlive the sensation of it all."

"True enough," Bethel replied. "We raised three lovely girls up there. Caroline is the oldest. She loved the land and remained, whereas the others went south. I was just returning from a trip to see them. That's why I was on the ship."

"We were heading home too," Leah said, unable to keep the longing from her voice. "My brother and I have lived in Last Chance for over ten years."

"Do you know the Kjellmann's, then?" Bethel asked.

"They are dear friends. Emma is like the sister I never had," Leah admitted.

"What do you do there?"

"In the past, my brother ran the mail in the winter. He was awarded the contract for several smaller villages, but this year he decided to forego it."

Bethel looked to Jayce, asking, "But why would you do that? What else will you do for a job?"

Jayce laughed. "I'm not her brother, but I think I can speak for him. He's been asked to help with an Arctic exploration. I was to be a part of that as well. I think Jacob plans to put things in order so that he can attempt that trip next year."

"We also run a trading post of sorts," Leah threw out. "We'll still have that, and Jacob will no doubt have to run for supplies throughout the winter."

Bethel seemed to consider this a moment, then turned back to Jayce. "If you aren't the brother, then who are you?"

"I hope to be the husband," he said, throwing a wink at Leah. "I haven't asked her yet, but I'm working up to it."

Bethel laughed. "I promise not to say a word."

Leah looked at Jayce in dumbfounded silence. Surely he hadn't just said what she thought he'd said. *Did he just say that he planned to marry me?*

Her heart pounded in her ears, blocking out Bethel and Jayce's conversation. After all they'd been through—all the pain and years of absence—had Jayce really just proposed in his roundabout way?

Chapter Twenty-Three

What do you mean we can't go out and search?" Jacob asked a man at the Sitka docks. "I'm willing to pay you good money."

Their trip from Nome hadn't been easy or fast, and now he was feeling the stress of not knowing if Leah and Jayce had survived. There had been no word. Bodies had been recovered, but identifying them was difficult. Jacob had gone to the makeshift morgue to see if any of them were Leah or Jayce. To his relief, they weren't among the dead, but that relief was short-lived.

"Look around you, mister," the older man declared. "This weather ain't right for being on the water. I know you're worried. Other folks here are worried as well. We'll go when things calm down."

Jacob knew the man was right. The ocean was pitching and roiling; he'd never have attempted such a sea at home. The chill in the air offered him no comfort as he thought of Leah being lost out there on the water—or worse. He tried not to think of all the possibilities.

For several moments he just stood staring at the angry gray waters. Somewhere out there, he fervently believed, Leah and Jayce were struggling to survive . . . and he couldn't help them. It had been nearly two weeks since *Orion's Belt* went down. How could he not know what had happened? How could he just stand idly by and wait?

When he came back to the hotel, Helaina was there to meet him. "What happened? Any word?"

"No," Jacob said. "The weather has made it impossible to search. Short of those boats that made it into various ports, there haven't been reports of other survivors. They aren't finding any more bodies. The search has pretty much been called off."

"I'm sorry, Jacob."

They sat down in the lobby of the hotel and said nothing for several minutes. Jacob didn't like the feeling of helplessness that washed over him. He had fought so hard to get this far, and now there was nothing he could do but wait.

"Have you had any word from your family?" Helaina prompted.

"Adrik is searching with some of the men from his area. He plans to work his way up the island coast and then in Sitka after that. He thought we could work together." Jacob stared off into space. Leah was smart and very capable. Jayce too. If they'd made it to a lifeboat, they would be capable of surviving. He was sure of it. He prayed for them—for all the passengers of *Orion's Belt*—but it didn't feel like enough.

"So where is God in all of this?" Helaina's tone told him that she wasn't merely trying to stir up trouble; she really wanted answers. Answers Jacob wasn't sure he could come up with.

"Sometimes it's hard to understand why things like this happen," Jacob said, trying to relax in the chair. "I know I've questioned God several times in my life, and I always see the answer later, or else God gives me a peace about it. Like when my ma died. I didn't see any good purpose in that, but later, I realized she'd always been kind of fragile and weak. She might have lived on like that and my pa would never have been able to endure it. I figure he would have left all of us—not because he didn't care about us, but because he wouldn't have been able to watch my ma die day by day. That would have broken my mother's heart. At least she died feeling loved and cared about."

"I still see no good reason for my parents and husband to be murdered. I know you say there is probably a good reason—something God wants to teach me in all of this—but I don't see it. Those kinds of lessons are cruel. Like now."

Jacob looked at her for a moment. She really was a beautiful woman. "Answers to our questions aren't always real clear—and frankly, I've learned that even when I know the whys and hows, it doesn't stop me from hurting."

"But it might help me stop reliving it," Helaina said in a distant voice. "Sometimes I imagine their final moments—even though I wasn't there physically. I read the reports and demanded all the details until the police were so tired of me they simply gave in. It was gruesome, and sometimes I wish I'd heeded their warning and left well enough alone."

"Did they ever catch the men who committed the murders?" Jacob asked.

"Yes, but it didn't help as much as I'd hoped. I had thought that once they were caught and tried, convicted, and punished, that my life would go on—that I would feel satisfied."

"But you didn't?"

"No. Well, my life went on, but the feeling of satisfaction was absent. No matter that the men were in jail—my family was still dead."

"That's why revenge never works."

"But I wasn't just seeking revenge. I wanted justice."

"There you go with justice again. I don't think you even understand the word. Justice suggests impartiality, and you show no signs of that."

She glared at him. "Justice is what our legal system is about—it's what this country was founded on. It's all I want in life—it's what I fight for." Jacob thought for a moment she might get up and leave, but instead she composed herself and squared her shoulders. "This isn't about me or justice—it's about Leah and Mr. Kincaid."

"I can't do anything about them right now, except pray—which I have been doing ever since we heard about the ship going down. But I think we need to go back to the issue at hand, and the point is, often people mistake revenge for justice. They think they'll feel better if they can see their offenders behind bars or even put to death. But it doesn't change the fact that they are hurting. I've found that offering mercy and forgiveness frees me from much of that pain. It also helps me to find a new direction for my life."

Helaina's voice took on a raw edge. "As I've said before, people who break the law deserve to face the penalty. Mercy is a matter left up to the courts. I will never understand your beliefs that people should just get off free and clear because they ask to be forgiven."

"Well, forgiveness is something we do on our part. We have control of forgiveness—whether we'll give it or withhold it. I can forgive the man who steals from me, but the court might still sentence him to time in jail. You could choose to forgive the men who murdered your family, but they would still need to pay the penalty for their crime."

"I could never forgive them," Helaina said bitterly. "And don't bring up that story from the Bible again. Just because God has decided to forgive mankind their sins if they accept His Son, doesn't mean that I should have to forgive as well. I cannot agree with that. It's just not that simple."

"I never said it was simple," Jacob replied. "Forgiveness is a decided effort. It doesn't come easy for most."

"I would venture to say it doesn't come to most . . . period."

Jacob fell silent. Helaina's pain was visible in her expression. He'd certainly never meant to hurt her, but at the same time, he believed God had put the two of them together for a reason. "Why did you come to Alaska? Honestly."

The pain left her face as a look of surprise seemed to cause her to tense. "You know why I came. You know all about the expedition."

"And I know you said that you wanted to make your husband proud, but I get the feeling there's more to it than that. I've always been rather good at discerning people, and you have hidden motives, Helaina. I've known that from the start, but I didn't want to say anything."

Her face flushed crimson at this comment. "I don't know what you're talking about."

"But you do. I can see that now, more than ever. If you can't be honest with me, then I'd just as soon you not come back to Last Chance. I hate lies, and now I feel confident that you are lying to me."

Helaina cleared her throat nervously. "Look . . . that is. . . . you simply do not need to pry into my life. I've done nothing but honor the agreement we had. I've learned to handle the dogs to the best of my ability. I ran your store and kept your house, again because of the agreement. I upheld my part of the bargain and gave you no reason to distrust me."

"You lied about the expedition. That much I already know." He looked at her hard, hoping she might feel intimidated.

"You're just upset because of Leah," Helaina said, crossing her arms. She was wearing one of her southern outfits, as Jacob called them. A blue wool skirt and jacket with a high-collared white blouse. She looked every bit the prim and proper lady.

"I am upset about Leah, but that isn't marring my judgment in the least. There was never a second summer expedition planned. The first expedition was in trouble, and they had to cancel and turn back by the middle of June."

"But the plan . . . prior to that trouble . . . before they cancelled their exploration, was to have a second expedition," Helaina said hesitantly.

"That's a lie, Helaina."

She said nothing, but Jacob could see she was uncomfortable. He almost felt sorry for her. Almost. "Helaina, there was no telegraph service in either Nome or St. Michael when you suggested you'd received word from the expedition association. Service was out—I know because I wanted to send a telegram. There was also not enough time for you to have received a post or letter, because there hadn't been a mail ship in for days when you suggested having heard from the group. I believe you made it up to serve some ulterior purpose. What I want to know is, why? Why were you so determined to get Jayce Kincaid to Seattle?"

Helaina stood up. "I don't have to take this. I will not sit here and be accused like some common criminal."

"It's a sin to lie. You know that, right? It's one of the Ten Commandments."

"The commandment you refer to states, 'Thou shalt not bear false witness against your neighbor,' " Helaina said angrily. "I did not bear false witness against anyone." With that she stormed off.

Jacob watched after her for several minutes. He had no more answers than when he'd started, but at least now she knew that he suspected her. It would be interesting to see what she did from this point.

Jayce and Leah struggled to row the lifeboat up the coast toward what they hoped would be Sitka. Leah thought she had never been so tired. She tried hard to keep up with Jayce's rhythm but knew it was impossible.

Bethel rested but was fully awake. She had continued to improve after several days of rest. Leah had found some plants to ease Bethel's condition, but the quality had been rather poor due to the onset of the cold weather. They had also been fortunate to gather enough fish to eat well. Eating something substantial had given them all renewed hope and energy, and now they were anxious to move on. By all calculations they had been missing for just over two weeks, and they knew that their families were probably frantic.

"We'll rest in just a few more minutes," Jayce promised.

"That would . . . be good," she gasped out, her arms burning from the strain.

Jayce seemed only then to realize how tired she was. "I guess we could rest now," he said. "I didn't realize how hard I was pushing you. I'm sorry."

"It's all right. I don't want our families to worry any longer than they have to. We've already been gone too long."

"I know the delay was due to me," Bethel said apologetically.

"We were all exhausted," Jayce answered. "I couldn't have gone on without food and water. None of us could have. Besides, the weather caused us trouble more times than not. It isn't a good time of the year to travel in Alaska."

"I know Jacob will understand," Leah replied, still trying to regain her wind. "Karen and Adrik too. They will all say we did the right thing in renewing our strength, waiting out the weather, and making sure Bethel had a chance to recover."

"My heart has always been weak. I suppose this will be my last trip of any consequence."

"Maybe your family will come to you now," Leah said smiling.

Bethel nodded, then seemed to think of something else. "I know Leah has a brother, but have you any siblings, Mr. Kincaid?"

Jayce frowned. "I do. I have an older sister and brother, as well as a younger brother. Well, he's younger, but not by much. See, we're twins."

"How unusual. That must have been interesting growing up."

"Especially since Chase insists on getting himself into trouble at every turn."

Leah looked at Jayce and shook her head. "I didn't know you had a twin."

"Well, it never seemed important to bring up. We're as different as night and day, even though we're identical in appearance. My biggest trouble is that Chase insists on blaming me for everything wrong in his life. He even blames me that he's the youngest. We have a rather unusual situation in fact. I was born at 11:57 P.M. on December 31st, in the year 1882. Chase was born at 12:04 A.M. on January 1st, 1883. We're twins born in entirely different years."

"That is quite interesting," Bethel declared. "But I thought twins had an unusual sense of connection. You two were never close?"

"Never. He hated me from the beginning. He blamed me for the trouble he had in school—for the problems he caused our parents. He even blamed me for the death of our mother."

"Why?" Leah couldn't imagine why a brother would act in such a way. "Why would he do that?"

Jayce began rowing again. "When my father died, my siblings went through their inheritances and then started taking what they could from our mother. My mother was rather naïve and gave generously to anyone who asked. By the time I realized what they were doing, she was nearly destitute. She had accumulated debts, and we had to sell her home in order to satisfy her bankers. Losing everything that reminded her of our father was more than she could bear. She was also distraught over the fact that Chase had gotten himself in trouble, and there was no money with which to bail him out. She grew quite sick with worry about him being in jail."

"And how does Chase figure that to be your fault?" Leah asked.

Jayce's face darkened. "Because I had the money to get him out, and I wouldn't do it. I knew he'd run if I did. I tried to reason with our mother and explain that jail was the best place for him—at least he'd be out of trouble there. But that wasn't the way she saw it, for Chase made certain her thoughts were in conflict with mine. He would send her horrible letters telling her how awful his conditions were and how badly people treated him. Mother pleaded with me to help him. I finally told her that I would take her to the jail and let her see the situation for herself."

"And did she go?" Bethel asked.

"Yes," Jayce said, looking past them as though he could see it all being played out in the skies overhead. "I took her there and she saw him . . . saw that he was living quite well, playing cards with the guards and eating high on the hog. When he realized what I'd done, Chase was livid. He rushed at me with the intention of killing me—at least I believe that was his plan. The guards had to pull him off, while our mother screamed for everyone to stop. I took her home, and she went to her bed, never again to get out."

"So Chase blames you for revealing the truth to her?" Leah asked.

"And for that truth taking her life."

"That is a sad story, indeed," Bethel said, clucking sympathetically. "What of your older siblings?"

"They blamed me as well. I was our father's favorite, and they hated me for that, seeking in turn to destroy my standing with our mother—although she thought equally well of each of us. It never bothered her to realize her children had taken advantage of her—or that she had given up everything she owned so that they would have whatever they wanted. She loved us all—right up to the end."

Bethel shifted and sat up to stretch her body. "A mother's love—the most precious of all earthly commodities. You cannot buy it or sell it, yet everyone desires it. Oh my! Look!"

Leah scanned the shores in the direction Bethel pointed. A dozen or so Tlingit Indians stood on the beach watching them. Leah stood. The boat rocked wildly, but she maintained her balance. "We need your help," she called in their native tongue. "Our ship sank, and we are trying to get to Sitka." She looked to Jayce and saw the relief in his expression. "We're saved. They'll know how to help."

Helaina paced her room in maddening steps. How dare he! How dare he accuse her of lying? She didn't care that it was true; she only felt that he had no right to interfere in her job. Now he would tell Jayce—if they found him at all—and her plans to talk him into heading to Seattle would be ruined. *Not that I have any real idea for getting Jayce there anyway,* she thought.

Not long after they'd arrived in Sitka, she had wired her brother with her concerns of whether Kincaid was even living. An hour ago she had added to the previous missives and told her brother that Jacob Barringer was suspicious of her—that he was now a real threat. Helaina hoped Stanley might offer her some insight or suggestion as to how to resolve it all.

Helaina had also mentioned her concerns about Jayce not being the right man. She had proof that suggested he'd been in two places at once. Not only with her information related to England, when Jayce supposedly stole from the British Museum, but also the situation with the *Homestead* and Jayce's supposed help with the dogs. The only answer was that there had to be someone who resembled Jayce. Perhaps a brother—maybe a cousin or someone else.

"The man I saw in Nome did not fit the patterns and attitudes of the man my brother wrote about. Jayce Kincaid seemed quite helpful and good. He showed no signs of breaking the law or of taking advantage of other people. Plus, he couldn't have been on the expeditions as Captain Latimore suggested. Jayce spent the summer with Leah," she said aloud, trying to organize her thoughts. "It just didn't make sense, unless there was another person."

She had shared these concerns with Stanley as well. Now she would just have to wait for some kind of direction from her brother.

A knock sounded on her door, and Helaina nearly jumped a foot. It came again, only this time harder and louder. "Open up, Mrs. Beecham."

Helaina recognized Jacob's voice and hurried to do as he said. "What's wrong? Have you had word?"

"No. They brought in a couple of bodies about an hour ago, but neither of them was Leah or Jayce. However, the weather has settled, and I'm going out in search of them."

"I'll change my clothes."

"You're staying here," Jacob replied without room for argument. "I just wanted to let you know where I'll be." He turned to leave, and Helaina followed him into the hallway.

"How can you just leave me here? I came to help you."

"I don't trust your help." With that he stormed off.

Helaina hurried to change her clothes. She might still catch him at the dock. She didn't want him going to hunt for Jayce and Leah without her. He would no doubt warn Jayce about her, and then the man probably wouldn't even return to Sitka.

Another knock sounded at her door. She smiled, anticipating his return. She sauntered to the door feeling rather triumphant.

She opened the door. "I thought you were . . ." It wasn't Jacob.

"I have a telegram for you," the young man declared. "In fact, I have three telegrams for you."

Helaina frowned. "Very well." She went to get her purse.

"I never saw anyone get three telegrams at once."

"Well, it's really none of your concern," she snapped, knowing she was losing precious time. She dismissed the boy quickly and opened the messages.

They were all from her brother, and he was not happy.

Get JK to Seattle. STOP. Use law in Sitka. STOP. I will notify. STOP.

The next one was just as insistent.

JK is a killer. STOP. Do not worry about his innocence or guilt. STOP. We have all the proof we need. STOP. Get him to Seattle. STOP.

The final one was more of the same.

Have wired the law in Sitka. STOP. They will assist. STOP. If JK is living take to Seattle immediately. STOP. Team will aid you there. STOP.

Helaina tossed the telegrams into the trash and grabbed her coat. She had to try to reach Jacob before he left town. If he reached Jayce first, there would be no hope of taking him in without a fight.

Chapter Twenty-Four

Jacob felt the crushing weight of defeat as their boat made its way to the docks in Sitka. He noted that the steamer *Victoria* was in the harbor and wondered if she might be heading to Nome. Soon no one would be risking a trip there.

Jacob sighed. The *Victoria* couldn't help him even if they were headed in the right direction. He still didn't know where Leah was. He had been out on the water for nearly forty-eight hours and hadn't found anything. It was as if the sea had swallowed up all evidence of *Orion's Belt* and her passengers.

"Will we go out again tomorrow?"

He looked at Helaina, not in the least happy to have her on board. She had come only moments before the ship's owner cast off and insisted she be allowed to help with the search. When she stood her ground and refused to leave the deck, Jacob finally relented but told her she was on her own. He wanted nothing more to do with her.

Even now he walked to the other side of the deck, anxious to be rid of Helaina. There were few things he despised as much as lying. The fact that she was caught in her lies and still continued to perpetuate them bothered him even more. Even on this journey she tried to explain away what had happened in Nome by telling Jacob that he'd misunderstood her meaning when she'd said that she'd gotten word about the expedition. She claimed she'd known that a second expedition was being planned even before coming to Nome.

Jacob was not swayed. He called her a liar and asked that she leave him alone. She had for a time, but then, like a bad penny, she just kept turning up.

"Jacob, please listen to me," Helaina now said, as she came up from behind him.

He clenched his jaw to keep from saying something he'd regret. He refused to play her game of words.

"Jacob, I know you're angry, but you don't understand—maybe you never will, but I'm not the person you think I am."

He drew a deep breath and continued gazing out at the Pacific. They'd soon dock and he'd be rid of her. For now, however, he'd have to ignore her pleading and hope that she got tired of trying to convince him of her innocence. He turned to her. "When we get back to the hotel, I want you to gather your things and get out." He looked out upon the water again.

"Jacob, I have to have a place to stay."

"Then pay for it yourself. I'll talk to the manager."

"I always intended to pay for the room anyway," Helaina answered in a rather defensive tone. "I have never asked you to pay for my needs."

"The *Victoria* is here. I'd just as soon see you book passage and leave. I don't need your help here."

"Jacob, you're being unreasonable," she protested. "I thought Christians were supposed to be forgiving and not judge without hearing the truth."

That got under his skin. Jacob turned slowly and narrowed his eyes. "I know the truth. I was in Nome, remember."

"But you don't know everything," Helaina said, her tone pleading. "Look, this is far more important than you know. There are things I cannot tell you." She gave an exasperated sigh. "I know it looks bad, but in a few days you'll understand. Just trust me until then. Don't say anything about this, and I swear I'll give you a thorough explanation."

"I don't want your explanations, and I certainly do not intend to spend any more time with you. My sister may be dead. My friend too. I don't have any interest in your stories or excuses."

"You're such a hypocrite," she said, putting her hands on her waist. "You are just as unforgiving as I am. But the difference here is that I don't claim to be a Christian or to value what the Bible says. You do."

She walked to the other side of the boat and sat down on a crate. Jacob refused to be troubled by her words. He knew she only hoped to rile him into arguing with her. He didn't understand what she hoped to gain by this, however. It wasn't like he could do anything about the lies she'd told, other than expose them. What seemed truly changed, however, was that she appeared for once to care what he thought.

As soon as the ship was tied off, Jacob exited without even looking to see what Helaina was doing. Hurrying up the dock, his heart nearly stopped when he found Adrik Ivankov waiting for him with several Tlingit natives.

"Is she dead?" he asked, his heart nearly breaking. His chest tightened and he couldn't breathe.

Adrik broke into a grin. "Not when I left her at the hotel."

Jacob closed his eyes and let the truth settle over him. "How . . . where . . . ?"

"We've been searching since word came to Ketchikan. These men and others have been helping." He motioned to the Tlingits. "We went out in a dozen boats and searched the beaches of nearby islands. We found her and Jayce and an elderly woman that they rescued. They were in one of the lifeboats and were trying to find their way to Sitka. Doing pretty well at it too."

"Jayce and Leah are alive?" Helaina asked, coming to join them.

Adrik looked at her oddly. "Yes, they are. Who are you, if you don't mind my asking?"

She extended her hand. "Mrs. Helaina Beecham."

"Adrik Ivankov." He shook her hand briefly. "The hotel was full, but when they told me Jacob had two rooms registered to his name, I knew he wouldn't mind our imposition. I've put Leah in one room, and Jayce in the other."

"Where are you staying, Adrik?"

"We have a camp down near the beach," Adrik told them.

Helaina seemed anxious to get back to the room. "I'd love to see them both, and I know Jacob longs to see for himself that Leah is safe. Let's go to the hotel." She pushed past Adrik and made her way up the street.

"Leah told me quite a bit about that one," Adrik said as he and Jacob followed after.

"She's up to something, but I really don't know what it's all about. I've caught her in several lies and had honestly thought she'd changed, but as soon as we got here and the focus was on finding Jayce, she started in again."

"Why does she want to find Jayce?"

Jacob shrugged. "I don't know. She's tried several times to get him to go to Seattle with her. I don't know what it's all about, but I've had a gut full. I've told her to get away from us. Now that we have Leah and Jayce safe, I plan to be rid of her for good."

"Will you come and stay with us awhile in Ketchikan?"

"Not if we're going to make it back before we're frozen out. As it is, we'll probably have to borrow a dog team and hike out for home once we reach Nome. There's just no telling. I know we can't afford to delay."

"I understand. Sure is good to see you, though." He put his arm around Jacob's shoulder.

"You too, Adrik. I wish I could have come and stayed for a visit, but there was too much work to be done this summer."

The older man scratched his bearded chin. "Just don't forget that life is about more than work. You need a little rest and fun now and then." He grinned and slapped Jacob's back. "Wouldn't hurt you to find a wife either."

Jacob smiled. "Maybe you could get one of the shamans to make me a potion. My natural charm and good looks don't seem to be doing the trick."

"Those only work on Tlingit people—they're much too powerful for the likes of you." He winked at Jacob and laughed.

By now they'd reached the hotel. Jacob dashed up the stairs to the rooms he and Helaina had taken. He went to the open door of Helaina's room. The two women were talking rapidly—both smiling.

"Leah!"

She turned to him and shrugged. "We took the long way home."

He crossed the distance and embraced her close. "Thank God you're safe."

"We were just talking about what happened," Helaina offered. "The ship actually blew up."

Leah and Jacob separated. "I know that," Jacob retorted.

"You seem to know a lot of things," Jayce announced from the door. "You all are making quite a ruckus over here. A man can't even get some much-needed sleep."

"Jayce, it's good to see you," Jacob said, going to his friend. "I can't imagine what you must have gone through."

"It wasn't easy, but your sister is quite ingenious. She had us eating well and living high off the land. That girl can dig for clams like no one I've ever seen, and the crabs she managed to cook for us had legs as big around as a dog's."

Leah rolled her eyes. "He exaggerates."

"Have you been here long?" Jacob asked.

"No," Adrik replied. "Just got in about thirty minutes prior to you. We got the older woman to the hospital. I hadn't even had a chance to let the authorities know they were alive."

"I could do that," Helaina offered.

Everyone looked at her for a moment, but it was Jacob who replied in a clipped tone. "I'm sure that would be a good idea. You go ahead. We're going to dinner. I'm starved."

"Well, you can go to dinner," Jayce replied. "I was just about to have a bath. Hot water and everything. Then I'm going to sleep in a real bed with real sheets."

"We are pretty dirty," Leah said, looking down at her clothes.

"Doesn't matter," Jacob replied. "I'm hungry and dirty. I wanna eat first."

Adrik laughed and headed for the door. "Then it's my treat. I know just the place. They won't care how dirty you are, and if you fall asleep in your grub, they'll just move you out of the way and bring the next person in."

Jacob let Leah go ahead of him to the door, completely ignoring Helaina. "Sounds perfect."

"You're welcome to come too, Mrs. Beecham," Adrik called.

Helaina seemed to consider it for a moment, then shook her head. "No, I'm not that hungry. You go ahead. It's only right that you have some time with your family."

Helaina knew she would have to act fast. Despite being dirty, she slipped into her regular clothes and hurried out of the hotel in search of the local law offices. They seemed to know all about her when she arrived.

"Got a telegram from a man in Washington, D.C. He says you're helping the Pinkerton Agency to apprehend a dangerous criminal."

"That's all true," Helaina said, nodding. "He was on *Orion's Belt* when it went down. I feared he might be dead, but he's returned to Sitka, and I need your help in apprehending him."

"Well, we can certainly do that," the man in charge declared. "What do you propose to do with him after we apprehend him?"

"I need to get him to Seattle as soon as possible. I'll have to book passage on the first available ship."

"The *Victoria* is here right now," a redheaded man threw out. He was haphazardly cleaning his pistol, making Helaina more than a little nervous.

"That's right," the older man declared. "The *Victoria* is headed to Seattle tonight. In just a couple of hours, in fact."

"I must be on that ship with Jayce Kincaid," Helaina said, realizing it would work the best for all parties concerned. If she could get him on that ship and out of town before Jacob and Leah realized what was happening, she could be assured of victory.

"Brett can run you down some tickets. You have the funds?"

Helaina nodded and opened her purse. "I believe this will cover it." She gave him several large bills. The boy put aside the gun and got to his feet.

"You take this money and get her two tickets. Make sure they don't put her in the hold. She needs a decent cabin—got it?"

"Sure, Walt. I ain't stupid."

"Well, that remains to be seen," Walt answered. "After you get the tickets, you go to the ship and make sure they don't pull out early. We'll be there directly." The young man ran out the door, whistling all the way.

"Well, little lady, I don't understand a country that allows its women to be arresting dangerous criminals, but I guess I have no say in the matter." He took up his hat and motioned her to the door. "After you."

"But we'll need more men. This is a dangerous, crafty, deceptive criminal. He's killed two men and wounded a third."

"Lady, I can handle him. Don't worry your pretty head about it." He reached to the wall and grabbed up some handcuffs and leg irons.

"But—"

He frowned at her, and for a moment Helaina was worried he'd changed his mind about helping her. Finally he asked, "Are we going or not?"

She nodded. "Very well. But I warned you."

Helaina felt as if her heart might pound right out of her chest. The end of her long ordeal was in sight. She would soon have Jayce Kincaid captured and on his way to Seattle. Then she could go home.

But even as she made her way to the hotel, there was a sense of unrest in her soul. Jacob despised her, and she longed to set the record straight with him. She wanted very much for him to know the truth, especially since he accused her so often of keeping it from him. Maybe she would write him a letter once she was back home.

"He's in the room at the top of the stairs," Helaina explained. "After we apprehend him, I'll need to gather my things. I don't have very much, so it will only take a minute."

"I can handle it," the man replied. He had a determined look on his face as he shifted the irons to his left hand and pulled out a revolver with his right hand.

He motioned Helaina to stand back as they reached the last step. He went to the door and knocked loudly, then stepped to the side. For a moment Helaina froze in place, then quickly jumped to the opposite side of the door. When no one came to answer the knock, she feared Jayce might have changed his mind and left for dinner.

The man knocked again, this time harder. There was some sort of reply from inside, but Helaina couldn't really tell what the muffled words were. She stiffened, pulling herself back against the wall.

"What's the matter, Jacob, forget your key?" Jayce asked as he opened the door. He yawned, then startled to realize there was a gun in his face. His eyes widened as Walt pushed the revolver closer.

"Now you raise those hands nice and easy, mister."

"What's this about? Are you robbing me, 'cause if you are, you're out of luck. I have nothing. I was one of those folks who was on *Orion's Belt* when it went down."

"I know who you are, Mr. Kincaid. Now don't cause me any trouble. I'm the law in this town, and I don't take well to folks who cause trouble."

Helaina stepped out as he managed to handcuff Jayce. She saw the look of surprise change to confusion as Jayce's eyes narrowed. "What is this about, Helaina?"

"I'm working for the Pinkerton Agency in Washington, D.C., Mr. Kincaid. You might remember a little scuffle you had with my brother on the back of a B&O Railroad car. You threw him off."

"You've got the wrong man." Jayce looked to the man who was even now checking his pockets for weapons. "She's got the wrong person."

"I have evidence that suggests otherwise," Helaina said, trying hard not to remember her own concerns about this case. Stanley was firm on what was to be done, so she pulled out the drawing of Jayce and unfolded it for him to see. "I was told to apprehend a man named Jayce Kincaid, who also fit this description."

"Looks just like you, mister," Walt declared.

"I'm telling you it isn't me," Jayce protested, trying to twist away from Walt. The older man held him fast.

Helaina put the picture back into her pocket. "You are under arrest for the death of two men, also agents, as well as for multiple theft and assault charges."

Jayce shook his head. "I've never even been to Washington, D.C. I'm telling you this is wrong. I'm not the man you're looking for."

"That's what they all say," the officer declared. He snapped the leg irons into place and straightened. "Come along, Mr. Kincaid. You have a ship waiting for you."

"I can't just leave without saying something to Jacob and Leah." He looked to Helaina for help. "Please, you know what I'm saying. I have to talk to them."

"I'm sorry," she said, her voice nothing more than a whisper. "We have to go."

"You'd best collect your things, Mrs. Beecham."

Helaina couldn't shake the feeling that this was all suddenly very wrong. "Yes, I'll go right now."

She hurried to the room next door and pulled the key from her purse. It was difficult to see in the darkened room. She went to the chair where she'd left her smallest traveling bag containing her personal items as well as her only other traveling outfit. Taking this up, she thought about her Eskimo clothes and decided against taking them. She'd have no need of them at home.

She rejoined the men and followed them down the stairs. Jayce protested every step of the way, alternating between pleading for Helaina's mercy and arguing his innocence.

"Helaina, I don't know why you're doing this. I don't know why you think me guilty of these things. I didn't do it. I'm telling you, I've never been to Washington, D.C."

She refused to even speak to him about the situation. Her conscience already bothered her more than she'd admit. There were too many inconsistencies, and she didn't know how to rectify the situation except to take Jayce back to stand trial. Then, surely if he was telling the truth, there would be evidence to support this and he would go free. If not . . . he would hang.

She swallowed hard at this thought. *What if we're wrong and he does hang? What if he can't get evidence in time?* She looked at Jayce as he hung his head. He wasn't fighting them—he wasn't even really trying to cause them any problems. It was definitely a surprise, given the other times the man had been arrested he'd turned ugly on his captors.

He hardly seemed like a killer. But then again, few killers looked as she had expected them to look. Especially the men who killed her family. They were hardly more than boys. Desperate boys. She shuddered. They had hanged, and Jayce Kincaid would hang as well. It was the price for his crimes.

Chapter Twenty-Five

Leah carefully balanced a plate of food for Jayce as they made their way back to the hotel. Darkness obscured the mountains and shadows hung ominously, then disappeared as patches of fog moved over the town. A sense of foreboding washed over her, but Leah tried not to think about it. Right now she was blessed to be safe and reunited with her family.

She smoothed the red checkered napkin over the plate and smiled. Jayce had been so exhausted, but Leah knew when he awoke, he'd be starved. The restaurant had prepared a nice plate with meatloaf and potatoes. There was even a piece of apple pie. Her heart nearly burst with happiness. It had taken ten years and a shipwreck, but Jayce had finally told her he loved her. God had brought him back to her, and now they would plan a life together.

"I just wish I could figure it all out," Jacob told Adrik. "I suppose we'll never know for sure what Helaina's been up to. Especially now that we'll be heading home to Last Chance. I told her she wasn't to join us."

"You can hardly keep her from showing up in the village," Adrik replied.

"You know how the people of those villages are. If a stranger shows up, they handle them with great caution, but if someone known shows up and others speak against them, they'll be turned away. She won't be able to survive the winter there without friends."

"It would probably be good to explain that to her before she tags along."

"I will."

They climbed the steps to their room, and Adrik suppressed a yawn. "I don't know why I'm following you. I need to be gettin' back to my camp. I'll come see you in morning, and we'll discuss your plans." He started to turn and head back down the stairs.

"That's strange," Jacob said. "The door to my room is open." He looked inside. The hall light revealed that Jayce was gone.

"Maybe Jayce went out for something to eat and didn't think to close the door," Adrik offered.

Leah felt her heart skip a beat. She glanced to the door of her own room. "Let me check my room."

She handed Adrik the plate and went to her door—it was locked. She used her key, and when she stepped into the room, a terrible feeling washed over her. There was no sign of Helaina, and her bag was missing.

"Anything?" Jacob asked as he came to the door.

"Helaina's gone—her bag's gone too. She left this," Leah said, holding up Helaina's sealskin pants and kuspuk.

"Well, maybe they went to supper together." Adrik balanced the plate in his left hand and pulled out his watch with his right. "It's getting late. Why don't we wait and see if they show up."

"She's done something," Jacob declared. "I know she has. She's planned all along to get to Jayce, but for what reasons I can only guess."

Leah's stomach churned in a most unpleasant way. "What are you saying?"

"I'm saying that Helaina has had an agenda ever since meeting up with us in Nome. I don't know what it's all about or why she's after Jayce, but there's something she wants bad enough to risk everybody's anger and a whole lot of danger."

"But what could that be?" Leah asked. "Do you suppose she's in love with him?"

"No. That honestly never crossed my mind," Jacob said. Leah's face must have shown the relief she felt, because he quickly added, "And it wouldn't matter if she were in love. I know Jayce loves you. There's no doubting that."

"Well, we may just be wrong on all accounts," Adrik reminded them. "I say let's wait and see what happens."

"But it's nearly nine o'clock," Leah said. "If we wait much longer we won't be able to ask anyone about them."

"Who do you propose we ask?" Jacob said, shaking his head.

Leah had no idea. She heard the sorrowful blast of a ship's whistle, and she couldn't help but think of *Orion's Belt* and the accident that took the lives of so many people. She had thought she and Jayce had survived for a reason—a reason that clearly involved a future together. Now she wasn't so sure. What if Jayce had deserted her? What if all of his words of love and devotion were just given because of the situation they were in? She bit her lip to keep from crying.

"I need to clean up," she told her brother. "Why don't you two wait in Jacob's room? I'll come over when I'm done."

"Bath is at the end of the hall," Jacob told her.

His words barely registered. The exhaustion of her ordeal began to overpower her. All Leah wanted was to run and hide and have a good cry.

As soon as Jacob and Adrik pulled the door closed, she let the tears come. A deep sob broke from her throat. "I can't understand any of this, Lord. I suppose it's silly to be worried already, but something's wrong. I just know it. I felt it even when Helaina showed up earlier. I could see in her eyes that she was watching Jayce with new purpose. I should have warned him. I shouldn't have left him alone."

She went to find her things, tears blinding her eyes. There had to be an answer—a reason for the things that were happening. Leah reached for her bundle of clothes Adrik had given her.

On the floor she saw a piece of paper. It seemed unimportant, but at the same time it beckoned her attention. She bent over to pick it up and noticed there were two other pieces in the trash can. They were telegrams. Taking all three in hand, Leah read the words addressed to Mrs. Helaina Beecham.

Leah read the words aloud. " 'JK is a killer. STOP. Do not worry about his innocence or guilt. STOP. We have all the proof we need. STOP. Get him to Seattle. . . . ' " She looked at the other cables and felt a wave of dizziness overcome her. What in the world was this all about? Who was JK?

Jayce Kincaid.

She hurried to Jacob's room and pounded on the door until he opened it. "Look!" She thrust the telegrams into her brother's hands.

"What is it?"

"These are telegrams addressed to Helaina. Jacob, she's taken Jayce away. She thinks he's a killer. Apparently someone else does too."

Jacob read the cables and handed them over to Adrik one by one. "I knew she had something going on. At least it explains her continued desire to get Jayce to Seattle."

"But what's this about him being a killer and not worrying about his guilt or innocence?" Adrik asked.

Jacob met Leah's eyes. "I don't know. I do know that Jayce Kincaid is no killer. I'd be willing to stake my life on that."

Adrik handed the paper back to Jacob. "It says the local law authorities are supposed to be helping her. My guess is that she has Jayce down at the jail. Why don't we get on down there and see for ourselves what this ruckus is all about."

"That's a good idea," Leah said, already heading out the door.

A million thoughts rushed through her head. Who was Jayce supposed to have killed, and why was Helaina involved in his capture? Had she really come to Alaska with the purpose of finding Jayce in order to take him back to Seattle?

"Hold up, Leah. You don't even know where you're going," Jacob called to her.

She stopped just outside the hotel, the fog much thicker now. At least Adrik would know where they were going. "It doesn't make sense," she said as the men joined her. "None of it. Why would the authorities send a woman to capture a man they believed was a killer?"

"That's a good question," Adrik replied, leading the way to the jail. "One that we'll hopefully get to ask her in just a minute."

Leah felt a surge of energy as anger encased her mind. She would tell Helaina Beecham what an awful person she was to force an innocent man to jail—a man who had just been rescued from a horrible ordeal. *The thought of that woman lying in wait at my home, just to capture Jayce, makes me want to throttle her.*

Adrik went into the jail first, with Jacob and Leah right behind him. Jacob put his arm out to keep Leah from rushing ahead. "Let Adrik handle it," he whispered.

"What can I do for you?" a large man asked. He leaned back in his chair and watched the three of them with a wary expression.

"I'm Adrik Ivankov. I'm wondering if you can tell me if Jayce Kincaid is here."

The man got to his feet. He was nearly as big as Adrik and didn't seem at all intimidated, as many people were when encountering the big man. "What do you want with him?"

"He's our friend!" Leah declared. "We just got back after nearly losing our lives on the *Orion's Belt*." Jacob held her tight. It was the only thing that kept Leah from charging the man.

"Well, your friend is in a world of trouble, missy. He's been arrested for murder."

Leah lunged forward, but Jacob held her securely. "He didn't do anything of the kind. Jayce Kincaid is no killer."

"The authorities in Washington, D.C., say otherwise. They've charged him with the death of their people. We received a cable earlier in the day asking us to assist the Pinkertons in his arrest."

"Pinkertons? Here?" Adrik questioned. "Who?"

"Mrs. Beecham," the man replied. "Not that I approve of women in such lines of duty, but it came all official. We helped her apprehend Kincaid earlier tonight."

"I want to see him," Leah said.

The man shook his head. "He's not here. He's on his way to Seattle."

"How? When?" She was terrified.

The man looked at them and crossed his arms. "Mrs. Beecham took him out of here on the *Victoria*. It just left the sound a few minutes ago. They're bound for Seattle with the last of the summer tourists."

Leah turned to Jacob and Adrik. "We have to do something!"

"I don't know what we can do," Jacob replied. "There isn't another ship available—at least not another steamer."

"Please, Adrik, we have to figure a way. Couldn't we get a message to the ship?"

"You people don't seem to understand. The Pinkertons were hired to take this man back for trial. You aren't going to stop that, and you sure aren't going to interfere with the *Victoria's* schedule. I'll arrest you myself on charges of obstructing justice."

"Justice," Jacob muttered. "That's what this is all about."

"What?" Leah turned to him. "What are you saying?"

"Helaina has this idea of what justice is. She believes that criminals should be meted out their full due without thought or consideration of the circumstance. She's without any compassion. She believes the law is the law, and there's no room for further consideration."

"She seems a good, law-abiding citizen."

Jacob turned to the officer. "She's angry and vengeful, and I intend to see her stopped."

Hours later the trio sat rather dumbfounded in Jacob's room. They had worn themselves out trying to figure what their next step should be.

"I think we can send a cable to Seattle," Adrik said. "We can contact the authorities there and suggest Helaina has the wrong man."

Jacob shook his head; his shoulders slumped in defeat as much as exhaustion. "But they'll want some sort of proof, and we don't have anything to offer."

"I think the man Helaina really wants is Jayce's twin brother, Chase," Leah said without warning.

Jacob looked at her. She was serious. "What are you talking about? Jayce has a twin?"

"Yes!" She suddenly seemed to regain her strength. "He told us about him while we were trying to get to Sitka. Me and Mrs. Wilkerson. He told us that he had a brother named Chase—that he was born just a few minutes after Jayce and that they are identical in appearance. Jayce said that his brother was always getting into trouble. That has to be the answer!"

"It could very well explain an awful lot," Adrik said, nodding. "But would that offer enough proof to the police?"

"I don't know, but I believe we have to try. Jayce said that Chase has been causing him trouble for years. The man even blames Jayce for the death of their mother, although she died because she was heartbroken over the misdeeds of Chase and the loss of her home and husband."

Jacob listened to every word, but he still found Leah's story difficult to believe. *And if I don't believe it—how can I expect the authorities to accept it as truth?* He blew out a heavy breath. "Look, I don't see how this is going to matter to the police. We can tell them whatever we want, but we can't prove any of it. I can't prove Jayce has an identical twin brother. I can't prove he has any family at all."

"We have to try," Leah said, tears forming in her eyes. "They mean to see him dead. They'll hang him for murdering those two agents. We have to find a way to help him, Jacob. We need to go to Seattle."

Chapter Twenty-Six

Jayce couldn't figure out what Helaina had planned next. She seemed quite nervous about the entire matter of docking in Seattle. Two burly sailors appeared at their cabin when the passengers were notified they could begin debarking. Jayce looked at the men, wondering if they were going to be the ones to escort him straight to jail.

"Look, my plans have changed," Helaina told Jayce. "There are a half-dozen Pinkertons waiting to take you from me when we set foot in Seattle. However, I would rather they not do that just yet."

Jayce sized up the men and then looked to Helaina again. "Why are you telling me this?"

Helaina pinned her hat securely and looked at the two sailors. "I will leave with the other passengers, and then I'd like for you to bring him along when the crew leaves the ship. I'll secure a carriage and meet you at the end of the docks. You said it would be about an hour—is that correct?"

"Yes, ma'am," the older of the two answered. "We'll have him to you in an hour or less."

"Very well. I'll go along now with the rest of the passengers." She turned to Jayce and met his curious expression. "If you want a chance to prove your innocence, then cooperate with me in this. These men have been paid well to see you do not slip away from my charge." With that she left, not even giving Jayce a chance to answer.

He looked at the two men. "So she paid you well, eh?"

"Very well." It was the same man who'd answered earlier. "She said you might try to promise us the moon, but that you didn't have a cent to your name."

"Well, she's right—at least I don't have a cent on me. I actually do have money in the bank. If you're open to negotiations . . . ?"

The men glanced at each other, then returned their gaze back to Jayce. "Sorry. We gave the lady our word. Besides, she has the law on her side. We don't plan to get on the wrong side of the law. She told us that if you escaped she'd put us in jail."

Jayce nodded. "No doubt she would. Well, fear not. I intend to go along with this plan of hers for the time being." And he spoke the truth. Just the fact that she was willing to consider him as innocent seemed worth the gamble.

An hour later the men delivered Jayce to Helaina. Her nervousness was palpable; she kept scanning the docks and motioning for the men to hurry. Finally Jayce was seated opposite her in the cab.

"What are you doing?" Jayce demanded as Helaina leaned over to unlock his leg irons. "I thought I was under arrest."

"You are," Helaina replied. "I just have some final paper work to get, and that may take a bit of time. Until then, we aren't leaving." She tossed the irons into her bag, then leaned back against the seat.

"So you're going to leave me in handcuffs indefinitely? These aren't exactly comfortable, you know. And I could use a bath and a shave."

Helaina stared out the window. It was obvious that she had a lot on her mind. And why not? Jayce had hounded her all the way from Sitka to Seattle. He told her about his brother, and while she had seemed notably surprised at this turn of events, she had refused to comment on the possibilities.

"I have a right to a lawyer," he now told her. "I want one now."

"No," she replied in a curt manner.

"You have no right to hold me against my will this way."

Helaina finally looked at him. "I have a warrant for your arrest. I can do as I please. I have legal authority by way of my association with the Pinkertons."

"Look, you have to believe me, Mrs. Beecham. I'm not guilty of these crimes. I have people in Vancouver who will testify to my being there during the times you've suggested I was elsewhere committing crimes. I've already told you that my brother Chase has been in constant trouble since the day he was born. He's been in and out of jails. Get in touch with the New York City police. They can tell you all about my brother."

Jayce looked at her for a reply. She seemed lost in her thoughts. Perhaps at last she was finally beginning to consider his innocence. "I'd like to help you catch my brother. The truth is, I saw him in Last Chance in June, just before the dog attack sent me to Nome."

She frowned. "The captain of the *Homestead* said you were with them in the Arctic prior to the time they had to leave because of sickness and other problems."

"But you know that I wasn't there," Jayce replied. "I was with Leah in Ketchikan, where I also have witnesses. I also took a trip to Juneau and have witnesses there as well."

"There's just no way to prove that you aren't the one responsible for killing those agents," Helaina said, shaking her head.

"If I can prove by the dates to have been somewhere else, then you would have to concede my innocence."

The cab stopped in front of the elegant Sorrento Hotel. Jayce could see it was a large, respectable place tailored in an Italian style. "How are you going to account for dragging me through the lobby in these?" He held up his manacled hands.

"We will drape my cloak over your arms," Helaina replied.

"And if I refuse to cooperate?"

She looked at him for a moment. "You don't have to cooperate. I can call the authorities and have you escorted to Washington, D.C., tonight. My brother will take his information against you and see you hanged. Or you can do what I tell you to do, and I'll continue checking out your story. It's that simple."

"But if I leave for Washington tonight, the authorities will also have to check out my story."

"Not necessarily, Mr. Kincaid. You see, I'm the only one who has found evidence of discrepancies that might show you to be innocent. Stanley might not be as likely to look into them."

"So you believe me?" Jayce felt a wave of hope.

Helaina shook her head. "I don't know what to believe. I do know that it isn't a simple matter any longer. I once thought it was very clear—thought I understood what I needed to do. But now it's different."

"I appreciate whatever mercy you might extend."

She frowned. "This isn't about mercy. It's about justice."

"How do you figure that?"

"Justice is seeing the right man punished for the crimes he's committed. That's all this is—nothing more."

The Sorrento stood as a remarkable tribute to the architect's desire to blend the warmth and luxury of Italy with the growing desire for elegance in Seattle. Jayce noted the dark mahogany walls. It almost seemed as though they had stepped into a men's club. Even the leather wing-backed chairs lent credence to this thought. Helaina seemed unimpressed. At least she made no comment.

They checked into the hotel as Mr. and Mrs. Beecham. Helaina explained to Jayce in a hushed voice that she wanted no trouble from the appearance of her, a widowed woman, sharing a room with a single man. Jayce heard her request a suite with a separate bedroom. She also demanded the bedroom have no windows. The clerk seemed rather confused by her stipulation, but he found exactly what she needed and concluded by asking her to have her husband sign the register.

She looked to Jayce as if expecting him to use this as an excuse to draw attention. Instead, he shook his head. "I'd prefer she sign."

He then looked away as if bored and indifferent with the entire process. Jayce heard the clerk mutter in a thoroughly annoyed manner.

"It's all right," Helaina declared. "My husband can be a bit eccentric. You must forgive him."

Jayce looked back to find her signing the register. The clerk then handed her the key and summoned a bellman. "Take their bags to room 212."

"We only have one small bag," Helaina said, smiling. "We can manage it ourselves."

The clerk rolled his eyes. "Very well."

They climbed the stairs to the second floor in silence. Jayce wanted to ask Helaina detailed questions about her plans, but he figured she would never reveal anything to him unless it suited her purpose. For now he'd give her the idea that he was cooperating, but if he felt things were getting out of hand, then he'd have to do otherwise. There was only one thing he would insist on.

Once they were secure in the hotel room, he tossed the cloak aside and faced Helaina. "You know that I could overpower you."

She looked at him for a moment and nodded. "No doubt."

"But I want you to understand and believe in my innocence. I want your help to clear my name. In return, I will stay here for a time. But I have two demands of my own."

"And what would they be, Mr. Kincaid?"

"I want a lawyer, and I want to write a letter to Leah. She's not going to understand my disappearance, and I won't have her misunderstanding this situation. I love that woman. I plan to marry her, and not you or the entire Pinkerton Agency is going to stop me."

She pulled off her hat and tossed it to a nearby writing desk. "I cannot allow you a lawyer at this time. If we involve anyone else—anyone—it will only jeopardize my ability to learn the truth."

"A lawyer could get to information you'd have no right to," Jayce protested.

"You are very naïve, Mr. Kincaid. I've been doing this for a long time. I have my connections and my processes for getting things done. I am willing to learn the truth about this and see your brother rightfully take your place. However, you must yield this to me. I need time. As it is, my brother is going to be livid. I took you off that ship right under the nose of a half-dozen Pinkerton agents. I couldn't see letting them take you, however, without at least trying to prove your claims one way or another. If I get you a lawyer, you'll have to go to jail and sit in a cell. Is that what you want?"

Jayce looked around him. The room was comfortably situated with a sofa and several chairs, a writing desk, and a luxurious fireplace. The bedroom door was closed, so he had no way to know what that room held. He had to admit a grand hotel room was better than a cell any day. "I suppose I can wait it out for a while. Will you in return trust me to be without these?" He held up his cuffed hands. "After all, we've already established that it wouldn't take much for me to overpower you—even manacled."

She considered this for a moment, then went to her purse. Producing the key, she drew a deep breath. "I hope you will not disappoint my trust, Mr. Kincaid. If you do anything to cause me difficulty, I will end my quest to prove the truth."

"I understand. If it helps at all, I give you my word that I'll remain here as you attempt to get your proof."

"Very well." She unlocked the cuffs and tucked the key in her pocket. "As for the letter," she said, crossing the room to open the bedroom door. "I suppose it will do no harm. I didn't want Leah or Jacob hurt in this situation. I know Jacob believes me to be a horrible liar, but I had my job to do."

"And that justifies telling lies?"

She reddened a bit at this. "Yes. Yes, I believe that I should use whatever means necessary to put evil criminals behind bars."

"Does that include breaking the law yourself—as you're doing now?"

She grew angry. "I'm doing this to help you. You'd do well to remember that. Believe me, I don't understand my own choice in this. It's all because of Jacob and the nonsense he tried to feed me about justice and mercy. If not for that, I'd just forget about the discrepancies and turn you over to the authorities. Furthermore, I'll let you write your letter, but for now this bedroom is your cell. I need to lock you in there to ensure that you won't escape while I'm out trying to gather information."

Jayce shrugged and walked to the door. Inside he could see a huge plush bed. "Suit yourself. I could use the sleep. Just make sure I have what I need to write that letter."

She went to the desk and took out paper and ink. "This should serve your purpose."

Jayce went into the room and waited for her to bring him the items. He stood at the far side of the bed so as not to unnerve her. Helaina placed the articles on the bed. "You should be able to use the nightstand for a table. I'll be back in a few hours. I'll bring you something to eat and drink at that time."

"All right. You have my promise that I won't try to leave."

She met his gaze. There was something almost sad in her expression. She seemed troubled and confused. Jayce figured it was an inner war—a battle within her that she'd never had to confront before. Apparently Jacob had given her cause to see the flaws in her logic. Jayce silently thanked God for this, because he was certain had Jacob not planted those seeds of doubt, he'd even now be on a train bound for Washington and a hangman's noose.

Helaina penned her words carefully. The telegram would cost her a precious amount of money, but she didn't care. She'd already requested more money from her bank in New York; after all, the Sorrento was far from inexpensive.

Stanley. Send me the fingerprint file for Jayce Kincaid. I believe he is innocent and the prints will prove this. Send a courier as soon as possible to the Sorrento Hotel in Seattle. Please don't be angry with me. I just learned Kincaid has an identical twin brother named Chase. We need to be certain which brother committed the crimes. Helaina.

She reread the words several times and afterward handed the paper to the telegraph operator. "I need this to be sent immediately. Here's the address."

The man looked over the message and nodded. "There's an extra charge for rush delivery."

"I don't care. This is a matter of life and death."

He looked at her oddly and nodded. "Okay, but it won't be cheap."

"It's already costing me everything," she murmured.

Leah settled down onto a pallet beside her brother. She would have laughed at her circumstance had it not been such a grave situation. The only transportation they could get to Seattle was aboard a freighter. There were no cabins or beds to be had. Just a quiet corner in the hold.

"We'll never get there in time," Jacob said. His voice was so full of regret that Leah instantly felt sorry for him.

"So much has happened to bring us to this place, Jacob. I know it isn't what either of us planned. We have to trust that God has everything in His hands."

"But what can we possibly hope to accomplish?" Jacob refused to look at her. "Leah, we're days behind them, and obviously Helaina had plans to be aided once she arrived in Seattle. Jayce is probably already gone."

"I know that's a possibility," Leah agreed, "but I don't feel like it's the reality. Besides, Karen promised to help. Her nephew is a private investigator in Seattle. Adrik has wired him, and he'll already be on the job before we arrive. God willing, he will have even found Helaina and Jayce and kept them from leaving Seattle. Remember, he has many friends to call upon for assistance."

"I know you're right. There is hope. There is always hope. I'm just . . . well . . . I guess I don't know what to think. Helaina told me there was more to her than what I thought, and I couldn't begin to guess the half of it."

"I think we have to put aside those kind of concerns and just focus on the future. I'm terrified for Jayce, but I know my fear will do him no good.

He'll need us now more than ever. I don't intend to give up my husband without a fight."

Jacob turned and smiled. "You aren't married yet."

"No, but my reputation is ruined just the same. After all, we spent all of that time alone . . . Well, Mrs. Wilkerson was there, but she was very sick," Leah said with a grin.

"Did you get to see her before we left?"

"Yes. She's doing better, but the doctor fears her heart is very damaged. She must always take it easy—lots of bed rest," Leah recounted. "I hope to see her in Nome when we return. It was her daughter's desire to get her back before the winter closed in."

"Wish we could be doing the same. I'm telling you, Leah, the thought of a city like Seattle unnerves me. I don't have any desire to go there, and we have no way of knowing what we'll encounter or how long it will take. I'll probably have to get some kind of job if it drags on too long."

"With a city that size, there is bound to be plenty of work. But don't worry about that just yet. Like Karen said, we can stay with her sister or one of the other relatives for a while. If things look like they will go on for a lengthy time, then we can reconsider what to do." She paused for a moment and grew thoughtful. "There's also another possibility."

"What's that?"

"Once we make it to Seattle and I'm safely in the care of Karen's family, you could return to Nome. There are more opportunities to get to Nome out of Seattle than Sitka or Ketchikan."

"I won't desert you. I won't desert Jayce either. I don't have to be happy about the circumstance to honor my commitment."

Four days later they docked in Seattle. Leah had never been so glad to see land in all her life. She wanted to run from the ship but comported herself in a ladylike manner down the gangplank. She wore a woolen skirt and coat, compliments of Karen. It felt rather strange to wear a dress after so many years, but at least she didn't feel too out of place.

The good thing about taking a freighter to Seattle was that they didn't have to endure the swarming crowds of a passenger liner. This made it much easier to spot the man who was to meet them.

"You must be Timothy Rogers," Leah said as a man approached them. He wore a stylish blue suit that complemented his tall, lean body and curly red hair.

He tipped his hat. "I am. Aunt Karen said you'd be arriving on the freighter, but I thought surely she was jesting." He looked beyond Leah to Jacob. "It's good to finally meet you both. My aunt has spoken of you as though you were her own children."

"In many ways, we were," Jacob admitted. "She has been a mother to us both."

Leah nodded but quickly changed the subject. "Tell me, have you any news of Jayce and Mrs. Beecham? Have you found them? Are they still here?"

Timothy smiled. "Indeed they are. I put my men to work immediately, and we searched every hotel in the downtown area. They are staying nearby, registered as Mr. and Mrs. Beecham. I've had them under surveillance now for days. He never leaves the hotel—the maid said he's always in the bedroom and the door is locked. Mrs. Beecham, however, has made some interesting trips."

"Such as?" Leah asked, casting a quick glance to Jacob before refocusing on Timothy.

"Such as wiring the Pinkerton agency in Washington, D.C., for a fingerprint file on Jayce Kincaid. It seems our gal is starting to doubt his guilt. She snuck him off the ship right under the noses of the agents her brother had sent to arrest Kincaid. It infuriated her brother, who sent a wire back telling her to forego this nonsense of worrying about whether or not Kincaid was the right man and that he was sending his men to arrest Jayce immediately. To which she sent the message that if he didn't help her and cooperate, she would disappear into the city until she had better answers."

"She cares about whether or not he's guilty," Jacob murmured.

"Yes, isn't that a change?" Leah said, catching Jacob's gaze. "Perhaps there's hope for Mrs. Beecham. Maybe she's learned that truth is more important than the letter of the law."

"And maybe she's finally learned what mercy is all about," Jacob said with a hint of a smile forming on his lips.

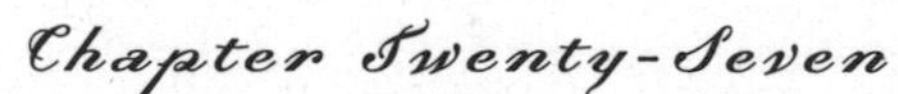

Chapter Twenty-Seven

Helaina had finally convinced Stanley to send the fingerprint files by courier. She breathed a sigh of relief and headed into the hotel. The past few days were beginning to take their toll. Jayce had been a well-behaved prisoner, but his attitude and actions only caused her more guilt and frustration.

I never would have worried about any of this before. Jacob Barringer has been a thorn in my side with his talk of mercy and compassion. Now I have Stanley angry and have jeopardized an important case . . . all in the name of mercy.

She made her way upstairs to the shared suite. For days she'd been sleeping on the sofa, and it had proved to be most inadequate. She longed for a bed but knew that it was better to keep Jayce imprisoned in the bedroom, rather than allow him free-range of the suite.

Unlocking the door to her room, she had nothing on her mind but to rest and rethink the information she'd gathered over the summer. But a roomful of people caused her to realize her plans were for naught.

"Mrs. Beecham."

Jacob stood by the windows and watched, as if waiting for her to do something dramatic. Beside him stood a tall, redheaded man. Jayce sat on the sofa along with Leah, while a fourth man sat at the writing desk.

"What's going on?" Helaina asked.

"We might ask you the same thing," Jacob retorted. "You kidnap a man in the dead of night and have the nerve to ask *us* what's going on?"

Helaina squared her shoulders. "I have a warrant for his arrest."

"So why isn't he in a jail, Mrs. Beecham?" the man at the desk questioned. He stood and came to where she stood.

"And who are you, sir?"

"Magnus Carlson, attorney-at-law. I now represent Mr. Kincaid."

Helaina eyed the man for a moment. He wasn't all that tall, and he carried an extra fifty pounds or more, but there was a certain presence to him. His pudgy face sported gold-rimmed glasses, from behind which icy blue eyes watched her every move.

"I see." She looked to Jayce. "I thought we had an agreement."

"I didn't bring them here," Jayce replied. "They found me."

"Might I inquire as to how you located us?" Helaina posed the question to Jacob.

"A private detective was hired by cable the night you left," Jacob replied. "He's been on the case ever since and brought us here to set Jayce free."

"I'm sorry, but that isn't possible," Helaina stated. She opened her purse. "I have the papers right here that entitle me to capture and arrest Mr. Kincaid."

"Then why hasn't he been properly remanded to the local authorities?" Carlson asked.

Helaina looked to Jayce. "Haven't you already told them this?"

"He has given his side of it," Carlson replied, "but we'd like to hear yours. This man's rights have been violated. Whether you have a warrant or not, he has constitutional rights."

"Yes," Helaina replied. "I'm very aware of that." She drew a deep breath. "There have been many discrepancies in this case. I chose this path to save Mr. Kincaid the drudgery of a jail cell while I researched and received the information I felt would help either convict or clear him."

"What exactly are the charges against Mr. Kincaid?"

Helaina looked around the room. "Why don't we sit down? This will take a while." She took her place in a wing-backed chair and smoothed the skirt of her new plum-colored traveling suit. Taking off her gloves, Helaina draped them across her lap while the others took their places.

Jacob joined Leah and Jayce on the sofa, while the other two men took up the remaining chairs. Helaina felt almost relieved to finally be able to explain to Jacob, but at the same time she could see the anger in his expression. He would never believe her. There would never be anything she could say to win his approval.

"Earlier this year my brother, Stanley, a Pinkerton man in Washington, D.C., captured a man calling himself Jayce Kincaid. The man was responsible for the death of two Pinkerton agents, as well as a theft of goods at the British Museum in London. There were other charges of thefts and assaults as well. Stanley took the man into custody and boarded a train for Washington, D.C. On the way, Mr. Kincaid managed to free himself from his handcuffs. When Stanley realized what had happened, they fought. Eventually, the fight took them out on the open platform of this private car. Mr. Kincaid was a powerful man whose larger size gave him advantage against my brother. After throwing several punches that nearly rendered my brother unconscious, Mr. Kincaid threw Stanley from the train. This resulted in Stanley being severely injured."

"I'm quite sorry for your brother, Mrs. Beecham, but how could he be certain that this man was the responsible party?"

Helaina opened her purse and pulled out the folded sketch. "Stanley had this drawing made." She handed it to Carlson and waited while he passed it along to the others. "Kincaid had never been photographed by the authorities, and this was the only thing we had to identify him. This and a set of fingerprints taken from the train car."

"Fingerprints?" Leah questioned.

"Each person has a unique design of swirls and ridges on their fingers," Helaina explained. "No two are alike." She looked at Jayce. "Even in the case of twins—although I have heard of twins having prints that were alike, but reversed in order."

"So the fingerprints will prove that Jayce wasn't the one on the train," Leah stated, her voice sounding quite excited.

"That is my hope," Helaina said honestly. "I've had a hard time convincing my brother to send a courier with the file, but I believe he is finally willing to do this."

"You cannot just hold this man against his will in the meantime," Carlson said. "You do realize I could have you before a judge on this matter."

Helaina swallowed hard. This whole case had caused her nothing but problems from the beginning, and now it threatened to cause her grief with the law. The law that she so thoroughly respected. "I suppose I do, but I hope you will also see the problem in my turning Mr. Kincaid over to the police. If I do that, the Pinkerton men my brother sent here will simply take him into custody and put him on the first train back to the Capitol. He won't have a chance to prove his case before they throw him into jail to await a trail. I had hoped to have the proof needed, by obtaining the print files, prior to acting further on this matter."

"But why, Mrs. Beecham? If you had a job to do, why did you delay in doing it?"

"Yes, please tell us about that, Helaina," Jacob said rather snidely. "You were trying to find ways to force Jayce back to Seattle from the first day we met you."

She grew uncomfortable under his scrutiny. "It is true that I had a job to do. I thought the evidence against Jayce Kincaid was strong enough to prove his guilt. But that changed. Other things came to light . . . situations developed that I couldn't just ignore."

"For example?" Carlson asked.

Helaina thought back to all that had transpired and began to list off the events that gave her cause to doubt. "I suppose it all culminated for me when I read a letter to Jacob from the captain of the *Homestead*." She glanced briefly at Jacob. "He mentioned how helpful Jayce had been on their short-lived expedition north. I knew Jayce was in Ketchikan with Leah. But, at the same time, here was a reputable man praising Mr. Kincaid's help with the dogs in the Arctic. I knew something had to be wrong."

"You must release this man until you have solid proof that allows you to arrest him. You cannot expect to keep him locked here in this hotel like some sort of animal."

"But if I release him, he will probably escape," Helaina replied. She was already convinced for herself that Jayce was innocent. But she had to, for the sake of Stanley's reputation and her own, prove that the fingerprints were not a match. "If Jayce leaves before I can check his fingerprints against the recorded prints, I will face serious problems."

"I won't leave, Helaina. I want to be proven innocent. As much as you want to know the truth, I want it more," Jayce said, his expression quite serious. "I have no reason to flee. I know what those prints will tell you."

"I don't know what should be done," Helaina finally admitted. "The file won't arrive by courier for a week or more."

"I have a suggestion," the redheaded man spoke up. He smiled at Helaina. "I'm Timothy Rogers, the private investigator who helped the Barringers—actually we're family." He turned and smiled at Leah. This caused her to nod.

"Anyway, I have a suggestion that might help all parties concerned. I can see that Mrs. Beecham has actually, out of the goodness of her heart, not imposed jail or the possibility of being sent east on Mr. Kincaid. She is trying to learn the truth in the hopes of knowing one way or the other if Jayce Kincaid was responsible for the deaths of other people. This is a critical issue. We cannot expect her to simply feel at ease in setting a possible killer free."

"Granted, Mr. Rogers, but there are laws to abide by. The law makes it very clear how these things are to be handled," Carlson said.

"And the law is the law," Jacob muttered, staring at Helaina with an unyielding gaze.

"That aside," Timothy continued, "I believe I have a solution. Since this should take no more than a week or two, I would like to offer my home. I have a large house with plenty of space for everyone. There is no Mrs. Rogers to be put off by my bringing home unplanned house guests, although my housekeeper might fret a bit."

"That is a very generous offer, Mr. Rogers," Helaina said. "But I'm not sure how that solves the situation."

"My thought, Mrs. Beecham, is that with everyone under the same roof, all parties may find the situation more agreeable. Mr. Kincaid will feel less like a prisoner. He has given his word that he has no plans to flee and desires the same thing you do. The Barringers are obviously interested in helping see Mr. Kincaid set free, so they are not planning to go until this thing is settled. And for you, the benefit would not only be peace of mind, but less strain on your budget. This hotel is quite expensive and my house is free."

"What say you, Mr. Kincaid? Would this meet with your approval?" Carlson asked.

"I would be willing to stay with Mr. Rogers. I'm even willing, for the sake of giving Mrs. Beecham peace of mind, to remain on the grounds until the proof is delivered and I am absolved of these charges. It would be my act of good faith, in return for hers."

Helaina knew they were all waiting for her to answer. "I suppose," she said after giving it only a moment of thought, "that this would be a better solution."

"Very well," Magnus Carlson said, getting to his feet. "Let us move our affairs to Mr. Rogers' house."

Helaina saw the others nod in agreement. All seemed pleased with the outcome—except Jacob. He continued to look at her as though she had been responsible for killing the agents herself. His contempt was evident, and for reasons that completely eluded Helaina, it very nearly broke her heart.

"But I think she's genuinely sorry for the things she's done," Leah protested.

Jacob had refused to hear a single argument in favor of Helaina. "I don't care how sorry she is—look at how she's treated everyone. Look at what she's done to cause problems for you and Jayce. Doesn't that bother you in the least?"

Leah looked at him and nodded. "It bothered me at first. You know how I worried about what she was up to—only I figured it to be some romantic notion. It never even occurred to me that she could be some kind of bounty hunter. But, Jacob, you can't just hold a grudge against her. It will hurt you more than it will her."

Jacob crossed his arms and shook his head. "I don't want to deal with her at all—ever again. Let her get her proof and then get out of our lives."

"But she needs your forgiveness."

He jumped up from the chair at this. "Hmph. She's never done anything to deserve it."

Leah laughed. "Jacob Barringer, listen to yourself. Since when do we offer forgiveness because someone deserves it?"

Jacob remembered the conversation he'd had with Helaina where he'd told her no one deserved forgiveness. He was trying to teach her about mercy, and now that she'd actually practiced a little of it, he was willing to condemn her without hearing another word.

"Just go talk to her," Leah said, coming to his side. "You more than anyone knows what it is to be shown mercy. Helaina merely wanted to capture the man who so brutally wounded her brother. She had the evidence and word of the Pinkertons, and she was doing an honorable job. We cannot hold that against her."

Jacob knew Leah was right, but it was hard to admit it. "I suppose I can hear her out, but I have no desire to be her friend."

"I don't see any reason why you have to be her friend," Leah countered. "But you have the power to give her peace of mind, to show her real mercy . . . the very thing you've desired for her to learn."

He felt a sense of calm wash over himself as he made up his mind to seek Helaina out. "I'll talk to her. I can't promise anything more."

"Then I'll pray for you, Jacob." Leah reached out and touched her brother's face. "Just as you prayed for me."

Deciding it was best to get the matter over with, Jacob headed to the door. "You'd better pray hard, then. I have a feeling I'm going to need extra help with this one."

Helaina sat reading quietly in the front parlor when she heard someone clear his throat from the doorway. Looking up, she saw Jacob. Her heart picked up pace a bit as she closed her book. "Yes?"

He seemed uneasy. "I came here to . . . well . . . I want to be fair and hear you out."

Helaina felt hope surge within. "Truly?"

He walked into the room in a rather aloof manner. "I wouldn't be here if I didn't intend to hear what you have to say."

She'd tried so hard to talk to him prior to this that for a moment Helaina thought she might be dreaming. She suddenly felt very guarded. "I suppose you should sit down. Confession sometimes takes a while," she said with the slightest hint of a smile.

Jacob did as she suggested, sitting on the edge of the green brocade chair opposite her. "I'm sitting."

She nodded. "Well, you know from our conversation at the hotel that I came into this case at the request of my brother. It seemed every time one of the Pinkerton men got close to Kincaid, he either ran or hurt someone. It was decided that Kincaid would never suspect a woman. I was encouraged to use whatever means necessary to get Jayce into a position where agents could come in and arrest him and take him into custody.

"There were eyewitness accounts and descriptions of the man who was a thief and a murderer. The proof seemed very solid, Jacob, or my brother would never have sent me."

"But the proof was wrong. There were other issues to consider."

"Yes, issues that no one had any idea existed. Who would ever suspect an identical twin?" she asked. "There was no information or background on who this man really was or where he was from. When I heard Jayce's story on the way to Seattle, everything finally made sense. You see, I had written to the exploration association in Vancouver, and they had confirmed Jayce's employment during the same time he was supposedly committing crimes on the east coast. It didn't make sense at the time, so I continued to dig.

"When I read the letter from Captain Latimore—the one I opened in your absence . . ."

"How could I forget?" His tone was still very guarded and edged with anger.

"As I said, when I read the captain's praises for Jayce Kincaid's help with the dogs, nothing made sense. I knew he wasn't on that expedition—well, at first I thought he might have figured out who I was and that he had given me the slip. But when I knew for a fact that Jayce was with Leah in Ketchikan, it changed everything. I knew that he couldn't be two places at the same time. I even wrote to my brother to suggest that something was wrong and that perhaps we needed to look into whether or not Jayce had a family member who was using his name—taking his identity."

"So why did you take Jayce from Sitka? If you were confident that you had the wrong man, why bring him here?"

She frowned. How could she hope to make him understand her turmoil? She wanted only to see justice served and Stanley's reputation restored. She wanted a killer behind bars, but she also wanted to make certain the man she put there was truly the right one.

"I know you have no reason to believe me. I did lie to you before, and for that I am sorry and hope you . . . well . . . that you . . . might . . . forgive me," Helaina stammered. She hurried on. "But I also need for you to understand that my brother was firm on what I was to do. He wanted Jayce brought to Seattle, and I didn't want to let him down. He's all I have left."

"Why didn't you just tell us that? Why all the sneaking around and secrecy?"

"Because Jayce is your friend. You wouldn't have believed me," Helaina said, getting rather angry. "I did my job, and at first I really didn't care what anyone else thought."

"At first?"

Helaina nodded and tried to restrain her emotions. "I honestly didn't care about your feelings or anyone else's when I first came to Nome. I was already unhappy because I'd lost the opportunity to capture Jayce in Seattle. But now . . . now I see how this wild chase has come about solely to teach me several things."

"What sort of things?"

She tried to figure out how best to word it. The last thing she needed was for Jacob to believe she was merely trying to sell him a bill of goods. She wanted—needed—him to believe her.

"You started talking about your faith, about your trust in God. You started telling me—showing me—about mercy and compassion. These were things I definitely didn't understand. I'm not sure I understand them even now. After all, the balance seems at odds to me. I'm breaking the law and disappointing my brother by not just taking Jayce to the Pinkerton agents and turning him over. I deserve to face the consequences for my actions, but at the same time, I want to make certain Jayce is really the guilty party before sending him off to my brother. I suppose you would say that is mercy. For me, however, it's this battle of duties and beliefs that I've never had to face before now."

Jacob seemed to relax and his expression softened. "Sometimes it's hard to understand how the balance works. Everyone struggles."

"Even you?" she asked with a bit of an awkward laugh. "You seem to have it all under control."

"I'm struggling now," Jacob said softly. "I'm fighting my own war right this minute—with you."

She cocked her head to the side. "How so?"

"I know you want my forgiveness, but frankly, Helaina, I don't want to give it. I don't want to extend mercy to you. Why? Because you have hurt me—hurt my friends and loved ones. However, I know what the Bible says about forgiveness and about my part in practicing such a thing. And even though you don't believe in following the Bible's teachings, I do. Therefore the responsibility comes back on my shoulders."

"I'm not saying that you don't have a right to be angry, Jacob. Because I truly believe you are entitled to that. I did lie. It was wrong, and yet I justified it as being necessary because of my job. Just know that my intention was not to hurt you."

"But whether that was your intention or not—it happened nevertheless."

"I know." She looked away, feeling so uncertain of what she was about to say. "You've taught me to look at life differently, Jacob. I still don't know what to believe or not believe about God, but on the issue of mercy, I have to admit to having a new perspective. I know you cannot begin to appreciate the ramifications of this, but it has changed my entire life. A few months back I would never have questioned Jayce's guilt. In fact, his innocence or guilt would simply have been the responsibility of someone else—not me. And if that truth wasn't proven, I was still able to distance myself and not care whether the outcome was good or bad. I had done my job. Now, however, I find myself questioning everything. I tell myself, despite the complications, I cannot send an innocent man to his death. I know that no one else cares to learn the truth in this matter as much as I do—they are angry at what they believe has been done to men of their own fellowship." She looked past Jacob, no longer seeing him. "Months ago, I wouldn't have defied my brother and the agency, and I certainly wouldn't have cared if you gave me your forgiveness." She paused and drew a deep breath before adding, "But I care now."

For several moments neither one said another word, then Jacob surprised her by getting to his feet. "This isn't easy for me, but at least I think I can understand this all a little better than before. I've treated you badly, even knowing that I was wrong for doing so. I guess what I'm trying to say is that I forgive you." He frowned and looked away. He seemed to wrestle with his own emotions, something Helaina thought quite unusual. Finally he added, "I hope you'll forgive me as well."

Helaina had not expected this or the sudden release of desire—need—from within her heart. Tears came to her eyes. She didn't understand what was happening to her, but the relief was so great that she couldn't do anything for a moment. He had asked for her forgiveness, when all the while she had been desperate for his.

"I forgive you," she whispered, hardly able to make the words form. She bowed her head and struggled to regain her composure. When she finally looked up, Jacob had already moved to the door. He watched her with a strange but guarded look on his face.

"Thank you," he said, then abruptly left the room.

Helaina buried her face in her hands and sobbed. *I don't understand any of this. What is happening to me . . . and why should his opinion matter so much?*

Chapter Twenty-Eight

"The city is quite intimidating," Helaina said as Leah accompanied her on a shopping trip. "It's the noise you usually have to get used to."

"And all the people. There are people everywhere." Leah looked at the swarming mass of humankind and shook her head. How could so many people live together in one place? The noise was oppressive. There didn't seem to be a single moment of silence.

"It does take a certain kind of person to endure it," Helaina replied. "But don't you find the choices to be far superior here?"

Leah considered this for a moment. "The numerous choices are almost as bad as getting used to the numerous people. I've lived a much simpler life in Alaska. Still, it's been a very good life." She pulled her woolen cape closer as raindrops began to fall. "I suppose I could say that I would rather not have the extra choices."

"But why? Wasn't it quite the adventure yesterday as we searched for new clothes? You look quite handsome in that afternoon suit."

"But Jacob and I have never spent our money foolishly. This outfit will only serve its purpose down here. And if we have our way about it, we won't stay here any longer once Jayce is cleared of your charges and set free."

Helaina grimaced. "They aren't my charges, and I'm sorry you and your brother equate them as such."

Leah heard the regret in her voice and took compassion on the woman. "I'm sorry; I meant nothing by that."

"I know," Helaina replied, motioning to a storefront. "Here's the place I want."

"A stationery store?" Leah noted that they advertised the largest inventory of writing supplies. "Why here?"

"I need quality paper and ink in order to make a good image of Jayce's fingerprints. We'll take prints from Jayce and then compare them when the courier finally brings the copies from Washington."

"And that will be the end of it?" Leah questioned. "Once you are able to prove that the prints are different, Jayce will be free to go?"

"Yes, I suppose he will be free," Helaina replied. "I'm hoping, however, he might help us in obtaining the true culprit. I need for Jayce to help me find Chase."

"You want Jayce to turn against his own brother?"

Helaina opened the door to the store and stepped inside. Leah was right on her heels. She couldn't imagine that the woman really expected any cooperation out of Jayce after all she'd done to him.

"Do you?" Leah reached out to halt Helaina in her steps. "I mean, you've put us all through a great deal. How can you possibly believe we'll just stay here and help you? I think that's asking entirely too much."

Helaina turned and looked at her as though Leah were being quite unreasonable. "You do want to see a murderer behind bars—don't you?"

"Not if it means having to stay here and force Jayce to hunt down his brother. That's the Pinkertons' job or the duty of the authorities. It isn't our responsibility."

"But you cannot think to just leave."

"You cannot think to make us stay." Leah shook her head. "You must know the pain we've endured. We simply want to return home and be done with this chapter of our lives. We need for God to heal the sorrows and pains of the past and look to the future."

"So you'll just leave when we get the proof?" Helaina questioned. "You won't help me at all?"

Leah shook her head. "I for one intend to go home."

"But how is that in accordance to what you believe?"

"What do you mean?"

Helaina pulled Leah to one corner of the store as another woman came into the shop. "The Bible is full of verses about helping those in need. There are verses—I've read them myself—that speak to bearing one another's burdens, to helping those who ask for it. What of that?"

Leah shook her head. "I can't speak for the others, Helaina. You'll have to take that up with them. I just wouldn't count on any of us remaining here once the truth is known. Jayce has already given you more information than he would otherwise have to give. He's told you all about his brother and where he last saw him. I cannot imagine he owes you more than that."

Jayce watched Leah from the parlor entryway for several minutes. She looked so different in her new clothes. She was as radiant and beautiful as he'd ever seen her, but also so completely out of place. As she studied the newspaper, Jayce could see the information there did not set well. No doubt she found news of the ongoing war to be very disturbing.

Jayce smiled to himself. He decided to put an end to her worries and give her something more positive to think on. He'd been waiting for just the right moment to speak to her about marriage.

He sauntered into the room, still limping ever so slightly from the dog wound. "Alone at last."

Leah smiled and put the paper aside. "Where are the others?"

"I heard Mrs. Beecham say she was going out for a time. Jacob and Timothy are deep in a conversation about the affairs of the world." He settled down on the sofa and reached out to take hold of her hand. "I think we should talk."

"I agree." She shifted her weight to face him. "What would you like to talk about?"

"Well, the obvious topic that comes to mind is us. Of course, if you have another subject more near and dear to your heart . . ."

Leah covered his hand with hers. "I suppose that will suffice."

Just then the front doorbell rang. Leah looked to Jayce. "Do you think the courier has arrived?"

"I certainly hope so." He got up and headed for the foyer. He turned abruptly. "I suppose our conversation will have to wait a little longer."

Leah followed behind, sounding quite disappointed. "I suppose so."

Jayce arrived just behind the butler. The man admitted their guest and nearly jumped a foot when he realized Jayce was standing right beside him.

"Sorry, sir. I did not see you there. This is Captain Latimore."

"Yes, I know the man well," Jayce said, extending his hand. "I see you got my letter."

"Indeed, I did. Mr. Kincaid, I'm glad you got in touch. You said Mr. Barringer was here as well?"

"Yes." He turned to Leah. "Have you two met?"

Leah nodded. "I met the captain in Last Chance—when you were injured."

"It's good to see you again, Miss Barringer."

"Leah, if you'll excuse us for a time, Jacob and I have business with the captain."

"Of course. Let me know if you need anything." She turned and headed back to the parlor.

Jayce smiled at the captain. "Why don't you come with me? I'll take you to Jacob and we can talk." Jayce led the way to Timothy's study. Knocking on the open door, he looked in expectantly. "We have a guest."

The men looked up, but it was Timothy who welcomed them in. "Come join us. We are always up for a guest."

"Captain Latimore," Jacob said, getting to his feet. "I'm glad to see you. This is our host and dear friend, Timothy Rogers."

The two men shook hands, then Timothy motioned to the butler. "Bring us coffee and something to eat. I'm sure we could all use a bit of something to tide us over until supper."

"How is your family, Captain? Did your wife enjoy the Arctic?" Jacob asked.

"I'm afraid the expedition was difficult for Regina to endure. Our son had just turned three, so he could not accompany us. She missed him fiercely. But of course you would remember that," he said, turning to Jayce.

"Captain, I wasn't with you. You mentioned my presence in a letter to Jacob, but that wound I suffered from the dogs kept me from joining you."

The captain looked stunned. "Then who was the man calling himself Jayce Kincaid? He was identical to you."

"I know. I believe it was my brother Chase—my twin. Although I'm uncertain as to how he knew I was expected on the *Homestead*."

"How strange," the captain said, shaking his head. "As I recall he showed up in Kotzebue. We were there trying to arrange native help. One of the men saw him and recognized him. After that he assumed your role without question. At times he seemed uncertain, fumbled around a bit, but I attributed that to your injury. I rarely spoke to him face-to-face, but when we talked, he answered as though he were you."

"I'm sure he did. He has always had a habit of pretending to be me. I hope he caused no trouble."

"None at all. That's why I was encouraged to ask for your return next year." The captain seemed troubled by this new turn of events. "I would still like for you to join us . . . since I know you studied and planned for the trip. Your geological skills would be much needed." He turned to Jacob. "Your dog handling skills will also be needed."

"You were speaking of your wife and her difficult time on the trip," Jacob interjected, seeming to sense the need to change the focus. "Will she accompany you next year?"

"No, I'm sorry to say she won't be able to, but I'm happy to announce we are expecting our second child in April."

"Congratulations," Jayce offered. "It's a troubling time for our world, but children are always a blessing."

"We were just discussing some of the war's conflicts. The Germans seem to have decided it would be in their best interests to play fair," Timothy said. "What say you, Captain?"

"I have had great concern about the affairs of this country. I worry that we will somehow be dragged into this matter, and that is really why I'm here today. I have no problem in interesting men in exploration—especially when it comes to the areas of the Arctic. Since the trouble with the *Karluk* and others, there has been a fascination for defeating the frozen north—taming the untamable, if you will. Even the army has approached me with interests for a mutual expedition, but they'd like for it to remain a secret. No sense stirring up the rest of the country in wondering what they're up to."

"What exactly are they up to?" Jacob asked.

"They believe this war will escalate. They desire that we be prepared to ward off possible invasions. Russia is having all kinds of trouble. They are fighting amongst themselves. It's the opinion of my government contacts that Russia may well go into a full civil war. If that happens, we may find them coming across the strait to attack or try to reclaim parts of Alaska. Many believe the sale was completely unfair, you know."

"But surely they know it would mean war with America if they were to attack Alaska," Jayce replied. "Fair or unfair, the deal was signed and paid for. The territory belongs to us."

"Exactly," the captain agreed. "However, it doesn't mean there won't be those who aren't motivated to change the situation."

Jayce considered this for a moment. If the captain's thoughts were correct, it could mean a great deal of danger to those living in the Seward Peninsula, so close to the Russian people. "So the army wants to form an expedition for what purpose exactly?"

"I'm not entirely sure of their complete objective, but the main one would be for the purpose of devising strategic locations for defense. They would want to explore the entire coastal region of the western boundaries of Alaska."

Jacob shifted to the edge of his chair. "And what would be your focus in this effort?"

The captain smiled. "I am still of a mind to explore for the purpose of seeing it all and knowing what else might be made of it. If there is potential for the military, then there is potential for towns and cities as well."

Jayce shook his head. "That land is raw and inhospitable. Life in the Arctic and along the Bering Sea is not an easy one. There isn't enough vegetation there to support large numbers of people, and planting additional crops simply won't work. This is not a good area of the world to raise food."

"Nor to build houses or roads," Jacob added. "The ground is permanently frozen just inches from the surface. Much of the area becomes impassable bogs and marshlands in the summer months as the top of this ground thaws. In the winter, the only travel by land is done with snowshoes and dogsleds. You won't get automobiles to pass over the frozen tundra with any degree of success."

Latimore frowned. "I thought you to be men of vision. You know that where there is a dream for such things, men will also figure out how to accomplish those dreams. I intend to be a part of that, and I would like you two to join my team."

"So you will definitely make another attempt at the north next year?" Jayce questioned.

"Yes, and we might even set up a winter camp in order to endure the elements and figure out what might be done to minimize the dangers and problems, with the hope of expanding villages already in place to become larger settlements—even cities."

"I've lived winters in the north," Jacob replied. "It's not for the faint of heart. One of the biggest things you're forgetting, besides the cold, is the darkness. For a great many weeks, we lose the sun all together. How do you propose to maintain cities in complete darkness? There simply won't be enough wood, coal or kerosene to keep things warm and lighted. There won't be flowing rivers for power stations so that you can string electricity in these proposed towns."

"Not to mention that the endless hours of darkness are even harder on a person than the summer's endless hours of light. It takes a special kind of person to live in the north," Jayce added.

"So you would defeat my project before it even starts?" the captain asked.

"Not at all," Jayce replied. "We would just suggest you be realistic."

"I think the men make good arguments," Timothy declared, "but I, for one, would be quite supportive of such a project. I think our pioneering grandparents and great-grandparents might never have settled this far west had they been unwilling to take risks. But there should also be a balance of caution."

Latimore nodded, rubbing his dark beard. "I completely agree. However, I will point out, if we don't go—someone else will. There have already been multiple trips to the Arctic by other teams. Some have not fared well, and others have. You have men talking all along the lyceum circuits about their exploits in the Alaskan wilderness. The passion is there, my friends. It's just a matter of figuring out who will go and then how to raise the funds to undertake such a project."

"I would definitely be interested," Jayce admitted. "But there are things about my life that have changed. I intend to take a wife." He looked at Jacob and grinned. "Although I haven't exactly had a chance to ask her yet."

"My first comment on that news is, congratulations," the captain replied, smiling. "And my second is, bring her along. We will have jobs for women as well as men. We plan to seek the help of the natives again—hopefully with better success this time. But we could always use a good seamstress."

"I'm sure Leah would love the adventure," Jacob admitted, "but while her sewing abilities are first rate, she's also a skilled healer."

"Wonderful! We could probably never hope to secure a doctor on such a trip, but if your sister is capable in this area, we would be quite well settled."

"How soon will you begin to assemble your men?" Jayce asked.

"I'm already at the task. That's why I'm here today. I can use a geologist and a man to handle the dog teams."

"I don't suppose you'll need a private detective," Timothy said, grinning, "but what of an investor?"

Latimore smiled. "There is always need for those, kind sir."

After refusing to stay for supper, Latimore took his leave. Leah then found herself in the middle of an animated table conversation concerning next year's expedition. Helaina, however, seemed quite unhappy with the topic.

"I see nothing of value in this; after all, there is a war going on in Europe. The expense is rather frivolous," she told them. "You could do your country a better service by helping me capture the killer who murders in your name."

Jayce looked at her and shook her head. "I never sought a career in the law. I'm sure there are plenty of men who would be happy to help you, but I'm not one of them."

"Leah said it would be your plan to head back to Alaska as soon as your name was cleared. I can't help but say that this a disappointment to me." She sliced into the beef and took a bite.

"Enough of a disappointment to keep you from clearing my name?" Jayce asked quite seriously. Every eye turned to Helaina, and they all waited for her answer.

She swallowed and seemed to consider the matter for a moment. "I wouldn't do that. I would never hold an innocent man just because he refused to assist me. I'm sorry you would believe that of me."

"But you've said in the past that you would do just about anything to get your man." Jacob looked at her hard. "Why would this not be an option?"

"Because it wouldn't be just," Helaina said, pushing back her plate. "But neither is it just for you to leave a guilty man at large."

"I've already given you all of the information I can," Jayce said, getting up from the table. Leah could see the anger in his eyes. "I've told you about my brother and the places I know him to go. I've told you about the company he keeps. I owe you nothing. Now if you'll excuse me."

"But wait! You would be the one person who might get close to him without arousing suspicions."

"How callous you are," Jacob interjected. "You honestly expect a man to turn traitor to his own family?"

"If his brother is guilty as he suggests, then yes, I do. It's the law. It's only right. Would you not turn your sister in if she committed murder right before your very eyes?"

Jayce only shook his head and stalked from the room.

Leah got up. "If you'll excuse me, I should go to him."

She left the room without another word. Helaina's insensitivity to Jayce's pain truly irritated Leah, but there was little she could say that she hadn't already said.

"Jayce? Are you all right?"

She found him in the front room, standing by the fireplace. He turned at the sound of her. "Do you think I should stay? Am I wrong?"

Leah went to him. "No. I think it's an unreasonable request."

"But what if he kills again, Leah? What if he kills someone, and I could have stopped him?"

"You don't know that you could stop him," Leah argued. "You don't know where he is, and there's no guarantee that you could ever find him. Like you told me once, when he wants to disappear, he disappears."

She could see the pain in his expression, knowing the war being fought in his heart was not one with an easy resolution. Someone would get hurt in this situation—no matter which side won out.

"Leah."

The way he spoke her name sounded almost like a plea. She put her hand to his shoulder and smiled. "I'm here for you, Jayce. I've always been here for you."

He took her in his arms and crushed her against him. "I love you. I think I always have." He paused, then added in a hushed whisper, "Marry me, Leah. Please marry me."

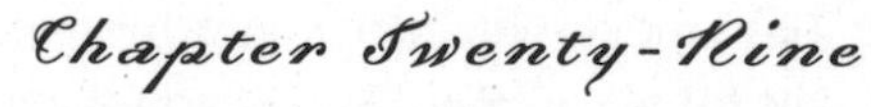

Chapter Twenty-Nine

Climbing the stairs to Mr. Rogers' house, Helaina paused at the sound of laughter coming from the front room. No doubt Jacob and Leah and Jayce were all caught up in an animated discussion. Helaina bit her lower lip and wondered if perhaps she should just come in through the back entry. At least then she wouldn't have to make the obligatory greetings and spend time in small talk with people she knew would rather she simply disappear from their lives.

The door opened, to her surprise. "Good afternoon, madam," the butler said in his stately manner. "Would you care for tea?"

He helped her with her coat and hat. "No thank you," Helaina replied. "I believe I'll just go upstairs and have a rest."

She crossed the highly polished oak floors, her heels clicking rhythmically as she passed the parlor door. Against her will she looked inside the room. Leah met her gaze and waved.

"How are you, Helaina? I've not seen you all day."

Helaina knew she had no choice but to pause. "I had to tend to business this morning. I've been back and forth, actually. I still have no word about the courier."

"Come join us," Leah suggested. "We were just talking about our wedding."

"Will it be soon?"

"Yes. Jayce and I are to be married before we return to Alaska."

The men seemed rather hesitant to join in the conversation. Helaina sensed their indifference at her appearance. "That's wonderful news. Congratulations," she said halfheartedly.

"Timothy is helping us to arrange things through his minister." Leah smiled at Jayce and added, "It will just be a small private service."

"I'm sure it will be lovely."

"We were also discussing our plans for next summer. We all plan to be involved in the expedition," Leah said. "I never would have believed it, but Captain Latimore said one thing they definitely could have used on this last expedition was a skilled seamstress. I can fit that bill easily. Not only that, but I can act as nurse to the expedition members."

"She is very good with a needle," Jacob finally joined in. "She can stitch up garments or men."

Helaina smiled, but an overwhelming emptiness inside threatened to consume her. "I'm glad for all of you. Now, if you'll excuse me." The men seemed relieved, but Leah appeared to be trying hard to make Helaina feel included.

"Are you certain you can't stay?"

"I'm afraid I'm quite tired. Thank you for the invitation, but perhaps I will see you at dinner." She edged toward the door the entire time. "Good day."

She headed upstairs, nearly running the remaining distance to her room. Closing the door behind her, Helaina felt hot tears stream down her cheeks. She felt so displaced. "What's wrong with me? I'm acting like a fool."

But inside, she felt as though her world were falling apart. Nothing fit anymore. She longed for something she couldn't even identify. In fact, when she thought of Jayce and Leah and Jacob just now, she knew they had something that she desired. Their companionship was so rich—so intimate. Yet it wasn't that alone that left Helaina feeling so empty.

"What is it? What do they have? What is it that I want?"

She moved to her window and pulled back the lacy curtains. Her room looked out on the backyard, and there she found Leah and Jayce walking hand in hand. From time to time Leah would look up and smile or laugh at something Jayce had said. While Jayce . . . Jayce seemed perfectly content to be imprisoned with the woman he loved.

"He must be innocent," Helaina reasoned. "His conscience is too clear. There is no anxiety in his heart. There can't be any guilt."

She let the curtain fall back in place. "But how can he know such peace?"

She thought immediately of Mrs. Hayworth. The older woman would have given her a motherly pat on the arm and said, "There. There. Chaos in life is given by the father of chaos, whereas peace comes from God alone. It's a special kind of peace that changes night into day and storm into calm."

Helaina sat down on the edge of her bed. "I don't know how God can offer peace when He allows such a world of conflict and hurt to go unchecked—unreined." She shook her head. "He cannot care about me."

"Leah, why did you fall in love with me?" Jayce asked as they walked in Timothy's fading gardens. "I mean back then—when we first met. What made you so certain that I was the man you would want to take as a husband?"

Leah shrugged. "There was no one thing. If anything, there was one thing that made it impossible for us to be together. Well . . ." She paused and smiled. "There were two things. One was you."

"Of course," he said, nodding. "I must have been crazy."

Her smile broadened. "The other was God."

"How so?" He enjoyed the warmth of her ungloved hand in his. How small and fragile Leah seemed at times—like now. But he knew her to be fully capable of taking care of herself—of enduring great trials.

"I knew I couldn't marry you unless you loved God. See, all of my life the people around me had encouraged me to love God and to put Him first. When I finally ended up in Ketchikan with Karen and Adrik, I came to understand the difference in a marriage where God was put first. I contrasted it against my parents, who had a great deal of love for each other but didn't have that common ground.

"My father was never happy. He was always restless. Always looking for some way to get rich and make his family comfortable. And in this pursuit, he knew nothing but failure and misery."

"What about your mother?"

"She was a godly woman, her only desire that her children seek God's purpose for their lives. As she lay dying, she didn't fear for herself or worry about the end. She cared only for us—that our hearts might be made right with the Lord so that she could one day see us again in heaven."

Jayce put his arm around Leah's shoulders. "She no doubt loved you deeply."

"She did, and that kept me going, even after she was gone."

"I know what you're talking about when you speak of how different Karen and Adrik's life was in contrast to others. See, my parents were God-fearing, church-attending, generous people. But their religion seemed rather shallow at times. When hard times came or something bad touched our lives, they were just as weak and frightened as people who had no place to go—no one to trust," Jayce said sadly. "I never saw them possess the kind of restful spirit that I saw in Karen and Adrik."

"That was what most impressed me," Leah said. "No matter how bad things got, they were always able to rest in the Lord. When you rejected me, Karen encouraged me to find peace in God. She told me over and over how God had a special plan for my life, and that I should never desire for anything but His perfect will. She reminded me that if I belonged to Him and sought to do things His way, I would always know the kind of peace that the Bible evidenced, even when things around me were falling apart."

"I can't begin to imagine the pain I caused you," Jayce admitted. He looked into her eyes as he pulled her around to face him. "I know it doesn't mean much, but I wish I could go back and relive those moments. I wish I knew then what I know now."

Leah put her hand to his cheek. "Jayce, I never thought I'd ever say this, but you were right to walk away. I was too young. I didn't know my own heart. I can't even believe I'm saying this now." She shook her head. "I was very immature. For all I'd been through, I was still very focused on myself. When something bad happened, I always weighed it in light of how it affected me—not others. I needed to learn a great deal before I was ready to be your wife. Sorry it took me ten years."

He grinned. "Are you sure two people who have a history of such poor choices can make a future together—a good future?"

"As long as we put God first," Leah said quite seriously. "And seek His will no matter our own desires."

"I know you're right. The wisdom of God's Word is definitely in that answer. I will try to be a good and godly man, Leah. But I know I'm flawed. I know there are serious problems in my heart—especially where Chase and my other siblings are concerned. Helaina Beecham doesn't understand how much I would like to see Chase punished for what he's done to me. She doesn't know how easy it would be for me to say yes to her request for me to help her."

"If that's what God wants you to do," Leah said softly, "then do it. I won't stand in the way."

"But I can't say that it is what God wants. Oh, He wants Chase to stop killing and stealing. He would also no doubt want Chase to pay for what he's done. But I can't discern if God is calling me to make it my campaign to hunt him down. I'm not certain about anything regarding Chase, except that this situation cannot be easily settled. I'm afraid it would only end in the death of one, or both, of us."

It was quite early in the morning, but Helaina found sleep impossible. Glancing at the clock, she knew that no one, save maybe the cook, would even be stirring at this unreasonable hour. She dressed quickly and made her way downstairs, hoping that the noise of her door opening and closing wouldn't awaken anyone else.

She had planned to make her way to what Timothy called the music room. The room was small and quiet, containing a piano that, as far as she knew, no one in the household could even play.

There were two chairs positioned in front of the window. They faced each other and yet gave the occupant ample view to the outside world. Helaina liked it here best. Early mornings were a peaceful time of day, and peace was what she desperately craved. She took a seat in a rather unladylike fashion, curling up in the chair with her legs tucked securely under her.

"Are you hiding out?"

Jacob's voice nearly sent her flying from the chair to do just that. Helaina quickly repositioned herself, her blond hair settling loose around her shoulders. "What are you doing up? It's quite early, you know."

He crossed the room and stared down at her for a moment. "I might ask you the same thing."

She looked away and shrugged. "I couldn't sleep."

"Seems to me you can't sleep a lot these days. You're up well into the night and then awake equally early in the morning—usually before sunrise."

"How would you know that?" She tried hard to sound as if his observations didn't matter.

"I know more than that. You're losing weight. You've hardly been eating this past week."

"That's none of your concern."

Jacob took a seat and crossed his legs out in front of him. He looked quite relaxed—almost as though he intended to be there for some time.

"I know something isn't right. I've tried to ignore it, but God keeps bringing it back to my attention. This morning I woke up about the time you started stirring, and I knew I was supposed to come down here and speak with you."

"How could you know that? Did God suddenly appear to you?" she asked snidely. His calm unnerved her, and Helaina didn't like that feeling at all.

"I suppose He did, in a sense." Jacob crossed his arms. "I know you're quite unhappy. I know you wish for this situation to be over with—for Jayce's brother to be found and put to trial for all his sins. But I think there's something else. Something you aren't even allowing yourself to realize."

"Who are you to suggest such things?" She narrowed her eyes. "I know you said you forgave me, but why come to me now, all tender and caring? You are a hypocrite."

"I treated you badly. That much is true. You see, God has always allowed me both the blessing and curse of being able to pretty well know a person from a first meeting."

"What do you mean?"

"I mean I can tell if they have good or bad intentions. A preacher once told me it's called discernment. It's a gift of God."

"And when you met me, you knew I was evil—right from the start."

"No, not evil. I knew you were up to something—something you weren't admitting. I knew there was more than happenstance that had brought us together. You came with a purpose—an agenda."

"True enough, but it's easy to say that now. Now that the truth is known to everyone."

Jacob nodded. "I suppose it would take something else to make you realize that God honestly cares enough about you to send someone into your life who could help you find your way back to Him. Something that no one else could possibly know."

"Like what?" There was no way she could believe this game of his. God might know everything that went on, but He didn't care about it, and He certainly didn't share that information with anyone else. Why should He?

"I've been praying for you for some time now," Jacob began, "and every time I pray for you, one word keeps coming to mind."

"And what would that be?"

He met her gaze and didn't even blink. "Guilt."

She swallowed hard and tried not to react. "Guilt? You must be crazy."

"Am I?"

She wanted only to get up and pace the room, but she knew this would be a dead giveaway to how close to the truth he'd struck. "If you're so confident that I'm consumed with guilt—and if God is the one giving you the information, then by all means share what you know."

Jacob drew a deep breath. "I believe you feel consumed with guilt because of the death of your parents and husband. I think you blame yourself."

She began to tremble. "Why . . . why . . . would I blame myself?" She didn't want to hear his answer, but at the same time she had to.

"Because maybe you were the intended victim? Because you should have been with them—died with them . . . died instead of them."

Helaina felt as though she couldn't breathe. She'd never told anyone how she felt about those things. About the truth of how the original kidnapping plot had been intended for her and her alone. She suddenly felt dizzy—her vision began to blur.

"Helaina. Helaina."

She could hear him calling her name, but she couldn't respond. She couldn't see him.

"Helaina, wake up."

She finally struggled against the grip of darkness and opened her eyes. Jacob stood over her chair, gently patting her face. "I . . . what . . ." She drew a deep breath. Jacob's words came rushing back to her. There was no pretense of defense left in her. She looked into his eyes, feeling as though he could see every secret in her heart. Surely the only way he could have known these things was because God had allowed him to know them. But why?

"I'm all right," she told him. She straightened and stared down at her shaking hands. "Anyone could have guessed about the guilt," she said in a voice barely audible.

"I suppose so," Jacob admitted, retaking his seat.

"But," she continued, "only a couple of people knew that the original plot was intended for me." She looked up against her will. "It should have been me."

"But it wasn't, and you find that impossible to live with. Don't you?"

She nodded very slowly. "I went to Europe on a whim. Robert couldn't get away, but I wanted very much to go shopping and to see friends. I talked my mother into taking over my responsibilities to host a charity event for the children's orphanage. It should have been me."

"But God had other plans, Helaina," Jacob said matter-of-factly.

"I know, and I hated Him for it. How could He be so cruel as to take those I loved and leave me behind? How could He allow those men to kill them? I don't understand that at all." She felt the tears begin to fall. "Robert was the love of my life. My mother was my best friend. And my father . . . well . . . he represented security to me well before I even knew Robert existed. They were there one day and then they were gone, and all because some amateur group of thugs decided they could best make a living by kidnapping me."

"What happened to make them kill your family?"

She could hear the confession of the youngest member of the group. "They got scared when there turned out to be three people in the carriage instead of one. Robert charged the men, and they fired their guns without regard. They were terrified, for they had no plan for what to do past stealing me away and demanding money." She wiped her eyes with the back of her sleeve. "I thought I would die when I heard the news."

"I think I know how that feels. When I got word about my father's death, it was unbearable."

"I felt so consumed with guilt. Because Stanley was working with the Pinkertons, I was given access to everything related to the file. I even saw photographs that I never should have seen. Pictures that never leave my memory."

"So you got involved with the law in order to ease that guilt?"

She looked at him and nodded. There was both a relief and a sensation of awe that he knew her so well. Could this really be because God had told him? "Every time I helped put a criminal behind bars, I felt a little bit of guilt slip away. I figured if I did enough—if I got enough people—then the hurt would stop and the emptiness would disappear. But it never has."

"And it never will," Jacob said. "Not that way. Only God can fill that empty place. Only God knows how much you hurt—how guilty you feel. Their death wasn't your fault, but you're carrying it as though it were, as though if you carry it long enough you might somehow bring them back to life."

She flew out of the chair and headed straight at him. She wanted to slap him—to silence him. "You don't understand. You can't understand. I have to do something. I have to right the wrong."

He jumped back in defense, then reached out and took hold of her wrists. Helaina crumpled to her knees in front of him. "You can't make anything right, Helaina. You can't change what has happened."

"Then why go on?" She looked up at him as he edged forward. "Why live—why try?"

"It wasn't your time to go, Helaina. God has another purpose—another plan for you. I don't know why your loved ones had to die, but I know that the injustice grieved God's heart just as much as it grieved yours."

"Why didn't He stop it? Why, Jacob? If He cares so much, why does He allow all this evil in the world? All this pain?"

"I don't have answers for that. We live in a fallen world and men will make bad choices—they will sin without regard to God or man. Why it has to be that way, I really don't understand either. But I do know that God has not left us as orphans. He promises to be with us always."

Helaina composed herself. She pulled away from Jacob and got to her feet. "I've heard those answers before. But they make no sense. God is supposed to be all-powerful and all-knowing. It makes no sense that He allows these things to happen to good people." She smoothed her skirt and wiped her face. "If you'll excuse me."

"I will," Jacob said as she moved to the door. "But I won't stop praying for you. God won't let me."

The words burrowed into her heart. She didn't want to admit that Jacob's concern touched her. "Do what you will," she murmured. "I don't believe it will help, but you do what you like."

Later that day the courier arrived from Washington, D.C. To Helaina's surprise, he turned out to be her very annoyed, very angry brother.

"I can't believe you're doing this. You know better. I've brought my men with me. They're waiting to take Jayce Kincaid into custody."

Helaina stood her ground. "No, Stanley. Not until we compare those prints."

"Helaina."

"No. I know without a doubt that this man is innocent. I want the prints as proof. I have his fingerprints all ready for the comparison. You cannot send an innocent man to prison or to be hanged. You would never forgive yourself."

Stanley calmed a bit at this. "Very well. I can't believe you're doing this, but since I have no choice, let's get the job done." He took a folder from his case. "Here they are."

Helaina nodded. "Come with me into the library."

"Where's Kincaid?"

She smiled over her shoulder. "In the library."

She saw her brother's reaction when he came into the room and stood face-to-face with Jayce Kincaid. For a moment his scowl deepened and his hands balled into fists.

"Kincaid," he muttered.

"I don't have the pleasure of knowing you, sir."

Stanley stiffened. His eyes narrowed as he stepped closer. He seemed to be searching Jayce's face—almost as if looking for proof. Helaina saw Stanley's expression change. "You aren't the right man. You look like him—but you're not him." There was a sense of awe in his tone.

Helaina looked at her brother curiously. "Why are you saying that now?"

"I cut the man who threw me from the train. I cut him deep across the left eye. It bled so badly that his blood covered me as well. It would have left a considerable scar." He shook his head. "You look just like him."

Helaina spread the prints atop the table and drew out a magnifying glass that Timothy provided. She looked at the set that she'd made. The ridges and lines were nearly committed to memory. Then taking the glass to the pages her brother had provided, she could finally prove the truth she'd known since leaving Alaska.

"They don't match," she whispered and looked up to meet Jayce's face. "Jayce Kincaid is an innocent man."

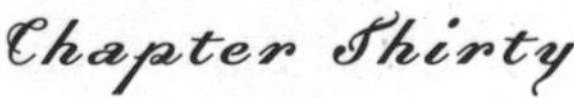

Jayce felt a profound sense of relief with those six words. Though he'd known the prints wouldn't match, to have legitimate proof of his innocence was almost overwhelming.

"But if it's not you . . . then who is it?" Stanley asked.

"My brother Chase Kincaid is probably responsible," Jayce replied. "He is my identical twin."

"Which is what I've been telling you since I arrived in Seattle," Helaina declared.

"Yes, yes. I remember well your list of discrepancies, though I'd disregarded them until now. Has Chase a record?" Stanley asked.

"He has served time, but overall, he's done a remarkable job of not getting caught. He has a long list of friends who are happy to help him in his endeavors because Chase has always been generous with money," Jayce answered.

"What is his goal, do you think?" Helaina asked. "For example, why steal from the British Museum?"

Jayce shrugged. "My guess is that he needed money first and foremost. Second, I would imagine that, rather than simply steal from someone's home or from individuals, my brother saw real excitement in taking things from the prestigious British Museum. He was always in pursuit of a good thrill. And of course, the chance to taint my name would add to the benefits."

Stanley seemed to consider this for a moment. "So where is he now? Do you have any idea?"

"Not really," Jayce admitted. "However, we might know someone who can give us some information. Captain Latimore is here in town. He is the man we spoke of earlier, who captained the ship Chase was on earlier this summer. The expedition met with problems and ended their trip early. Latimore can at least tell us where he parted company with Chase."

Stanley nodded. "Very well. How do we reach this Captain Latimore?"

"I've already sent for him," Helaina said with a smile. "We figured that he might prove helpful."

Stanley squared his shoulders and eyed Jayce. He shook his head as if he still couldn't believe his eyes. "I must say, the resemblance is uncanny. Had I not been assured that my cut left its mark and had the fingerprints not proved your identity, I would have seen you hanged."

"Captain Latimore has arrived," the butler announced.

The group turned to await the captain. Jayce both dreaded and looked forward to what the man might have to say; his own gut ached as he struggled over his dilemma with Chase. If he refused to turn Chase over to the law, he was allowing a vicious criminal to go free. But if he saw to Chase's capture, he was turning over his own flesh and blood to die.

"Captain Latimore," Helaina said in greeting. "Thank you for coming."

"You said it was urgent," the man replied. He looked to the group and nodded. "I came as soon as I could."

Jayce stepped forward. "We need some information regarding my brother Chase and his affairs while with you onboard *Homestead*."

The captain nodded. "I'll give you whatever I can."

Leah reached out for Jayce's hand, and he felt strengthened by her support. She had never once doubted him. Neither had Jacob. This thought gave him courage to face what he knew must be done.

"Captain, my name is Stanley Curtis. I'm a Pinkerton agent. I live in Washington, D.C., and have been on the trail of a dangerous criminal for some time. We had thought the man to be Jayce Kincaid but have since learned that it is probably his twin brother, Chase. I understand you had opportunity to employ Chase this summer."

The captain rubbed his beard for a moment. "I did employ the man—thought he was Jayce. We had met a couple of times prior, and the man seemed exactly as I remembered Jayce. I had no reason to doubt him when he agreed that he was Jayce Kincaid."

"Did the man in question have a scar over his left eye?" Stanley asked.

The captain seemed excited at this question. "Yes. Yes, he did. Although I hadn't really thought about it until now. It was positioned just above the eyebrow on the left side. The scar was not that old; it hadn't faded as a scar will over time."

"Yes," Stanley said, looking to Jayce. "It must be him."

"So what do we do now?" Jayce asked in return.

"Sir, when did you last see Chase Kincaid?" Stanley questioned.

The captain considered this question for a moment. "When the expedition broke company, we returned the natives to Kotzebue, but Chase asked to be taken to Nome. The rest of the crew returned to the States or to Vancouver."

"You left Chase in Nome?"

Latimore nodded. "Yes. I believe that would have been in early August. He told me he planned to spend the winter there."

"So he may still be there," Jayce said. He exchanged a brief glance with Leah before letting go of her hand and getting to his feet. "We'll have to return to Nome as soon as possible."

"Why would Chase Kincaid remain in Nome?" Stanley didn't sound at all like he believed this possibility.

"He must think it best to lay low and hide out for a time. He might have even gotten wind of what was happening with your search and how you were after me," Jayce said.

"That's impossible," Helaina replied. "I was very careful with my investigation."

"True enough, but I wouldn't trust that he counts himself safe for the time."

"Does he know much about Alaska—about survival up there?" Stanley asked.

"I wouldn't have thought so," Jayce began, "but then, I wouldn't have expected him to handle the dog teams like a professional. Captain Latimore said he was quite proficient with the teams."

"Well, he was clumsy at first, but he quickly recovered and then took on real proficiency. We were well into the northern reaches of the Arctic where the ice never thaws. Some of the team had discussed staying throughout the winter. We had plans to locate one of the Canadian islands for this purpose when we started having so much trouble. But Mr. Kincaid was perfectly capable with the dogs and even volunteered to be one of those who stayed behind."

Jayce knew it was his brother's way of thwarting the law. "I'm going to Nome," he stated firmly. "If he's there, I will capture him and take him to the authorities."

"I'll send my men with you," Stanley said. "I have at least two who won't mind the trip and have no family to hold them back."

"I'm going too," Helaina suddenly declared. "It was my job to catch him—I don't intend to fail at this mission."

Jayce intervened. "No. You cannot go. Chase is too dangerous. He'd have no regard for the fact that you're a woman."

"He's right," Stanley added, "this is too dangerous."

"It wasn't too dangerous when you sent me out here five months ago," Helaina remarked.

Though Jayce sensed her anger, he couldn't let her go along with them—not after realizing the extent of his brother's ruthlessness. "It wouldn't be right, Helaina. Chase may already be onto you. If he's heard about a woman hunting me down, then your cover will be no good. You won't be safe."

"Besides, you had your chance at this," Stanley said firmly. "You figured out that Jayce wasn't the right man. That doesn't make you a failure at this mission. You succeeded in saving an innocent person from the gallows."

"But it's not enough," Helaina replied. "I want to see the right man caught. I want to be the one to capture him."

Jayce shook his head. "It doesn't matter who catches him. It only matters that he be caught."

Helaina said nothing, but Jayce knew she was seething. He hoped she might learn to trust him again, as she had before, when she'd needed him to remain her prisoner.

"So we need to book tickets to Nome," Jacob said, shaking his head. "That won't be easy. The season is nearly over and most captains are going to be unwilling to risk their ships and the lives of their crew."

"It's not impossible, though," Latimore stated. "I could probably be persuaded to help."

As Latimore, Jacob, and Stanley circled together to make plans, Jayce felt more confused than ever. He believed he was doing the right thing, but his conviction troubled him more and more. Chase was in Nome. Chase, the murderer—the thief. *But he's also my brother.* Jayce felt as though his heart were torn in two.

Helaina fumed over being excluded from the upcoming trip. She had worked hard on this job, and now Stanley wanted to keep her from being a part of actually apprehending the right man. It infuriated her.

She sat at the music room window staring out at the pouring rain. There had to be a way to maintain her role in this situation. She knew herself to be a woman of means, not only financially, but mentally. She had often come up with crafty, witty plans for catching criminals. So why couldn't she take charge now and make it all work to her benefit? Chase Kincaid might have heard of a woman's involvement, but it was doubtful he'd recognize her. Jayce and her brother were simply being too careful.

"I know you don't agree with my decision," Stanley said from the doorway to the music room. "I hope in time, however, that you will see it as sensible."

Helaina knew in that moment she had to be cautious. If she was to be successful in managing to maintain a role in the capture of Chase Kincaid, she would have to convince Stanley that she had given up her part. "I'm just disappointed," she finally replied. "I know it's possible that Chase could know about me, but I doubt that he does. I understand your fears for me, but at the same time I hope you understand how very much I wanted to be a part of the team that caught Chase."

"I know. I know how disappointing it is because I'd like to be a part of that group myself," he said, crossing the room to where she sat. "No one wants this man behind bars more than I do."

She sighed, knowing he had a valid point. He had suffered far more embarrassment and physical pain than she had. "I know, Stanley. He wronged you, and you have a right to see him taken—to take him yourself."

"I'm sorry that I ever got you tangled up in this. I knew at the time I assigned it to you that it was dangerous. I suppose to my way of thinking, if I couldn't be there to get Kincaid—you were the next best choice."

Helaina understood. "So do you intend to leave for Washington right away?"

"Yes. Probably tomorrow or the next day, although it might be nice to see something of Seattle. This is my first time here—probably my only time. Perhaps you could show me something of the town and then we can head back to Washington together."

Helaina hadn't counted on that. She forced a smile. "But of course. That would be wonderful. We could spend the travel time catching up on things. Do you already have the tickets?"

"No."

She got to her feet. "The trip home will be taxing, so you should rest. I'll go get tickets; I am quite familiar with the station, as I've been there several times." At least that much was true. Helaina had gone there every day this last week checking on the courier.

"Thank you. That would be great."

She kissed him on the cheek. "Then I'd best get to work. I'll see about the tickets, and after I return we can go out into the city. I know several wonderful restaurants. The seafood is incredible here."

Stanley smiled. "I think I would like that very much."

Helaina headed to her room to change her clothes. She threw her day dress on the bed and took up a lightweight blouse of white lawn. The simple lines and high neck matched her desire to appear businesslike and less the vulnerable female. She then chose a dark brown wool suit—her plainest and least feminine article of clothing. Though the war crinolines with their full bell skirts and wide-collared bodices were more popular, Helaina could not get used to the shorter skirt lengths. Why, some fashions were edging up as much as eight inches from the floor. It seemed rather scandalous—just asking for unwanted attention.

She looked in the mirror, pleased. She had business to tend to. Business at the station where she would buy her brother's ticket home, and business at the docks where she would hopefully book passage to Nome. Passage she hoped would get her there before the others.

Chapter Thirty-One

Leah stood beside the fireplace in the front parlor. She wore a beautiful white muslin creation that Jacob had insisted she buy for the occasion. "A woman only marries once," he told her. "She should have something beautiful to call her own and to always remember the day by."

I'll have no trouble remembering this day, she thought. Her stomach churned as she waited for the minister to finish complimenting Timothy on his house and get to the job at hand.

"I was glad to see that the rain had stopped," the older man said as he took up his Bible. "It's always a pity to have rain on a wedding day—not that I believe in the wives' tales of rain representing the number of tears a bride will cry during her years of marriage." He laughed as though even suggesting such a thing was completely out of place.

"We were glad to see it stop as well," Jayce said, coming to stand beside Leah. He winked at her. "You are beautiful. More beautiful than I could have ever imagined."

Leah felt her cheeks grow hot. "I feel rather silly," she whispered. "It would have been more appropriate to wear sealskin and mukluks."

He laughed and took her hand in his. "You'll be wearing them again soon enough. But it does my heart good to know that you still desire that kind of life after living in the comfort of this lovely home."

She looked into his eyes. "The only home I desire is the one we share together. I really don't care where it is—so long as you are there and happy."

"I feel the same way."

"Shall we begin?" the pastor asked.

"Posthaste," Jacob declared, surprising them all. "Let's not waste any more time."

"Helaina and Stanley never came back?" Leah asked as her brother and Timothy took their places as witnesses to the wedding. The butler, cook, and housekeeper had also come to join the festivities at Timothy's request.

"No," Jayce said. "When I told them the wedding was to be this afternoon, Stanley informed me that he and Helaina had plans. I think they both felt out of place."

Leah nodded. "Then let's start." She turned to the pastor and smiled. "I've waited ten years for this."

Jayce pulled her close against his side. "And I have waited a lifetime."

The wedding proceeded in the simplicity and joy that Leah had always imagined. She could hardly believe that, after all this time, God had brought about her dreams. So many years had been spent in the bleak hopelessness that the one man she dearly loved would never love her. Now all of that had changed.

"Will you, Leah, have this man, Jayce, to be your lawfully wedded husband?"

The words blurred in her ears. *Of course I will have him.* She trembled as she gazed up to meet Jayce's face. *I will have him and love him forever and always.*

"You know," Stanley said as they allowed the cab to drive them through Seattle, "I'm sorry I doubted your intuition about Kincaid."

"It really wasn't intuition," Helaina replied. "I can't say for sure what it was. Jacob Barringer kept talking to me about mercy and compassion. I told him I believed in justice, and he accused me of seeking nothing but revenge."

"Sometimes I think we do seek revenge. I know I have felt that way about Kincaid. I wanted him to pay for not only what he did to me, but what he did to my fellow agents. I know it's better to remain at a distance when dealing with these criminals, but I couldn't help it."

"Still, the law is the law," Helaina replied. "I've always felt confident that, in serving the purpose of the law, mercy was unimportant. I suppose this case has changed my mind somewhat. But I'm still uncertain as to how the two are reconciled without someone paying a steep price."

She considered her next question carefully. "Stan, what are your thoughts on God?"

"What in the world causes you to ask something like that?" he replied. "God is God. What else can I say?"

"Do you see a need for Him in your life? Have you ever thought to turn your life over to Him?"

"In what way?"

She shrugged. "I'm not completely certain. Jacob and Leah, and even Kincaid—they are all Christians. But not just the kind of people who go to church on Sunday, making sure they're seen by all the right people. These people really believe in God—in doing what He wants them to do. They read their Bibles every day, and when people are troubled and hurting, they talk about things from that Bible. They use Scriptures to help each other overcome difficulties."

"Some people need that kind of crutch," Stanley answered. "I suppose I see nothing wrong with it, but neither do I feel a need for it."

"So you've never felt the need to turn your life over to God?"

Stanley strained to see something out the window, then eased back against the leather upholstery. He looked at Helaina and shook his head. "No. I believe man has to make his own way in the world. We alone are responsible for our actions. We can't be blaming things on supernatural beings—be they divine or evil."

"Then God plays no part in your life?"

"I've never really considered it, to tell you the truth. Why would He care about me?"

"Jacob says He cares about all of us. That He showed us mercy even before we existed on this earth and sent His Son to die for us."

"I've heard all of that, but I think it rather pretentious to imagine that God would sacrifice His Son for us lowly sinners. Why would He do that? Why not just make everything right with the snap of His finger?" Stanley smiled. "If God has fingers."

He shook his head. "No, I'm confident that man controls his own path. He must. He must make choices good or bad. When he makes bad ones, then I get involved."

Helaina had heard it all before, but in the back of her mind she was confused. She had hoped in hearing it again that her convictions might be reestablished. But instead, Stanley's words only troubled her more. Because in spite of Stanley's assurance in his theories and thoughts, Jacob Barringer seemed far more confident of a truth that was not of his own making.

"These are the men I promised you," Stanley said. He turned to introduce the larger of the two first. "This is Big Butch Bradford. He's been in the service of the Pinkertons for nearly ten years. He's a good man to have in your corner."

Leah watched as her brother and Jayce shook hands with Big Butch. The man's thick barrel chest and broad shoulders reminded her of Adrik Ivankov.

"And this is Sam Wiseford, and the name is quite appropriate. He is very wise—too smart for his own good. He'll be a good asset to you. He's only been with the Pinkertons for a year, but he's already distinguished himself several times."

Leah thought the man looked too young to even be allowed a job as a Pinkerton. He was athletic in appearance with sandy brown hair that fell in a boyish manner across his face. She smiled when he realized she'd been watching him. He blushed furiously.

"Where's Helaina? We'll be late if she isn't ready," Stanley said.

Leah looked around the room, realizing for the first time that Helaina hadn't joined them. "I'm sure she's just packing last-minute things. Let me go see if I can lend her a hand."

Leah heard Stanley grunt an approval and continue talking about his men and what their duties were to be. Leah could hardly contain her joy at returning to Alaska. She missed the summer in her village and now longed for her friends and little house. She particularly missed Ayoona and Emma.

"Helaina?" she called from outside the woman's closed door. "Helaina, Stanley says you must hurry. Can I help you pack?"

She knocked when there was no reply and found that the door was open. Looking inside, Leah called again. "Helaina, are you here?"

There was no sound. Leah went into the room and looked around—all of Helaina's things were gone, and there was no sign of the woman anywhere. Leah noticed a folded piece of paper on the nightstand and saw a name on the outside. *Stanley.* The script was flowery and feminine, no doubt from Helaina. Leah got a strange feeling that trouble was on the horizon. She hurried downstairs and held out the note to Stanley.

"I found this, but it appears Helaina is gone."

"Gone?" Jacob asked. "Gone where?"

Stanley read the note and growled. "Gone to Alaska. The foolish ninny has bribed passage on a freighter bound north. She left last night."

Jayce looked to Leah. "She's gone after my brother."

"She's gone to get herself killed, is what she's done," Jacob declared, his anger evident. "I can't believe she'd put herself in harm's way like this."

"Oh, she thrives on it," Stanley replied in disgust. "I can't begin to tell you how many times she's done things like this."

"So what do we do now?" Jayce asked.

"We don't have a lot of choices. Captain Latimore won't be ready for another two days," Leah replied. "I think we'll simply have to try to catch up with her before she finds trouble."

"I'll find her—I promise you that," Jacob told Stanley. "We'll do what we can to keep her out of trouble, but knowing your sister, she'll probably attract it to herself like a magnet to metal."

Stanley shifted his weight. "I wish I could come with you, but I'm needed in Washington. My supervisor wasn't happy I even came here."

Stanley handed him a card. "Here's the address where I can be reached. Please let me know as soon as possible if she's all right. Then send her home. Hog-tie her if need be."

"I doubt we'll get her out of Alaska until next spring. We'll be lucky if we can just get ourselves into Nome without great difficulty," Jacob said, taking the card. "But I assure you we will get there."

Later, Leah found Jacob in the music room. He hadn't seemed himself for days, and she chalked it up to him being out of his element. But after seeing his reaction to Helaina's secret departure, Leah couldn't help but wonder if there wasn't something more to this.

"Are you all right?" she asked her brother.

"I'm about as mad as a person can be with Mrs. Beecham."

"She's really managed to . . . well . . . attract your attention."

"I'd like to give her some attention all right. She wouldn't like it, of course."

"Jacob, what's this all about? Why are you so upset with Helaina? Sure, she's thrown the wool over our eyes and set herself up for trouble, but she's a grown woman. She's done jobs like this before. Why torment yourself over her getting to Nome first?"

"Because if she gets there first, she just may get herself killed. Jayce has told me that once his brother feels threatened, he'll stop at nothing to be rid of the threat. He wouldn't think twice about killing Helaina."

"I wouldn't want to see her come to harm either, Jacob. I didn't mean to sound calloused. I just think your feelings for her are stronger than you'd like to admit."

Jacob looked at her oddly for a moment, then let out a heavy sigh. "I fear she's in trouble. She used to have her firm belief in the law and justice to drive her through times of peril. But I've been talking to her about the Lord's mercy and compassion. It's given her a lot to think about, and I know she's troubled by it. I'm afraid it might affect her judgment in dealing with Chase Kincaid."

"But you did nothing wrong, Jacob. You shared God's truth with her. That's what we're supposed to do. She still has to make her own choice. If she decides against choosing God, it won't be your fault any more than it will be to your credit if she does choose Him."

"I know all of that, but . . . well . . . I feel that before she had an inner strength that made her fearless and capable of dealing with desperate situations. I'm not sure she still has that. She's doubting herself now, which is good on one hand but may end her life on the other."

Leah began to see his reasoning. "I think I understand. But even in knowing this, we are helpless to do anything but pray. And you know even better than I do that prayer is our most powerful tool." She took hold of Jacob's hands and squeezed them tight. "Jacob, you need to stop feeling guilty and use that energy to pray."

He nodded. "I know."

Leah could see that she'd accomplish nothing more in talk. She would pray for Jacob and trust God to guide his heart. So many times in life they'd done this for each other. . . . It had never failed her.

Chapter Thirty-Two

The rocking motion of the *Homestead* nearly sent Leah from the bed. In fact, had Jayce not held on to her tight, she might have found herself sleeping on the floor.

"The weather is getting rougher," she said, snuggling against her husband.

Jayce pulled her close and murmured sleepily. "Soon we'll be home and we won't have to worry about it."

"But there's a lot to do before we get home. I hope you know how proud I am of your decision."

Leah looked up as Jayce opened his eyes. "Having you at my side gives me a strength I don't think I would have otherwise had. I feel so mixed in my decision. On one hand, he has to be stopped. He's a killer and seems to have no regard for anyone. But he's also my brother."

"I know. I kept thinking to myself: how would I respond if this were Jacob?"

"But there's a difference. You and Jacob grew up close to each other. You cared for each other and stuck it out together. Chase has avoided me since we were five. He's always gone his own way and has spent most of his life blaming others for his problems."

"Well, I'm proud of you for not hating him. You've treated him well, considering how he acted toward your mother—not to mention others."

"Not always. When I saw him in Last Chance this summer, I hid from him. I was so stunned to find him there. I figured he would only cause me trouble. I would like to know how he learned of my whereabouts, but I suppose he'll never tell me."

Leah sighed and placed her head on her husband's shoulder. "I never thought I'd say this, but I'm homesick."

"Your taste of big-city life and fancy clothes didn't change your mind about remaining in Alaska?"

She laughed. "Just like it changed your mind? After all, you got to sleep in a plush bed in a warm house with servants. You never once had to hunt or look for wood to fuel your stove."

Jayce kissed the top of her head. "I'm at home wherever you are," he whispered. "I just never realized it until now."

Jacob knew Captain Latimore was deeply worried about his ship. They'd reached Nome, but the waters had roughened considerably, and now early ice was threatening to keep the ship from returning to Seattle.

After overseeing the last of the loads being taken into Nome, Jacob went to meet with the captain. "It seems to me," Jacob told him, "that unless you are hard-pressed for a return on your money, you should leave that in our hands. We can arrange sale of the goods and collect the money for you. Of course, it might be spring before you see it." He grinned.

"I'm agreeable to you handling the procedure and keeping ten percent of my share for your troubles."

Jacob reached out and shook hands with the captain. "Consider it done."

"Then we will endeavor to leave as soon as possible. Pray for us to make it safely back."

"I will. Oh, and they tell me there are a group of passengers who have asked if you will allow them to return with you. A couple of them are hoping to get to San Francisco, but most are content to get to Seattle."

"I would be glad to do so. It hardly seems like a sound business decision to return empty."

Jacob looked down the shoreline. "I'll let them know they should talk to you. You can settle on the cost of passage and such." He shook hands once again with the captain. "I'll see you in June."

Jacob went about the business of arranging for the sale of the goods. It took some time to manage the account and inform the proper authorities of how they might contact him and arrange the sales.

"I'll take all the canned goods you have," a merchant told Jacob as he checked his invoices. "Of course, with all the trouble of late, we might see a lot of people leave this town, and I'll be left holding the goods."

"What kind of trouble?" Jacob asked, counting the remaining inventory.

"Didn't you hear? We just had a double murder and a kidnapping. Two of our deputies were gunned down—ambushed. A lady who'd just arrived in town was taken hostage by the madman."

Jacob looked up. "Was the woman's name Beecham?"

"I don't recall. I just know it's scared a good many people. Maybe not bad enough to leave Nome, but bad just the same."

Jacob tried to focus on the transaction but found it impossible. "Look. Here are the tallies." He showed the man his papers. "I can let you have all of this."

"I'll take it. Come by in the morning, and I'll have a draft for you."

Jacob nodded. "I'll do that."

With business concluded and his heart full of dread, Jacob hurried into town to find Leah and Jayce. When he caught up with them at the hotel, there was no doubting they'd already heard the news.

"A woman's been taken hostage," Leah said in a hushed voice. "The police chief was injured and two men were killed."

"So what do we do?" Jacob asked Jayce.

"We were just heading over to the jail. The Pinkerton men are already there. I want to talk to the police chief and see what insight he can offer. I'm sure the offender was Chase, although I suppose I could be wrong. Fights and killings go on all the time up here."

"But kidnappings don't," Jacob nearly growled. "I just know that ninny got herself taken hostage."

Jayce and Leah exchanged a look and nodded. "We do too," Jayce replied.

The police chief confirmed their fears. "We were approached by Mrs. Beecham two days ago. She showed us her documentation and discussed the situation at length. She said it was imperative that we catch Chase Kincaid as soon as possible."

"So what happened after that?"

"Well, we helped her find the man. He was calling himself Jayce Kincaid. Mrs. Beecham said this was normal procedure for him." Jayce nodded and sighed. The chief continued. "He seemed to have a penchant for playing cards, so I arranged a game with a couple of my deputies. There were also a couple of other townsmen in on it too. Mrs. Beecham insisted on being involved as well."

"I'll bet she did," Jacob muttered.

The police chief shrugged. "There didn't seem to be any harm in letting her at least be there. I figured she could identify the man. We set it up in the hotel lobby last night—gaming goes on there all the time."

"So what went wrong?" Jayce asked.

"Kincaid seemed to know what was going on." He looked hard at Jayce. "I've never met twins before. It's almost spooky."

Jayce nodded. "In more ways than you know."

The chief seemed mesmerized for a moment, then continued his story. "Like I said, Kincaid seemed to know what we were up to. It was like someone had given him the information for the entire plan. We let the game play out for most of the night. Thought he'd be drunk and tired by the time we jumped him. But instead, he seemed just as fresh as when he'd sat down.

"A couple of the guys left the game. They cut their losses and exited the hotel, as did I, to maintain a position from the street. Pretty soon it was just my men and Mrs. Beecham. She was sitting close to the front of the room reading a book. When my men decided the time was right, they went into action. But Kincaid was two steps ahead of them. He shot them both on the spot—dead on, right through the heart. That brought the hotel owner running. Kincaid winged him and sent him diving for cover. Mrs. Beecham, however, was not to be undone. She pulled a derringer and pointed it right at Kincaid's head. According to the hotel owner, the man didn't seem at all disturbed by this. In fact, as he handed over his gun, he smiled at her."

Jacob barely held his temper. He felt a rage burning inside that he couldn't even begin to explain. Maybe he did care for Helaina more than he should. Maybe she had somehow wormed her way under his skin.

"Well, Mrs. Beecham thought she'd march him to jail holding that derringer on him. Kincaid pretended to go along with it at first. I was in the street, trying to position myself to catch him when he came out. But when I called to him, it distracted Mrs. Beecham and Kincaid took control of her gun and grabbed her as a shield."

"And then what?" Jacob sounded more demanding than he'd intended. "Where did he take her?"

"I'm really not sure. There was a bit of a crowd gathering in the streets by this time, and Kincaid threatened to kill anyone who followed. I tried to talk him into letting her go, but he ended up shooting me in the foot as a warning. He took off with Mrs. Beecham and disappeared into the darkness. Wounded as I was, I had to let him go—at least momentarily. I knew I'd need to put together a posse of men to go after Kincaid, and that was going to take some time."

"Did you ever go after him? I mean if this just happened last night, what's going on now?" one of the Pinkerton men asked.

"No one wants to get involved. Kincaid was so brazen and callous, they fear for their lives. I've asked around, but nobody has seen a thing. I can't just up and leave Nome to go hunting him down—not with my foot like this. I've put the word out that he's out there and dangerous. I've given his description and the description of the woman to people coming in and out of town and sent information out on the telegraph, but you know how slowly things happen in Alaska. You can't expect that we'd know something this soon."

"I'll go after them," Jacob said, getting to his feet. "People don't just disappear. There have to be clues—tracks."

"I'll go too. It's my brother on the loose."

"You aren't leaving me behind," Leah told them.

"That's where you're wrong," Jayce said firmly. "I can't have you risking your life out there. You need to stay here or arrange to get back to Last Chance. Those are the only options you have."

"He's right, Leah. You can't be in the middle of this."

"But you can?" she asked her brother.

"We're going too," Sam declared.

Jacob shook his head. "No. You'll just slow us down. Wait here and then you can take him from us when we return."

"Wait a minute," the police chief called out. "If you two are serious about going after that man, I should deputize you both. That way anything you have to do will be in the name of the law."

The law. Jacob would have laughed at that comment had it not been such a serious situation. Helaina and her love of the law had gotten them all into this situation to begin with.

"That's fine by me," Jayce said, standing.

Jacob came back to the chief's desk. "Me too. Let's just get it over with so we can be on our way." He glanced at Leah. She gave him a glaring look that told him this matter was far from settled.

The police chief swore them both in. "I wish I could give you a file full of information, but like I said, nobody is saying a word. I think they're all running scared."

"That's all right," Jacob said, once again moving toward the door. "I'll find out what I need to know."

"You do know," the chief called out, "he's to be taken dead or alive."

Jacob turned and met Jayce's tight-jawed expression. His friend's eyes had darkened to almost black. "We'll bring him back however he chooses. If he cooperates, then he'll be alive," Jayce murmured.

Jacob had never felt sorrier for anyone. He couldn't imagine the pain this new situation had caused his friend. How could a man hunt down his own brother—knowing that it might well end the life of one or the other?

They walked in silence toward the restaurant to eat and make plans. The weight of the world seemed upon all three, and Jacob knew that somehow he and Jayce still had to convince Leah to remain behind.

They sat down to a table and ordered coffee and roast beef sandwiches. Jacob toyed with his knife as he waited for Leah to offer her protests. When he looked up, however, she was doing the one thing he hadn't expected—she was crying.

He looked to Jayce, feeling helpless against her tears. "I can go alone," he offered.

"No." Jayce put his hand out and took hold of Leah's arm. "I think Leah understands the seriousness of this situation. She's had time to think about it."

"That doesn't change the fact that I don't want you going out there without me. What if one of you gets hurt? You know I'm good at tending injuries."

"And what if you're the one who gets injured?" Jayce asked.

"Or what if one of us gets injured because we had to worry about you?" Jacob questioned.

Leah met his gaze and seemed to calm a bit. "I hadn't thought of it that way."

"You know if you're out there, you'll be our first concern. I would constantly be wondering where you were and how you figured in to the situation. What I can't bear to think about is Chase taking two hostages."

Leah looked to the table as the waitress brought their order. Jacob smiled at the woman. "How are you, Sally?"

She smiled shyly. "I'm good. Be better soon. I'm getting married."

"Congratulations," Jacob offered, taking the plate she held out. "I hope he's a good man."

She nodded. "Sure. He's plenty good."

She finished serving them, then disappeared into the back room. Jacob offered a blessing on the food and then started to eat. He'd barely taken a bite when Leah spoke.

"All right. I'll go home. I don't want to stay here in Nome indefinitely. If you can get word to John or someone in our village to come and help me, then I'll wait here for them."

"Maybe you could stay and help the doctor again until John can get here," Jayce suggested. "That way you'd have a safe place to stay and you'd feel useful all at the same time."

Leah nodded. "But then I want to go home."

He smiled and touched her cheek. "I know you do. I want to go there too."

"No worse than I do," Jacob added. He reached across the small table to touch Leah's hand. "Thank you for understanding. I couldn't bear it if something happened to you."

"I do understand. But sometimes, understanding isn't enough to calm your heart."

Leah watched her brother and husband prepare to leave Nome. They were packing as if for a hunt, only this time they were hunting man instead of bear or seal. She felt a sense of dread—almost panic. What if they were killed like the other two deputies? What if she never saw them again . . . never knew what happened?

She tried to reason that someone had to go—that Helaina couldn't be left in the hands of such a ruthless man. But in her heart, she wished it could be someone else.

Oh, Father, please keep them safe. Please bring them back to me. I love them so much. I need them with me. The prayer did little to calm her spirit.

"I've arranged to get word to John," Jacob told her. "A couple of natives are headed to Prince of Wales. They can drop off word on the way. As soon as he can, I'm sure he'll be here to help you get home. There's a load of goods I set aside from what we brought up from Seattle. Take those back with you."

Leah nodded and hugged him close. "Please be careful, Jacob. I'm so afraid for you."

He kissed her forehead and pulled back. "It's all in God's hands. You know that. If it's my time, it won't matter if I'm hunting down Chase Kincaid or resting in my bed."

She knew this was true, but it didn't help matters. Jacob picked up a large rifle and slung it over his shoulder. "You need to have faith, little sister. I'll see you soon."

He left Leah alone with Jayce. This good-bye was even harder. She looked at her husband and felt the tears well in her eyes. She hadn't wanted to cry. She didn't want to burden either Jayce or Jacob with her tears.

" 'The Lord is my portion, saith my soul; therefore will I hope in him. The Lord is good unto them that wait for him, to the soul that seeketh him. It is good that a man should both hope and quietly wait for the salvation of the Lord,' " she whispered.

Jayce nodded. "Lamentations, chapter three."

She smiled. "I've often taken comfort in those verses."

"As have I."

She rushed into his arms. "I love you, Jayce. I cannot bear the thought of losing you. I know I told you how proud I was of your willingness to help in this, but now I wish you'd both just refuse and go home with me."

"I know. I wish I could. For your sake and the sake of our future, I wish I could walk away. But it's because of you and our future that I *must* go after Chase and see this thing end, once and for all."

"I know." The words were barely audible as Leah buried her face against his neck.

He pulled back slightly and lifted her face to meet his gaze. " 'The Lord is my portion, saith my soul; therefore will I hope in him. The Lord is good unto them that wait for him, to the soul that seeketh him.' " He stroked her chin with his thumb. "Hope in Him, Leah. Wait for Him. He's never let you down."

She nodded. "I know. He brought you back to me when it seemed impossible to ever hope that such a thing could happen."

"He never punishes obedience. Remember that too. We are seeking to be obedient, Leah. God will honor that and see us through. You . . . me . . . Jacob . . . even Helaina and Chase. The Lord has a plan. We have to trust Him for the outcome."

She felt her strength renew. "Yes. I will wait for Him. I will wait for the Lord's salvation."

Jayce kissed her passionately, his warm mouth claiming hers in a way that promised forever. She cherished that brief moment and could have cried when he dropped his hold and walked away. He joined Jacob in the street as a new snow started to fall.

Leah knew he wouldn't look back. He couldn't look back and leave her. With all the strength she could muster, Leah closed the door and walked back to her room in the hotel. The Lord had given him to her after years of loneliness and regret. The Lord would hold Jayce safely in His hand now. She had to believe that—to trust that.

She thought of another portion of Scripture in the third chapter of Lamentations. Quoting it from memory, she smiled at the assurance it offered.

" 'It is of the Lord's mercies that we are not consumed, because his compassions fail not.' " She straightened her shoulders and drew in a deep breath. " 'They are new every morning: great is thy faithfulness.' "

She smiled and wrapped her arms around her body. A peace settled over her that defied the situation. God was faithful. He would see to her—no matter what. No matter her lack of understanding or the madness of the moment.

"You were faithful yesterday . . . and today, Lord." She raised her arms to the ceiling in an act of praise. "I know you will be faithful tomorrow and the next day . . . and forever."

ALASKAN QUEST

Under the Northern Lights

To Merrill,
with love for your friendship.
You are a dynamic daughter of the King,
and I'm a better person for knowing you.

Chapter One

Last Chance Creek, Alaska

Home."

Leah Barringer Kincaid sighed the word as the settlement they called Last Chance Creek came into view. It felt as if she'd been gone a lifetime instead of just months. But even as the relief of familiarity settled over her, another thought shadowed her joy.

"But it's not really my home anymore," she whispered as the dogsled drew ever closer to the village. She had just recently married, and though she and Jayce had talked about different possibilities of where they might make their home, nothing had been settled. Not completely.

This village—this house—was one she had shared for many years with her brother, Jacob. She could hardly expect that he would leave now, especially at this time of year. It wouldn't be prudent or beneficial for any of them to set out on their own in the face of the Arctic winter. A million thoughts rushed through her mind. So much would change now. She and Jacob had often talked about what they would do when one or the other of them married. Leah had always figured the house would belong to Jacob and she would move off to her husband's home, but where would that be? Jayce had spent time living all over Alaska. He spoke with fondness for Last Chance, but did he love it enough to remain?

"Lay-Ya! Lay-Ya!" Ayoona's voice beckoned to Leah. The squat old native woman waved and pushed her fur-lined parka back just a bit to reveal her brown face as she called to her son. "John! You look hungry. We got you supper."

Leah felt awash in emotions. Seeing Ayoona was like seeing her own grandmother. How she had missed her home. *And to think, there was a time when I wanted to be anywhere but here*. She remembered the restlessness as easily as she remembered her own name. The isolation of the Seward Peninsula was sometimes daunting. Winters were hard and long. Summers were fraught with dangers and endless sun.

John pulled the sled to a stop in front of his mother. "I need to see to the dogs, and then I'll eat."

Leah climbed out of the basket and hugged the old woman. "I've missed you so much. It's good to be home." The woman smelled of seal oil and smoke, and the combination made Leah smile as she pulled away.

"You got married," Ayoona stated. "Your man is a good man?"

"Yes," Leah said. "He is a good man. I love him very much."

"And he loves you. I know." Ayoona grinned, revealing several missing teeth against her weathered lips.

John interrupted their revelry. "I'm going to leave your things at the house," he told Leah. "I can help you get them inside after I feed and water the dogs."

"Don't worry about it. I can get the boxes inside," Leah answered, glancing toward the house. "I'll be fine."

"Your man can help," Ayoona said matter-of-factly.

"My man? Jayce is with Jacob. They're tracking down Jayce's brother Chase," Leah explained to Ayoona. "That's why John had to bring me home. Chase took Helaina Beecham at gunpoint. Remember her? She was the woman who helped Jacob last summer."

"I remember her," Ayoona said, nodding. "She didn't like it here. She strange—lived in your *inne* even when it was full of water." Ayoona referred to the summer ritual when most of the Inupiats moved into tents as the permafrost melted and caused flooding in the subterranean houses. Ayoona shook her head. "She didn't like our ways—our people." The words were matter-of-fact, and there was no condemnation in the woman's tone.

Leah smiled at the thought of Helaina Beecham up to her ankles in water. "I don't think she understood the people here, Ayoona. I honestly don't think it was a matter of like or dislike. She was probably terrified and uncomfortable with such a drastic way of life."

Ayoona nodded. "Not like you."

"No, not like me." Leah had always loved the people here, even if the place had grown wearisome.

John moved the dogs out. "I'll see you at the house, Leah."

"I'll be right there." She gave Ayoona another quick hug. "When I get things put away, I'll come tell you all about my time in Seattle."

"You bring your man too. We eat together."

Leah shook her head. "My husband isn't here, Ayoona. Like I said, he's trying to find his brother. The man is a killer and kidnapper."

"Your man is here." Ayoona pushed her parka back even farther. Her expression revealed absolute assurance that her words were true.

"Jayce . . . is here?" Hesitating, she shook her head. "He's here? You're sure?"

"He just got here. He came this morning," Ayoona stated with a smile. "Needed more dogs. Better dogs. Said he was only staying for a few hours, then going."

Leah felt her heart skip a beat. Jayce was here. They would have a few moments alone, and he could tell her what they had discovered so far. "I have to go," she told Ayoona. "I need to find him."

Ayoona grinned. "You won't have to look for long."

Leah fairly ran the distance from Ayoona's inne to her own home. The little structure of wood and sod had never looked more inviting. John had just finished offloading the crates from the sled. "I'll see you for supper," he told her.

"Thank you for coming after me, John. Ayoona said that Jayce is here. He came for more dogs. Jacob probably wanted his own dogs, though why he sent Jayce instead of coming himself is beyond me. Anyway, we'll be over in a bit."

"Jayce!" she called as she opened the door and went down the few stairs. The houses in this part of the world were partly buried in the ground for insulation and protection against the wind. She and Jacob hadn't buried theirs quite as deeply as the natives usually did their homes. Leah didn't like the feeling of being in the ground. She had also gotten Jacob to build their house with a shorter entry tunnel than those of the natives. Tunnels gave her a feeling of being closed in—trapped. She shuddered as she opened the second door to their house.

"Jayce! I'm home!"

She looked into the store on her left. There was no one there. The kitchen would be the likely place. The wood stove kept the place nice and warm and required the least amount of work. "Jayce?" She pushed back the heavy fur that acted as a door.

And there he was. Her heart skipped a beat as he turned from the stove. "Jayce," she sighed.

"Welcome home . . . Leah."

It was only then that she realized it wasn't Jayce at all.

It was Chase.

"You are Leah—aren't you?" he asked. His resemblance to Jayce was uncanny, but there was something about him that set him apart. Something raw and cruel. Something very, very evil. The skin on the back of her neck prickled, and Leah swallowed hard and leaned back against the doorframe. "What are you doing here?"

"Now, that's no way to welcome your husband." He grinned wickedly at her and took up the coffeepot.

"You aren't my husband." She turned to leave. Surely she could outrun this man. She'd get John, and he could take Chase in hand.

"I wouldn't go, if I were you. Otherwise your husband and brother, not to mention your dear friend Mrs. Beecham, might all be killed. I'd really hate to do it, but I will."

Leah froze in her steps. She turned very slowly. "What are you talking about?" How could he possibly have Jayce and Jacob?

He poured himself a cup of coffee and gave a nonchalant shrug. "I suppose we could discuss that over something to eat."

"Ayoona is expecting us. She thought you were Jayce."

"Just as I hoped she would. I find that being an identical twin has its advantages. The heavy winter clothing doesn't hurt either. It's easy enough to hide a man's face when needed. But since it wasn't needed . . ." He let his words trail off.

Leah felt a shudder go through her. A million questions came to mind. "How did you even know about me—about this place?"

"Mrs. Beecham has been most helpful—without really meaning to be, of course. Not only that, but I've watched Jayce most of his life—or had him watched. Getting information on a man who is doing nothing to hide himself really isn't that difficult. I have well-paid friends who always seem happy to share their knowledge for a price. As for this place, I've been here before."

"How did you know about me—about Jayce and me being married?"

He looked at her and laughed. "You really are quite naïve—aren't you? You've certainly done nothing to hide your marriage. Besides, Mrs. Beecham told me about it—told me about Seattle and her clearing my brother through the use of fingerprints. She loves to talk, and I figure, why not let her? It's not costing me a cent, and it's valuable information."

Leah could have throttled Helaina. She had done nothing but cause trouble from the beginning. Now Chase was here, threatening everyone Leah loved, and there seemed to be nothing she could do but play along.

Leah felt a shudder go through her. "What have you done with my husband and brother?"

Chase took a seat at the table. "They're safe enough . . . for now."

Leah felt her anger overcome her fear of the man. "Where are they?"

Chase took a long drink, then settled back against the seat. "Look, you must be a fairly smart woman. I doubt Jayce would marry a ninny. He always did have to have the best of everything. But be that as it may, being smart, you must know that I'm not about to divulge any secrets that might help you to betray me. All I will say for now is that they are safe. Safe for the time. What you do or don't do will determine if they continue being safe."

Leah decided it couldn't hurt to temporarily play his game. "What do you want?"

"I want dogs and provisions. Mrs. Beecham eats a lot, and we left town in a hurry—as you probably know—not exactly prepared for this sudden change of weather. I figured to get blankets and warmer clothes. You know, sometimes a person's survival depends on little things." He swept her body with his gaze.

Crossing her arms against her chest, Leah wished fervently she could wipe off the smug expression Chase wore. He clearly had the upper hand. If she told the village that he was Chase instead of Jayce, he would most likely be taken into custody . . . but not without a fight. But more important, she might never find Jayce and Jacob. Or even Helaina. Leah felt bad that she held very little concern for the woman, but with her brother's and husband's lives at stake, Helaina ran a distant third—especially considering all she had blabbed to Chase.

"So how do we resolve this?" Leah finally asked.

"You do what I say and no one will get hurt. We will pack a sled and head out in the morning. I figure a night of rest and . . . warmth will be to our advantage." He dropped his voice low. "I'm very much the same man as my brother. So it would hardly be wrong for us to . . . well . . . enjoy each other's company."

"You're nothing like my husband. Jayce is a good man with a strong conscience to see right win over wrong. He loves God, and you clearly love only yourself," Leah said, shaking her head. "I might help you get dogs and supplies, but I won't betray my husband by allowing you any part of me."

"And if I insist?"

Leah's knees threatened to buckle. She was shaking so hard she was certain Chase could see her tremble. With a false sense of bravado, she squared her shoulders. "Then I suppose we all die."

He studied her for a moment. "Keeping your marriage bed untainted means that much to you? What has Jayce done to deserve such loyalty?"

Leah refused to back down. "He's a trustworthy man, and he's had my heart since I was nineteen. I love him very much, and I won't betray him, even to save my own life."

"But what about doing it to save his life?"

It was then that Leah realized this was all a game to him. He was enjoying the play of emotions on her face—the frustration and fear in her voice. He seemed to feed off of it.

Leah could stand no more. "I have supplies to bring in and put away. The villagers believe you are my husband. For now I'll let them believe that. But if you do anything to cause me grief, I'll tell them all, and you'll be imprisoned."

"Not without a fight," Chase said, laughing.

"I think we both realize that," Leah replied. "But you do not know these people like I do, and there you are at a grave disadvantage. You'd do well to remember that. Now I'm going to bring in the supplies—otherwise everyone here will know that something is wrong."

She hoped her words sounded believable. She certainly didn't feel convincing. Walking back out of the house, Leah contemplated what she could do. The options seemed so few. She didn't want to risk the lives of the people here, but she didn't want to give Chase any advantage.

"So where does this stuff go?" he asked.

She hadn't realized he'd followed her out, but it made sense. He wanted to keep track of her—to keep an eye on her so that she couldn't cause him any harm. "It goes into the room on the left."

He easily hoisted one of the heavier crates. It drove home the point to Leah that this was no city-born dandy. Chase was strong and well muscled, or he'd never have been able to handle that box. There had to be at least one hundred pounds of supplies in that crate, and yet he acted as though it weighed no more than a pair of *mukluks*.

She followed after him, carrying a smaller pack of goods. She tried to pray but found the words were jumbled and made no sense. Surely God would understand the situation and know her heart. Leah feared for her brother and Jayce. She longed to see them again—to know they were safe.

While Chase went back for the last of the goods, Leah began to put things away. How had Chase managed to capture Jacob and Jayce? No doubt he had used Helaina as bait. Leah suddenly felt very angry with the younger woman. She'd been nothing but trouble from the moment they'd met. *If not for her, things would be different. If not for Helaina, we would never have had to endure the trip to Seattle and the fear of Jayce hanging for offenses committed by his twin.* Leah seethed. The rise of her anger fueled her body as she tore into the crate. None of this had been their fault. Everything could be squarely placed on Helaina Beecham's shoulders.

"This the last of it?" Chase asked as he put a small wooden box on the counter.

"Yes." Leah hoped her clipped tone would indicate her unwillingness to discuss anything further.

"We need to establish how things are going to be. Especially since we don't want to give anyone here the wrong impression," Chase stated. He leaned against the counter and watched Leah. It gave her an uncomfortable feeling, almost as if he could see through her layers of clothing—even past her flesh and bones to her very soul. It was like he could read her every thought.

"You need to act as though nothing is wrong when we go to eat with your friends."

"I'll fix us something here. I don't want you around my friends."

"That will never do. If you reject their hospitality, they will assume something is wrong. We can't have that, now, can we?"

Leah stopped putting cans of milk on the shelf and looked at Chase. "I'm not going to give you away." *At least not yet.*

"Good. I'm glad to hear you say that. I'd really hate to have to hurt you—or them. But I can hardly sacrifice my life because of sentiment. I haven't survived this long by letting my heart run the show."

"I seriously doubt you have a heart, Mr. Kincaid," Leah said, returning to work.

"Ah, but there you are wrong, my dear sister-in-law." He came up behind her and took hold of her shoulders. She froze in place. "I have a heart, and I can be quite considerate—when extended the same respect." He forced her to turn toward him, then reached out to lift her chin so that she would look him in the face. He stroked her cheek and seemed to study her reaction.

Leah steeled herself against his touch. She wouldn't tremble and give him the pleasure of seeing her fear. "I won't play your games, Mr. Kincaid. I will give you as much respect—as you put it—as I can, but I won't dishonor my husband or my God."

Chase laughed and let her go. "So now God is your sole possession? I thought He was available for everyone."

Leah nodded very slowly. "He is. But since I'm the only one in this room who hasn't rejected Him, I figured it suited the situation well to claim

Him as my own. You are more than welcome to surprise me and prove me wrong."

He walked away, chuckling. "I would never attempt to prove you wrong on this point, Mrs. Kincaid. I hardly have need for God, much less one that you claim possession of so fervently."

Leah watched him walk away, and for the first time since learning about Chase Kincaid and the things he'd done, she felt sorry for him. It was little wonder he did the things he did. He had no use for living a righteous life. He had made his bed in hell, and it seemed to suit him just fine.

Chapter Two

Jacob held up the pot of coffee. "Want some more?"

Jayce looked inside his mug at the settlement of grounds and shook his head. "Nah. I think I've had enough."

They'd taken shelter from the strengthening wind and had decided to make camp among some dwarf birch and shrub willows. Snow had fallen off and on for the last two hours, but it was the bone-chilling wind that had the dogs sleeping with their noses buried between their hind legs. Jayce was glad for the warmth of their tent. The camp stove helped considerably, as would the furs and wool blankets they'd brought from Nome.

"The dogs aren't going to last long," Jacob said matter-of-factly. "I've been checking them over. They weren't in the best shape to start with, but they were all we could get on short notice. I figure, however, we're not that far from Last Chance. It might be wise to head that way and put together a couple of good teams."

"But what about the trail? We'll lose it altogether if we leave."

Jacob put the pot back on the stove. "This wind and snow is burying the last of it, anyway. I seriously doubt we'd be able to pick up on it in the morning. If we get fresh dogs and better provisions, we might be able to hit the trail again and find someone who's actually seen Chase."

Jayce considered this idea for a moment. "What about Helaina?"

"Look, I don't like it any better than you, but I'm telling you, these dogs aren't going to last long. If we spend any more time attempting to run Chase down, I think it will kill half of these beasts."

"How far do you figure us to be from Last Chance?"

"Probably two, maybe three, days."

"And the dogs will hold out that long?"

Jacob shrugged. "Most will. I think there's one that might not. We can always put him in the basket."

Jayce nodded. "I guess it makes sense. We'd also get to see that Leah made it home safely. I hated sending her back on her own."

"I'm sure John got word to come for her. There were a good number of people heading north to Teller, and I'm sure they would have rested at Last Chance. Some have family there, and you know they wouldn't have missed a chance to share some time together."

"Sure. It'll put my mind at ease, nevertheless, to see that she made it home without any trouble."

Jacob smiled. "Me too. I can't imagine life without her. Of course, now that she's your wife, I guess I'll have to."

"I never had the kind of relationship with my siblings that you two share. I was born into a brood of vipers. They were all about what they could get for themselves. My father used to say that if his casket had gold plating, my brothers and sister would pry it off before putting him in the ground. I suppose I'm the odd man out in the family. Although I'm hardly a saint, as your sister will attest. I had my selfish ambitions as well." Jayce looked out into the darkness. "It's just that I seemed to realize, as I grew up, that selfish ambitions were hardly the way to live amicably with family or friends. Of course, I came to Alaska because I had no desire to live with my family—amicably or otherwise."

"Were you and Chase never close? I thought twins were always . . . well . . . like one soul or something." Jacob almost seemed embarrassed to have asked such a question.

"Chase was ambitious from the start. Mother used to tease that the only reason I'd been born first was because I was bigger and had blocked Chase's way." Jayce smiled at the memory. "I told you, didn't I, that we were born on different days in different years?" Jacob nodded and Jayce continued as if he needed to explain. "I was born at the close of the calendar year at three minutes till midnight in 1882. Chase was born four minutes after midnight on New Year's Day. He had to be cut out. He was all wrapped up in the umbilical cord, and he and our mother nearly died. Somehow, Chase has had to do things the hard way ever since."

"Some folks are like that," Jacob admitted. "I know I've had my hardheaded moments. Still, it's difficult to imagine two such different brothers."

"Like I said, my other brother and my sister are no different. Eloise always acted like she had somehow been robbed in being born a woman instead of a man. She was the firstborn, treated like a pampered pet. I remember she actually talked of going to college to simply irritate and offend our mother. I knew nothing would ever come of it, however. Eloise was lazy and concerned only with finding a wealthy husband who could spoil her as father had done."

"What about your other brother?"

"Clyde? Well, he's really just a more subdued version of Eloise. He demands his own way, but he's more subtle in controlling situations." Jayce shifted, as if the ground had suddenly become unbearably hard. "I don't suppose it really helps matters now to speak ill of any of them. It's enough to say we weren't close. I envy you the relationship you've had with Leah."

Jacob smiled. "Leah is loyal to a fault. She will never bear you a grudge or desert you. You've got a good woman in her. I will miss her, but I couldn't be happier for her to have found true love in you."

Jayce only missed Leah more at Jacob's warm description. "I wish I hadn't wasted so many years." His words were laced with regret.

"You can't go around bemoaning the past," Jacob said sternly. "It won't serve any good purpose. God had a plan in all of it."

"I suppose He has a plan in all of this, too, but it's sure hard to see it for myself."

"I really admire you for your willingness to go after your own brother, Jayce. I know I've said it before, but I figure you deserve to hear it again."

"Well, at least a dozen times a day I find myself wanting to turn around and head as far away as I can get from Chase."

"You know, I can go on without you," Jacob suggested. "After we get back to Last Chance, you could stay there with Leah and care for the dogs and store—maybe get in some good trapping. I can go on and find Helaina and Chase."

Jayce considered the proposition for only a moment. It was tempting, but he knew he couldn't leave Jacob to bear a burden that was clearly his responsibility. "No. I have to do this. I'm grateful for your help, but if you want to stay in Last Chance, I wouldn't hold it against you."

"No. I'm in this for the duration. This likely isn't a surprise, but Helaina . . . well, I've come to care for her a great deal. I don't know what her feelings are, but I feel I must try to save her from Chase."

"I figured as much, even without Leah mentioning it," Jayce said, smiling. "But Helaina's not like us. I seriously doubt she'll ever stay in Alaska. Are you prepared to go to the States for her?"

Jacob shook his head. "I don't know how to live down there anymore. I can't see myself doing that."

"So what will you do?"

"I don't know," Jacob answered honestly. "I suppose I'll let her go once we find her. I just pray she's safe and that Chase hasn't . . ." His words faded off, but Jayce understood the fears Jacob had. Chase had proven he had no regard for life; what would stop him from assaulting a woman's virtue? Still, that had never been Chase's style in the past. No one had yet accused him of such things.

"I don't think Chase would . . . hurt her." He drew a deep breath, pondering his further response. "Everything Chase has done up until now has been against men. Helaina got in the way and made herself an easy target. I'd honestly be surprised if she's even with him now. I figure Chase has probably set her free somewhere along the way. As soon as he felt safe and out of the reach of the law in Nome, I'm thinking he probably dropped Helaina off at the nearest village. He wouldn't want to be bothered with her—she'd serve no useful purpose. He'd probably just consider her inconsequential."

"Not if she ran her mouth," Jacob said, frowning. "You know Helaina. She holds no fear of men like Chase. I think she actually gets her energy from encountering them. If she goes on telling him about her connection to the Pinkertons and how she's there to catch him, Chase might get the idea that he can hold her for some kind of ransom. He might even believe the Pinkertons would trade him his freedom for Helaina."

"I suppose it's possible. I can't be sure from one minute to the next what Chase will get a mind to do." Jayce wondered what he could say that would offer his friend some measure of comfort.

"We may have made a mistake in leaving those Pinkerton agents in Nome." Jacob leaned out the tent opening and tossed the remains of his coffee. Cold air rushed in, causing Jacob to hurriedly close the flap. "There's strength in numbers." He secured the tent and crawled back to his pallet.

"True, but they would have become a liability to us. They're not cut out for an Alaskan winter. They weren't even wearing decent boots. They would have slowed us down—or worse, died on us."

"That's probably true, but I can't help feeling we would be better prepared to deal with your brother if we had more men."

"There's no way of telling what we need in order to deal with Chase," Jayce admitted. "But I know we've made better time on our own. Those agents will be just as happy filling in for those deceased officers, and the police chief seemed real happy to get the help."

"I suppose you're right."

Jayce laughed. "Of course I'm right. After all, this is the same argument you gave me back in Nome."

"Thought it sounded familiar," Jacob said with a smile. "Besides, I guess the objective is to stop Chase. I can't keep second-guessing everything else or I'll never be focused enough to get the job done."

"Chase has a way of stealing a man's attention. It's like . . . well . . . sometimes I swear he can read my mind—even from a thousand miles away."

"Hope not. That would give him too much advantage in this situation."

Pulling up a thick wool blanket and heavy fur, Jayce settled in to go to sleep. "You know, I remember a time when Chase wasn't so bad. He was about eight years old and he'd come down with the measles. He was pretty sick. I guess we all thought he might die. Chase was pretty scared, but he kept telling our mother that he didn't want her to take care of him because he was scared she'd get sick and die too. Mother was undaunted by the threat, telling Chase that he was her child, and she would see him through this crisis as she had seen him through others. Chase told her that if he lived, he would be a better boy."

"So what happened?" Jacob asked, nestling into his own pallet.

"He was good for a time. Really seemed to have a changed heart. Up until his bout with the measles, he'd often lied and cheated at school, was even given to petty thievery and assaults to get what he wanted. My father was at his wits' end trying to figure out what to do with him. I think Chase was close to being sent to a military academy.

"For a few months after his recovery, Chase walked the straight and narrow. Then one day he just seemed to put it all aside. He grew angry and hateful, and none of us ever knew why. It just got worse after that. Father threatened him, Mother cajoled him, Mrs. Newfield, our cook, promised him her best goodies. Nothing worked. Chase just seemed to go bad."

"Something must have happened to make him that way. Especially if he had been good for a time. He had to have seen that being good accomplished more than being bad," Jacob countered.

"But see, that's the thing," Jayce said, shaking his head sadly. "I don't think it did merit him more. I think people still treated him like the same old Chase. They expected the worst from him, and I think after a time, he just decided to meet their expectations."

"I guess I can understand how that would happen. Expectations are hard to live up to—or live down, in this case. It's always hard to imagine what causes a person to choose the wrong path. I know even for myself, some choices just seemed a little short of good—not really bad. You know what I mean?"

Jayce nodded. "I've been on some of those paths myself. I knew a decision wasn't completely in keeping with what was right, but it wasn't really all that bad. Just tilted the wrong direction a little."

"Yeah, and you can convince yourself that they aren't tilted at all if you try hard enough. I know when I ran away to go find my father, I convinced myself that it was a good thing I was doing. See, we'd gotten word that a man killed in an avalanche might be our pa, but we couldn't be sure. People carried letters back and forth for folks all the time, and this man had a letter from our father. I needed proof—one way or the other—of whether our father was alive. Never mind that I had to defy all of my authority figures to do it, and hurt my sister. She confronted me about it too. Leah was never one to just let you out of a situation—not if she thought it was for your own good. I gave her a necklace and told her I didn't want her to give up on the dream. I needed for her to keep dreaming, because all of my dreams were gone." Jacob sighed.

"I'll never forget the way she looked at me the day I left. I knew she'd forgive me in the long run, but there was such a sense of betrayal in her expression that I very nearly didn't go. Still, I left because I felt I had a good and righteous mission. Maybe a lot of bad choices are made that way."

"Maybe, but that can't be Chase's excuse. He's broken the law so many times that he cannot doubt his choices are wrong. Maybe when he was eight years old or even a young man of thirteen, those choices were not clearly understood. But a man of nearly thirty-three must surely know the difference. My only hope is that in going after him—in capturing him and turning him over to the authorities—I might see other people safe from his antics."

"It won't be easy when the time comes," Jacob said.

Jayce stifled a yawn and nodded. He closed his eyes. "I've had a hard time coming to terms with potentially killing my brother, but if it saves the lives of innocent people, then there really is no choice."

"You're not the one killing him," Jacob said softly. "He's made his own choice to live this life. He's bearing the consequence of those choices—or will bear it. You had nothing to do with that."

"But I have everything to do with hunting him down." Jayce rolled to his side and tried not to see the image that had haunted him since leaving Nome. It was the shadowy picture of his twin hanging from a gallows. Even more unnerving was the fact that the scene only served to remind him that Chase would have allowed Jayce to suffer the same fate and probably have had little regret for it. The thought angered Jayce, but it also gave him cause to check his heart.

This cannot be about revenge, Jayce told himself. *Chase has caused me unknown damage and heartache. He's given me a reputation I did not deserve. But this cannot be about revenge. I could never live with myself if I found that to be the motivation of my heart. It has to be about justice and saving other people from my brother's threat. Nothing more or less.*

Chapter Three

Leah finished packing food provisions in a crate just as Chase came into the store. She hadn't been able to get all of the supplies put away because Chase had forced her to come and help him handle the dogs.

"Are you nearly done?" he asked, sounding strangely nervous.

Leah looked up as she secured the pack. "Yes. Did you see to feed for the dogs?"

"Yes," he murmured, not sounding at all like the confident man she'd been dealing with.

"Good. Take this and load it on the sled. I need to grab a couple of traps and the rest of my things. Then we can leave."

"Traps? Why are you taking traps?" He sounded suspicious, but Leah could hardly be bothered. If she allowed herself to think for even one moment about the gravity of the situation, she might well back out and expose Chase.

"We'll need to stretch our supplies as far as we can. Especially where the dogs are concerned. If the pulling gets hard or the distance extensive, the dogs will need more food. Then there are Jayce, Jacob, and Helaina to consider. Have you provided for them? If not, we'll need to see to that as well. I have no way of knowing where you are taking me or when you plan to let us go. We can hardly survive for long on what we can carry out in one sled basket." She thrust the heavy bag at him. "This will last us a couple of weeks at best, even a shorter time once we join the others."

"Should be sufficient for two," Chase said, easily hoisting the bag to his shoulder. "I have a place up north. Near Kotzebue. We shouldn't have too much trouble reaching it before supplies run out."

"But what of the others? If this is sufficient for two, what about Helaina, Jayce, and Jacob?"

He shrugged. "I don't figure to take an entourage with me. One hostage will suffice."

Leah felt her knees tremble. Somehow she knew she'd be the one hostage he'd choose. She drew a deep breath to steady her nerves. "Nevertheless, I'll take the traps. Fresh meat will keep us alive and the furs will be useful for trading or even using in our clothes." She went to where she stored the traps and pulled out two. One larger and one smaller. Checking them for defects or problems, Leah was finally satisfied that she had all she needed.

"Lay-Ya!" Ayoona called from the front door.

"That's what I hate about the north," Chase declared, turning to go. "Nobody ever knocks."

"There's no need when you care about each other as if they were family," Leah replied. "Just go load that, and let me deal with business here." He cocked a brow but said nothing.

"Lay-Ya, are you here?" Ayoona pushed back the fur. "Oopick is with me."

"Good. I need to go over our arrangement and make sure you have everything you need." Leah watched as Chase allowed the women to come into the room before edging carefully around them.

"You ladies are looking lovely today," he said with a devilish grin. "If I weren't already head-over-heels in love with my wife, I would surely come a-courting." Oopick smiled, but Ayoona ignored him. She was far too intent on speaking to Leah.

"Lay-Ya, it's not a good time to travel. There are bad storms coming. You should stay."

"I know," Leah said, nodding. She had seen the signs herself. "Chase . . . Jayce is of a mind that it won't cause us any real trouble." She hoped neither woman would think it strange that she'd stumbled over Jayce's name. "I've taken good provisions and a sturdy tent. We should be all right."

"You won't get far today. The wind is going to blow in plenty soon," Ayoona said matter-of-factly. "Tent won't do you good. You tell your man to find something better."

"I will," Leah replied. She knew Ayoona was worried. "Oopick, thank you so much for being willing to watch the store. These last couple of crates are what's left to put on the shelves." Leah pointed behind the women. "Just write down what everyone buys and pays. We'll go over the books when I get back." *If I get back*. The thought startled Leah, but she held fast to her calm façade.

"John and I will take care of everything," Oopick replied. "He will take good care of the dogs, and I will run the store."

"And you'll both stay here, right?" Leah questioned. She knew that Oopick and John would be hesitant to enjoy the Barringer hospitality. They were never ones to take pay or reward for simply offering a neighborly service.

"We will stay, but we will bring our own supplies. You will need yours for the winter. John plans to hunt tomorrow, so maybe there will be plenty more meat when you come back."

"When you be back, Lay-Ya?" Ayoona asked.

Leah shrugged. "I don't know."

"Where you go?"

She shook her head. "I don't know. Likely Kotzebue. Jayce wants to surprise me. He has a place up north," she told them, hoping that if her husband and brother escaped and showed up in the village, someone might be able to help direct them to where Leah and Chase had gone.

Ayoona shook her head. "Bad storms there too."

Leah knew the old woman was probably right but said, "I'll be back before you know it. Take care of each other." She hugged Ayoona and then Oopick. She didn't want to admit it, but deep in her heart, the situation felt bleak and increasingly hopeless.

Ayoona and Oopick had barely gone before Emma Kjellmann showed up. As a missionary to the frozen north, Emma seldom made it to the States. She was eager for a discussion with Leah.

"Is the coffee on?" she asked as she popped her head in.

"I think there's a bit left," Leah admitted. She knew Chase would be in a hurry to leave, but she hadn't had a chance to even visit with Emma since coming home. She led the way to the kitchen, holding back the fur for Emma as she passed through.

"I heard you were heading out again and figured I'd better come over before you left. I wanted to hear all about Seattle and about your wedding.

I saw your husband outside, and he sure seemed happy. Guess our prayers were answered and God worked all things together for good."

Leah buried her surging emotions, hating to mislead her dear friend. She wanted to believe Emma's words with all of her heart, but at this point that thought would not even begin to register in her brain. Nothing seemed to be for good at this point. "God does know what He's doing," she replied, more for her own sake than Emma's. Leah took up a cup and poured Emma a cup of coffee. "Hope it's warm enough. We let the fire die out since we're leaving."

"I'm sure it will be," Emma said, taking the mug. "Say, I heard you brought back supplies. I hope you thought to bring sugar. I never did get enough in my shipments. They were always running short, and I hate to think of going through the winter with no more than I have."

"I did bring some, but it probably won't be enough to suit the likes of Bryce and Nolan."

"Ja, my boys, they like their treats," Emma admitted. "I spoil them too much, but their papa is just as bad."

"I'm sure he is, but he's a good man."

"Your man is good too. I remember our talk last spring," Emma began. "I remember how you worried he might never understand your heart—never love you. But God knew what would happen." She was grinning from ear to ear. "Did you have a lovely wedding? Oh, I wish you would have gotten married here so I could give you a party."

"It was a nice but very simple ceremony," Leah remembered fondly. "I wore a beautiful white muslin dress. I brought it back and will show it to you sometime. It seemed silly to buy such a thing, but Jacob insisted. He felt I deserved a special dress for my wedding day."

"Ja, I agree. A woman only gets married once. She should look as pretty as she can. My mama and sisters made me a beautiful gown. It was white with tiny bluebells embroidered around the hem."

"That sounds lovely," Leah commented.

"I'm sure you made a beautiful bride. I'm surprised your husband can bear to be away from you at all."

Leah suddenly felt very compelled to tell Emma the truth. She opened her mouth, determined to explain the situation, then closed it again. Chase had no scruples, no fear . . . and would take Emma if necessary. He would even kill her if she got in his way. Leah couldn't risk that.

"So was it a pretty day?"

"Hmmm?" Leah looked at Emma. "Oh, the wedding. Yes and no. It had rained in the morning, but it cleared off and that made everything seem lovely and clean. The autumn weather there was quite nice. Not too cold or too warm."

"Oh, I almost forgot to tell you," Emma interjected. "My little sister, Sigrid, is coming to live with us next spring. She's agreed to come and teach school."

"That is good news. Where is she now?"

"She lives in Minnesota with my parents. She teaches there at a big school. She's very good."

"What caused her to agree to come here?" Leah couldn't imagine a young woman just up and coming to Alaska to teach school.

"I begged her," Emma admitted. "I miss my family so much. Bjorn said we could go back next spring, but he wanted someone to be here to take care of the house and such. Sigrid agreed to come for that purpose, and then the more we wrote back and forth, the more she realized it might behoove her to come and teach. She checked into the requirements and will come through the government. Isn't that wonderful?"

Emma's delight was contagious. "Yes, I am sure you will enjoy her visit," Leah said, laughing. "So you plan a trip home next year?"

"Ja. My parents are anxious to see the children. They've never met Nolan or Rachel. I just want to sit on my mother's porch and snap beans and talk about the old days. I want to eat her cooking and have a mound of fluffy scrambled eggs for my breakfast. Oh, and my mama's fresh curds and whey."

"It all sounds wonderful. We certainly enjoyed our share of delicacies in Seattle. I'd almost forgotten what beefsteak tastes like. And, I have to admit, I ate more than my share of eggs and fresh fruit. Oh, the oranges and bananas were incredible," Leah remembered. "The man whose house we stayed at had a taste for both, and the house was never without them. I could only wonder at the cost, but he insisted we all partake." Leah offered Emma a grin. "I didn't have to be asked twice, but I'm sure they were expensive."

"Ja, I can imagine. I sometimes miss those things enough to leave here forever."

"I hope you won't," Leah admitted.

"Probably not. Bjorn says there's much of God's work to be done. He sees good changes in the people. Less drinking and fewer superstitions. The village is more peaceful. Remember the murder that took place the year we came?"

"I remember not only that, but the ones that came before your arrival. Up here the law means very little to some. And to others . . . well, Inupiat justice is sometimes very swift and without concern for white man's ways."

"We've tried to teach respect for the laws, but when you've lived here for generations and haven't had to worry about the government, it must be hard to have to take on someone else's ways."

"It's hard to know what's right," Leah said thoughtfully. "Eventually more people will come to this area. Alaska will probably be made a state soon. They're already working hard to see that happen. Once they convince people to move north, Alaska will fill up like the States. I fear for the natives then."

"I do too. My grandparents were missionaries to some of the Indian peoples in Montana, before it was a state. They told us stories of how the whites lied and cheated those peoples."

"Adrik . . . you remember he's married to the woman who helped raise Jacob and me?" Emma nodded. "Adrik is part Tlingit, and he's talked of the abuses he's seen his people endure. Of course, there are good white people." She smiled. "I try to be one of those myself."

"Ja. It's sometimes hard to gain their trust," Emma said, finishing her coffee. "I sometimes feel we have accomplished very little."

"You've both done great work here. The north needs you." Leah would never want to keep them from going wherever God directed them, but at the same time, she didn't want to lose her friend to the south.

"There is other news," Emma said, smiling. "We're going to have another baby. I'll probably deliver in May, just before breakup. Then we'll travel to Minnesota in June."

"That is wonderful news. Maybe it will be a little sister for Rachel."

"I'd like that. Rachel doesn't seem so much a baby anymore. She's walking and talking. Always running after her brothers."

"I wish I could see her. I wish I were going to be here longer," Leah said with regret evident in her voice. "I would love to have a nice long talk, for there's so much to tell you about. My visits with Karen in Ketchikan, the ship blowing up on my trip home . . . God really showed me a great deal. I hope we'll get a chance to discuss it when I get back."

"Where are you going?"

Leah knew she would have to be careful. She wanted to give as much detail as possible without endangering Emma. "I'm not entirely sure, but Jayce says we'll head north—he has a place up there somewhere. He mentioned the area around Kotzebue."

"You aren't going to move there, are you? I couldn't bear it if you left us for good. And it's such a long way to travel."

"I don't plan to be gone long, and I certainly don't plan to move there," Leah said. "Truth is, I've had enough travel to last me a lifetime. Now I'd just like to settle down and stay put."

"So why go?"

Leah thought for a moment. Maybe if she shared some of the true details, it would help to save her life—and the lives of her brother and husband. "Jayce has a twin brother—an identical twin brother." She said the words with a strong emphasis on *identical*. "Chase is a criminal, and he's kidnapped a woman and she must be rescued." She again emphasized her words, this time focusing on *kidnapped* and *rescued*.

"Chase is very dangerous. He has killed several men. Two police officers were gunned down in Nome before he took this woman. Jayce and Jacob went after her." Leah lowered her voice and spoke even more slowly. "They will need to hurry or Chase may get beyond their reach."

"Leah, we need to go," Chase said as he bounded into the kitchen, looked momentarily at Emma, then back to Leah. "I didn't know you had company."

"Oh, I snuck in while you were admiring Qavlunaq's baby." Emma gave him a big smile. "Maybe you'll have your own baby to admire this time next year."

Chase laughed. "I certainly would enjoy that."

Leah felt her face grow hot. "I wish I could visit more, but like Jayce says, we need to head out. Bad weather is moving in, and Ayoona says we'll need to find some reasonable shelter before we get too far."

"You can always put the trip off another day or two."

"No," Chase said firmly. "It's important we leave now." He came up behind Leah and took hold of her shoulders. She couldn't help but stiffen. Chase and Emma didn't seem to notice as Chase continued talking. "There's something that needs my attention not far from here. If I don't leave today, it could be too late."

Emma laughed and got to her feet. "I usually find there's nothing that cannot wait another day. But, of course, Alaskan winter changes everybody's schedule."

"He's right. This is really important," Leah said, remembering Chase's hostages. She broke away from Chase's hold and went to hug Emma tight. "Pray for me. Pray for us."

"Ja, I will pray. God be with you." She headed out without another word, but there was a strange look on her face that gave Leah hope that perhaps Emma had noticed things were not exactly right.

Leah turned to Chase. "I'll grab my pack." She hurried to her bed and picked up the bag. Throwing it on her back, Leah couldn't help but frown. She had hoped to arm herself with a gun, but Chase had cleared those out prior to her arrival. She cast a quick glance over the room, wishing there might be something else that could aid her on the way.

"I'll take your bag," Chase said.

Leah nearly jumped out of her skin. She hadn't realized he'd followed her. "I can manage it just fine." She jerked away from him and set out for the door. He took hold of her arm, however, and pulled her back. Leah resisted him as he tried to draw her closer.

"I certainly hope you didn't say anything to your friend that would . . . well . . . slow our progress."

"I wouldn't risk Emma's life that way," Leah said, growing very still. She met his gaze and narrowed her eyes. "I'm not a fool, Chase Kincaid. You'd do well to remember that."

He looked at her oddly for a moment. "I have never figured you for one, even if you did marry my brother." He let go of her arm. "Is it true the old woman believes the weather will turn bad on us?"

"Yes. She's seldom wrong. You can see the signs for yourself. The wind has shifted and increased, the temperatures are colder, and the skies are growing darker on the horizon. Anyone can see it bodes ill."

He shrugged and turned toward the door. "Then we'd better hurry. We've got a lot of distance to cover and apparently a shorter time to do it in than I had planned. Come on."

Leah followed him, but all the while her mind searched for ways she could leave her husband and brother a message, if they returned. She hoped fervently that if they did show up, they would be able to follow the signs. Signs. Leah thought of the word for several seconds. Hurrying back to her chest, she threw open the lid and reached for a red checked tablecloth. It had been placed here for mending, but now Leah thought its purpose would be better served in tattered pieces.

"Leah, come on!" Chase called. His voice betrayed his frustration with her.

Leah took the tablecloth and stuffed it inside her parka. The layers would add warmth when the weather turned bad, and hopefully she could find ways to leave pieces of the material along the trail for whoever might come to her rescue. *If* anyone even realized she needed to be rescued.

Chapter Four

By the time Leah got to the sled, Chase was studying the western skies. She could sense that things were not shaping up well, and apparently he was pondering the same thing. Looking at him as if his answer didn't matter, Leah asked, "Are you sure we have to leave today?"

"Unless you want your loved ones to die," he replied in a gruff manner. He didn't sound the least bit happy.

The dogs yipped and danced anxiously in their harnesses. They loved to run and couldn't understand the holdup. Behind them, some forty other dogs yelped and howled at the injustice of being left behind. Trying to forget the situation for a moment, Leah leaned down and scratched the lead dog behind the ears. Marty, who had been a fun-loving pup, had turned into a first-class leader.

"So what's it to be?"

Leah was surprised he'd asked her opinion. "You know the answer to that." Leah didn't even bother to look at Chase. "I'm willing to brave the dangers."

"Are you sure ten dogs will be enough?"

Leah looked at the team. They were some of Jacob's best, known for their strength and predictability. "These are some of the strongest. They are very experienced, and I wouldn't expect trouble from them. Some of the others are less reliable."

"I suppose I'll have to take your word on it. My own experience has taught me much, and they seem capable." He acted as though he was about to walk away, then turned back to her. "By the way, I want you to drive the dogs. I want you busy," Chase said, climbing into the basket. "Besides, they know you better. No sense starting out with animal troubles."

Leah straightened and eyed him with a frown. "But I have no idea where we're going."

"North. I told you that much. Head north as if you were traveling to Mary's Igloo—you do know where that's at, don't you?" Leah nodded and he continued. "I'll let you know when it's time to veer off the trail."

Leah pulled on her sealskin mittens. There was nothing to do but cooperate. She pulled her pack from her back and secured it in the basket beside Chase. It would be far easier to manage the dogs without the cumbersome weight on her shoulders.

She freed the anchoring hook and jumped to the runners in one motion. "Ho, Marty! Hike!"

The dogs began to bark in earnest as they strained against the weight and pulled the sled into motion. Leah felt the wind against her skin and realized she'd forgotten to wrap a scarf around her face. She considered trying to manage it and the team but knew that would never work. The dogs were just starting out, and their enthusiasm was much too high. She would need all of her skills and focus to control them.

Besides, it's not that cold, she reasoned. *We'll stop for a break soon enough, and I can deal with it then.* But Leah knew that normally she wouldn't have forgotten such a precaution. Alaska was a harsh companion at times, and often unforgiving. Jacob had always reminded her that a person had to pay attention to every step, every inch of land, every breath. There were just too many potential problems.

If I hadn't been so upset with this situation, she told herself, *I never would have forgotten to secure my scarf.* She pulled the parka farther down, cutting some of the chill. Her mind flooded with questions and thoughts. She wondered how she might facilitate an escape once she found the others. Timing, no doubt, would be one of the more critical issues.

Having made the trip to Mary's Igloo many times with Jacob, Leah was somewhat familiar with the territory. The coastal flatlands broke into small hills from time to time, and in the distance the mountains created a daunting barrier to the interior. Of course, there were ways through those places as well. There were always ways around obstacles—if a person paid attention.

Leah had lived in this area for over ten years, and in that time her training had been intense. She thought of the ways Ayoona had assisted her in learning the vegetation, especially beneficial herbs. She and Oopick had also worked to teach Leah about watching the weather, the seasonal signs, and even animal tracks and behavior. Living successfully in Alaska was all about observation.

Leah was glad for the opportunity to drive the sled. The work gave her something to think on other than her circumstance. But even with this job, she couldn't help but let her thoughts drift. Jacob and Jayce were out there somewhere. Chase knew where they were and knew what he planned to do with them. Leah, too, wanted to make plans—to think ahead to that moment when they might all be free again.

"Lord, I don't know what I'm supposed to do in this," she whispered, knowing that Chase would never hear her with the wind and his own insulated parka distorting the sound. "Please help us, Lord. Keep Jacob and Jayce safe and help them get free from whatever place Chase has put them. Help Helaina too." She said the latter almost as an afterthought. Her feelings toward Helaina were still too emotional and raw. She blamed Helaina for all this, and it was difficult to feel sympathy for the girl. *I've defended her so many times—to so many people. Just yesterday I defended her to Ayoona, and now I feel so angry.* It wasn't easy to consider Helaina, however, without thinking of her brother.

Jacob cares for her very much, Leah reasoned. *What if he rescues her and decides to marry her? I'll have to accept this woman as family.* The thought made Leah uncomfortable. Helaina was a woman who loved the noises and the smells of the city, who talked often of her home in New York and of the life she missed. Jacob would never want to be a part of those things. Jacob loved the land and the wide-open spaces.

Leah sighed. Maybe nothing would come of Helaina and Jacob's relationship. After all, she couldn't see either one of them coming to terms with where they might live. And if they couldn't come to terms on something that simple—how could they ever hope to make a marriage work?

They stopped the dogs and had a small lunch nearly three hours later. The winds were growing fierce and the skies had turned a leaden color. Winter had come early to the Seward Peninsula, and the snow and cold were more intense than usual. It felt and looked more like January than nearly November. "We should find a place to take shelter. It would be good," Leah said, "to find a nook away from the direct flow of the wind."

"Do you have a suggestion?" Chase asked, finishing the last of the boiled seal meat Leah had given him.

"I haven't been up this way in some time," Leah admitted. "But I'm thinking we need to hurry. It's already starting to snow, and the wind will soon whip it into a blizzard."

Chase got to his feet. "Then let's move out. Get us as far as possible, and if a good place to camp presents itself, then take it. Maybe we'll make better time tomorrow."

Leah nodded and readied the dogs. They needed little encouragement. They were still eager to move ahead, and Leah found their enthusiasm matched her own. Perhaps they knew they were going to find their master soon.

By early afternoon the snow still fell and the temperatures had lowered even more. But the wind held back, almost as if God blocked it with His hand. At least that was how Leah liked to think of it. Thoughts like that helped her feel less lonely.

Leah was about to give up hope of a shelter when she spotted a place between a couple of small hills. She urged the dogs in that direction and felt only moderate relief when the cut seemed to offer perfect protection.

"Help me get the tent up or we'll both be in for it," Leah called as the wind seemed to pick up a little. "I can't do this by myself."

Chase didn't hesitate, much to her relief. He took up the canvas and held it in place while Leah drove the stakes into the frozen ground. It wasn't easy to do, but in about ten minutes they were able to raise the pole to secure the tent. The wind whipped at their refuge in a merciless fashion, despite the hill's meager protection.

Leah finished securing the dogs while Chase took their needed supplies into the tent. Listing the tasks in her mind, Leah realized there would be much to do before she could rest. She needed to melt snow for the dogs to drink, as well as some for herself and Chase. Next she'd have to fix food for them all. Perhaps she'd just throw the dogs some frozen fish and worry about something warm later.

She crawled into the tent as the snow grew more blinding. There was no hope of keeping the snow completely out of the tent, but Leah tried her best. "I'm glad you agreed to stop," she said, securing the tent flap.

"It's no problem for me," Chase said, lighting a seal oil lamp for warmth. "I'm not the one waiting for my return."

Leah frowned. "How can you be so callous about human life? About the death of others?"

"Everybody dies, Leah."

She looked at him as she pushed back her parka. "Yes, that's true enough." She pulled her mittens off and let them dangle on the cording that attached them to her coat. "You just seem intent on helping some of them die sooner than they might ordinarily have."

He shrugged and gave her a cold-blooded smile. "We all have our jobs to do."

Her anger spilled over like the river during spring breakup. "I've never met anyone as evil as you."

He looked almost hurt. "Evil? You have the audacity to call me evil? Your friend Mrs. Beecham runs all over the world trying to catch me for the purpose of putting me to death. Why is it acceptable for her to kill me, but not the other way around? Then, too, what about the world at war? Soon America will no doubt be a part of that European fiasco. What about that evil? Will you so readily condemn those who fight, as you condemn me?"

"They fight for a cause—for their countries, for their homes."

"And I, too, fight for a cause," Chase protested. "My cause—me. I've never had an easy or simple way. Yet I find a way that works for me—an unconventional way, I suppose you could say."

"What way? Thievery? Murder?"

Chase's expression seemed confused for a moment. He considered his words, then shook his head. "I don't expect you to understand. You've set yourself against me and will not be persuaded to feel sympathy for my cause."

Leah could hardly believe his words. "Is that what you want from us? Sympathy?"

Chase again shrugged. "Sympathy is a start. At least sympathetic people do not have the tendency to seek your life."

"I'm sympathetic when one of the dogs gives birth to pups that aren't healthy enough to live. But I still put them out of their misery." Leah's words were delivered in such a cold, even manner that they frightened her. When had she become so lacking in compassion for the life of another human being? How could she call herself a Christian and still feel such hatred?

Hoping Chase would drop the subject, she reached for one of the food sacks. "Dried salmon and crackers should make us a decent supper," she muttered.

"So are you trying to tell me that you would kill me if you had the chance?"

Leah looked up to find Chase watching her. She considered his words for a moment, then shook her head. "I wouldn't kill you. You're the only one with the knowledge of where my husband and brother are. Not to mention Mrs. Beecham. If I killed you, I'd have to go find them myself."

Chase laughed. "That's very true. I'm glad you realize that I have the upper hand in this situation. The people you love so much will die if you fail to completely cooperate with me."

Leah felt a chill run down her spine. Chase had a way of taking the fire from her anger. "I never said I wouldn't cooperate with you."

Chase studied her for a moment and nodded. "Just so long as you remember the facts. I feel as if I must constantly remind you."

"I need no reminding. I need my family back safe and sound."

They existed in silence after that. Chase seemed to doze off and on, while Leah recited Bible verses and poetry, and prayed. An hour or so later the snow abated and the winds calmed. Leah found herself surprised by this turn of events. She had fully expected the storm to rage on for hours, even days. The thought had grieved her, leaving her worried for Jacob and Jayce.

"I need to feed the dogs," she announced. "I'm also going to set some traps. Hopefully we'll have fresh meat in the morning."

Chase leaned up on his elbow and narrowed his eyes. "Remember, if you try to get away from me, I'll kill them all. Then I'll go back to the village and kill your friends there."

"I gave you my word, Chase. I told you that I would cooperate until I knew that Jacob and Jayce were safe." *But only until they're safe.* "I'm not going to do anything to jeopardize them."

With that, Leah pulled on her mittens and secured her parka hood. The chilled night air hit her face and lungs and took her breath momentarily, but it quickly refreshed and invigorated her in a way she had not anticipated. She felt strength replace the defeated spirit she'd known only moments before.

Leah held up a lantern to see in the darkness. She fed the dogs, then walked well away from the camp to set and bait the two traps she'd brought. There was always the danger of encountering a wild animal, but at this point, the risk was worth taking. Chase wasn't about to see her armed for protection.

"I don't know why he's done this," she said, trudging through the snow with her traps and lantern. Finding a promising spot, Leah stopped and set to work. She prayed as she hid the mechanisms in the snow. "Lord, I don't know what we need, but you do. Please help me to help Jacob and Jayce—even Helaina. Please show me what to do—and when to do it."

Walking back to her tent, Leah was startled by a sound that rose up behind her. She turned quickly, half expecting Chase to have followed her. Instead, the noise sounded again, only this time her gaze went heavenward. There in the night skies danced the northern lights in impressive displays of reds and greens and whites. The sky was ablaze in color.

For a moment, Leah felt her breath catch. The northern lights were one of the most beautiful sights she'd ever known. She'd never gotten tired of this wonder. She remembered seeing them for the first time as a teenager; one of the sourdoughs in Dawson City had told her that if you whistled the lights would move faster, but though she'd tried it, Leah didn't think it worked. Still, she had to admit that the display was breathtaking. It made her feel as though God himself were swirling the skies with some heavenly paintbrush.

"Oh, Father," she whispered. "It's almost as if you are speaking directly to me—as if you want me to know for sure that you are here for me." Leah felt her heart grow warm in her chest. "It is a sign for me; I'm certain of it. A sign that I shouldn't give up hope. You are here." Her voice lowered to a barely audible whisper. "You are here for me."

A peace she'd not known since finding Chase in her house at Last Chance washed over her in waves that matched the pulsating rhythm of the aurora. She had no idea how she would deal with Chase once he finally reunited her with her husband and brother, but Leah felt more confident that, when the time came, she'd know instinctively what to do.

The evening passed quickly, despite Leah's discomfort with such close quarters. When she announced her desire to sleep, Chase tied her hands and feet together, then secured the rope loosely, but effectively, behind her back. Leah didn't protest his actions. She knew he needed the reassurance that he would remain in power. She wanted him to have no reason to doubt her full cooperation.

"You're a beautiful woman, Leah," he said as he pulled a fur around her. He touched her cheek. "We could really benefit each other nicely on this trip."

Leah tried not to react as her stomach churned at the very thought of Chase's intentions. "I have nothing to offer you, Chase. I belong to your brother."

He frowned but moved away from her. "That can always change," he muttered. He said nothing more, nor did he try to touch her again.

Leah drifted off to sleep feeling her peace of mind slip away. If he came to her in the night, she would be defenseless. *God, please keep me in your care. Guard me through the night.*

When she awoke in the morning, Leah felt stiff and achy from having been stuck in pretty much one position all night. Still, she was determined not to complain. Chase slept soundly in front of the tent opening. No doubt he thought this would be just one more barrier to keep Leah from escaping.

"Chase, wake up. I need to check the traps and get the dogs readied for the day," she said as she struggled to sit up. It was impossible. "Would you please untie me?"

"It's still dark outside," Chase muttered.

Leah laughed. "It's going to be dark for several more hours, but I still need to tend to things. Unless, of course, you don't plan on our leaving before it's light."

Chase yawned and unfastened her bonds. "If it were up to me, we'd forget about the others all together."

His words frightened Leah. She suddenly thought, for the first time, that perhaps he would do just that. "I don't want to forget the others. You know that full well." She pulled the rope away from her feet and hands. She decided to say nothing more. "I'll get a fire going. If we've managed to catch something in the trap, I'll do a quick skinning and cleaning and put the food to cook for our breakfast."

Leah didn't wait for a response. Instead, she hurried to secure another oil lamp to light her way outside, then left Chase to his own devices. The dogs stirred and began to whine for their breakfast. She gathered dried brush and took pieces of driftwood that she'd packed on the sled to start a fire. Once that was going, she put a pot of snow on to melt, then set off to check her traps. By the time she returned, the snow would be melted and she could add more to the pot.

There was no other sound except for the sorrowful howls of the dogs. They were grieved that she would go off along the trail without them. Especially Marty. She could hear his distinct cry even as the others joined in.

The first trap revealed a fat fox. Leah smiled. She would save the skin for trading, should they come to a village, but feed the meat to the dogs. It would stretch their meager breakfast and make a hearty addition to the frozen fish. The other trap revealed a hare. Not as fat as the fox, but a good enough size to feed Chase and herself a couple of meals. She would boil the animal, and they could drink the broth and have some of the meat for breakfast. Later in the day they could have the remaining meat for lunch. The skin would be nice to save as well. If she didn't sell it, Leah knew it could be useful to them for lining their clothes or making additional protection for their feet or hands.

She had been working for nearly an hour when Chase finally came outside. It was still very dark, not even hinting at dawn.

"What time is it?" he asked, yawning. "I fell back asleep. Good thing you're a woman of your word." He stretched and sniffed the air. "What's that?"

"Snowshoe hare. I caught one in the trap, as well as a fox. The dogs made quick order of the fox meat, but our rabbit will make two nice meals for us."

"Smells delightful. I guess your traps came in handy."

Leah looked up from the camp stove. "Yes. They always have in the past. If you're ready for something to eat, I can pour you some of the broth. I figured we'd drink the broth and eat a bit of the meat, then save the rest for lunch. Does that meet with your approval?"

"I'll tell you after I see how full I get on broth," Chase replied, sitting down on the ground beside her.

They ate in silence, but all the while Leah kept wondering where they would travel and how far they would have to go. "So are you holding my husband and brother at Mary's Igloo?" The tiny town, if it could even be called a town, had once been a fairly well-populated place. It had originally been called Kauwerak, but when gold came to the area in the early 1900s, a name change had come about due to an Eskimo woman named Mary who offered refuge and warm meals for the miners who were in need.

"They aren't there," Chase said flatly.

Leah felt the food stick in her throat. She quickly grabbed some water to wash down the lump. "Why are we going there, then?"

"I didn't say we were. I just said that was the direction you needed to go."

Leah drew a deep breath and let it out slowly. "I see. So how much farther will we go? Surely it does you no harm to tell me now. We're far from Last Chance. There's no one for me to give the secret to."

"I suppose not," Chase replied, "but I know you to be a very ingenious woman. After all, your survival skills rival mine or any other man I know. If I were to tell you where we were headed, there would be little to keep you from doing me in and slipping away to find them on your own."

"But I gave you my word."

"A lot of people have given me their word before, Miss . . . excuse me . . . Mrs. Kincaid. I don't trust you or anyone else."

"Maybe that's your problem," Leah replied rather flippantly.

"Well, now it's yours as well," he answered, getting to his feet. "Be ready to leave in ten minutes."

Leah watched him walk away. She had no idea where he was headed, but no doubt he'd keep an eye on her the entire time. With a sigh, she quickly went about breaking camp. Within the requisite ten minutes she was ready to roll out. As Chase made his way back into camp, the skies overhead revealed signs of dawn.

"Let's be on our way," he announced, motioning her to the basket. "But this time, I'll drive the dogs."

Leah had no choice but to accept the arrangement. But as she settled into the basket, she felt a despairing chill settle over her once again. Gone was the peace from the night before, and in her heart she cried out again for God to help her.

I'm not a very faithful child, Lord, but I'm trying. Please help us. Help me . . . help Jayce and Jacob. Lord, I don't know what else to do. I just need for you to show me.

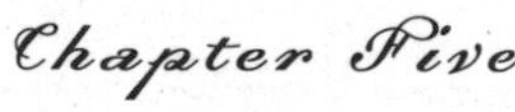

Chapter Five

"What are you saying, Emma?" Jacob looked in disbelief at the woman. "Jayce hasn't been here until now. Not since last summer."

"But he was here. I saw him. He was here with Leah. They left together."

Jacob looked to Jayce. "It must have been your brother."

Fear for Leah mingled with anger—no, rage—at Chase. Jayce clenched his fists. "I'm sure you're right. Which way did they go?"

Emma shook her head. "I don't understand any of this." The bewildered woman took a seat at her table. "I thought Leah wasn't acting herself, but since she'd just arrived and was so tired . . ."

Jacob sat down across from her. "Emma, think back. Tell me everything."

Jayce joined them. He feared any kind of delay, but it was evident they needed more information.

"Well, Leah came home with John. They only arrived a few days ago. The man we thought to be Jayce arrived a few hours ahead of her. We thought from the things he said that he was you. He seemed to know us—at least he acted as though he knew us."

"My brother is a consummate actor. He has fooled an entire nation into believing we are one and the same."

"He was very nice," Emma said, shaking her head. "I would have expected . . . well, he didn't seem bad."

"Chase has a way of putting people at ease and making them believe whatever he wants them to believe," Jayce said. "Don't feel bad."

"Well, he certainly had me fooled. He seemed quite kind and very loving toward Leah. Are you sure she would know the two of you apart?"

Jacob laughed. "Leah would know. She was probably under some sort of threat. At least that's my guess."

Emma nodded. "She did tell me that your brother was in trouble. She mentioned his kidnapping Mrs. Beecham."

"What about Mrs. Beecham—Helaina? Was she here as well?" Jayce questioned.

"No, there was no one but your brother."

Jayce and Jacob exchanged a look of concern. "That's probably how he gained her cooperation." Fear for Helaina edged Jacob's tone. "Leah knew your brother had taken Helaina. If Chase played on this—well, she would probably have done whatever he asked her to do."

"Which was what?" Jayce looked to Emma again. "What were their plans?"

"Leah said they were going north—Kotzebue was mentioned, but she didn't know anything for certain. She said he had a place up north. I asked if she was going to move away from us, and she assured me she wasn't. Oh, I wish I'd paid better attention."

"Chase spent last summer with the *Homestead* exploration group. They were in Kotzebue for some time trying to get native help. You don't suppose he really has a cabin up there, do you?" Jayce turned to Jacob for answers.

"I can't imagine Chase being open enough to confide any such news. If he told her Kotzebue, it's probably just a diversion."

Emma began to twist her hands. "I can't believe this. It's so awful. Leah with a murderer."

Jayce's fear and anger mounted. Chase had gone too far this time. What little sympathy Jayce might have mustered for his brother fled in the realization that Leah was now in jeopardy.

"I wonder what he did with Helaina," Jacob muttered.

Jayce realized Jacob was now pacing instead of sitting with them at the table. "I'm sure she's fine. Chase would have had no way of knowing Leah would return to the village. If he came here merely to get supplies and new dogs, he probably put Helaina somewhere for safekeeping. Somewhere with friends or someone he could pay to watch over her. Maybe he promised them extra food or needed supplies."

Jacob stopped. His face appeared to be chiseled in granite. The expression was one of barely contained rage. "He could have just killed her."

"I don't think he'd do that," Jayce said, shaking his head. "Think about it, Jacob. He knows someone is after him. He had to figure that a search team would be assembled. Besides, Helaina would have told him that we would personally come for him. She knew we were only days behind her arrival into Nome."

Jacob seemed to consider this and calm. "That's true enough. Still, I don't trust your brother."

"I don't trust him, either, but I trust his sensibility when it comes to self-preservation. He won't do anything to jeopardize his safety and survival. Keeping Helaina alive while he gathered supplies and dogs would be in keeping with his manner of doing things," Jayce assured. He could only pray that he was right. It did seem reasonable that Chase would conduct business in such a manner, but it also seemed just as much like Chase to eliminate any extra problems. Jayce would not tell his friend that, however.

"So he came here, and they took ten dogs and supplies," Jacob reiterated. "Emma, did Leah mention how many supplies they were taking? Did she perhaps say that Chase had told her to pack a certain amount of stuff?"

Emma frowned and closed her eyes. "I don't think she ever mentioned it. We only talked briefly. I told her my sister was coming in the summer and that I was expecting another baby. I told her we had plans to go to the States in the summer. I just ran on with talk about me. I feel so ashamed." She opened her eyes, revealing the tears that had welled.

"Emma, this isn't your fault," Jacob said. He came to her and put his hand on her shoulder. "No one blames you for this. Now tell me, did anyone else talk to Leah before she left?"

"Ayoona and Oopick did," Emma recalled. "You might talk to them about how that went. Ayoona's a very astute old woman. She might have noticed something amiss."

"That's true," Jacob said, looking to Jayce. "She might have known something was wrong but not been able to figure out what it was."

"We'll talk to her," Jayce said. "So let me get this right. They left two days ago with ten dogs and a sled packed with goods and headed north—but you know nothing more."

Emma nodded. "I'm really sorry." From one of the other rooms a baby began to cry. "That's Rachel. She's not been feeling well. If you'll excuse me, I need to tend to her."

"You go ahead, Emma. Jayce and I have bothered you long enough. Thanks for helping us."

"I wish I knew more," Emma said, getting to her feet.

"It's all right. It's more than we knew before this," Jacob replied.

Jayce nodded. "It's very useful."

Walking away from the missionaries' house, Jayce couldn't help but feel a tremendous sense of frustration. It had been such a surprise to arrive at Last Chance and find Leah wasn't there. The first people they spoke with had no idea where Leah had gone, but then they'd happened upon Emma as she was hauling in chopped driftwood for her stove. Jayce wished that Emma's comments had given comfort instead of dread.

"We'll find her," Jacob said. "We'll find them both. We're smarter than Chase, and we know this land better than he does."

"But you don't know him. He has an uncanny knack for learning and surviving. I mean, look how long the Pinkerton agents were after him. He knows how to take care of himself, but he doesn't have any regard for others. Now he has Leah and Helaina. I want to be encouraging about this, but I don't know how."

Jacob nodded. "I know. I feel the same way. But if we despair, we might be inclined to admit to defeat and give up."

"I'll never give up." Jayce was resolved to the pursuit of his brother. "If I have to follow Chase all over the world, I won't give up. He's made this more personal than merely pretending to be me. He's taken the woman I love. He's taken the very heart of me, and I won't stand for it."

Karen Ivankov awoke with a start. She sat up in bed and tried to listen to the silence around her. It wasn't even light yet, but something felt very wrong. And then she remembered: She'd had a horrible nightmare about Leah falling through the ice. She was a young girl again—about the age when Karen had taken over guardianship.

Leah was flailing against the water and Karen had tried desperately to reach her, but it was impossible. Then in her dream she saw Jacob walk out across the ice to help his sister. Karen called to him, admonishing him to crawl on the ice to better distribute his body weight. But Jacob wasn't listening and fell through the ice as well.

"Are you all right?" Adrik asked with a yawn.

Karen turned. In the darkness she could only make out her husband's outline. "I had a bad dream about Jacob and Leah. I can't seem to shake the feeling something's wrong."

She could feel Adrik turn over. He reached out to her. "Come here. I'm sure it was nothing."

"I don't know." She snuggled down in his arms. "It seemed so real. Leah fell though the ice, and then Jacob fell through. I couldn't help them, and they were going to . . . well . . . die. I just knew they were going to die."

"Sweetheart, they've already been through life-threatening circumstances. You're probably just dreaming this because of what happened this last summer. Leah and Jacob are no doubt doing just fine. Besides, Jayce is there to help Leah now. He'll help Jacob as well. Don't worry about them. God has it all under control."

Karen cherished the warmth of her husband's arms and felt a small amount of relief as he pulled her closer. Perhaps he was right. It was, after all, just a silly dream.

"So what do you think about my taking that railroad job?" Adrik asked, changing the subject.

"What exactly would you do for them?"

"I'd help the teams that are planning out the route. I'd hunt and trap for them and help them find their way through the forests and such. The governor doesn't want to see the line fall apart again, for there's been a great deal of money put into this venture. The project has halted twice now, and if it stagnates again, he's afraid it will never be completed. He trusts a handful of his old friends to help get the track . . . on track." He grinned at his play on words.

"But you'd be gone for a long time," Karen said, thinking in earnest about the job offer.

"Well, that's what I wanted to discuss with you. I've been thinking about it, and well, I think you and the children should come with me. Move to Seward at least, or better yet, north to the mouth of Ship Creek. There's a huge population there—nearly two thousand people. It's mostly tents, but I'd build you a house."

"I thought you said it would only be temporary."

He frowned. "It would be temporary."

"Temporary as in years? No one is going to build that railroad overnight. Then, too, there's talk about setting aside lands for a national park. No doubt they'll want you to stick around and help with that. Before I know it, they'll decide to run the line all the way to the Arctic, and I'll be wearing a fur parka year-round."

Adrik laughed. "The Arctic would be a very ambitious project to say the least. There's an awful lot of rough terrain between Seward and Fairbanks; just getting it that far would be a miracle. I'm not completely convinced that a railroad line would ever be prudent in Alaska. The marshy ground in the summer would never support the tracks. They'd have to figure something out to ensure its endurance. Just look at all the trouble the earlier builders had. They used green wood and lighter rails. There are a great many places where the line will have to be rebuilt before they can ever move forward to new land."

"But they'll find a way. I know they will." Karen's tone held a sound of resolve. "They built the train over the White Pass," she reminded her husband. "That train line has lasted since 1898, and from all I've heard is still in decent order."

"But most of it is on solid rock. This project is entirely different. I'm not sure what the politicians and railroad barons have in mind, but it's going to take more money than any of them can possibly imagine. Supplies too. I had a letter from Peter Colton just the other day. He's been commissioned to haul supplies from San Francisco to Seward for the railroad. There's going to be good money in it for him, but he agrees that the men involved are really underestimating the cost. Thirty million dollars was originally invested, and those men haven't seen a dime of profit yet. I figure once they get further along, they'll see just how expensive this project is going to be. And to what purpose is it all being built? It's not like this line will truly amount to much."

"Maybe they figure more people will come and settle the territory if they offer more civilized means of transportation," Karen offered.

"Maybe, but if you want my opinion, they're asking a lot. Most folks in the States aren't going to be able to adapt to the isolation. Most are used to the bustle and comfort of city life. You remember those comforts."

"Chicago was a long time ago."

"Not long enough. Now Ashlie talks of nothing but going to the States—to cities where she can enjoy all that the world has to offer."

"Our daughter craves adventure," Karen replied. "It's in her nature to be that way. She has a father who constantly seeks such things."

"Ah, as if her mother never enjoyed those things at all. Wasn't it just the other day you were telling me how bored you were?"

"That was just for the day. I thought a trip to Ketchikan would provide a nice diversion. I wasn't planning trips to Chicago."

Adrik laughed. "Just think about it, Karen. I won't take the job with the railroad if you're against moving to Seward. I can't be that far away for that long. I want my family near me."

Karen leaned up and kissed Adrik's bearded face. "I want to always be near you, my love." She felt much better now. She could almost laugh at her earlier fears. Almost. "Adrik?"

"What?"

"Would you pray with me for Jacob and Leah?"

He chuckled. "You know I will. In fact, you know the moment you spoke of your fears, I prayed for them."

"I know," she sighed. "I just want to hear the words out loud."

Jacob's anxiety was causing him to make mistakes. Mistakes, he figured, that might cost him his life if he didn't start paying attention. But as he loaded the sled for their trip to find Leah and Chase, Jacob found it nearly impossible to focus on the task at hand. His sister was in grave peril. Helaina too. It was bad enough when only Helaina was at risk, but now Leah faced an uncertain future.

I don't know why any of this is happening, Lord, but I pray you'll give me the strength to overcome Chase and his plans. Jacob prayed on but felt little comfort. Sometimes he wondered if he lacked the faith to make things happen. Sometimes he just wanted to sit down with the Bible and not get back up again until all the answers were clear. But even as he'd think these things, Jacob knew there were no easy answers and sometimes, even when a man put forth all kinds of effort, God's ways were still a mystery.

"Jacob, some of us have been talking," John said as he brought Jacob a requested dog harness. "We want to help find Leah."

Jacob took the leather strapping and met his friend's sober expression. "John, that's more than I can ask of anyone."

John shrugged. "So you didn't ask. We decided on our own. We're going to go with you."

"But there's a lot still left to do to make sure the village will get through winter."

"We dried a lot of salmon, more than we ever have in the past. We have seal and whale meat. We're doing good for the winter. We can't let Leah die."

Jacob felt the words cut to his heart. "No. We can't let Leah die."

"So we want to go and help get this man. He needs to go back to the authorities and leave us all to go on with our lives. He's caused a lot of problems."

Jacob nodded but was silent.

"What about that other woman?" John asked.

"Helaina?" Jacob shrugged. "She's in danger too. Chase Kincaid is a ruthless man. He doesn't care who he hurts so long as he gets his own way."

"If he kills them," John said sternly, "I will hunt him like *nanook* and kill him too."

"I don't want you to make pledges like that," Jacob replied, shaking his head. "Chase is as crafty as the bear, but he doesn't need to be gunned down by us. We need to let the law take care of it."

"Sometimes the law can't help you up here. Sometimes the law can't help you at all."

"It may seem that way," Jacob answered, "but God still expects us to obey the laws of the land. Unless, of course, the legal authorities want us to go against God's law. Then we have reason to make a stand." He sighed. "No, we have to trust that God will see us through this, John."

"I don't want to see Leah hurt. She's a good woman," John said, turning to go. "We'll be ready to head out when you are."

"John, I'll only agree to your coming if you promise to head back if we don't pick up the trail within the week. Will you promise me that?"

John waved. "I give my word. I think we'll find them, though. We've got the best tracker in the village going."

Jacob laughed. "And who would that be?"

John gave a sly smile as he glanced back over his shoulder. "Me, of course."

Chapter Six

The cold cut through Helaina and numbed her hands and feet. The old man who watched her vigilantly night and day seemed not to notice her misery, although Helaina had mentioned it more than once.

"Please could I have a blanket or a fur?" she asked once again. "Just something, please. I'm freezing."

She knew the temperature had dropped steadily since Chase Kincaid had taken her from Nome. She had tried hard to keep track of the days, but the darkness was confusing, and the old man seemed to keep no clock or watch.

To her surprise, the man brought her an old wool blanket and dropped it on the ground beside her. With her hands and feet bound, she had great difficulty in wrapping the warmth around her body.

For days now she had plotted and planned how she might escape, but the problem of her clothing always ruined her plans. She was hardly dressed for Arctic winter, yet that was what she would face. She really had no idea of where they were, but Chase had told her he was taking her north, and from what she could figure by watching the sun, it seemed to be true.

The other thing that concerned her was her own health. She felt weakened by the meager meals and poor conditions he'd forced upon her. Her head ached and she'd developed a cough. It wasn't going to be easy to escape under any circumstance, but if she truly were ill, it would make matters much worse. One thing she could count on: Chase would have little, if any, sympathy for her situation.

Helaina tried not to think about what would happen when Chase returned. He'd been nothing but a problem since her brother, Stanley, put her on Chase's trail. Stanley had warned her that Kincaid was a master at keeping himself out of the hands of the law, but Helaina hadn't taken him seriously enough.

She thought back to the high price she'd paid to get the ship's captain in Seattle to take his freighter into the dangerous waters of the far north. She had given him the ridiculous amount of money he'd demanded, although she thought, in some ways, the man saw her request as a challenge. Could he get his ship up and out of Norton Bay before the winter froze him in?

She might have been able to talk him into undertaking the mission for a lower price by challenging his abilities, but Helaina had not had time to appeal to the man's ego. And so she had paid his price and had gotten to Nome ahead of Jacob and Jayce and the Pinkerton agents her brother had sent along.

I wanted to redeem myself, yet now here I sit. And I can't even be sure Jacob and Jayce even know anything about my kidnapping. They may have no idea that Chase took me, and even if they do, they may have no desire to come after him and save me. The thought sunk in as a crashing wave of defeat. What if no one cared that she'd been taken? After all, Stanley was thousands of miles away and still recovering from the wounds Chase had given him earlier in the year. What if Jacob, Jayce, and Leah arrived in Nome and realized Helaina's fate, but upon talking it over, decided to head home instead?

"This is impossible," Helaina muttered.

"You talkin' to me?" the old man questioned.

"No. Not really." She thought to appeal to the man's sympathies. "What if Chase doesn't come back? I'm out here—wherever here is—all alone. Will you help me to safety?"

"No," he replied quite simply.

Helaina frowned. "No? Just like that—you won't help me?"

"Can't help you."

"But why?"

"Chase said to keep you here. I keep you here. You stay here, and then Chase come back for you."

"But," Helaina argued, "what if he doesn't come back? What will you do then?"

"I kill you," the man said with a shrug. "Chase said to kill you if he don't come back."

Helaina couldn't hide her shock. "What? What are you saying? You would just murder me in cold blood? What kind of man are you?"

The old man shook his head. "I go trapping. You talk too much."

"Please don't go. I need to talk to you about this. Look, I'm a very wealthy woman. I could pay you generously if you let me go."

The man just continued pulling on his parka. He appeared to have no interest in Helaina or her money.

"Wait, please. I need to talk to you. I need you to help me. Please . . ." Helaina's words faded. The old man had never given her his name, so she couldn't even appeal to him by using the smallest expression of familiarity.

"Can't help you."

He headed out the door, leaving Helaina so overwhelmed that she burst into tears. Why was this happening? What had she done to deserve such consequences?

She thought about Jacob's faith in God and wished for at least the twentieth time that she had such a faith of her own. At least then maybe she wouldn't feel so alone. She thought of her housekeeper in New York. Mrs. Hayworth had a deep faith in Jesus. She often spoke of the love of God—a love that followed her out of church on Sundays and accompanied her throughout the week, as Mrs. Hayworth loved to say. But for Helaina, it had never seemed real—never important. Now, however, alone in the wilds of Alaska . . . alone with a man who planned to kill her should her murdering captor not return, Helaina thought God seemed very important.

She gazed around at her surroundings, then attempted to adjust the blanket around her shivering form. Jacob would laugh if he could see her now. He would chide her for showing up in Nome without sealskin pants and a fur parka. He would note the silly leather boots she wore—quite suitable for Seattle's weather, but most inadequate for Alaska.

Drying her tears, Helaina pulled and tugged against the knotted ropes that held her fast. She had rubbed her wrists raw, leaving blood on the rope as a constant reminder that she was helpless to overcome this obstacle—this adversary. When had she ever known such a situation? When had money not been able to buy her out of difficulties?

The door to the cabin opened and an old woman Helaina had never seen entered the room. She held in her arms a stack of fur clothing. "This for you," she said, placing the garments on the dirt floor in front of Helaina. "You dress more warm now."

Helaina held up her hands. "I can't get dressed trussed up like this."

The woman stared at her for a moment, then went to the door. She called out in her native language, and it was only a moment before the old man reappeared. She jabbered for several minutes, the old man arguing her comments. Then finally he waved his hands as if to shut her up and went to Helaina. "I untie you, but you get dressed very fast."

"I will," Helaina assured him. Getting loose of her bonds and being given warm clothes seemed like a momentary victory for her situation.

Helaina did as instructed, hurrying to don the heavy pants and parka. There were no mukluks to help warm her feet, but at this point Helaina decided to be grateful for what she had. As the old man replaced her bonds, Helaina thanked him for the clothing.

"I appreciate your kindness. I wish you would tell me your name. I think that as much time as we've spent together, we should at least know one another's names. I'm Helaina Beecham."

The old man looked at her and grunted. "I don't talk to you. You go back and be quiet now. I get our food."

Helaina tried not to be upset. She shrunk back against the wall to the blanket and pallet that had become her prison. Cherishing the warmth, she actually dozed off. She tried to reason a plan for escape as she fell asleep, but the pain in her head seemed to intensify, and her chest hurt when she breathed deeply. The symptoms were starting to worry her. *What if I grow ill and die? Will anyone ever find me? Does anyone even care?*

Leah felt more frustrated as they traveled. Chase not only wouldn't share any details of his plan with her, but for the most part he refused to let her out of his sight. Leah had wanted to leave bits of cloth in case someone, preferably Jayce and Jacob, tracked after them. Her constant prayer was that by now they might have escaped and that they would learn the truth and rescue her. And they would need her to mark the way.

But with Chase continuing to watch her, Leah had a hard time marking their route. She did what she could when Chase allowed her private moments, but mostly she left great messes when she trapped animals. She tried to make sure the site appeared somehow very human in origin so as not to be mistaken for a mere animal kill. Still, she knew the odds were against her.

Leah had more than enough time to let her mind wander, which of course was very dangerous. She began to consider the situation in greater detail and worried that perhaps Chase had already killed Helaina and that he'd never taken Jayce or Jacob captive. What if it had all been a lie? A lie given because of his surprise at finding Leah in camp before he could slip away. This filled her with dread. Chase had no proof of holding Jacob or Jayce, and yet he was smart enough to know that Leah would fully cooperate with him if she thought that complicating the situation would endanger their lives.

That night as they made camp, Leah prayed to better understand her adversary. She figured that a conversation with the enemy might best serve her purpose.

"Why do you hate Jayce so much?"

The question clearly took Chase by surprise. He didn't even take time to try and hide the truth from her. "Because he's made my life unbearable."

"How?" she fired back.

He studied her for a moment, but Leah lowered her gaze and busied herself with food preparation as she expanded her question. "How could one man make you so miserable that you would do the things you've done?"

"You have a brother. Hasn't he ever made you mad? Taken something that belonged to you?"

Leah frowned but refused to look up. "No. Jacob wouldn't hurt me that way."

"Well, Jayce would—and he did. He hurt me by means of his very existence."

"How so?" She dared a quick glance. Sometimes seeing the man look like such a mirrored reflection of her husband was uncanny and unnerving. It was best not to look at him for overlong.

Chase grew quiet for several minutes, then finally spoke. "My brother was the perfect son who grew up to be the perfect man. He could do no wrong. At least he could do no wrong in the eyes of my father, while I could do no right."

"Would you share an example?" She braved the question only because she was hopeful it would somehow help her case.

"My entire life was an example. Jayce learned quickly and easily. Jayce was fearful of punishment and obedient to the laws, whereas to me laws seemed to only be in place for the purpose of breaking. I thought it all rather silly. Jayce had his way of looking at life, and our parents praised him for it and his accomplishments."

"But they didn't praise you?"

Chase looked at her hard. "No. I cannot remember a single word of praise. I remember once when I startled one of the scullery maids as I came down the servants' stairs in the kitchen. She dropped an armload of dishes and I helped her clean up the mess. My father came in as we were finishing up and demanded to know what had happened. I explained and even took full blame for what had happened. I wanted him to see that I could be responsible. Instead, he chided me—no, he yelled at me—for having come down the servants' stairs. He told me I knew better and that this had been caused by my disobedience. I was never so angry with the old man as I was in that moment. It changed everything . . . forever."

He grew quiet and closed his eyes. Leah felt sorry for him and opened her mouth to speak, but closed it as he continued. "My father could have chosen to praise me for helping the maid, for being a man and owning up to my mistake, for being honest. But instead he condemned me. I have an entire lifetime of similar circumstances that play themselves out in my memories. But things were always different for Jayce. Jayce made good marks in school. Jayce saved his money and made wise purchases. Jayce showed ambition and a flair for business. I had none of these abilities, and it only caused my father to hate me more."

"I cannot imagine a father hating his child."

"Then you didn't know my father." Chase's words were full of venom and bitterness. "It wouldn't have mattered who held me in esteem. My father would have used it against me or to show me some object lesson."

"I'm sorry," Leah murmured. And in truth she was. She felt sad for the little boy who must have tried his best to please.

"I don't need your pity," Chase countered.

"That's good," Leah said, handing him a plate of food, "because I offer you none."

He raised a brow. "You are a queer woman, Leah."

"I suppose that could be said of me," she responded. "But I'm also honest. I don't lie."

"Everybody lies, Leah. It isn't possible to live life without lies."

"That is where you are wrong, Chase. Honesty is the only way to live life. If I wrap myself in lies, I'll have nothing but misery. My mother taught me at an early age to cherish the truth—and I do."

"Then tell me the truth now."

She looked at him and shook her head. "I don't understand. Tell you the truth about what?"

"Why did you marry my brother?"

She actually chuckled at this. "Because I love him. I've loved him since I was nineteen."

"That's your truth?"

Leah thought about the question a moment. "No. It's not just *my* truth. It's *the* truth. Jayce is a generous and loving man. He has worked hard to earn a good reputation, for which he's had to fight equally hard to clear—thanks to you. I suppose that's what bothers me the most," Leah said thoughtfully. "For hating a man as much as you claim to hate Jayce, I can't help but wonder why you would so clearly associate yourself with him. Associate yourself so much, in fact, that you take on his personality, his likes and dislikes, even come to Alaska. I think rather than hate Jayce, you truly esteem him—love him. I think you desire more than anything to be like him."

"Hardly that," Chase said, looking away. "I competed with Jayce all of my life. First for our parents' affection and later our teachers' attention. I have known nothing but misery from him, and frankly, it would not bother my conscience in the least if he were to meet with a terrible accident. An accident that ends his life."

Leah tried hard to keep the fear from her voice. "But that's where I believe you're wrong, Mr. Kincaid. I think that you'll go forward in life only so long as Jayce goes forward. I think when you come face-to-face with the prospect of killing your twin, you won't do it, because there is just too much of yourself in Jayce. It would be like killing yourself."

"But we're all killing ourselves in one way or another, Leah. So what if my standards are different from yours?"

Leah shook her head. "You are wrong, Mr. Kincaid. I'm not killing myself. I'm trying hard to survive—no thanks to you."

Chapter Seven

Leah found it impossible to know exactly where they were. She had tried her best to keep a mental picture of their trail—mapping the route in her mind as they continued north and east. To the best of her knowledge, Leah figured they had skirted Kotzebue Sound by some distance and now were moving into interior lands, away from the sea. The weather had calmed somewhat, but from the look of the skies overhead, Leah figured it would begin to snow most anytime.

The other thing that had her worried was the fact that winter had come rather early and hard. She was concerned that the bears would be desperately hunting for food to fatten themselves for winter. She saw signs of bear from time to time but said nothing. If Chase was as smart as he claimed to be, then he'd no doubt see the tracks and scat.

But more than the bears, Leah feared the natives. The tribes that lived farther inland were often warring with the coastal people. There were very few members on either side who would tolerate the others. Some had pacts and agreements that allowed for one or two specified people to come and trade goods, but this had been born out of desperation for foods and furs, not because of any great love between the nations. Now as she and Chase moved farther from the coast, Leah couldn't help but wonder if there would be repercussions for this intrusion.

"You do realize, don't you," Leah began as they readied to move out after a modest lunch, "that the tribe in this area isn't very accommodating toward strangers."

"I have friends in these parts," Chase said, completely unconcerned. "I wouldn't worry about it."

"But I do." Leah pointed to the sled and then to her own clothes. "They will clearly associate us—or at least me—with the coastal natives. There are many hostilities going on between some of these people. They may not realize you are friendly to their party until it's too late."

"By my calculations, we have less than two, maybe three hours to go. I'm telling you it isn't a concern."

Leah shook her head. "We have two or three hours until we reach the others?"

"That's right."

"And what are your plans for us then?"

He shrugged. "I'm not entirely sure. I have a place up north, but this was where I left Mrs. Beecham."

Leah frowned. "What of the others?"

Chase laughed and gathered his things. He checked the rifle he always kept close, then motioned her into the sled basket. "There are no others."

Leah froze in place. "What are you saying?" The tightness in her chest made her realize that she was holding her breath. With a loud exhale and gasp for air, she questioned him again, aware her greatest fear was unfolding. "What are you saying to me? Where is my husband—my brother?"

"I have no idea." He again motioned her to the basket. "I haven't seen either of them."

"But I don't understand. You came to the village knowing they wouldn't be there—otherwise you wouldn't have posed as Jayce."

"I came there because it was close enough to get the supplies and dogs I needed, and Mrs. Beecham had already informed me that my brother and yours were after me. I figured the last place they would look for me would be in Last Chance."

Leah was completely confused. She momentarily considered pushing Chase to the ground and attempting to take off with the sled, but she found she could not move.

"We're wasting time, Leah. Now get on that sled. I'm taking us to where Helaina has been kept. If she's still alive, I'll decide then what to do with the two of you."

Leah moved slowly to the sled. "*If* she's still alive? What do you mean by that? Why wouldn't she still be alive?"

"Because she's a woman, much like yourself, who asks way too many questions. Frank has probably grown quite tired of her by now. It wouldn't surprise me at all if he's already killed her."

Leah swallowed down the bile that threatened to rise in her throat. "Who is Frank?"

"He's a murderer and a thief. Much like myself. You could say that we're kindred spirits. I met him on my trip north last summer. They call him Cutthroat Frank because he likes to do just that—especially while people sleep."

Leah didn't know what to think. For all she knew, Chase could be lying to her again. She took her place in the basket without asking anything more, knowing she needed to formulate a plan. The situation had changed. Helaina was the only person at risk now.

No, that's not true, she thought with a heavy sigh. *I'm at risk, and I have no one but myself to blame for believing a man who's made it his goal to be the best of liars.*

"Is it much farther?" Leah called back to Chase. "The snow is growing worse, and before long we won't have any light at all."

"It's just over the next ridge, if I have my bearings," Chase shouted over the wind.

Leah could see that the dogs were tired. They hadn't had a decent meal all day because Chase had been unwilling to allow Leah to feed them more than a few scraps of frozen meat. For all he seemed to know about driving a team, Chase acted rather unfeeling—even ignorant of their care. When one of the dogs had slowed his pace due to sore feet, Chase had merely shot the dog rather than let him be taken off the line for rest and Leah's ministerings. The act had grieved her greatly, but it once again served to drive home the realization that Chase had no regard for life, human or otherwise.

As they topped the ridge, Leah could see a small cabin. There was a light in the window—a traditional method of helping weary travelers to find their way to safety. But this cabin didn't represent refuge. This might well be the place where Leah and Helaina would meet their fate.

Oh, God, Leah prayed, *help us now. Help us to be wise about our choices—to see what we should do and when.*

Chase brought the team up alongside the cabin and threw out the hook to anchor the dogs firmly. Leah didn't think at this point it was as needed as other times. The dogs were spent. They were more than happy to collapse on the ground for rest.

"Get inside," Chase commanded. He grabbed hold of Leah as she jumped out of the basket.

"I need to take care of the dogs."

"No. Get in the cabin."

"But . . ." She saw something in his expression that halted her words. "All right." She turned toward the cabin door, surprised when it opened and light spilled into the dusky twilight.

"Frank, it's me," Chase called. "Come take care of these dogs for me. I'm half frozen."

The old native man looked at Leah, then grunted. She could see he wasn't happy with the task but nevertheless appeared to accept that it had to be done. Up here, dog teams were the difference between life and death at times. Surely this man understood the need to see the animals well cared for.

Chase pushed Leah through the door of the cabin. She might have fallen, but as if pulled up straight by unseen hands, Leah steadied herself and lifted her eyes to gaze straight into the face of Helaina Beecham.

"Leah!" The woman's expression seemed to be one of hope, until she caught sight of Chase. "You."

Chase laughed. "Miss me, darling?"

Leah stepped to the side. She could see that Helaina was bound by ropes. She could also see that the cabin was small and held few places where escape might be possible.

"You are despicable. Do you realize how long you've been gone?" Helaina questioned before falling into a fit of coughing.

"Well, it sounds as though I've been gone long enough that you've talked yourself hoarse and grown ill in the process."

"Why is she here?" Helaina questioned, regaining her wind.

"She's my additional insurance against my brother's attack. See, after listening to you, I'm just not all that convinced that Jayce will care at all what happens to you."

Leah saw Helaina's expression fall. "But my brother will care," Leah quickly threw out. "He's the one you need to fear in this situation. You've not only taken his sister, but you've taken the woman he cares for."

Helaina looked at Leah oddly, but Chase seemed not to notice. He laughed, but it sounded rather nervous to Leah. "It seems I'm always paying for someone's affair of the heart. Well, let him come. I have a rifle and plenty of ammunition, thanks to your store in Last Chance. I'll deal with him when he gets here—if he gets here."

He motioned to the corner where Helaina sat. "Leah, I want you to sit there and wait for my return. I'll tie you up if I need to."

Leah shook her head. "You don't need to. You know I've pledged my cooperation."

Chase narrowed his eyes. "That was when you thought I had your husband and brother. Now that you know I don't, there's really no reason to expect your good nature. Still, it's enough for you to know that I will kill you and Mrs. Beecham if need be. Now sit there while I bring in some of our supplies."

Leah immediately sat and said nothing more. She didn't want to give Chase any reason to believe her anything but obliging.

When he'd gone, Helaina turned to her. "I don't understand any of this. How did Chase capture you?"

"It's simple enough. He came to Last Chance thinking it would be the only place people wouldn't expect him. He took you at your word that Jacob and Jayce would be after him. You've really got to learn the benefit of keeping some things to yourself. Anyway, he figured no one would be at our home in the village. So he went there to secure dogs and supplies. Apparently he'd been there before because he knew his way around—at least in part. He very nearly pulled it off without a hitch, except I showed up and caught him in the act."

"But why were you there? Where is Jayce . . . and . . . Jacob? Where are the agents my brother sent to Alaska?"

"Jayce and Jacob thought it too dangerous for me and asked that I remain in Nome until someone from the village could come take me home. Jacob sent word via some relatives of our villagers who happened to be heading north. It took longer than I'd hoped, but John finally came for me. As for the Pinkertons, they're in Nome. The two officers Chase shot in Nome died of their wounds. The police chief wasn't in great shape, either, and needed help. My brother felt the agents would be liabilities as he and Jayce moved out across the territory. The agents were ill-equipped and knew nothing of survival in the frozen north. It seemed the best decision."

Helaina nodded. "No doubt. So there's only Jayce and Jacob to come for us?"

Leah leaned back against the cabin wall. For so long she had figured her brother and husband to be prisoners, and while she had hoped they might escape, she hadn't really believed this scenario to be possible.

"They'll come," she said softly. "I just don't know how soon or in what manner. They may have headed back to the village to restock and reorganize."

"But they'll not give up?"

Leah heard the desperation in Helaina's tone. "No. They won't give up."

"Because of you," Helaina said, sounding rather defeated. She, too, fell back against the wall. "They hate me, don't they?"

Leah considered the question. "They aren't happy with you, Helaina—that's for certain. Your actions caused problems for everyone. It caused the death of two good men, and now it's risking the lives of other good men. What in the world possessed you to leave ahead of us and pull that stunt in Nome?"

"I had a job to do."

"Your brother had relieved you of that job, as I recall."

Helaina was undeterred. "You are just as determined a woman as I am. I know that if you were given a task, you would seek to accomplish it no matter the cost."

"I wouldn't risk the lives of other people. Not just to satisfy my ego."

Helaina opened her mouth to speak but instead fell into a fit of coughing.

Leah could hear the hacking, unproductive sound. "Does your chest hurt—down deep?"

"Horribly. Every breath cuts me like a knife, right here." Helaina pointed to her lower ribs on the left side.

"It's probably pneumonia. I have some herbs, but I don't know if Chase will allow me to treat you."

For several moments Helaina said nothing, and then she surprised Leah with her question. "Why did you say that Jacob cared for me?"

Leah was quiet a moment before saying, "Because I believe he does, even though it wasn't my right to say so. I said it because I wanted to ensure that Chase knows you are as important to my brother and husband as I am. Otherwise, I'm afraid he might very well kill you simply to be rid of the responsibility."

Helaina nodded. "I'm afraid he might just do that. He has no conscience."

"Be that as it may, we have to figure a way to outsmart him."

"Yes!" Helaina seemed to gain momentum. "We have to capture him and get him back to Nome, where my brother's men can take him into custody."

Leah eyed her for a moment. She was completely serious. The thought of capturing Chase was far from Leah's mind. "I meant only that we need to find a means of escape. Turning the tables on Chase and taking him hostage is not in my plan."

"But it must be. He's a criminal. He's the reason your husband nearly died for crimes that were not his doing."

"No, Helaina. You are the reason my husband nearly died for crimes that were not his doing."

Helaina looked stunned by Leah's words. "You can't mean to hold that against me. I was doing a job. I realized there were discrepancies and I worked to resolve them. I am also the reason your husband's name was cleared."

"I suppose so," Leah replied, "but I still fail to see why I need to play bounty hunter. I have no desire to risk my life to capture Chase Kincaid. I want to figure a way out of here and do it as quickly as possible. Either you're with me or you're against me. What's it to be?"

"Please listen to me, Leah," Helaina said, lowering her voice. The pained expression on her face indicated the cost of talking so much. "I know this is a difficult situation, but I need you to help me. Chase must be taken into custody or he will continue to kill. He's proven that over and over."

"My point exactly. We need to get away from him and let others who are more qualified take that matter into hand."

"But I am qualified."

"You're also desperately sick. If you don't get treatment . . . and soon," Leah said quite seriously, "you'll most likely be dead within a week."

Helaina shook her head. "That cannot be. I'm not that sick."

"You are. You're burning with fever—it's clear by the glazed look in your eyes."

"I'm freezing in here. I can't possibly have a fever."

"You're chilled because of the fever. I know it makes no sense, but you can trust me on this one. I know medicine, and I know you're sick." Leah reached out her hand and touched Helaina's forehead. "You're burning up."

Helaina refused to give up. "Leah, I know I can make it with your help."

"But the only help I'm offering you is for escape. I'll gladly help you to sneak out of here and head home. But I will not lift a finger to help you apprehend Chase. Do you understand me?"

"No. I don't understand any of this. My brother nearly died at the hands of Chase Kincaid. Your husband nearly faced the gallows because of this man. Now your own brother will put his life in jeopardy to save you and me, and you selfishly worry only about saving your own life."

Leah had taken all she could stomach. Her anger toward Helaina had only grown as the woman continued to argue her point. Folding her arms against her chest, Leah closed her eyes and prayed for strength to hold her tongue and not lose her temper completely.

"You can't just ignore this and hope it will go away," Helaina said in a gruff whisper. The men were returning and at the sound of the door crashing open, Leah startled. "They aren't going to just leave you alone to plan our escape."

Leah threw a glare in Helaina's direction, hoping that Chase and Frank would be too inundated by the winds to hear what the ninny had just said.

"If you don't hold your tongue," Leah said, leaning against Helaina's ear, "I'll only plan *my* escape."

Chapter Eight

God bless our girl," Jayce said, holding up a strip of red checked material. "I don't know how she's managed to do this with Chase no doubt watching her every move, but I'm glad she did."

"She's resourceful," Jacob agreed. "It's evident she's been trapping along the way. The kills have been clearly made by humans. There are trap marks by the tree."

"So she's at least allowed that much freedom," Jayce said, analyzing the situation. "Still, I wonder why she hasn't tried to get away from Chase."

"No doubt he's keeping her tied up most of the time," Jacob offered. "I can't see him allowing her any real freedom. He has to know she's dangerous—at least in the sense of being able to care for herself."

"I'm betting he's threatening her as well." Jayce shook his head and walked back to the sled. "He's probably told her that if she so much as raises a finger against him, he'll kill her."

"But Leah wouldn't be afraid of that." Jacob came to where his own dog team waited. "I'm guessing that if there's a threat, it's against us or Helaina. Leah wouldn't be cautious in regard to herself, but she would endure hell itself to see you or me safe."

"Yeah, you're probably right." Jayce was in no mood to contemplate his brother's way of doing things, but he knew it was important that they keep a clear picture in mind when dealing with Chase. The more they considered what was driving him and why, the better off they'd be in the long run.

"Where do you suppose he's going?" Jacob asked.

"I keep asking myself that. We know Chase spent time up north this past summer; he must be returning to a place he's familiar with."

"I can't figure out how he knows so much. It's almost as if he can read your mind. He's able to mimic your interests and abilities enough that he took your place on the *Homestead* last summer."

Jayce nodded. "All I can figure is that he's been watching me. Maybe shadowing me throughout Alaska. Maybe he's even lived up here for a time."

"Well, we know he hasn't spent all of his time up here. After all, you've been sighted all over the world . . . or rather Chase has been sighted."

"I know." Jayce sat on the edge of the basket and pulled out some jerked meat to eat. "I guess none of it makes sense—maybe it never will."

"Right now the only thing I care to make sense out of," Jacob said, moving toward his dogs, "is where he's heading and what he plans to do once he gets there."

Leah took the bowl from Frank and nodded. "Thank you."

"Why are you thanking him. That . . . that . . . meat," Helaina said in a tone that wavered between disbelief and disgust, "is spoiled."

Leah waited until Frank left the room before answering. "It's seal meat and yes, it's gone a little rancid, but it will give you strength. It's part of the supplies I brought, and it won't be that bad. You need to eat it."

"I won't." Helaina turned up her nose and fell back against the wall.

"You have to or you'll never have the strength to leave when the time comes."

"I already told you—without Chase, I won't go."

Leah frowned and popped a piece of the seal in her mouth. "Suit yourself."

Helaina said nothing for several minutes, then finally she reached out to take a piece of the seal. "I can't go without him, Leah. You need to understand this and help me."

"I won't risk our lives to capture him. That is a job I'm happy to leave in the hands of Jacob and Jayce. They are stronger and better equipped to deal with someone like Chase. I would think that by now you would have learned that lesson. Your brother and several other Pinkerton agents were unable to keep up with Chase, much less capture him. You should know it won't be easy to turn the tables on him and take him captive. He has ammunition and weapons, and he's not afraid to do what he must in order to serve his own purpose."

"It doesn't matter." Helaina coughed quietly. "I can't leave without him."

"Then you'll most likely die on the trail."

Chase chose that moment to come into the cabin. Leah was relieved to see that he'd brought her pack. "Is this what you wanted?"

Leah nodded. "Feel free to go through it. I have no weapons. There are just herbs and remedies that I thought we might need on the trip. I believe Mrs. Beecham has pneumonia, and I would like to give her some medicines to help her. Would that be all right?"

Chase opened the bag and began to rummage through it. "I don't know why you should bother." He looked up at Helaina, his expression void of emotion. "If she dies naturally, it's one less murder in my name."

"You can't just keep killing, Chase. You have to stop this madness and—"

"And what? And they'll overlook the other murders and let me go? If I let you save Mrs. Beecham, will they show me mercy and only put me in prison to rot away the rest of my life instead of hang me?"

"I can't say what they'll do or not do," Leah admitted. "I just thought maybe you were tired of such things. Wouldn't you like to stop killing?"

He threw her the bag and laughed. "Killing people is no more or less important to me than any other survival skill. Do you tire of trapping and killing animals for meat or does the possibility of an empty belly or death on the trail keep you going? I won't be taken alive—you both must know that by now. I'm backed into a corner by those who hunt me. And you, Leah, above all others, should know what trapped animals are capable of doing."

He was right. She did know. A trapped animal was capable of chewing off its own leg to get itself out of the trap. Chase Kincaid was the kind of man who would do whatever it took to keep himself free.

"Fix her whatever you have to, but then we're going to be on our way. I can't just sit around here and wait for Jayce and your brother to catch up to me. I figure once we put a few more days and storms behind us, they will be hard-pressed to find any kind of tracks."

Leah knew the storm from the night before had probably obscured any sign of their trail. She could only hope that the bits of cloth she'd tied to the dwarf birch near their camp the night before had survived the winds and snows.

"I'll need some hot water," Leah said before Chase exited the house.

He turned to look at her, sizing up the situation. "I'll have Frank bring you some."

With that he was gone and Leah took up the pack to search its contents. "Well, are you any more convinced of the futility of staying?"

Helaina shook her head. "I cannot go without him. You do what you have to do, and I will do what I have to do."

"If you're still alive to do it," Leah said rather dryly.

"I've been thinking about what you said regarding the railroad job," Karen said as she poured Adrik a cup of coffee. "I think if you believe it to be the best thing, we should do it. I think the boys might actually enjoy going north. Ashlie will be difficult about it, but she would give us trouble even if we did nothing more than stay here."

"I'll talk to her," Adrik said, smiling. "She'll come around."

"When do you want to make the move?"

"We should probably go before it gets too cold. We don't have to worry about the harbor freezing, but the waters will get rough. I don't want to place anyone's life in jeopardy."

"Well, after praying about this, it seems to be the right thing to do," Karen said.

"I think we have to accept the very real possibility that Alaska will be a completely different place in a few short years. We might as well do what we can to have a say in its development. After all, we know the land better than those from the States."

"True. I think there are those, however, who won't care what the truth is about this land. Besides that, what about the war in Europe? It shows no signs of letting up and being resolved. Did you see the article in the paper from Seattle? The one about that English nurse the Germans murdered?"

"How could I not?"

"What kind of people does it take to kill a woman who worked to help so many? Edith Cavell was the head of the nursing staff there in Brussels."

"Yes, but she aided the enemy, as far as Germany was concerned."

"She helped her countrymen and others to escape prison camps and certain death. I know she was an enemy to the Germans, but she's a hero in this country. I just can't believe that anyone would put a woman to death for simply helping people to live."

"The situation seems to be escalating out of control. Boys are dying and the world seems to be in the fight of its life. Makes me glad to be so far removed."

"But with aeroplanes and trains coming to Alaska, it won't be that way for long."

Adrik tossed back the coffee and got to his feet. "No, I suppose it won't. Still, I'd rather have some kind of say in what's happening than to turn away and pretend it won't come if we ignore it."

"I agree," Karen said with a sigh. "I just wish it weren't the case. I've truly come to love the north, just as my parents loved it. Their missions work up here to the Tlingit people was something I didn't completely understand. In my youth I thought them rather mad for leaving the comforts of the real world." She grinned at this reference. Ashlie often chided her parents that she deserved to at least try life in the "real world" before being forced to spend the rest of her life in the frozen north.

"The real world," Adrik repeated and nodded. "I can't say I've ever seen such a place, other than what we have right here." He frowned and looked at Karen. "Perhaps we should consider sending Ashlie to live with some of your family in the States."

Karen could see he was serious. It was the first time they'd really discussed the possibility. "She won't be happy with the move to Seward—that much is true. Still, I hate to see our family separated."

"She's almost grown. Maybe we could get her into a regular school down there and let her see just how the *real* world operates."

Karen considered it for a moment. "If you think it's for the best."

"What do you think?"

Karen got to her feet and came to where her husband stood. "I think Ashlie will leave us no matter what. Perhaps if we send her on our terms and with our blessing, she'll feel less rebellious and more appreciative of what she already has."

Adrik nodded. "Why don't you send a telegram and make some arrangements? We'll send some extra money with her. That should see to her physical needs."

"My family would never take money from us—you know that." She was still surprised by Adrik's sudden turnaround. Never before had he advocated sending their daughter south. Perhaps it was all God's timing, she thought.

"Well, try to send it anyway. If nothing else, tell them to keep it for Ashlie's return trip home."

Karen sighed. "If she ever does come home."

Leah helped Helaina into the sled basket. Chase had demanded they leave immediately, and while Leah knew Helaina was in no shape to travel, there was nothing she could say or do to persuade Chase to stay.

"My brother will be closing in. I can feel him coming."

Leah shook her head. "He won't stop just because you keep pressing on. You've crossed a line this time. You have to know that."

Chase shrugged. "I was always crossing lines as far as Jayce was concerned." He motioned to Helaina. "Is she going to make it?"

"I doubt it," Leah stated matter-of-factly. "You're taking her out into the elements, and the trip will only get rougher. She's very sick. I think you should leave her here."

"I can't. Besides, Frank would kill her for sure. He says she talks too much. He'd cut her tongue out at the very least."

Leah refused to show any shock at what Chase said, but inwardly she shuddered. "Very well. I'll do my best to help her. But it won't be easy."

"Nothing in my life has ever been easy," Chase said bitterly. "I don't know why this should be any different."

"Did you get my traps repacked?" Leah asked, looking at the sled basket.

"They're near the back. Can you both ride in that basket?"

Leah looked at the sled and nodded. "It'll be hard on the dogs. The going will be slower."

"I've added the dogs I stole out of Nome. They aren't the quality that your brother has raised, but they'll get by and give us a better time of it—at least for a while."

"All right, but they're also going to require more food. Does Frank have some for you to take along?"

Chase laughed. "Frank has very little to spare for any reason. We'll get by. You'll trap us something nice and perhaps I can shoot us a caribou or bear. Bear seem to be plentiful around these parts, and they make good eating."

Leah nodded. "It'll take a bear to keep this brood in decent shape to make the trip. I don't know where you plan to take us, but be advised, these dogs won't last long without a decent supply of food."

"It's duly noted. Now get in that basket with Mrs. Beecham. Perhaps your added warmth will help her to heal."

"And if she dies?" Leah questioned.

"Then let me know so we can dispose of the body." His callous attitude reflected the deep void in his soul. "I'm sure the dogs would love it."

They moved out quickly, Chase sparing no consideration of the team. Leah felt sorry for the brood. They were well rested, but their rations had been quite meager. Chase hadn't even allowed Leah to care for them; instead, he'd relegated her to play nursemaid to the fading Helaina.

"Where does he intend to take us?" Helaina asked groggily. The medicine Leah had given her had caused her to breathe a bit easier, but it also induced sleep. Frankly, Leah was glad for the silence.

"I don't know. I tried to get him to leave you behind. I thought maybe Frank could get you to safety, but Chase insisted you be a part of this journey."

"Good." Helaina nodded. "I can . . . watch . . . him that way."

Leah shook her head and eased back against the basket. "You can hardly watch the passing scenery, much less keep track of Chase Kincaid."

"I haven't found anything," Jayce said in complete frustration. "How about you?"

Jacob studied the landscape a few more minutes, then answered. "There's nothing here. Maybe John will have had a better time of it. He really is the best tracker. He should be back soon."

Jayce pulled off his eye protection and stared out across the white landscape. He was grateful for the little wooden slit goggles Jacob had given him, but at the same time he felt they restricted his vision too much for close-up work like tracking. "There's got to be some signs . . . somewhere. Two, three people can't just disappear without a trace."

"The storms have wreaked havoc with the trail, Jayce. You know that as well as anybody. We might as well just sit it out and wait for John. Hopefully he'll have some good news for us."

They waited for nearly an hour before John and most of the others returned. "We killed a bull caribou two miles up. I left a couple men to prepare the meat. We need to feed the dogs." John smiled and added, "Need to feed me too."

Jacob nodded. "Any sign of the trail?"

"I think so. I found some tracks buried deep. Looks like they went that way." John pointed toward the northeast. "I know some people up there. Bad folks. Not good."

"Just the kind of company my brother prefers," Jayce said, repositioning the goggles. "How about I head out that way on snowshoes, and when you get the dogs taken care of you can catch up to me. The day is clear and bright. You shouldn't have any trouble tracking me."

"It would be better if we stayed together. We don't need to lose you as well."

Jayce picked up his gun. "We can't let them get much farther, Jacob. You know that as well as I do."

Jacob put out his hand and touched Jayce's shoulder. "I know. But I also know there is strength in our numbers. We have food and we have good trackers. We need to be sensible about this. You and I know this territory to a point, but John and his men know it even better. This is their homeland. Not for five or ten years, but for a lifetime. We have to trust them."

Jayce understood the logic in what Jacob said, but he didn't like it. Leah was out there somewhere, and Chase was her captor. He cringed when he thought of what might have already happened. He didn't trust his brother to be honorable . . . even though he said otherwise to keep Jacob from worrying about Helaina. Chase was a man who would take whatever pleased him, but he was also a man bent on revenge. How better to avenge the wrongs he considered done him? He would know that in hurting Leah, he would hurt Jayce more than any other way. He would also know that Jayce would never stop coming for him if he did hurt Leah. And perhaps that was what Chase wanted more than anything: He wanted Jayce to come for him. Maybe he even wanted Jayce to end this whole miserable thing. There was no way of telling.

Turning away in defeat and frustration, Jayce waited for Jacob to finish securing the dogs. *Lord, this isn't easy. In fact it's the hardest thing I've ever done,* Jayce prayed. "I ask that you protect Leah from my brother. He's evil and he cares nothing about anyone but himself."

"Did you say something?" Jacob asked, coming alongside Jayce.

"I was just praying," Jayce said. He drew a deep breath and let it out slowly. "Are we ready to move out?"

"Yes."

Jayce started to walk away, but Jacob stopped him. "John says we're very close. He doesn't think they're very far now."

Jayce nodded without turning around. "Good." He said nothing more. In his mind he wondered how the matter would resolve itself when they found Chase. Jayce hated the thought that he would have to kill his brother in order to free Leah, but deep inside his heart, Jayce was convinced that it would probably be the only way. "Let's get going."

Chapter Nine

The weather cleared, but the shortened days gave them less and less sunlight by which to traverse the land. Leah constantly looked for landmarks that might help her find her way back home. She tried to memorize the trail, as well as figure out ways in which she might actually escape Chase. She needed dogs and a weapon. Those things would ensure her success. Without either, she wasn't convinced she could make it.

Helaina seemed no better. The herbs were causing her to sleep, but she was still feverish. Leah could only pray that God would help them. There was very little chance that Leah could get the sickly Helaina away from Chase, even if a moment of escape presented itself. Of course, Helaina had already stated on several occasions that she would not go.

Chase stopped them for the night and, after allowing Leah to help him set up camp, tied her up with Helaina. "You don't need to trap tonight. We need to leave no sign of our being here. I won't even have a fire." He stared out into the growing darkness as if sensing his brother's presence.

"I'm going to backtrack and make sure we've left no signs along the way," he told her. He gathered a small pack and slung it on his back. "Keep quiet."

"What if we're attacked?" Leah questioned. "You've seen the bear tracks, not to mention wolf and lynx. There are plenty of animals out here—no doubt hungry animals."

"The dogs will raise a ruckus if anything comes near. If that happens, I'll hear it and come back. I won't let anything happen to you." He leaned down and touched her cheek. Leah jerked back, causing him to laugh. "I could make you just as happy as Jayce has."

"Hardly," Leah replied.

He eyed her for a moment, then glanced at the sleeping Helaina. "In time, I'll prove it to you. We could be quite happy up here together. You know the land and the people. I have skills as well. Once Jayce and your brother are out of the way . . ." He let his words trail off.

Leah looked away lest he see the tears that were forming. She had noticed Chase watching her more closely. His eyes held a kind of hungry look that she had never seen. Chase frightened her more and more, and she knew her escape must come soon or he might well act upon that hunger.

Helaina stirred and opened her eyes a short time later. With Chase gone, Leah leaned down to speak. "We have to get out of here soon," she told Helaina.

"I told you, I can't go." Helaina fell into a spell of coughing and gasping. The pain was evident with each breath she drew.

"You can't stay," Leah replied. "You're very sick. I need to get you to safety."

"I'm feeling much better. Look, while we're on the trail it should be easy to overpower him. There are two of us."

"Two of us who are tied up. What do you suggest? Should I gnaw through the ropes?" Leah's sarcasm was not lost on Helaina.

Helaina struggled to sit up. "I am better. I feel stronger. Just help me in this. We can overpower him. Then you can get us back to Nome."

"No. I want no part in taking Chase prisoner. I've told you that before. I won't risk our lives that way. We need to get away from him."

"I've been thinking," Helaina said. "We can knock him over the head while he sleeps. Then we can tie him up."

"Again, how do you propose to do this when we are tied up nightly?"

Helaina nodded. "I've been thinking about that too. You are allowed to prepare dinner each evening. You could hide your *ulu* and retrieve it after he goes to sleep."

The thought had already occurred to Leah, but Chase always kept close track of the tools she used. Especially in skinning the animals and preparing the meat. "Chase said that I can't trap tonight. He's not even going to allow us a fire for supper. He's too worried about Jayce and Jacob spotting us."

"Well, he'll want food sooner or later. When he does, you can hide the knife. Or wait . . ." Helaina said, glancing around. "What about your herbs? Might you have something in there that could put him to sleep? That would be perfect. You could put it in his food."

"How do you propose I do that without putting it in our food as well?" Leah questioned. "Chase is hardly going to eat food that we refuse to touch. What then?"

"There has to be a way, Leah. I'm sure of it."

"Like I said, he's not even allowing for a fire tonight, much less for me to prepare food. We'll probably eat nothing more than dried salmon and crackers until he feels we're safely out of Jayce and Jacob's reach."

"Just keep it in mind, Leah. Sooner or later he's going to want something hot again. I'm sure of it. Just be ready for the moment."

Leah thought about Helaina's suggestion long into the night. By the time they were on the trail several hours before dawn, she was beginning to think there might be some merit to Helaina's plan. She could put herbs in the food, after setting some food aside for herself, then drug not only Chase, but Helaina as well. It wouldn't be easy to pull off, but so far it was the best plan Leah could come up with.

When they stopped again the next evening, Chase seemed far less concerned about being spotted. He allowed Leah to go set her traps but followed her at a distance. His gaze never left her and Leah hated the feeling. When she walked back to where he was standing, Chase seemed quite lost in his thoughts. At least she'd thought him to be. When she walked past him, however, Chase reached out and pulled her without warning into his arms.

"Let me go," she said, struggling against him.

"You're really very beautiful. I can see why my brother would fall in love with you. I can see why he would hunt me down to take you back."

Leah fought his hold, but Chase was much stronger. "Leah," he murmured against her ear. He slipped his hand inside her parka. "I want you."

The lust and desire in his voice froze Leah in place. "Let me go, Chase. You have no right to touch me like this."

He pulled back to look in her eyes. In the growing darkness, Leah could barely see his face, but she could feel the intensity of his stare. "I've always taken what I wanted," he said, his voice edged with anger. "I want you, Leah. And I mean to have you." He forced her to the ground and threw himself on top of her to hold her still. "We can do this the easy way or with great difficulty and pain. It's up to you."

"It's never been up to me," Leah said, still struggling against him. "You took that choice from me back in Last Chance."

Jacob stared out across the landscape as the first hint of light touched the horizon. Their progress had been slow but steady. The day before they had managed to find the cabin where Chase had held Helaina and Leah. They had waited in the dark, keeping watch, and when the old man tried to sneak into their camp, John had wrestled him to the ground. The old man had admitted everything. He had told of knowing Chase from encounters with him earlier in the year. He had admitted to being well paid in supplies to hold Helaina while Chase went for additional goods and animals.

Jacob wasn't at all sure what they should do with the man and his wife. He knew they couldn't leave them unrestrained or they might well come after the party. On the other hand, they couldn't just tie them up and leave them to die. Finally John had come up with a solution. He arranged for two of his men to transport the couple to the nearest village. John had an arrangement with a village just to the west of where they were situated. He felt certain that once his men presented the couple and explained the situation, the village elders there would take the matter under consideration and keep them prisoner until the proper legal authorities could arrive to arrest the old man.

"I know they're out there somewhere," Jacob muttered. He gazed to the skies. "You know where they are, Lord, and I'm just asking that you keep my sister and Helaina safe, and that you would guide me to their hiding place. We need your help now more than ever."

"He's getting better at covering his tracks," John said as he joined Jacob on the ridge. "But he's not as good as he thinks."

This caused Jacob to smile. "How far ahead of us are they?"

"Three, maybe four, days. They're still following a straight path," John said, pointing. "Heading north. Just like they've been doing since they left that old man's place."

Jacob nodded. "We're not gaining on them quickly enough. Dare we push on, even in the dark, and trust that they will continue this path?"

John looked north across the horizon. "I cannot say, Jacob. If we trust that and they go west or east, we will lose a lot of time."

It was the very thing that Jacob had already considered. "But if we don't start taking some chances soon, we'll never catch up with them. They have the lead and the advantage of knowing where they're headed. We can't just follow at this slow pace and hope to overcome them."

"Then I would go north. We can keep pushing . . . travel during the night. When light comes, I can check for signs."

"I think that's our best chance," Jacob said.

"Our best chance for what?" Jayce asked, joining them.

"We're going to press on through the night. We'll change out drivers and rest in the basket as the other one drives. When light comes, John will check for signs and see if we're still on the right trail."

"But that's a big risk," Jayce countered. "What if we lose the trail in the night?"

"We were just discussing that," Jacob admitted. "But if we do nothing, we'll never gain any ground. We've noted that they are moving steadily north. Hopefully they will continue that way, but even if they don't, we can always backtrack and find where they changed course. I'm just afraid if we don't take a chance, we won't catch up with them until Chase reaches wherever he's headed and has a chance to dig in and defend himself against us. We'll have a much better situation if we can catch him out here on the open trail."

Jayce nodded. "I suppose you're right. I trust your judgment in this."

"We need to go," John stated firmly. "We will go fast and travel round the clock. I'll get the dogs ready." He headed back to the teams and Jayce followed after him.

Jacob watched them walk away. He wished fervently that he had a better feeling about their situation, but he couldn't muster up much hope. He felt a deep sense of dread and frustration. The old man back at the cabin had told him that Helaina was very sick and he figured she'd die. The thought of it troubled Jacob's heart like nothing else. If she died, he knew a part of his heart would die as well.

Leah tried not to think about what Chase had done to her. She had hoped . . . prayed that he would not take such liberties. She had wanted to believe that there was some good in Chase—something buried down deep inside that would keep him from hurting her. But she'd been wrong.

Now as she sat in the basket with Helaina, she wiped at the tears that would not stop flowing. How could God let Chase rape her? She'd tried her best to be kind and share God's love with Chase. She had presumed that in return, God would keep her from harm. Wasn't that the way it was supposed to be? If she trusted God, put Him first, and did everything in accordance with the Bible, God would protect her. But He hadn't.

Trembling, Leah tried to regroup her thoughts. It was bad enough to feel hatred toward Chase, but worse still to feel such isolation from God. She tried to rationalize that what Chase had done needn't change her—shouldn't steal away her peace and faith in God's goodness—but the more she thought about what had happened, the more she could still feel his hands on her body. And the more she relived what Chase had done, the more she longed to kill the man.

She drew a ragged breath and forced down the lump in her throat. *How can I ever face Jayce again? How can I ever hope for him to comprehend what this means? He'll never understand or want me after this. Chase has been nothing but a thorn in his side since they were young. Now this has happened.* She shook her head. Jayce could never want her back after this. She would be better off dead.

Chapter Ten

Karen struggled with her fears for Leah and Jacob. She couldn't shake the premonition that they were in some kind of danger. She tried to pray about it, but often she felt her prayers reached no higher than the ceiling. Adrik offered comfort and support, but Karen knew it was a burden she would carry until she found out for certain they were safe. Now standing at the Ketchikan dock, preparing to bid her firstborn good-bye, Karen didn't know if anything would ever feel safe or normal again.

"Mama, you mustn't worry," Ashlie declared. "Cousin Myrtle said she would take good care of me."

Karen tried to smile. Her elderly cousin had written an enthusiastic letter upon learning that Ashlie had a desire to travel south. Myrtle had pledged to be the best of chaperones, assuring Karen that Ashlie would be properly dressed and arranged in the third pew of the First Seattle Lutheran Church every Sunday. Furthermore, she would pay for the girl to attend a very fine finishing school there in the Seattle area.

Knowing that Myrtle was left a wealthy, but childless, widow, Karen had no doubt that the old woman was lonely and in need of someone to spoil. Ashlie, on the other hand, was a young woman in need of an adventure. The two seemed mismatched, but Karen felt a peace about sending her daughter to the older woman. At least as much peace as a mother could have when parting with her only daughter.

"I know you'll be fine," Karen said. She reached out to touch an errant wisp of her daughter's strawberry blond hair. Ashlie had pinned it up in a very adult manner and topped her coiffure with a dainty hat she'd actually made. Karen was impressed with the girl's skills but knew it wouldn't matter now if she complimented her on such. Ashlie's mind and heart were set on the journey to come.

Karen forced a smile. "I can't say this is easy. One day you may be a mother, and you will know just how difficult such a separation can be."

Ashlie hugged her mother tightly. Karen thought perhaps she did this more for herself than for Karen. "I know it's not easy for you, Mama. I'm just grateful you are allowing it." She pulled back and looked into her mother's eyes. "I don't want to appear as though I don't care about your feelings . . . but I'm just so excited. I feel as though everything good is about to happen to me all at once."

Karen nodded and smiled. How could she not be enthusiastic? The child's excitement was almost contagious. Even her brothers were jostling around the pier in animated wonder.

"Well, as soon as your father returns with the Reverend Mulberry, I suppose you'll board the ship." Karen looked across the crowd of people to where the southbound *Horatio* was docked. "You mind your manners and listen to whatever the reverend tells you. I don't want any bad reports on how you caused him undue worry."

"I will be as good as the boys on Christmas morning," Ashlie teased. "But I still don't see why the reverend has to travel with me. I'm almost sixteen."

"Ashlie, this is not a civilized land. For all of our pretenses at being one, we hardly come close. Of course, from what I remember of so-called civilized lands, they could be far more dangerous than anything you've grown up knowing." She hugged Ashlie close again. "Oh, you will be careful, won't you?"

Ashlie laughed. "Of course I will. Now stop worrying. Remember what you said about worry being a sin? You said it was like saying that God couldn't do what He had promised. It was like calling God a liar."

Karen drew a deep breath and nodded. "I guess I thought you weren't listening to such things."

Ashlie grasped her mother's arm. "I was listening to that and a whole lot more. Please . . . don't be afraid. I'll come and see you soon. You'll see."

Karen knew she had to be brave. She squared her shoulders and drew in another deep breath. "I know you'll have a wonderful time. Don't forget to write to me and tell me everything."

"Papa's coming!" nine-year-old Christopher declared. "See! There he is with the reverend."

Karen turned to look in the direction her son pointed. Sure enough, there was her bear of a husband towering over the rather petite Reverend Mulberry. They looked almost comical in each other's company. As they approached, Karen put on her bravest smile. "Reverend, it's good to see you. I can't thank you enough for acting as a traveling companion to our daughter."

"It is I who am blessed," the older man said, pushing up wire-rimmed glasses that perpetually rested on the end of his nose. "How could I refuse such sweet company? Or such a generous donation to bettering my own quarters. I don't believe I've ever had a stateroom to myself. I think it all so fortuitous that I should be traveling home to Illinois just when you needed a companion for your daughter."

Karen looked to her husband and back to the reverend. "God knew exactly what we needed, and it was our pleasure to improve your journey. You are, after all, guarding one of our most precious gifts."

He nodded. "Indeed, Miss Ashlie is a remarkable girl. I've no doubt she will excel in her finishing school."

"You have the address and money I gave you to hire transportation to Myrtle's house?" Adrik asked Ashlie.

"It's all right here," Ashlie declared, patting her small purse. "I shall keep it with me at all times."

The final boarding was called for all passengers bound for Seattle. Ashlie looked momentarily panic-stricken, and then the expression was replaced by one of sheer joy. "It's time!" She threw herself into her father's arms.

Karen watched the scene play out, feeling almost as though she were watching from a dream. Ashlie tousled Christopher's hair and then embraced him for just a moment. The boy was clearly embarrassed by the whole thing and squirmed out of her hold. Oliver, suddenly quite somber, allowed the hug and even offered Ashlie the briefest peck on the cheek.

"I'll miss you both," Ashlie told her brothers before turning back to her mother. "I'll miss all of you, but I've wanted to do this for so long."

Karen smiled and embraced her daughter one final time. "I know you're happy, and that pleases me. But I feel as though I'm sending a part of my heart away. Guard it well." She felt tears fall and didn't try to hide them. She needed Ashlie to understand the importance of this moment.

"I promise I will, Mama," Ashlie whispered against her mother's ear. She pulled back and saw the tears. Instantly her eyes dampened. "We're a fine pair," she said, barely keeping her voice from quivering.

Karen nodded. "A fine pair indeed."

The reverend had moved to the gangplank, where he waited patiently for Ashlie to join him. Adrik prayed for their safe journey, then handed

Ashlie's small bag to her. "I'll miss you, my girl. Don't forget to write to us in Seward, care of the railroad. We leave the day after tomorrow."

"I won't forget."

And then she was gone, moving up the gangplank, Reverend Mulberry at her side. They appeared to be chatting comfortably, neither one too concerned about the people they were leaving behind.

Adrik came and put his arm around Karen's shoulders. She felt comfort at his touch, but her tears would not stop flowing.

"Are you all right, Mama?" Christopher asked. He patted her hand as if to help. Oliver came to stand in front of her beside his brother. He simply looked up at her, as if ascertaining her well-being.

"I'll be all right, boys." She hoped her voice sounded reassuring. She wiped at the tears with her handkerchief, then spied Ashlie and the reverend at the rail. They were waving good-bye along with many other people. Karen waved her handkerchief rather than shouting her good-bye because words would not come. *How can I let her go, just like that? Send her thousands of miles away . . . Oh, Ashlie . . . please be safe. Please be happy.*

"Your boots are smoking," Chase said, sounding rather startled. "Do you not see it?"

Leah looked at the mukluks and realized her fate. Sitting beside the fire, she'd not even noticed that her mukluks were being singed by the flames. She pulled her feet back and powdered them with snow. Bitterness corrupted her thinking. She was making mistakes at a time when she couldn't afford to make them. She could feel Chase watch her; still, she did her best to ignore him—to pretend he simply didn't exist.

"How is Mrs. Beecham today?" Chase asked.

Leah said nothing. Helaina was still quite ill, and Chase already knew it. He was simply trying to engage her in conversation. Leah felt certain he regretted what he'd done to her. But he could never regret it as much as she did.

Leah stared at the fire, her shoulders hunched, her face kept down. As Chase squatted down beside her, she cringed inwardly but held her ground.

"Look," he began. "I don't know what to say. I can't change what happened. I . . . well . . ." His voice faded as he seemed to consider what to say. "I didn't intend for it to happen. Not really. I know I've acted inappropriately since we first met, but . . . well . . . you must understand, what happened wasn't a reflection on you at all."

Leah's head snapped up. This was nothing like the man who'd tormented her since forcing her from Last Chance. She looked at him in disbelief. "You sound as though you're offering conversation over tea and cakes. As though the offense was something as simple as a stolen kiss. You didn't intend for it to happen . . . it isn't a reflection on me. Is that supposed to make me feel better? Is that supposed to make it right?"

Chase shook his head. He no longer looked as much like her husband as he had when she'd first met him. Worry, fear, even exhaustion marred his features, and the beard he'd grown on the trail also altered his face. He seemed to hold less power over her now. . . . It was almost as if he'd done the worst to her that he could, so what was left to fear? Death would have been a kindness, as far as Leah was concerned.

"I know it can't make things right," Chase said, getting to his feet. He paced out a space on the opposite side of the fire. "I don't know why I did what I did. I wanted to hurt you . . . but not really even you. I wanted to hurt him." He looked at her hard. "I wanted to hurt Jayce."

"I don't care," Leah said evenly. She had never intended to get into a conversation with this hideous creature. She looked down at the fire again.

"You should. The hate between us will probably kill us both."

She shook her head, still not looking at him. "The hate has already killed you. You aren't a human being anymore. You're an animal. You kill and maim at will. You are like a rabid dog gone mad and you need to be eliminated."

"So the good Christian now wishes me dead?"

This caused an anger in Leah that she had not expected. Leaping to her feet, she jumped the fire to claw at his arrogant face. "You have no right," she said, flailing as he fought to control her. "You lost your right to compassion and kindness when you took from me what you had no right to take."

"But that's what I'm trying to say." He pushed her back, almost pained at the contact of even touching her. "I took from Jayce. Not from you."

Leah saw the emotion in his eyes but didn't care. She balled her hands into fists. "I am Jayce and he is me. When you harm one of us, the other bleeds. You are a fool. You have no idea what you have done. The war between you and your brother has only grown more intense . . . more destructive. Jayce will never let you live now. Not that I care. I only hope your actions don't get Jayce hurt in the process."

She could hardly believe her own venomous words. There was nothing of the love of Jesus in her heart at that moment. Her anger and wounded spirit refused to be calmed by the comfort she knew could be hers.

Chase seemed genuinely stunned by her reaction. Perhaps he had thought to merely apologize and seek her forgiveness. Maybe he believed her a simpleton because of her religious beliefs. Whatever his reasoning, there could be no doubting her thoughts now.

Chase straightened. "I can't undo what's happened. What's done is done."

His matter-of-fact words served only to further irritate Leah. "Oh, it's not done, Mr. Kincaid. Not by a long shot. Jayce will come for you. He will come because of Helaina and because of me. And when he finds out what you have done to us . . . he will even the score."

She turned and walked away, going to the tent where Helaina slept. Leah was certain the woman was dying. There simply wasn't proper medicine to treat her sickness. Leah crouched down and crawled inside the tent. It was surprisingly warm. Leah had lit a pot of seal oil for light and heat, and the results were quite satisfactory. Reaching out, Leah touched Helaina's forehead and felt that the fever still raged. If she couldn't find a way to ease the temperature, Helaina would no doubt die.

Leah shook her head. If only Helaina would have done what she was supposed to do. If only the woman would have been obedient to her brother.

"This is all your fault," Leah said, shaking her head. "I hate you as much as I hate him. I don't care whether you live or die. You've brought this on yourself."

Leah regretted the words the minute they were out of her mouth. But perhaps more than that, she regretted the ugly hate that festered, out of control, in her heart. There seemed no way to overcome it. She was a prisoner to those feelings, as much as she was a captive of Chase Kincaid.

Chapter Eleven

Leah's mind was made up. Botanist Teddy Davenport, dear friend from the gold rush days, had sent Leah a nice shipment of herbs that weren't available in her part of Alaska. He knew of her medical work in Last Chance and had kindly sent the herbs, along with instructions for their use, to help in her cause.

She had some of these herbs with her now. One of them was belladonna—deadly nightshade, as some called it. A little bit could be used to relieve respiratory spasms. In fact, she had used some to ease Helaina's cough. A little higher dosage could be used as a sedative for surgery. More still could cause death.

Leah would simply slip some belladonna into the food that night and put Chase to sleep. Once he was asleep, she would take Helaina and they would head out. She'd tried to focus on the trail as Chase pushed them ever farther north and into the interior. She'd never journeyed this direction and hadn't even heard Jacob tell tales of such trips. It would be difficult to escape and make an easy path home, but to do anything else might well end her life . . . or Chase's.

The rage she felt toward Chase terrified Leah. She tried to calm her spirit, but she found there was no reasoning with herself at times. Just as soon as she'd convince herself that everything would be all right—that Jayce would still love her and that she would heal from the damage done by Chase—her anger would resurface, and Leah found herself wishing fervently that she could exact her revenge.

The days were shorter than ever. Leah had lost track of the time but knew that if they continued north they would soon have no daylight at all. That would make travel very dangerous. She felt certain Chase couldn't be all that capable in such circumstances.

Chase brought them to a stop earlier than Leah had expected. He'd grown careless of late—no longer going back to see that the trails were obliterated, nor concerned about having a fire at night. He had even allowed Leah to begin trapping again, although the catches had not been good.

Tonight, Leah thought, *tonight I will end this one way or another.* She tried to think of exactly how to handle the situation. She would set the traps and hope that perhaps something could be caught before she needed to leave the area. She would prepare Helaina's medicated broth and while measuring out those herbs, would add the belladonna to the main dish. The trick would be to put aside some food for herself—food that hadn't been tainted. She couldn't risk putting herself to sleep along with Chase and Helaina.

"Will you set the traps tonight?" Chase asked in a gentle tone. Since the assault, he had strangely gone out of his way to ease the tension between them, but Leah wanted no part of it.

"Don't I set them every night? At least every night that you aren't too fearful to let me out of your sight?" She wished immediately that she could take the words back. Perhaps she should force herself to be nice to him—just long enough to put her plan into motion. *No,* she thought just as quickly. *He'll know that something's going on if I treat him well. I have to continue with things just as they are or it will ruin my plans.* She looked at him from the corner of her eye and set her jaw. "So are you letting me set them tonight?"

"I see no reason to do otherwise." He seemed rather thoughtful for a moment. "You always manage to make us good meals. You're a good cook."

She hated his patronage. She knew his words were only intended to sooth his own guilty conscience, and Leah refused to give him such comfort.

"Your flattery means nothing." She glared at him. "You are still worse than an animal. I'll not absolve you of your sins."

"But what of forgiveness?" Chase asked, surprising her. "Doesn't your God require you give forgiveness when people seek it?"

"Lately my God has required a great many things of me," Leah answered. "If He wants me to forgive you, however, He's asking too much."

She stomped off toward the sled basket, where Helaina slept. The traps were tied to the side toward the back. Leah reached out and touched Helaina's forehead. To her surprise it seemed the fever had lessened considerably. Leah checked the younger woman's breathing. It appeared much less labored, more even. Perhaps Mrs. Beecham was on the mend.

"How is she?" Chase asked, coming up behind Leah.

Leah jumped and moved away as though he might touch her. "She's very sick. I've already told you that."

Leah turned to go, but Chase questioned her again. "Should I put her in the tent?"

Leah hated that he was asking her opinion. He was doing this only to force her into conversation, thinking she might crack under his kindness and give him what he seemed to crave more than anything: her pardon.

"I think she'll be warmer and more comfortable in the sled." Leah kept her answers short and without emotion. She walked away without waiting for him to respond and was glad when he said nothing.

With the traps set, Leah went back to their cache of food and began to unwrap the supplies. She thought of what she was about to do and realized that she had no concern for Chase's well-being. She knew the herbs she would use could kill if too much was consumed. She knew, too, that some people reacted violently to the medication. She'd seen a man die in their village when he'd had such a reaction. But her heart was hardened. If Chase died, she'd consider it justice and nothing more.

The wind picked up, causing the flames to dance in their campfire. Leah watched the show and thought of a time long ago when she had sat at her mother's knee before their hearth. She could almost feel her mother brushing out her hair . . . almost hear her speak.

"Leah," her mother had said, *"sometimes life is very hard. It doesn't mean God no longer cares. It's just the way things are at times."*

"But it seems unfair," Leah had replied. *"If God loves us so very much that He would send His Son Jesus to die for us, then why not keep the bad things away from us?"*

Her mother had leaned down and kissed her on the top of her head. *"I wish I had an easy answer for you, my love. God has His reasons. They sometimes seem cruel, I know. But I promise you, Leah, even when things seem confusing and wrong, God loves you. He's still by your side, holding your hand—guiding you through the painful times."*

Leah didn't realize she was crying until droplets fell onto her hands as she prepared the hare she had saved from the previous night. She wiped at her cheeks with the back of her sleeve and tried not to think about the memory of her mother. The thoughts would not leave her, however.

Life might have been very different had her mother lived. Leah might never have come to Alaska. She might never have known the sorrows and betrayals that had haunted her days. Jayce Kincaid might never have entered her life, and without him there would certainly have been no Chase.

But would I trade away the good along with the bad? The question permeated her hard façade. There were many wonderful things that had also come her way. The love she knew with Jayce had been the fulfillment of everything she had hoped for. Would she throw that away as well?

"But that's all ended now," she said, not meaning to speak the words aloud. She looked up, wondering if Chase had overheard her. Yet he was nowhere in sight. Sometimes he took himself away from the camp, but never for long. Often he was trying his best to hunt food, but for some reason the game was quite scarce in this area.

Leah turned her attention back to the broth. Ayoona had given her some dried *mazué*—Eskimo potatoes. Leah had hoarded them away for times when the food was scarce. The mazué were good by themselves and could even be eaten raw with seal oil. This time, however, Leah thought the added treat might entice Chase to eat more than a small portion. Cutting the roots with her ulu, Leah made a list in her head of things she needed to do in order to make her escape plan work.

I will need to hide the knife so that I can cut my bonds if Chase ties me up tonight. Her hope was that the belladonna would work quickly and Chase would fall asleep long before he thought of securing Leah for the night.

I will also need to collect the traps and anything that might be in them. She glanced at the basket. Helaina continued to sleep, but Leah figured to wake her and get some of the drugged broth down her. She couldn't risk having Helaina awaken and raise a fuss about their leaving Chase behind.

Leah portioned out some of the broth and left the rest of the soup to cook. She put another dose of belladonna in the mixture and stirred it for several seconds. This should keep Helaina asleep and cooperative.

Going to the basket, Leah arranged things so that she could sit beside the sick woman. "Helaina, wake up. I have some broth for you."

To her surprise, Helaina managed to open her eyes. "Are we there yet?"

"Where?" Leah was surprised by the woman's question.

Helaina shook her head. "I don't know. I can't remember. I just . . . wondered . . . why we'd stopped."

"We've stopped for the night, and no, we aren't there—wherever there might be. We're still in the middle of the wilds." Leah lifted a spoonful of broth. "Now take this. It will make you feel better."

"I do feel better," Helaina replied. "I don't feel so cold."

"I think your fever broke. I can't be sure that it will remain gone, but for now it seems to have passed. That's why you must take your medicine."

"Thank you for taking care of me." She swallowed the broth and closed her eyes. "That's very good. What is it?"

"It's just a concoction of things," Leah replied honestly. "I used what I had available. You have to keep up your strength."

"I know you . . . are . . . unhappy with me," Helaina said before taking more of the soup. "I'm sorry for the . . . trouble I've caused. I hope you'll forgive me."

Leah grimaced. Yet another person asking for forgiveness, as though that might suddenly make everything fine. She spooned more soup into Helaina's mouth, hoping to silence her, but it didn't work.

"I know your faith is strong. I know you will forgive me, but . . . well . . . sometimes I think I don't deserve forgiveness."

Leah focused on the bowl. "There are times when everyone feels that way. I think people especially feel that way when they know just how wrong they were to begin with."

Helaina shook her head. "I know I went about things in the wrong . . . way." She yawned and Leah knew the herbs were working.

"Forget about it. You need to stop talking and eat."

Helaina gave up the discussion and Leah breathed a sigh of relief. She hadn't had to lie and tell Helaina that she didn't feel like forgiving her and then wrestle with some argument about why Leah was obligated to forgive.

By the time the bowl of soup was gone, Helaina was once again unconscious. Her heavy breathing suggested a very deep sleep. Leah felt a huge sense of relief as she returned to the fire and checked the soup. Everything was ready. All she needed now was for Chase to return. Leah pulled out the portion of meat and broth she'd hidden for herself. She slipped a few pieces of root into her own mixture and stirred it before sampling.

"It smells marvelous," Chase said, once again slipping into camp without a sound.

"It's ready."

Leah continued eating her own portion, hoping he'd sit down and serve himself. To her surprise, he did just that. She tried not to look anxious as he began to eat. He ate nearly half a bowl before commenting further.

"It tastes as good as it smelled. I could eat the entire pot."

"Do as you will. I have all I want." Leah hoped her words sounded indifferent. She didn't want him to suspect a thing. Not until she was long gone.

Chase dished himself more food and sat back. Leah finished her bowl and grew nervous about what to do next. She had slipped the ulu under the fur on which she sat and hoped Chase wouldn't ask for it as he usually did after their meal was concluded.

"You know, when I was a young man we ate very well. After my father made his fortune, we had the best of everything. I remember sumptuous meals. Huge roasted baron of beef, five and six side dishes with gravy and sauces that made your mouth water just to see them on the table. Oh, and the bread . . . Our cook could make the flakiest rolls—nothing like the sourdough we get up here." He yawned but continued eating.

Leah thought to show him that she felt just as tired. She faked a yawn of her own and forced herself to lean in a relaxed manner near the fire. Chase seemed completely at ease as he continued with his memories.

"My favorite things were the desserts. Oh, we had such wonderful creations." He smiled. "I'm sure I'm boring you—that's why you're so tired. I'll get the tent set up as soon as I finish here."

"Don't bother on my account," Leah said with a yawn. "I plan to sleep in the basket with Helaina. She'll need my warmth. I've no desire to share the tent with you any more than I have to."

Chase frowned. His eyelids seemed heavy. "I'll have to tie you up."

"Why should tonight be any different?" Leah asked sarcastically. She changed the subject then, hoping to keep his mind occupied elsewhere. "How long must we continue this journey? Where are you taking us and when will we finally be there?"

Chase shook his head and downed the last of his meal. "Not long now. I have a cabin not far from here. It's on the river. It's plenty warm with lots of wood. It'll keep us well through the winter."

"You expect to keep us there all winter?" Leah questioned. "Then what?"

Chase seemed to struggle to think. Leah thought he looked almost puzzled at her question. "I don't know what we'll do then. We have to deal with Jayce first. I know he will come. It might take him a while, but eventually I'll have to deal with him."

"Jayce will hunt you down. You can be assured of that."

Chase put the bowl down and rubbed his eyes. He couldn't quite keep them open. "What . . . what have you done? What have you put in the food?"

Leah laughed, but the sound was choked and unnatural. "I've put in deadly nightshade, some mazué, and the last of our snowshoe hare."

"Nightshade!" He tried to get up but fell back down. "You've poisoned it. You've . . . decided . . . to kill me."

"Kill you? Why, Mr. Kincaid, as much as I would love to see you pay the ultimate price for your crimes, I have done no such thing. I certainly don't need your death on my conscience."

He fell sideways and struggled to keep awake. "I should shoot you now." He pulled the gun from his coat, but it fell from his hands even as he attempted to raise it.

Leah sat up and watched him fight against the herbs. "It's no use, you know. Belladonna is quite potent. You will be asleep for several hours. More than enough for me to take Helaina and the dogs and leave."

He let his head fall hard against the ground. The jarring prompted him to open his eyes for just a moment. "You'll leave me to my death."

"Maybe," Leah said, getting to her feet. She came to where he rested and picked up the gun. The temptation to put a bullet through his head was strong. The smell of his breath against her face, his hands on her body, his pleasure despite her pain . . . the memories begged for her to kill him.

For a moment Leah wrestled with her conscience. She wanted nothing more than to put an end once and for all to this miserable chapter of her life. But would it end? If she killed him now, no one would blame her. They would take into consideration the kidnapping and the rape, and the great possibility that Chase had planned to kill both her and Helaina.

But even as Leah fingered the cold metal of the revolver, she knew she couldn't shoot a defenseless man. She looked at Chase, his expression now relaxed in sleep. He deserved to die, but she'd leave that for someone else.

Without another thought, Leah slipped the gun into her pocket and went to work. She collected her things and loaded them in the sled. She thought to leave Chase without anything, but she couldn't do it. She knew the cruelty of the north. She portioned out a few supplies and left him a knife. There was no possibility of leaving him the rifle or the revolver. It would be dangerous for him to be left without a gun, but Leah couldn't risk it.

The traps were empty, just as she'd figured they'd be. There hadn't been enough time. She gathered them, securing the bait for another time, and tied the traps back on the sled. Her last order of business was to offer Chase some sort of protection from the elements. She stoked up the fire, then took one of the furs and a wool blanket and secured them around his body. It wasn't much, but she couldn't bring herself to do more. In several hours he would awaken and his fate would then rest solely in his own hands.

The dogs sensed that the journey was about to take a new turn as Leah adjusted their harnesses. They moaned and yipped as she rubbed their heads and spoke to them in soothing tones.

"We're almost ready, boys. Come on now, don't fight me." She pushed one of the big wheel dogs back into place as he tried to dance around her. He bumped up against the basket and yipped but finally obeyed Leah. It took only a few more tries before she finally had him strapped securely in place.

With this done, she hurried to light a lantern. It wouldn't help much, but it would give her a sense of the path and their surroundings. Hopefully it would be enough to ward off any dangerous breaks in the trail.

Leah felt her heart racing as she rocked the sled to release it from the ground. The crusty snow gave way easily. She then released the snow hook. "Hike!"

The dogs pulled against the weight easily. Leah circled them around the camp, her gaze resting only momentarily on the sleeping form on the ground.

It's what he deserves, she told her guilty heart.

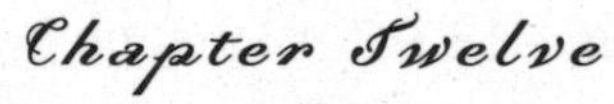

Chapter Twelve

"The tracks head back to the west," John said, coming to join Jacob and Jayce. "We were lucky the dog went lame or we'd have missed it for sure."

Jacob scratched the dog's head. "Well, Brownie can't pull anymore. He'll have to ride." The dog yipped as if to contradict this statement.

Jayce looked to John. "How far behind them are we now?"

"I think maybe just a day or so. Those trails were pretty fresh."

Jacob straightened. "What about villages? Did you find anything in the area?"

John nodded. "Just north and west of here. Not far."

"Do you think they might have seen them?" Brownie strained against Jacob's hold. "Do you think Chase would have gone there?"

John shrugged. "If the villagers were out, they might have seen them, but I don't think Chase went there. Tracks keep going west. I don't think it's a trick."

Jacob considered the words for a moment. "Well, why don't we go there? The dogs need to rest. We've been pushing them pretty hard. We can drop off Brownie, and maybe someone there will know something more. Hopefully they'll be friendly and offer us a meal as well."

"I don't see the harm in it," Jayce replied. "As long as it doesn't take too much time. If John thinks we're just hours apart, I think we need to push on as soon as possible."

"I agree," Jacob said. "I think we'll have an easier time of it without having to worry about Brownie. We can always pick him up on the way back or even trade him for supplies. He's a good dog and he'll heal just fine."

"Maybe they trade information too," John said with a grin.

"We should be cautious." Jacob turned to lift Brownie into his basket. "I've heard rumors that the tribes around here are fighting amongst themselves."

"I'm willing to take the risk," Jayce said, moving to his dog team. "Let's go."

Jacob tied Brownie in the basket. The poor dog was miserable and began howling up a storm as Jacob resumed his place behind the sled. The injustice of it all left Brownie miserable, but he finally settled down in the basket.

They approached the village cautiously. Heavy clouds were blocking what little sun could be had, but it was easy to see that the people were not feeling in the leastwise threatened by the appearance of Jacob and their party.

They exchanged greetings, and Jacob listened as John fired off a rapid line of questioning to the man who seemed to be in charge. The man shook his head vigorously, and John continued with additional questions.

Though the dialect seemed a little different than that of the natives of Last Chance, Jacob caught a good portion of the conversation. Apparently the man had not seen any strangers in the area, and especially not any white people. He would have remembered such a thing. Jacob and Jayce were, in fact, the first whites he'd seen since summer.

Then one of the other men spoke up. He had seen a sled moving west, and it appeared there were at least two people, but he had no idea whether they were white or not.

"How long ago was this?" Jacob asked in the man's tongue.

The older man smiled and replied, "Yesterday morning."

Jacob turned to Jayce. "That has to be them. We should give it all we have to finish the job."

"I agree. I say we let the dogs rest a short time, then immediately put ourselves back on the trail."

"I have to fix my sled runner," John threw in. "I don't need long." He headed off toward his sled.

Jacob went to work seeing to the dogs. Several villagers brought him hot water, and one even prepared a nice fire for him. Jacob began mixing a hot meal for the teams, but all the while his mind went back to the time he'd spent alone with Helaina while they were in Seattle. He thought of how irritating she could be—how headstrong. But at the same time he couldn't help but feel sympathy for her. She had endured so much, and all she really wanted was a way to fill the emptiness left by the tragedies of life.

If she could only come to terms with the fact that God loves her, that she needs Him. But of course that would take time . . . and maybe seeing it with her own eyes, instead of hearing stories about it. Jacob had known many people who were that way. They could hear people's stories all day long, but until something actually happened to them personally, it just didn't make any sense. He figured Helaina would be that way.

As the wind picked up and the temperature grew colder, Jacob wondered if Helaina and Leah were warm enough. Leah knew about this land and had no doubt dressed appropriately. Ayoona had mentioned that Leah had packed the sled, so Jacob felt confident she would have taken ample supplies. But Helaina knew very little of the far north.

With the dogs fed and resting, Jacob noticed John was finishing up with his sled runner. John had been more than a brother to him, offering to take time away from the village and his own family in order to find Leah. So much time had passed, however, that Jacob felt he needed to release John from any obligation.

"You need help?" Jacob questioned as he came to where John sat working.

"No. It's not too bad. I got it fixed now."

Jacob looked around for some of the other natives. "John, I think it's time for you to head back. We've been gone a lot longer than you'd planned."

John's round brown face took on an expression that suggested he was considering the comment. "No. I won't go," he finally said.

"But you have a lot of people depending on you."

"They got others to depend on too. We had great hunting this summer and the salmon were good. We dried a lot of fish. Leah only has you and her husband . . . and us. We stay and help you."

Jacob knew the act came as a sacrifice, no matter what John said. He was deeply touched. "You're a good friend, John. I won't forget this."

John looked at him and nodded. "In Alaska you don't forget."

Leah sensed the dogs' excitement. Something was urging them on. They had picked up the scent of another animal—perhaps a hare or fox. She held fast to the sled, working her best to slow and direct them. She felt their anxiousness. They were headed home—they were free. She wanted to put as much distance between herself and Chase as was possible, but she knew the dogs were her lifeline. She couldn't let them wear themselves out.

"Whoa, Marty!" She felt the pace slow. Then without warning the dogs picked up speed again. They began to bark and fuss as they raced across the snow.

Leah feared she might lose control of the animals and decided to show them who was boss. Her muscles were weary of the work as she fought to manage the sled and team. "Whoa, Marty! Whoa!" She stepped down on the brake hard.

Again Marty heard her command and lessened the pace. This was all Leah needed. They were good dogs, generally as eager to please as to have their own way. Putting her full weight on the brake, the team slowed and finally stopped at Leah's insistence.

Leah anchored the sled and stretched her aching shoulders. She tried to calculate the time. Heavy clouds were making the day gloomy and nearly as dark as evening. It seemed they had been traveling for at least four hours since their last stop. Leah could always tell because of the way the middle of her back began to hurt after that amount of time on a sled.

"Where are we?" Helaina asked groggily. She tried to sit up, but Leah wasn't ready yet to do battle with her.

"Stay where you are. We're taking off in a minute. We're just resting the dogs."

Helaina stretched up. "I think I feel better. It doesn't feel so hard to breathe."

"That's because of the medicine I've been giving you. I have some more you should take." Leah went to where she had what remained of the stinkweed concoction. "It would probably taste better hot, but you need to drink this down."

"Is it going to put me back to sleep? I don't want to sleep. I need to make plans for capturing Chase. Where is he, anyway?"

"It isn't important." Leah shoved the bottle into Helaina's hands. "Drink this now." She pushed Helaina's hands toward her mouth. "Hurry. A storm is moving in and we need to get going."

Helaina drank the mixture and yawned. "Leah, you aren't making any sense. What's going on?"

"Look up and you'll see for yourself. The clouds are thickening, the wind is picking up. Already the temperature is much colder than it was just a few hours ago. Now settle back down. We need to be on our way."

Helaina had no sooner eased back on her furs than Leah wrapped a scarf around her neck, adjusted her parka hood down, and called to the dogs. "Up, up, boys! Hike!" She pulled the hook and gripped the sled as they once again headed down the trail.

Leah thought that Helaina was trying to say something to her from the basket, but she pretended not to notice. She figured that once Helaina realized the full impact of what Leah had done, there would be little or no peace. For now, Leah just needed time and distance to feel safe.

But safety wasn't to be had. The dogs began frantically barking. They pulled toward the right, but Leah held them fast. "Haw! Haw! Marty, haw!" And then she spied something coming out from the side of the trail. It was nearly fifty yards ahead, but the outline was one Leah recognized immediately.

"Whoa!" She held fast to the sled and jumped on the brake at the same time. "Stop, Marty!" He had no interest in stopping. Leah did the only thing she could think to do. She threw one of the snow hooks and prayed it would catch and halt the team.

At first it didn't catch, but the drag helped enough that Leah could get the team under control. Finally the hook caught in a snow-covered tussock, jerking Marty backward as it did. They were stopped. And none too soon.

A grizzly stood not twenty yards from them. He seemed very interested in the dogs. Much too interested. Leah figured he was a young male who hadn't made it to a den prior to the snowfall and storms. Sometimes the animals were confused and remained out of their winter dens, seeking additional food.

Leah reached for the rifle and squared it against her shoulder. The meat would be good to have. She'd hate to take the extra time to dress out the beast, but it would definitely benefit them. After all, she had no idea how many days it would take to reach home. She had no idea which path would get them there in the most direct route.

Breathe, she reminded herself. Jacob was always chiding her for holding her breath whenever she was about to shoot. She forced a deep gulp of air into her lungs and sighted the swaggering animal.

Breathe. Just breathe.

The dogs were frantic now, pulling at the sled, trying to get to the bear. The bear lowered his ears and then his head. Leah wasted no time. She squeezed the trigger before he could charge. The bullet hit the grizzly in the shoulder. She worked the lever to eject the casing. The reassuring click of the next round loading gave her renewed confidence. She took aim again and fired.

This time the bullet grazed the bear's head. He'd had enough, but rather than drop, he turned and ran. The dogs howled in sorrow that they could not give chase. Leah, however, was fretful over what she should do. A wounded rogue bear was nothing to leave running free, but she was limited on ammunition and on knowledge of the area. If she left this trail to follow the bear, she might get hopelessly lost.

She took in a deep breath and relaxed the rifle. Her heart was pounding so hard she could feel it and hear it in her ears. There was no time to waste, she reminded herself. She put the rifle away and reached for the hook. They needed to press on.

Chapter Thirteen

With the village nearly three hours behind them, Jacob noted the thickening clouds. They would have to either press on or make camp. He felt a deep sense of frustration. The terrain was unfamiliar to them and the threat of complications were everywhere. He brought the dogs to a stop, hoping to rest them and confer with the others as to what they wanted to do. As if he didn't already know.

"Why are you stopping?" Jayce asked as his team came up behind Jacob.

"Look at those clouds—a storm's gathering. I figured we should discuss what to do. Do we press on?"

"Of course we press on," Jayce declared as John came to join them. The other men waited with the sleds.

"If Brownie hadn't gone lame we would have missed them turning west," Jacob offered. "What if they change direction again? We might waste a great many hours."

"I can check the trails," John offered. He looked up at the sky. It was just starting to snow. "Looks bad."

"Feels bad too." Jacob didn't like the sense of foreboding that permeated the pristine beauty around them.

Then the silence was broken by the sound of a single shot ringing out. All three men looked toward the north. It wasn't that far away. A second shot rang out. Jacob stiffened and looked to Jayce.

"Let's go!"

The other men ran for their sleds while Jacob offered a prayer and pulled his sled hook. He felt sick in the pit of his stomach. He couldn't help but wonder if Chase had killed Helaina and Leah.

Two women.

Two shots.

Jayce could hardly bear the images racing through his imagination. Chase had to be responsible for the gunfire. He could believe no other explanation. Never mind that it could be a hunter from the village foraging for food. His gut told him that Chase was somehow involved.

If he's hurt her, I'll kill him.

Jayce thought only of his wife. His heart seemed to beat in a rhythm that called her name.

Le-ah. Le-ah. Le-ah.

He tried not to think of how reasonable it might seem to Chase to end the lives of his hostages now that he was this far north. No doubt Chase figured he'd thrown off any pursuit. *If he thinks that, then he doesn't know me at all,* Jayce thought.

He clenched his jaw. Throughout this pursuit and search he had tried hard to keep an even temper. He'd tried to pray that somehow God might turn his brother to the truth before his life ended. Now that Jayce had put his faith in God, he hated to think of his own brother dying and going to hell. His entire life had been spent worrying about and dealing with the trouble Chase got into, but this was something he couldn't help him with. Chase would face his Maker on his own. Maybe sooner than he planned.

Jayce might even be the one to end Chase's life. Especially if he just killed Leah. A fire started somewhere in the pit of his stomach and spread. Why had this happened? Why couldn't Chase have been caught by someone else? Jayce felt so torn. He knew this had to be done. Chase had forced Jayce's involvement when he posed as his brother during his crimes. But still, it seemed so unfair—so unnatural that one brother should turn against another in this way.

They moved along the trail for two, maybe three, miles when a dog sled team came into sight. The view was somewhat obscured by the snow. The team approached them from the opposite direction and there seemed to be only one person on board—and that was the driver.

Jayce did nothing to slow his dogs. He wanted to close the distance as quickly as possible. If the driver was his brother—if Chase had done the worst—Jayce knew the responsibility should be his to bear.

But as he drew closer, Jayce realized the figure was too small for his brother. Disappointment washed over him as he figured the driver to be a local native. He was ready to give up hope when Jacob called out, "That's Marty in the lead. It's them!"

Jayce looked again and realized that the driver was a woman. "Leah." He barely breathed the name. He stepped on the brake and called to the dogs. "Whoa! Whoa now!"

The dogs were none too eager to stop; after all, there were other dogs to meet up ahead. But Jayce got them stopped in short order. He was in no mood to brook nonsense. He secured the hook and stepped from the sled. He allowed the other driver to approach and pushed back the hood of his parka as he waited.

The driver stepped from the sled and pushed back the shielding hood that kept her face obscured. Jayce instantly recognized his wife, although she looked quite tired. She locked gazes with him and shook her head ever so slightly. Jayce covered the distance between them in long, easy strides. He pulled her into his arms and held her tight.

"Thank God you're safe. I feared the worst." His voice broke. Jayce buried his face against Leah's hair and silently thanked God for her return. Leah said nothing at all. She stood rather stiff in his arms, neither embracing him nor rejecting him.

Jayce finally pulled away and took Leah's face in his hands. "Are you all right?"

Leah looked at him for several seconds. She almost seemed to be searching him for some answer. "I left Chase drugged. He's back to the north—at least he was. That was last night."

"We heard gunshots," Jayce began. "I feared the worst."

"I shot a bear. It only wounded him."

"But you weren't harmed?"

"The bear ran off. He didn't have a chance to attack me or the dogs."

Jayce felt a strange sensation wash over him. She hadn't answered his question. She looked away from him as Jacob came up. Something wasn't right.

"Leah. You're a sight for my eyes," Jacob said, hugging her. Again Leah remained rather stiff, almost as if she were separating herself from her brother.

"Helaina's very sick. She's there in the basket. She's better than she has been, but I think she has pneumonia."

Jacob went immediately to the sled. Jayce moved closer, mainly to be at Leah's side, but he figured he might as well see Helaina for himself.

"She's had some stinkweed tea. She should be waking up soon," Leah said in a rather monotone voice. "I had to keep her sedated or she would never have cooperated."

Jacob looked at his sister. "What do you mean?"

"She intended to take Chase into custody. She wanted me to drug him and bring him back for her. I refused."

"I'm glad," Jayce said, putting his arm around Leah. "Chase is very dangerous. He might have hurt you."

Leah looked at him as if she might comment, then turned back to Jacob. "I'm out of herbs. I can't help her anymore. She's been so ill, I thought for sure she would die."

Jacob knelt down on the sled. He put his hand to Helaina's cheek, but she didn't stir. "There's a village a ways back. We can get her there. Maybe they have medicines to treat her."

John finally interrupted them. "The storm is bad, Jacob. We should make camp. After that, I can look for a closer village."

"There's a rogue bear out there somewhere," Leah reminded them. "I shot him twice. Hit him both times, but the second shot was just a grazing blow to the head."

John nodded. "We'll find him. Bear like that will be dangerous."

Leah shrugged. "I've got a tent. I'll set it up."

Jayce watched her, sensing that there was something very wrong with his wife. Perhaps it was just that the entire ordeal had worn her out. She had endured great physical demands, as well as emotional ones.

Leah was already pulling the tent from the sled as Jayce joined her. "Let me help you." She cringed slightly as he reached toward her. "Are you angry at me?"

Leah looked surprised. "No. I'm . . . I'm tired. We need to get the tent up quickly."

He nodded but said nothing. What could he say? What should he say? Leah seemed a completely different woman. He helped her put up the tent while Jacob and John were busy putting up their own shelters. When they finished, Helaina was starting to rally. Jacob lifted her from the sled and took her to Leah's tent.

"Why are you bringing her here?" Leah asked. She was already busy unrolling the bedding, while Jayce worked to set up the oil stove.

"I don't suppose it would be appropriate to have her lodge with me," he said rather sheepishly. "John's tent is already pretty crowded, so I figured some of the guys could share my quarters. I know you and Jayce would probably like your privacy, but this seems the best solution."

"She can stay with us," Jayce replied. "We'll soon be home and have all the privacy we need. It's all right. She'll need Leah's help."

"She wouldn't have needed anyone's help had she just listened to her brother," Leah snapped. She quickly turned away.

Jayce exchanged a rather confused look with Jacob. Leah's attitude puzzled them both. "I see she's waking up."

Helaina moaned and struggled to open her eyes. Jacob gently positioned her on one of the pallets Leah had just arranged. "Helaina, it's me, Jacob. Wake up."

Helaina murmured something and tried to stretch. "I hurt so much." She opened her eyes and seemed startled to find Jacob. "Where are we?"

"I'm not entirely sure," Jacob said with a grin. "Alaska is about the only answer I have."

"That's a very big answer," she said, rubbing her neck. "Oh, I'm so sore. Everything hurts. It has for days—maybe weeks. How I long for my warm feather bed in New York. I think I'd sell my soul to be back home."

Jayce saw the sobering affect this had on Jacob. "Look," Jayce interjected, "we need to finish caring for the dogs. The storm is really building."

Helaina looked past Jacob to where Jayce was kneeling. She studied him for several moments, then looked back to Jacob. "That's Jayce—right?"

"Right." Jacob appeared to recover his good nature. He smiled again. "You don't think I'd let Chase share a tent with you if I had any say over it."

She relaxed a bit. "Where is Chase? I hope you've tied him up good."

Jacob looked to Leah and then to Helaina. She hadn't missed the exchange. Fighting to sit up, she squared her gaze on Leah. "You did tie him up—right?"

Leah narrowed her eyes. "I told you for days that I had no plan to help you capture Chase at the cost of our success. I left him on the trail. I left him there drugged and asleep. He has a knife and a pack of food, a fur, and a wool blanket."

"Leah, how could you!" Helaina's voice was weak but clearly angry. "I had a job to do and you interfered." She began to cough.

Leah balled her fists. "You nearly died. I should have let you, for all the gratitude you show." With that, Leah left the tent.

Jacob and Jayce were stunned by Leah's words. They had never known her to be so ugly with anyone.

"She blames me for all of this," Helaina said. The coughing dissipated and she fell back against the pallet. "I deserve it, but I don't like it." She closed her eyes. "I can't believe she let him go. Now I'll have to start all over."

"You have to get well first," Jacob said firmly. "You're still very sick."

"I'm going to help Leah," Jayce said, noting that Jacob had the situation under control. Jayce slipped from the tent and felt the blast of Arctic wind against his face. The darkness and storm made visibility nearly impossible. "Leah?"

"I'm here," she said. "Getting the supplies from my sled."

He walked against the wind, feeling the icy particles against his face. Jayce pulled his parka hood closer.

Leah met him halfway. "This is all we need."

"Let me take it." She gave the box over to him without protest. "Hold on to me while we make our way back. This weather is not going to show us any mercy, and I don't want to lose you again."

"I'm fine. Just get the supplies to the tent." She spoke out against the wind, but to Jayce it almost seemed to be an angry demand.

Rather than argue, he pressed forward. They were soon back in the tent, but Jayce was completely uncomfortable with the way Leah was acting. She wanted very little to do with any of them. Something had happened; he was certain of it. He put the box on the tent floor beside the stove and considered his options. If he took issue with her now, she would have to explain in front of Helaina and Jacob. Obviously that would be most uncomfortable.

"Do you have anything for Helaina's cough?" Jacob asked as Leah rummaged through the box.

She shook her head, not even looking up. "I told you. I gave her the last of the tea. I'll put some water on the stove. The steam will help her. Otherwise, she needs to just rest and not talk."

Jacob nodded, but Jayce noticed Leah's attention was focused on the stove. The wind howled mournfully outside. The small tent shook rather violently but held fast.

"What do you have to eat?" Leah asked no one in particular.

Jacob replied before Jayce could answer. "We have some fresh reindeer meat. We traded for it back at the village. I'll go retrieve some from John. We can definitely feed you well."

Leah plopped down on her pallet as Jacob opened the outside flap. Cold air rushed in, causing the seal oil lamp to flicker and nearly go out. Jayce watched as she did her best to protect the flame. His glance then went to Helaina, who watched him very closely.

"It really is me—Jayce," he told her. "I'm not sure how to convince you."

"It's uncanny how much alike you two look. With the beards, it's even more difficult to distinguish who's who."

"Jayce looks nothing like Chase," Leah said angrily. "His eyes are completely different. Their mouths and noses aren't alike at all."

Jayce laughed. "We're identical twins, Leah. Of course we look alike."

She devoured him with a look that nearly froze him to the ground. "Don't ever say that again. There is nothing about you that is like him. Chase Kincaid is evil. He's an abomination with no conscience—no concern for others. You might have come from the same mother, at the same time—but that doesn't matter."

Jayce held her gaze for just a moment, but it was long enough to see the terrible pain in her eyes. In that moment he was certain that his brother had deeply wounded Leah. How deeply and through what means, he couldn't be sure. Unfortunately, his imagination ran wild enough to believe Chase capable of most anything. And that frightened him more than he cared to admit.

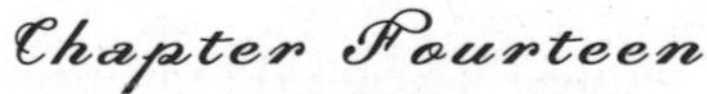

Chapter Fourteen

Jacob watched Helaina's labored breathing and felt dread wash over him. What if she died? What if the storm lasted for weeks instead of days and they couldn't get her help?

Jayce had suggested that Jacob remain in their tent so that he could keep an eye on Helaina, and for that Jacob had been very grateful. He struggled with his feelings for this woman. Helaina still didn't understand the need to turn her life over to God, and without that, Jacob couldn't be more than friends. Now with her fighting just to stay alive, he worried that she would die without having found God's peace for her soul.

But Leah's attitude troubled him deeply as well. She was strangely quiet and aloof. She had cooked for them but then went to her pallet, turned her back on the rest of them, and went to sleep. Now, nearly ten hours later, she was still sleeping. Her behavior was unlike anything he'd ever known.

"Coffee?" Jayce asked him.

Jacob looked up and realized he'd been staring at Leah's back. He saw in Jayce's eyes that he held some of the same worries. Jacob looked again to Leah.

"Do you think she's all right?"

"I don't honestly know. I was hoping you'd tell me. You've known her a lot longer."

Jacob shook his head and lowered his voice. It was a big tent, but not that big. The last thing Jacob wanted to do was offend Leah for talking about her as if she wasn't there just six feet away. "I've never seen her act this way. Not even when you left her back in Ketchikan. She's always spoken gently—kindly—of everyone. Even when she was angry, I've found her to hold her tongue."

Jayce nodded. "That's what I figured. I don't know . . . I mean . . ." He fell silent. "Forget it." He still held the coffeepot. "Want some?"

Jacob extended his tin cup. "Sure. Doesn't seem to be much else to do while we wait out this storm."

He sipped the brew slowly, enjoying the warmth. Just then Helaina stirred. Her fever had returned in the night—no doubt because they had nothing with which to stave it off. She opened her eyes.

"When we reach the train station," she said in a low, raspy voice, "will you see to my bags?"

Surprised by her request, Jacob said nothing for several moments. "Helaina, it's me—Jacob."

She narrowed her eyes as if to see him better. "I'm sorry. What did you say?"

Jacob leaned a little closer. "It's Jacob. I'm here to help care for you."

"Oh, I was having the strangest dream. I was riding in a buggy and . . . we . . . we . . . well, I can't remember."

He smiled. "It doesn't matter. Would you like a drink? I have some tea for you. It's not the same as what you've been drinking, but it will help warm you."

"Tea would be nice."

Jacob turned to Jayce, who immediately went to work making the tea. When he returned his attention to Helaina she seemed to be a little more coherent, so Jacob asked, "How are you feeling? Is it still difficult to breathe?"

"No, not as much. I don't know why . . . I'm still sick."

"Leah thinks it's pneumonia. That's very hard to overcome. I know—I had it once myself. I wound up in bed for three weeks."

"I don't have three weeks. I need to get better so I can finish my job."

Jacob shook his head and took the cup of tea that Jayce offered. He helped Helaina sit up and steadied the tea for her to drink. "There is no job for you to finish, Helaina." He tried to keep his tone gentle.

She drank some of the tea, then fell back against Jacob's arm. "I've let Stanley down."

"He doesn't feel that way. He's worried that you'll be hurt."

She closed her eyes. "I don't know what to do. I'm just so tired."

"You needn't worry about it, Mrs. Beecham," Jayce said. "I plan to go after him myself. You need to recover, and maybe by the time you are well we will have Chase in the hands of the Nome authorities."

Jacob wasn't sure if Helaina heard this or not. She seemed to have gone back to sleep. He loved the feel of her cradled in his arm. She seemed so vulnerable and helpless—not at all the bossy, arrogant woman he'd first met in Nome.

Just then John peeked in through the inner tent flap. "I'm gonna water and feed the dogs. You coming?"

Jacob placed Helaina back on her pallet. "Yeah, I'll be right there." He pulled a blanket over Helaina, then reached for his gloves. "You'll keep an eye on her, right?"

"You know I will. I'll watch them both."

"I'm worried about them," Jacob admitted, "but I keep trying to pray through it. God has a reason even in this, I keep reminding myself. I just wish I understood better why any of this had to happen."

"Sometimes we don't get answers," Jayce said, looking sadly at Leah. "I guess we just need to be patient. Sometimes the only thing to do is wait."

"I guess," Jacob said, but his heart couldn't accept this. There had to be something more he could do to help his sister and Helaina.

Leah listened to her brother and husband's conversation. She tried to take comfort in their words but found she couldn't. She felt such a mix of emotions: guilt for having left Chase on the trail and feeling he deserved nothing better; anger that God would have let things get so out of control—that He would take her to a place where she was helpless to keep bad things from happening.

She felt sorrow for the way Chase had ruined things for her and Jayce. Bitterness for the loss of a good future—for truly she did not know how she could go on with Jayce once he learned the truth.

She finally rolled over after Jacob left to help John with the dogs. Jayce was watching her as she opened her eyes.

"Hello," he said softly. "Did you sleep well?"

Leah thought the question absurd. How could she sleep well in the middle of the horrors that had become her life? Nevertheless, she tried to be civil. "I suppose."

"Would you like some coffee?"

She sat up and stretched. Her body ached from the long hours in one position. "Yes." Coffee actually sounded quite good.

"Are you hungry? I can warm you up something, or we have jerked meat and smoked salmon." He smiled and handed her a tin of steaming coffee.

"I'm not hungry." She drank the coffee slowly, happy to have something with which to occupy her mouth so that she wouldn't have to talk.

"You look better. The dark circles are gone from your eyes."

Leah didn't know what he wanted her to say. She could barely look at him without being reminded all over again of Chase and what he'd done. She longed to just go home, but she could hear the wind still wailing outside their shelter. Who knew when the storm might abate?

"Can you . . . well . . . talk about what happened?" Jayce asked hesitantly.

Leah felt sorry for him. He seemed almost afraid of her. "There's not much to say."

"Jacob and I went back to Last Chance for dogs and supplies. We learned that you were gone and that everyone thought I had already been there. I take it Chase told them I was your husband?"

Leah looked at the cup. "Yes. He wasn't expecting me to arrive in the village. I think he thought I would be with you."

"I'm sure he thought he could fool everyone."

"He did. No one suspected a thing," Leah replied. "Not that I would have wanted them to. If they would have known it was Chase instead of you, they might have gotten hurt."

"I suppose that much is true. Chase wouldn't have cared who he harmed. We followed your tracks and found the markers you left us."

"I couldn't do much. He watched me all the time."

"I don't understand why he took you."

Leah gave Jayce a look of disbelief. "For protection—to keep the others from learning who he was and coming after him. Because he's a selfish, evil man. How many more reasons does he need?"

"I suppose those things crossed my mind, but it seems that traveling with one woman, let alone two, would slow him down. We honestly worried that he would kill Helaina as soon as he got far enough away from Nome to feel safe."

"She nearly killed herself."

"I can see that. But I can understand that she wanted to complete her job. I don't like what she did, but I can reason through why she would take those chances."

"She did what she did because she's as selfish as Chase," Leah said matter-of-factly. "None of this would have happened if she'd just gone home with her brother."

"But that's not true, Leah. I would have gone after Chase even if she had gone back to Washington. You know that I labored over that decision, but I felt it was my obligation. I'd hoped that it would help keep other people from suffering at Chase's hand. I still feel that way."

Leah nearly dropped her cup. "What are you saying? You can't still plan to go after him."

"I have to. This must come to an end. Chase has hurt too many people. Why, he came in and stole you right out from under the noses of people who'd known you for ten years. He hurt you as well. That's easy enough to see."

If you only knew, Leah thought. She drank the last of her coffee. "You can't go. He hates you. He plans to kill you. Frankly, I think he means to put an end to your life and assume your place in society."

"But obviously that would be difficult."

"Why? He's performed all of his heinous acts under your name. If he convinces people that *you* were the evil twin, then there will be no reason to cause him further grief."

"Leah, listen to yourself. You aren't making sense. Helaina's brother has no doubt already shared the truth with the Pinkerton Agency. They know the fingerprints they have on file belong to Chase and not to me. As they compare evidence from all of Chase's crime scenes, they will have other proof as well. Chase can't win in this situation, and I won't live in his shadow all of my life."

"That's the way he feels about you. That's why I know he will kill you." Leah tried to contain her frustration at Jayce's ignorance. "You can't go through with this. You can't."

"I'm sorry you had to endure so much," Jayce said, suddenly changing the subject.

"I don't want to talk about it," Leah replied. "I want you to promise me that you won't go after Chase. I need you to just be done with this here and now."

Jayce's expression told her his answer before he spoke. "I can't. You know I can't. Especially now."

"Why especially now? Why should it matter so much?"

"Because he took you. Because he will go on believing himself capable of taking whatever he wants. You know it's true."

Leah did know, but she wasn't about to admit it. Not if it meant Jayce would risk his life to go after Chase. "Maybe so, but I also know his hatred will drive him to destroy you. He told me stories, Jayce. Stories of when you were young. He hated you even then. He blames you for everything wrong in his life. You can't fight against that. He only cares about seeing you dead."

"And you think me such a poor example of manhood that I couldn't be the one to put an end to this? Do you honestly give him more credit for ability and brains?"

Leah heard the hurt in his voice. "No. I don't give him credit for those things. I give him credit for his blinding hate. There is a rage and hate so fierce inside of your brother that he will never stop trying to satisfy it. But the only thing that will ever ease it will be your blood—or his."

The storm eased the next day. Leah awoke to a strange silence in the absence of the wind, then immediately noticed the missing warmth of Jayce sleeping next to her. He hadn't tried to be overly familiar with her, and for that Leah was grateful. She felt strange in his arms, almost confused. She knew it was her husband—knew that Jayce and Chase were two different men—but at the same time there were just too many similarities. It was as if Chase had cursed her somehow. Could she never again be alone with her husband without remembering what Chase had done—how he had touched her? She shuddered and closed her eyes tight against the memories.

I can't live like this. I have to find a way to get beyond this—to no longer remember anything about it.

Sitting up, she pushed back the blankets and looked to where Helaina slept. With a heavy sigh, Leah went to the woman. She didn't want to hold such fierce anger toward Helaina. The woman was sick and needed help. If Leah didn't offer her healing skills, Helaina might yet die. That was something Leah knew she couldn't live with on her conscience.

"Helaina?" Leah felt the woman's forehead. It was cool. "Helaina?"

Helaina stirred and opened her eyes. "What's wrong?"

Leah shook her head. "Nothing. I just woke up and wondered how you were doing. It sounds as though the storm's abated. Jayce and Jacob must be outside readying things for us to leave."

"But if we go, we'll lose track of Chase."

Leah squared her shoulders. "Haven't you learned your lesson about that? What in the world possesses you to continue with such nonsense? Chase Kincaid is a dangerous man who wouldn't think twice about killing you."

"But he had every chance . . . and he did nothing," Helaina said in a weak voice.

"He did plenty." The bitterness was evident in Leah's reply.

"So you're awake," Jacob declared as he entered the tent. He had a tin plate of steaming meat. "John's enjoying the calm after the storm. He cooked this up for you."

"Where's Jayce?" Leah questioned, moving away from Helaina.

Jacob's joyful expression contorted to a frown. "He said he left you a letter explaining."

"Explaining what? What are you talking about?" Leah looked back to her pallet. Jayce's things were gone, but a folded piece of paper was propped up against Leah's mukluks.

The answers came to her without Jacob speaking a word or without opening the letter. Jayce had gone after his brother. Leah shook her head and yanked on her boots. "Fine. If this is the way it's to be, I don't know why I even bothered to marry him. It's obvious that we are totally wrong for each other. He doesn't trust me to know the truth of this situation, and he won't listen to anything I have to say."

"Maybe it's more an issue of honor," Jacob suggested. "He has a job to do—he's pledged himself to do it."

"She said the same thing," Leah said, pointing her finger at Helaina. "But you don't want her going out there after Chase. What's the difference, Jacob?"

"The difference is, she's a woman and she's very sick. Jayce and Chase are brothers. You know how Jayce has suffered over his decision to go after Chase. It's not easy for him."

"It hasn't been easy for me either," Leah countered. "You probably just urged him on. That's it, isn't it? You wanted to keep Helaina safe, so you encouraged Jayce to get out there and capture Chase."

"You're talking crazy, Leah. No one has more influence over Jayce than you. You know very well that he's struggled with his decision to get involved in this. You told me so yourself, and now you're acting as though it's the first time you've heard it."

"I'm not the crazy one here. Crazy is going after a man who wishes to see you dead. A man who hates you so much he would stop at nothing to hurt you. Nothing."

"That makes it all the more logical for Jayce to want to go after him. He can't very well spend the rest of his life looking over his shoulder for Chase, now, can he? You're being completely selfish about this, Leah."

Leah could hardly believe Jacob's words. "You don't understand any of this. You never will." She pulled on her parka and stormed from the tent, ignoring Jacob's comments and protests.

The sun shone in a washed-out manner against pale blue skies, but Leah hardly noticed. She looked across the small camp noting Jayce's dog team and sled were gone.

He's really gone. He's left me to hunt down his brother—not even knowing what Chase has done. Chase has taken my virtue, my purity, and now he will take my husband as well.

Leah actually tried to pray. *Please, God, keep Jayce from death.* The words seemed to echo in a hollow manner within her worried mind. She wanted to believe that God still cared—that He was truly faithful and knew exactly the wrongs that had befallen them. Leah wanted to trust that He was able to deliver her and Jayce from this nightmare, but it hurt so much. She felt betrayed—deserted. Her soul ached from trying to battle the demon that threatened to completely destroy her heart and mind.

She sunk to the ground. "Oh, God, help us. Help me."

Chapter Fifteen

Jayce pushed north in the direction from which he'd seen Leah come. The snowfall had covered the trail, but he was certain that if he continued in this manner, he would find some sign of his brother. The crisp air stung his nostrils and ice formed on his mustache and beard. It was considerably colder than when they'd first started the journey. He wondered how long they'd actually been gone; he'd managed to lose track of the days in his worry over Leah.

Slowing the dogs, he tried to find some sign of the trail. There was nothing, even though this had looked to be a main thoroughfare, according to John. The snow had clearly buried the evidence, and the dogs were tired from battling the trail. Jayce knew it would be easier for them if he cut the trail for a while. Jacob had taught him this during one of the other storms.

Jayce halted the dogs and let them rest while he took up his snowshoes. It wouldn't be easy to break the trail, but it would help the animals, and that was of the utmost importance.

"Come on, boys," he said, taking hold of the gangline. Jayce worked to clear a path wide enough for the dogs, all the while looking for any sign of his brother having passed this way.

He tried not to think of how angry Leah would be when she awoke and found him gone. After her comments the night before, Jayce knew there would be no reasoning with her. A weight settled over him. Marriage was hard work, and he and Leah had scarcely had time alone together since their wedding. Chase had come between them in so many ways.

"All of my life you've caused me trouble," Jayce declared, as if Chase could hear him. "All of my life you've tried to exact some kind of revenge on me, and none of it has ever made sense."

Eventually the snow evened out and Jayce could see that it wasn't as deep. He took off his snowshoes and positioned himself behind the sled once again. The dogs were happy to have their head again. The lead dog, especially, seemed to have renewed energy for the day as he pulled eagerly against the weight.

The next morning Jayce felt his cause rather hopeless. There was no sign of Chase. Any tracks he might have left had been covered by the wind-driven snow. Jayce studied the landscape for any discrepancies and found none. He thought perhaps Chase had taken a different direction. If so, Jayce would be hard-pressed to figure out what direction he'd gone.

"Lord, I need your guidance. I need to know where to go and how to find my brother."

Jayce continued to search the trail. There was an abundance of dwarfed birch and willows. Rounded tussocks, dangerous to the sleds when hidden in the snow, were barely visible in areas where the wind had drifted the snow. It was a lonely, desperate country.

Clouds moved in, subduing the light. Soon it would be night and another day would pass without Jayce having anything to show for it. He let his mind drift to Leah. He knew Jacob had promised to get her back to Last Chance. Jayce could only hope she'd been cooperative and sensible. He couldn't endure it if she tried to come after him and got hurt.

Up ahead the trail seemed more notable. There looked to be signs of activity. There were numerous animal tracks. Snowshoe hare, fox, and even a wolf or two. Jayce felt for his sidearm. It might be nice to hunt something down for his supper. He didn't relish the idea of eating smoked salmon and crackers once again.

Then he noted other tracks. They were human.

Chase.

Jayce didn't dare even breathe the name lest it somehow jinx his search. Once again he halted the sled. Leaving the dogs anchored and resting, Jayce walked ahead, following the tracks. There seemed to be something wrong. The tracks were staggering first in one direction and then another. There was no real sense to their pattern. If they did belong to Chase, perhaps he'd grown ill or was hurt.

Glancing back, Jayce could see he was a considerable distance from the dogs. He didn't like that idea and retraced his steps back to the sled. Once again he took hold of the gangline and led the dogs himself.

The dogs were agitated. They were good at sensing trouble, and Jayce couldn't help but wonder if he was walking into an ambush. It would be like Chase to feign illness or some other trouble. Jayce pulled out his revolver just in case.

The tracks veered to the west. The path was more open here, but the tracks were just as strange. It almost seemed as if the one who'd made them had been dancing instead of walking. What could it mean?

Another ten yards and a stand of stunted spruce revealed that someone had taken refuge beside them. A blanket remained behind as evidence. Jayce anchored the dogs and went to retrieve the piece. He held it up against the dimming light and felt his breath catch. Blood!

Jayce looked around him, searching past the spruce and the other vegetation. Someone was injured. If not Chase, then someone else. Either way, they would clearly need some kind of care.

Jayce hurried back to the dogs and pulled the hook. "But what if it's a trick?" he questioned. The lead dog cocked his head and gave a whine, as if to question Jayce in return. "What if Chase left this and it's just animal blood?" His mind raced with questions. "But why would he do that? What would he hope to gain?"

Jayce moved out with the dogs, still wondering at the situation. He felt his skin prickle. Every sound seemed magnified—every movement was suspect.

The path came to a creek. The ice looked solid enough, but just as Jayce was about to cross it, he noticed that there was a smaller trail that ran alongside the frozen water. For reasons that were beyond him, Jayce turned to follow the path. It wound back and forth as it followed the outline of the creek. Snow had drifted here and hid any tracks.

Jayce stopped the dogs and knelt several times to see if he could brush away the snow and spy any clues. There appeared to be nothing and he pressed forward cautiously. The dogs sensed his concern and began to whine. One of the swing dogs let out a mournful howl that caused Jayce to seriously consider turning back. Something just didn't feel right.

When they rounded the next bend, Jayce spied something on the trail up ahead. He stopped and strained to see. It appeared rather furry. He thought of Leah's wounded bear and drew a deep breath. Perhaps the thing had come here to die. Then again, maybe it wasn't dead yet. Jayce gripped the rifle tighter and began to walk slowly forward.

As he drew closer, however, he could see it wasn't an animal at all, but rather a man. Native, from the looks of his clothing. *But it could be Chase,* he thought. He felt a catch in his throat. He held his breath. Was this a trap?

Halting the dogs, Jayce secured the sled, then gingerly made his way to the man on the ground. "God help me," he murmured as he poked at the man with his toe. The man didn't move.

Carefully, Jayce reached down and rolled the man over. He jumped back at the reflected image of his own face. Only this face had been cut—sliced several times by some sort of animal. The pattern suggested bear. Perhaps Leah's rogue bear.

"Chase, can you hear me?" Jayce leaned down to ascertain if his brother was yet alive. There was a faint heartbeat and shallow breathing. The man was barely alive.

Helaina's recovery was slow but steady. Leah managed to secure healing herbs at the small village where Jacob had left Brownie. She faithfully tended Helaina, saying very little and offering nothing more than medical care.

"You can't just go on like this," Helaina said that morning as they prepared to head out once again. Jacob and John were busy with the dogs, so she thought it the right time to speak to Leah.

Although Leah looked up from her packing, she said nothing. Her expression seemed to challenge Helaina to continue. "I know you're angry at me, but if anyone has a right to be mad, it's me."

"And how do you figure that?" Leah was clearly intrigued.

"We had Chase Kincaid at hand, and you let him get away. Now he's off doing whatever he pleases."

"It's not enough that this obsession of yours has cost me everything I care about," Leah said frankly. She stared hard at Helaina, and it was easy to see the disgust in her expression. "I wouldn't even be here if it weren't for you. You have no right to condemn my actions."

"But you have the right to condemn mine? I hardly see where that is fair."

"Nothing about this trip has been fair. Fair doesn't even enter into the picture. You are a selfish, self-driven woman, Mrs. Beecham. Had you not had to have your revenge on the world for the loss of your husband and parents, you might have done the sensible thing and settled down to remarry and have a family."

"This isn't about my family," Helaina retorted angrily.

"No, but it is about mine," Leah countered. She squared her shoulders and put her hands on her hips. She appeared to wait for Helaina to comment on this. Instead, Helaina refocused on Leah's role.

"You have to understand—by leaving Chase, you put us days behind in his capture. He might even escape all together. All you had to do, once he was drugged, was tie him up and throw him in the basket with me. It should have been fairly simple."

Leah looked at her oddly but said nothing. Helaina continued. "He'd be here now, on his way to justice, and your husband would be at your side. Do you not see how you are the cause of your own misery?"

"You are by far and away the most ruthless and uncompassionate woman I've ever known." Helaina bristled at this but allowed Leah to continue. "Your own brother suffered because of you. You weren't there when he discovered what you'd done. He was heartbroken to realize you would probably end up dead. How he must be suffering even now—not that you would care."

"I care," Helaina said, surprised at Leah's words. She'd tried not to think of Stanley or how she'd disappointed him.

"You care only so long as it doesn't cost you anything—as long as you can get your own way in a matter." Leah pulled her long dark hair over her shoulder and began to braid it in a furious manner. "You are a spoiled woman who is used to having her own way. You have a separate set of rules designed for yourself. The rest of us have to do your bidding or you use your rules against us."

"I don't have any idea what you're talking about. I've only worked to see justice done."

"You've worked for revenge. You've worked to prove something to yourself and to your brother. I'm not even sure you know what it is you're trying to prove, but it drives you on—and God help the man or woman who gets in your way."

Helaina felt the words stab deep into her heart. Was this truly how Leah perceived her? How others perceived her? "You don't understand—"

"Nor do I want to," Leah interrupted. "I spent far too long trying to understand. Trying to forgive you and give the matter over to God. I tried to pray for you, to help you get well, and now I have to contend with your condemnation once again."

"I'm not condemning you. I merely wished that you hadn't left Chase behind." Helaina's words came out rather stilted. "I might have a different way of doing what I think to be right, but that doesn't mean I can't appreciate your position."

"It's not my position that worries me now," Leah replied, securing her braid. "My husband is out there facing that monster. Jayce is a kindhearted, loving man who has labored with the decision to track down his own flesh and blood. You only care about getting the job done, but my husband has to face that he's sending his own brother—his twin brother—to his death. Imagine someone asking—no, demanding—that you send Stanley to his death."

Helaina felt tears come to her eyes. Leah was right. She hadn't really cared about Jayce's feelings or how it might affect him to hunt down his brother like some kind of rabid dog.

"I'm sorry," she whispered.

Leah looked at her for a moment and shook her head. "Sorry doesn't change anything. It doesn't bring Jayce back here safely, and it doesn't return the things that have been lost or stolen in this."

Helaina had no idea what Leah meant, but she tried to ease the tension. "Look, sorry may seem to just be an empty word to you, but I truly mean it. I'm not one to offer it lightly. I know I've been demanding in this matter, but look at the harm Chase has done. Do you want to be responsible for his continuing to kill and wound? I couldn't live with myself if I didn't at least try to see to his capture."

"There are a lot of things I can't live with," Leah replied in an eerie calm that unnerved Helaina even more. Leah grabbed her parka and left the tent without another word.

Helaina, much to her own surprise, burst into tears and buried her face in her hands. "What have I done? What do I do now?"

Leah felt as though a noose had tightened around her neck. Every word, every thought that had been exchanged with Helaina had drained Leah's sanity and energy. She hated herself for the things she'd said, for purposefully trying to make Helaina feel the same depth of pain that she herself felt.

"I would be better off dead," she whispered as she stalked off away from camp. She looked to the skies overhead. "Why not just kill me? Why must I suffer more? You've proven your point. You've shown me how wretched I am. I already believed it. I'd already asked for your help and deliverance, and here I am—angry and ugly. It's no use for me to go on. I can't be helped this time." She began to cry, the tears that she'd held back on the trail refusing to abate.

Leah fell to her knees. She pounded her fists against her thighs and let out an anguished sob. It was all just so hopeless. How could she ever be alone with Jayce and not see his brother and remember what he had done to her? Those memories would never fade—they were permanently planted in her mind like hidden dynamite that would go off when she least expected it.

Her nature had fought against the anguish and sorrow in order to survive, but Leah no longer wanted to survive. What was the point? If she couldn't love Jayce and give herself to him without fear of the past, what was the sense in living?

Chapter Sixteen

Helaina heard someone come into the tent and presumed Leah had come back to continue her attack. Looking up, she was surprised to find Jacob instead. "What are you doing here?"

"I heard you crying. What's wrong?" He knelt down beside her. "Are you feeling worse?"

"I feel terrible, but not because of my health." She wiped her eyes with her hands. "Your sister thinks I'm a horrible person."

"Leah said that?"

"Well, not exactly that." Helaina looked away and tried not to remember what Leah had said about Jacob loving her. She saw no proof of that, and she figured now that Leah had been lying in order to worry Chase.

"Then what did she say?"

Helaina bit at her lower lip. She wasn't entirely sure she wanted to have this conversation. A part of her reasoned that Jacob might offer comfort, but at the same time another part suggested that he might confirm Leah's statement.

"Please tell me. I want to help if I can," Jacob said, reaching for her hand.

Helaina pulled back quickly. "She said I was selfish. She said that I was the cause of all of this." She waved her hand. "She blames me for everything—for her being kidnapped, for Jayce being forced to go after his brother, for . . . for . . . everything." The tears came again. "I only did my job. I only did what I thought was right. No one seems to understand my motivation. . . . my reasoning in this."

Jacob sat cross-legged a few feet away but said nothing. It was almost as if he needed to hear more before he could comment.

"I know that no one wanted me to leave Seattle alone, but I had to show Stanley that I was still trustworthy and capable. He had given me a job to do, and I had done it fairly well to that point. After all, I'm the one who figured out that Jayce Kincaid was not the man we were after."

"That was a good thing, Helaina, but had you just talked to some of the rest of us—even questioned Jayce himself—you probably would have learned that without having to send us all the way to Seattle."

"But that's not how things are done in apprehending criminals. All criminals suggest they are innocent. Every man or woman who ever broke the law has some excuse as to why it wasn't their fault or why they shouldn't be charged." She pushed back her long blond hair, wishing fervently she'd at least attempted to attend to it before Jacob's arrival. It had been so long since she'd had a bath or any chance to clean up. She knew she must appear a frightful mess. Perhaps that was why Jacob looked at her with what seemed a suspicious expression.

"Even guilty," she continued, "Jayce Kincaid would have declared that he had nothing to do with those crimes, and his statements would have been no different than any other criminal I've helped to apprehend. So you see, it isn't quite as easy as you'd like to believe. I had a job to do, and I did it."

"All right, so we set aside your deception from last summer and focus on Seattle," Jacob said softly. "Your brother relieved you of your job. He forbade you to go to Nome. Yet you disregarded his decisions and went ahead on your own. You didn't even wait for us."

Helaina realized she couldn't deny his words. She thought for a moment. It suddenly seemed very important that she make him understand. "Have you never felt responsible for something? Something that you had to see through to completion?"

"Of course."

"Well, this was no different. I knew Stanley had relieved me because he felt the job too arduous for me. Perhaps he even felt that I wasn't as cunning and smart as Chase Kincaid."

"You know that isn't true. He took you off the job because he finally came to his senses and realized you could be killed in the process."

Helaina painfully got to her knees. "But he knew that from the beginning. He was always nervous about sending me, but Chase had already defeated several agents. He'd nearly killed Stanley, so he knew something had to be done. He figured Chase would never expect a woman."

"No doubt that was true," Jacob replied. "But it wasn't sensible. Chase is much too dangerous . . . as you've learned the hard way."

"So you think Leah is right? You think I'm just selfish and self-centered?" She felt tears stream down her cheeks and hated herself for such weakness.

Jacob looked to the floor. "I think you were wrong."

"Explain yourself."

He lifted his gaze to meet her eyes. "I think you acted out of a desire to accomplish something for yourself. You were motivated not by justice, but by a need to fulfill some imaginary mark you had set for yourself."

"It wasn't imaginary and it wasn't just for me," Helaina argued. "Chase is a dangerous man who needs to be stopped. I felt responsible—I needed to finish the job. I wish you could understand that."

"I wish you could understand my point of view on this as well."

She looked at him questioningly and sank back to her pallet. "What do you mean?" She suddenly felt drained of all energy. Her illness had definitely taken its toll.

Jacob didn't answer right away, and for several minutes Helaina thought he might refuse to speak. Finally, just when she'd given up hope, he began.

"I don't think Leah has a right to put this all off on you. However, I do believe Leah innocent of any wrongdoing. I don't think you have a right to blame her for not apprehending Chase. It wasn't her obligation or desire. She was afraid for her safety and for yours. She knew that without proper treatment you would die. You do realize that, don't you?"

"I know I was sick, but I've always had a strong constitution. I would have recovered."

Jacob shook his head. "Do you honestly think you're invincible? That you'll live forever? Because without accepting that Jesus died for your sins and that He wants you to repent of those sins and turn to God, you can't live forever."

She stiffened. The last thing she had expected was a sermon. "I asked you if you believed your sister was right in calling me selfish and self-centered. I didn't ask for a theological discussion."

Jacob looked sadder than Helaina had ever seen him. She instantly regretted her words but knew there was no way to take them back. She opened her mouth to speak, but Jacob beat her to it.

"I don't want to have a theological discussion either. You know, I feel sorry for you, Helaina. People care about you—genuinely care—but you push them away because you're terrified of being disappointed . . . hurt. God genuinely cares, too, but you've lumped Him in with the rest. You're afraid He'll disappoint you as well."

"This isn't about God. It's about your sister."

"No. It's about you."

Leah fell asleep despite the rough ride. In her dreams she saw Jayce and couldn't help but feel joy at his affection. He told her how much he loved her, but as Leah started to reply, his image faded. Soon there were other faces. Ayoona and Oopick, Jacob and Karen. Leah felt as though they were all trying to tell her something, but she couldn't make out the words. It was as if they all spoke a language she couldn't understand.

Then the dream shifted and Leah was a little girl running in the mountains. She felt free and exhilarated by the mountain air. She thought for a moment she might lift right up into the air and fly. It was a marvelous sensation.

"Leah?"

She knew that voice. Turning, Leah found her mother. She smiled and waved. "I'm here, Mama."

Her mother smiled. "Leah, do not forget who loves you."

"I won't forget, Mama. Look, I've picked you some flowers." Leah held out the bouquet, but the blossoms withered and blew away. She frowned. "They used to be beautiful. Now they're ruined." Leah began to cry. "I'm ruined too."

"No, Leah. You aren't ruined. You are beautiful, and you are loved. No one can change that." The voice was no longer her mother's; rather, it was a deep, comforting voice that seemed to come from the skies. Could it be God?

"But Chase did those horrible things to me," she sobbed, suddenly seeing herself as a grown woman in rags. "Look at me. He's destroyed me."

"Chase had no power to make you, and he has no power to destroy you, Leah. You have already chosen who holds power over you. Remember?"

Leah awoke with a start. For a minute she feared everyone in the party had experienced the same voice she had heard. She pushed aside the furs and came up from her place in the sled. Buried there in her warm cocoon, no one knew whether she was awake or asleep. She glanced over her shoulder to John. She had chosen his sled so that Helaina could ride in Jacob's. John didn't seem to even notice her there. No one paid her any mind.

No one had heard the voice. She realized she was panting and eased back into the furs. Could the words have come from God? The bitter pain that had hardened her heart felt lessened.

"Chase had no power to make you, and he has no power to destroy you, Leah. You have already chosen who holds power over you. Remember?" She heard the words echo in her head as though they were being freshly spoken.

"Chase has no power over me unless I give it to him," Leah murmured. Her heart picked up speed. "I know who holds power over me." A tiny spark of hope began to burn. Chase had only touched her physically because he had imposed that upon her. She had no choice. But she was allowing him to touch her spiritually and emotionally, and she had a choice in that.

"I won't give him that power," she whispered. "I won't give him that part of me." The words gave her renewed strength. The shackles seemed to fall away. The ember of hope burst into a flame. "I'm not ruined." Tears fell hot against her cheeks. "I'm not ruined."

Later that night, Leah felt she had to face Helaina again. She had hoped Helaina could stay by herself so Leah could share Jacob's tent, but Jacob insisted the women stay together. Knowing this, Leah knew she had to apologize for having lost her temper.

"I've brought you supper," she said as she came into the tent.

Helaina looked up. "What is it?"

Leah put the tin plate on the floor in front of her. "Reindeer stew. It's the last of the meat. John and one of the other men plan to scout ahead and hunt. I'll be driving John's sled tomorrow."

"It smells good," Helaina admitted and sat up to eat.

"Look, I want to say something," Leah began. She sat down, hoping Helaina would understand that this wasn't just a quick, insincere comment. "I need to apologize for losing my temper this morning. I was wrong to do that."

Helaina looked up in surprise. "Were you also wrong to say the things you said?"

Her tone seemed rather hard—almost smug, but Leah refused to let it put a damper on her newly found peace of mind. "No. I meant what I said this morning." Helaina's expression fell and Leah continued. "I spoke the truth."

"Maybe your truth." Helaina pushed back the plate and shook her head.

"Truth is truth. You're the one who believes the law is the law. Why should it be so hard to understand that it's no different for truth?"

"Laws are established and written down. There is only one interpretation—one meaning."

"Then why must there be judges—Supreme Courts to review the laws and the cases involving those laws?"

"Look, this isn't about that. You called me names—said I was selfish and self-centered."

Leah easily remembered her words from the morning. "And your actions have proven to be such. You focus on yourself—not God or anyone else. I apologize for getting angry about it and saying things I might otherwise have kept to myself. But that's all."

"So this is about God. Just because I don't believe the same things you believe, I'm wrong?"

"Helaina, I'm not here to condemn you. I don't even want to argue with you." Leah got to her knees. "But I hope someday you will understand that vengeance belongs to the Lord. You will never find satisfaction in your schemes for revenge—at least not the same kind of satisfaction you could find in belonging to someone who will never change—never disappoint."

"How many times do I have to tell you or your brother, I'm not in this for revenge?"

"Do you suppose if you say that often enough, it will be true?" Leah didn't wait for an answer. "Helaina, I wish you would truly consider the matter with an open heart. You want revenge for Stanley—for the pain caused him. You want revenge on Chase because he's the one assignment that you've failed to fulfill. You couldn't catch him. Just like you couldn't keep your family from being killed."

Helaina gasped. "How dare you? You have no right to bring them into this."

"Maybe not, but I think if you consider it, you'll see the truth for yourself." Leah got to her feet and moved to the door. "I'm sorry if I've offended you, but rather than worrying about yourself, I'd start thinking about poor Stanley. All he knows is that you've disappeared into the wilds of Alaska chasing after a madman. If the Pinkerton agents were able to get word to Washington from Nome, then Stanley will truly be grief-stricken. He won't know if you're dead or alive, but given Chase's record, he'll assume the worst. Instead of worrying about the one that got away, it might be good for you to remember those you still have."

Leah left Helaina to ponder her words and hoped that the younger woman would see and understand. Walking toward the fire, Leah met Jacob's questioning expression.

"Was she hungry?"

Leah shrugged. "I don't suppose she has her appetite back just yet."

"What about you?"

Leah sat down beside him. "I ate. It was quite good."

"Are you feeling better now? You seem . . . well . . ."

"Less caustic?" she asked, throwing him a smile. "I'm sorry for the way I've acted. This little adventure in my life has taken its toll. I'm ready to go home and be quiet. I'm still not myself, but I'm trying to regain some peace of mind."

"God can give it to you, if you let Him."

Leah nodded. "But we've been at odds lately. I feel frustrated that He would allow all of this misery into my life. If He loves me, how can He allow me to suffer so much?" She genuinely wanted answers.

Jacob gazed into the fire. "But God didn't spare His own Son misery and sorrow. Why would He spare us?" He turned toward his sister. "Look, I think that things happen—all things—for a reason. Those reasons are sometimes painful to deal with . . . to understand. I think, however, that it's all a part of trusting God more. It's easy to trust Him when things go right. Then your faith has no need to grow. Understand?"

"I think so. I guess I just didn't want to grow that much." She forced a smile. "So many times in my life, I've had to grow up before I felt I was ready. Like when Mama died, and then Papa died, or when Jayce refused my love. Now with all that's happened, I feel that again I've been made to face things that I wasn't ready for."

"But God will take you through it. He will never leave you nor forsake you. The Bible says so. These problems are only momentary. They won't last forever."

Leah nodded. "I know you're right. I need to look forward to my future with Jayce instead of looking back at the sorrows of the past."

"Exactly." He shifted his position and suppressed a yawn. "Look, I've been thinking about that as well. I want you and Jayce to take the house. I'll build a small place close by. It'd be nice if you'd still cook for me from time to time." He gave her a rather pathetic look that suggested pleading.

Leah smiled. "You know I will, but we could surely work out something so that you don't have to go building a house in the dead of winter."

"Maybe I'll stay with someone until spring."

"You can stay with us," Leah countered. "We can set up a room for you in the store. There's plenty of room in there. So long as we learn to respect each other's privacy, I don't think there will be any problems."

"Well, maybe until spring," Jacob said, nodding. "You should know, though, I've actually thought about returning to Ketchikan."

"Why?" Leah was genuinely surprised by this statement.

"Adrik asked me to consider it. He says there's going to be a lot of new job opportunities. The government is going to pick up that plan to build a railroad to Fairbanks. They've already gotten started and have asked Adrik to come in and help them."

"Help them do what?"

"Hunt for the workers, mainly. I think he'll also help with the natives."

"But he's Tlingit and Russian," Leah replied. "The railroad will go into Athabascan country."

"I know, but Adrik said he has friends there and feels he can offer help as an interpreter. He suggested I come and take care of the homestead in Ketchikan or even come work with him."

Leah considered this for a moment. "It's hard to imagine you leaving Last Chance."

"Well, I haven't completely decided. Captain Latimore still wants our help with the Arctic exploration. I wouldn't mind giving that a chance either. I know Jayce is still very interested. We talked about it on the trail."

"I guess I hadn't thought about either of you leaving."

"You were invited as well."

Leah shook her head and reached her hands out to the flames. "I've had enough excitement to last a lifetime. I don't want any more."

For several minutes, Jacob said nothing. "What happened out there? With Chase?"

Leah swallowed hard. The old feelings tried to creep in, and she closed her eyes. "Please don't ask me." Her voice was barely audible. "I can't talk about it. Not now—maybe never."

Chapter Seventeen

Jayce managed to get Chase into the tent before the wind picked up and the temperature dropped. He carefully arranged his brother's injured frame, then went to work melting snow for water.

The weather threatened more snow, and Jayce worried about finding his way back to the village at which they'd stopped. He'd seen no other sign of civilization and given Chase's desperate state, this furthered his concern. For all he knew there could be a village just over the next hill, but then again, he might head off in the wrong direction and be hundreds of miles from any kind of help.

As Chase's body began to thaw, he started to move and then to moan. Jayce moved to his side with a bit of melted water and one of his old shirts. He ripped the shirt into strips that he could use to dress Chase's wounds. The only problem was that there were many cuts.

"Chase, can you hear me?"

His brother's head moved, but he didn't open his swollen eyes. Jayce took one of the strips and dipped it in the water. He touched the cloth to Chase's bloodied lips, hoping to trickle a little of the clean water into his mouth.

"Chase. It's me, Jayce. I'm trying to help you, but you need to wake up."

With a tenderness he didn't truly feel, Jayce lifted Chase's head ever so slightly. How could this man have gone so wrong in his life? How could he have forsaken the training and upbringing of good people to live a life of crime and murderous hate?

"Chase, I'm going to give you a little water." He squeezed the cloth onto his twin's lips. Some of the water ran into his bloodied beard, but a little made it inside.

Lowering Chase back to the pallet, Jayce began to tend the wounds. All the while he talked to his brother.

"I don't know why it had to come to this. It seems such a senseless waste of a life. You were always clever and good with mastering skills when they were of interest to you."

Jayce felt certain the nasty rips in Chase's face and upper body were made by a bear. Perhaps it had been Leah's rogue bear or one of the Arctic polar bears wandering inland. If it was Leah's bear, he would have been wounded and more dangerous. He would most likely attack without provocation. Chase would have only had a knife with which to defend himself. The fight would have definitely been unevenly matched, even if the bear was injured.

The water bloodied in the bowl rather quickly, and Jayce found himself in a dilemma. If he tossed it outside, it might attract the killer bear to join them. If not the bear, then perhaps wolves would be attracted to the scent. On the other hand, Jayce hadn't brought a lot of supplies and utensils with him. The bowl was much needed and Chase required more care.

Jayce finally decided he had no choice. He braved the wind and cold to walk some twenty yards from the tent. He carried the bowl and lantern in one hand while balancing his rifle with the other. He wasn't about to take a chance that the bear was still in the vicinity, just waiting.

The night was amazingly quiet. Only the wind offered any sound across the frozen tundra. The skies were heavy with clouds. No stars. No moon. Yet Jayce's thoughts were focused solely on his situation: He was in an unfamiliar area of the territory and his brother was fighting to live. Neither of them were in a good position. Jayce still needed to figure a way back to civilization, and Chase . . . well, as best Jayce could tell, Chase was dying.

"But you were coming here to take him to his death anyway," Jayce spoke to the silent landscape. "Isn't it better to see him die here than wait for him to be hanged?" There was no comfort in such thinking; what Jayce really wished could never be. He would trade most everything he had to see the years turned back and his brother's heart remade. "But that isn't going to happen. This is the life we have chosen. He chose his way, and I chose mine. It can't be undone now."

He made his way back to the tent and refilled the bowl before sitting back down at Chase's side. His brother lay very still. Jayce wasn't even sure he was breathing. He put his hand on Chase's chest and felt the very shallow rise and fall. At least he was still alive.

But to what purpose? Jayce felt almost torn in nursing his brother's wounds. He felt certain that without the medical attention of a doctor, Chase would most likely not make it through the night. It seemed heartless to pick and prod at his wounds. Even as Jayce contemplated this, Chase began to stir and then to cough.

Jayce heard him make a gurgling sound and rolled Chase slightly to his side. Blood poured from his mouth, causing Jayce to jump back a bit, while Chase struggled to regain consciousness. His eyes opened slowly. They were lifeless dark pits that seemed to see nothing.

Jayce put his hand on his brother's shoulder. "Chase, it's me. It's Jayce. You've been wounded." He helped Chase ease back on the pallet. "Can you hear me?"

"I . . . do." The words were barely audible.

The wind picked up, blowing fiercely against the tent. Jayce was glad for the small refuge but couldn't help wishing he could close his eyes and wake up in another place—another life. He suddenly hated where this one had taken him.

"You've been attacked by something. You're in bad shape."

"I . . . know."

"I'll make you some tea in a minute," Jayce said as he went back to tending Chase's face. "These cuts are very deep. I'll have to make a salve for them and see if we can keep the bleeding from starting up again. The head wounds are the worst. Whatever got you seems to have chewed on your head."

"Bear." Chase looked Jayce in the eyes. "Big bear."

Jayce nodded. "Leah said there was one moving around."

Chase tried to smile, but it looked most macabre. "Leah safe?"

Jayce was surprised by the question. "Yes. She and Helaina met us on the trail. Jacob and some of the men from the village took them home."

"Not you."

It wasn't really a question, but Jayce felt as though Chase were asking why he hadn't gone with them. "I had to find you. You knew we'd come for you."

Chase closed his eyes and drew a couple of wheezing breaths. Jayce set aside the bowl of water and went to the stove. He made a cup of strong tea and tested the temperature. He worried that it would be too hot for Chase to handle and went to the tent flap to retrieve some snow. He only opened the very bottom of the flap to keep the cold from stealing away the warmth. Stretching out, he grabbed a handful of snow and quickly plopped it into the cup. The tea sloshed over the sides, burning Jayce's hand momentarily. The pain caused him to remember Leah. There was so much he wanted to know—needed to know. How had Chase hurt her? What had he done and said that left her so devastated?

Jayce secured the flap and came back to Chase. His brother had opened his eyes again and watched him intently. "I have tea. I'll help you sit up a bit. It should help to relax you."

Chase gave the tiniest shake of his head. "No."

"Look, I'm just trying to make this better for you. Contrary to what you believe, I don't want to see you in pain."

"Lot of pain."

"I'm sure you're in a lot of pain," Jayce replied. "This tea should help."

"No."

Jayce felt a sense of frustration but put the tea aside. "Have it your way. You always have."

Chase tried again to smile. "Never had . . . it . . . my way."

Jayce sat back and shook his head. "I don't know how you figure that. You've done nothing but run our family for years. You know it's true. Now that you're finally incapacitated, you have no choice but to listen to me. And since the weather has turned foul on us, we have nothing better to do than talk."

"You were . . . the perfect . . . one."

"No, I wasn't perfect." Jayce toyed with the sinew that attached his mittens to the parka. "I didn't have time to be perfect. I was too busy trying to clean up after you. You were always causing me trouble, and I really resented it. I guess now that I have turned to God for my answers, I should ask your forgiveness for the hatred I felt toward you all these years."

"God . . . doesn't . . . care."

Jayce looked at the wounded man. "He does care. He cares more about you than you've ever cared for yourself. You were always taking chances with your life—with the lives of those around you. You've lived a reckless existence, and now you've no one to blame but yourself for this mess you're in."

"Can blame . . . you."

Jayce laughed and shrugged. "Sure. Go ahead and blame me if it makes you feel better. I doubt it will, however. Why you ever believed that made things better is beyond me. You've blamed me all of your life for one misery or another. And you know what's sad? In most cases I was your defender."

Chase's eyes seemed to widen a bit. "Didn't . . . ask you . . . to be."

"I know that."

"Hated . . . you . . . doing it." Chase grimaced and closed his eyes against the pain. Jayce leaned forward, and Chase immediately opened his eyes again. "Don't . . . touch . . . me."

"Don't be ridiculous. You'll die if I don't help you."

"I'll die . . . anyway. You'll . . . see . . . to it." He was panting the words, yet they came out stronger than the others.

Jayce said nothing for a moment. What could he say? He knew Chase was implying that Jayce would see him hanged. And if the rest of the family ever found out the part Jayce had played in this strange little play, there would be no living with any of them. Not that he would anyway. It was one of the reasons Jayce had chosen to hide out in Alaska. His siblings had no desire to follow him here. Only Chase had braved the elements.

"When did you first come to Alaska?" Jayce found himself asking.

"When you came." The words came out all run together.

Jayce cocked his head to one side. "That was a long time ago. You mean when I first came here after Mother died?"

"Yes."

"But how did you follow me? I didn't even know where I was going."

"You . . . weren't trying . . . to hide."

"That's true enough. Still, why would you do it?"

Chase tried to lick his lips, but the effort, coupled with talking, seemed too much. Jayce, without waiting for Chase's approval, took one of the clean strips and dipped it in the tea he'd made. Coming back to Chase, he put it to his brother's lips and dampened them.

Chase made no protest, so Jayce took the opportunity to do it again. That seemed to be enough and Chase raised his left hand ever so slightly as if to wave off his brother's efforts.

Jayce presumed the conversation would end. Chase was in no shape to continue, and it would probably be best if they both got some sleep. "We'll need to get out of here at daybreak. Better rest for now." He started to clean up the area.

"Had to leave . . . you were leaving."

Jayce turned at Chase's comment. "I don't understand."

"If I stayed . . . they would know . . . who I was."

Jayce thought a moment, then realization dawned. "You mean if you stayed with everyone knowing I had gone, and continued to pull your pranks and commit crimes, there would be no doubt that you were the culprit. Is that it?"

"Yes."

Jayce shook his head. "So even then you were planning a life of crime?"

"It . . . suited me."

"But why? You were wealthy. You had a good inheritance from our father. All of us did. I never understood the way you each squandered what you had instead of investing it or buying something useful like a home."

"You . . . were . . . the perfect son." His eyes narrowed, and Jayce clearly saw the hatred there. "Turned . . . Mother against me."

"But I wasn't trying to be perfect, and it had never been my intention to turn Mother or anyone else against you. You did that all on your own." Jayce felt his ire grow. "I was merely trying to do the right thing. Our mother was alone and needed protection from all of you. You robbed her blind. She loved you and you took everything she had."

"I . . . never . . . did."

"I know you did. She gave you her inheritance. She gave money to each of you after you went through your own fortunes. She ended up so deeply in debt that she had to sell the house in order to make things right with her creditors. Don't tell me you didn't do that. Don't lie to me—not now."

"I . . . would have . . . helped her."

"It doesn't matter now what you would have done. It's in the past." Jayce took a deep breath to ease his anger. There was no sense in getting mad at a dying man.

"You'll . . . soon have . . . your way . . . your revenge."

Jayce looked at his brother and shook his head. "I never wanted revenge. That's never been what this was about. I wanted to keep you from hurting people. You'd already killed, and then in Nome you killed again. I couldn't let that go on for the sake of those innocent people. But it's never been about revenge."

"It . . . will be." Chase gasped for air and seemed to fight against some imaginary grip as he clutched his chest as best he could.

Jayce feared Chase might die any moment. "You need to make your peace with God. You cannot die without making things right."

"No." Chase moved his head from side to side, the movement ever so slight.

"Chase, God wants to forgive you your sins. The Bible says that He sent His Son, Jesus, to die for those sins so that you could have everlasting life. He can wipe away the blood and thievery. You can die a forgiven man with a clean slate."

"And . . . you?"

"I don't understand. What about me?"

"You . . . forgive . . . me?"

Jayce thought about it for a moment. He had wrestled with such thoughts while on Chase's trail. Could he forgive his brother for stealing his life . . . ruining his reputation . . . kidnapping his wife? It would take a supreme effort on his part, but Jayce knew he had to try.

"I want to forgive you, Chase. I won't lie to you and say it's easy. You've given me nothing but a life of misery and heartache. You've grieved me at every turn. We could have been close. . . . I really resent that we couldn't have that. You might have been my most trusted confidant, but you chose instead to put a wall between us. You destroyed what might have been. What I hoped could one day be salvaged, you destroyed by your deception and lawless acts."

Jayce rubbed his bearded chin and held his hand against his mouth for a moment. When he pulled it away, he gave a heavy sigh. "I want to forgive you, because it's the right thing in God's eyes. God will forgive you if you ask, and I must as well."

Chase gave a strange laugh. "You won't . . . forgive."

Jayce narrowed his eyes. "Why would you say that? You know nothing of who I am, Chase. Through God's power, I can do all things. The Bible says so. And since I believe that to be true, I have to believe that with God's help, I can forgive you."

Chase shook his head. This time the movement was more pronounced. "I . . . had . . . Leah." Jayce saw him watch for a reaction. Even in the midst of his pain and suffering, even though he was dying, Chase was commanding the moment. "I . . . forced her."

Jayce couldn't move. He couldn't breathe. To hear his brother's declaration—his admission of guilt—was surprising and devastating. Jayce had suspected this bitter truth, but to hear his brother's confession made him want to strangle the remaining life from him. He thought of his wife and how she must have suffered. *No wonder she didn't want me to touch her. No wonder she was changed.*

Jayce took his time and spoke in a measured fashion. "I knew you had hurt her. I could see in her eyes that she had been deeply wounded. I suspected . . . that you . . ." His words trailed off. He wanted to cry for Leah but knew he had to be strong. He was determined that Chase not have the upper hand in this matter.

"You . . . can't . . . forgive." Chase paused and fought for air. "God . . . can't forgive."

God, help me, Jayce prayed. He wanted to hate Chase. He wanted to let the hatred fester up inside and give him the strength to deal with the matter man-to-man. In that moment it seemed like retribution was the only thing that would get Jayce through the pain. Yet even as he thought this, he knew that it wasn't the right answer. God wanted Jayce to rely on Him. Though the trial was worse than any he had ever known, God would be the one to see him through—not anger or revenge.

Jayce looked at his brother and found his eyes closed. He thought for a moment that Chase had succumbed to the pain and lost consciousness, but then it became obvious that this wasn't the case.

Jayce leaned over and touched his hand to Chase's chest. There was no movement. Jayce quickly felt for a pulse. There was none. He sat back in stunned silence.

Chase was dead. He was dead and Jayce had not forgiven him . . . nor had Chase turned to God. A dark cloud settled over Jayce. He wanted to believe that Chase's death signaled the end of misery for him and Leah, but he knew it wasn't true. Chase had come between them in the only way possible. Jayce could hardly bear the moment.

"I've failed. I've failed Chase. I've failed Leah. And I've failed God."

The anguish rose up inside him like the rushing winds outside. With a scream born of pain more intense than a human being should have to endure, Jayce clawed blindly at the tent flaps and staggered from the tent into the dark Arctic cold.

Chapter Eighteen

Leah resented the time Jacob spent with Helaina. Watching them now as Jacob helped Helaina to warm herself by the morning fire, Leah knew she would have to figure some way to separate them. Jacob already cared much too deeply for this woman, and Leah knew that Helaina would only hurt him.

She's a selfish woman who would never stay in Alaska for him, Leah reasoned. *I cannot let Jacob fall in love with her. It will be no different than the pain I suffered with Jayce when he didn't return my love.*

Leah tried to imagine how such a rejection would alter Jacob's sweet nature. He possessed such a strong faith in God that no doubt he would turn to the Lord, but Leah also felt confident that he would sequester himself away from everyone, and she couldn't bear the thought of losing him that way.

She gathered her things and started repacking John's sled. He'd gone on ahead of them to hunt. Leah prayed he'd be successful, as her traps had proven less and less fruitful as they'd drawn near the Kotzebue Sound.

"You're sure quiet this morning," Jacob said, coming to help her take down the tent.

"Well, you aren't." Leah regretted that her voice held such a snide tone.

"What's that supposed to mean?"

Leah stopped and looked across the short distance to where Helaina sat. Leah lowered her voice. "She's nothing but trouble, Jacob."

"Let me be the judge of that." He pulled up the tent stakes using the end of a small pick.

"But I'm afraid you won't be a very good judge this time."

"You know me to be a cautious man when it comes to dealing with people," Jacob countered. "You should trust me to be the same this time."

"But your heart may not listen to your head."

Jacob laughed. "What makes you think that all my decisions and choices are made with my head?"

"I suppose that I don't, but this is one of those times when I think it will be dangerous for you if you let your heart rule. She's not for you."

"I think I'm old enough to decide these matters for myself. I didn't come to you and tell you that Jayce wasn't right for you. And I think I would have been well within my rights to do so. After all, I knew the pain he'd caused you all those years and how much it had altered your life."

"This is totally different."

"Is it really?" He pulled out the remaining stake and looked up at her. "I don't think it is."

Leah walked a short distance from the camp and motioned to her brother. Jacob finally got up and followed her. He shoved his hands into his pockets and waited for Leah to speak.

"Helaina has done nothing but lie to you and me. She's caused us so much trouble. You cannot let yourself fall for her schemes. You were the one who warned me about her in the first place. Go back in time to those first minutes you met her in Nome. You know that she's going to cause you nothing but trouble. If she plays on your emotions, it will only be to benefit herself and capture Chase Kincaid."

"You think so lowly of me? A woman can't fall in love and be kind to me because of that love?" Jacob sounded genuinely hurt.

Leah shook her head. "You know that's not what I think. You are a wonderful man with a big heart and a loving nature. I don't want to see you used for any reason, but especially not for her games. Helaina Beecham is another story. She's manipulative and self-centered. She's here for just one reason, and I don't trust her."

"But you don't have to. This is really up to me."

"Look," Leah gazed back over her shoulder as Helaina began to cough. "She's sick. Let's leave her at the next village. Someone there can help her. They can treat the sickness, and when spring comes, they can get her out on the mail ship."

"Listen to yourself. You would deny the woman our Christian hospitality just because you fear I'll lose my heart to her? That isn't like you, Leah. You used to be far more compassionate."

"I used to be a great many things. All of that has changed now. This trip has cost me too much."

"I know," he said softly. He reached out to touch her, but Leah pulled back. "I wish you'd tell me what happened. Maybe talking about it would help you to get over it."

Leah pushed the old feelings aside. She had to fight this—had to overcome. Chase didn't have power over her unless she gave it to him. "This isn't about me. It's about you and . . . her."

Leah paced a few steps farther from the camp. She was desperate to help Jacob see the truth. "Look, all she's been able to talk about is going back up north. She wants to catch Chase to prove to her brother that she can do the job. She's obsessed with it. She will do whatever is necessary to get the help she needs. If that includes duping you with emotions and flowery words, then she'll do it. I've no doubt in my mind."

"Leah, this isn't your business." His words were stern and his expression held such a serious look that Leah felt instantly reproved. "I'm a grown man. I know how to look out for myself. If it's of any comfort to you, I have no plans to take a wife just yet. But even if I did, I would hope you would respect my wishes and be happy for me, no matter the circumstance."

With that he gathered the stakes and tent poles and rolled everything into a neat bundle. Leah stood watching him. She couldn't make herself join in. She was fearful of what she might yet say, and Jacob had made it clear he wanted no more advice.

They broke camp about twenty minutes later. One of the men from the village led the way in his sled, while Leah followed and Jacob brought up the rear. Leah couldn't help but wonder how she might yet put distance between Jacob and Helaina. She didn't trust anything about the younger woman and figured that even now, Helaina was plotting how to get Jacob's cooperation.

"I have to stop her," Leah whispered against her scarf. "There has to be a way."

There has to be a way to get Jacob to help me, Helaina reasoned as the sled moved easily over the trail. She knew he cared about her physical well-being. He'd checked on her many times since finding them, and he was always happy to share her company. Helaina had not yet broached the subject of hunting down Chase Kincaid, but she was watching for her opportunity.

He will help me. I know he will. He wants to see this matter resolved. I'm sure of it.

She pondered the situation, wondering how to set it all in motion. She had no confidence that Jayce would find his brother, let alone capture him and bring him back for the authorities. It wasn't that she didn't think he wanted to see justice served, but Helaina figured he had no real motivation to try too hard. After all, as Leah had already pointed out on many occasions, it was very hard for Jayce to decide to pursue his brother.

Perhaps I can hire Jacob as a guide, she thought. *I have more than enough money, and if he knows that I'm determined to go with or without him, maybe the promise of wealth will entice him.*

But even as she contemplated this, Helaina knew that Jacob Barringer was not a man to be purchased—not at any price. To be honest, she liked that about him. He wasn't easily swayed by feminine wiles or cold hard cash. She found that refreshing. In fact, when she'd first met him in Nome, it had been a challenge just to get him to talk to her, much less put any trust in her.

Snuggling down deeper into the furs, Helaina smiled at the memory. Jacob had wanted nothing to do with her. He had hardly been willing to look her in the eye. She'd thought then that it was due to some criminal intent or complication in his life. Usually the men who avoided such contact were up to something devious, but with Jacob it turned out to be more of a protective issue.

She yawned and let the pleasant memories spill into her planning. Last summer Jacob had been so good to help teach her how to work with the dogs and how to keep house in the Alaskan wilderness. She could still remember the trials she'd faced enduring the smells of butchering and then tanning the hides. She was mortified to learn that Ayoona wanted her to save urine in order to pour on the hides. This would cause the hair to fall out and leave them with a clean skin. Helaina shuddered still to think of the stench.

It was definitely a strange existence in Last Chance, but Jacob had made it all bearable. The only truly bad times she'd known were those days when he was gone off hunting or delivering dogs. Those were lonely times for Helaina. She hadn't been able to connect with anyone else in the village, save Emma Kjellmann.

Knowing there was little she could do at this moment, Helaina allowed herself to doze. As Leah kept saying, rest would see her well faster than most anything else.

They stopped around one o'clock to rest the dogs and eat a little lunch. They were near water, but Helaina had no idea where they were. All she knew was that every hour took her farther and farther away from Chase Kincaid.

"So where are we?" she asked Jacob as he helped her from the basket.

"On the Kotzebue Sound," Jacob answered. "We'll follow it around a ways, at least as far as Kiwalik, and then maybe south to Candle. There are some good trails, and if the rivers are frozen solid they'll make a good path for us."

He walked to the small fire that Leah had built. Helaina followed him as he added, "It won't take us long to get back to Last Chance if the weather holds. We know this territory at least. It's always slower going when you don't know where you are."

Helaina sat down on the ground. She had no strength and was frustrated by her weakness. *There was a time when I could walk five miles without even getting winded,* she thought. *Now I'm reduced to collapsing after just a few feet.* Still, she refused to show Jacob any weakness.

"I feel much better," she told him. This much was true. "I'm sure I'll soon be able to—"

"Look, it's John and the others," Leah called.

Helaina looked in the direction Leah pointed. Sure enough, John and two other men were making their way to camp. They were dragging something behind them.

"We were blessed," John announced. "On the ice we got a seal. He was sunning himself. He's small, but he'll taste good."

Leah clapped her hands together. "That is a blessing. How wonderful. The dogs will eat well and so will we."

Helaina watched as the men approached the fire. Jacob helped John with his pack. The Inupiat stretched. "We'll have to butcher him fast in case nanook comes to see."

"Nanook?" Helaina said, trying the word. "Bear?"

Leah turned with a look of exasperation. "Yes, bear. The polar bears will be tempted to take away our little catch. Here, near the water, there's a greater danger. There could even be other bears and animals who'll smell the kill." She turned back to the men. "I'll get the pots out and cook up some of the meat."

"I'll help you get it cut up," Jacob said, crossing the camp. The dogs began to catch the scent of the seal and started to bark and whine. "They want to help too."

John laughed, as did Leah. Helaina merely sat back and realized she truly didn't belong in this country. She felt as though she were an uninvited guest in a party of strangers.

I can fit in too. I am strong and resourceful. I can do what I have to do. She tried hard to convince herself that she could belong anywhere she chose to belong.

"I'll start gutting him, John," Jacob said. "You all get some coffee. I'll have Leah fry up the liver for you."

"Too bad it not summer," John said, picking up a tin cup. "We'd make soured liver. Good eating."

Helaina shuddered. The thought of eating the seal meat wasn't as troubling as it used to be, but she remembered Ayoona making the soured liver. They put it in a dish and left it in the sun for days. After it had soured—or spoiled, as Helaina believed was the case—the older people would relish the flavor. Trying not to show any displeasure, she turned to Leah, who was busy filling pots with snow.

"Do you . . . well, that is . . . is there any way I can help?"

Leah looked at her for a moment, then shook her head. "No. You're still sick. You'll just have a relapse if you start working too hard."

Helaina didn't argue with her. She had no strength for work and was glad for the directive to remain idle. After all, it would give her time to continue thinking on a plan. She had to figure a way to convince Jacob to help her return to the north. There had to be a way.

Jacob worked quickly with the others and soon had all of the dogs fed and watered. As he sat down to enjoy some boiled seal meat, he found Helaina taking an unusual interest in him. He felt a warning bell go off in his brain.

"You look really tired," she began. "Can I get you anything?"

"I'm fine, actually. And I'm not that tired. Maybe you're just seeing me through tired eyes." He smiled, hoping she would take the joke in a good-natured fashion.

She smiled, and he went back to eating as she spoke. "I think lying around doing nothing makes a person tired. I shall endeavor to exercise a bit more when we make our stops."

"Just don't overdo it. You have plenty of time to rest up and regain your strength."

"Yes, but I want to help more. I know I've been a terrible burden."

"You haven't been a burden at all," Jacob replied. He didn't want Helaina to feel bad; after all, she couldn't help that she'd caught pneumonia.

He ate in silence for a time after that. It seemed that Helaina was content to rest and enjoy the quiet of the day. Jacob knew they would be pushing out soon, so he motioned to the sled. "We'll be heading off in about fifteen minutes. You might want to get yourself comfortable."

Helaina nodded. "I have some urgent personal matters to see to first." She got to her feet rather slowly. "Don't leave without me."

Jacob laughed. "We couldn't do that." He watched her move away. "Don't go too far. We don't want you having to deal with nanook."

"Indeed not," Helaina called back, "for you would have to come to my rescue, and you've already worked very hard today."

Leah approached him as Helaina left the camp. "See what I mean? She's flirting with you."

"So what? There's no harm being done to either of us." He finished the meat and handed Leah the tin plate.

"It's dangerous and you know it. She's going to presume a relationship with you that doesn't exist."

"You worry too much. I'm a grown man, Leah. I wish you would stop worrying over me like a mother bear with cubs."

Leah wiped the plate with snow. "Jacob, I think we should leave her in the next village. We can always make arrangements for her once we get home. Or you could even go to Nome and contact those Pinkertons, and they could make arrangements for her."

"Leah, we've discussed this before. You aren't being reasonable."

"Neither is she. Mark my words: She'll try to force you to help her with Chase. If we just drop her off at one of the coastal settlements, there are bound to be missionaries who can help get her back to the States."

"You know that Helaina wouldn't be comfortable with that."

"Be comfortable with what?" Jacob and Leah turned in surprise to find Helaina had already rejoined them. "What wouldn't I be comfortable with?"

Leah took a deep breath and exchanged a glance with her brother. "I was telling Jacob that for your sake, we should leave you in the next village. We can get you better care, more herbs, and warm accommodations. Then we can arrange to have you picked up when the mail ships are running again."

"No!"

Jacob shook his head and got to his feet. "No one is being left behind. We'll get Helaina back to Last Chance and then send her home in the spring. We can surely find someone who can put her up for the winter. Emma has that new addition for her sister, so maybe she would let Helaina stay there in return for helping with the children. Leah, didn't you tell me she's expecting another baby? Emma would probably love the help."

"I don't want to stay in Last Chance," Helaina said firmly. "I need to get to Seattle or San Francisco. From there I can get in touch with my brother—perhaps even take the train back to Washington, D.C., and rethink our strategy."

"See, I told you she wouldn't be content to remain in Alaska," Leah said, packing Jacob's plate with the others.

"I need to get more help," Helaina admitted. "I need to convince Stanley that I can handle the situation and secure more agents to assist in Chase's capture. Then I'll return to Alaska."

Jacob frowned at Helaina's statement. He tried to ignore the woman and returned to readying the sled for travel, but she followed him. Leah came along as well.

"Jacob, I can't just leave this matter to Jayce Kincaid. He won't be able to bring Chase in. Not if he was as tortured by the situation as you made it seem."

"My husband can handle the matter," Leah replied sternly. "You need to remember your place."

"Bringing Chase to justice is exactly my place."

"No it's not," Jacob said. "Look, you were relieved of your duties. You are still sick and very weak. Don't think I don't know it's taking every ounce of strength you possess just to stand here."

"I'm much better. By the time we get to Last Chance, I'll be perfectly able to travel to Seattle."

Jacob shook his head. "But there will be no transportation south. We're frozen in until spring breakup."

"But I have money."

"Helaina, your money won't matter. There are no ships into Nome this time of year."

She was undeterred. "Then where is the nearest year-round port? Take me there. You have dog sleds, and you told me once before that you've made the trip across the interior. So I'll pay you to take me now."

"Jacob isn't going to risk his life trekking out across the interior of Alaska for your selfish needs."

"Leah, I can handle this." He saw the look of anger that crossed his sister's face. She wasn't one who liked to be reprimanded, much less in front of someone like Helaina. He held up his hands. "Ladies, we're wasting time. Leah, you need to finish loading up John's sled and get yourself settled in the basket. He can drive now. Helaina, you need to get settled here."

"Fine," Leah declared, stalking off toward John's sled.

He thought the matter settled and turned to go, but Helaina had taken hold of him. "You can't just leave me stranded like this. I need your help to get south. I need more men to go north on the search with me."

Jacob felt a deep sorrow. "Helaina, what you need and what you want are two entirely different matters."

She looked at him oddly. "I don't know what you mean."

He gave a sigh. "I know you don't, and that's your biggest problem."

Chapter Nineteen

That night Jacob found himself actually contemplating Helaina's request to go across the interior. Adrik had suggested Jacob come to Seward and join him working for the railroad. If he took Helaina, she could catch a ship out of Seward and head south. The harbor never closed and would be the perfect place to get transportation to either Seattle or San Francisco, given the large volume of goods that were being shipped back and forth in association with the railroad.

He went as far as to take out pencil and paper and try to figure the cost of such an expedition. It would be harsh and difficult to deal with the weather and unpredictable land. There were mail trails that could be followed, but even these would present dangers.

"What are you doing?" Leah asked as she joined Jacob at the fire. Most of the others had retired to their tents and sleds.

"I was just thinking about getting Helaina to Seward."

"What? Are you crazy?"

He rubbed his bearded chin. "Not the last time I checked."

"Jacob, you can't do this. It's much too dangerous. It's not like this is any real emergency."

"But maybe it would be better for everyone concerned to get Helaina on her way. You want her away from me, after all." He watched her frown.

How could she argue such a point—she was, after all, the one who had made such a big issue of it earlier.

"I want her away from you, not isolated with you for a month or more." Leah sat down and tried to reason with him. "Jacob, it would be costly and dangerous. You know it would. The dogs would be pressed to their very limits, as would you. The winter has come early and the weather has been unpredictable. You could find yourself in trouble within days."

"Again, thank you for the vote of confidence."

Leah slapped her palms against her sealskin pants. "You know this isn't about you and your ability. It's about it being November—nearly December in Alaska. You wouldn't suggest anyone else take such a risk, so why take one yourself?"

"I didn't say that I would. I'm just trying to think of what would be best for everyone concerned. Helaina won't give us any peace so long as she's determined to get to the States."

Leah's jaw clenched. "Helaina needs to learn some manners."

"Be that as it may, you should remember your Christian charity. You were the one who gave me such a difficult time of it when I wanted nothing to do with Helaina. Now you're angry because I'm being kind."

Leah blew out a heavy breath. "I'm not trying to be difficult, Jacob. I'm just worried."

"You needn't worry about me. I've been through much worse than Helaina Beecham." He grinned and added, "If she's the most difficult thing I have to contend with, then my life will be rather simple."

"I seriously doubt that."

"I was just thinking that I could take her by sled to Seward. It would be a long and arduous trip, but Adrik would like to have me join him there anyway. We talked about the potential of it when we were in Sitka."

"But you also have the Arctic exploration to consider. Have you given up on that idea? Captain Latimore will return in June and expect you to be a part of his team."

"I know. I haven't given up on such plans. I want to pray and seek what God wants me to do in regard to both options. I feel that God has a purpose in presenting both possibilities. I need to consider which might be best for all parties concerned. Including Helaina's desire to get to a ship."

"Helaina desires a great many things. Too many, if you ask me. She wants Chase captured. She wants to show the Pinkertons how capable she is. She wants you to make all of her obstacles go away."

Jacob actually laughed at this. "I wish I could. I wish I could set her free from the shackles that bind her, but only God can do that. She thinks she needs so many other things, when what she really needs is Jesus. She has no peace of mind—no hope for anything past the performance she can give."

Leah frowned. "I suppose I haven't been too concerned with her spiritually, though I did seek her forgiveness for my mean spirit."

"Then you should understand," Jacob replied. "I want to help her see the truth. It isn't a matter of allowing her to manipulate and have her own way. I want her to see that Chase and the original job she was given to do are no longer the reasons she's still here. She focuses on this because it's all she has. She doesn't know how to be fulfilled any other way."

Leah put another piece of driftwood on the fire and stretched out her hands to the flames. "I can see the truth in that. I've suggested as much myself. I told her I believed she was seeking revenge for the past."

"As have I." Jacob leaned forward. "I don't know what the Lord would have for me regarding Helaina. I do care about her . . . deeply. I never thought I would, given our initial introduction."

"But she's—"

"Just hear me out." Jacob looked at her hard. "I care about her. I can't help it. I won't pursue it because she doesn't love God. She sees God as some sort of adversary. I couldn't pretend that doesn't matter. You know me well enough to realize that."

Leah nodded but remained silent. Jacob gazed into the flames and tried to figure out how to say what was on his heart. "When we were in Nome, you helped me to understand that often I allow my ability to discern people and their motives to keep me from caring about them—about their souls. I know that isn't why God would give me such a gift. Helaina is hurting. She's still trying to figure out why she was left behind when all that she loved, short of Stanley, was taken from her. She needs to understand that God isn't the enemy here, and that terrible things will often happen to the children He loves, but it doesn't alter His love for those children."

Leah still said nothing, and Jacob looked up to find her crying. "Leah?"

She looked to the ground. "I'm sorry."

"Don't be." He scooted closer and hesitantly put his arm around her. She didn't push him away and Jacob breathed a sigh of relief. "Talk to me."

"I don't think I can."

"Of course you can. I love you. You're my little sister. We made promises to each other a long time ago. Remember? We promised to be honest with each other and to take care of each other. Of course, Jayce has the job of caring for you now, but I will always love you."

Leah sank against him and he tightened his hold on her. "I used to think God would keep me from bad things. I remember asking Mama why God didn't protect us from evil men and evil things. I asked her if God wasn't strong enough. She told me that God was always able but that sometimes things happened as a means to bring Him honor and glory. Like remember when we were at that revival meeting and the minister talked about the missionaries who had been killed by the natives when they went to Africa?"

"I remember. He said the missionaries hoped that their story would bring people to God."

"Yes, and even as they were being tortured to death, they praised God. That did inspire me, Jacob. I thought how wondrous it would be to have that kind of faith. To be put in the flames—to die for the cause of taking the Word of God to people who had never heard it. But at the same time, I couldn't understand it. I still don't. Those people were serving God. They were living for God, trusting Him for direction. They were being good to other people, and . . ." Her voice broke. "They were trying to do the right thing."

"But still they died. Died in God's service," Jacob whispered. "And you were trying to do the right thing. You were living for God and trusting Him, and yet Chase came and took you away."

"Yes." She grew very quiet. For several minutes she said nothing, so Jacob merely waited. Finally, she looked up. "He forced himself on me, Jacob."

The words were delivered matter-of-factly. Jacob had no doubt they were true. "I'm so sorry, Leah. I wish I could have kept you from that."

Leah bit her lower lip and drew several ragged breaths. "He . . . well . . . I . . ." She shook her head and leaned back against her brother.

Jacob simply held her for several minutes, waiting until she felt able to speak again. He knew it would be important for her to talk.

"I didn't tell Jayce," she finally said. "I couldn't."

"You'll find the strength when the time is right. Jayce will understand."

"How can he? I don't." Leah sat up. "I don't understand why God would allow that to happen. I even tried to help Chase know more about God—about salvation. I tried to be helpful to Helaina even though I blamed her for our even being in that situation. I tried to have a good heart. Do you think my anger at Helaina caused God to punish me?"

Jayce shook his head. "I don't think God works that way, Leah. I think what happened was the result of Chase's evil ways. This is a corrupt world. There is evil that lurks and waits to cause harm in the lives of the innocent."

"But we pray for God's protection. The Bible is full of examples of people who were protected in times of trouble. Why not me, Jacob? Why not? What did I do that was so terrible that God wouldn't hear my prayers?"

Jacob felt a lump form in his throat as he looked at Leah. She pleaded with him for answers that he didn't have. "I believe God heard, Leah. I don't believe He rejected your prayers. Remember that even while there were times when people were protected in the Bible, there were other times when they were not. Paul went through many trials. He was stoned and thrown in jail. He was shipwrecked and beaten, yet Paul loved God and God loved Paul. And what about Job? Job was a righteous man and God allowed him to be stripped of everything but his life. And Job wished that had been taken, as well, because of his physical infirmities."

"He promised that though God had slain him, Job would still trust Him. I remember that verse," Leah said. "And I do want to trust God. I didn't at first; I felt angry. I felt that God couldn't possibly care about me anymore—that He didn't love me. I know that's not true, and I still love Him, but I don't understand any of this."

"And God has never promised us that we would understand. He has His plans, and ultimately they will deliver us into a peaceful and perfect place. But, Leah, that place isn't here on earth."

She nodded. "I know. I guess that's why I would just as soon have died."

Her words pierced Jacob's heart, but he didn't reprimand her for them. Her pain was already so great. "I don't know if I could bear that loss," he said simply.

"You know, Chase was actually sorry afterward. I couldn't believe it, but he was. He kept trying to find a way to get me to let go of my anger and absolve him of his guilt. It was almost like nothing else in his life had ever made him feel the need to make a thing right. But I couldn't deal with him."

"I can understand that."

"I honestly wanted to kill him, Jacob. That really scared me. I've never wanted to end anyone's life. Never. How can I be such an awful person? I left him out there to die."

"He is already a dead man, Leah. One way or another, he will pay the price for the things he's done."

"Jacob, what am I going to do? When I look at Jayce, I see Chase. How will I ever be able to . . . be a wife to Jayce again? I just keep thinking of that and I can't reconcile it. Chase didn't just steal a part of me; he's taken what's most important to me. He's taken my happiness with Jayce."

"They might look alike, Leah, but they aren't the same man. You know that better than anyone. Jayce has a heart that is full of love for you. You should have seen him when he realized that Chase had kidnapped you. He was a driven man. He wouldn't rest or even consider turning back, no matter how hard things got. He loves you."

"But once he knows the truth," Leah countered, "that love may fade."

"Then it isn't love at all, because the Bible says that love endures all things."

"Maybe, but I think it's asking a lot of Jayce."

Jacob laughed, surprising them both. "Sorry, but I think Jayce would say that loving you is easy. I know he'll be angered by this, but his anger won't be directed at you."

"I realize that. I figure his anger with Chase will be greater than ever."

"Maybe to a point, but his real rage will be directed at himself."

"Himself?" Leah shook her head. "But why? This wasn't his fault."

"But he will feel like it is. He'll second-guess his decisions and choices. I know I would. He'll think that if he'd only gone back to Last Chance with you instead of going after Chase, you wouldn't have gotten hurt. He'll think that if he would have just told someone sooner about Chase being in Alaska, then Helaina might actually have caught him early on. He'll have a million questions that have no answers, and all of them will point to his failing you. You have to be ready for that."

"But he didn't fail me."

"You don't need to convince me, Leah. You'll need to convince Jayce."

The next morning Jacob found a moment to be alone with Helaina. "I want to talk to you."

"Good. Have you thought about getting me to Seward?" Her expression was hopeful and her tone excited.

"I have considered it," Jacob began, "but the answer is no. It would be a very dangerous and expensive trip to make."

"But I have plenty of money."

Jacob smiled. "That still leaves it dangerous, and I doubt you have any tricks in your bag that would prevent that."

"But you know this land and the people. I trust you. I believe you could get us through without any mishaps."

Jacob looked back at the camp. He had purposefully asked Helaina to walk with him to get away from the others. Now as they readied the dogs and sleds, Jacob knew he couldn't waste time.

"I appreciate your trust in me. I'm honored that you think so highly of my skills and abilities. But that belief won't keep things from happening to us. You know how difficult this trip has been, and John has known the people and most of the terrain. Yet still some of the men have suffered injuries, and you are fighting to recover from pneumonia. Leah had to shoot a bear. There are just too many unknown factors."

"So don't take me to Seward. Help me instead."

"Help you?" He knew what she would say, but he couldn't help but ask the question.

"Help me capture Chase. I'll pay you. You can hire other men to help us. We can get supplies and head back to where we left him. Surely there's a good enough tracker among you all that he could pick up the trail again."

"Helaina, you need to let this go. You can't continue like this." He looked at her and saw the set of her jaw. She was in no mood to hear him out—at least not on this subject. Jacob let his gaze travel to her lips. He wanted nothing more than to kiss her. Kiss her and make her think about something other than Chase Kincaid.

"Jacob, I'll pay you whatever you want. I have more than enough money."

"Helaina, this isn't about money. It's about the fact that I care about you. I care too much to be the one to help you risk your life. I care too much to help you continue this unhealthy obsession to find Chase Kincaid. I won't do it. Not for ten dollars or ten thousand." He left her to contemplate his words and walked back to the sled.

Helaina stood frozen in place as Jacob walked away. Normally she would have gone after him and tried to argue her point, but given what he had said about caring about her, Helaina found it impossible to move. What did he mean by those words?

She watched him speak to Leah and then go to check out the lines on his dog team. He was a handsome man. She'd conceded that some time ago. And she had to admit that no one had ever taken as much time to reach through her façade of self-sufficiency.

She heard the words in her head. *"It's about the fact that I care about you."*

She shook her head in confused disbelief. "But what did he mean?"

Chapter Twenty

Leah felt exhilarated at the thought that they would arrive home that evening. John and Jacob had discussed their location and felt confident that if they didn't stop too long for rests, they could have the group home not long after nightfall. The very idea appealed to Leah in a way she couldn't explain. It seemed like she had been on this journey forever instead of just weeks. She supposed it was due to having been gone all summer, only to return and be forced onto the trail by Chase. It really had been months since she'd been able to just sit down and work on her sewing and enjoy the sights and sounds of her own little house. Now it was nearing December, and she longed only for the peace and comfort of Last Chance. She wanted to celebrate Christmas with Emma and Ayoona, and she desperately wanted to feel the peace that she'd once known.

Feeling rather useless with the packing done, Leah walked away from the camp just far enough to crest a small hill. She looked over the frozen valley and sighed. Alaska was a beautiful and diverse territory. She thought of growing up near Ketchikan. The thick forests and large amounts of rain left the area lush and green. The temperatures were mild year-round compared to other parts of the territory. Their gardens grew delicious vegetables and the fruit bushes were plentiful with salmonberries, raspberries, blueberries, and many others. It was there among the Tlingit people that Leah had learned about healing herbs and how to treat wounds.

She had also lived in Skagway and Dyea, farther up the inside passage. The pines and spruce were plentiful there and the mountains were impressive. Going north into Canada had been such a great adventure for a little girl. Leah had been a young teenager when she'd experienced the gold fever. Living in Dawson had taught her the dangers of con men and greed, but it had also shown her what wealth could buy.

Leah had experienced much in her life, but this trip had taken the biggest toll. Now all she longed for was the refuge of home and her friends. She missed Ayoona and Oopick and Emma. She wondered how the village children were doing—if they were studying hard and getting excited about Christmas. Emma and Bjorn always made Christmas such a special time.

Leaving her solitude, Leah slowly walked back to the camp. She heard Helaina's voice on the other side of the tent and stopped in her tracks.

"I need to know what you meant when you said you cared about me."

Leah bit her lower lip to keep quiet. She knew Helaina was talking to Jacob. The poor man. How could he have just opened his heart up to tell her that he cared?

"What do you suppose it means, Helaina? I care about you. I've come to care a lot about your well-being, both physically and spiritually. I want to see you happy. I want you to know the peace that comes in trusting God to watch over you and to lead you. I want you to believe in something bigger than yourself, because I know from experience that when the world is crashing down around you, you need something bigger."

"So this is just about preaching to me? You care, but only about my soul?"

Leah wanted to step in and declare that this was indeed the only interest Jacob had, and then steal her brother away before he could open his mouth.

"I care about you, Helaina, but that's all I can do so long as you put this wall between us."

Leah had no desire to listen anymore. She walked away, hoping that Jacob would not hear her footsteps. She pitied her brother for having given his heart to a woman who despised his faith. She pitied Jacob for the pain she knew he would endure when Helaina refused to give up her battle for Chase.

"Oh, God," she prayed softly, "he needs you so much. Please keep him from the misery that will no doubt follow him so long as Helaina's involved."

———

Jayce had done his best to secure a grave for Chase. The ground was frozen solid, but by using a series of fires to thaw the earth, he'd managed to dig down a short way into the ground. After placing Chase in this shallow grave, Jayce went to work finding rocks to stack on top of the body. He could only hope and pray that the animals wouldn't dig up his brother's remains.

Work seemed the only way to ease his anger. Jayce tried to pray, but while it comforted his heart to a degree, he would inevitably begin to think about the pain Chase had caused, and soon the comfort was lost.

Jayce simply couldn't reconcile the fact that Chase was dead or that he'd raped Leah. It all just seemed impossible to accept. Why had these things happened? What purpose did they serve? It seemed like one of the strange nightmares Jayce had had as a boy. Nightmares where everyone he loved had been lost in house fires or floods. He supposed those things had been borne out of his worst fears, but this was no dream. He couldn't just wake up this time and have it all fade away with the night.

When the grave was finally complete, Jayce packed up his gear and readied the dogs. He had been fortunate in his hunting efforts and would return to Last Chance with two wolf pelts, three fox, and four rabbit furs. The meat had provided well. The dogs seemed particularly fond of the wolf meat. The bear that had killed Chase never materialized again, however, much to Jayce's disappointment.

Moving out, Jayce tried to imagine what he would say to Leah when he saw her again. He wanted no secrets between them and planned to just tell her that he knew the truth. He hoped it would be less painful for her this way. He reasoned that if she didn't have to come to him it would be less humiliating for her. Still, Jayce couldn't help but wonder how they would overcome this obstacle.

How can I help Leah? How can I ever make this right for her? How can she forgive me for not saving her from Chase, when I can't forgive myself?

The questions continued to nag at him all that day. Every time he attempted to clear his mind and refuse to dwell on the matter, something would come along to steal his peace. He knew it was foolish to let his mind wander. The trails were deadly and full of surprises. There were creeks and rivers to cross or follow, as well as obstacles buried under the snow that could wreak havoc with his dogs and sled. Still, it was only by forcing his mind to comply that Jayce managed to even see his surroundings. Leah was all he wanted to see—to think about.

With no little difficulty, Jayce found the native village where they'd left Brownie. He'd gone in the opposite direction twice as he lost his bearings but finally came around right. He was welcomed and cared for, as were the dogs. The people seemed to sense a great sorrow had come upon Jayce. One of the elders asked for his story and Jayce shared his tale with the man. He said nothing about Leah, however, seeing no reason to bring her into the story.

"My brother is dead. A bear attacked him. I buried him the best I could."

The man nodded. "It bad thing. I am pained to hear you speak."

Jayce tried to suppress a yawn. "I thank you for your hospitality—for your kindness."

"You rest here. This good house to sleep in. I know." He smiled and motioned to a woman whom Jayce knew to be his wife. "We let you sleep now." The man pointed to where his wife had created a pallet of blankets and furs.

"Thank you. I will rest very well." Jayce gave them a slight bow and went to the makeshift bed.

Lying there awake well into the night, Jayce knew that he needed a good night's sleep. But he was restless and sleep wouldn't come. He tried to pray, to reason with himself, to force his body to relax—but it was no good. He felt like the biblical Jacob, having wrestled all night with something not of this world. He finally fell asleep just as the man and woman began to stir. His last conscious thought was of Leah. How he longed to hold her—to reassure her that his love for her hadn't changed. He could only pray her love for him had stayed the same, because if she didn't love him anymore—if Chase had driven that from her heart—Jayce didn't think he could bear it.

Leah had never been so happy to see a place in all her life. In the distance, light shone in the windows of a dozen or more houses. Home. Last Chance Creek had never looked more wonderful.

"It's past suppertime," Jacob said as he pulled the sled to a stop. John pulled his sled up alongside, while the other men were already dispersing for their homes.

"My wife will cook for us," John said. "I'll take the dogs. You can take the women."

Jacob laughed. "I think the dogs might be easier to care for."

"We can hear you perfectly well," Leah said, getting out of John's sled basket. Dogs around the village began to bark and yip. "Well, now everyone will know we're here."

It wasn't long before Ayoona came from her inne. "Lay-Ya! You are here."

Leah went to embrace the old woman. "Yes, I am. I am home."

"You come in, and I feed you. We have walrus stew. You like it plenty."

"I do," Leah admitted. "It sounds wonderful, but I'm so tired, I don't know that I can even crawl down your tunnel."

"Leah! Jacob! You're home!" Emma Kjellmann came running across to greet them. She waved her lantern back and forth. "I've never been so happy to see anyone in my life. Where's Jayce?"

Leah squared her shoulders. "He's gone to find his brother."

"Oh, when we heard it was Chase and not Jayce who'd taken you, we were sick. Bjorn called a prayer meeting and we prayed well into the night for your safety. And here you are, safe and sound. Oh, I'm so blessed. God is so faithful to answer our prayers." She hugged Leah tightly while Leah exchanged a glance with her brother.

"Ayoona was just offering to feed us walrus stew," Leah said, pulling back more quickly than Emma was prepared for.

"Oh, bring the stew to my house. We have fresh sourdough bread and white-fish soup. Please come, Ayoona."

The old woman grinned. "We come for your bread."

Emma laughed. "Oh, what a grand celebration. We should invite everyone, but they'd never fit in our house."

"Speaking of your house," Jacob said, "we wondered if you might be able to put up a houseguest for a time. Like maybe until spring thaw."

Emma looked from Leah to Jacob. "You, Jacob?"

"No. Helaina Beecham." He pointed to where Helaina was just now getting out of the sled. "She's been sick with pneumonia and needs time to mend."

"I'll be fine," Helaina protested. "Stop fussing over me."

"Of course she can stay with us. We have all that extra space, and Sigrid won't come until next June. Of course, Helaina can stay on if she needs because Bjorn and I will take the children south to see their grandparents. Sigrid will have the big house to herself, so Helaina is more than welcome to stay."

"I won't be here that long," Helaina told her. "In fact, if I have my way, I won't be here long at all. I need to get back to the States."

Emma laughed. "Well, unless you have one of those aeroplanes to take you out of here, you'll be hard-pressed to find another way."

"Well, I understand there are men who for hire will take me by dogsled. I intend to find one of them since no one here seems to care enough."

Leah frowned. "It's a matter of feeling the risk to life isn't worth the price," she interjected. "Sometimes the price required is too high."

"Look, it's cold and we're hungry," Jacob said. "Let's discuss this over food."

"Ja. Where are my manners? I'll send Bjorn to help with the dogs."

"No need. I'll have Kimik and Seal-Eye Sam. They help." John moved to take the lines for both teams. "Jacob, pull the hooks."

Jacob quickly released the sleds, and John led the dogs away. They were feisty, but John was quite capable of keeping them in line.

"I get Oopick and we come," Ayoona told Emma.

"Good. Come along, you three. You can wash up before you eat. I have warm water."

They followed Emma to the house, and Leah couldn't help but laugh at the reception they got as they entered the mission home. Bryce and Nolan rushed her and hugged her so tightly that Leah thought for sure they would break her in half. Even Rachel came dashing across the floor to see what was happening. Leah knelt down, but the little girl shyly took hold of her mother's dress.

"She doesn't remember me."

"Of course she does, Leah. She's just going through a stage. She does this with everyone. Even Ayoona." Emma scooped up her daughter and grinned. "She'll be playing with you soon enough. She has to have everyone's attention eventually."

"I'll be right back. I just want to make sure John has enough help," Jacob said, taking off before the women could answer him.

Emma bounced Rachel on her hip. "Helaina, why don't you come with me? I have some clothes that I think will fit you. You can wash up and change from those things and we'll get you tucked into bed. Then I'll bring you some soup and bread. Leah, I have plenty of herbs if you want to mix up something for Helaina's sickness."

"You don't need to fuss over me," Helaina declared as Emma led the way to the back side of the house.

Leah nudged Helaina along. "We just want to get you back on your feet so that you can be on your way. That's what you wanted as well—to get back to the States. Now don't argue with the pastor's wife."

The room they'd added was no bigger than eight foot by six, but it seemed wonderfully large to Leah. A small rope bed stood in one corner. It had been constructed from driftwood and looked quite sturdy.

"It has a feather mattress," Emma said proudly. Rachel fought to get down, and Emma conceded and put her on the floor. In a flash the toddler was off and running. "I plucked enough ptarmigan and duck feathers to make a pillow as well."

"Oh, it sounds divine," Helaina said, rubbing her stomach. "I wonder if you might help me with something else."

Leah and Emma looked at the woman and nodded. Leah felt apprehensive of what Helaina might request, but at this point it would be good just to have the woman settled and out of her hair.

Helaina looked beyond the two women and took a step closer. "I think my monthly time is due. I have terrible cramps."

"Oh, not to worry," Emma said with great assurance. "I have everything you need. I'll bring you tea with the soup. Now you just get out of those things. I'll bring you hot water and something to sleep in. Leah, you come with me to my room. I'll bring water for you too."

Leah hardly heard Emma's words. She followed her slowly, trying desperately to calculate the last time she'd had her own monthly time. A sickening feeling washed over her. It had been just before her marriage to Jayce. She'd not had her woman's time since then.

Feeling weak in the knees, Leah sank onto the nearest chair. She could hardly bear the thought of what it all meant. She might very well be pregnant.

"Are you all right?" Emma asked, her voice heavy with concern.

"I'm fine . . . just tired. The trip was exhausting."

"Well, you were gone for so long."

Just then Ayoona and Oopick arrived, their arms full of goodies. "We are here, Lay-Ya."

Leah looked up and forced a smile, while Emma rushed to help the women. The reality of the moment was almost more than she could bear.

I might be with child. The thought was startling. Worse still was the question that followed.

I might be with child, but who is the father?

Chapter Twenty-One

Leah and Jacob settled into their house and a sort of familiar routine emerged. Jacob rose daily to care for the dogs and later went to hunt or help in the village, while Leah cooked and preserved, tended the store, and worked with hides and sewing. The store took less and less time as the supplies gave out. Most winters Jacob would have already made a trip to Nome, but given the events of the last few months, their regular schedules were completely altered.

"Most of the folks have traded clothing items and furs for the store's food and tools," Jacob said as they finished a breakfast of caribou sausage and oatmeal. "I need to get into Nome and exchange them for goods. We brought some cloth up with us on the *Homestead*. I put it in storage so that we'd have it later. Would you like me to bring some back? I think it might be useful in making shirts and *kuspuks*."

"That would be very useful. Will you leave right away?" Leah saw it as a good way to get Jacob away from Helaina and her constant nagging to help get her to the States.

"Not for Nome," Jacob replied. "I need more furs. One of my suppliers in Nome is big on furs. He has some group in New York that pays him top dollar—especially for beaver, wolf, fox, and such. Oh, and I should lay in a good supply of meat for you before I leave. There's no telling how long it will be before Jayce returns. No sense making John hunt for you as well as his own family."

"No, he's already done so much for me. I still haven't found a proper way to thank him for helping you come after us."

"I'm sure he'd love some of your baked goods," Jacob said, smiling. "I know I would."

"Well, when you bring back supplies, make sure there's plenty of sugar and lard. Nothing ever tastes right when I use seal or whale fat."

Jacob nodded and grew quite serious. "I want you to know that I won't leave if you don't want me to. If you want me to wait for Jayce to return, I will."

"No, there's a greater need for you to be gathering supplies. I'd rather you go. I know it could be some time before Jayce returns, but then again, maybe he'll come back tomorrow. We can't be certain." Leah wanted to keep

Jacob focused on his trip. She hoped his interest in Helaina would wane if the two were separated for a time. "Will you go with someone?"

Jacob drank the last of his coffee and got to his feet. "Nutchuk wants to go hunting with me, and I think it will serve him well. His grandfather is constantly giving him trouble over becoming a Christian."

"Well, since his grandfather is a shaman, it isn't surprising. I'm sure our ways seem just as strange to him as his ways are to us."

"I wish their superstitions wouldn't bind them so strongly. It's hard for Nutchuk to be in that family with his new faith. I know God will give him the strength he needs, but I think getting away on a trapping trip will give Nutchuk a much needed rest from the rhetoric. We can spend time reading the Bible every day, and hopefully his faith can grow."

"I'm sure you're right. I'll put some things together for you."

Jacob nodded and pulled on his parka. "I need to finish up with the dogs. Oh, and we have a new batch of puppies. Angel gave birth last night."

"How many?" Leah asked as she moved to gather the breakfast dishes.

"Six. They all look good and healthy. Not a real runt in the bunch."

"I'm glad to hear it. I hate it when we have to put them down. Seems so cruel, yet I know fighting for an existence out here is also cruel when you're smaller than the rest."

"I don't want you having to be responsible for the dogs while I'm gone, so I'm gonna pay John to help with them. Of course, he won't want to take money, but I figured I'd promise him a couple of Angel's pups for all he's done."

"I think that's a good idea. The dogs will give him better service than my baked goods," she said, smiling. "But I'll get some of those prepared as well."

"Oh, I nearly forgot," Jacob said, turning at the door, "I'm gonna need some new mukluks. These are nearly worn through."

"It's no wonder with you traipsing all over the territory. I'll check around the store and see what we have, and if nothing's large enough, I'll go talk with the women in the village. Ayoona may have even made some for you. You know how she likes to give you something special at Christmas."

"Well, I'd hate to ruin her surprise."

"But you can't go out there on a long hunt without good boots. Let me see what I can find. I think the trip will do you good, and no doubt the furs and meat will keep us well through the winter. I hope you find some caribou. I've really wanted some caribou steak."

He smiled. "That does sound good. I'll see what I can do."

"I know you—you'll probably bring home a whole herd." She wanted to sound as positive as possible about his trip. Leah didn't want Jacob to worry about her or do anything that might delay his leaving. The sooner he left, the sooner he would be away from Helaina, and Leah felt that was the most important thing of all.

Jacob had actually been surprised to find Leah so receptive to his leaving again. He feared she'd be uncomfortable staying alone, and maybe worried, too, since Jayce hadn't returned. Instead she was practically pushing him out the door.

He checked on Angel in the partially open birthing shed he'd made for such occasions and found her happily nursing her pups. "Just look at you, little mama," he said, bringing her fresh water and food.

Angel was hungry and quickly shook off her babies to come to where Jacob poured her a bowl of food. It was a strange concoction of mixed meats and commercial dried dog food, something Jacob didn't use often. "Here you go."

The dog, a large powerful animal who held a wheel position on the sled line, devoured her food quickly, then looked to Jacob as if to question if there'd be more. Jacob gave her a rigorous petting. "You're a good dog, Angel. But now you need to go back and tend to your babies."

She yipped at him as he started to go. Jacob felt sorry for her. She needed more approval and attention than he could offer her right now. He checked the gate of the shed. It was designed to deter intruding wildlife but wasn't all that sturdy. Of course if anything did approach, the dogs would raise a ruckus and someone could deal with it before anything managed to get to the animals.

He thought about how he still needed to talk to John about the dogs' care and make sure he was willing to take on the responsibility with Leah. She would be hard-pressed to see to everything, and Jacob didn't wish to leave her overburdened. Perhaps Helaina could also come over and help. After all, she'd spent the previous summer learning how to care for the animals. But then he remembered she was still recovering from pneumonia.

The thought of Helaina made Jacob momentarily uncomfortable. She didn't yet know that he planned to leave the village. That would be a difficult thing for her to accept. He pondered how he might break the news as he finished with the dogs.

"She won't be happy," he muttered to Marty. The dog cocked his head and gave a little whine as if to agree.

That afternoon Jacob finally made his way over to the Kjellmann house. He brought with him a six-month-old sled dog pup that he'd promised to give to Nolan and Bryce. The pup had broken a leg in a fight with an older dog. The leg had not set right and so he walked with a limp. The boys, however, didn't care. They wanted a pet and Limpy, as they called the pup, seemed the perfect solution. Jayce had promised that as soon as the dog healed completely, he would bring him to live at the mission house.

"Jacob!" Bryce declared at the door. "You brought my dog."

"Doggie!" Nolan called and came running. "Mama, come see!"

Limpy squirmed and yipped as the boys flooded him with attention. Emma soon arrived and laughed at the antics of the boys and dog.

"I hope this isn't a bad time to bring him. I'm going to be leaving for several weeks and wanted to make sure the boys got their dog first."

"Of course it's not a bad time," Emma said. "Come in. Would you like some coffee? I have some good Swedish coffee—strong and black."

Jacob nodded. "Sounds good." He glanced toward the back of the house. "Is Helaina awake?"

"Ja. She'll join us pretty soon," Emma replied. Her Swedish cadence seemed particularly noticeable this morning. "So, you are going away?"

"Yes, I'm heading out to hunt and trap. We need to lay in some of our own supplies for winter, although Ayoona and her family have taken great pains to see us provided for."

"They are good people, as are most in this village," Emma said, bringing Jayce a cup of coffee. "Have a seat. I'm sure Helaina will join us."

Jacob did as she suggested and laughed as the boys rolled about the floor with the dog. "I'm glad you wanted a pet. I worried about whether I'd have to put Limpy down. Up here everything has to be useful."

"He'll be a good watchdog for the boys, I think." Emma looked to where her sons played. "I worry about bears and such when they go out to play. A dog will help guard them."

"I think that's true. These dogs are good about bonding with their owners. He should make a useful pet."

Helaina chose that moment to make an appearance. "I thought I heard voices." She had carefully pinned her blond hair into place and looked quite sophisticated, despite her native clothes.

"I just stopped by to bring the boys their dog before I go." He saw her frown and waited for her comment.

"Are you going somewhere?" She joined them at the table. A smile suddenly lit her face. "Are you going to take me to Seward?"

He focused on the coffee and took a long drink before answering her. "No. I'm going on a hunting and trapping trip. I'll be gone for a while. At first I'll probably just try to get a couple of caribou, and if I do, I'll be back in a couple of days—maybe a week. Then I plan to go out and trap with Nutchuk. We'll probably be gone several weeks."

"But why?" Helaina sounded a little panicked. "I wish you wouldn't go."

Rachel began to fuss and cry from the other room. Emma got up. "Sounds like she's up from her nap. She woke up at four-thirty this morning and wanted to play. Then, when it was a decent hour to wake up, she was ready to sleep again. If you'll excuse me."

"Of course," Jacob said, getting to his feet. "I should probably go."

"No. No. Sit and drink your coffee. There's plenty more."

She left them, pausing only long enough to help the boys with their coats as they headed outside with Limpy. "You stay close to the house," she commanded.

Jacob shook his head. "They'll soon be venturing out everywhere. I can't believe how those boys have grown."

"Jacob, you can't go," Helaina said, not in the least bit interested in the boys.

"I beg your pardon?" He looked at her oddly. "I can go and I will."

"I thought you cared about me. Were those just idle words?"

"This has nothing to do with my caring for you."

"Of course it does. You're deserting me when I need you most."

"I'm providing for my family—for you as well. Emma and Bjorn can't be expected to feed you and keep you without some kind of compensation."

"I'll pay them," she said in a flippant manner.

"Helaina, have you not yet learned that your money can't buy everything or everyone? Up here money is useful, but only when there are products and goods to be had. We are self-supportive people in this territory. We hunt, gather, or make most everything we need. If we don't, we do without in many cases."

"You can't really care about me and just walk away like this."

"I don't recall our marriage," he said sarcastically. "You don't own me, Helaina."

"I didn't suggest we were married, but you said you cared."

"And I do. But that concern is rooted in your spirit right now." He paused. "Well, at least most of my concern is there."

"So this is just about getting me right with God, is that it? You only care so far as helping me to see the error of my ways. You're worse than a preacher."

"Why do you say that?"

"At least preachers are open about the numbers they seek to gather for their cause. You are deceptive with your plan."

"I don't need to listen to this." He got up and headed for the door. "Tell Emma thanks for the coffee."

Helaina followed after him. "Fine. Be like that. At least it tells me what I need to know."

Jacob turned and found her only inches away. "Which is what?"

"That you only care about yourself. That I don't matter to you."

Jacob had had all he could take. Without thinking, he grabbed Helaina in his arms and pulled her hard against him. Then he lowered his mouth to hers and kissed her long and passionately, just as he'd wanted to do for some time. Then just as quickly as he'd begun, he pushed her away. "There," he said. "Think about that while I'm gone and tell yourself that it's just your soul that matters to me."

The house seemed quite empty with Jacob gone and Jayce not yet returned. Leah fell into a routine of work that included finishing off many sewing projects she'd started the summer before. It was hard to believe she'd been gone from home for nearly half a year.

There were plans in the village for a big celebration in honor of Christmas. In years gone by these were always festive occasions where the village would gather at the big community house. Here they would share copious amounts of food and stories, as well as enjoy traditional singing and dancing. The children would show off some of their school papers and put on skits related to Christmas. It was a wonderful time of sharing and fellowship. Even the non-Christians would join in to celebrate the birth of the White Jesus, as they sometimes called Him.

There would also be an exchange of gifts. Usually these were very little items—trinkets, really—that would show respect and consideration for those in the village. Leah always tried to have a little something for everyone, but it would be very difficult this year. Having been gone so long, she would be limited on what she could make or provide. She had planned to bring back jelly and preserves from Karen, but those were all lost when the ship had gone down on Leah's return trip.

But always, even in the midst of planning for the festival, Leah couldn't help but worry about Jayce and wonder about her own physical condition. There was still no sign of her monthly cycle, and Leah was growing more certain that pregnancy was a very real possibility. There had even been moments of nausea.

Against her beliefs, Leah contemplated the herbs that she knew would induce a miscarriage. If she were pregnant, there was no way to be certain of whose child she carried. She couldn't bear the thought of not knowing, but neither could she reconcile the idea of killing her own baby.

"But I don't know for sure that I'm carrying a child," she reasoned. "If I take the herbs to bring on my monthly time, it wouldn't be wrong." But even as she spoke the words, Leah knew it was no excuse. She couldn't pretend that she wasn't pregnant, because the odds were too great that she was.

"Why is this happening, Lord?" she prayed as she worked on a shirt for Jayce. "I'm trying so hard to put what happened behind me—to find a way to not let it come between Jayce and me . . . and now this. How can I bear this blow?"

She had always figured that when she married and became pregnant, it would be the most joyous moment of her life. While cuddling the village infants, Leah had often imagined what it would be like to hold her own baby. With every baby she'd helped deliver, Leah had paid close attention to the things that worked best for mother and child. She wanted to learn so she'd be prepared when her time came.

Just that spring, with the arrival of her thirtieth birthday, Leah had wondered if she would ever know the joy of motherhood. But it wasn't a joy to her now. The very thought sickened her with despair.

"It isn't fair." She looked to the ceiling. "God, this just isn't fair."

Though a visitor was the last thing Leah wanted, when a knock sounded, she opened the door to find Helaina Beecham.

"What do you want?" Leah asked without any real interest.

"I need to talk to someone . . . to you."

Leah shook her head. "I really have no time. I'm quite busy."

"Please, Leah."

Her tone sounded different—almost desperate. Leah knew she'd probably regret her decision, but she opened the door fully and stepped back. "All right, come in."

She directed Helaina to the kitchen and closed the door. Leaning against it momentarily, Leah couldn't help but wonder what Helaina was up to. "Do you want some tea?" she offered.

"No. Please just come and talk with me. I feel so confused."

Leah raised a brow. "You? The epitome of confidence?"

"Don't mock me. It was hard for me to come here."

Something in Leah's spirit softened. "All right. Tell me what's wrong."

Helaina looked distraught. "I can't stop thinking about things Jacob has said to me."

Leah cringed inwardly. If Helaina wanted to talk about her brother's attraction to her, Leah wanted no part of it. "I don't think I should be the one you talk to. Why don't you wait for Jacob to come back?"

"Because I need answers now."

"But how would I have any of those answers?"

Helaina folded her hands and pressed them to her lap. "Because you are a women who believes in God."

Leah frowned. "What does that have to do with anything?"

"I have questions about God. I never used to care about such things, but ever since I met your brother, he has challenged me with such things. You have as well. I suppose I've simply had too much time to contemplate it all, and now I find myself confused."

Leah felt a sense of frustrated anger. Why should God bring Helaina here? She was living in the missionaries' house after all; why not ask Emma?

"Why do you come to me?" Leah looked at Helaina and saw desperation in the woman's face.

"Because I trust you. You've been through a great deal—mostly because I've caused it, I realize—but your faith has never wavered and you seem to completely understand what God is doing."

Leah laughed out loud at this. "Oh, Helaina, if you only knew. I've been sitting here for days trying to understand why God has allowed certain things to happen to me. Believe me, I'm not the best one to talk to about this."

"But you seem so strong. Even after Chase forced you to join our trip north. You were always talking to him about God's love and His desire for Chase to be forgiven his sins."

"Not that it ever made a difference." Leah contemplated how much to share with Helaina. The woman was still so focused on going after Chase that Leah wondered if it would make a difference. "Let's sit down." She went to the table and motioned Helaina to a chair.

Sitting, Helaina considered Leah's words. "Well, Chase seemed to respect you at least. I think he knew your faith in God made you different."

"Chase respected no one." Leah took a seat and tried to sort through her emotions. She wanted to tell Helaina the truth and hoped that in sharing she would abandon her pursuit of Chase—especially if it involved Jacob. There seemed no easy way to share what had happened, however.

"Helaina," she began, "you were too sick to know what was happening, but one night when he was particularly angry, Chase . . ." She paused and drew a deep breath. "He raped me."

Helaina covered her mouth as a small gasp escaped. Leah decided to press on. "Worse still, I may be pregnant, and I don't know if the baby belongs to Jayce or to his brother."

Leah couldn't comprehend why she was sharing this news with Helaina, but the words just kept pouring out. "Do you understand now why I had to get away from him? I couldn't bear the sight of him. I feared what I might do to him. I couldn't understand why God would allow such a thing to happen to me when I was trying so hard to live a good life for Him. I still don't understand, but . . ." She fell silent and tried to collect her thoughts.

"Leah, I didn't know. I didn't know. I'm so sorry." Helaina had tears in her eyes. "You've often said that I was selfish and thought only of my needs, and you're right. I can't bear it. I never even considered the possibility. I suppose because Chase didn't seem like a threat to me in that way, I assumed he'd be no threat to you."

Leah shook her head. She hadn't expected Helaina to respond with such compassion. What was happening to change Helaina's heart? Leah decided to continue. "I haven't told anyone but Jacob about the rape. I didn't mention the idea of being pregnant to Jacob, because until you spoke of your monthly time when we first arrived at Emma's, I hadn't even thought about it. I tell you this not because I have some great confidence in our relationship, but rather because I am desperate for you to stop your pursuit of Chase Kincaid. Especially if you plan to involve my brother. Don't you see? Now that Jacob knows what Chase did to me . . . well, if he agrees to help you track and capture Chase, he will be guided by his anger and need for revenge. I can't let that happen."

Helaina leaned back in her chair. She appeared to be deep in thought. Leah could only hope—pray—that her words were finally helping the younger woman to understand.

"What will you do?" Helaina finally asked. "How will you trust God, when all of this has happened? See, these are the things I cannot understand.

I've heard lofty sermons given by pious men all of my life. I saw no need for such things in my life. Now, in the midst of all you've endured, I need to understand how believing in God works. Tell me in a concise and logical manner."

"I don't know if I can explain it in a logical manner, Helaina. I'm not sure God works in what mortals consider logical ways. All I can tell you is what I know. When I was a little girl, the Bible was respected as God's Word. The people around me believed that God was their final authority. My mother helped me to see, as a child, that trusting God is a matter of faith. My faith is rather damaged right now, but I'm doing my best to let God help me nurse it back to health. I remind myself that oftentimes things happen that we cannot understand. For example, why would God allow so much of the world to be involved with war right now? Why did the *Titanic* sink and take so many lives? Why must children get sick and die? I don't have answers. All I have is my belief that God is good and just—that He will honor His promises."

"But that's exactly what I'm talking about. How do you do that? How can you believe in a God that allows such horrible things? How can I turn to God when He allowed my mother and father and husband to be killed?"

Leah's heart softened toward the woman. They weren't so very different after all. Although they'd been raised in very different worlds, peace of mind and spirit were still dependent upon letting go of all that seemed secure and putting one's faith in God.

"I suppose as far as logic and reasoning go, I would have to ask: What are your other choices? What are the alternatives to trusting God? You could put your faith in money or possessions, but those things aren't any more eternal than human life. We can put our trust in other people, but they, too, will fail us. And when they fail us we're left empty—wounded."

"Jacob said long ago that only God could fill that emptiness," Helaina said, growing thoughtful. "I never believed him, but the last few days I've had a great deal of time to think. Emma won't let me do anything but rest, and I find I'm not very good at sitting idle." She smiled. "I think it has mostly to do with the fact that I don't like myself very much, and when I'm alone and quiet, I only have myself for company."

Leah couldn't help but smile to see Helaina bare her soul and seek help as she reached out to God.

"I want the kind of faith you have, Leah. I want to know how to have the kind of trust in God that you have. The kind of trust that can love Him and believe in Him even after being mistreated as you've been by Chase. I want to know how you go on believing, even when you might be carrying the child of your rapist."

Chapter Twenty-Two

Leah looked at Helaina. "The Bible says that God sent His Son Jesus for all—that none should perish. Jesus died on the cross to be a supreme sacrifice for the sins of men—to give us a means of returning to the Father. When we admit our sins and ask God to forgive them, He does. He sees us not in our sinful nature, but through the blood of Jesus and gives us everlasting life."

"And then we'll be perfect?"

Leah shook her head. "I wish I could say that were true. I was just asking God to forgive me for the way I've felt toward you."

"Me? Why me?"

Leah got up and stood behind her chair. Gripping the back, she tried to measure her words carefully. "Helaina, my life seemed fairly well ordered until you entered it. It seemed you put a completely new set of complications to our existence in Last Chance, and frankly, I resented the intrusion. But I really resent and worry about the way you use my brother to try and get what you want."

"I have been wrong about that," Helaina admitted. "It's just that . . . well . . . I'm so confused. I've always been, as you said earlier, confident and capable. All of a sudden I feel that I'm no good for any purpose. I hate the thought of people being disappointed in me."

"I can understand. I just fear that Jacob will get hurt in all of this. But we can discuss that another time. I don't want to deny you your desire to come to peace in the Lord. I can tell you that my belief in who God is and what He's already done for me is all that has gotten me through these bad times. I've been very angry, however, with everyone—God included—for the things that happened. It's hard not to blame someone for what happened, when I feel so clearly that I did nothing wrong. I see no other choice I could have made . . . but then I remember I could have exposed Chase from the beginning. I could have said something to the people here, but I feared for their lives."

"So you sacrificed your own life because of your love for them. I think that's admirable."

Leah looked at the wall past Helaina. "Sometimes there are no clear answers. What happened with Chase is done. I can only pray now that Jayce is not hurt or killed as he pursues his brother."

"And I'm definitely to blame for that," Helaina admitted. "I'm sorry, Leah. I'm starting to see all of this with new eyes. Like I said, your brother has given me much to think about."

Leah extended her hand. "Helaina, forgive me. I've wronged you by holding bad thoughts against you."

Helaina took hold of Leah's hand and gave it a squeeze. "I've always known about justice—about seeing the law observed—but now I need mercy. I do forgive you, Leah, and I hope you will forgive me in turn."

Leah smiled. "I do. And now all you need to do is ask the same of God."

Jayce wearily drove the sled the remaining few miles to Last Chance. He felt an overwhelming sensation of guilt upon first viewing Leah's house. How would he face her? What would he say? He wanted to make up for the evil Chase had done but knew there was no way. He couldn't take away what had happened, and he couldn't erase her memory.

"Jayce!" Jacob saw him first and came running. He looked at the nearly empty sled basket. "No luck finding your brother, eh?"

"I found him. He's dead."

Jacob's face contorted. "Did you have to . . ." The words trailed off.

"No. A bear attacked him. Might have been Leah's wounded bear. It cut him up pretty bad. When I found him he was half frozen and nearly dead."

"Were you able to talk?"

"A little." Jayce drew a heavy breath and closed his eyes. "Enough."

Jacob put his hand to Jayce's shoulder. "I'm sorry."

"Where's Leah?"

Jacob shook his head. "I don't know. I just got back myself. I'm only here for a short time, then I'm heading out again. I need to get back to camp before I lose all the light. I'm just here to bring in a caribou kill."

Jayce looked to the house again. "I guess I'll start there."

"You go ahead. I'll take your dogs. John's back there helping unload the caribou. We'll get the dogs fed and put away."

"Thanks. That would be great."

"I'll be over directly with some fresh meat. You might let Leah know. Oh, and if she's not home, she might be visiting Ayoona or Emma."

He nodded. "I'll check it out."

Jayce stomped the snow from his boots as he made his way down the stairs to the door. He prayed silently for guidance, then went inside. He heard voices in the kitchen and pulled back the heavy fur. "Leah?"

He saw her startled look. She seemed immediately fearful, then calmed. "Jayce?"

He gave her a slight smile. "It's me." He raised the errant hair that fell across his left brow. "See, no scar."

She appeared to relax. "I'm so glad you're home." She moved to him as if she knew it was expected.

He held out his hands. "Don't come too close. I smell pretty bad."

She smiled. "This time of year most everything does."

"So what about your brother? Where's Chase?" Helaina asked, getting to her feet. "Did you find him? Is he here?"

Jayce looked at the woman who had caused him so many problems. "He's dead."

"Dead?" the women questioned in unison.

Jayce looked first to Leah and repeated. "He's dead. I buried him myself."

"But how? Did you kill him?" Helaina questioned.

Jayce turned back to her. "No. He was attacked by a bear."

"A bear," Leah murmured. "Probably the one I wounded." She went to the chair and sat down rather hard. "It's all my fault. I should never have left him without a gun."

"That's not true," Jayce said, coming to the table. He halted, remembering that he didn't want to frighten her. "If he'd had a gun, he would have come after you."

Helaina came to his side. "Tell me everything. I want to know the details. I'll need to let Stanley know in Washington."

"There isn't that much to tell, Mrs. Beecham. I found him on the trail; he was nearly dead already. He'd bled a great deal. I managed to set up a tent and unthaw him a bit, but the wounds were too serious. As he warmed up, the bleeding started in earnest. He regained consciousness for a time, then died."

"What was the date?"

"What's today's date?"

"December tenth," she said matter-of-factly.

"Then I suppose the best I can figure is . . . the twenty fifth of November."

"I'm so sorry, Jayce." Leah stared at the table wide-eyed. "It's my fault he's dead."

"No, it's not, Leah. You can't go blaming yourself over this."

"But if I'd tied him up and taken him with us, he'd be safe. If I'd just done what Helaina wanted me to do in the first place—he wouldn't be dead." She buried her face in her hands.

Jayce put his hand on her shoulder. He hoped she wouldn't jump or refuse his touch. "Leah, you did the right thing. Chase was too strong and too cunning. If you'd have taken him with you, he would have found a way to escape your hold, and then he probably would have killed you both."

"I just wanted to get away—needed to get away."

"And you were right to do so."

"Yes, you were," Helaina offered.

Leah looked up and met her eyes. "What?"

"You heard me. It was the right thing to leave him behind. I know I've said otherwise before now, but I feel differently. In thinking about the situation and what Chase was capable of, I think you had to do exactly as you did."

Helaina looked to Jayce. "Thank you for letting me know what happened. I'll go write it up for my brother. Leah, thank you for praying with me. I know it will make things better."

"But not perfect," Leah said softly.

Helaina smiled. "No, not perfect."

Once Helaina was gone, Jayce knelt beside Leah's chair. He hoped his position would make her feel less threatened. "You should know your brother is back for a short time. He's had a successful caribou hunt but plans to head out before nightfall."

Leah looked at him intently. "Thank you for letting me know. It will be good to have fresh meat."

"I thought so too." He gave her a hint of smile.

"Jayce," she said seriously, "I'm sorry for what you had to go through."

"I'm sorry for what *you* had to go through. My struggles don't compare to yours."

She looked at him oddly, then shook her head. "You know . . . don't you?"

"Yes." His voice was barely audible. He felt his words stick in his throat. What should he say? How could he tell her that it didn't matter to him—that Chase couldn't hurt her anymore?

Leah looked at her hands as she twisted them together. "I've worried about how to tell you, and you already know."

"Chase told me."

Her head snapped around. "He told you?"

He heard the disbelief in her voice. "Yes. He was dying. I was talking about God, encouraging him to ask forgiveness. Chase asked me if I could forgive him, and I told him that while difficult, I wanted to try. He challenged that I wouldn't want to try once I knew the truth."

"Then what happened?" Leah asked, her eyes wide.

"He told me he had forced himself on you." Tears welled in Jayce's eyes. "I'm so sorry, Leah. I'm sorry for the pain he caused you—for the torment. I don't know how to say the things I want to say, but please know it doesn't change my heart for you. I'm so afraid that it will change your love for me."

She held his gaze, confusion racing in her expression. "I felt ruined, but God has tried to tell me I'm not ruined."

"You aren't ruined. You are my wife and I love you. Nothing will change that."

Leah shook her head. "There's something that might."

"No. There's nothing. I will always love you. We will forget about Chase and build a new life together. We are just getting started. We can go anywhere and do anything you like. We can live wherever you want to live and—"

"I'm pregnant."

He looked at her in stunned wonder. "A baby? Leah, that's wonderful." He could see she was frowning. "Isn't it?"

"Jayce . . . I . . ." She swallowed hard and he could see this was taking all of her strength. "I don't know who the father is."

And then the realization of what she was saying dawned on him. "You don't know . . . because of Chase?"

She nodded, her gaze never leaving his face. "I have no way of knowing."

"Leah? Jayce?" It was Jacob.

"In the kitchen," Leah called.

"Does he know?" Jayce asked, quickly getting to his feet.

"Not everything—not about the baby," she managed before Jacob entered the room with a chunk of caribou meat.

"I've brought you your steaks, Leah. You'll just have to cut them up yourself."

Leah got up from the table and went to get a baking sheet. "Here, let's set it on the table." She put the pan down first and Jacob put the meat atop it.

"I'm not staying long. I plan to eat and get back to camp."

"Will you eat with us?" Leah asked. "I can get some of this meat frying up in just minutes." She went to the stove and added driftwood.

"That was my plan, unless Jayce minds. I know you two probably have a lot to talk about."

"Stay," Jayce said. "I wouldn't want you out there begging a meal." He smiled and added, "I need to clean up."

"I'll get you some hot water. You can go to the main room. No one will bother you there," Leah said as she took a bowl down from the cabinet. She dipped out hot water from the reservoir until it filled the bowl. "There's some soap in the chest by our bed."

"Our bed?" Jayce asked.

"Kimik made us a bed while we were gone," she replied. She'd turned away so Jayce couldn't see by her expression what she thought of this arrangement. "It's a good bed—very comfortable. I think you'll like it."

Jayce looked to Jacob and nodded. "I'm sure I will."

The dinner table was quiet as they sat down to have their lunch. The caribou steaks were thick and juicy, the canned peas Leah served with them seemed the perfect balance, and the sourdough bread tasted better than anything Jayce had had in a long time.

He couldn't help but watch Leah from time to time. She was more beautiful than he'd even remembered. But even with this, in his mind he kept hearing Leah tell him that she was pregnant. That she didn't know who the father was.

The baby could belong to Chase. The baby might be a result of that unholy, evil union forced upon his wife. How could he love and regard the child as his own in such a case?

On the other hand, the baby could be his.

"I have no way of knowing," Leah had told him, the resignation heavy in her voice.

No way of knowing. How could there be no way of knowing? Surely there was enough time between Jayce's last night with his wife and Chase's rape. Surely these things could be calculated and figured. He looked across the table to where Leah sat eating in silence.

I cannot voice my fears about this, he thought. *She is already tortured enough. If I say anything it will only add to her misery—her burden. But, God, how can I bear this?*

"Will you be back in time for the Christmas festival?" Leah asked her brother.

"I doubt it. Nutchuk has plans for us to get into the mountains. He's heard there's good trapping to be had there. I'm guessing we'll be back in January. And I'll leave for Nome soon after checking in here."

"That's good. Supplies are low. There's plenty to eat, but things like molasses and sugar are completely gone. Oh, and canned milk too."

"Make me a list. I'll get whatever I can. Nome should be in pretty good shape given the load we brought in on the *Homestead*. Plus, we still have the things we put in storage."

"I'll ask around and see if there are any other items people need," Leah replied before turning her attention back to the steak.

Jayce admired her calm. He wanted so much to comfort her—to hold her. He wondered if she'd ever let him hold her again. It pained him to think she might reject his physical touch.

They finished dinner in relative silence. Jacob got up and threw Leah a smile. "Good grub, sis. I'll be thinking of this nice warm meal for a long time. Jayce, I'll see you in a month or so." He pulled on his parka. "Oopick says we're in for a bad winter. Be sure and tell her I said thanks again for the mukluks." He glanced to his feet. "They're sure warm."

"We'll remember you in our prayers." Leah's voice seemed hollow and sad.

"And I'll remember you." Jacob answered Leah, but he looked at Jayce and gave him a slight nod. "God will get us through. We have to have faith."

Jayce nodded. *Faith is all I have.*

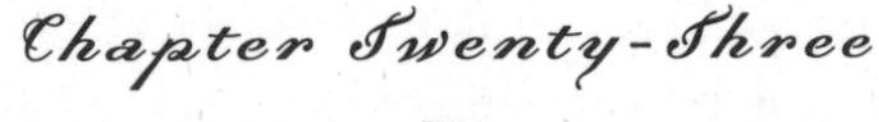

Chapter Twenty-Three

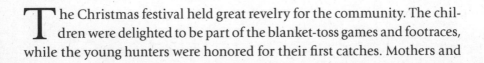

The Christmas festival held great revelry for the community. The children were delighted to be part of the blanket-toss games and footraces, while the young hunters were honored for their first catches. Mothers and grandmothers had carefully preserved whatever animal their young had managed to track down and now presented it to the gathering as confirmation of the new hunter's ability.

Leah found herself enjoying the native dancing. She watched as the men and women moved in rhythm to the beating of the skin drums. Everyone seemed to enjoy the stories told in the dances, even though they were usually the same stories told year after year. The older folks seemed to be particularly delighted by the abundance of food. Everyone would bring bite-sized portions in huge bowls, and servers would offer them throughout the evening. It was a great time of fun for all ages.

Perhaps the crowning joy of the entire evening was when Bjorn shared the Christmas story with his congregation and with the other villagers who chose not to attend his little church. Afterward gifts were handed out and shared throughout the community. The wealthier would bring in more substantial presents, sometimes offering large pieces of fur or clothing, while the poorer gave only the most meager offerings. It didn't matter, however. No one belittled the poor. In this community they looked out for each other and took care to provide for those who could not provide for themselves. It was the way things were done from generation to generation. Leah loved that about the Inupiat people. They were good to each other. The elderly were cherished and revered, unlike in many white communities. Leah had heard horrible stories from Karen and her relatives in the States.

Days after the celebration, Leah went to see Emma and got the sad news that she'd miscarried. The news took Leah by surprise.

"I'm afraid I'm not good company," Emma said, her eyes still wet with tears. "I was so looking forward to another baby."

Leah had still not told her about her own pregnancy, but realized it was not yet the proper timing for such an announcement. "I'm so sorry, Emma. I wish I could do something to help."

"There's nothing to be done. I told Bjorn last night, and he was ever so reassuring. He said before I knew it, I would be carrying another baby and that we shouldn't mourn too greatly. I know he means well, but I will miss my little baby."

Leah thought of how she'd almost prayed to miscarry. A miscarriage would seem like a gift from the Lord, given her circumstances. If God took her child, then Leah wouldn't have to feel guilty for her thoughts or her negative heart.

"So you seem very well," Emma said, drying her eyes. "I heard about Jayce's brother dying. It's a tragic end, but God's ways are often more than we can understand."

Leah could only nod. She didn't feel that she could yet explain things to her old friend.

"Did he have a family? A wife—children?"

Leah felt the words stick in her throat. Did Chase have children? That was what she needed to know. "No," she finally said. "There was no one like that. He has another brother and a sister too. I'm told they live back east. Jayce tells me the family has never been close."

"Pity. But on the other hand, it's probably best Chase didn't leave a family of his own behind." Emma picked up some crocheting and began to work.

"No doubt," Leah replied softly. Anxious to change the subject, Leah asked about Emma's planned summer trip. "Will you still go to Minnesota to visit your families next summer?"

"Oh, ja. I'm looking forward to it. I can hardly believe how the children have grown. I'm looking forward to showing them off and shopping for them. The mission board has promised us an extra stipend for supplies." Her spirits seemed to lift. "We've taken turns talking about what we'd like to buy. There's always so much to consider."

Leah nodded. "I can only imagine. I was so overcome when we were in Seattle. I guess I'd really forgotten what it was like to be in the city. The choices were more than I could even imagine. There are so many manufactured goods to be had."

"Ja, my sister Sigrid writes to tell me of new inventions and improvements on things already in existence. She's always good to tell me of such things. She's not good to tell of the war or of other things, however."

"Do you think she'll like it here?" Leah questioned. "It will definitely be different from a city like Minneapolis."

"I've told her as much. I've written long letters to explain how her days will be spent up here, just to be sure she still wants to come."

"And does she?"

"Ja. She's certain the wild open spaces will agree with her. She wants to learn to hunt and fish Alaskan style. She loves to do both in Minnesota. She's quite an earthy girl. I suppose her real passion is teaching. She loves to teach school, which is not something Bjorn and I enjoy as much."

"She sounds like a very resourceful woman," Leah admitted. "I will do my best to help her feel welcome. We'll have to have a party for her when she arrives and introduce her to everyone."

"I think that would be great fun," Emma said, glancing up from her work. "I know you two will get along well. I have even wondered if she would be a good match for Jacob, but I think I told you that. Could be they might find a fit in each other."

"I'm certain I would prefer that to the current possibilities."

"Helaina Beecham?"

Leah nodded. "I don't think she really cares for him, but Jacob has lost his heart to her. I'm sure that now this situation with Chase is settled, she'll be bound for the States as soon as possible. She misses her cities and life of ease."

"She does seem to be a good woman, however. She is trying hard to learn what she can."

"I know that's good, but I don't see her being willing to give up everything to live here in Alaska. It just doesn't seem to be her way." She stood up. "I should get back home. I'm working to make some undershirts for Jayce and Jacob."

"Leah, don't worry overmuch about your brother and Helaina. Helaina has been a good help to us. She has the children off on a Saturday adventure. They love her very much. Who would have thought it?" Emma said, shaking her head. "I am glad she's at peace with God." She gave a little laugh and added, "Well there's some peace, and some frustration. She asks poor Bjorn questions day and night."

"She asks me a fair share, as well, and believe me, I'm trying not to worry." Leah hugged Emma. "Come and visit me when you can."

"And you come back when you can stay longer," Emma declared.

Leah nodded. "I promise, I will."

Jayce worked to make lashings out of caribou sinew. He braided the pieces together and felt satisfied at their strength. He was making a new *umiak* for summer trips on the water and the lashings would have to be strong to hold the sealskin to the wooden frame.

As he worked, his mind kept returning to the same subject: his marriage to Leah and the baby that she now carried. Jayce found himself burdened with the idea of fatherhood. Would he make a good father? Could he be a loving parent to a child that might not even be his own? He tried to shake off such thoughts, tried to reason that even if the baby were Chase's it would look no different. Jayce and Chase were identical in appearance, and therefore the child could have features that would be the same no matter the father.

Jayce sighed and put his work aside. He didn't want it to matter. He wanted to be the bigger man—the hero of the story. He wanted Leah to feel comfortable and loved. He wanted them to put questions about the baby's parentage behind them. But he couldn't help himself. He dwelled on the issue constantly, and Jayce knew it would only be a matter of time before he said something.

"God, what do I do?" He left his work and decided a short walk would be in order. He took up his Bible and rifle. In case anyone asked, he would just tell them he was out to scout something fresh for supper. Then if the moment presented itself, he'd be ready.

He walked away from the village, heading south along the shoreline. His mukluks crunched against the crusted snow. A storm had come in only days earlier, pushing the salt water over the ice just beyond the shores. This, in turn, pushed the ice toward the beach, forcing it up, breaking it and piling it in what Jayce knew to be pressure ridges. These could be quite dangerous and most people avoided them.

Farther out on the ice he saw several men working with seal nets. They would dig holes in the ice and string nets from one hole to the other underwater, all in hopes of catching fresh meat. Jayce had only learned how this was done a few weeks back. It sometimes proved very fruitful, and other times it was days and days before anything could be caught.

Moving farther away from the village, Jayce's thoughts returned to Leah and the baby. They hadn't talked about the child since she'd told him she was pregnant. It seemed to be an unspoken agreement between them, but Jayce knew it couldn't continue. Soon Leah would begin to show, and everyone would know about the situation. If she and Jayce were not able to deal with this in a joyful manner, there would be further explanations due. Explanations that would no doubt leave Leah feeling ashamed.

Jayce found a spot to sit and placed his rifle across his knees. Reaching inside his parka, he pulled out his Bible and opened it. He went to Matthew, remembering that Bjorn had read from here when telling of the Christmas story. There were verses here that Jayce felt drawn to—Scriptures that told of Joseph dealing with Mary's news that she would bear a child. A child that did not belong to Joseph.

Then Joseph her husband, being a just man, and not willing to make her a public example, was minded to put her away privily. But while he thought on these things, behold, the angel of the Lord appeared unto him in a dream, saying, Joseph, thou son of David, fear not to take unto thee Mary thy wife: for that which is conceived in her is of the Holy Ghost. And she shall bring forth a son, and thou shalt call his name Jesus: for he shall save his people from their sins.

The words comforted Jayce as he read and reread them. Joseph had trusted the Lord and had taken Mary to be his wife. He had raised Jesus as his own child—loving Him and teaching Him, despite the fact that he knew without doubt that this baby was not his own flesh and blood.

Jayce, on the other hand, might well be the father of Leah's baby. He knew this and knew that he had to make a decision here and now that, no matter what, this child was his. This would be his son or daughter and nothing would ever change that.

Looking again at the verses, Jayce felt renewed. *And she shall bring forth a son, and thou shalt call his name Jesus: for he shall save his people from their sins.* Jesus had saved them from their sins. They had asked for His forgiveness and sought His eternal redemption. Neither Jayce nor Leah had done any wrong in the conception of this baby. Furthermore, the child had done nothing wrong. Jayce could not punish an innocent life for the crimes of someone else.

He smiled as a peace settled over him. "Thank you, God. Thank you for showing me the truth." It might not be an easy situation, and there would no doubt be questions to deal with from time to time, but the important thing was to heal and grow in their love as a family.

With renewed vigor, Jayce raced for home. He needed to see Leah—to tell her of what he'd read and reassure her that they would have a wonderful life together, and that their child would be a blessing.

"Leah!" he called as he rushed into the house. "Leah!"

"What is it?" she asked as she came from behind the kitchen fur. "What's wrong?" Her face was ashen.

"Nothing is wrong," he said, pulling her close. He'd momentarily forgotten to be more gentle, but he couldn't help it. "I have something good to tell you."

She smiled. "I'm all for good news."

"Come, sit with me." He led her into the main room of the house. The small table and chairs there would make a good place to talk. When they were both seated, he began.

"I know we've avoided talking about the baby." He saw her eyes widen just a bit as she nodded. "But I need to talk about the baby now. I need for you to understand something."

"All right."

He smiled, hoping that she would be put at ease. "Remember when Bjorn taught about the birth of Jesus?" She nodded and he continued. "He talked about Mary learning that she would bear a son, and of Joseph learning that Mary was with child. Joseph knew the baby wasn't his, yet God sent an angel to encourage Joseph. He told Joseph that it would be all right—that Jesus was God's Son and He would take away the sins of the world."

"I remember that." She seemed to consider his words.

"I was humbled by the fact that Joseph, even though he knew he wasn't the father of Jesus, became the earthly father and raised Jesus as his own son." He reached out and took hold of Leah's hands. "We might not know for certain whether this child was conceived during our time together or not, but there is a good chance that he was."

"So now it's a boy?" she asked, a hint of a smile on her lips.

"Boy or girl, it doesn't matter. This baby is mine."

She cocked her head to the side and raised a brow. "Just like that?"

"Just like that," he said firmly. "I am the father. I will always be the father. The past doesn't matter. We were innocent of any wrongdoing, but even more so, this child is innocent."

Tears formed in Leah's eyes. "I . . . I . . ."

He shook his head and put a finger to her lips. "The past is gone. We are free from its grip. Chase is dead, and he cannot hurt us anymore. We are starting a new life—a new adventure as parents to a wonderful child who will give us great joy. Jesus came to save His people from their sins, and I believe this baby will come to save us from our sorrows and regrets."

Leah took hold of Jayce's hand and placed it against her cheek. "I want that very much. I want to be happy about this baby. Emma just told me that she miscarried her child. She was so devastated, and I felt so guilty hoping God might do that for me as well. Please forgive me for thinking in such an unloving manner."

He got up from the table and pulled her into his arms. "Leah, I forgive you. Please forgive me for having any doubts about this child. Everything will be all right—you'll see. We'll tell everyone in the village that we're going to have a child, and we'll celebrate."

She nodded and lifted her face to his. Jayce saw the invitation in her eyes. It would be the first time they had kissed since returning to Last Chance. Slowly, so as to let her change her mind if needed, Jayce lowered his mouth to hers. The kiss was tender, lingering, and filled with the love he held for her.

Jacob and Nutchuk returned after the start of the new year. They brought a plentiful harvest of skins, as well as fresh caribou meat from a kill made just the day before. The village celebrated and immediate preparations were made for Jacob to make a trip to Nome.

Jacob had done a lot of thinking while away from the village. He'd spent much time reading his Bible and praying for guidance, and now he felt he knew what needed to be done. He approached the Kjellmann house with determined steps. He needed to talk to Helaina.

"Why, Jacob, I thought you'd still be sleeping after our festivities last night. Such a happy time. We were so excited to learn about Leah having a baby," Emma said as she greeted him. "You will be an uncle, ja?"

"Yes, indeed. It's a happy time."

She nodded. "So what brings you here?"

"I need to speak with Helaina. Is she in?"

"Ja. She's putting Rachel down for a nap. Come in. Can you stay to drink some coffee?"

"Well . . . maybe just a bit. I need to talk privately with Helaina."

"Ja, I understand. I was just heading over to help Bjorn with school. Helaina is watching Rachel, and the boys are playing down the way at Seal-Eye Sam's. He's teaching them to catch seals." She grinned. "Bryce was certain he would bring one home tonight."

Jacob laughed. "Never underestimate a boy's spirit and drive."

"I won't. It wouldn't surprise me to find a seal on my doorstep when I get back."

"Jacob!" Helaina nearly gasped his name as she came from the back room. "I didn't know you were here."

"I came to speak with you—if you have a moment."

She nodded. "Would you like coffee?"

"You sound like Emma now. That Swedish hospitality has worn off on you, eh?"

"She'll make a good housewife," Emma declared and moved to the door, where her parka hung. "I'll be back after school, ja?"

"That's fine. I'll feed the boys lunch when they come home."

Emma nodded and pulled on her coat. "I'm thinking Sam will feed them. He's probably feeding them all day long. They will be too fat to fit through the door if Sam and his wife have anything to say about it." The trio laughed and Emma quickly departed.

Jacob watched Helaina as she moved comfortably around the kitchen. She seemed somehow changed. Softened. He sensed a newfound peace in her. "I wanted to talk to you. I didn't see you last night at the celebration."

"I stayed here and kept Rachel for Emma." She brought the coffee to the table. "Be careful—it's hot."

Jacob warmed his hands for a moment on the mug. "Well, I'm sure you've heard that I plan to head out for Nome. I'll probably leave tomorrow at the latest. We're out of so many supplies, and while there is still plenty for everyone to eat, it would be nice to have some of the things that spoil us."

Helaina nodded. "I agree. Sometimes I miss fresh fruit more than I can say."

"Well, that's why I'm here. I think you should come with me to Nome. You can get word to your brother, hopefully, and make plans for the spring. Nome will have more to offer you, and while you'll have to pay for room and board, you won't have to worry about feeling too isolated or lonely."

She frowned. "I wasn't feeling isolated or lonely."

Jacob looked down and suddenly felt very confused. He wanted to tell her that she had to go—had to get away from him so that he wouldn't lose his heart any more than he already had. But at the same time he wanted to declare his love for her and plead with her to stay.

"But," she continued, "if you feel that this is what I should do, then I'll go."

Jacob looked up. He started to tell her that he didn't feel that way at all, but something held him silent.

"I suppose I can be ready tomorrow. I don't have that much that belongs to me. In fact, most of my things are still in Nome. At least I hope that the hotel had the decency to hold on to them for me."

Jacob didn't know what to say. He was surprised by her cooperation. There was definitely something different about Helaina Beecham. "I'll be ready to leave by six. It'll still be dark, but I know the trails well."

"All right." She turned away from him rather abruptly and busied herself with something on the kitchen counter. "I'll be ready."

Jacob finished his coffee and got up. "I'll go now."

He walked back to Jayce and Leah's, all the while wondering if he'd made a mistake. With Chase dead, there was no reason for Helaina to remain in Alaska—no reason for her to be in Last Chance. No reason at all.

Chapter Twenty-Four

Helaina thought she could be strong and cooperate with Jacob's decision to take her to Nome, but with each mile they passed, she was less certain it was going to work. She'd completely surprised herself by falling in love with Jacob Barringer. What she thought at first was just infatuation with the tawny brown-haired man had turned into something different.

As they traveled she thought of her late husband, Robert, and how he had been her heart and soul. Robert had made her feel protected and loved. She had been a delicate possession in his care. Jacob, on the other hand, expected her to have skill and endurance. While he offered her protection, he also expected her to be independently capable of fending for herself. She liked that. While she'd never thought it possible to fall in love again, that was exactly what had happened.

To her surprise the sled slowed and Jacob leaned down. "There's a storm moving in. See the heavy clouds to the west and south?"

She looked and nodded. The dark clouds and the sea had closed on the horizon and the wind had picked up, dropping the temperature. She recognized the signs. "What do you want to do?"

"We'll need to make camp for the night—or as long as the storm lasts. I've seen them last for days up here," he announced. "I'll look for a good spot and we'll stop."

In another mile he made good on his word as he brought the sled to a halt. "This will give us as much cover as we can hope for."

Helaina glanced around at the barren landscape. There wasn't much in the way of protection. "I'll help you set up the tent," she offered.

"That would be good. We'll get it done much quicker, and then I can see to the dogs. I think we'll have an hour or so before things get really bad.

I'll start a fire first and see about getting some snow melted and some food thawing. It'll be much faster than just relying on the oil stove."

Jacob was quite proficient in his tasks. At times Helaina could almost swear there were two of him. "I'll need you to gather more driftwood once we have the tent up," he told her. Helaina nodded her agreement, all the while checking the skies to see how close the storm might be.

They worked well together. Jacob showed her how to scrape snow from the camp to make a little indention for their dwelling. He talked of using the snow for insulation. "I've been out before with John and we cut ice houses. He's very good at it, and I can hold my own, but it isn't easy. It's not fast either. They are, however, surprisingly warm."

"I was amazed to hear that so many people lived in tents during the gold rush in this area. You said you were a part of the Yukon gold rush. Did you live in a tent?"

"We did," Jacob said. "The tents were pretty large, and we had bigger stoves than the little ones we use here. There were times when we lived with a lot of people in one tent. Other times there weren't but a few. People lived in those tents even when it was forty below."

"I can't even imagine. Everything up here seems so extreme—so unusual."

"It's definitely a life of sacrifice. But I wouldn't be anywhere else. I love Alaska."

She said nothing, not sure that she could respond without giving away her feelings.

"You've probably noted that most of our tents have floors," Jacob said as he fought the frozen ground to secure the stakes. "That's Leah's doing. She felt more secure and definitely warmer. She bought duck canvas and put it together herself."

"I do prefer it," Helaina admitted. "I feel less exposed. It was ingenious. Leah really ought to patent the idea and sell it to Sears, Roebuck and Company."

Jacob laughed. "I'll tell her she can be a tentmaker like Paul."

"Paul who?"

Jacob looked up. "He's in the Bible. He wrote much of the New Testament."

"Oh, the man who was called Saul. The one who persecuted the Christians?"

Jacob nodded. "I'm impressed. You've been reading."

"I've been asking a lot of questions too." She worked to get the tent poles positioned. "Did your sister tell you that I made my peace with God?"

Jacob seemed surprised. "No. No, she didn't. I suppose I really didn't give her a lot of time to tell me anything. I heard about the baby, though. That's very exciting for her. Exciting, too, that you would give your heart to Jesus. What changed your mind?"

"You did. You and Leah both. I was amazed at how you handled difficulties and trials. You always seemed to have such peace. It was quite maddening, actually." She grinned and got to her feet.

"Come on, let's get this thing up so that we can unload the sled. We can talk about this all night if need be." Jacob manhandled the tent into shape and soon had it erected. "There. That ought to hold us."

Helaina gathered driftwood while Jacob saw to the dogs. They were quite efficient, she thought. We would make a good team—a good husband and wife. She looked up suddenly at the thought—almost fearful that Jacob would have heard her.

"I've got to stop thinking that way," she murmured to herself. Refocusing on her task, Helaina felt her hands trembling. She tried to pretend it was simply the cold, but her fingers were plenty warm inside her sealskin mittens. She looked to where Jacob finished watering the dogs. The wind was starting to blow harder and it made her steps more uncertain. Jacob didn't seem in the least bit bothered by the weather. He took it all in stride, as though it were nothing more troubling than an ocean breeze.

I've never planned to remarry. I've never wanted to risk loving someone again. This is a dangerous land. It would be easy to lose him up here—see him killed by a bear. Just like Chase. But it had been simple enough for thugs to kill her parents and Robert in an affluent New York neighborhood. Perhaps life was fraught with dangers no matter where you were, and a person just had to endure.

"That's enough wood," he called above the wind. "Go ahead and get in the tent. Get the oil stove lit. That will help to warm up the place."

Helaina slipped inside the tent. It wasn't much more than seven by seven and smelled of old seal oil. She thought of the close quarters and wondered how she would ever rest comfortably knowing that Jacob was just a few feet away. When they'd planned this trip he had figured to sleep in the sled, but with a storm approaching, she wondered if he would spend the night with her in the tent. He would at least take refuge here for a time, and that would put them in very close proximity to each other.

By the time Jacob joined her she had the stove going and the chill off the air. It was still cold, but not so much that she couldn't discard her mittens.

"Feels a lot better in here. Oh, it's starting to snow. I think we've had more snow this winter than most." To her surprise he pulled off his parka and set it aside.

"Won't you get cold? I mean colder?" she asked, motioning to his coat.

"Momentarily, but if I keep it on I'll start to sweat, and that could be deadly. It's important to layer yourself properly up here and pace your work so that you don't sweat. Otherwise you risk freezing even if you're amply dressed. It's a mistake a lot of people make up here."

"It is a completely different world." She thought about her own parka and finally decided to take it off. "I feel foolish," she said, carefully putting it aside.

He laughed. "You won't. You'll warm up with both of us in here and the stove going. You'll see."

She rubbed her arms for a moment, more out of nervousness than cold. "Emma and Leah helped me dress, so I suppose I'll be fine."

Jacob nodded and started to put together their supper. "I hope you don't mind more caribou."

"Actually no. I prefer it to the seal and whale meat. I suppose we all have our preferences. I can't imagine what my friends in New York will say when I tell them of the things I've eaten. They might even think such things delicacies, but I doubt I'll ever see *muktuk* on the menu at Delmonico's."

"What's that—a restaurant?"

"Yes. A very popular place at one time. Although that poor establishment is having a fierce time of it. The war has changed everything."

"Truly? Even though we're not at war here in the United States?"

Helaina nodded. "It's more felt on the East Coast, I'm sure. The businesses in New York and Boston that were dealing heavily with imports from the European countries are suffering. It affects our economy even if we aren't involved. Although, sadly, I believe we will be involved before much longer. I'm not sure how we can avoid it."

"I guess the war doesn't seem very real here in Alaska. I read up on it in Seattle, but even there it seemed almost the stuff of fables."

"I assure you it's not. I was in England and France at the outbreak and then later when fighting was well under way. It's a horrible situation—one that will require clear heads to prevail. I don't know if that will include American heads or not, but it seems that we must do something."

Jacob warmed the stew Leah had prepared for them, then took out two tin plates. He'd managed to unthaw some sourdough bread by the fire and placed a big piece on each plate before pouring the thick stew alongside. "This should definitely warm us up."

They ate in relative silence while the wind gathered strength and the storm moved ashore. Helaina worried about their safety and about whether the dogs would be able to endure, but Jacob assured her those animals had survived much worse.

"I remember a time when a blizzard held us captive for two weeks. It was something else. I'd tie a rope onto myself and then to the house, and every day go out like that to feed and water the dogs."

"Why didn't you just bring the dogs inside?"

"There were over sixty of them, for one thing," Jacob mused. "But they would also lose their conditioning if I let them live inside. They were fine outside. They all have little houses, as you know, but usually they just sleep outside. They have thick coats and they sleep with their noses tucked against their bodies and their tails wrapped around them. I'm sure you've seen it. They're a hardy bunch to be sure."

"The people are hardy too," Helaina replied. "They are incredible. I wasn't sure how to take them at first. They seemed very quiet and not at all interested in me."

"You were a snob at first," Jacob countered. "You acted rather poorly toward them."

Helaina thought back on it and nodded. "I suppose I did at that. I don't feel that way now."

"God has a way of softening our hearts. You'll find that things are different, and they'll keep changing as you grow closer to the Lord. That's where I see God making a difference in our everyday life. Having eternal salvation is one thing, but letting God make you a new heart for the day-to-day living is something else."

"It's like seeing life through someone else's eyes," Helaina said. "I don't know how it will be once I'm home again."

Jacob frowned, then looked away quickly. "I'm sorry you'll have to wait so long. It will probably be June before the first ships make it up to Nome."

Helaina regretted even mentioning returning to New York. She wanted to take the words back as soon as they were out of her mouth. "I'm in no hurry" was all she could say.

The hour grew late, and once dinner was concluded and everything cleaned up and put away, Helaina felt rather awkward. "Will you . . . are you . . . staying here tonight?"

Jacob looked at her sheepishly. "I hope you don't mind. I'm a very honorable man, however. I'll sleep in the sled like I promised . . . if that makes you feel better."

"No, it's all right that you're here. I couldn't send you out there. It would be too cruel."

"I've slept in the sled on many occasions," Jacob replied. "In fact, I wouldn't have even brought a tent had it not been for you. It just cuts down on my ability to bring back goods to Last Chance. Of course, I could store the tent in Nome since you won't be coming back with me."

Helaina felt heartsick and turned away. "I'm tired. I suppose I'll try to sleep."

"Probably a good idea. If the weather clears we can get an early start."

She nodded. She started to say something about not wanting him to go back to Last Chance without her, but it seemed completely inappropriate, so she said nothing.

Days later in Nome, Jacob was still thinking about how uncomfortable it had been staying with Helaina alone in the tent. He was awake for a long time that night just listening to her breathing and wondering if there could ever be a future for them. There was so much he didn't know about her world—so many ways he didn't fit in. And she certainly had trouble adapting to his world.

To Jacob's relief he found Nome still had a plentiful supply of goods. He left the furs and gave his list to one of his more trustworthy suppliers, then went in search of the Pinkerton agents they'd left behind. He went to the last place he'd left them and found them both still gainfully employed by the Nome police department.

They were content with their jobs and lives in Nome. Maybe too content. Each man indicated he had no desire to leave for the States.

"This is proving to be a good town for me," Butch Bradford told Jacob. "I got me a wife and little place to live. I plan to stay."

"I'm pretty sure I'm stayin' as well," Sam Wiseford added. "I like the isolation."

"What about Mrs. Beecham?" Jacob questioned. "She'll need an escort to the States come summer. Wouldn't one of you be willing to accompany her?"

"Summer's when they'll need us most. I won't be goin' anywhere," Bradford said. "Sorry." The smaller man nodded in agreement.

Jacob spent the rest of his time in Nome trying to figure out what should be done about it. He didn't feel comfortable leaving Helaina to fend for herself until spring, but he also didn't feel that he could take her back to Last Chance.

He sat at dinner, wondering how in the world he could fit all the pieces together, when Helaina came in to join him. He hadn't been sure she would come, but now that she was here he felt mesmerized by her beauty. She was dressed in her Inupiat clothes, which rather surprised but pleased him.

"I figured you'd be anxious to dress in your old things," he said, getting up to help her be seated.

"It's too cold for that." She took her seat and added, "I'm not the same woman I was last summer."

He nodded. "I know." His voice was barely audible.

"Did you order?"

"I did. They have a nice caribou roast, vegetables, and pie for dessert."

She nodded and motioned to the waitress, who looked old enough to be her grandmother. "I'll have what he's having. As well as some hot coffee. I see you've already had some."

Jacob's cup was already empty. "It's good. Pretty strong, though."

Helaina waited until the old woman walked away before beginning the conversation. "Jacob, I came here to say something, and I hope you'll hear me out."

He leaned back in his chair. She had that look on her face, that same determined look she always got when she was up to something. This time, however, it made him smile. "I guess I don't really have a choice, now do I?"

She shook her head. "No, you don't. If you won't listen to me here, I'll follow you all over Nome until you do."

He laughed. "Then you'd best get to it."

"Well," she began, folding her hands and striking a serious pose, "I want you to take me back to Last Chance when you leave tomorrow."

He met her blue eyes. She held his gaze and continued, though he barely heard her words. "I can't stay here, especially when every place I've checked out is costly and hardly concerned with safety. I would be much better off in Last Chance. If I go back with you, I can help Leah and Emma through the winter and then head home in the spring. I could even accompany the Kjellmanns when they leave and be perfectly safe."

"I hadn't really thought of that," Jacob admitted.

"Emma said I was more than welcome to stay with them through the winter. The children are fond of me, and frankly, I've grown quite fond of them."

Jacob knew that what she said made sense. "Are you sure you wouldn't feel more comfortable here? You would have more access to supplies."

"I would be very lonely. Please, Jacob, don't leave me here."

He dropped his gaze to the table. *How can I take her there and stay too?* He wondered for a moment how he might live in the same village—in the same close company—and not make himself completely miserable or act the fool. He was already in love with her, yet he knew she would never be able to adapt to life in Alaska and forsake all she was accustomed to. And he would never leave Alaska. There was no reason to continue the relationship—it would only cause them more pain in the long run.

"Jacob, I need for you to do this for me."

He looked up. "Why?" Something in her tone told him she had something completely different on her mind—something she wasn't saying.

Helaina was the one to look away this time. "I . . . well . . . I know I can stay strong there."

"Strong?"

She nodded but still didn't look at him. "Strong in the Lord. On my own, I'm not sure. I just feel like I need time. Time to better understand and learn. I know I can do that in Last Chance. Spending these last couple of days on my own, I've found myself with questions that have no answers. I look in the Bible, but I don't know how to really understand what I'm reading."

"There are churches here. Pastors can help you to better understand Scripture," he countered.

"I don't know these people. I don't trust them. Please, Jacob."

He knew he was losing this argument rather rapidly. It felt like the time he had slid down the embankment of the creek and broke through the ice. He was not on a firm foundation. "Life isn't easy in Last Chance. You know how it is there."

She looked up again and nodded. "I do, and I don't mind. Please take me home . . . with you."

He knew she wasn't asking him this to help with any job or obsession as she had before. At least he couldn't imagine what obsession it might be, if she were actually using him in that manner. He knew he couldn't refuse her.

"All right," he finally said. "I'm not sure it's wise, but I'll take you back to Last Chance."

She smiled and it lit up her whole face. "I promise you won't be sorry."

Jacob sighed. *I already am.* But of course, he couldn't tell her that.

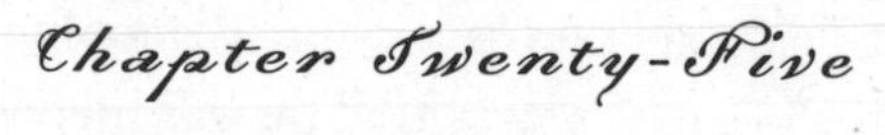

Chapter Twenty-Five

Winter passed with Helaina actually enjoying her life at the Kjellmann residence. She enjoyed talking with Emma and Bjorn over supper each night and found they generally had answers for her questions. The idea of trusting God didn't seem nearly as foreign to her now. Emma had been good to point out that learning to believe God to be who He claimed to be would come first through faith, and second by letting God prove himself day to day.

"It's no different than learning to trust the man you will marry. Think back to when you met your husband," Emma had told her.

Helaina had done just that. The memory of that developing relationship helped her to understand that learning to love and trust God was no different. She couldn't love and trust someone she didn't know—so she made it her priority to get to know God as well as she could.

Night after night she spent time studying the Bible. With Jacob gone so much, she really had little else to hold her attention. Bjorn led his family in daily devotions, so Helaina used these to be the basis for her studies. That way it was easy to ask Bjorn questions regarding the matter.

Sunday services were another place Helaina thrived. She learned rather quickly that it wasn't just about coming to a place to hear the Bible preached; there was much more. Why she'd never seen it until now was beyond her, but attending church seemed to be like a special refreshment. Maybe it was just because they were so isolated and there was nothing else to do, but Helaina seriously doubted that was all there was to it.

Week after week, Helaina found herself looking forward to the gathering. She longed to be with the people—to sing hymns and to hear Bjorn teach on the Bible. She would never have thought it possible to enjoy church as much as she did now.

June brought the excitement of spring breakup. The villagers were eager for true Alaskan summer, as they knew it, to begin. Helaina, however, dreaded it. Breakup meant the ships would return and the Kjellmanns would head south to visit their family. Helaina would have no choice but to go with them.

It was hard not to be discouraged by this thought. After all, Helaina had hoped to spend the winter getting to know Jacob better, but he'd seldom been in the village. Leah had said he was busy trapping and working with his dogs, but Helaina began to worry that he was merely avoiding her. But why? He'd said that he cared. Didn't he want to know her better—maybe even consider a future together?

"There's so much to do before we go," Emma said, rushing around the little house while Helaina cleaned up after breakfast. "I can't believe we'll leave in just a few weeks or that Sigrid will soon be here."

Helaina nodded and dried the last of the dishes. "I can't believe the time has already come. It really didn't seem that winter was all that long."

"This wasn't a bad winter. Even if it started early, it didn't torment us as some have," Emma said.

"I think the church services and parties helped too," Helaina said with a smile. There had been several celebrations throughout the dark, lonely months. Emma had told her that these were purposeful parties meant to keep spirits up and prevent the people from becoming too bored.

"Oh, ja. The gatherings are always good. Otherwise we tend to spend too much time thinking of ourselves. When that happens, things can get dangerous. I remember one time right after we came here there was a murder. A man had slept with another man's wife, and when her husband returned from hunting and learned what had happened, he grabbed up his gear and went hunting after the man who'd defiled his marriage bed."

"But what of the woman?" Leah asked. "Did he also kill her?"

"No, but he might have if he wasn't caught first. He killed the man and then some of the villagers found him. They took him to the legal authorities, and he was eventually executed. Bjorn said that we would work to keep the people busy with other things so that they wouldn't turn to such mischief. But you know, people are people. They will do as they please."

"I think you've done a good job. Especially having monthly parties to celebrate all the birthdays that fall during that time. That has been great fun."

"We do what we can."

She seemed to be searching for something, so Helaina dried her hands and came to help. "Have you lost something?"

Emma held up one of the boys' socks. "The mate for this. I'm afraid Bryce is still very bad about picking up after himself. He tries, but boys are boys. My mother often said of my brothers that they knew the clothes hamper only as an obstacle to leapfrog over."

Helaina laughed and helped in the search. "I can well imagine. My brother, Stanley, was none too neat himself. My mother was particularly grieved by the way he would manage to completely ruin his clothes with his rough games. I was, on the other hand, her china doll. She loved to dress me in frilly clothes and have my hair curled. Which," she added, touching several straight strands, "was no easy feat."

"I'm looking forward to having my mother and sisters fuss over Rachel that way. It will do me little good to buy her all manner of frippery. Can you see her dressed in ruffles to run across the tundra?"

Shaking her head, Helaina felt almost sad. Hadn't this been something she'd thought of in regard to herself? She missed her finery. She missed dressing up for parties and being the belle of the ball.

They soon discovered the missing sock under Bjorn's favorite chair. "Here it is," Helaina said, holding it up. "The sock also has a friend." She pulled out one of Rachel's tiny shoes.

"Oh, but I had given up hope of finding that. I thought I'd lost it somewhere outside." Emma laughed as she took both items. "The lost has been found. Always a good thing to declare in a preacher's home."

Helaina straightened up the living room as Emma bustled in and out, her arms always filled with a variety of things. "We won't take all that much," she declared at one point, "because we always bring so many things back with us. Still, I must have clothes for the children."

Helaina nodded, her thoughts filled with images of stores and establishments in New York. She tried to think of what it would be like to remain in Alaska and never have easy access to shopping and the latest fashions.

But even as these thoughts crossed her mind, she looked at her own outfit. She wore sealskin pants under one of her old skirts. Her blouse was very worn and could hardly be considered fashionable as it might have been just the year before. But here in Alaska function and practicality always won out over decorative style.

Helaina had to admit there was a part of her that was homesick. She longed to relax in her bedroom suite. The room itself was larger than Emma's house. The fireplace alone would take up the space held by Emma's entire kitchen.

Helaina began to prepare tubs with hot water for the wash, yet her thoughts continued to return to New York. She really did miss it. She longed for a thick beefsteak and fresh vegetables. The thought of wearing silk again nearly drove her mad. There were so many things she desired. But even as she thought of these, Jacob's image filled her thoughts. She desired him, as well, but there seemed to be little hope of resolving that problem.

The more she thought about it, the more Helaina needed an answer. Jacob was due back any time now, but it wouldn't be for long. Leah had mentioned on more than one occasion that her brother had made up his mind to honor his commitment to Captain Latimore. He would head north when the good captain came with his ship. Helaina had contemplated imposing herself on the trip. Perhaps if she reminded Captain Latimore that she was to have been assistant to the map maker, she, too, might gain passage on the *Homestead*.

There simply seemed no easy answers. If she went north with the men, she'd never make it back to New York this year. Despair dogged her every step. There was no way to resolve the matter without the need to forsake something she loved.

Why does this have to be so hard?

Leah moved slowly around the house. Advanced in her pregnancy, Leah felt more confident than ever that the baby must be Jayce's child. Just the fact that she was already showing signs of being ready to give birth made this even more certain. By her best calculations, if she'd gotten pregnant on her wedding night, the baby would be due in late June or early July.

Throughout the winter Leah had worked to ready her life and her home for the arrival of this new life. She and Jayce both agreed the house was not big enough for their family, so plans were in the works to build a new house and leave this one to Jacob.

"I've got the money," Jayce had told her. "We might as well use it for our own comfort." And with that he'd accompanied Jacob to Nome to place an order for supplies.

But Leah wasn't sure that Jayce could be totally happy in Last Chance. There wasn't much in the way that he could do to gainfully employ himself, and while he had money in the bank from his inheritance, they certainly couldn't live off of it the rest of their lives.

It troubled Leah, for she knew in her heart that a man needed to have a job that he could call his own. Thoughts of having to move from Last Chance to live in Nome or one of the larger Alaska settlements like Sitka or Seward tormented Leah. She would miss the people in Last Chance, but worse yet, she would miss Alaska if Jayce decided there was no other answer but to move away.

Another troubling thought was how to help Jacob deal with the loss of Helaina Beecham. He'd been gone a great deal throughout the winter, but as he'd told Leah on his last trip home, now nearly a month past, he always knew Helaina would be waiting here and that comforted his heart. But soon she would go back to New York, and Jacob would have to face the fact that she would never come back.

"He can't live there and she can't live here," Leah said sadly.

Leah had never seen Helaina as an ideal woman to be Jacob's wife anyway. Helaina was so willful and headstrong, although that had been tempered by her spiritual growth. Still, Helaina was used to having things her way and living a life of luxury. She was a wealthy widow with a home in both New York and in Washington, D.C. Neither place could Jacob ever call home.

"It seems we are all in a dilemma regarding our home," she told herself. She glanced around at her meager surroundings and realized that deep in her heart, she did want more. She wanted a regular house and a yard where her children could play and have adventures. Of course, the Alaskan wilderness provided the biggest yard of all, but Leah knew the dangers there. Only last week one of the village children had gone wandering off, not to be seen again. The family was still out searching for the three-year-old, but there wasn't much hope of finding him alive. That sorrowed Leah deeply, for the family, like all families in Last Chance, was precious to her.

"Leah, are you here?" Helaina called from the outside door.

"I'm in the main room," Leah replied.

Helaina came through the hall and lifted the fur that divided the room from the rest of the house. "Do you have time for a chat?"

Leah nodded. "I was just getting ready to sew more clothes for the baby." She patted her belly. "It won't be long now."

"I know. It's all so very exciting. I'm hoping you'll have the baby before I . . . leave." Helaina frowned and took a seat at the table. "That's what I want to talk to you about."

Leah brought her sewing basket and awkwardly lowered herself to the chair. "About leaving?"

Helaina seemed to consider her words for a moment. To Leah she seemed quite troubled. "Yes. About leaving and about Jacob."

"What about Jacob?"

"Leah, I'm in love with your brother. I know that sounds ridiculous."

"Why? Why should it sound ridiculous for someone to fall in love with Jacob? He's a wonderful man."

"He is," she said, leaning forward. "He's the most amazing man I've ever known. He's smart and trustworthy too. He never fails to amaze me with his knowledge."

Leah smiled. "He is quite incredible. He's taught me a great deal. He tried so hard to be both father and mother to me, but as I told him long ago, I preferred he just be my brother, for that was what I needed from him most."

Leah picked up a small gown and began to work on the hem. "But I'm sure," she added, "that you did not come here to hear stories of brothers and sisters. Why don't you tell me what's on your mind?"

"Well, as you know the breakup has started, and the ships will soon arrive."

"Yes. We can expect the first ones within the next couple of weeks. Everyone always gets so anxious for that first ship," Leah said with a grin. The memories of nearly a dozen years flooded her mind. Even the natives had come to appreciate the appearance of the revenue cutters.

"Well, I'm not anticipating it like I thought I would. Truth be told, I'm quite torn about leaving."

"Because of Jacob?" Leah asked.

Helaina nodded and looked at the table. "I long for my home in New York. I sometimes miss it so much that it's all I can think about. But then I think of Jacob, and I know that leaving him will hurt me . . . maybe more than I can bear." She got up and began to pace. "I never planned to fall in love again. Robert was everything to me. To my way of thinking, he was perfect. But now I believe Jacob is perfect, and strangely enough, the two men are nothing alike."

"Jacob is far from perfect, and it's never good for a woman to consider a man in that light. We are all human, Helaina. We will disappoint each other at some point. If you put my brother on a pedestal, he will fall off of it."

"I know that. I know he's just a man, but he's the man I've grown to love. I know you can't understand my point, but when Robert died, a part of my heart died too. I became guarded and protective of myself. I had so many men come calling—all wanting to be my suitor. Most were more interested in courting my bankbooks than me, but all were ever so concerned with my being left a widow." She gave Leah a bittersweet smile. "See, I'd not only inherited Robert's money, but Stanley and I split a huge estate left by my parents."

"I knew you were quite wealthy simply by the way you were able to afford outfitting the *Homestead* last fall before we returned to Nome."

"Money has never been a problem. The problem is my heart. I want to stay with Jacob. I want him to fall as deeply in love with me as I am with him, but I know he loves Alaska."

"And he won't leave," Leah said, knowing her brother's thoughts on the matter. "He might relocate to other parts of the territory, but he won't go back to the States. You might as well know that."

"I do," Helaina replied sadly. "I suppose that's why I'm here."

"I don't understand. Do you want me to convince him to go?" Leah put down her sewing. "Because I won't do that."

"No." Helaina shook her head and retook her seat. "You misunderstand me. I suppose I just need . . . well . . . I guess I don't know what I need." She sighed.

Leah felt the woman's sorrow. There were no easy answers for her in this matter; Leah had already contemplated the situation many times. "Helaina, at first I really didn't want you having any part of Jacob's life. You were troublesome to me because of your job and your focus on justice at any price. Now, however, you've really changed as you've gotten to know the truth of God's Word. Your heart is completely different."

"But you still don't like the fact that I'm in love with your brother."

"It isn't that," Leah said, meeting Helaina's intense stare. "It's that I know Jacob will never leave Alaska, and you seem just as unwilling to leave New York and your old world behind. Jacob would never fit into that world. You need to know that. He would never be comfortable in the city. He hated Seattle and seldom ventured from the house where we stayed. He hates the noise and the traffic—you surely remember that."

"I do," she said in a barely audible voice.

"He's not going to suddenly change and love it all as you do."

"So what you're saying to me is that I must either give up New York and my life as I knew it, or I must give up Jacob."

Leah nodded. "I see no other alternative."

"But if Jacob loves me . . ." She paused and looked away. "Wouldn't he at least be willing to try?"

"At what price?"

"I don't know. I suppose he would have to come with me to New York and sample the life there."

Leah shook her head and got up. "Helaina, he knows what city life is all about. He hates it there. Would you, loving him as you do, cage him like that? He might be willing to try—he might in fact love you so much that he would leave Alaska. But I think that in time it would kill him, and if not that, it would destroy your love for each other. Could you live with that?"

Helaina's shoulders slumped forward. "No. I couldn't hurt him that way." She looked at Leah with tears in her eyes. "I suppose the right thing to do is just go home without telling him how I feel."

Leah's heart nearly broke for the woman. She was truly in love with Jacob—apparently enough to let him live the life he needed to live. Leah had to admire that. She knew from the past that it wasn't easy to let go of a dream—especially when that demanded you also let go of your heart.

Chapter Twenty-Six

Jacob returned two days later. Helaina watched him from afar at first. She busied herself with Emma's children and tried to pretend that it didn't matter. *Leave him alone,* she warned herself. *Don't give him any reason to think you care as much as you do.*

But when Saturday rolled around and the village joined together to celebrate the spring breakup, Helaina couldn't avoid his company.

"I haven't seen much of you," Jacob said as he came to stand beside her. Native dancers were just starting to perform.

"I've been helping Emma with the children and packing. We leave in a few days, you know."

Jacob frowned. "Yes, I know. I wanted to talk to you about that. I've been doing a lot of thinking out on the trail. Isolation gives a man plenty of time to consider what's important."

Helaina felt a band tighten around her chest. The last thing she wanted was for Jacob to declare his undying love or, worse yet, tell her that he'd changed his mind and was mistaken about his feelings.

"Oh, look. There's Leah. I didn't think she'd be able to make it," Helaina said. "Come on, let's go help her."

Jacob opened his mouth to speak, but Helaina didn't wait. She moved through the people seated on the ground and prayed that Leah would keep Jacob from further serious talk.

"Leah, I'm so glad you were able to make it," Helaina said, putting an arm around her. "Where's Jayce?"

"He's coming with the food. Jacob, maybe you could help him?"

Jacob looked to Helaina and then Leah. "Sure." He sounded disappointed, but Helaina said nothing.

After he'd gone, Helaina turned to Leah. "I think I'd better stay with you. It seems Jacob wants to talk seriously."

"I wondered about that. He mentioned giving a lot of thought to his future," Leah said, putting a hand to her back. "I'm so tired. I think it may have been a mistake to come."

"Here. There are a few chairs over here. You should sit." Helaina helped lead Leah to a chair. "Can I get you something to eat or drink?"

"No. I'm fine. I'm just tired. I can't believe how big I am. I feel like I'll explode at this point." Leah pushed back a strand of wavy brown hair. "Ayoona assures me it will soon be over and I will be blessed beyond anything I could imagine."

"She seems to be a wise old woman. I think you can trust her to be right. I still worry that you should have a doctor. I mean, what if something goes wrong?"

"The women of this village have been helping each other give birth for generations. There have only been a handful of stillbirths or babies dying during delivery since I've come here. I doubt that's much different than where doctors are readily accessible."

"Still, it's frightening to think that you won't have someone more knowledgeable."

Leah laughed. "Ayoona has helped to deliver over forty babies. Oopick has helped with at least half of those. I think I'm in good hands."

Helaina knew that it was reasonable to believe this. After all, many of the women in the States delivered their children at home with midwives.

The men returned with several bowls and a tray. Leah turned to Helaina and motioned. "Jayce has a tray I think you will be interested in."

"Oh, and why is that?"

"I actually made some chocolate cake."

"Truly? How did you manage it?" Helaina could almost taste the delicacy. Just last month at the birthday celebration she had mentioned craving chocolate cake.

"I managed to hoard some cocoa, and Oopick brought me eggs from their trip up the beach. I wasn't sure I had the energy for such a thing, but it came out quite well, if I do say so." She grinned. "However, once it's learned what's under that dishcloth, you may not have a chance of getting a piece. I think you should go right now, if you want some, and grab a piece before they start to distribute it."

Helaina nodded. "I think I'll do just that. I'll bring you one too."

"Oh, don't. I've sampled enough while making it. I'll yield my piece to someone else."

Jayce and Jacob were heading their way, so Helaina took the opportunity to make her way to the table via a different path. She knew Jacob was watching her, but she tried to ignore him. Instead, she went to the cake and took a piece. Leah had cut the dessert into very small pieces so that more people could have a taste. Helaina popped the morsel into her mouth and smiled. It was like a little piece of heaven. Oh, how she missed succulent meals and fancy desserts. She would make it a priority once she was back in New York to go to all the best restaurants.

Helaina tried hard to encourage herself in this manner. Whenever she was sad or worried about leaving, she reminded herself of something wonderful that she missed. Something that she could have in New York but not in Alaska.

Jacob tried two more times to talk to her privately as the celebration wore on, but Helaina managed the situation with great finesse. She knew it would only hurt them both if Jacob revealed his heart. As the party came to a close, Helaina volunteered to get the Kjellmann children home to bed—something Emma quickly took her up on.

"You're so good to me," Emma told her. "I'm glad you'll be traveling with us. I'm certain to need the help."

"They're dear children," Helaina said, taking a sleeping Rachel from her mother's arms. With Bryce and Nolan in tow, she hurried for the Kjellmann house and the refuge she would find there.

"Please don't follow me, Jacob."

"What did you say?" Bryce asked with a yawn.

Helaina shook her head. "Never you mind. It's not important."

"I think Helaina's avoiding me," Jacob told his sister. Leah turned from the stove, where she worked on making breakfast for Jayce and Jacob.

"She's pretty busy right now. She leaves tomorrow."

"Yes, I know. That's why I'd hoped we might have time to talk."

"Talk about what?"

Jacob drew a deep breath and shook his head. "Apparently nothing."

Leah shrugged. "Well, this caribou sausage is just about done, and the biscuits are ready. Why don't you call Jayce? He's out back sharpening his axe."

Jacob did as she asked, but all the while his mind wandered. Apparently Helaina had no interest in talking to him about their situation. The only explanation for that was that she had considered his words and kiss, and she just didn't feel the same way. After all, she was returning to New York. If she cared, she'd be making plans to stay.

"Jacob!" Emma called from across the way. "The ship has come with my sister. Tell Leah!"

Jacob looked past Emma to the harbor. Out in the water was a three-masted vessel that had also been fitted for steam. "I'll let her know."

"Come for supper. We'll be making merry. It'll be the last time we'll all be together for a while."

Jacob thought of Helaina and knew it would be the last time he'd see her. "We'll be there," he said without enthusiasm.

Sigrid Johnsson blew in like a late season blizzard. Her spirit of excitement was nearly contagious as Helaina watched her flit from one room to another.

"It's a perfect house. I love what you've done with the rooms," she declared to her sister.

Emma beamed. "Helaina has been good to help me make new curtains and rugs. I'm glad you like them."

Sigrid looked to Helaina and laughed. "Well, someone that pretty is bound to have marvelous taste."

Helaina didn't know what to think of such praise. She smiled but couldn't figure out what to say. Sigrid didn't seem to mind, however. She continued talking at such a maddening pace that no one had a chance to interject a word.

"Life in Minneapolis has grown so predictable and dull. It's terrible when you come to hope for a summer cyclone just to have a little excitement. Oh, I hope you enjoy your stay there, but I'll bet you'll be ready to return home within two weeks. Last Chance seems like a marvelous place. I'm so excited about the children. How many are there? What are their ages?"

She turned to inspect the kitchen, but even as Emma opened her mouth to explain, Sigrid went on. "Oh, you know Mama. She has sent me with plenty of supplies. Lots of preserves and lutefisk. I don't know how many times I have to tell her I despise the latter." She made a face, sticking out her tongue like a wayward child. "Then I got to thinking that the natives here eat far worse things than lutefisk. I'm sure they'll enjoy it. Anyway, I'm glad Bjorn is arranging for all the crates and baggage. I know I should never have been able to bring it all up."

Helaina felt exhausted by the time Sigrid paused to draw breath and Emma managed to speak. "We're having a special supper tonight. You'll get to meet my dear friend Leah. She's expecting a baby soon and she's promised to help you in any way she can. Her brother, Jacob, will be here too. He's the one I wrote to you about. I think you two will enjoy each other's company."

Helaina looked at Emma as though she'd lost her mind. Realizing how she was responding she hurried to cover her mistake. "I just remembered that I promised to help Ayoona." It was true enough. She'd promised to help the old woman look for early berries.

"Oh, I wish you didn't have to go," Sigrid said. "I'd like to have more time with you both."

Helaina nodded. "I wouldn't mind sticking around myself, but . . . well . . . duty calls." She wasn't sure what kind of explanation she'd offer if Sigrid asked what duty she was speaking of. But Sigrid quickly moved on with the conversation.

"I would very much like to go on some of the hunts. Will the men allow me to come? I think it would be marvelous to go whaling. Do you suppose they would take me with them?"

Helaina quickly slipped out of the house and made her way toward Ayoona's. The thought of Jacob spending time with the vivacious and beautiful Sigrid was almost more than she could stomach. The girl was positively a chatterbox. Jacob would never fall for someone like that. Would he? She stopped midstep and stared at the Barringer-Kincaid house. Maybe she should allow Jacob to speak to her. Better yet, maybe she should just explain the situation. It was hardly fair to go off without a word. How honest would that be?

She thought about how hard it had been to come to the conclusion that she should leave—leave without sharing her heart. *How can I tell him how I feel and still be able to go? How can I hear him speak of love or worse . . . ask me to stay?*

She twisted her hands. *It just isn't fair. Why should life be so difficult? Why can't Alaska and New York be close together? Why couldn't we just live in both places?*

But Leah's words came back to reaffirm Helaina's choices. Jacob was miserable in the city. He hated the noise and the traffic. Helaina knew this firsthand. She had often seen him in Seattle in the gardens at the back of the house, trying to seek quiet and solace.

"Are you all right?"

She looked up to find Jacob watching her. He was leading two young dogs on leashes. "I'm fine. I . . . well . . . I was coming to see you."

"Me? Why me?"

"I . . . uh . . . I know I haven't been very good company. I know you've wanted to talk to me, but I've been so busy thinking about my trip home. I'm sorry if I've hurt you or caused you grief."

Jacob opened his mouth to speak, then seemed to reconsider. For a moment he just looked at her. "I'm fine. You didn't hurt me. I just didn't understand why you didn't want to talk to me. I think I do now."

"Truly?" She wondered what he meant.

"Well, I know your mind is occupied with thoughts of this trip and no doubt seeing your brother again. I know you've wanted to explain everything to him. I'm sure you're homesick, and you desire to be back where you belong."

Where I belong? I don't know where I belong—except with you. She pushed the thought aside. She wanted so much to tell him the truth. "Jacob . . . I . . . well, you should know—"

"I think I know what I need to," he interrupted. His voice sounded gruff. "Look, I have a lot of work to do before supper tonight. Maybe we can talk more then."

Helaina nodded and Jacob took the dogs and left. She didn't realize how she'd balled her fists in frustration until after he'd gone. *Why can't I just tell him how I feel and be done with it? Why can't I let him know that I love him, but that I love him enough to leave him in Alaska?*

Supper that night was misery for Helaina. She watched Sigrid captivate and amuse Jacob with her stories and suggestions for her summer activities. He seemed to think the woman quite amazing as she told tales of rescuing one of her students from a well and saving her young nephews from burning in a fire they accidentally set in the barn.

"Children are amazing wonders," Sigrid announced, "but they are dangerous and destructive too. Especially to themselves. They need a firm hand of guidance and an education as early as possible. And I'm not just talking books. Children need to know their place and to grow in that place. I'm always troubled by the people who hide their children away for nannies and governesses to raise."

Helaina knew many of those people. She had good friends who had children cared for by nurses. "I suppose," she offered, "that their way of life dictates that they provide for their children and enjoy them whenever they can."

"Hogwash," Sigrid proclaimed, renouncing the idea. "It's selfishness, pure and simple. If you're too busy to be a mother or father to a child—then don't have them."

That caught everyone's attention, but Sigrid didn't seem to mind. "I'm quite serious. You all look at me as though I've suggested we burn down the capitol building, but I assure you, I know what I'm talking about. I worked at a very prestigious school for girls just before coming here. Those young ladies were miserable. They'd spent an entire lifetime barely knowing who their parents were. They had a stronger bond to their nannies."

"That doesn't mean their parents don't love them," Helaina protested.

"Perhaps not, but why then do their parents have no time for them? You see, I believe time spent together equals love. If you love someone, you want to be with them." She smiled at Jacob, who surprisingly enough nodded in agreement. Helaina wanted to throw something.

"It's very easy," Sigrid continued, "to say you love someone, then go about your merry way. Love requires a commitment. It requires sacrifice and sometimes a little bit of disorder in one's life. If you cannot give it, you needn't expect it in return."

Helaina felt as though the wind had been knocked from her. Sigrid seemed to be speaking right to her. It was as if she knew Helaina's situation completely.

"Well, I've always been glad for the time I spend with my children," Emma threw in. "I know Leah will enjoy her time as well. After all, you've had to wait all these years to become a mother."

Leah nodded. "I can't imagine waiting so long and then giving my child over to someone else to raise. After all, what could be more important than being there to love and nurture my own baby?"

"Exactly!" Sigrid declared enthusiastically. "Nothing is more important than future generations."

"Speaking of future generations," Jayce began, "what of the war in Europe? Have you read much on it—will America go to war?"

Sigrid frowned. "I've avoided immersing myself in that sorry affair. There is much to concern ourselves with regarding the war. I feel that one way or another we will find our men dragged into this fight, but I certainly cannot approve it. It's a waste of human lives."

"Do you have specific news?"

Sigrid shook her head. "None that I care to discuss at a joyous occasion such as this." She smiled graciously. "I would much rather stay on positive topics."

Like nannies raising children? Helaina wondered. She toyed with her food and suddenly felt very frustrated. She used to be just like Sigrid. She thought nothing of stating her opinion and laying out her values for all to see and evaluate. Perhaps that was what irritated her most about Sigrid. It was the reminder of who Helaina had once been.

She glanced again at Jacob, who seemed to be captivated by Emma's sister. And why not? The petite young woman was charming and beautiful. She was also well educated and loved to talk about the things she enjoyed. The conversation had now turned to a trip Sigrid had made to Sweden. She was telling of their relatives and the life they lived in various cities and towns.

"Of course, our family is very close," she said, looking to Emma, who nodded. "We have always been that way and always will be. Nothing will break our ties. We cherish family too much. That's why I shall miss you all so much when you've gone away. I've hardly had time to get to know the children and you will leave tomorrow."

Emma dabbed at tears. "But we shall be back in late August. We cannot leave for too long, after all. The people here need us."

"Yes, we do," Leah agreed. "I'm so sorry, Emma, but you will have to excuse me. I'm afraid I'm completely worn out." She turned to Jayce. "Would you mind if I went home?"

"If you plan to go alone, then I mind very much." He got to his feet and helped Leah from the table. "Emma, Helaina, the food was wonderful. Thank you for inviting us to share in this."

"Yes, it was a great time," Leah agreed. "I was very fond of the strawberry preserves. I haven't had any in some time."

"I shall bring you an entire jar as a gift for the baby," Sigrid said, smiling. "And since babies cannot eat jam, you will have to take care of it for him . . . or her."

"Thank you, Sigrid. You are very kind. I know we shall be good friends," Leah replied.

Helaina had taken as much as she could stand. In her mind she pictured this wonderful little group—so close and congenial—while she stood on the outside. She was a stranger here, even though she'd spent an entire winter with these people . . . even though they'd gone through hideous life and death experiences together.

A lump formed in her throat, and Helaina knew tears would soon follow if she didn't busy herself with something else. "I'll clean up," she said, reaching out to gather several dirty dishes.

"No," Sigrid said, putting her hand atop Helaina's. "That is my job now. It will be my home, and I will care for it. You must have a wonderful time on your last evening here. Take a walk. Go say good-bye to old friends."

"I'll help Sigrid," Jacob said as he gathered his own things together.

Helaina swallowed hard. All she could do was nod. She wasn't needed here. She'd been replaced.

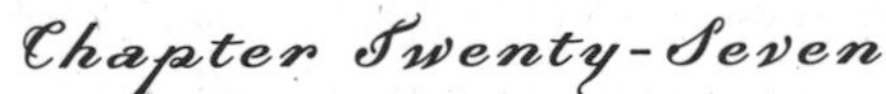

Chapter Twenty-Seven

Jayce looked at the missive in his hand, then raised his gaze to meet Leah's face. "Well?" she asked.

Jayce turned to Jacob and shook his head. "The letter says that Captain Latimore intends to be here next week. The letter was mailed in early May. He's expecting Jacob and me to join him for his northerly adventures. His plans, it seems, have changed again. Now he has someone funding a trip to the Queen Elizabeth Islands. Apparently these are Canadian islands some distance north and east of the Yukon Territory."

"That's a long distance away," Jacob said. "How does he plan to go exploring and get back before he gets frozen in?"

"Well, according to the letter he is merely escorting this team of archeologists, botanists, and geologists to the islands, where they plan to work for the next four years. He has been commissioned to bring them supplies over that time period. He'd like to include us in the project because we speak some of the native languages, you know dogs, and I'm a geologist."

"Will his wife accompany him again?" Leah asked.

Jayce shook his head. "No. Sadly enough she has passed away."

"What? But how?"

Jayce hesitated to say. He took a deep breath. "It seems she died in childbirth."

Leah's hand went to her overextended stomach. "No. How awful. You certainly would not expect such things to happen in big cities where doctors and hospitals are available."

"Nor do I expect them to happen here," Jayce reassured. "Don't let this make you overly sad or worried. It wouldn't be good for you or the baby."

"I feel so awful for Captain Latimore. He's a good man and seemed to love his family very much," Leah said. "And his poor little son is now without a mother."

"It is indeed sad." He paused and looked at the letter again. "It also says that the *Homestead* caught fire and completely burned last winter. He has replaced that ship with a new one and has called it the *Regina,* after his wife."

"I suppose what remains to be discussed," Leah said, looking to her husband, "is will you go?"

Jayce desired to head north and continue the adventure he'd tried to begin last year. But looking at his pregnant wife, he didn't see how that was any longer possible. He was a married man with a child on the way. Those kinds of obligations changed a man's choices.

"I can't leave you like this. The baby won't be born for another few weeks by your own calculations. How could I go without knowing if I have a son or a daughter?"

Leah frowned. "But I know what this means to you. I also know there is very little for you to do here this summer and certainly no employment short of ensuring our own survival. I've already been praying about it, lest I fret over such matters."

"My employment is not your concern, my dear. That is solely my responsibility. I wouldn't have you worrying over it."

"But you do desire to go, don't you?" Her words were quite matter-of-fact.

Jayce wouldn't lie to her. "I would like it very much."

"Then I want you to go. Whether the baby has come or not, you need to do this. Besides, it's just for a few months. The summer will be so busy for me, I'll probably not even notice that you're gone," she said with a smile.

Jayce knew better. "You're a poor liar, Mrs. Kincaid."

Leah laughed. "I'm not lying. Not really. I know that with the baby, I'll be quite busy. Not only that, but I'll help with the fishing and smoking of salmon and seal. I'll help pick berries and greens and look for medicinal herbs and roots. You haven't been here for my summer routine. There is much to do."

"But we were to build a new house this summer. The supplies are to be shipped here by July."

"So I will hire help to see it built," Leah replied. "We have good men here in the village, or I can bring in others from Nome. I'll see it done, or if you prefer, it can wait. The baby won't be so big by next summer that a larger house can't be postponed until then."

Jayce folded the letter and put it in his pocket. "I'll pray about it."

Leah smiled and turned to Jacob. "You must convince him. He needs this adventure—I'm sure of that."

"It would be easier if the baby were already here," Jayce said. "Then I'd know that you were safely delivered and doing well."

Leah laughed and struggled to her feet. "Then I shall pray for God to begin my labor."

Jayce chuckled and jumped up to help his wife. "You go rest and pray then, my love. I want you doing little else."

"I'm much stronger than you give me credit for," Leah declared. "I wouldn't want to drive a dog team, but I can clean up my house."

"Jacob and I will see to everything. And if that isn't good enough, we'll hire one of the girls to come and help you." He accompanied Leah to a bed couch that had been recently delivered from Seattle, a wedding present from Karen's relatives.

Leah stretched out. "Well, maybe I'll rest for a little while. My feet have been swelling miserably of late, and this might do them some good."

Emma and Bjorn's trip was delayed by several days when the ship developed some kind of problem with its steering. Helaina was grateful for the chance to spend more time in the small community. She thought perhaps the ship's problems were divine providence—God himself intervening to give her time to change her mind.

Watching the village come to life under nearly continuous sun, Helaina remembered her time the previous summer. Jacob had been a hard taskmaster then, but he'd driven her only so that she might survive. He'd taught her much about the dogs and helped her adjust to life in such an isolated environment. She'd begun to learn the native language, although the natives wanted little to do with her, and she'd learned their culture. Jacob had reminded her over and over again that if she were to live in the village, it would serve her well to learn the ways of its people. Jacob had been right.

Now, however, he seemed just as focused on teaching Sigrid Johnsson. Helaina tried not to be jealous as she watched the couple. Jacob was showing Sigrid one of the dogs, and she was happily petting the animal as though it were her long lost friend.

Helaina couldn't help but remember that she had been quite afraid of the beasts. They were so wild looking—especially the huskies with their intense dark-rimmed eyes. Helaina always felt she was being watched by those eyes. After a time she had come to enjoy the dogs. She loved the puppies, and once she lost her fear of the older dogs, they had come to trust her and love her as well.

Sigrid laughed and straightened. Helaina saw that Jacob seemed amused by the girl's antics. Helaina envied Sigrid's ability to balance her whimsical nature with her more academic and serious side. There was nothing playful in Helaina's nature whatsoever.

With a sigh, she walked away from the scene and berated her heart for its inability to be less attached to things from her past.

"It will be all right," she told herself. "Once I'm in New York, I won't even think of this place. Jacob will be nothing more than a memory." But she knew that was a lie, even as she spoke it. Glancing overhead to the icy blue skies, she sighed. "Lord, I don't know how to get through this. I know Emma says you can see us through all adversity, but I'm more troubled by this than I even know how to pray about."

"Helaina!" Emma called as she came hurrying up the path from the shore. "We leave with the tide. Bjorn was just given the word. We need to get our things together so the men can load our bags on the ship."

So this is my answer, Helaina thought. She nodded and followed Emma home, but her heart was so heavy that it made each step more difficult than the previous one. *I'm leaving. I'm leaving Last Chance and Jacob forever.*

Throughout the day, Helaina helped Emma make sure that they had everything they would need. Sigrid came home shortly after the news had been delivered about the departure. Helaina found she could hardly bear the woman's company.

"I am so looking forward to all the different foods," Emma confessed. "I long for fried chicken, pork roast, and thick gravy."

Sigrid laughed. "You'll be as round as a barrel when you return."

"Yes, but because I won't have a chance to go home again for some time, I'll surely work it right back off."

Helaina helped to get Rachel's little button-top boots secured, then smiled as the child attempted to dance around in them as she had her furry mukluks. She fell down several times as she tried to adapt to her aunt's gift.

"I don't think she knows what to make of such shoes," Emma said, laughing. "You were good to bring them to her, Sigrid. And the dress too. Now she won't go to our parents looking like such a savage."

"Mama wouldn't care if she came naked as the day she was born," Sigrid replied. "You know that very well. Besides, she has been sewing up a storm for the children and will have many outfits ready by the time you arrive. Never fear."

"Oh, it will be so good to see family again."

Helaina felt a twinge of envy at the comment. She would see Stanley in Washington, D.C., but once she went home to New York, there was no one save her household staff. No one would be there to care whether she might come or go. No one would chide her for staying out unreasonably late. Mrs. Hayworth, the housekeeper, would be happy to hear of Helaina's new faith in God, but it wasn't the same as having family waiting.

I should settle down and create my own family, she thought as she gathered her own two bags. They'd already sent the Kjellmanns' things to the ship, but Helaina had figured to take these herself. They were stuffed full of her native clothes and a few gifts from the villagers who'd finally befriended her. Somehow Helaina couldn't bear to leave them behind.

"Is everyone ready?" Bjorn asked as he came bounding through the door. His sons were on his heels.

"We're going, Mama. The captain is ready for us to board." Bryce's authoritative voice commanded attention.

"Ja, I know," Emma replied. "I am ready for us to board as well."

Helaina stepped from the house, unwilling to put herself through the tearful good-byes that Emma and Sigrid would share. She had hardly taken ten steps, however, when Jacob called her name.

She turned to find him coming toward her. Placing her bags on the ground, Helaina forced a smile. "So you've come to see us off?"

He stopped about three feet from her and said nothing. Helaina thought he looked very much as though he'd like to say something, but he remained silent.

"Is Leah feeling well this morning?" Helaina finally questioned. She couldn't bear the tension between them. She feared if she didn't keep the topic of conversation neutral, she might very well plead with Jacob to join her.

"She's feeling very tired. Jayce has made her stay in bed. She sends her best wishes for a safe trip."

Helaina nodded. "Please thank her for me and give her . . . ah . . . give her my . . . best."

"I will."

The silence fell awkwardly around them. Helaina thought she might just take her bags and go, but something in Jacob's expression looked so forlorn and sad that she couldn't help but whisper, "I will miss this place . . . and the people."

"You know . . . I have wanted to tell you—"

"So you're here," Bjorn said as he came out of the house with Rachel in his arms. "I'm glad to have you see us off."

Helaina could have screamed. She longed to know what Jacob would have said. She picked up one bag and toyed with the latch as she waited, hoping Jacob would renew the conversation once he'd bid the Kjellmanns good-bye.

"We'll miss you," Jacob said, "but I know the trip will do you good. I wish you safe journey."

"Thank you, friend," Bjorn replied. "And you'll look after our Sigrid, won't you?"

Jacob nodded. "We'll make sure she's provided for and doesn't grow too bored."

Helaina felt her heart sink even further. She longed only to be gone—to be done with the good-byes and the heartache. She moved away from the group as Emma came out the door. Didn't they know she cared for Jacob—that her heart was being ripped in two?

You've done a good job of hiding your feelings, she told herself. *No one knows how you feel, save Leah. And she won't say anything. She loves Jacob too much to see him hurt because of me.*

"Helaina!"

It was Jacob again. She froze in place, willing herself not to run. What would he say? If he declared his love for her, she wouldn't know what to do.

"Helaina?"

She finally turned. "Yes, Jacob?"

He met her eyes and for a moment said nothing. She felt her heart begin to race. She longed for another kiss—even if it was to say good-bye.

"You . . . ah . . ." He held up her other bag. "You forgot this."

Disappointment washed over her. Helaina reached out to take hold of her case. "Thank you." Their fingers momentarily touched as Jacob released the handle to her hand. She wanted to say a million things, but the words wouldn't come.

The rest of her traveling companions were walking toward them. Helaina feared that if she didn't leave now, she might not ever go. "Good-bye, Jacob." She hurried away, not even hearing if he replied.

Don't look back, she told herself. *Don't look back.*

Leah could hardly bear the pain of her contractions. "Ayoona, it hurts so much."

"That the way, Lay-Ya. You get great pain, but also great joy. You push now and the baby will come."

Oopick wiped her head with a damp cloth. "It will soon be over."

Leah bore down. She could feel the baby pushing through, fighting to be born. There was something so wonderful and terrifying at the same moment. What if something happened to the baby? What if he or she wasn't strong enough to withstand the birthing? What if Leah was too weak to live afterward?

Leah screamed as the child was expelled from her body. She fell back against the bed, tears flowing down her cheeks. The sound of the baby's first cry only made her cry harder.

"It's a boy, Lay-Ya. A nice boy. His father be very proud," Ayoona said.

Leah breathed a sigh of relief but almost instantly felt the pains tear at her once again. "What's wrong?" she gasped, grabbing her stomach.

"You have twins, Lay-Ya." Ayoona spoke the fact in such a nonchalant manner that Leah could only stare at her in stunned amazement.

"What?" She cried out against the pain, struggling hard to draw a breath.

Ayoona handed the baby to Oopick. "You gotta push again. You gotta push hard or this baby could die."

"I don't understand." Leah had never once considered herself to be carrying twins. There had been a tremendous amount of activity with her baby, but she had nothing to compare it to and had figured it to be perfectly normal.

The contractions increased in severity, and Leah held her breath and pushed with all her might. Gasping, she drew in another deep breath and pushed through the pain.

"This baby got itself backwards," Ayoona said with a chuckle. "Just like my son John. Comin' to the world the back way."

Leah had helped with breech births before. She knew the dangers—knew that the birthing canal could close in around the baby and strangle it before birth. She found herself praying for God's intervention. She had no idea that she'd carried twins, but now that she knew, she couldn't bear the idea of losing either baby.

The infant came quickly and was smaller than her brother. She had a lusty cry that commanded attention long after her sibling had quieted. Leah stared in wonder as Oopick and Ayoona cleaned her children and dressed them for the first time. Twins. It was almost more than she could comprehend.

An hour after the ordeal, Jayce stood beside his wife and shook his head. "Two babies. I can't believe it. Did you know?"

"I had no idea, though I suppose we should have considered it," Leah said. "After all, you are a twin, and twins tend to run in families."

"They're beautiful, and how congenial that you would give me one of each—a son and a daughter." He grinned at her and gently stroked her face. "Leah, you are the most beautiful woman I've ever known. Thank you for my children."

She tried not to let her fears steal the joy of the moment. They were Jayce's children. As he had told her so many months ago, he would take care of these babies and be their father. They would look like him and her, and they would grow up without questioning their parentage.

"So I suppose the names we picked out for a boy and a girl can both be used," Jayce said, looking at his son. "William Edgar after our fathers. We'll call him Wills."

"And Meredith Patience for our mothers," Leah said, looking at the tiny bundle in her arms. "We can call her Merry."

Jayce nodded. "I like that. Wills and Merry. Perfect additions to our family."

Chapter Twenty-Eight

Captain Latimore showed up four days later on the twelfth of June. He was a shadow of his former self, having lost a great deal of weight. It seemed he had aged well beyond his nearly fifty years. Leah felt sorry for the man. His pleasant, almost humorous demeanor was gone, and in its place was a gruff, hard man who didn't care about the pleasantries of life.

"This is an ongoing job for me," he announced to Jacob and Jayce. "The Canadian company that put this plan together intends to see their men living in the Arctic for no fewer than four years. They believe this will garner much knowledge about the north. I will make a yearly run of supplies to them, and given the distance, it will take all summer."

"So the plan this time around is simply to take the party north, help establish their camp, and then leave?" Jayce questioned.

"That and gather a few samples for some of my American scientific friends," Latimore announced. "That's where you come in, Jayce. I will rely upon your geological and botanical knowledge to help retrieve a list of samplings. We will, however, say nothing about it to the others. No sense ruffling feathers since they are paying the bulk of the expenses."

Leah sat in her bed across the room while the men discussed their plans at the small living room table. She wished she might join in but sensed that Latimore wanted nothing to do with her, given the fact that she'd just given birth. He looked at her with an expression of disdain, then nodded and turned away. No doubt she was a sad reminder of his dead wife.

"I have left the Canadian team on the ship. They want to purchase two teams of dogs from you, as well as sleds, harnesses, and any other gear you can spare."

"Well, I have dogs that can be purchased but not many that are trained well enough," Jacob said. "There are quite a few yearlings that show great promise and we might incorporate some of those into a team. We also have eight teams of pups that are being trained to pull, but they'll take time and I'd rather not take any of them. And regarding the gear, I don't have that much that I can afford to spare, but I'll ask around. I know that John had some extra things, and perhaps he could part with one of his sleds for a reasonable price."

"We did purchase one sled and some harnesses and lines in Nome," Latimore told him, "but you know those things are going to wear and it will be necessary to replace them."

"Yes, of course," Jacob replied. "I'll do what I can."

"How big is the team of men you will leave behind?" Jayce questioned. He offered Latimore coffee, but the captain waved him off.

"There are a total of six. Two are archeologists. They believe there will be signs of some sort of ancient life on the islands. Personally, it sounds like nonsense to me, but they pay well. There is also a botanist, a geologist, a medical doctor, and a meteorologist who is working for the Canadian army, which is surprising given Canada's deep involvement with the war."

"Which brings up another question," Jacob interjected. "What happened to the U.S. Army and their interest in military sites in Alaska?"

"I'm sure the interest remains, but their sight is now fixed on Europe. Things are not looking good. Back in March the Germans torpedoed a French channel ferry called the *Sussex*. That in turn caused an international crisis. Twenty-five of the fifty killed on that ship were Americans."

"How awful," Leah said from her bed. Latimore seemed not to even hear her.

"President Wilson immediately condemned the act and those responsible. He threatened to sever diplomatic relations with Germany. The Germans abandoned their U-boat campaign immediately. They are terrified, in my opinion, that we will come into this war and put an end to their bullying."

"And you believe that to be the case?" Jayce asked.

"I do. That is another reason I've committed my ship to a four-year plan. If there should be a war, and should they need my vessel, they cannot confiscate my ship without compensating me quite well. I would even have the ability to protest any kind of government interference based on the fact that lives would be at stake should I be unable to fulfill my contract."

Leah thought he seemed pleased with himself, and in actuality she couldn't blame him. The idea of sending Americans into a foreign war was outrageous to her. She hadn't understood the Spanish-American War, and she certainly didn't understand this European war.

"There is also the Battle of Verdun. It began last February," Latimore continued. "The fighting goes back and forth between the Germans and French, sometimes with one side winning and then the other. It's a battle for the hearts of the French, as I hear it. Verdun is quite special to them. There appears to be no end in sight, however."

"I am sorry to hear that," Jacob said, shaking his head. "I'm sure many lives will be lost before this war ends. Tragically, I wonder if the people even understand what they are fighting for."

Latimore rubbed his bearded chin. "That remains to be seen. My purpose is to remain in service to myself. We shall leave on the morrow. Can you be ready?"

Jacob and Jayce looked to each other and then nodded. "We'll be ready."

"Wonderful. Now why don't you show me your dogs." It was more a command than a question. Latimore got to his feet and nodded toward Leah. "Mrs. Kincaid, I wish you the best."

Leah thought him without emotion or feeling, and the next morning she had a chance to prove that her summation was correct. She was up from bed finally, tired but needing to show Jayce that she was fully recovered from the birth of their children. She hated knowing that Jayce would leave that day and be away for several months. It was apparent to Leah that he would remain behind should she ask him to do so, but she knew how much he desired to go on this quest. He had talked of nothing else since the sun had returned to last the length of a normal day.

In her heart Leah felt there was little choice. She had to let Jayce go, and she felt almost comforted to know that he and Jacob would look after each other. She would worry less with the two of them together, but in some ways she would also worry more. If anything happened to the ship and crew, she might lose them both.

"Good morning, Mrs. Kincaid," the captain said as he entered the kitchen. "Is your husband here?"

"He will be shortly. He's gone to see someone. Why don't you have a seat and I will fix you breakfast."

"No, thank you. I ate aboard the ship. I have a fine cook there."

She smiled and felt it necessary to speak about her husband's involvement. "I hope that you will make every effort to keep my husband and brother safe. They are all I have now besides the children. Given your loss, I'm sure you can understand. You are all that your son has now."

"My son is no longer my concern. I have given him over to my sister to be raised. I seriously doubt that I will ever see the boy again."

"But how can you say that?" Leah questioned.

"I don't believe I will be long on this earth, ma'am."

The words startled Leah and she found herself gripping the back of the chair as though it were her lifeline. "Why would you believe such a thing? You're not that old, and while you appear thinner than the last time I saw you, you surely are in very good health or you'd not venture north."

"I have no idea of whether my health is good or bad. I simply feel that my days are numbered."

"No doubt you are mourning the loss of your wife. You may feel different in a year or two," Leah offered in a sympathetic tone. "Your sorrow must be great indeed, for I remember the way you spoke of Mrs. Latimore. You held great fondness for her and for your son."

The captain met her gaze and for a moment Leah thought he might contradict her statement. Then his features softened, but only a bit. "I do mourn Regina's passing, but perhaps that is why I have no fear of my life coming to an end. If I am to rejoin her soon, then this interlude will become nothing more than a brief nightmare."

"But if you die, you'll leave your son an orphan. Would it not be better for him to at least have a father than to be without both mother and father?"

One of the twins began to fuss and Latimore took this as his cue to exit. "I will wait for your husband outside. We sail with the tide."

Leah watched the man hurry from the house. He wanted no part of answering her question or of seeing her children.

"Such a sad man," she murmured, making her way to the tiny box bed where her babies slept.

She found Wills awake and quite angry. He was wet and hungry, as usual. Leah changed him, using diapers she'd borrowed from Emma. "There you are, little man. Now come and get your fill while your sister sleeps."

It was there, feeding her son, that Jayce found her. He smiled from the doorway and simply watched her for a moment. "This is the image I will take with me to the north. My daughter sleeping soundly and my wife nourishing our son."

Leah smiled. "I'm certain there will be many such scenes."

He frowned. "And I shall miss them."

"You won't be gone forever. Wills and Merry will still be quite small when you return in September."

He came to sit beside her. "And we might be back as early as the latter weeks of August." Jayce reached out to touch his son's downy hair. "He's so small. It amazes me that we all start out this way." He looked up, their faces only inches apart. "I still battle against myself about going."

"You need to go," Leah countered. "I know that this is important to you, and if you do not go, I fear you will always regret it. And in turn, you may come to resent the children . . . and me."

"Never. You're my life. I cherish you as I do my next breath." He grinned. "I should tell the captain that I need larger quarters and bring all of you with me."

"I doubt Captain Latimore would agree to that. The man is bearing a terrible burden of grief. He has sent his son away to live with his sister and believes his life is not to be long on this earth. That troubles me because I fear he will endanger the lives of his men if he has no concern for his own life."

"Even if that is the case, Jacob and I are strong capable men. If need be we'll reason with the man and help him to see the truth. Pray for us while we're gone, and I'm sure things will work together."

"I haven't stopped praying since you and Jacob decided to go forward with this adventure," she admitted. With Wills satisfied, she placed him in the crib with his sister.

"When the innes begin to flood, you will go to the mission house and stay with Sigrid, won't you?"

She smiled. "I've already promised you that I would. You worry too much."

He laughed. "It's usually me telling you that very thing. Still, I guess I can't help but be worried. You are my responsibility, and now there are three of you. If there are storms or other problems, I won't be here to help."

"Nor will I be there to help you when problems come," Leah said softly. "Oh, Jayce, for years I mourned losing you. I won't mourn your departure this time. Before, there wasn't even the hope that you would return, but now I know without a doubt that you'll come back to me."

He took her in his arms and peered down at her. Leah sometimes still remembered the awful things Chase did to her when looking into his eyes, but the memories were fewer and fewer. Jayce had been a most compassionate, tender husband whose mercies knew no limits. He had never rushed her to intimacy, and in fact had offered her nothing but his undying patience throughout her pregnancy. She couldn't begin to put into words what that meant to her.

"I know you've come to tell me good-bye," she said softly, "but I wish you would not say the words. I'd rather hear that you love me—that you'll be thinking of us."

"Every minute of every day. Probably to distraction."

She laughed. "I don't want that. I wouldn't want you failing to pay attention to some detail and find yourself overboard."

He put his hand to her cheek in a tender fashion. "I promise I will not fall overboard." He kissed her forehead. "I love you so very much. We've been through a great deal, I know. But we've faced it together, and after years of bearing such sorrows on my own, I can honestly say that it is so much easier to walk through life with someone at your side.

"When Chase . . . took you away—when he . . . hurt you—I feared that I had lost you forever. That I would have to go back to living a lonely existence after finally knowing what was missing in my life. I cannot tell you how I struggled with that. I knew I couldn't impose myself upon you and force you to deal with a constant reminder of the man who had done those awful things, but neither could I lose you."

"You'll never lose me." She put her hand against his. "It hasn't been easy. I won't pretend it has. I know that we agreed you are the father of these children, but it seems that Satan can use this one thing to disrupt me more than anything else. But I am trying, and I'm fighting against such disparaging thoughts."

Jayce leaned down and kissed her nose. "You are a strong and incredible woman, Leah Barringer Kincaid. I will pray that you never stop fighting such lies. I am the father of our children—only me—always me."

He kissed her soundly on the mouth, his arms wrapped around her in a protective embrace. Leah found no fear in his touch and momentarily lost herself in the memory of their first kiss. *There is nothing of Chase in this man,* she reminded herself. *Nothing of the pain and sorrow that I once associated with the name Jayce Kincaid. There is only love.*

"Did you hear me?"

"Hmm?" She opened her eyes and sighed.

He laughed and put her at arm's length. "You weren't even listening to me."

Leah straightened rather indignantly. "I was busy."

"I suppose I'll let it go . . . this time." He walked to where the babies slept and shook his head. "I can't get over having two at once."

"Wait just a minute—what did you say that was so important?" Leah asked.

"Hmm? Oh that." He turned with a nonchalant shrug. "I merely said that I loved you—that I would love you forever."

She frowned. "Oh. That." She couldn't hold the look, however, and began to giggle. "I love you, too, and I shall count the days and hours until you come home to me—to us."

Jayce carried that moment with him as the ship weighed anchor and steamed away from Last Chance. He didn't bother to stand at the rail and wave good-bye. He knew from their agreement that Leah wouldn't be on the shore.

"I'm a fool," he told Jacob as he stretched out on the bed in their cabin. "I shouldn't be leaving them."

Jacob looked at him for a moment, then shook his head. "So why are you going, then?"

Jayce consider the question. "Because your sister is wiser than both of us put together. She knows this trip is important to me. I think it's possible she understands me better than I understand myself. It's at her insistence I go."

"I know how Leah can be," Jacob admitted. "She is wise. Maybe the time apart will do you both good. It will give her extra time for healing. You know what they say about the heart and being absent."

"Indeed." He laced his fingers behind his head. "For my heart is already fonder of her, and we've barely begun our journey."

Jacob threw a pillow at Jayce, hitting him full in the face. "I'm not going to room with some lovesick cow the whole trip. Let me know now if this is how it's to be and I'll go sleep with the dogs."

Jayce laughed and tossed the pillow back to Jacob. "I'm a new father; you must indulge me. I will miss many things in the months to come."

"Yes. Dirty diapers and colicky stomachs," Jacob said, counting them off on his fingers. "Crying in the middle of the night to eat, and crying to be held when they feel neglected. I tell you what: In keeping with your new fatherhood and all the things you will miss, I shall put you in charge of the dogs. They have messes to clean and whine when they need to be fed. It will be just like caring for infants."

"Ha-ha," Jayce said, closing his eyes. "I am so very touched by your compassion. I shall remember it in my letter home to your sister. No doubt it will deepen her regard for you, just as it has mine."

Chapter Twenty-Nine

After a brief encounter with a very busy and preoccupied Stanley, Helaina found herself safely ensconced in her New York estate. In this house—mansion, really—Helaina had known many pleasant memories. She tried to find comfort in that as she moved in silence from room to room. For weeks now she'd tried to readjust herself to this once-familiar setting. Everything was just as she'd left it. Having wired ahead to let Mrs. Hayworth know of her return, Helaina found that the furniture had been uncovered, the dust dealt with, and the windows freshly washed. The entire house smelled of oil and polish.

New York society was also as she had left it. They ushered her back with open arms, although there was an underlying attitude that hinted of a mother scolding her wayward child. Helaina found herself making the circuit, explaining her travels much as she might explain her misguided purchase of property in an unfashionable neighborhood.

Some of the men immediately began to fawn over her, telling Helaina what a drudge their life had been without her in the city. Others suggested a desire to come calling, which Helaina quickly declined, much to their disappointment.

There were parties and teas at which she was made the guest of honor and could not refuse to attend. Much of New York had taken their leave to cooler, less hectic climes, but many of the old guard remained and took it as their personal responsibility to see Helaina properly fitted back into society. To Helaina it was all rather mundane and exhausting.

The house, Helaina thought, seemed larger than she'd remembered. Now as she walked its hallowed halls, she felt a sense of sadness wash over her. She was queen over her domain, but it was a very empty domain, and she was a very lonely queen.

She walked into the main receiving parlor. The room was some thirty feet long and twenty feet wide. Fitted with heavy gold damask, the floor-to-ceiling windows allowed a great deal of light to brighten the otherwise dark room.

Helaina smiled as she thought of the blinding bright sunlight she'd known in Alaska. It was easy for a person to lose their vision, at least temporarily, from overexposure to sun on snow.

Helaina touched her hand to the ornately carved table. Here, delicate silver frames displayed photographs of her family. She couldn't help but pick up the picture of Robert. The side view of her mustached and serious-faced husband did not do justice to the fun-loving soul she had known.

"So many things have changed," she told him. "You would hardly recognize me."

"Am I interrupting?"

Helaina looked up to find Mrs. Hayworth.

"Cook said you wanted to see me," the housekeeper added.

Helaina smiled. "Yes. We haven't had a chance to sit and talk since I arrived home. I thought if you had a moment . . ."

Mrs. Hayworth smiled. "Of course, deary. You know I always have time for you."

Helaina crossed to one of the brocade sofas. Her plum-colored silk day dress swirled gently at her ankles. It was a marvelous piece, one that made Helaina feel glamorous. "I have missed our talks."

"Truly?" Mrs. Hayworth took a seat on the sofa opposite Helaina's. "It touches me to hear you say that."

"Well, it's true. I know I was unbearable at times, and for that I must apologize. I know that you were only trying to help me in my grief." Mrs. Hayworth nodded, and Helaina continued. "I've had a remarkable year to be sure, but perhaps the most important part is that I have come to understand God's love for me."

"Oh my. It's what I have prayed for." Mrs. Hayworth leaned forward. "Please tell me what happened."

Helaina thought back to the first time she'd met Jacob. "I met a man and his sister." She began her story and tried to cover all of the important details. Mrs. Hayworth was her captive audience, just as Helaina had known she would be.

"I kept hearing some of the same things you had told me, repeated in their conversations. For the longest time, however, I couldn't reconcile it with what I felt was true. I felt the law should be observed at all cost, but Jacob and Leah taught me about mercy. Mercy that extended to me, even though I didn't deserve it. In fact, I'm sorry to say that my actions caused that sweet family much grief."

"But even that can be forgiven," Mrs. Hayworth interjected. "I'm sure such loving folk would never hold you a grudge."

"No, Jacob and Leah don't hold me a grudge," Helaina said, feeling rather sad. "Leah was somewhat vexed with me for a time, but knowing the truth of all that happened to her, I cannot blame her. Still, I have her forgiveness, and she has mine. Although truly there was nothing I needed to forgive."

She sighed and leaned back, feeling the tight constriction of her stylish new elastic corset. Despite the freedom offered by the rubber webbing, Helaina had not worn such restricting undergarments in Alaska. She found the missing liberty to be quite a loss.

"You seem troubled, if you don't mind my saying so," Mrs. Hayworth offered.

"I suppose I am. I feel . . . well . . . misplaced. Does that sound odd to you?"

The older woman smiled. "Not at all. Your old life here may seem in conflict with your new life in Christ."

Helaina nodded and leaned forward again. "Yes. Yes, that's exactly the problem. Remember the party I attended the night before last?"

"The one given by the Chesterfields?"

"Yes, that's the one. I remembered them as having the most incredible gatherings. Food and orchestras to rival the best families in New York. I remember the witty dialogue and the pleasure of simply being seen in my elegant clothes and jewelry. But it wasn't the same. It didn't satisfy me at all. Yet, while I was gone, New York and my life here were all I could think on."

"The greener grass," Mrs. Hayworth said with a chuckle. "While you were in one pasture, another seemed better."

"I was certain while in the Alaskan wilderness that nothing could possibly be more to my dislike. There were vast open fields of nothing. No people—no buildings. It was an incredible place. In the village where I lived last summer, I endured the most hideous meals, flooding of the little house where I stayed, and people whom I couldn't understand until I learned their language. I never felt more alone or miserable."

"But to my way of thinking, this was just God's way to get you to a place where He could have your attention. Perhaps here there were just too many distractions."

"I suppose you're right. Just getting into my clothing here takes more time and effort than I ever exerted in Alaska. Although there I was trying to learn how to actually make some of my own things. Goodness, but I wish I'd been more attentive when being taught to sew."

Mrs. Hayworth laughed heartily at this. "I never thought I'd hear you worry about such things. You were far more concerned with the designers who made your gowns or the quality of the crystal on your tables."

"I was nothing more than a snob. God has made that clear to me."

Sobering, Mrs. Hayworth grew thoughtful. "But you miss Alaska, don't you?"

"I do. I find myself thinking of it constantly. And of Jacob. I never thought I would ever fall in love with another man, but I have."

"That's marvelous."

Helaina shook her head. "No. Not really. Jacob could never give up his life there. Alaska is in his blood."

"Sounds to me as if it's in yours as well."

"I think it is, but it would only be worthwhile to me if Jacob were a part of my life there."

The chimes rang from the large ebony grandfather clock. "Goodness me, but it's already five o'clock," Mrs. Hayworth declared. "Aren't you attending the Morgan dinner tonight?"

Helaina sighed. "I completely forgot about it. I'm supposed to be there at seven and I still need to take a bath."

"I'll have one of the girls draw it immediately. I've already seen to your gown. You'll be quite dazzling in that peacock blue creation."

Helaina nodded, but her heart wasn't in it. Mrs. Hayworth surprised her by coming to her side. She gently reached out to touch Helaina's shoulder. "I'm delighted to know you've come to trust the Lord. Lean on Him in this as well. Pray about what you should do. It's very likely that the right thing is to go back."

"But if I do, I would probably have to sell this house and all of my things, because I doubt I would return here. Certainly not to live."

"And what would be so wrong with that?"

"Where would you go?" Helaina reached up to take hold of her housekeeper's hand. "I won't put you on the streets."

"You wouldn't. I've been trying to think of a way to tell you that I'm giving my resignation at the end of the summer. My daughter in Milwaukee wants me to come there and help her with the children. Her husband recently died after a long illness and she needs me."

"I'm so sorry. I didn't know," Helaina said. She got to her feet and faced Mrs. Hayworth. "I will miss you."

"Not as much if you make your way back to Alaska," the older woman said with a wink. "I have a feeling once you are back in the company of your Mr. Barringer, you won't be thinking of this old woman."

Helaina surprised them both by embracing Mrs. Hayworth. "I shall always think fondly of you. You were the first to brave telling me of Jesus. You were the only one who loved me enough to stand up to my nasty disposition and try to explain what was missing in my life. You've been such a dear, dear friend, and I thank you."

Mrs. Hayworth had tears in her eyes as they separated. "You've been a blessing to me as well. Now don't forget what I said. If you are still so very miserable here, perhaps it's because you no longer belong here. God will show you."

That night at the Morgan dinner, Helaina enjoyed the attention of most every single man in the room. She made a striking figure in her gown of blue silk. The high-necked lace inset of her bodice had been trimmed in a braided cord of silver. It seemed a perfect touch with her silver elbow-length gloves.

"Mrs. Beecham, we have positively languished without your company," the gentleman at her right began. "I heard you were traveling extensively. Perhaps you would care to tell us of your travels."

"Mr. Broderick, you are kind to ask," Helaina said, reaching for her water glass. "I did travel extensively as you suggest. In fact, I spent considerable time in the Alaskan Territory."

"Seward's Icebox?" he questioned. The men close by perked up and leaned toward them.

"Tell us about it," the young man across the table insisted. He bent his head to try and peer around a large display of flowers and fruit. "I've heard it's filled with wild animals and nothing but snow."

"It's a very diverse land. I spent time in the far western sections of the territory, as well as some of the southeast islands. It's amazing that they even exist in the same territory, but you must remember the vast number of miles between locations."

For some time Helaina told of the landscape, people, and the day-to-day existence that she'd known. "I cannot imagine another wholly unspoiled place in all the earth."

"It sounds as though you were smitten with Alaska, Mrs. Beecham. Perhaps you will journey back one day."

Helaina smiled. "I think that is quite possible."

"But what of the food? Surely there was nothing as marvelous as this meal," Mr. Broderick said, lifting a piece of veal to his lips.

"This truly is a delightful meal," Helaina agreed. "I thought often of such meals while suffering through seal meat and oiled greens. Sometimes I thought I would perish of hunger because of the unpleasant things served. However, I grew to actually enjoy the food. Well . . . there were things I still did not care for, but many other dishes I came to enjoy. For example, caribou is quite a tasty piece. When the steaks are fried up, as you would a beef-steak, the meat is most enjoyable."

"But what of the luxuries you have here?" the woman sitting opposite Mr. Broderick asked. "Surely you wouldn't forsake such finery. I know you to be a woman of impeccable taste. Your wardrobe is praised in the highest circles and your jewelry rivals that of our best families."

Helaina thought about this for a moment. These were the things she was known for. Praised for her clothing and jewels. Leah, on the other hand, was loved and regarded for her healing touch and giving heart. *I've wasted my life.*

"It has always been a comfort to have every luxury at my fingertips," Helaina began slowly, "but I've come to realize that there is much more to life than those temporary things. I believe God would also have us reach out to those in need and offer ourselves as well as our money. The people in Alaska taught me that. There were so many times when I tried to buy my way out of conflict or trouble, only to realize that money means very little to those people." She couldn't help but remember Jacob's words on such matters.

"I wouldn't want to live where money couldn't buy me what I needed," the woman said with a bit of a laugh.

Helaina made a pretense of eating her dessert. The thick piece of chocolate cake was smothered in a rich raspberry sauce and topped with mounds of fluffy whipped cream. It was delicious, but no more so than the cake Leah had made for the breakup celebration. She pushed the dish back.

"Everything has been wonderful," she announced as the guests began to rise and move into the various rooms for after-dinner drinks and conversation.

The men took their brandy and cigars into Mr. Morgan's study, while the ladies retired to the music room to be entertained by some of the guests. Helaina found herself rapidly growing bored with the gossip that seemed to titillate the other women.

"I'm told that Mr. Hutchinson was seen that very evening with his gardener's daughter," one graying matriarch announced.

"No!" gasped one of the other women. "Did his wife ever find out?"

The matriarch laughed. "It was his wife who told me about it. She spied the entire affair from her bedroom window."

"How scandalous. What did she do?"

The matriarch shook her head and sobered. "Poor dear could do nothing. It's her husband's money, after all." The women all nodded sympathetically.

Without warning, however, the woman turned to Helaina. "You are blessed not to have to concern yourself with such matters. A woman of means need never be slave to a man's wants and demands."

Helaina shook her head. "Perhaps I am blessed financially, but I cannot say that my money has staved off the loneliness of an empty house. I would very much like to have a husband—a family."

"Why, my dear, you could have your pick of any single man in New York," a rather fragile woman declared.

"And half the married ones too," the matriarch announced. "But, my dear, you mustn't let yourself get taken for your money. You must find a man who is just as rich as you are. You'll never respect him otherwise."

Helaina thought of Jacob and smiled. He owned very little, yet Helaina had never respected anyone more. Pretending to stifle a yawn, Helaina rose. "You must forgive me. I'm still quite exhausted from my travels. The dinner was marvelous," she said, turning to her hostess. "Mrs. Morgan, I thank you for such a delightful evening."

"But we have not yet started the music. Wouldn't you at least stay and play a song or two for us?"

"No, really I must go." Helaina patted the woman's gloved hands.

"I do hope we will soon see you holding one of your famous summer balls," the matriarch declared. "Your parties were always the talk of the town. You can easily dismiss those lonely evenings with a masquerade."

"No doubt. The people in this town truly love to wear their masks." With that Helaina exited the room. She knew the women would gossip horribly about her after her departure. Wasn't that the way she had always known it? And having often been one of the last guests to leave a party, she knew this practice better than most.

Once she was safely in her own house, Helaina reflected on the evening and the comments of her companions. She began to undress and was surprised when Mrs. Hayworth showed up with a cup of hot tea.

"I thought you could use a bit of chamomile to help you sleep."

"You know me very well," Helaina replied, fighting to release the clasp that held her gown closed.

"Here, let me help you. I dare say you were the highlight of the evening, no? The men were probably captivated by your striking figure."

"I suppose so," Helaina said, slipping the gown from her shoulders. "I, on the other hand, have never been so bored in my life." She gave a little laugh. "I felt as though I were playing dress-up in someone else's clothes. I simply didn't belong there, Mrs. Hayworth."

Her housekeeper looked on her with great compassion. "My dear, it really doesn't matter how many places you don't belong. What counts is that you figure out where you do belong."

Helaina let the expensive gown fall to the floor. "You know, you are absolutely right. I think I know exactly where I belong." She drew a deep breath. "We've got our work cut out for us, Mrs. Hayworth. I have an estate to sell, along with a world of goods. Then there's Stanley. I'll have to deal with him, as well as the townhouse in Washington."

Mrs. Hayworth smiled in such a way that Helaina felt the older woman's approval. She picked up Helaina's dress and walked to the door. "I'll bring your breakfast at seven."

"Better make it six."

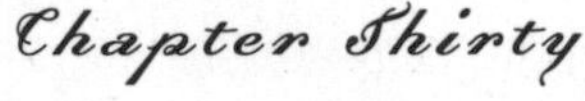

Leah enjoyed the warm August day as they gathered berries. With her twins sleeping on a blanket nearby, Leah couldn't help but feel as though she were the happiest woman in the world. It hadn't been easy taking care of her babies without Jayce—the twins demanded much of her time and still weren't sleeping through the night—but with the help of Mary, Seal-Eye Sam's youngest daughter, Leah managed to get enough rest. The fifteen-year-old was a great help to Leah, but so, too, was Sigrid. Sigrid seemed to dote on the infants as if they were her own.

Sigrid had adapted well to the long hours of sun and the lack of amenities. She often talked of her family and friends in Minnesota, but not in a way that suggested she was homesick. Rather she seemed to use the tales in a sort of honoring remembrance that always tied into something she was experiencing in Alaska.

Leah had asked her at one point if she thought Alaska could ever be her home, and Sigrid had given her a blank stare and responded, "It already is my home."

So with both Sigrid and Mary being quite devoted to the babies, Leah felt herself blessed. Of course there were times when Leah enjoyed time alone with her children. It fascinated her to watch them develop; already they had grown physically and were developing personalities. Wills was very demanding, whereas Merry seemed content to wait her turn. Wills seemed to grow bored with everyone, but Merry appeared happy to watch and listen for long periods of time.

Today was their first outing out-of-doors. Leah had decided it might do all three of them good to enjoy the warm summer day. This also fit well for Mary, who was busy washing clothes back at the mission house and Sigrid, who had decided to can some of the early berries they'd already collected. Ayoona and Oopick, along with several other women, had come with Leah. The day promised to be very productive.

It was nearly time to stop for lunch when the twins began to fuss. They were both ready for their lunch and that suited Leah well enough. She'd actually gotten the trick of feeding both babies at the same time. Sitting cross-legged on the ground, Leah smiled at her children.

"So you decided to wake up," she said, drawing Merry to her breast. Merry's dark blue eyes seemed to watch Leah's face in wonder. Wills would have no part of this. He cried with such intensity that there were actually tears around his eyes.

"Poor boy," Leah said, securing him to feed. "Did you think you'd been forgotten?"

A little ways down the hillside, Ayoona and Oopick were fixing lunch for everyone. Ayoona, though elderly, was quite fit, and Leah was constantly amazed at her stamina. It seemed the old woman could often work long hours after others had worn themselves out completely.

"I bring you food, Lay-Ya," she called, giving a little wave.

"That sounds wonderful."

Leah looked down at her babies. They nursed eagerly, seeming otherwise oblivious to Leah. Even Merry had closed her eyes as if relishing the moment.

If Jayce were here, it would be perfect, Leah thought. She missed her husband more than she could say. She'd heard nothing since early July, when he'd managed to send a missive out from the Point Barrow area. At that time things were going well, but Latimore, it seemed, kept more and more to himself. Jacob had found himself responsible for encouraging the men and keeping morale high.

Jayce, on the other hand, had taken over meal preparations when the cook had fallen ill and had taken to his bed with a fever. As of the time Jayce sent the letter, the man had not yet recovered. Jayce encouraged Leah to pray for them, as the seas were rough and the farther north they went the more ice they would encounter.

Leah tried not to think of the *Karluk* and other vessels that had been trapped in the ice only a few years earlier. Most of the crews had been lost to the elements and starvation. She couldn't bring herself to even consider that the same thing could happen to her husband and brother.

A sound behind Leah caused her to stiffen. There was a rustling in the grass that wasn't being made by the women she'd come with. With her children at her breast, Leah found it difficult to turn but strained to see what might be coming behind her.

Uff.

The grunt sounded not but about ten feet from Leah. She froze. It was a mother bear with a cub that seemed intent on wandering ever so close to Leah and the twins. Uncertain how best to protect herself, Leah started to get up, then decided against it. She had both babies in her arms, and no doubt if she made a sudden move the mother bear would take this as a threat to her cub.

Dear God, help us. I don't know what to do. She didn't even feel that she could call out to the women below for fear of further agitating the bear. The cub gave a whiny grunt and walked within two feet of Leah as he made a beeline for his mother.

Uff.

A low growl followed, and Leah could see that the mother bear had flattened her ears. A sure sign she meant business. She watched Leah with determined intensity.

Leah closed her eyes. She had left her rifle with her other things near the place where Ayoona prepared lunch. It was foolish, she now realized, but she'd felt safe.

Father, you closed the mouths of the lions that threatened Daniel. Please close the mouth of this bear.

Wills, sensing Leah's tension, stopped feeding and began to fuss. Leah felt frustrated, not knowing how best to help her son. If she moved, it might be seen as an aggressive act. Just then a loud boom resounded in the otherwise silent morning. Leah's head shot up as she twisted around to see Ayoona, still shouldering the Winchester 45-90 that Leah had brought along for protection.

Behind her a dull thud sounded as the beast hit the ground. The cub went to his dead mother, while Leah moved quickly to get off the blanket with her babies.

Ayoona walked over to meet them. "Lay-Ya, you finish her. I take babies."

The old woman placed the rifle on the ground and reached out for the children. Oopick was immediately at her side to help.

"Ayoona, you saved our lives." Leah gasped the words, feeling herself near to tears. "I didn't even know you could shoot."

The old woman shrugged. "John teach me. He say it might be useful." Her old weathered face broke into a grin. "Guess he smarter than I figured."

Leah drew a ragged breath and picked up the gun. She looked up the hill, where the cub pawed at his dead mother and was beginning to raise a fuss. "I'll have to kill him too," she said, feeling overwhelmed by the entire matter. "He'll die out here anyway if I don't. I wish Jayce were here."

"We have good meat," Ayoona stated matter-of-factly. "And we get good hide. God has provided."

"The skins will be yours—your reward." She knew the old woman would cherish the grizzly hide.

With new resolve, Leah worked the lever of the rifle to eject the spent shell and went back to where the sow lay. Without giving it another thought, she fired another bullet into the head of the bear, then worked the lever again. She looked at the cub and felt immediate regret. Although this baby would grow up to be just as threatening as its mother, he was just a new addition to the world and quite precious.

Leah took hold of the lever and gave it no further consideration. By the time she'd finished killing the cub, all of the women had gathered not far behind.

"Now we work," Ayoona said, as though the day had suddenly turned perfect. "Leah, you rest. You do enough. Take care of your babies and shoot more bear if they come." She handed the infant in her arms to Oopick and went for her knife.

Leah tried to relax as the women began to skin the bears. She'd nearly been killed—her babies too. *This country holds no mercy for anyone—especially the young,* she thought as she watched the women butcher the cub. *It is a cruel and hard land. How can I raise my babies here?* She shuddered and went quickly to her children. When Emma came back from the States, Leah would have to get her advice on raising infants in the Alaskan wilds. For now, she had already decided this would be the last time she brought the children with her on food-gathering excursions.

"You're to be married?" Helaina asked in surprise. A giddy Stanley—quite a departure from his usually serious demeanor—had arrived to pick her up at the train station that warm August day. When she questioned him, he'd explained his matrimonial plans.

"I know it's rather sudden. Perhaps even more so given that we plan to wed in just a few days."

"Is there a problem . . . a reason that you must rush into marriage?"

He took hold of her arm. "Just that we're in love. She's a marvelous woman. A widow with a young daughter. I shall have an instant family instead of just a wife. She's very smart—you'll like that about her. And she's very beautiful."

They walked to where Stanley's car awaited them. "Do you like it?"

Helaina eyed the contraption. Already the noise of such things was annoying to her. "When did you learn how to drive?"

"Oh, earlier in the year. I just bought it last week, but I'm already proficient."

They were soon wending their way through the busy traffic of downtown. Dodging pedestrians seemed to be one of the bigger challenges. People seemed absolutely oblivious at times to the monstrosities that shared their streets. Helaina was still uncertain as to the value of such a machine. "I think I prefer a dogsled," she said honestly. "In fact, I know I prefer less noise."

"This is the way of the future, my dear sister. You used to see the necessity of such things. I remember your being quite enthused about a more rapid means of transportation. Then there was your argument about how automobiles wouldn't leave behind droppings or kick at passing strangers."

"I suppose I remember saying those things, but Alaska has changed me." She looked at him and figured now would be as good a time as any to mention her plans. However, Stanley was not inclined to let go of his own interests.

"I hope you don't mind, but I thought we'd have lunch with Annabelle." He grinned. "Don't you just love that name?"

"You sound like a lovesick ninny to be sure," Helaina laughed. "But I completely understand and would love to have dinner with your intended."

"I'm glad you agree. We're to meet at her father's house in Georgetown. It's not far from your townhouse. Annabelle moved there after her husband died. She was expecting little Edith when her husband caught the measles and passed on."

"So how old is your Annabelle?"

"Twenty-two. Edith is now two years old and quite the handful. She adores me, though." Stanley fairly glowed with pride.

"I'm sure you'll make a wonderful father." Helaina could see how much her statement pleased him by the way his grin seemed to broaden and his eyes sparkled in delight. "They must both be very special. Where did you meet?"

"We met through her father, Erwin Taylor," Stanley said, maneuvering the automobile through a particularly narrow side street. "He's one of several aides to President Wilson. He made a good fortune for himself in land prospecting. He's just gone abroad on government business, and it worries Annabelle sick, what with the war. He's given us his blessing, however."

"So when are you to marry?"

"On the tenth. I do hope you'll be in town that long."

Helaina considered the timing. "Well, that's just three days from now. I don't see why it won't work out. I should be on my way shortly after that, however."

"Where are you bound this time? With a war in Europe I'm certain you aren't heading there."

"Actually, no. This may come as some surprise to you, but I've fallen in love as well." Stanley turned in dumfounded silence. Helaina pointed to the road. "Stanley, you should watch where you're going!"

He looked back to the road but shook his head. "Who have you fallen in love with?"

"Jacob Barringer."

"The Alaskan? Is that what this sudden sale of your New York estate is all about? Are you planning to move north?"

She drew a deep breath and lifted her chin. "Yes, I am. I wanted to come here and say good-bye, but I also wanted to see if you would handle the sale of my townhouse. I can't afford to wait around. The last ships to Nome will sail late this month, and I must be on one if I'm to get there before the ice makes it impossible."

"But this is all so fast."

"No more sudden than your engagement," she countered.

They passed through impressive gates and up a well-manicured drive that spoke of wealth and sophisticated taste. Helaina was impressed but forced her attention back to the conversation.

"I love him, Stanley. I know it sounds crazy. I never thought of myself as a person who could live in the Alaskan wilderness, but I miss it almost as much as I miss Jacob."

"But it's so isolated," Stanley said, bringing the car to a stop. "I nearly died worrying over you last winter. How will it be when I can only hear from you once or twice a year?"

"Now who's not looking to the future? They are building a railroad to cross a good portion of the state from south to north. There is talk of air travel, and as that industry takes off, who knows what it will afford us? And with so many people moving to settle that territory, the government will continue to speed up the mail. You needn't fear, Stanley. I'm sure we'll be in touch."

"But I . . . well . . . I thought you would be close at hand. I wanted you to be a part of our life here in Washington."

"I'm not saying that I'll never come back to visit. Goodness, I'm a wealthy woman—or did you forget?" She gave him a smile and reached out to pat his arm with her gloved hand. "Stanley, I need to go to him. He plans to return at the end of the month—September at the latest. I need to be there—to see if we have a future. If he doesn't feel the same way, then I'll be back. Probably to move in with you and your young bride."

He laughed and got out of the car. "Then perhaps I won't sell the townhouse right away."

"I think Latimore is wrong," Jayce told Jacob as they settled into their cabin after supper. "He's been frivolous with the supplies, and since the ice has slowed us considerably, I think we should talk to him about conservation."

Jacob had already been gravely concerned about the trip. They'd been able to deliver the Canadians, but the trip had taken much longer than Latimore had considered. They were now heading back to Nome, but it was late in the season and Jacob believed they were in serious danger.

"Perhaps if we remind him of the *Karluk,*" Jayce added.

Jacob thought of that poor ship and the disaster that had ensued when they found themselves trapped in the ice some three years earlier. Many men had lived to tell about that adventure, but others had died. The last thing they needed was a repeat of such a tragedy.

"I'm not sure reminders of anything would help. Latimore is, as Leah pointed out, a broken and defeated man. He has little will to live. I thought in all seriousness that this trip would give him a new direction—a desire to break the bonds of his grief. But if anything, I think it's only worsened. I think he's completely unconcerned with our situation."

"The ice is thickening near the shores. Daily we're moving farther from land, and you know that isn't wise."

Jacob stretched out on his small bunk. "He thinks to follow the open lanes of water—believing that this will be our easiest passage home. He tells me the ship has a thick bow and will easily break the thinner ice, but I'm not sure how much the *Regina* can endure. She wasn't created for this purpose."

Jayce sat on the edge of his bed and shook his head. "Jacob, I think we're in serious trouble here. We have a dwindling amount of supplies; no dogs, should they be needed for land travel; and a crew that knows little of survival in the north."

"Add to that a captain who would just as soon die as live," Jacob threw in, "and it spells disaster for sure. I've been praying about it and have even tried to counsel Latimore. However, I'm inexperienced in such matters, according to our captain. He points out that he has successfully navigated the Arctic and dismisses me as if I were a whining boy."

The ship rammed hard, nearly knocking the men from their beds. Jacob shook his head. "We've hit ice again."

Jayce steadied himself. "I've got a bad feeling about this. I think I should have stayed home where I belonged."

Jacob laughed, but there was no joy in it. "Little late for that now." He thought of his sister and the babies, but mostly he thought of Helaina Beecham. He wondered if he'd ever see her again. *I'm a fool,* he thought. *A fool for ever coming on this expedition and a fool for letting her go. When we get back—if we get back—I'm going to find her. She has to know how I feel.*

Chapter Thirty-One

Helaina sat rather uncomfortably as her brother and new wife exchanged their vows. No expense had been spared for the small but elegant wedding. Hundreds of lilies and white roses had been used to decorate the formal parlor of the Erwin Taylor mansion. The bride, dressed in pale pink silk, looked at Stanley as though he were her knight in shining armor. There was no doubt to Helaina that this was a love match. She found herself envious, wishing it might be her wedding instead.

What if I go to Jacob and find that Sigrid has already won his heart? What if I arrive and find that in my absence, Jacob has come to realize he doesn't care for me at all?

The day had turned out quite warm, and Helaina longed for the cooler temperatures of Alaska. She began to think back to the winter and realized she had not even minded the extreme cold as much as she hated this stifling heat. Of course, the fashionable green creation Helaina had chosen for the occasion didn't help. The long, fitted sleeves and high neckline seemed to hold the warmth of the day to her body. She waved her ostrich feather fan, but it did little but move the damp, warm air around her.

When the ceremony finally concluded, the entire group was ushered into the main dining room for a wedding luncheon. Helaina found herself swarmed with friends of the happy couple as she made her way through the house. She tried to offer reasonable small talk, but her mind was ever on the train she would board that evening.

"Your brother mentioned at supper last night that you intend to leave us," a young man in a navy blue suit declared. His accent bore a distinct southern flavor.

"I'm afraid so," Helaina replied with a smile. "I will take a train bound to San Francisco tonight."

"I hate train travel," said the maid of honor, Amorica Smythe. She seemed bored with the entire matter. The spoiled young woman was the exact opposite of Annabelle, whom Helaina had found to be simple and unpretentious.

"Well, my dear Amorica, you'd hate wagon travel worse," the young man replied. He looked to Helaina and smiled. "My manners are atrocious. I'm David Riley."

"Very nice to meet you. I'm Helaina Beecham."

"Yes, we all know. Your brother has told us much about you, including the fact that you've worked in the past for the Pinkertons. That must have been most sensational."

Helaina could see that several other gentlemen had joined her circle. They all seemed very much interested in knowing about her adventures. "I wasn't a true agent. I merely helped Stanley with some select cases. My finest adventure was in Alaska. And I found that I enjoyed that dear territory so much that I'm heading back tonight."

"To Alaska?" Amorica asked in surprise. "I've heard there's absolutely nothing there. Is that true? Where will you live? How will you manage?"

Helaina shook her head. "The territory is vastly unspoiled by man. There is great beauty and riches beyond compare."

"Yes, they still have great veins of gold, I'm told." David seemed quite excited. "Perhaps I will come and visit you there."

"Your mother would never let you leave the area," one of the other men teased. "You know how she dotes on you."

"She'll have to part with him if we go to war," another said.

"Hardly that," Amorica countered. "She'll merely buy his way out of that responsibility like she does all others."

David seemed rather hurt by this. "She needs me—I'm all she has."

The others laughed as though in on some big joke.

Helaina saw that Stanley was by himself and excused herself. "I must apologize for ending our conversation, but I need to speak privately with my brother."

They were noticeably disappointed but nodded their consent. Helaina was never so glad to be away from a group in all her life. They seemed so much younger, although she doubted David was more than a year or two her junior.

"You look handsome," she told Stanley, standing on tiptoe to offer him a kiss on the cheek.

"Thank you. I'm so hot, I thought I might well give up the ghost during the ceremony. Maybe it will rain and cool things down," Stanley said, pulling at his collar.

"Perhaps. It would be nice for you." She noted the clock. "I'm going to have to be on my way. Would your driver take me to my townhouse and then to the station?"

"I've already arranged it," Stanley said, sounding sad. "I do wish you would stay. At least for the luncheon."

"I can't. I'll be late for my train."

"But I worry about you. I don't want to see you get hurt."

"I know, little brother." She smiled. "But I have to follow my heart, just as you did. I pray you'll both be very happy."

"I hope Jacob is worthy of your sacrifice," Stanley said, shaking his head.

Helaina laughed. "I suppose because I love him so much, it doesn't feel like a sacrifice at all. The sacrifice would be in staying here."

"Well, if you are sure of this." He frowned but leaned down to kiss her cheek. "I give you my blessing."

"Thank you. And put your mind at ease. I've never been more sure of anything in my life."

Chapter Thirty-Two

September arrived without any word of the *Regina*. Night after night Leah waited and prayed, always hoping that the dawn would reveal the return of her husband and brother. The nightmares made her wait more difficult. She often dreamed of bear attacks—huge white polar bears that would come out of nowhere to devour Jacob and Jayce. Other times she saw them drowning in icy waters—their ship crushed to kindling in the background. Her worst fears were confirmed when a whaler bound for Dutch Harbor made a stop in the Last Chance harbor.

Leah had heard of the ship's arrival and left the babies with Mary and Sigrid to make her way to the shore. She hoped the ship's captain might have seen or heard of the *Regina* and have some news to share. What he had to tell her, however, was not what she wanted to hear.

"We heard tell the *Regina* ran into trouble west of Point Barrow. She's stuck there in the ice, out to sea. She's moving with the floe but has no chance of breaking free."

"Is something being done?" Leah asked. "Has the government been notified to send help?"

"There's no help to be sent now. No one's going to risk their vessel to save a few foolhardy explorers. They should have known better."

He had little else to offer, and Leah walked back to the mission house feeling a great sense of dread. Stories of the various ships stranded in the Arctic came back to haunt her.

"Well, did you get word?" Sigrid asked. She sat on the floor, playing with Wills, while Merry slept peacefully nearby.

"The captain said he'd heard that the *Regina* is stuck in the ice."

"Well, that would explain her delay," Sigrid said, smiling. "Surely it won't be long before they manage to break free of that."

Leah shook her head. "No, this is most serious. It won't be possible for them to get away from the ice—not now. The season is too far gone. The temperatures have dropped drastically up there, and ships won't be able to maneuver." She sat down and tried to figure out what might be done.

"Do we know for sure that they're stuck? You said the captain only heard this. Maybe it's just a rumor."

"I suppose that could be true, but there's been no other word from them. I would have expected them to return by now. The open water lanes won't be available much longer. If they are free to maneuver, they would be headed to warmer ports by now."

"I suppose you're right. What then can be done? How would you go about finding out for certain that the rumors are true?"

Leah shook her head. "I suppose I shall have to go to Nome. That will be the closest place where I can get reliable information. They may have heard more official reports. If the government ships have seen the *Regina* or taken reliable accounts of her fate, they would report it to the officials in Nome." She looked to her children and knew she couldn't risk taking them with her. Oopick and Ayoona would no doubt be willing to care for them. Mary, of course, could also offer a hand.

"I need to speak with John. He'll be able to help me. We can make a supply trip and bring back goods." Leah got to her feet. "I'll be back in a few minutes. Will you stay with the children?"

"Of course."

Leah hurried to find John. She was breathless when she reached him where he sat working on building a sled. "John, we have a problem," she panted.

He looked up, his round brown face appearing serious. "What's wrong?"

"I was just talking with some men from a southbound whaler. They said rumor has it that Jayce and Jacob's ship is stuck in ice. He didn't know anything for certain, and I must have news. I'd like to make a trip into Nome. I know there isn't enough snow to take the dogs, although I would expect it soon enough. Still, I need to get there. Do you suppose we could go by umiak and bring back supplies as well?"

"Sure. We can get there pretty fast that way. It won't freeze over too bad if we go quick."

"I can be ready within the hour. Will that suit you? Can you arrange for the dogs?"

"Sure. I'll get Kimik to take care of them."

She nodded. "I'll speak with Oopick and your mother. I'll have to leave the babies." Even the thought of being separated from her twins left Leah questioning the sanity of this trip. "I'll meet you on the beach."

Leah hurried to attend to every matter. She spoke at length with Oopick and Ayoona, who assured her that they would care for her children.

"You no worry, Lay-Ya. We keep them safe and feed them plenty. They can chew muktuk soon."

Leah smiled. "I'm sure Wills would love that. Sometimes I worry that he's not getting enough to eat. I've been supplementing their nursing with bottles of canned milk for weeks now, but they always seem hungry." She sighed. "I shall miss them so much, but I have to know what's happened to Jayce and Jacob. I see no other way."

Leah wrestled with her decision from the time she left Last Chance until she stepped foot in Nome. This was the first time she'd been separated from her babies for any length of time and it felt completely wrong.

Seeking out information, Leah made her way from the harbor to the telegraph office and then to the military officials.

"We have no official word, ma'am."

The officer was sympathetic but completely useless, as far as Leah was concerned. "I need to get information about the *Regina,*" she reiterated. "If the reports are true and she's stranded in ice, those men will need a rescue."

"I can understand your concern, ma'am, but if they are moving with the ice, we have no way of knowing their exact location. Furthermore, the dangers are too great to risk a rescue. The situation would probably just leave two ships stranded."

Leah clenched her fists. "But my husband and brother are on that ship."

"Yes, ma'am. You told me that."

Leah finally gave up and went back to find John. "Nobody knows anything officially," she told her friend. "Everyone has heard the same rumors and believes them to be true, but they cannot act upon them. It's too risky."

John's expression never changed. "Alaska too risky, but I don't see them leaving."

Leah smiled, despite her worry. John always had a way of easing the burden. "I suppose I'll check into the hotel. It's kind of late to head back. I'll be ready bright and early. We'll tackle the goods together."

Walking with less enthusiasm than she'd known earlier, Leah made her way to the hotel where she and Jacob had stayed the year before. The place hadn't changed. There was still a musty odor of cigars and unwashed bodies.

"I need a room," she told the man behind the counter.

"Just you?"

"Yes. And just for tonight."

"Sign the register."

Leah turned the book to sign her name. She saw only two names listed on the page above hers. One belonged to a man, and the other was Helaina Beecham. She thought for a moment she was imagining the words. Leaning down, Leah looked again.

"Helaina Beecham." She looked to the man. "Is she still here?"

"Sure. She's in room 211. You want a room next to hers?"

Leah nodded. "I'd like that very much." Hope surged anew. Helaina had money and contacts. If she was back in Alaska, it could only mean that she'd come here to be with Jacob.

Only Jacob isn't here.

Leah knew once Helaina realized the situation, however, she would take charge and figure out what needed to be done. Leah might know the wilderness and be able to treat a case of pneumonia, but Helaina would know how to cut through the bureaucratic nonsense of government and get some answers.

Racing up the stairs, Leah didn't even bother to stop at her own room. With her pack sack in hand, she went straight to room 211 and knocked.

"Who is it?" Helaina called from behind the closed door.

Leah could have cried for joy. "Helaina, it's me. Leah!"

"Leah?" Helaina immediately opened the door. The women embraced. "I can't believe you're here," Helaina declared. "I have been trying to secure some type of transportation to Last Chance. This is answered prayer. What brings you here?"

"We have a problem—a very serious one," Leah said. "May I come in?"

"Of course." Helaina stepped back and opened the door wider.

Leah smiled to find the woman dressed in native fashion. "Where are all your pretty city clothes?"

"Back in the pretty city," Helaina said with a laugh. "I have a great deal to tell you. Is Jacob here too?"

Leah frowned and shook her head. "That's what we need to talk about."

Helaina closed the door and leaned against it. "What's wrong? Where is Jacob?"

Leah put down her pack. "You know that Jayce and Jacob went north with Captain Latimore."

"I knew that was the plan."

Leah heard the questioning in Helaina's voice. "They've never come home, Helaina. The ship is missing somewhere in the north."

Helaina moved her bags from the only chair in the room. "Sit down and tell me everything." She placed herself on the edge of the bed.

"I'm afraid what I know isn't much. No one seems to have any real knowledge. I've talked to all the officials in the area, and while they've heard rumors that the *Regina* is trapped in ice moving with the floe, they have no other proof or information about her location."

"When was she last heard from?"

Leah shook her head. "No one can tell me. It's almost as if the ship doesn't exist."

"I'm used to dealing with that kind of thing," Helaina said with a wave of her hand. "We won't let that slow us down. First things first." She pressed one index finger down on the other. "We will talk again to the officials. Sometimes you don't get the right answers because you don't ask the right questions. I know it may sound strange, but sometimes details are easily forgotten. There might be some information to be had that we just haven't learned about."

"I knew when I saw your name in the hotel registry that you would know what to do," Leah said, tears forming. "I can't manage this on my own. I have to get home to the children."

"Children?"

Leah nodded and forced a smile. "I had twins right after you left. A boy and a girl."

"Oh my. That must have been quite the adventure."

"It was. They are such dear babies, and I'm anxious to return to them." She shook her head. "What are we going to do, Helaina? Winter is no time to get things accomplished up here, and the snows and storms will soon be upon us. Communication will be difficult at best."

"I didn't sell everything I owned to move here only to see my dreams crumble. I've come too far to lose Jacob now," Helaina replied. She met Leah's gaze. "I won't give up. I'll wire Stanley and use whatever resources are available to us. I don't care if we have to go to President Wilson himself."

"You know the president?"

"Not exactly, but Stanley just married a woman whose father is an aide to the president. I'm not afraid to use family ties to get help in this situation. Those men can't manage a winter out there alone—without supplies."

Leah considered the stories she'd heard. "It has been done before. That's the only thing that gives me hope. They can hunt on the ice and Jacob knows plenty about that. Jayce even knows something of it. They are both very knowledgeable about surviving the harsh temperatures and storms that accompany life in the Arctic. I have great faith in their ability."

"I have faith in their ability too," Helaina agreed, "but I also know it doesn't hurt to work on things at this end. I can't sit idly by and do nothing."

"But what if that's all we have until spring?" Leah asked seriously. She'd already given this plenty of thought and knew the odds of any kind of winter rescue would be difficult, if not impossible.

"I don't know, Leah. I suppose we'll deal with that when we know there is nothing else to be done. Either way, I have plenty of time and money to put into bringing our men back safely. If we have to purchase our own ship and outfit it for the Arctic, then that's what we shall do."

Leah couldn't help but smile. "And you can be the captain and I'll be first mate."

"Whatever it takes," Helaina replied with a grin. "For as long as it takes."

"There must be something we can do," Jacob said as Captain Latimore sat reviewing his log.

"I know of nothing. This is the end for us. I've read too many other accounts of ships crushed in the ice. We can't hope the *Regina* can last long."

"Then we should make ready to abandon ship when the time comes," Jacob countered. "We should start setting out supplies on the ice. We can even pitch our tents there." The ship moaned as an awful cracking sound echoed in the cabin. "See what I mean? One of these times the ice will break through. You can't just sit here and do nothing."

"I am the captain. A good captain stays with the ship until the bitter end," Latimore said.

"Well, I'm not the captain. With your permission, and even without it, I intend to see our evacuation begun." Jacob got to his feet and looked at the poor man. "I'm sorry it's come to this."

Jayce waited for Jacob outside the door. "Well?"

"He's given up. He no longer cares. I told him it was time to off-load as many supplies as we are able to handle. I suggested we pitch tents and get away from the ship in case she caves in and sinks. He's oblivious to it all. Says he's the captain and he'll go down with the ship."

Jayce shook his head. "The crew has gathered to eat. Shall we go and speak with them?"

"It's mutiny."

Jayce met Jacob's eyes. "I don't think we have any other choice."

Chapter Thirty-Three

As the end of October approached, Leah waited anxiously in Last Chance for John to return with Helaina. In Nome the women had agreed that it was best for Leah to return home to her babies while Helaina waited for any information Stanley might be able to garner for her. John returned to Nome around the twentieth of October to bring Helaina back to Last Chance. Hopefully she would have some idea of how they could best help the men of the *Regina*.

It was already dark when Leah heard a commotion in the village, signaling Helaina and John's return. She had kept food warm on the stove every night for the last few evenings, thinking they would be back any day. Tonight's meal would be pleasing to Helaina. Leah had fixed canned roast beef with potatoes and gravy. It was a far cry from the usual Inupiat fare.

Checking quickly on the children, Leah made sure they were asleep before heading outside. Helaina met her at the door, her bags in hand. Leah reached out and took the larger one.

"Come in. I have supper for you."

"It turned kind of cold this evening," Helaina said, a bit of shiver to her voice. "Otherwise we had a good time of it. We're delayed because I was waiting for information from the coast guard; they seemed to be the ones who would have the most official word."

"Come into the kitchen and tell me everything."

Helaina pulled her parka off once inside the house. Her long blond hair fell from its once carefully arranged bun. She began pulling the rest of the pins and put them on the table while Leah went to get her food.

"I hope you like this. It's roast beef—not seal or walrus."

"Sounds divine. I had John bring back more food supplies. I just can't help but think it's better to have too much than not enough."

Leah put the plate on the table and Helaina gasped. "Those aren't potatoes with gravy—are they?"

"Yes. I figured you should have something special. I've had some ready every night for the last three nights. When you failed to show up, I simply ate them myself." Leah brought Helaina a hot, wet towel. "Here, I thought you might like this to wash up with."

Helaina sighed. "This feels wonderful." She began to wipe her hands and face. "Do you want the good news or the bad news first?"

Leah felt her heart skip a beat. "There's bad news?" She drew a deep breath and steadied herself. "I'd rather have it first."

Helaina put the towel aside and sat down at the table. Leah joined her. She could see that Helaina was quite tired, but there would be time for sleep later. Right now, Leah needed to know everything.

"There is still very little information and nothing can be done until warmer weather. That's the worst of it. Not knowing and not being able to do anything.

"I've had communication with everyone possible, and no one can say for certain that they know anything more than we do. The coast guard, which now runs the revenue cutter service, does have an official report of the *Regina* being stuck in ice and moving westerly with the current. The confirmed word states that they were last seen on August fifteenth."

"That's over two months ago," Leah said, shaking her head. "A lot could have happened between then and now."

"Exactly. Especially since they were still moving with the ice."

Helaina began to eat the roast, a smile touching her lips. "This is wonderful. I was already tired of dried salmon. I don't know how I'll ever adapt to the food here, but I will."

"So what's the good news?" Leah braved the question.

Helaina sipped her coffee before answering. "The good news is that we have everyone from the president in Washington, D.C., to the governor of the Alaskan Territory involved. Stanley is leaving no stone unturned. He's even managed to reach some of the men from the *Karluk*. He's hoping with the help of that ship's log, as well as that of another ship that was stranded just last year, they might put together a chart of currents and events that took place and help establish where the *Regina* might have drifted."

"But we can't help them at all until spring? That's a long time." Leah knew that the Arctic would be ruthless and that the lives of the men were in grave danger.

Helaina stopped eating. "I know. I've wrestled with this myself. It's so hard to imagine that nothing can be done, but as everyone, even my brother, pointed out—where would we start? Even if you managed to put together a team of natives and dogs with plenty of supplies, where would we even begin to search?"

Leah slumped back against her chair. "I know. That's already gone through my mind—because believe me, I did have all kinds of plans in the works."

"They could be clear over on the Siberian coast by now."

"I just don't understand why this happened," Leah said, shaking her head. "I keep trying to reason it out, but it makes no sense."

"Well, the word I was given was that the temperature dropped sooner than expected. Everyone figured to have at least until September before things turned truly bad, but the ice came early and cold weather set in so as to drive everyone south. Even the revenue cutters and whalers returned well ahead of schedule. You probably saw that for yourself. Apparently Latimore didn't realize how dangerous the situation had become."

"Or he didn't care," Leah replied. "I know he was grieving his wife's passing. He should never have led this expedition."

"No, that's for certain."

Helaina continued to eat while Leah thought on the problem at hand. "I know Jacob and Jayce will be able to take care of themselves and anyone else. But even that will depend on supplies. I don't know how well situated they were for Arctic survival. Latimore probably gave it no real consideration."

"But Jacob would have," Helaina said. Her voice revealed that she had no doubt of this fact. "Jacob wouldn't go off without making sure that they had adequate supplies and gear."

Leah nodded. "That's true. And Jayce would have insisted on no less. Between the two of them, Latimore would have had to listen. At least we know they have that much."

"What do you mean we don't have any ammunition for the 30-30?" Jacob asked. He'd had the men taking a meticulous inventory of what goods were still available on the ship.

"All I can find is just under a thousand rounds for the shotgun," a young man they called Bristol announced. "I know the captain has a revolver, but I couldn't say what kind of extra rounds he keeps."

"There's got to be ammunition for the 30-30. We'll never be able to take down large animals with the shotgun." Jacob looked at the list of equipment and inventory that they should have had. "Do you suppose the Canadian team took more ammo than belonged to them?"

Jayce shrugged. "It's always possible, but I say we keep looking. It's easy to miss something on a ship this size. It could have been stashed somewhere just to get it out of the way."

"We need to find it, then. If things get bad and we have to abandon ship, we'll need those rounds."

Jayce nodded. "I'll make it my job to find them."

Jacob looked to Elmer Warrick, the first officer. The tall, skinny twenty-four-year-old had also served with Latimore on the *Homestead*. "What can you tell me about the food supplies?"

"It's a little more encouraging," Warrick reported. "We have ten cases of smoked or dried salmon, five cases of tomcod, and one hundred fifty cases of sea biscuits." He looked up and grinned. "Hardtack, as you land-lubbers call 'em."

Jacob smiled. "Go on."

Warrick nodded. "There's nearly a dozen cases of canned peaches, thanks to the captain's love of 'em. There's ten casks of beef, six cases of dried eggs, twelve barrels of molasses, enough coffee and tea to float us home, and an odd assortment of canned goods, flour, pemmican, and seal oil. I can get you exact counts on those things later."

"All right. Be sure that you do." He turned to Jayce. "What did you find regarding some of the other equipment?"

"Well, we have the obvious bedding supplies we've each been using. There are also another two dozen blankets in storage, along with two wood stoves, two coal stoves, two sleds for which we have no dogs, thirty cases of gasoline, a case of matches, and three hundred sacks of coal." Jayce looked down to the list he'd made. "We have a good collection of tools—axes, hammers, shovels, a couple of saws—all of which I figure could serve us well in ice fishing and even making ice houses."

"If we can find some solid land instead of ice floes," Bristol interjected.

"All of this gear will help us in some manner to stay alive," Jacob said. "We have to remember that nothing goes to waste. When the time comes that the ship is destroyed, we will need every bit of it. Even wood from the ship itself."

"What about water?" one of the other crewmen asked. "We can't live without water."

"Very true," Jacob said. "The natives taught me a most valuable lesson. The old ice floes can be used for drinking water. Something happens from their long exposure to the sun—somehow the salt is drawn from it. We will melt ice from the older floes and keep our water source until we manage to find land."

"But how will we survive, Jacob?" Bristol asked. "The captain's gone mad and we can't even find half the supplies we should have. We have no dogs to take us by sled, and the lifeboats are useless to us without open water, which we probably aren't going to see again until June."

"We will survive by trusting first in the Lord and then in the wisdom we each have. All of us know things that can help in our survival. I've lived in the frozen north since my teen years. I'm not about to let this stop me. I hope you won't let it stop you either." The men around him nodded. "We will have to work together—to trust each other and to be trustworthy. There can be no thievery. No hoarding. We must share and share alike. Do I have your word on this?"

The men nodded again, and Jacob could see that they were desperate to have hope. He smiled. "Physically, we are good, strong, healthy men, but I've seen such men defeated because their spirits were not also strong." Jacob dropped to his knees. "I, for one, will not be weak spiritually."

The crew joined him on their knees. Not a single man protested as Jacob began to pray. "Father, we seek your guidance and wisdom. We ask for direction and knowledge as we deal with the days to come. Watch over us. Keep us in your care. Let our minds be clear and our bodies strong. Renew our spirits and our hearts, that we might be generous with each other, practicing kindness and mercy. Lord, the way looks so very difficult, but we know that you are a God of infinite power. We trust you now for all that we need. In Jesus' name, amen."

Jacob heard the men murmur in agreement. Opening his eyes, he looked overhead and saw the aurora dancing in a brilliant display of color. Some might consider it a bad omen, but Jacob felt as if God were answering him, reassuring him that all was not lost.

"Leah's out there . . . somewhere under the northern lights," Jayce said as he and Jacob walked to the ship's rail. "She's worried about us and probably mounting up an army to come find us."

"If I know my sister, she'll be trying to lead the whole bunch."

Jayce sighed. "If I know my wife, she'll not rest until we're both back safe and sound."

Leah stood under the northern lights, watching the show as if it were the finest entertainment in the world. Helaina soon joined her, awestruck by the display.

"They're truly beautiful," she told Leah. "I've never seen anything like it."

Leah thought of all the times she'd seen the aurora before. She never tired of it, but tonight they left her feeling rather sad. "The natives have a legend about the lights. They say they are caused from the torches of spirits who are looking for the souls of the dead. The people believe there is a narrow path to follow over to a land of plenty. It's their heaven—where there is no sickness or hunger. They believe the noise made by the aurora is because the spirits are whistling to them. Some of the people believe they can send messages to the dead through these spirits." She sighed and wrapped her arms to her body. "But always they think of those who've just died. This is their light home."

Helaina put her arm around Leah. "But it isn't Jacob's light home, nor Jayce's. They aren't dead—I know they aren't."

Leah looked to Helaina and nodded. "I know it, too, but I don't know anything else. I don't know if they can hang on—or if they have the things they need to live. I don't know if they are sick or if . . ." She let the words fade away.

"You taught me, Leah, that faith is believing even when it's hard to see anything to believe in. We both know that God is with us—just as He's with Jayce and Jacob. God must have a purpose, even in this."

"You sound so wise," Leah said with a smile. "Almost as if you'd spent a lifetime believing in God."

"I have. For I didn't really live until I found Him."

Leah embraced her friend. "Thank you for coming. I think I might lose my mind if not for you."

"We will keep each other strong," Helaina said. "We look to the only light that matters—the true light."

Leah looked back to the skies. "They're out there . . . somewhere . . . under the northern lights. And they're thinking of us—hoping to see us again, just as we hope for them to come home."

"And we won't give up hope," Helaina whispered. "Because they won't give up."

Leah thought of her babies and of the comfort they had already offered her. God had a way of loving His children through other people. He had sent her Helaina, a woman Leah had once considered her enemy. A woman she now called friend.

"Nothing happens by chance," she murmured. "Not even this."

"Especially not this," Helaina replied, looking to the brilliant display of lights. "I think the aurora is God's way of reminding us that He's still in control—that we aren't forgotten. That they . . . aren't forgotten."

Leah felt strength anew. "I think you're right." She smiled and warmth spread throughout her body. "No . . . I know you're right."

ALASKAN QUEST

Whispers of Winter

To Sarah Long for all you do;
the books are better because of you.
Thank you for being a blessing to me.

Chapter One

MAY 1917

"Ayoona is dead."

Leah Barringer Kincaid looked into the face of Oopick and saw there was no exaggeration in her statement. "Dead?" The word stuck in her throat.

Ayoona's daughter-in-law nodded. "She went to sleep last night and . . ." Tears began to flow down the brown weathered cheeks of the Inupiat woman. "John stayed with her but told me to come let you know."

Leah shook her head. The news was unexpected; no doubt it had shocked John to have his mother suddenly taken from them. Ayoona was old to be sure, but she'd been so full of life, so capable just the day before. An emptiness settled over Leah. It wasn't that she didn't know where Ayoona would spend eternity—the old woman had believed in Jesus since attending a missionary school as a youngster and had often been a great source of encouragement when Leah's own faith had seemed weak. But this loss, coupled with the burden and grief she carried for her missing husband and brother, had Leah feeling overwhelmed.

Last year her husband, Jayce Kincaid, and brother, Jacob Barringer, had journeyed north on a ship called *Regina*. The captain bore the world a grudge for the death of his wife. Still, he had an interest in the Arctic, though perhaps he had hopes of losing himself there. At best he seemed to presume the frozen north could make him forget his woes. Instead, his carelessness or forgetfulness had caused the ship to get caught in early winter ice floes, which took the ship hostage and locked them in tight. Whalers returning south for the season had shared of seeing the *Regina* trapped in ice and headed in a westerly current toward the Russian boundaries. But no one seemed to know exactly where the ship was now or if its crew and passengers had survived.

"I'll miss her so much," Leah said, forcing her thoughts back to Ayoona. "Just two days ago we were making plans to sew seal skins for a new *umiak*."

The small skin boats were a tremendous asset to the Inupiat people, who sought much of their sustenance from the Bering Sea.

"We will sew the skins and remember her," Oopick said, wiping her tears. "We will tell stories of her life and be happy for her."

Leah hugged her friend close. Oopick was probably fifteen years her senior, but Leah loved her like a sister. "We will do just that. You let me know when to come, and we will sew the skins for Ayoona."

Just then one of Leah's twins began to cry. Leah released her hold on Oopick. "I'll come help with the body as soon as Helaina returns to watch the children."

Oopick nodded. "I need to tell Emma and Bjorn."

Leah knew the missionaries would be devastated to learn of Ayoona's passing. The old woman was greatly loved by the people of the village, and her loss would be sorely felt for years to come. Oopick departed as Wills joined his sister, Merry, in crying for attention.

"Poor babies," Leah said, walking to the homemade crib her children shared. Both were soaking wet and in need of a warm bath and fresh diapers. Leah already had hot water on the stove and, despite her children's miserable howls, went in pursuit of the copper bathtub and towels.

She knew she was more fortunate than most in the area. The new house she and her husband had ordered from the States had arrived in pieces last year. When Jacob and Jayce failed to return from their summer mission to explore the Arctic coast and islands, Bjorn Kjellmann had organized men to build the house in Jayce's absence. The Swedish man of God knew no lack of enthusiasm for helping his fellowman, and because Leah and Jacob were much loved in the community, help was readily available to see Leah and her children properly housed for the winter.

It was Bjorn, in fact, who had helped them to figure a way to assemble the foundation on a system of stilt-like supports to keep the permafrost from melting and sinking the house. The house had settled some, but Bjorn assured Leah it would be fairly easy to remedy each year by adding or subtracting wedges under the house. All of this would hopefully keep the structure of the new home stable.

Once completed, their house brought the natives visiting in throngs. Everyone wanted to experience the store-bought house. They laughed at the way it sat up off the ground. Their *innes* were built into the earth in order to provide insulation and protection from the wind. The fact that they flooded out each summer seemed insignificant; they were a nomadic people during the warm season anyway. It was the one thing Leah had never quite gotten used to in all her years on the Seward Peninsula. She longed for stability, consistency, and a sense of permanency. None of that could be had when a person constantly traveled.

Leah poured hot water into the tub, then added a measure of cold water until the temperature felt just right. With this accomplished, she threw a few more pieces of driftwood into the stove. Although it was finally May and spring breakup had begun, the air outside could be quite cold and could chill the house. She wanted nothing to threaten the health of her children and therefore kept the dwelling as warm as possible to afford them every benefit. The north was not kind to those who were weaker—children and the elderly often suffered the most.

Leah thought again of Ayoona. How strange it would be not to have her around to talk to. Ayoona had taught Leah so many things. Things that no doubt had kept her alive over the years.

With the water ready, Leah went to the twins' bedroom and noted that their tears had stopped. They were now quite caught up in playing with the sheet on their homemade mattress.

"Come, babies," Leah said softly. She opened her arms and smiled.

The twins eagerly pulled themselves up and balanced their walks by holding on to the railing of the crib. Leah could hardly wait until they could toddle on their own, yet she also feared that time. One baby would be hard enough to keep up with; she feared two would be nearly impossible.

She lifted her children in unison and made her way back to the kitchen, where the copper tub waited. Placing them on the table, Leah talked and cooed while undressing first one and then the other. The children seemed captivated by her voice, and it never failed to thrill Leah to realize they were her own flesh and blood. Of course, in the back of her mind she still felt haunted by the uncertainty about their parentage. Her husband was always good to assure her that such things didn't matter, but to Leah it was an ominous rain cloud that hung over her otherwise perfect party.

Looking at the twins, Leah couldn't imagine that anything so perfect might be the result of a hideous rape. There was simply too much joy and love to be had from these precious gifts from God. She sighed, unable to free herself from the memories of Jayce's brother Chase. The man had ruined her life in so many ways. . . . But despite his assault on her and his subsequent death, Leah fought to retain a hopeful future for her children. She couldn't let Chase's destruction perpetuate.

Leah pushed the memories of bad times aside and lifted her naked children. "Here we go. It's time for our bath." Her singsong voice suggested a great outing was upon them. And for the Kincaid twins, such a thing could be said. They loved their bath time, and Leah enjoyed it as well, finding a certain comfort in the morning ritual.

Placing each child in the water, she laughed as they adjusted to their new surroundings and began to splash and play. Merry was far and away the more shy of the two, but she seemed to find her own measure of bravery here in the water. Wills, always the adventurer, sometimes stuck his face right down into the water only to pop back up as if surprised that he couldn't breathe in the liquid.

Leah let them play until the water began to cool off. She then took soap and quickly bathed each one. With the bath ritual drawing to a close, Leah wrapped the babies in warm towels that she'd kept on the back of the stove. It was just then that Helaina Beecham appeared.

"It's a glorious day," she announced. "I wouldn't be surprised to see the ice completely melt or drift out to sea."

Leah secured diapers on her babies, then began the arduous task of dressing them. "I hope you're right. The sooner the ice clears, the sooner help can be had for Jacob and Jayce."

Helaina pulled off a thick woolen hat and pushed back loose strands of blond hair. "I'd like to get to Nome and see if Stanley has sent any further word." She had been a good source of encouragement to Leah.

Helaina's brother had been faithfully helping the women get any available information on the *Regina*. Unfortunately, there hadn't been much the Washington, D.C., Pinkerton agent could offer. No one could travel north, and after a winter of waiting and praying, Helaina and Leah had reached the end of their patience.

"I would have suggested John could take you down, but we've just had bad news," Leah said, remembering her friend's death. "Ayoona passed away in the night."

Helaina's expression turned to one of disbelief. "I just talked to her yesterday. She showed me how to clean and cook a goose."

"I know, but she's gone." Leah tried not to cry in front of the children. The twins weren't quite a year old, and anytime Leah cried, they were very sensitive to their mother and began to cry too. Leah often had to save her tears of despair for the dead of night when the household was asleep.

Helaina took a cup and poured herself some hot coffee. "I can't believe she's gone." Sitting down at the kitchen table, she shook her head, then took a long sip.

"Oopick was just here. I told her I would help prepare the body if you could watch the twins. If you don't have time, however, I could ask Sigrid. There's no school today, so she won't be busy teaching."

"Nonsense. I can watch them. Besides, Emma will probably want her sister with her. Won't they also help with the body?" She pushed her coffee aside as Leah got to her feet.

"I suppose so." Leah finished with the children, then handed Wills to Helaina. "Please hold on to him while I secure Merry. They seem to be everywhere at once these days."

"Come see Auntie Helaina," she coaxed, and Wills eagerly launched himself into Helaina's arms. She had become a special member of the family to Leah's twins. To Leah too.

It was hard to believe that this woman Leah had once hated had become so important to her now. Leah honestly loved Helaina. The woman had spent tireless hours helping to gather wood off the beaches, caring for Jacob's dogs, and working at the small store Leah ran from her old inne not twenty yards away.

Leah placed Meredith into a crudely constructed baby chair, then scooted her to the table. Next was Wills' turn, but he was so intrigued with pulling Helaina's hair from its pins that he had nearly forgotten his hunger.

"Come along, son. You can charm the lady another time."

Helaina chuckled and reached again for her steaming mug. "I'd say he'll be charming all the ladies one day. He's quite the handsome young man."

Leah took a dish towel and tied her son in place. She'd learned the hard way that if she didn't secure the children in such a manner, they were only too happy to climb out.

"I have oatmeal on the stove for their breakfast. There's canned milk, too, and a precious little bit of sugar."

"I'll see to it," Helaina said, getting to her feet. She pulled off her coat and hung it on a peg by the door. "I think I'm finally warmed up enough to function."

"How did you sleep?" Leah watched her friend for any negative reaction. Helaina had just taken to sleeping in Leah and Jacob's old home the last few days.

"At first I was a bit unnerved. I kept thinking about that first summer I spent here, when you and Jayce were in Ketchikan. I hated it then. I was sure the house would cave in or that some animal would tunnel its way through the dirt and sod. But this time . . . well . . . it just made me feel closer to Jacob."

Leah felt sorry for Helaina. The woman had given up everything in the States, her home, her career helping Stanley catch criminals for the Pinkertons, even her social life—and all to pin her hopes on a man that might or might not return her affections. But Leah was almost certain he would return them, otherwise she would never have encouraged Helaina.

"I'm glad it had that effect," Leah said as she pulled on her parka. "Soon enough it will flood out, but until then you might as well enjoy the privacy."

"I lived in it all summer, even when it was flooded," Helaina said, laughing. "The villagers thought I was crazy. I think I might have been at that, but the prospect of living in a tent in a land full of bears and other wildlife hardly appealed. I slept on the table."

Leah laughed. "Well, you won't need to do that this time. When the ground starts to thaw, just come back here. You know you're welcome."

"I do, but I also want to help you with the store. I have the inventory complete, and by tomorrow I should be able to finish the list of who owes how much."

Leah smiled. "I knew you'd be quite efficient. Jacob always admired that about you."

"Well, let's pray my efficiency will help get them home safely. As soon as we finish with Ayoona's funeral, I want to find a way to get to Nome. Even if I have to hike there by myself."

"You won't have to. I'll go before I send you out there blind to the trail." Leah headed for the door as Helaina pulled bowls down from the cupboard, and after a quick glance at her children, she walked to Ayoona's.

The day was beautiful, just as Helaina had said. The crystal blue sky was cloudless, and in the distance she could make out definite signs of spring.

"Lord, please let us find the men. Let us find Jacob and Jayce and the others. Please bring them home safely."

She couldn't count the times she'd prayed these same words over and over. She had never felt more helpless than when she'd realized last winter that she could do nothing to help her husband and brother. The winter had seemed to last forever, with one storm after another leaving them more and more isolated. With each blizzard, each stormy day, Leah thought of the men and wondered if they were enduring similar hardship.

Leah tried hard not to get discouraged, but it hurt to be without the people she loved most in all of the world. Jacob had been her mainstay through the years—especially when Jayce had refused her love long ago. But now that she and Jayce were married, Leah had quickly turned her focus on her husband. Jayce was the love of her life—her hope for the future—her heart's desire. If she lost him now, Leah wasn't sure what she'd do. If she lost them both . . . well . . . she couldn't even let her mind consider such a possibility.

Helaina had been an amazing tower of strength throughout the winter. When despair threatened and discouragement whispered in Leah's ear, it was Helaina and her faith in God that strengthened them both. Helaina hadn't always cared about what God wanted. After years of doing things on her own—relying on self-knowledge and preservation to see things through—Helaina had come to experience the same emptiness as others without God. Leah had known that the answer to her misery would be Jesus, but Leah also knew that until Helaina found such a thing for herself, it would do no good to force the issue.

So that was why it was a special joy to reflect on Helaina's love and consistent reading of the Bible. Many had been the night that Helaina had read from the Scriptures while winds raged outside and the twins howled inside. Leah and Helaina had discussed passages at length, sometimes even taking notes in order to ask Bjorn Kjellmann on a later date. He had laughed the first time they'd come to him with a list of questions, but after laboring over that same list and searching to give answers, Bjorn stopped laughing. He now said they were the iron sharpening iron—the students who caused the teacher to search deeper.

But Leah knew that book learning and heart understanding were two different things. She tried not to worry about the situation anymore than she needed to, but at times like this, she felt rather hopeless.

Her dear friend and mentor had gone home to be with the Lord.

Her brother was lost somewhere in the frozen Arctic.

And her husband might very well never return home.

Chapter Two

Jacob Barringer looked out across the frozen waters of the Arctic. There was no real sign that spring breakup was upon them, but in his heart he felt certain it was coming. He could almost feel it in his bones. The winter was over—at least technically speaking.

He thought about all they'd gone through. He and the rest of the crew of the *Regina* had been fortunate to find the missing ammunition for the 30-30, as well as another rifle and pistol. A supply of medicines meant for the Canadian scientists they'd taken north had been located, and Dr. Ripley had been delighted. It had given them all hope for survival. Now that the winter was over, the men were anxious to get home. Tempers were flaring, and Jacob was worried about how they would endure much longer.

"What do you see?" Jayce Kincaid asked as he joined his brother-in-law.

"Nothing that wasn't there yesterday," Jacob admitted. "I know the thaw is coming, though. By my calculations it's got to be near the end of May. It won't take long for the ice to break free once things start warming up. I've seen mornings back home where we woke up with the ice and by evening it was gone. Once the ice is gone, the searchers will come."

"At least the ice had made the seal hunting easier."

"True. We've eaten pretty well thanks to that."

Jayce shook his head. "We've eaten well because you've taught us how to survive up here. Most of these men had no idea how to live in this cold, much less thrive. And with no help or encouragement from Captain Latimore . . . well, let's just say the responsibility has fallen hard on your shoulders."

"Yours too. The men look to you just as readily as they look to me. Once we landed on this island, you were the one who taught them how to build those snow-block houses."

"Only because I learned it from you," Jayce said with a laugh. He gazed out to the ocean and sobered. "I know they're out there, rescuers . . . Leah." He sighed heavily. "I know they are, but what I can't figure is if they know we're here."

Jacob nodded. "I'm hoping they'll remember the *Karluk* and figure the current might have taken us in the same direction. We'll be all right if they consider that. At least they'll close in on us."

"I pray you're right."

The next morning around five, Jacob awoke to storm clouds gathering on the horizon. The men went about camp, tying down the things they'd managed to secure from the *Regina*. Jacob had helped direct the evacuation of the ship when the ice broke her apart. For weeks they had lived with nothing but several feet of ice between them and the Arctic waters. They were definitely blessed to have found land—even if it was desolate.

"Looks like a snow coming in," Jacob told one of the men. He pointed to a stack of cut driftwood. "Better get some of that inside. No telling how bad or how long this one's going to last."

"Latimore's missing," Jayce said as he came up behind Jacob.

"Missing?"

"No one's seen him since last night. When Bristol woke up this morning, he realized Latimore hadn't called him for his watch."

Jacob considered the situation for a moment. "Bristol was scheduled to take the four-o'clock watch, correct?"

Jayce nodded. "I looked around and found tracks that headed off toward the west along the beach. I'm thinking Latimore might have gone off that direction. Maybe he heard or saw something that caught his attention."

With continual daylight upon them, Jacob knew it should be easy enough to find the man if they spread out and searched. "We should be able to locate him if we split up. Gather the men, and we'll do what we can. He may have become confused or snow-blind."

Jayce quickly retrieved the men. They had long ago turned to Jacob as their leader, especially given Latimore's despondency toward life and his crew. "Look, it seems the captain disappeared last night. We don't know if he saw something that took him from his post or if he simply wandered away." Jacob didn't want to further demean the man, so he quickly continued. "There have been many bear tracks as you well know, so it wouldn't be wise to just assume Latimore is unharmed. Go in pairs, and take one of the firearms. If you haven't found anything in an hour," he said, gazing to the southwest, "return to camp. The skies are looking mean, and we'd best be settled back here before it hits."

"All it ever does up here is snow and be cold," nineteen-year-old Bristol grumbled. "I never knew you could have temperatures as cold as this place."

"Oh, stop complaining," Elmer Warrick, former first mate, commanded. "We haven't got time to list all of our problems."

Originally there had been fourteen men who'd abandoned the *Regina* when she sank. They'd lost four in accidents—accidents that had awakened the rest of the team to just how serious their station had become. Now with Latimore gone, that left nine men. They were a good bunch, as far as Jacob was concerned, but they were starting to get sick and irritable. It would only be a matter of time before they started feeling the desperation of their situation. Especially if help didn't come soon.

As the men paired up in teams, Jacob considered the lay of the land and each man's ability. Some were growing weak from the lack of a good diet, and Jacob didn't want to further risk anyone's life by making their trek too arduous. The snow was difficult to navigate at times, and unfortunately, many of these men were from southern states that saw very little cold or ice.

"Travis, you and Keith go north. Dr. Ripley and Elmer go west and follow the tracks Jayce found. Jayce, you and Bristol head east and Ben and Matt go northeast." Since they stood on the southern shore of the island and were able to see for some miles to the south, no one felt the need to head in that direction. Besides, the ice was far too unstable.

As the men gathered some supplies and split up, Jacob decided to head northwest, away from the shoreline. There was no telling if the tracks Jayce had found belonged to Latimore or to one of the other men. The captain could have gone any direction, for any reason. Jacob sighed. Latimore hadn't been much use to them since getting stuck in the floes, but he couldn't be forsaken—no matter the risk to the rest of them.

"What I wouldn't give for a few good dogs," Jacob muttered.

The landscape of their island offered some diversion. There were hills and cliffs where nesting birds had provided good meals for the team, but dangerous crevices and ice heaves were plentiful and difficult to navigate, and snow depths were often deceptive due to the drifts. It was truly an inhospitable wasteland. God forgive the leader of the *Karluk* expedition for calling it "the friendly Arctic." Vilhjalmur Stefansson was well known for declaring that the Arctic was merely misunderstood and that with proper training anyone could live quite easily in the frozen north. But Jacob knew better. Life up here was a matter of God's grace and common sense. Lose either one and you were doomed.

The glare from the constant sunlight was blinding. Jacob could only pray that the men were practicing wisdom and using their sun goggles. Jacob had shown each of them how to make the wooden glasses by carving tiny slits out of driftwood masks. They were crude but efficient, and the man who forgot to wear them quickly learned not to do it again. Several of the men had become snow-blind and suffered brutally; the pain caused by the condition was intense and would last for hours, even days. Now that their normal treatment of zinc sulphate solutions was nearly exhausted, the men were becoming far more cautious. No one wanted to endure such a fate.

Besides the lack of scenery, the monotony of their routine had nearly driven them all mad at one time or another. Bristol had a deck of cards that the men shared, but Dr. Ripley would have nothing to do with it, swearing they were the devil's tool of destruction. Dr. Ripley would therefore bury his face in one of three medical books he'd managed to keep with him after leaving the ship.

Travis, Ben, and Keith were quite good at singing and often entertained the group with their renditions of old folk songs and hymns. Travis, a meteorologist, kept records of their conditions, and Keith planned to keep similar botany records once the ground thawed.

Jacob often read from the Bible, sharing stories that the men knew from their childhood days in church. Besides botany, Keith was well versed in church history and the Bible, and Jacob had enjoyed dialoguing with the man from time to time. Ben and Matt also enjoyed such conversations, as did Travis. The others, however, avoided religious discussions.

Generally speaking, the men were a good lot. Jacob had feared there might be troublemakers in their group—men who would steal or kill in order to survive. He was glad to say that hadn't been the case so far.

Yet despite the men's good natures, Jayce was Jacob's mainstay. Together the two talked of home and of Leah. They remembered times spent in Ketchikan and of Karen's cooking and Adrik's stories. Their conversations sustained Jacob's hope of seeing home again.

He also often thought of Helaina Beecham. He wondered where she was and how she was doing. Had she gone back to work for her brother? A dangerous job such as bounty hunting should never have been allowed for women. Still, the world was changing.

Jacob thought of the war going on in Europe. He could only wonder if the war had extended to include America by now. So many people seemed to think it would happen that way. Still, it was possible the European countries had worked out their differences and had ended the war. That would be the best they could hope for, but somehow Jacob doubted it had happened. There had seemed no end in sight the summer before.

He trudged through the ice to crest one of the bigger hills and scanned the landscape in all directions. Using his binoculars, he spotted a great herd of seals on the ice. They were sunning themselves at the edge of a break—open water clearly available to them should a bear or man make an unwanted appearance. The water was a good sign. Perhaps the breakup would come sooner than Jacob anticipated.

There was no sign of Latimore, but the storm clouds were thickening and moving toward the island at an alarming rate. Jacob could feel that the temperatures had dropped significantly as the wind picked up and blew in the storm. He hurriedly scanned the rest of the land. There was nothing to suggest that a man had passed this way recently.

Making his way down the opposite side, Jacob tried to calculate the distance he and the men might cover in an hour. To press for more time would surely risk being out in the storm. He wondered if he'd be forced to leave Latimore to the elements rather than endanger the lives of everyone else.

The men, however, wouldn't consider this the loss of a leader. That had happened back in January when Latimore had sunk into a deep depression, isolating himself from most everyone. Jacob had taken it upon himself to hide the firearms from the captain for fear he might take his own life. With each small decision, the men began to think more and more of Jacob as their leader. Even the captain's first mate, Elmer Warrick, yielded all authority to Jacob. It wasn't exactly a responsibility Jacob had wanted, but having it thrust upon him out of necessity, he hadn't turned them away.

It had been clear that he and Jayce would be the only hope these men had. Most knew nothing about living in the Arctic; they had no training in hunting, neither were they very knowledgeable about survival off the ship. When fresh water ran desperately low, it was Jacob who taught them that good water could be had from the oldest parts of the ice floes, where ice could be chipped out and melted for a decent cup of water. With the fear of thirst defeated, the men then began to listen to Jacob in earnest for ways to survive the cold.

There Jayce had been equally helpful. They worked with the furs they'd managed to collect from their hunts, for prior to leaving the Canadian team at the Queen Elizabeth Islands, the crew had managed to shoot several bears, multiple caribou and seals, and a few fox. The furs came in handy as Jayce helped teach the men how to fashion warmer clothes for themselves. It was imperative they learned to keep their hands and feet warm and dry and their chest well insulated against the icy winds.

Jacob felt the wind blow hard against him and turned to observe the approaching storm once again. The mass was picking up speed, and the light was diminishing quickly as thick gray clouds descended. He checked his watch. They still had another twenty minutes before they'd agreed to return to camp. Jacob picked up his pace and decided to parallel camp just to the north. It would allow him quicker access to safety and give him the optimum time to search.

He crossed a frozen stream, hoping that the ice was still solid enough to hold him. Hours in the sun had weakened the foundation, however, and Jacob nearly fell through twice. He noted to go well downstream as he returned home, knowing that there he'd find a narrowing short enough to jump.

Time passed quickly, and soon the hour was up, but tracks that seemed fresh drew Jacob farther north and away from camp. Certainly they had to belong to the captain. Snow began to fall, and the wind blew hard against his back as Jacob topped another hill and strained against the pelting ice to see. He pulled his snow goggles up just long enough to put the binoculars to his eyes.

There, against the gray skies and snowy hills, was the unmistakable blue of Latimore's coat. Jacob called to him, but the man didn't hear. Hurrying, Jacob stumbled and slid most of the way down the hill. He jumped to his feet, sore but unhurt, and raced across the field to where Latimore seemed to wander in circles.

"Captain, are you all right?"

"I was not informed of the situation," he muttered. His face showed signs of frostbite and his lips were rather blue. "I can't seem to find the engineer."

"Sir, we have to get back to camp. There's a storm upon us. If we hurry, we might yet get back before the worst of it."

"You are not coming to the party, then?"

Jacob shook his head. Latimore had clearly lost his mind—at least temporarily. Not only that, but his eyes were nearly swollen shut from exposure. Jacob sighed. "Come, sir. The party is this way."

Latimore seemed momentarily appeased, but when Jacob pulled him along at a merciless pace, the man protested. "I cannot force the children to walk this quickly."

"The children will manage," Jacob replied, his gaze ever to the skies. If they kept this pace, they might make it back within half an hour. That would be just enough time, Jacob surmised. He absolutely couldn't allow the captain to slow for any reason.

"I haven't seen Regina. Is she here?"

The captain's mention of his wife surprised Jacob. "She's back at the camp, sir. She's waiting for you there," he lied, not knowing how else to ensure Latimore's cooperation.

This did the trick. "Then let us make haste. She is not one to be kept tapping her toes. She loves to dance, and the party will do much to raise her spirits."

The snow was blinding by the time they reached the camp. Had it not been for Jayce standing in the storm with one of their ship's lanterns, Jacob might have wandered out to sea. It was a danger he had often warned the men about. In the eternal darkness of Arctic winter, it was impossible to be certain where land began and ended without strict attention to detail. In an Arctic blizzard, it was just as difficult to gain your bearings.

"I see you found him," Jayce called above the winds. He reached out to take hold of Latimore's arm. "Let's just take him to our shelter."

"Have the others safely returned?" Jacob pushed Latimore while Jayce pulled.

"They have."

They reached the shelter of their makeshift house. The house had been built of pallets and wooden boxes from the ship's supplies. Around this they'd packed ice and snow, and it served them remarkably well. With the small camp stoves continually heating the shelter, they had survived sixty-below temperatures with only minor discomfort.

Jacob pulled off gear and helped Latimore to the stove. Keith and Ben got up to assist their captain, although it was easy to see they were disgusted with the man.

"He's confused and blind. I found him wandering in circles."

"I find the Atlantic abominable to navigate," Latimore stated as they helped him sit. Jayce brought several blankets and wrapped them around the man while Ben poured a cup of tea and handed it to Latimore. The man's hands shook so much that he couldn't hold the tin, so Ben gently held the cup to his lips.

Latimore drank, then eased back. "We shall never see Scotland again." He sighed the words, then passed out and fell backward against Jayce.

"Will he live?" Ben asked.

Jacob shook his head. "Not if he doesn't want to."

Chapter Three

"I'll take you to Nome."

John's statement startled Helaina. She'd been working to feed the dogs and hadn't even heard the native man approach. She straightened, ignoring the ache in her back. John's expression was emotionless, yet his eyes bore great pain. His mother's passing had not been an easy thing to bear.

"That's very kind of you. How soon can we leave?"

"Right now, if you can be ready."

"If you're sure. I don't want to . . . well . . . I know you're grieving."

"We are all grieving, but not just for my mother. I grieve for my friend Jacob. I grieve for Leah and her children. We must go and see what is to be done."

It was the moment Helaina and Leah had waited for all winter. "Let me get my things packed. I shouldn't need more than ten minutes."

"Meet me at the water."

Helaina nodded. The ice was gone and they would take the umiaks to Nome. It would be a blessing to the whole village, for she knew they would bring back ample supplies from her storehouse and that of any new shipments from Seattle and San Francisco. That was, if any of the ships had made it north yet.

She hurried back to the Barringer inne and gathered her things. The warm weather was already causing the ground to thaw, and it would be only a matter of weeks before the house started to flood. Still, she liked the place. Liked it because it reminded her of Jacob. She could see him here—smell his scent, hear his voice. Here she felt an unusual sense of peace that he would return to reclaim his home—and she hoped he might claim her as well.

Helaina hurried to pack a small bag of necessities for the trip, then threw everything else into her trunk and placed it up on the kitchen table. She would ask about having someone retrieve it and take it back to Leah's home. Maybe she'd just mention it to Leah when she told her good-bye.

Rushing for the Kincaid house, Helaina was glad to find that Leah was already waiting outside with the children. "John told me about the trip. I've packed you some food." Leah handed Helaina a gunnysack. "Hopefully the good weather will hold and you won't have to stop before reaching Nome."

"You're so thoughtful. I do appreciate your thinking of this," Helaina replied, slinging the sack over her shoulder. "I've packed up the rest of my things and left them on the table in my trunk. Could you have someone bring them here when you have time? I'd like to keep them from the water."

"Of course." Leah turned away from the toddling twins. "Please get word to me as soon as possible." The longing in her voice matched that in Helaina's heart.

Helaina reached out to touch her friend. "You know I will. No matter what. I'll let you know what's going on."

Leah nodded. "No matter what." The words were spoken with a kind of ominous resolve.

Helaina turned without another word and headed to the boats. John helped her in and tucked her things at the back with the rest of the supplies. Helaina knew the men wouldn't allow her to help row, so she settled in and tried to ready herself for whatever news she might encounter.

There's always the possibility, she rationalized, *that the men of the* Regina *managed to find help and get to land before too much trouble set in.* But in her heart she knew the chances were remote. Of course, the news could be that the revenue cutters had already gone in search of the men. After all, the ice had been gone several days now. This would be her prayer, Helaina decided. She wanted only to hear that a rescue ship was already en route and that everyone was certain of the *Regina*'s location.

She dozed off as the sun warmed the air. Her thoughts were of Jacob and her hope that he would be happy to see her in Alaska. She had prayed so often that he might still love her as Leah believed he did. There was no regret in her decision to come north, but Helaina knew that if Jacob refused her love, there would be no reason to stay. That thought saddened her more than she could bear, for then she would truly belong nowhere.

You'll always belong to me, a voice seemed to speak to her heart. She felt an immediate hope that grew every day as her knowledge of God grew.

Yes, she thought. *I belong to Jesus. I belong to God, and I will always have His love, even if Jacob has none to give me.*

In Nome Helaina learned that the war in Europe was not going well. American casualties were high, and no one had any idea of when the conflict might end. She worried about her brother, knowing that Stanley's patriot heart would cause him to want to sign up. His leg would keep him from being accepted—of that she was certain. After Chase Kincaid threw him from the back of a moving train, Stanley had never been the same. The leg had been shattered and other bones broken; Stanley had been lucky to survive. She shook her head slowly as she remembered it all. Had it not been for the Pinkertons' desperation to capture Chase Kincaid, she might never have met Jacob Barringer.

Helaina looked at the small building in front of her and tried to put worries of Stanley aside. Since it was Sunday and there would be no chance of receiving news or information from the army or other officials, she had decided to spend her time in church. The woman at the hotel had told her about a tiny church and of the love the people held for one another. It sounded like just the thing to lift Helaina's spirits.

"Are you lost?"

Helaina turned to find a determined older woman looking her square in the eye. "No. I was just planning to attend church."

"Well, you're in the right place." The woman offered a huge smile, along with her outstretched hand. "I'm Mina Bachelder, and we're glad to have you. Are you new to Nome? I don't think I've seen you here before."

"I've been here on several occasions. In fact," Helaina leaned closer, so as not to make her next comment a public announcement, "I was the woman kidnapped when the deputies were shot and killed."

"Oh, mercy me. And here you are safe and sound. I guess I'd heard you went back to the States."

"I had, but . . . well . . . there was something and someone I needed to come back for."

Mina grinned and her whole expression lit up. "You should tell me all about it over dinner. I'm serving up a good caribou stew. Please join me."

Helaina nodded. "I'd like that."

After a wonderful church service, Mina led Helaina to her house on Second Street. "Will you be in Nome long?" she asked.

"No, probably not," Helaina said. "I came for information. My . . . well . . . a dear friend of mine has a husband and brother on the *Regina*." In church the pastor had asked the congregation to pray for the men of the *Regina*. It had blessed Helaina to hear the pastor offer up prayers for the men, comforting her in a way she couldn't explain.

Mina reached out to touch her arm. "So that's why you're here."

"Yes. I'm hopeful that the army or the Coast Guard can give me information as to whether any rescue ships have been sent north. I know it's early, but those men have endured a cold winter." She hated to even think of what kind of fate might have befallen Jacob and Jayce.

"Well, we've certainly been praying they've endured."

Helaina stopped in midstep. "They must have. They were good men—strong and knowledgeable. They wouldn't take chances."

"Seems they took a chance when they went north," Mina replied. "Here we are." She walked up a few steps and opened the door. "Just hang your coat on the hook. I'll get the dinner on."

Mina disappeared through yet another door while Helaina pulled off her fur parka. The house proved to be nice and warm. Apparently Mina had stoked up the fire before heading to church. Helaina closed the door behind her and observed the tiny living room. There was a colorful rag rug, several wooden chairs, and a horsehair couch that had seen a great amount of wear.

"Here's a cup of tea for you to sip on while I set the table. I hope you don't mind tea. I don't drink coffee."

Helaina smiled and took the offering. "Tea is just fine. I'm very fond of it." She sipped from the cup as she continued to study the room. A small fireplace had been trimmed with a simple wooden mantel. This in turn held pictures of people Helaina guessed to be Mina's family. She leaned closer for a better look.

Several of the pictures were obviously wedding photographs. Women who appeared a decade younger than Helaina peered out from white gowns and veils with sober expressions. They would have the viewer believe the day was nothing more special than any other—that having the photograph taken was a commonplace event that left the subjects fighting off moments of ennui. But Helaina knew better. This was the day most of them had waited for, prayed for. This was the beginning of a new life. A day so important that they had to commemorate it, no matter the cost, with a photograph.

Helaina thought momentarily of her late husband, Robert Beecham. The marriage seemed to have taken place a hundred years ago. She didn't dwell there long, however, as Jacob's image came to mind.

"I see you've found the children."

"Are all of these your children?" Helaina asked in surprise. There had to be at least a dozen different couples or families.

"Indeed. I bore my husband seventeen babies. Fifteen lived to see adulthood."

"Where are they now?"

Mina smoothed her colorful apron. "Some live right here. Some live down in the States. A couple made their way to other parts of the territory.

They're all good to write—especially the girls. I have ten daughters, so they keep me well apprised of what's happening in the family."

"It's an impressive family to say the least."

"They're my blessing from God. And they all love the Lord as much as I do, so I can stand before Him on judgment day with a clear conscience."

Helaina heard the pride in the woman's voice. It was quite an accomplishment to raise such a large family in the wilds of Alaska, but an even greater feat to see them all come to a spiritual understanding of biblical truth. Helaina wondered what the woman's secret might be.

"How did you do it?"

Mina grinned. "Sit down with me and I'll tell you all about it."

Helaina did as she was instructed, listening to Mina offer a simple prayer for the meal, as well as for the men of the *Regina*. The sincerity of her words made Helaina feel the woman genuinely cared about the plight of those men.

"I always told my children," Mina began, "that whether or not they chose to believe in God—He was still God. He wouldn't make any special deals with them just because they were stubborn or confused. I told them that the good Lord had given them God-fearing parents for a reason, and that reason was to bring them up in the way they should go."

"And that caused them to believe?"

"That and the constant reminder that hell was a very real place where you would spend eternity in misery and absolute separation from all hope and love. My husband led devotions at breakfast and supper every day. We talked about the people in the Bible as though they were family. There wasn't a story my children didn't know, but their daddy was good to remind them that it wasn't enough to just know those lessons in their head. They needed to take them into their hearts and heed the message."

"Still, that's a big accomplishment to see fifteen children learn to trust God and believe in Him. I was late in coming to believe. It was very hard for me."

Mina looked at her sternly. "Were your people believers? Did your folks take you to church?"

"Oh, we attended church—but you must understand, I lived in New York. In our circle of friends, church was a place to be seen socially rather than for the sake of your soul."

"Goodness. I can't imagine that."

Helaina smiled. "Think of this: One of the churches I attended held row after row of highly polished mahogany pews. You earned the right to certain pews by nature of who you were associated with and how much money you gave the church. The closer to the front, the more important you were—the more you were valued."

"That's awful. Teaches a bad lesson."

"To be sure." Helaina sampled the stew. "Mmm, this is wonderful. Thank you so much for inviting me."

Mina handed her a platter with biscuits. "These are a couple of days old but should crumble up nice in the stew."

Helaina took one and followed Mina's example of tearing it up in her hands and mingling it with the caribou and vegetables. "How did you come to live here in Nome, Mina?"

"My husband brought us here when there was little more than natives around. It was long before the gold rush—such a difficult time." She tutted under her breath and focused on her food. "Nome has always had its problems, and those were grim days to be sure."

"Why did your husband want to live here?"

"We were missionaries, ministering to the people of this region. When my husband passed on, there must have been more than two hundred natives from Nome and the surrounding area at his funeral. They loved him."

"If his hospitality was equal to yours, then I can definitely see why," Helaina replied.

"The Lord calls us to hospitality. The Bible says you never know when you might be entertaining angels, so I try never to pass up a chance to invite a newcomer."

"Well, for me this was an unexpected treat. I'll remember it for some time to come."

"You'll come back and see me too, won't you? When you come to Nome, you're more than welcome to stay with me. You can leave that hotel and come here now if you like. I have a small room off the back that has a spare bed and its own stove. It'll keep you quite comfortable."

Helaina had never seen such generosity in New York. Life in Alaska was much different; people knew to look out for each other. To do otherwise might cause someone's death, and no one wanted that on their heads.

"I think it would be very nice to stay with you, Mina. If my time in Nome extends to several days, I will seek you out."

Mina nodded, satisfied that Helaina was telling the truth. "Eat up. I have a cobbler waiting for your attention."

The next day Helaina was still remembering the sumptuous meal with Mina when she came face-to-face with Cheslav Babinovich, a Russian man she'd met the previous year. "Why, Mr. Babinovich, is that you?" she asked the frightened-looking man.

"Ah, dear lady. It is I." He glanced over his shoulder. "Your name escapes me."

"Helaina Beecham. We met last year when you were seeking assistance. I introduced you to Dr. Cox."

"Ah, I do remember you." He rubbed the back of his hand against his thick black mustache. "I fear the despair of the last few months has left me greatly distressed. I am no good at remembering much other than the terror being experienced by my dear czar and his family."

"I've heard things in Russia are quite grim where the royal family is concerned. Someone mentioned the royals have been imprisoned."

"It is all true." He moaned and turned away. "I am desperate to assist them. I fear they will all be killed if I do not negotiate their release."

"Can you do that? Can you negotiate with their captors?"

"If I have enough money," he said, turning back to face her. "Money is the only thing that speaks in my poor country."

Helaina watched as several men approached. Babinovich ducked his head against his coat and turned toward the storefront window, as if making himself invisible to their scrutiny. When the men were gone, he once again faced Helaina. "One cannot be too careful. Spies are everywhere. They will hunt down all of us with royal ties and see us dead."

"Who will?"

"The new government in my country. The Bolsheviks. But I mustn't speak of it. There is too much danger." He lowered his voice. "I have jewels to sell. But for now, if word got back to our enemies that royal jewels were smuggled out of the country and sold to help the czar and his family—well, just let me say heads would roll."

Helaina frowned. "I wouldn't want to be a part of that."

"But you might be interested in purchasing some of my jewelry?" he asked hopefully. "You are such a good woman, you surely could not stand to see the children left in the hands of such vicious people. The czar's daughters are quite beautiful, and little Alexi is such a dear lad. They have no doubt been horribly misused."

Helaina frowned. The man's story was quite compelling. "I suppose I might buy a few pieces," she found herself saying.

Babinovich nearly forgot himself as he reached out for her. He stopped before actually taking hold of her. "Oh, Mrs. Beecham, you have made me most happy. I am sure we can save them now."

Helaina arranged for the man to meet her in the lobby of the hotel later that day, then turned her attention back to her destination. She needed to know what had been done for the *Regina* and her men.

Latimore rallied as Jacob spooned hot coffee, heavily laden with sweetened condensed milk, into his mouth. His eyes were less swollen, and it seemed to Jacob that perhaps he was regaining his vision.

"Captain, can you see me?"

Latimore squinted. "Just a bit." His voice was hoarse and his breathing labored.

"Good." Jacob set the cup aside. "You've been quite ill. It's been nearly a week."

"You should have let me die," the man said matter-of-factly.

"And what good would that have done your son?"

Latimore frowned and looked away. "I have no son."

"Saying it doesn't make it true. I could tell you that we were not lost in the Arctic, but rather had been found and were even now enjoying the luxuries of a Seattle hotel, but it wouldn't be our situation."

"I am of no use to the boy."

"Not like this. But there was a time when the Captain Latimore I knew would have been quite valuable to any child."

"That man is long gone."

"I don't believe that. I think you've merely buried him alive."

Latimore looked back at Jacob. He narrowed his eyes, then started to rub them. Jacob prevented the action. "That won't help, and in fact it could do more harm. Do you feel like eating some duck? We've cooked one and have a nice broth that might suit your stomach."

Latimore shook his head. "Why are you doing this? You would get along just as well—if not better—should you let me die."

Jacob leaned back and folded his arms against his chest. "I'm not in the habit of giving up on people. You have a great deal to live for, despite your loss. You must stop deceiving yourself and see this. God hasn't allowed you to live without reason. You have a job to do, but you are avoiding it. Running away from your son is not going to give you the peace you crave."

The last remnants of Latimore's strong walls began to crumble. "But when I look into his face . . . I see Regina."

Jacob nodded. "I'm sure you do. But perhaps that will eventually prove to be a blessing instead of a curse. You mustn't forsake your son, Latimore. He needs you. Regina is gone and she has no earthly need, except that you care for the child she gave you. You must draw on your strength and return to him. You must."

Latimore shook his head. "I don't think I can. I'm too far spent—too sick."

Jacob grinned. "I'm not giving up on you, Latimore, and I refuse to allow you to give up on yourself."

Chapter Four

Leah watched her twins with a proud heart as they toddled around, exploring the new growth of wild flowers just beginning to bloom. Most of the snow was gone, but that didn't mean the storms were behind them. She knew that snows could come suddenly and without warning. They were always on their guard for such surprises.

"Come along, Wills—Merry," she called and clapped her hands together. The twins immediately took note and waddled toward her in their awkward baby way. "We're going to see Sigrid," she said, lifting both children at once.

Wills kicked his legs immediately, wanting to get down, while Meredith snuggled her head against Leah's shoulder momentarily. Today the women were working on the sealskins for the umiak. Ayoona was to have led the group, but now they would work without her. Oopick promised, however, they would tell stories about the old woman and sew to her memory. The idea of such a gathering encouraged Leah's rather raw heart. She longed for the comfort of her loved ones—of Jayce and Jacob. She missed Ayoona's mothering and wisdom.

Sigrid had offered to watch the very small children so the mothers could work unhindered. Several of the Inupiat girls would help her as well. It would keep the mothers from constantly having to run after their little ones, and it would keep the children away from the oily skins.

"Good morning," Leah called as she entered the school. Sigrid was already busy playing with some of the children.

"Oh, hello, Leah. I see you've brought me two more friends." Sigrid got to her feet and came over to take Wills. He immediately grunted and pushed against her to be put down. "This one's ready to play."

"He's always ready to play," Leah said, laughing. She put Merry on the floor, but the baby didn't seem inclined to explore further. She clung to Leah's leg and hid her head. "Merry, on the other hand, is probably ready to be rocked to sleep."

Sigrid put Wills down and reached for Merry. The child went hesitantly but didn't cry as Wills darted off across the floor to play with the toys and other children. Sigrid cuddled Merry and cooed to her softly.

"Will you have enough help?" Leah asked. She saw that two of the older girls were here to assist but wondered if that would be enough.

"I have another couple of girls coming. They're quite excited to help. Emma has promised them each a special gift. I'm not even sure what it is, but the girls were quite excited."

Leah nodded. "I'm sure Emma will make it special. She has a way of doing that."

Sigrid grew sober. "Has there been any word from Helaina or John?"

"Not yet." Leah tried not to let her disappointment show. "It's only been a short time, however. I'm sure they'll be back as soon as they have news."

"I know they will. They won't have you wait too long if they have word."

Leah drew a deep breath and let it out slowly. "Waiting has never been something I have borne well." She frowned. "I suppose it's a lesson I'm still learning."

"Well, hopefully the wait won't last much longer."

Leah could see the sincere concern in Sigrid's eyes. "I pray you're right."

Leah left the children and walked slowly to the community building. Glancing beyond the building, her attention was drawn to the sea. Glints from the water sparkled hypnotically, beckoning her.

Forgetting the women for the moment, Leah walked to the edge of the water. She gazed longingly across the surface to where the sky met the sea.

"You're out there somewhere," she murmured. The aching loneliness nearly sent her to her knees. How could Jayce be so far away and yet so close—connected by the very water that touched her shores?

Leah knelt and touched the Bering Sea. Maybe somewhere her husband was doing the same. Sometimes the days went by so incredibly slowly that Leah thought she might lose her sanity. Other days she was so consumed with the children or other people she had little time to mull over her situation. But in truth, her heart was in a continual state of breaking. Every night she went to bed lonelier than the night before. And each day Leah awoke to the harsh reality of her situation all over again, and every day it hurt just as much as it had when she'd first realized Jayce and Jacob weren't coming home for a long, long time.

She hadn't yet allowed herself to believe they wouldn't come home at all, however. She couldn't. The pain of that thought could not even be comprehended. Leah feared the truth—feared that they might never know the truth, feared that the truth might not be what she wanted to hear. It was a terrible dichotomy. Pushing an errant strand of brown hair away from her face, Leah straightened.

"Father, please bring them home. I cannot bear this burden much longer. My children need their father and uncle. I need Jayce to return. I need Jacob." She wiped at the tears that came. "I trust you in all of this, but, God, I don't understand why this had to happen. Things had finally worked out. I was still troubled by what had happened with Chase, but now . . . now I just want Jayce back. Those old wounds have healed, but these new wounds never will unless they come home. Please, God—I can't make it through unless you help me."

The women were seated on the ground already wearing waterproof gear when Leah arrived. She pulled on her own protective garments and took a place between Oopick and her daughter-in-law Qavlunaq. Emma Kjellmann sat across from them, laughing at something one of the other women had said. She looked up and smiled at Leah. "I'm so glad you came. I wasn't sure if the twins would be well enough. I heard they were teething."

"They are, but today they seemed quite fit. In fact, so fit that they were running circles around me." Leah picked up a needle and pulled the oily skin closer. They were sewing several large sealskins together to make the exterior wrapping for the umiak. Skin boats were the life of the village; they would use this large open boat for whaling.

Leah used her needle with confidence. They would have to be very careful with their stitches in order to make the boat watertight. Leah had participated so many times in this ritual that she was actually more skilled than some of the native women.

"We were just discussing village news," Emma continued.

Leah nodded knowingly. These gatherings were always a place where the women shared news of their families and friends.

"Mary was just telling us about her family in Teller. They have had several deaths among the children. It sounds like it might be diphtheria."

Leah couldn't suppress a shudder. "I pray it isn't." She caught Mary's worried expression. "We will pray for your loved ones."

Epidemics were feared everywhere, but perhaps more so in remote areas. It seemed the villages were always dealing with one health issue or another. Sickness swept through uninvited, stealing away whole families. Last Chance Creek hadn't seen the likes of such for a while, but everyone knew it was just a matter of time.

Emma changed the subject. "It looks to me that there will be a large amount of wild berries to pick this summer. The bushes and ground berries are blooming in abundance. I think we would all do well to make special plans for canning and drying."

The women nodded, and so the conversation continued. Leah found herself only halfway listening to the comments. She thought of the short summer and how few months there would be before the ice once again made northern travel difficult, if not impossible. Would there be enough time for a rescue of her men? Would the government even approach the matter with any degree of seriousness?

Pressing her leather thimble against the needle, Leah caught Emma's announcement that she was expecting. "The baby is due in November, as best I can tell." She smiled proudly. "We're praying God will see fit to let this one come to us."

"That's wonderful news," Leah said. She knew how hard it had been on Emma to miscarry during her previous pregnancy. "I have lots of little clothes to share with you. Some of them are yours from before."

Qavlunaq smiled shyly. "I'm having another baby too. We will have them together."

"Congratulations," Emma said. "The baby is due in November?"

"Yes, the same time as you."

Leah tried not to seem upset or unhappy as the revelry of the other women resounded in the large open room. She was quite happy for her friends to expand their families, but at the same time it only served to remind her of her own circumstances.

"I promised Leah we would speak of Ayoona and her days here in the village," Oopick declared. She looked to Leah and nodded.

"Ayoona was a good woman." The other women nodded, including Lopa, Ayoona's other daughter-in-law. Lopa was the second wife of Seal-eyed Sam, Ayoona's elder son. She was not nearly as sociable as Ooopick, but she'd come here today with her seventeen-year-old daughter, Mary, as Mary and her betrothed were the ones who would receive the boat as a wedding gift.

"Ayoona taught me to do many things better than my own mother taught me. She taught me to make better stitches for sewing the skins. She taught me about forgiving others their wrongs," Lopa shared.

Leah knew the truth of that. Ayoona had been a woman of faith, and she had given Leah much encouragement during lonely and difficult times. Just weeks earlier Ayoona had told Leah that she shouldn't worry and cry over her man.

"God will bring him home when the time is right, Lay-ya. You cannot be tellin' God what to do."

The memory made Leah smile. *No, I can't be tellin' God what to do, but I can certainly try to persuade Him.*

"When Ayoona was a girl, she ran faster than anyone in the village. Her mother always told her not to run so much. She was afraid it would make the spirits angry. Ayoona told her mother that the spirits could not catch her, even if they were angry." Oopick smiled and added, "Her running was a blessing later, when she surprised a bear. Ayoona told me she was just seventeen and she was picking berries for her mother. A bear was there picking berries too. She said they were both so surprised they started to run. But they ran the same way. The bear wasn't really chasing her—he just happened to go the same way."

Everyone laughed at the thought of the bear and Ayoona. Leah pictured the old woman running side by side with the animal. Leah had no doubts as to who would win, although bears could outrun most people—at least in short distances.

Another woman shared a story about Ayoona dancing some of the village story dances. Leah listened as one after another told their stories and shared their love for the old woman. Ayoona would be sorely missed in the village—of this there was no doubt. But maybe more important, Ayoona had left a legacy of love and knowledge. She had taught every woman present something about survival in the village. She had helped deliver most of the babies these women had birthed. Ayoona was more than just a part of the village—she was the village. In many ways she had sculpted and molded the village to reflect her loving heart.

Later that afternoon Leah worked quietly in her house while the twins were sleeping. The last thing she expected was to hear a ruckus in the yard. The dogs were barking madly, as if something or someone had come into their territory. Leah took up a rifle and slipped out the front door and around the side of the house. Jacob's dogs were yipping and whining as if their master were home. Leah felt her heart skip a beat as she picked up her pace.

She crossed the yard and went to where Jacob's inne stood. There, much to her relief and surprise, were Helaina and John. They'd just returned.

"I was coming over as soon as we secured the dogs," Helaina said, embracing Leah. "John bought several new dogs while in Nome. They're good, solid animals. I think Jacob will like them."

Leah cocked her head. "You have news, don't you?"

Helaina smiled. "Well, some news. Not exactly the news we want, but it's good. There's a revenue cutter already searching in the north for the men. I got word while in Nome, and we headed home as soon as we were convinced we'd done everything we could to aid the cause."

"Do they have any idea where the *Regina* might have gone?"

"Just what we've sent them and what the sightings encourage," Helaina declared. She pulled her jacket away from her body and shook her head. "I need a bath."

"Come to my house—your things are there anyway. I've got lots of hot water. I'll get more on the stove."

Helaina glanced at John. "Do you have everything under control?"

"Sure. Go on." He was a man of few words, but he was clearly happy to dismiss the women. "I'll bring those things you wanted after I get the other items packed in the store."

"It's flooded in the inne," Leah said. "Maybe you should just bring them to my place."

John straightened. "We never did before. Not much sellin' goes on in the summer, anyway. Not when the hunting is good. We'll be moving up north pretty soon."

"You make a good point," Leah replied. "Just do it the way we always do."

"I've brought home some new material. There was a nice shipment brought in just before I left," Helaina announced as they walked toward Leah's house. "I think you'll really like what I have."

"What I'd like even better is to hear everything," Leah said as she pulled Helaina along. "What did you find out? Was there any news at all?"

"There was one other report. Apparently a couple of Russian fishermen spotted a camp in the distance on one of their islands. The Coast Guard services feel confident that it will prove to be the men of the *Regina*."

"Oh, I pray they find them soon. Summertime is so fleeting in the Arctic."

Helaina nodded and followed Leah into her house. "They've been out working their way north even before the ice was gone in Nome. They may have had to wait it out here and there, but they're trying to reach them."

Leah heard the excitement in Helaina's voice and felt hope surge anew. "I pray they hurry. I can't bear to think of what those men have endured."

"But they're smart. Smart and strong and they trust in the Lord. At least our men do."

Leah smiled at the way Helaina claimed Jacob as her own. She prayed her brother's love for this woman had not faded over time. "You're right. It's been hard at times to remember that God has always known where they are—even when I didn't." The thought offered comfort for the first time in a long while.

"The twins are asleep in their room, but I'll have your bath ready in your old room. Go ahead and start undressing. There are fresh towels and soap in the drawer." Leah turned to go, but Helaina stopped her.

"They're coming home, Leah. I just know it."

Leah felt her enthusiasm. "I know it too. I feel sure of it now. Even if I didn't before."

Chapter Five

On the eighth of June the village celebrated the first birthday of Leah's twins, and the children reveled in the attention. Wills went from person to person, never staying very long in any one place. He appeared to enjoy being the life of the party and laughed and clapped so much Leah was certain he would wear himself out. Even Merry was more outgoing than usual. She smiled shyly and accepted the gifts and food people offered.

There were several native dances offered to honor the twins. Both twins tried to mimic the steps, causing the adults to laugh at their efforts. Leah thought it all quite nice, but she couldn't help thinking about how much Jayce would enjoy the babies. She wondered if he was safe, if he had food to eat. Here they were stuffing themselves on all sorts of goodies, and Jayce and Jacob might well be starving.

When would Jayce come home? When could their lives move forward together?

Time was passing by, but Leah felt as though she were frozen in place. Only seeing the twins grow from babies to toddlers proved to her that the calendar had truly changed dates.

The day after the birthday celebration, a large number of the villagers packed up their tents and supplies and migrated to the north. Many birds and ducks had been sighted, and the promise of eggs and meat other than seal and dried salmon beckoned. Leah had gone on several of these bird-hunting excursions and had been amazed at the proficiency some women had with a bow and arrow. In fact, she remembered a time when Qavlunaq had been just a girl of eleven and had wanted to prove to her father that she was capable of hunting as well as her brothers. She accompanied her family as they hunted and managed to climb onto a ridge where she waited for the geese. As they flew by she took her bow and arrow and shot the largest of the birds. Her father had been quite proud of her that day. Leah still pictured the little girl grinning proudly and holding up her goose. Now that girl was a grown woman with a child of her own and another on the way.

Two days after the first group of villagers headed off, another group prepared to go. John and Oopick were among those who planned to leave. A part of Leah wanted to take the children and follow along for the sake of company and something to do, if nothing else. But the hope of Jayce and Jacob being rescued and returning to Last Chance kept her in place. After all, what if they came home to an empty village, with no one and nothing to celebrate their survival?

The day dawned bright and clear, but by nine o'clock a heavy sea fog rolled in without warning. One minute Leah could see across the open sea, and the next she couldn't see more than ten feet in front of her. She was used to these fogs but hated them nevertheless. They were terrifying out on the open trail. Once when she and Jacob were returning from Nome, a fog came in fast and thick. Jacob had been wise enough to hold up and wait out the fog despite his knowledge of the trail, but Leah would never forget the isolated feeling of not being able to see. She kept expecting someone to reach out through the fog and grab them. Jacob, sensing her fear, had told her stories of Colorado and their childhood. Stories Leah had forgotten.

"The fog is bad," Oopick said, entering Leah's house unannounced. The village was like a large extended family, and no place was considered closed to them.

"Will you still go today?" Leah asked, pouring Oopick a cup of tea.

"John says we can wait until tomorrow. He sees it as God telling him to take more time." The older woman smiled.

"I'm glad you'll be here at least another day," Leah admitted.

Oopick took the tea. "It's not too late. You can come with us. You could return early."

Leah weighed the suggestion. "No. I wouldn't want them to come back and not have me here to greet them."

Oopick lowered her gaze. "It could be months, Leah. Maybe until the ice comes again. You . . . well . . ." She took a long drink from the cup as if to silence herself.

"Oopick, you speak the truth, and that's never wrong. I've thought of the possibility that they won't be found until late in the summer . . . maybe not even then." Leah had to force the words. "Still, I want to stay. There will be a few of the oldest people here, and they may need my help. Plus, Emma and her family will be here. I just feel like it's the right thing to do."

"What's the right thing to do?" Helaina questioned, coming from the back room.

"Staying here instead of going north with everyone else."

Helaina exchanged a look with Oopick. "I think she's right. We'll be fine."

"I have a lot of good seal meat thanks to John and Kimik, and soon the salmon will run in full. I'll venture out to catch as many of them as we can get from the river," Leah promised. "You'll see. I'll have the drying racks full before you even get back."

Oopick smiled. "You always work hard. I know you will do as you've said, but we'll see who brings home more fish."

Leah grinned. "That sounds like a challenge. I accept." She knew Oopick and the other women would gather far more fish, but it didn't matter. She liked the lighthearted banter; it helped to put her mind on other things. "Besides, it won't be long and you'll be back. Don't forget we'll have a lot of berry picking come next month."

"We'll have good pemmican," Oopick said, nodding.

"Jelly and jam too," Leah added. "I've ordered extra sugar for just such things."

"John will like that. He thinks that's a good treat. He likes to spread jelly on the salmon sometimes." Oopick laughed. "I tell him he better be careful or he'll turn into a white man."

Leah had never known a white man to put jelly on salmon, but she laughed nevertheless. So did Helaina, who quickly added, "I've never tried that, but maybe I will. Sometimes even the best food gets old."

"John says we'll come back to check and see if you have news." Oopick finished her tea and handed Leah the cup as she turned to go. "He wants to know about Jacob. I want to know too."

Leah nodded. They all felt the misery of not knowing the men's fate. John had been worried enough to consider a trip north on his own; it hadn't been that long ago that he had said he might put together a search party. Leah had almost encouraged it, figuring that somehow—some way—she, too, would go on the search. But then reality set in, and Leah knew it wasn't wise for either of them to try such a thing. There was no way for them to be sure where the *Regina* had ended up, and they might only find themselves stranded in similar fashion. And, of course, there were the children.

Leah knew she could never leave them that long. It was one thing to make a trip to Nome—that was quite far enough when facing a separation from the children she loved. Considering that a search team could easily spend all summer looking for the missing ship, Leah knew the role of rescuer did not belong to her.

Helaina had agreed, encouraging Leah to trust the government to go after them. She had further stressed that should the ongoing war in Europe keep the government from searching, her brother, Stanley, would arrange a private search out of Seattle or San Francisco. Helaina's healthy bank account could afford such a venture. This comforted Leah to some extent.

The fog cleared around two o'clock, presenting a beautiful landscape that looked as if it had been freshly washed. Leah decided to leave her napping children with Helaina while she went to gather some herbs on the mushy tundra hillside not far from their home. To her surprise, she found a ship docked out in the deep water. There were already launches heading into shore. She held her breath and watched—hoping, praying that Jayce and Jacob might be among the men coming to Last Chance.

Shielding her eyes against the light, Leah studied the forms as they drew closer. No one looked familiar, and given the way some of the men were holding up bottles, Leah knew her husband and brother would not be among their numbers. These were whalers who unfortunately added to their business ventures by selling whiskey to any native who would buy it. Leah turned away in disgust. She hoped Emma's husband, Bjorn, would dissuade the remaining village men from giving in to the temptation. Furthermore, she hoped he would encourage the whalers to move on.

Leah lost track of time as she searched through the vegetation. There were a great many plants that were useful to the village's medicinal needs. Leah often found that natives who were Christians sought her out to help with particularly bad cases. Others, who held no use for the white man's faith, went to their shaman. Ayoona had once told Leah that such superstitions were difficult to let go of when you had been taught all of your life that they were true. She told Leah to think of how hard it would be for her and Jacob, should someone come declaring that Christianity was wrong—that everything they'd learned all of their lives was nothing more than a collection of stories perpetuated by a group of people who were ignorant to the truth.

This single statement, perhaps more than anything else, had taught Leah great patience and tolerance in living with the Inupiat. She often remembered Ayoona's words and knew that it would be quite impossible for her to accept any other beliefs as truth. Why should it not be equally as hard for the natives of Alaska? Emma and Bjorn had agreed with such thoughts and told Leah that living an example of Jesus' love was the best way to encourage the people to believe. When the natives saw the hope and joy that the whites had in life—especially in adversity—they would become curious and seek answers. This had proved true over and over.

Realizing that she needed to get back to the twins, Leah gathered her sacks and started back down the hill. She had no idea what the time was but figured it was probably late in the afternoon. With the summer in nearly continual sun, it was always hard to gauge the time.

Leah heard her stomach rumble and was glad to know that she'd left a stew simmering on the stove before heading to her gathering task. She hoped that it would be an appropriate time to set a supper table and enjoy her efforts.

Leah reached her small catalogue house, smiling as she imagined Jayce's reaction when he set eyes on the place for the first time. The house seemed quite out of place in the village. Except for Emma's house, everything else was built partially underground in Inupiat fashion. The Kincaid house was a pleasant enough sight, but it did stick out as a rather strange anomaly on the seacoast. She knew Jayce would like it, but even this would pale in light of seeing his children.

His children. The old thoughts trickled back to haunt her. *Are Wills and Merry truly Jayce's flesh and blood? Why can't I just let this go? Why can't I just be glad for what I have and stop worrying about the past?* She shuddered and pushed the memories aside. There was nothing positive to be gained by remembering those terrible things. There was nothing good to be had in asking questions for which she could not give conclusive answers.

Wills and Merry were Jayce's children. That was all there was to it. Leah would not think of it any other way.

A ruckus on the beach drew her attention even as Leah climbed the steps that led to her home. A sudden chill rushed through her body. She set the sacks down on the step and felt herself inexplicably drawn to the sounds of men fighting.

Reaching the community building, Leah could see that several of the natives were drunk. These were good men—she knew them well, but liquor had clouded their senses. They were angrily raging at each other, and one man was waving a gun. She knew this wouldn't end well; someone would no doubt get hurt. The whalers with their liquor appeared to be nowhere in sight.

"Put down the rifle," John commanded as he stepped toward the man.

"He stole my axe," the man declared.

"He tried to take my wife," a man named Charlie replied. "I'm going to give his axe back—right in his gut."

"I didn't want your ugly woman," the man shouted in Inupiat.

Leah felt someone at her side and turned to find Oopick. They could only stand and watch the situation play out. Some of the other native men joined in commenting on the situation, some taking Charlie's side, others taking the side of the armed man.

"You got to put the rifle down, Daniel," John demanded. "Somebody's gonna get hurt."

Then, as if John's words were prophetic, the rifle went off with a loud cracking sound. Everyone fell silent as Charlie grabbed his stomach and sank to his knees. He looked up, then collapsed on the sand.

Leah put her hand to her mouth. To witness this awful affair, a situation that might never have come about but for the whiskey, was more than she could fathom.

"That's enough. Give me the rifle."

"You're gonna kill me." Daniel's eyes were wild with fear.

John shook his head. "No. I'm gonna take you and hold you until the *Bear* shows up. When those government officials come, then I'll turn you over to them."

Leah shook her head. There was no telling how long it would be before the revenue cutter returned. Charlie's family would return to the village for revenge. This could be counted on.

"I won't go," the man said, leveling the rifle again. Before anyone could do anything the man began backing away. "I won't go."

John approached him, matching each of the man's steps in equal pacing. "Come on, Daniel. You know it's the way."

"I can't. I won't." He backed up another step and stopped. "You go on now, John, or I'll . . . well . . . I'll have to shoot you."

John shook his head. "Don't do it, Daniel. They'll see you dead if you do."

"They'll see me dead anyway."

John reached for the barrel but had no time to push it away before the gun fired. Leah screamed and Oopick went running. The bullet hit John in the stomach. The big man didn't fall immediately; instead, he seemed to contemplate the situation as several men rushed Daniel and wrestled him to the ground. Oopick reached her husband's side just as his body seemed to register what had happened.

Leah was just paces behind Oopick. She'd thought at first that maybe John hadn't been struck, but when he fell to the ground she screamed, "No!"

Oopick knelt beside her husband, pulling at his clothes to see how bad the wound was and exactly where it was located. Leah helped her, forgetting the others around them.

The wound, located just six inches in from John's left side, bled profusely. Leah pulled off her *kuspuk* and pressed the soft cotton cloth against John's abdomen. "We need to get him home," she said, looking up. "Is anybody sober enough to help?" Her tone held great anger.

"We can help," several men announced in unison. They came forward to await instruction.

"We need to be careful with him," Leah commanded. "One of you will need to hold this cloth to the wound while the others carry him. Can you do that?"

The men nodded and Leah stood. Oopick was sobbing uncontrollably, reluctant to leave her husband's side. Kimik, her son, appeared and helped the men lift his father as Leah took hold of Oopick.

"Come on. There will be time for tears later," Leah encouraged. "Right now John needs us both." Oopick looked into Leah's eyes as if trying to comprehend her words.

Leah knew the next few moments would be critical. "Oopick, John needs us to keep him alive. Come along—we have work to do."

Chapter Six

The ice is melted enough," first mate Elmer Warrick declared. "I see no reason for us to sit here and wait for a rescue that might never come."

Jacob shook his head. "It's very risky to consider heading out, not having any idea of where we are."

"We have a good idea that we're close to the Russian Territories," Dr. Ripley replied. "Not only that, but as the crew's physician, I have to interject my opinion on the matter. We all have scurvy in various stages. Our diet is so imbalanced that most of us are dying of malnutrition. Not to mention that the captain has developed trouble with his heart and Bristol is sporting three toes that we're going to have to remove tonight or see him dead in a week."

"We're all dying?" Matt questioned. He cast a quick glance at Jacob, as if to ascertain the doctor's truthfulness.

Ripley shrugged. "If not exactly, then we soon are to be. Our bodies need a balance of vegetables and fruits. Foods that are obviously missing from our diet. Exposure to the elements is another issue entirely."

"But to head out without any idea of where we're going," Jacob began, "is risking death as much, if not more, than staying here."

"I agree with Jacob," Jayce said, looking to each of the men. "We have shelter here and enough food for the time being. I propose a compromise: Rather than just sit here indefinitely, what if we agree to remain here until July tenth? That will still give us plenty of time to head out and risk the open water."

The men considered this for a moment while Jacob posed a question. "Dr. Ripley, since you are concerned about the issues of our health, would this be an acceptable compromise to your way of thinking?"

Ripley rubbed his bearded chin. "That's not much more than a month. I suppose it would be acceptable. Although I will say that every day we wait, we grow weaker from our lack of proper nutrition."

"I agree," Jacob said, nodding. "Captain Latimore is a very sick man, even now. I know Ben and Travis are suffering a great deal as well." Those two hadn't been themselves since developing a bronchial infection two months back. "It's not my desire to keep any of us here a moment longer than needed. You must understand me on this point, if nothing else. I desire to be home as much as anyone here. I won't keep us here any longer than necessary. You have my word on this."

The men met his earnest gaze and one by one nodded in agreement of his words. Jacob knew their longing for home was strong—as was his own. He wanted nothing more than to wake up in his own bed and be among friends and family. The crew needed to see that he was just as connected to this goal as they were.

"Very well. We shall stay here until July tenth. If rescue hasn't come by that time," Jacob announced, "we will set out on our own."

He walked away from the group, feeling a mixed sense of frustration and relief. He was glad that Jayce had suggested the compromise but worried about what would happen if no one found them by the tenth of July.

"I hope you didn't mind my suggestion back there." Jayce came alongside Jacob and matched his stride. "I wasn't trying to usurp your authority."

"I'm glad you thought of it, Jayce. Someone had to come up with something to calm them down." Jacob stopped and looked back at the waters of the Bering. There was still ice here and there. A great many floes dotted the otherwise tranquil waters.

"They just don't know what they're asking for. I've been out there in an umiak when the village was hunting whale. It isn't easy even when you have healthy, experienced men who know the lay of the land and the currents. These are men whose bodies have been compromised by the elements and lack of proper food. They are weak, and their minds are not as clear as they need to be." Jacob turned back to Jayce. "None of our minds are working as well as they should. I found myself struggling with a column of figures this morning that normally would have been easy to add."

"I know what you're saying is true, but we can't give up hope." Jayce pointed out across the water. "There are a lot of seals with pups out there. The fishing has been decent, and now that we've located the area where the birds are building nests, we can have eggs. All of these things will keep us alive and well fed, even if they don't offer the balance the good doctor wishes us to have."

Jacob shook his head. "My teeth are loose. My gums are spongy."

"Mine too," Jayce admitted. "So we have scurvy. It's to be expected."

"It'll kill us if we don't find better food or someone to rescue us."

Jayce shrugged. "We can't sit around worrying about it. Someday something is going to kill us. If we just dwell on it, we'll only manage to hurry it along. Frankly, I think we've come through Arctic winter in good order. I honestly believe help is on the way. We're going to make it."

"I can only hope and pray that we've gotten through the worst of the weather," Jacob muttered. "I know for sure we can't go through another winter unless we prepare."

"We aren't going to need to go through another winter," Jayce declared. "You agreed to the compromise. If rescue hasn't come by the tenth, then we'll head out."

Jacob tried to imagine making it back to Alaska. "Jayce, do you hear what you're saying? Do you understand the dangers and the near impossibility of such a trip with these sick men?"

Jayce grinned. "But you taught me that we serve a God of impossibilities. Are you suddenly changing your mind?"

Jacob sighed. He felt wearier than he'd ever been in his life. "I don't know what I'm doing. I'm tired, and like I said, I'm not thinking clear. I think heading out will be death, but I can't blame them for wanting to get home."

"We all want to get home, but we need to make sensible plans," Jayce said, matching Jacob's stride. "We can do this, but as you've said over and over, we need to work as a team. If you desert us now, the team will fall apart."

"But what happens if no one comes for us by the tenth?" Jacob looked at Jayce without stopping, then just as quickly turned his attention back on the hill they were climbing. "Those men will expect me to produce a miracle. A miracle I simply do not have."

"Since when have you ever been in the miracle business?" Jayce asked sarcastically. "You aren't God, Jacob. Stop trying to be Him."

This caused Jacob to pause. He felt his anger rise as his hands automatically balled into fists. He wanted to punch Jayce, but just as quickly he calmed, knowing that Jayce had done nothing wrong. He'd spoken the truth. Jacob squared his shoulders and walked a few more steps to the ridge. "If no one comes, we will load up the boats and head out. But to where? To what? How will we make our way if the storms come? You can't ride out a late-season blizzard in an umiak."

"I don't have all of your answers, but we can pray and trust that God will send us what we need. If not a rescue ship, then surely Latimore can be of help. He's sailed the waters of the Bering before."

"If Latimore survives he might be able to offer some insight, but by his own admission, he has never been in this area. We may be in the Chukchi or even East Siberian Seas. There's no real way for us to know."

At the top of the hill, Jacob sat down on a rocky outcropping. "I keep looking for a sign—something to tell me where we are. Are we on Wrangell Island or Skeleton Island or something else entirely? We found signs of that one camp, but we don't know that it had anything to do with the men of the *Karluk*. I was under the impression that some kind of marker had been left behind."

Jayce eased onto the rock with a bit of a moan. Jacob had forgotten that Jayce had twisted his back just days earlier as they wrestled a seal onto the shore. He seemed to still be quite sore, and that only made Jacob feel more guilty for his rapid ascent to the top of the ridge.

"How's the back?"

"It's better. Truly." Jayce added the latter as Jacob cast him a look of doubt. "I think a nice hot bath would help." He grinned. "Maybe a Turkish bath with steam and eucalyptus branches."

"And a soft bed," Jacob added.

"And Leah to give me backrubs." Jayce picked up a rock and gave it a toss. "I miss her more than anything else. I can't help but wonder what the little ones are doing now."

"They aren't so little is my guess," Jacob countered. "They're a year old. I thought of that the other day. If we've managed to keep proper records, then they've had their first birthday."

"I know. I realized that too," Jayce's voice was filled with longing.

"I've been doing a lot of thinking. When we get back . . . I'm leaving Alaska."

"What?" Jayce shook his head. "What are you talking about? You told me Alaska was in your blood—that you'd never leave."

"Helaina Beecham's in my blood too," he answered softly. He had her face emblazoned on his memory. "She's all I think about—she's all I really care about."

"But leave Alaska?"

Jacob leaned his arms against his knees. "She said Alaska was too hard for her. That life there was too isolated. How could I go seeking her as a wife, knowing that she'd only be miserable there?"

"But to give up your life for the love of a woman—that's kind of dangerous. You know it could spell trouble in the years to come. When things are hard, you'll blame her. You might even end up pining away for what might have been and come to resent her for taking you from all that you knew."

"I could never feel that way about her. Could you feel that way about Leah?"

Jayce sighed. "That's a bad question to ask me—or maybe I should say a good question. I'm the one who avoided a relationship with her not only because of her age, but because I figured she'd leave Alaska and I didn't want to. Even the summer before we married she was talking of going to Seattle to hunt for a husband. That put me at odds again. Would she really leave Alaska? Would she ever come back? I knew I would never have planned to be at odds with her if we married and she suddenly wanted to leave the Territory. Neither would you set out to feel that way toward Helaina, but it could come later in life. You have to be realistic about this and not just think about it with stars in your eyes and your heart all aflutter. You're talking about a life change that you would never consider for any other reason."

"But I love her," Jacob said softly, and in his heart he could only think of his need—of the emptiness without her in his life. "I was so happy when she came to believe in Jesus. Her anger and misery over the past was like a burden that weighed her down. She blamed herself for her family dying—for her husband's death. She carried that inside and it nearly killed her. She wanted only to be free, but she honestly believed it was her punishment—her grief to bear for eternity."

"Sometimes we torture ourselves with things like that," Jayce agreed. He shifted ever so slowly, and Jacob worried that perhaps his friend was in more pain that he'd let on. "Sometimes we choose to take on the responsibility of something when God never expects or wants us to."

"You mean like my leaving Alaska for Helaina?"

Jayce shrugged. "I mean only that you should be certain that it's the Lord's leading and not your loneliness. Once you make a decision, you will have a price to pay no matter what."

"I have prayed about it. I continue to pray. I've told God that if I get out of this alive, I'll do whatever I can to win her over."

"You told God, huh?" Jayce grinned. "What happened to asking Him what He wanted for your life? You used to tell me that was the most important thing for a man to do."

Jacob blew out a loud breath. "I know, and I'm not saying that I haven't *asked*. It's just that . . . well . . . the Bible also talks in Proverbs about making your plans and trusting God to direct you. I have to believe that the plans I'm making are His direction. They seem right. They feel right."

"I'm not saying they aren't right," Jayce said, stretching to rub the small of his back. "I'm just cautioning you. Take it slow and really think things through. Otherwise you may be sorry. Sorry in a way that can't be fixed in a day or two."

Jacob thought a great deal about Jayce's words long after they'd returned to camp. He knew his friend was only concerned with his well-being. He didn't want to keep Jacob in Alaska for his own purposes or desires. He cared about Jacob like a brother and wanted him to make the right decision.

"But what is the right decision?" he murmured, glad to be alone in the shelter. He yawned and leaned back onto his pallet. With the worst of winter weather having eased, they had moved camp and set up new dwellings. The room around him had only recently been created using some of the boxes and tent canvas that they'd brought with them from the *Regina*. The doctor had thought this good for the health of everyone. Jacob had thought it good to keep them occupied.

Now he wrestled with what to do and how to do it. Jayce had offered wise counsel. Jacob felt that a lack of good food and decent living accommodations had left him addlepated at times. Could he even make the right decision?

The decision had to include Helaina, he told himself. If she wasn't a part of the matter—then his life wouldn't be the same.

But why would you want her if the Lord doesn't also want her for you?

The thought came unbidden, and no matter how hard Jacob tried, it wouldn't leave his mind. What if Helaina wasn't the right woman for him? Would he really want to impose her with a life of misery if he weren't the man for her?

Jacob fell asleep with these troubled thoughts. He pulled a seal fur around his body and over his head to block out the light. Somehow—some way—he knew God would direct his steps. He only hoped the path led him back to Helaina.

Jayce prayed for Jacob long into the night. Except there was no night. Not these days. The light in the sky at one in the morning might as well have been one in the afternoon. Jayce had been unable to sleep and had decided a short walk might help. But it hadn't.

"Couldn't sleep?"

Jayce looked up to find Keith Yackey. As was often the case, a Bible was in his hands. One of the rifles hung casually over his shoulder. It appeared to be his time at watch.

"I needed to pray. For a friend."

Keith nodded. "I'd love to join you. I can guard camp, watch for ships, and pray all at the same time. God will still listen even if I don't close my eyes."

Jayce chuckled. "I can be sure of that. I've prayed a great deal while pacing or driving dogs. I didn't close my eyes then either."

"I've been memorizing some Scripture," Keith told him. "I figured to go back to civilization with a big portion of the Bible memorized."

"And is it working?" Jayce asked.

"I've got most of the New Testament done. I'm working on Isaiah now."

"That's impressive." Jayce glanced back at the shelter. "I have a friend who has a difficult decision to make. A life-changing decision. He trusts God, but this is a matter of the heart."

"Which always complicates matters," Keith added.

"Have you ever been in love?"

Keith laughed. "I still am. I have a wonderful wife and three beautiful children."

"You must miss them very much. I know I miss my wife and the twins."

"I knew you had twins. I heard Jacob talk about them. You're married to his sister, right?"

Keith's knowledge of his situation only served to make Jayce feel worse about not having gotten to know the man better. "Yes. Leah is Jacob's sister. She's an amazing woman."

"She'd have to be to live in Alaska."

"Where is your family?"

"California."

Jayce smiled. "Where it's always nice and warm."

"Well, most of the time," Keith admitted. "We have our storms and our problems, but nothing like this."

"Will your wife despair over what's happened?" Jayce asked cautiously. "Will she believe you to be lost—dead?" He forced the final word.

"Janessa? Never. She's not one to give up easily. That's one of the things I love about her. She has great faith and hope." Keith opened his Bible and started to say something more but was quickly hushed.

"You dirty rotten . . ." The sound of men fighting spilled into the peaceful moments Jayce had been enjoying with Keith.

Both men turned to look toward one of the other shelters. Bristol and Elmer were arguing about something. Then without warning Elmer raised a pistol and fired it over Bristol's head. Things had taken a deadly turn.

"What's going on?" Jacob asked as he came outside.

"I don't know," Jayce answered. Keith was already heading off to see what was going on. "It just started. Elmer fired the pistol at Bristol, but just over his head."

"I heard it. I thought maybe the war had come to us."

Another shot sounded. Jayce narrowed his eyes as Jacob checked his own revolver to make sure it was loaded. "Come on. We'd better see what this is all about."

Chapter Seven

Elmer! Bristol! What's the problem?" Jacob called as he approached. He didn't want to startle the men and have them turn on him, so he slowed his pace and tried again. "Elmer, put down the gun and tell me what's wrong."

"He said I was stealing. Called me a thief."

"You are a thief!" Bristol countered. He could barely stand due to his bad foot. "I saw you get into the food locker. You were taking what didn't belong to you."

"Food belongs to all of us. I went out on the last hunt and brought down the biggest seal. That ought to count for something."

"There's no call for using a weapon against a man. Not here. We're too few in number, and we need every man just to survive." Jacob kept a tight grip on his revolver. "Put the gun down, Elmer, and let's talk about this like civilized men."

"This ain't a civilized place," Elmer replied. "Neither is he a civilized man. I don't see how losing my weapon will help the matter."

The other men had gathered by this time. Dr. Ripley rubbed his eyes. "I thought we were under attack. Are you men absolutely certain you wish to give me more work to do—under the circumstance?" He turned to Elmer. "Good grief, man. Have you actually lost your senses?"

"He accused me of stealing, and I ain't lost my senses."

Ripley shook his head. "Well, at least have the decency to shoot off those three bad toes if you have to shoot him at all. That way maybe I won't have to perform two surgeries." Bristol frowned, looking momentarily confused, but Elmer merely steadied his aim.

"Just put the gun down and we can talk about what happened," Jacob interjected.

"What happened," Bristol said in a heated manner, "is that he thought we were all asleep and went to help himself to an extra portion of food. He's a thief."

"Am not. I was just hungry!"

"Enough!"

Everyone turned to find Captain Latimore struggling to make his way to the two men. He pushed past Jacob and Keith and went directly to Elmer. "Give me that weapon."

"Uhh . . . Captain, I . . ."

"Hand it over now." Latimore stared at him hard. "We will discuss this in my quarters, but we will not be armed to do so."

To Jacob's surprise, Elmer handed the pistol over. Latimore turned to Bristol. "Come with me now." The younger man nodded, looking almost sheepish. He limped toward the captain.

Latimore headed back to his tent with the two men following behind. Jacob exchanged a glance with the captain as he passed. It was evident the episode had cost him every bit of strength. However, there was a look to his countenance that suggested he had regained the will not only to live but to take back his command.

After the men had disappeared, Jacob turned to Jayce. "It's good to see Latimore take the matter in hand."

"Yes. It's obvious the men have needed him."

Keith nodded. "He's a good man. A fine captain. I was sorry to see him so grief stricken, but perhaps now things will be righted." He walked away to join the other crew members.

Jayce turned to Jacob. "He's right, you know. If Latimore is able to rally his men, we may see positive spirits restored."

"I hope you're right." Jacob yawned. "I suppose for now we should head back to bed. We've had enough excitement for one night." He watched Keith pass the rifle to Travis. "They're good men—the demands of survival have been too much for them."

"God will see them through. Just as He'll see us through, Jacob. You know it's true. Rest in it."

Eight hours later, Jacob sat across from Latimore. The captain looked better than Jacob had seen him since the *Regina* went down.

"The problem is that the men do not have enough to keep themselves busy with. Do you have suggestions, Jacob?"

"I do, but you may be no happier to hear about it than they will be."

Latimore eased back against a pile of furs. "You'll have to excuse me; I still have great weakness."

"Please feel free to rest. We can discuss this another time."

"No. I think we should talk now. If Elmer were kept busy, I don't think he would be so fearful about starvation. You see, as a boy he was quite impoverished. He went hungry most of the time. It's haunted him into his adult years. He's not really a bad person, but his fears are causing him to make bad choices."

"I can understand that, but the men are angry about it. They feel he's cheated them of food that should rightfully be shared. Starvation is something we all fear."

"I am not making excuses for Warrick, merely pointing out the truth of the matter. I have confined the man to my presence when he's not busy with required duties. Which brings me back to that situation. My men are used to hard work. They need to have a purpose."

"We need to lay up food," Jacob said. "Between you and me, there is always the possibility that help will not come. A compromise was struck that we would leave the island on July tenth if rescue has not reached us. Still, whether we wait it out here on the island or take the umiaks and try to make our way back to Alaska, we will need food. The men don't seem to understand this or respect it. Well, perhaps I should say a few of the men do not see the merit. Some are quite cooperative."

"I will speak to them. Hunting and butchering are not their best skills, but they must do this for the sake of their own survival. Perhaps, too, if they see this as a goal toward leaving the island, they will be encouraged to help."

Jacob could see the wisdom in the captain's words. "We could also let them know that rescue may come in the form of the Russians or Inupiats. They will be much easier to deal with if we have something to barter in return—such as dried meat."

"That is a good point. I will mention it as well."

Jacob looked hesitantly over his shoulder before leaning toward the captain. "I cannot in good conscience say that I wholeheartedly agree with the plan to leave the island on our own if help fails to reach us. I did agree to the compromise, but it was very much against my better judgment."

Latimore considered this for a moment. "I know I've been a burden to you, Jacob, but you've always proven yourself to be a man of sound reasoning. I trust you to know best in matters of this Arctic survival. That said, how can we hope to exist another year in this environment? The winter has been cruel."

"You're a man of the sea," Jacob interjected. "You know the dangers out there in a large ship like the *Regina*. Imagine trying to survive a storm in one of the skin boats. We would perish for certain. The men are weak—most are suffering more than one affliction. Trying to navigate our way home would be difficult at best and deadly at worst."

"What would you want from me in the matter?"

Jacob thought for a moment. "I suppose I would like for you to override the decision regarding the compromise. You weren't there to put in your vote and you are the captain of this expedition. Now that you are recovering, the men will again look to you for decisions. You could explain that you've been apprised of the matter, but believe it lacks . . . well . . . sound reasoning, I suppose."

Latimore nodded and rubbed his bearded chin. The white, which had once dotted his hair and beard, now appeared quite prominent. "Let me think on the matter. It could be that it will resolve itself. If the time grows near and there is no sign of rescue, I will speak to the men."

"I hope so." Jacob knew he didn't sound entirely convinced.

Latimore looked at him for a moment, then cleared his throat. "About the rescue, Jacob."

"What of it?"

"Do you believe it will come?"

Jacob thought back to the time years earlier when the *Karluk* had disappeared. Everyone presumed they were lost forever. No one expected the men to actually make land and survive the winter. There were other ships that had gone missing as well. Ships that had never turned up. But then he thought of Leah. Leah would never let them go without a fight. She would believe the very best until proof told her otherwise.

"I believe there are people looking for us even now," Jacob admitted, wanting to be optimistic. "My sister is a determined woman. She will use whatever means available to seek our rescue. She won't give up—no matter how bleak it might seem."

"But you are concerned. I see it in your eyes and hear it in your speech."

"We don't know where we are. The searchers don't know either. They will have to cover a large territory in a short amount of time. The ice will freeze this area over in a matter of months—it might be even better gauged in weeks. Arctic summer forever holds a whisper of winter."

"I can imagine that to be true. Still, you speak greatly of the powerful effects of prayer. I presume you have been praying about our rescue as fervently as you prayed for my recovery." He smiled at Jacob's raised brow. "I heard you pray over me when I was in a barely conscious state. God has surely heard those prayers—why not the prayers for rescue?"

Jacob felt rightfully taken to task. "You are right. I have been rather faithless. It just seems the closer the time comes to what might be our salvation, the more despair I feel."

Latimore nodded knowingly. "It's rather like when I take to sea. If we pass far from land and spend many weeks isolated from our loved ones, I sometimes feel a sense of anticipation—even despair. There is always the lingering question of whether or not we'll make it back again. I suppose my despair has been greater on this trip than any other."

"But you had other circumstances to consider as well. Losing your wife, leaving your home and child—those are strong influences for any man."

Latimore shifted and crossed his arms against his chest. "I still find it difficult to imagine my life without Regina."

There was such a sorrow in his voice that Jacob thought he ought to change their focus of conversation. He'd opened his mouth to speak when Latimore interrupted. "Have you ever been in love?"

Jacob felt a dagger of pain pierce his heart. "Yes. I am in love."

Latimore smiled. "But you haven't yet wed?"

"No, the timing wasn't right." Jacob shook his head. "No, it was more that the place wasn't right. She hated Alaska."

"Hate is a powerful thing, but so too is love." The captain sighed. "Regina hated my being a sea captain. She said it took me away from her too often. That's why she sometimes traveled with me. She was miserable on my ship but happy to be in my company."

Jacob realized they shared more in common than either had suspected. He dared to ask, "Do you regret not having given up the sea for her?"

Latimore's eyes narrowed. "I regret that she died. I regret that she could not safely give birth to the baby she so loved. I regret that we didn't have more time. So I suppose in many ways, I regret not having given up the sea."

"Could you have been a good husband—a happy man—if you'd given up the life you loved for her?"

Latimore chuckled. "So long as she was in my life, I would have found a way to be happy. Sometimes love requires sacrifice. Often we're too blind to see that we can lose something seemingly important in order to gain something infinitely more valuable."

" 'He that findeth his life shall lose it: and he that loseth his life for my sake shall find it,' " Jacob quoted.

"What's that?" Latimore leaned up as if the conversation had suddenly become quite important.

"It's a verse from the book of Matthew. The whole chapter is full of so many good things. Jesus is sending out His disciples and He tells them what to do and not do. He instructs them to be on their guard. He warns them of persecution when people hear the Gospel preached. He tells them not to be afraid of those who can only kill the body, but rather to fear God, who can destroy both body and soul. It also shows that Jesus knew His ministry would divide people."

"How so?"

"In the passage I was quoting, Jesus also says that if you love your father or mother, son or daughter more than Him, you aren't worthy of Him. He wants us first and foremost. It isn't that we can't have the other people in our lives, but we cannot put them first."

"As I did with Regina," Latimore said regretfully. "Perhaps that is why He took her. He is a jealous God, is He not?"

Jacob reached out and put his hand atop Latimore's. "I do not believe God is as cruel as that. He is a just and loving God also. People die, Captain. They are born and they die, and that is how it is in this fallen world of ours. I do not believe God would sneak in and steal your Regina away because of your love for her. But I do know that God wants our loyalty, our faithfulness.

He wants us to seek Him above all others—first . . . always." The words comforted Jacob even though he had hoped to comfort Latimore.

He continued. "Sometimes we are called to lose the things we hold most dear. Obedience is sometimes painful."

Latimore nodded. "Indeed. It is no different than the child who must choose between following his own path or that of his father's instruction. One path may seem easier, quicker—but experience might tell him that the more difficult path will be better, safer, more fulfilling."

Jacob took the words deep into his heart. What path was God sending him on where Helaina was concerned?

"It seems you are contemplating weighty matters," Latimore said before falling back against the cushion of furs. "Perhaps too weighty for me to impart any wisdom that would be of use."

"You've already helped me more than you realize," Jacob replied. "I'm glad to have you back. I'll pray for your continued recovery. The world needs more men like you."

"Perhaps not so much the world," Latimore replied, closing his eyes, "as one little boy."

Chapter Eight

John hovered near death for days. Leah and Oopick worked together to help his body mend, but he'd lost a lot of blood.

Fever and infection had been their biggest concern, and both had come with a vengeance. Leah knew their herbal remedies were good ones and that her own training was useful, but still she wished they had a doctor and a hospital.

"If John were stronger, I'd suggest having Kimik take him to Nome," Leah said, looking up to meet Oopick's and Kimik's fretful gaze. "But the trip would kill him. I feel certain of it."

"I think we should get the shaman," Kimik declared. His defiance toward God had been building since the shooting. "My father deserves to have the care he's always known."

"Kimik," his mother began, "you know your father no longer believes the old ways. I cannot go against his wishes, even if he cannot speak them now."

"Your father believes in God's ability to help him," Leah offered. "God would not want you to yield to superstition. Put your faith in God, Kimik."

"God didn't keep my father from getting shot."

"Neither did God shoot your father," Leah countered. "Whiskey caused another man to do that. If you want to do something positive for your father and this village, then convince the men to keep whiskey out. It's not supposed to be here—so why not make a stand to enforce the law?"

"She's right, my son." Oopick put her hand on Kimik's shoulder. "Your father would not want you to lose faith in God. He believes that God is powerful. He believes God loves us all."

"Letting him get shot isn't very loving. Why would God let this happen? Why would He not protect someone who loves Him?" Kimik sounded like a frightened boy instead of a grown man.

Leah felt sorry for her friend, knowing how hard it was to keep faith in the face of adversity. Hadn't she asked these same questions regarding Jacob and Jayce's disappearance?

"Kimik, who are we to question God? He does not think like we think. Your grandmother would tell you to clear the mud out of your ears and listen to what God tells you. He will not forget you. He has not forgotten your father."

Leah saw tears come to Kimik's eyes, and she longed to comfort him.

"I hate this," Kimik finally said. Anguish was replaced with anger. "God is not fair. He is not merciful. If He were, my father would not be dying." He stormed from Leah's house.

"I am sorry for Kimik's words," Oopick said. She reached for a rag and began to wipe her husband's brow. "He felt such sorrow over Ayoona's passing. I think he's afraid that same sorrow will come if his father passes."

Leah mixed a bowl of herbs that she would use as a cleanser for the wound. "I think it's fear that overwhelms him right now. Fear often makes me angry." She pulled back the poultice they'd put on a few hours earlier and surveyed the wound. "It looks better." And it did. Much of the inflammation was gone, and the swelling had lessened. "Let's clean and dress this side, then see how it looks on the back side."

The bullet had gone completely through John's abdomen. Leah could only pray that it hadn't caused problems with his internal organs, for there was no possible way she could perform the surgery necessary to heal that kind of injury.

Once the wound was redressed, Leah looked at the clock. "I'm going to get some rest. You should too." Earlier she'd set up a small bed for Oopick right alongside John. "I also want to see the children."

Oopick nodded. "I will rest. I will call for you if something happens. You have been a good friend to John—to me."

Leah smiled and went to embrace the older woman. "I love you both so much. You are like family to me. I couldn't bear to lose either one of you."

Oopick's brown-black eyes swelled with tears. "You are my family too."

Leah wiped her eyes and stretched as she left the dark quiet of the room she'd given to Oopick and John. Helaina was there to greet her, as were the twins.

"Ah, there's Mama," Helaina said, pointing Wills in the right direction.

Merry had already spotted her mother and came running. Wills joined her just in case there was something of interest. Leah dropped to her knees and embraced them both.

"How is he? I saw Kimik storm out and feared the worst."

Leah met Helaina's concerned gaze. "John's actually doing better—at least in my estimation. The wound seems less infected. The fever is nearly gone. I see those things as positive signs of healing."

"Has he regained consciousness?"

"Only for very brief moments. Oopick wanted to keep him sedated as much as possible so that the wound would heal. We're worried about how much damage that bullet did internally. There's a possibility it managed to miss the most vital spots, but on the other hand, it could have injured a great deal and we'll never know it until it is too late."

"I'm sorry. I know this must be very frustrating to you." Helaina began to pick up around the room.

"You have been a great help to me," Leah said. Merry toddled off to play with her doll, and Wills seemed oblivious to everything but the new puppy Leah had allowed them to have. She thought it would be wise for the twins to have a guardian—especially for those times she couldn't be everywhere at once. Champion—so named because she hoped he would take that role on behalf of the twins—was nearly the same size as Wills. Champ seemed delighted to be the boy's playmate; the two were already inseparable. Merry was afraid of the dog at first, but even she was warming to their new companion.

"As I bathed them last night, I thought about how it would be to have my own children. I imagined a home of my own and . . ." Helaina fell silent and turned away to pick up a towel that had somehow fallen to the ground.

"That day will come, Helaina. I'm sure of it. You'll have a family all your own."

"If that's what God has for me." Helaina turned and shook her head. "But what if it's not? What if Jacob—"

"Don't say it," Leah said, holding up her hand. "I couldn't bear to hear it right now."

Helaina gave her an odd look. "I wasn't going to say what you think. I was merely suggesting that it's possible Jacob will return and have no feelings for me."

Leah let out a sigh of relief. "I'm sorry. I'm just so tired of the unknown. So many people asked me over the winter and now into the summer, 'What will you do if they don't come back? What will you do if they're found dead?' I just couldn't stand the thought of hearing it again."

Helaina came and put her arm around Leah. "I know, but that's one question I will not ask. They are coming home. I know they will."

"I just can't stand the waiting. And now the only person who might have taken me to them is lying wounded in my spare room. It's just more than I can bear." Leah felt tears slide down her cheeks. "I feel as bad as Kimik. He was questioning why God would let this happen to his father, and I feel no different. I know God must be so disappointed in me. Where's my faith? Where's the peace that passeth understanding?"

"Leah, we all have our times of doubting and discouragement."

Leah pulled away. "But I know better. God has proven himself to me over and over. It seems I never learn. Why can't I just understand and accept that whatever happens, happens. That He has been in control all along and that I need not fear the future."

Helaina drew a deep breath and sighed. "I keep reminding myself the same thing. But, Leah, even Jesus, knowing what His purpose was in coming to earth, asked to be let out of it."

Leah thought about that for a moment. "That's true. He even knew what the outcome would be—and still He died for me."

"And rose again," Helaina replied. "I know you're discouraged, Leah. I am too. I know it may seem I'm being strong and accepting, but it's been so hard. I believe they'll come home safe and sound. I don't know why I believe it, but I've never been more confident of anything. What I don't know is what Jacob's heart will feel for me once he gets here."

"I know he loves you," Leah offered.

"Maybe. But adversity sometimes changes people."

Wills ploughed into Leah's legs and laughed as though it were a special game. Champ was right at his side. She looked at her son and saw the startling reflection of his father's face staring back up at her. "That's what I'm afraid of," she whispered. She lifted Wills into her arms, and for once he didn't try to flee. Instead he took hold of her face, almost as though demanding she see him for who he was. Champ whined for a moment, then went to check on Merry.

"I sometimes get so afraid that they aren't his children. I try not to think that way, and most days I'm all right. But I keep wondering what if he's decided that they aren't his? What if all this time he's been pondering the situation and has decided that the twins are from Chase?"

"You can't dwell on that. You know this. We've talked about it over and over. Leah, it doesn't matter. They're your children first and foremost. Your flesh and blood. You cannot worry about anything more. Jayce loves you and he loves the twins. He won't deny them—not even after this long separation."

Leah gently touched Wills' hair. "But he hasn't been here to watch them grow—to love them and know them. He hasn't endured their tearful nights or sicknesses, nor enjoyed their sweetness." Wills let go of her face and snuggled against her in uncharacteristic fashion. He seemed to sense her need for comfort.

"You worry about whether or not Jacob will love you, but I have the same worries," Leah admitted. "What Jayce has endured may have changed him. I have to accept that possibility."

"That's nonsense. Has it changed your heart toward him?" Helaina asked, putting her hands on her hips like a scolding mother. She cocked her head to one side. "Leah Kincaid, you know better. This is just the devil trying to get the better of you."

"I suppose you're right. I'm so tired right now it makes no sense to even try to have a proper conversation." She looked up and smiled. "I'm sorry to be so gloomy. Is there anything to eat? I need to sleep, but I also need food. I feel as though I haven't eaten in weeks."

Helaina laughed. "I have a nice caribou steak for you. With that are some fried potatoes."

"Potatoes?" Leah's mouth watered. They hadn't seen potatoes in so long.

"Whiskey wasn't the only thing the whaler brought us. I secured these for us. The natives might not miss such things, but I do on occasion."

Leah ate while Helaina prepared her tea. Once the cup was in front of her, Leah knew she wouldn't last much longer. She took a long drink of the warm liquid. "Thank you for all of this. I suppose I should go rest now."

"You do that. I'll save this for you," Helaina said, picking up Leah's plate. "Your appetite will be stronger once you get some sleep."

Leah nodded and got to her feet. "Call me if anything happens with John."

"You know I will."

Helaina watched Leah head off to rest. She admired Leah like no other woman. She could easily remember their first encounter and Leah's kindness. Later, however, Leah had wanted nothing to do with her. She'd resented Helaina's interest in her brother and blamed Helaina for all of them having to risk their lives in the wilds.

Helaina felt they were only right to blame her. She had known their forgiveness and God's, but she wasn't sure she'd fully accepted that release. So much had changed in her life these past years, and now the one question that continued to haunt her was the one thing she couldn't answer. Not until Jacob came home.

"Either he loves me or he doesn't," she told herself. "If he loves me, then all is well. And if he doesn't . . ." She felt a wave of despair wash over her. "If he doesn't . . . then . . ." She thought of her words to Leah and smiled. She had to take such negative thoughts captive. "If he doesn't love me still, then I shall make him fall in love with me all over again."

Chapter Nine

July brought beautiful sunny days and a healing in John that gave new hope to Leah. With John on the mend, Oopick insisted they move out of Leah's home. Kimik set up a tent at the beach for them. He seemed less angry with God, but Leah worried that a barrier remained between him and the God of his father. Kimik's wife, Qavlunaq, helped Oopick, freeing

Leah to focus her attention on her family. Unfortunately, that caused her to feel an overwhelming sense of grief as the days continued to pass without word from Jayce or Jacob.

July also brought a letter from Karen and Adrik. They were coming with their children to be with Leah for as long as needed. They had been so upset to learn of the *Regina*'s disappearance the year before. Adrik, Karen wrote in her letter, had nearly loaded up a sled and team to reach Leah across the interior.

" 'He still thinks himself a young man,' " Leah read aloud from the letter. " 'Of course, our rather rowdy boys are good at reminding him he is not.' " She grinned. "I know how that goes. Wills and Merry leave me exhausted most days."

Helaina motioned to the letter. "Does it say when they intend to leave or arrive?"

Leah read on. "She says they'll leave at the end of June. That means they should be here soon. No telling what kind of storms or fogs might have slowed them down, but even so, it's already the eighth."

Helaina got to her feet. "I'll pack my things and move back to the old place. The flooding isn't that bad, and I could always use one of the tents. That way you'll have the extra room for them."

"I hate to have you go. We can surely just fit everyone in."

"No, I think it's better. I go there to take care of the dogs anyway. Besides, I like it there."

Leah laughed. "Good thing, too, since you may call it home for a good long while."

Helaina paused at the door. "I'd love nothing more."

The salmon run proved to be abundant. Leah spent her free time catching as many salmon as possible and drying them for winter. Each evening they enjoyed fresh salmon for supper and even managed to have a few early bog blueberries.

Leah kept as busy as possible, knowing that this would help the time to pass more quickly. She read the Bible every day, washed and mended, played with her children, and helped with the dogs. She hunted for eggs and berries and caught salmon to provide for their needs, and she managed to work with Helaina to see the store had the supplies necessary for winter.

There was a great deal to do, but while this occupied her hands, Leah had to force her mind to be otherwise engaged. It was so easy to dwell on what she didn't have instead of focusing on what the Lord had given.

Karen and Adrik arrived four days after their letter. With their baggage and crates sitting on the beach, Leah offered them a quick tour of the village on her way home.

"It's a very small village, as you can see for yourself, but the people are very efficient. Some of the people have moved off to Teller or around Nome, but those who have stayed are just like family."

Wills seemed in awe of Karen and Adrik's boys. He didn't run ahead in his characteristic manner but rather kept pace with the older boys, laughing and babbling as if he were giving the tour in his own way.

Leah looked at Karen's children and shook her head. "I can't believe how you've grown. Why, you're nearly grown men."

"I'll be thirteen on August eighth," Oliver declared proudly.

Christopher frowned. "My birthday doesn't come 'til December."

Leah laughed. "We'll have to celebrate enough for both of you. I doubt you'll be here on your birthday, so maybe we can pick a day and celebrate ahead of time."

Christopher perked up and looked to his dad. "Could we?"

Adrik seemed to consider the matter seriously for a moment. "Well, I don't know."

"Please, Papa. Please!"

Adrik finally couldn't keep the stern look in place. Laughing, he answered, "I don't see any reason why not. I'm always game for a party."

Merry seemed quite happy in Karen's arms. "She's so beautiful. Wills too. You must be so proud of them."

Leah nodded. "They are truly a blessing."

"A blessing out of sorrow," Karen murmured. "How like God to give such a special healing."

Leah considered Karen's words. She was still haunted by the question of their parentage and whether or not Jayce would love them, but she often forgot how much they had helped her to focus on the future. Of course, they were also bittersweet reminders of the past.

"I can't believe how big they are. I wish I could have seen them sooner."

They came to stop in front of her home. "This is it," Leah said.

"This is quite the house, Leah. You say you ordered it from a catalogue?" Adrik asked.

"Yes. All the parts and pieces came on a ship. It was quite an ordeal putting it together." She leaned toward the man. "We had an amazing number of pieces left over and have no idea where they go."

Adrik let out a powerful guffaw. "Well, it seems to be holding up well enough. I especially like the way you've built it up on pilings."

"Jayce learned about it from some men who had experience with houses in Boston, of all places. Apparently they've reclaimed some of the land closest to the ocean, and to build on it, they've put the houses on pilings. It's more complicated than that, but it caused Jayce to start thinking, and this is what he planned."

"But he wasn't here to build it?" Karen questioned.

"No, but he had left drawings. John and some of the others worked together and figured it all out. Anyone who says the native people are ignorant can't possibly have spent any time with them."

"I certainly agree with that." Adrik had not only spent a good deal of his life around the Tlingit people of southeast Alaska, he was part Tlingit.

"The house has been harder to keep warm, of course," Leah continued. "The people build into the ground around here for a reason. When the winds come up, we get a good chill. I think we'll have to insulate better, but I like not living underground. It was the one thing I could never quite get used to. I always felt buried alive."

"When will the villagers come back?" Karen asked. She put Merry down to play with the others.

"I've heard that the hunting has been good. Some have come back to set up drying racks and such. Others will wait until August. The berries around here look like they'll be abundant, so many will want to be sure and get in on that. The village people are so good about helping each other. Like with us—Helaina and I can't very well hunt seal for ourselves, and that is a staple of our diet out here, as well as a mainstay for clothing, oil, and such. John and his family have always been good to supply us with our share. Same with the whaling. The men will bring me my portion. They know they can count on me to trade store goods that the ships have brought me. We have a good system here."

"It definitely seems that way. Nevertheless, the boys and I will do our best to help out while we're here," Adrik said, looking around.

"How long can you stay?"

"As long as you need us," Karen said softly. "If things . . . well, if the worst should happen . . ." Her voice trailed off. She lifted her eyes to meet Leah's gaze. "You always have a home with us. You know that, don't you?"

Leah nodded and offered a weak smile. "I know that." She wanted to maintain her composure, but just having family with her once again made Leah feel weepy.

"Where are your trees?" Christopher asked.

Leah immediately turned her attention to the boy. "They all blew away. At least that's the story I've heard the natives tell. The winds from the sea blew so hard that they blew all the trees to the east."

The boy shook his head and looked at the open landscape with disapproval. "It doesn't look very pretty this way. I'd miss not having trees."

Leah surveyed the treeless landscape. "I do miss them from time to time. I remember living with you in Ketchikan and the tall firs and pines. Oh, the aroma was heavenly. I'll never forget the long walks in the forest. I always felt so protected there."

Wills and Champ wandered over. "Eat, Mama," Wills said, pulling on Leah's skirt.

Leah nodded. "I would imagine everyone is starved. Helaina has been cooking for us, and lunch is likely ready. Why don't we go inside?"

Christopher helped carry Merry, while Leah took Wills by the hand. Champ seemed excited and happy just to be included and bobbed along at Leah's heels. Inside, the delicious aroma of salmon and vegetables filled the air.

"Oh, I nearly forgot," Karen said as they gathered around the table. "We brought several crates for you."

"For me?" Leah's surprise was evident. "You certainly didn't need to do that."

"We wanted to. We didn't want to just show up empty-handed, but we also had gifts we wanted to bring just for the fun of it—including some new books for you."

"Books? How wonderful." Leah had seen very little in the way of new reading materials since the twins were born. Not that they would be very fond of letting her read. Leah struggled just to find quiet moments when she could read her Bible.

"The boys and I will go down after lunch and bring them up," Adrik said, rubbing Oliver's head in a good-natured manner. "You should just see how strong these boys of mine are. They can be good help."

"I'm sure." Leah helped Helaina finish setting the food on the table.

"I've already eaten," Helaina announced. "I'm going to head over to the store and tidy up."

Leah looked at her oddly. "No, stay with us. You're practically family."

Helaina shook her head, and Leah noted the sorrow in her eyes as she whispered, "Practically isn't good enough." She hurried from the room before anyone else could question her.

"What was that all about?" Karen asked as Leah took her seat between the twins.

"She's in love with Jacob. She gave up everything and came back here, hoping that he would return that love—which I'm confident he'll do. However, she's feeling quite uncomfortable right now. She knows you will remember her past and what she did to Jayce and the trouble she caused."

Karen helped mash some vegetables for Merry while Leah did the same for Wills. "But that's all in the past. Surely Helaina knows we won't hold the past against her. Not when she's sought forgiveness."

"Eat. Eat," Wills declared.

"I think she's reminded of the shame," Leah said, handing Wills a cracker to still his ranting.

"Maybe we should bless the meal," Adrik said, joining hands with his sons. Leah and Karen did likewise with the twins. Adrik prayed thanksgiving for the food, for their safe journey, and then asked God's hand to be on the missing men of the *Regina*.

"Amen," they murmured in unison after Adrik ended his prayer.

Before Leah could say anything, he picked up their conversation as though it had never been interrupted. "We all have things in our past that we're ashamed of. Helaina is no different. I'll talk to her after we've eaten. Maybe she just needs to know we don't hold her a grudge."

"Oh, these fabrics are wonderful!" Leah held up a bolt of blue flannel. "This will make nice warm shirts."

"I thought the same when I saw it," Karen replied. "And look at this. Sturdy canvas. You could make all sorts of things with this."

Leah noted the dark-colored cloth. "To be certain."

"I brought you some of my preserves and jellies," Karen said, reaching into one of the other crates. She pulled some straw packing out and with it came a jar of dark liquid. "I even made some syrup for flapjacks."

"I still have the sourdough starter you gave me," Leah said proudly. "It's amazing to be making bread and pancakes from starter over twelve years old."

"It's older than that now—at least the original piece was. I brought it down with me from the Yukon." Karen pulled one jar after another from the crate. "I think they may have all survived. Adrik was so meticulous in caring for this crate. He wouldn't let anyone else touch it."

"This is certainly generous of you. It feels like Christmas."

"Well, it's not over yet." Karen pulled off the pried top of another crate. "I made a few things for your new house." She took out a large, thick quilt. The squares were done in shades of blue, yellow, and white. It was quite bright and lovely—like an Arctic summer day.

"Oh, it's . . . it's beautiful." Leah touched the corner in amazement. "I've never seen anything so pretty."

"There's no sense in not having pretty things. A gal needs them now and then. So what if you have to put a fur underneath it to keep warm enough? Better yet, just snuggle up closer to Jayce when he gets home." Karen's blue eyes seemed to twinkle in amusement. For a woman who'd just turned fifty in May, she was amazingly young at heart.

"I also made clothes for the children," Karen said as she reached into the box again. "I knew you would make plenty, but it was just so much fun. It'd been ages since I'd had any reason to make such tiny things."

"Maybe Ashlie will marry soon and you'll have grandchildren."

"That's always possible. She's having a wonderful time in Washington. She thinks she might like to become a nurse. Wouldn't that be grand? To have her return to the territory and help sick folks?"

"What if she doesn't want to return? Does she still talk about roaming the world?" Leah inspected the little dress Karen had just handed her. "Your stitching is always so perfect."

"Ashlie loves the city. She's told me that many times. But she also talks about the things she misses most about home. I know there's a part of her heart that still belongs in Alaska."

"Are there any romantic possibilities?"

Karen handed Leah another outfit, this one for Wills. "She's attending a school for young ladies, so there aren't any young men on a regular basis with which to have conversations or outings. However, church seems to be another story. There are a great many young men there who have been quite intrigued with her. They have a regular Sunday school class for her age group, and apparently there are far more boys than girls."

"It wouldn't be so bad to meet the man of your dreams in church," Leah said with a smile.

"Not at all." Karen winked. "Maybe even better than meeting him in the wilds of the Yukon."

"Or Alaska," Leah countered.

"You sure hurried off at lunch," Adrik said, coming upon Helaina as she worked with the dogs. She'd donned an old pair of Jacob's work clothes and tucked all her hair up under a cap.

She wasn't surprised to find him there, but apprehension filled her. "I thought you all deserved time alone. I know it's been a while since you had time to visit."

Adrik leaned against the birthing shed and studied her for a moment. His gaze made Helaina uncomfortable. "I'm keeping Jacob's dogs." She offered the information as if he'd asked.

"Leah tells me you're very good with the animals. That Jacob trained you the summer she and Jayce came to stay with us."

"Yes. I had to earn my keep," she said with a small smile. "I don't mind at all, however. I love the dogs."

"Love Jacob, too, as I hear it."

This startled her. "I . . . uh . . ." She turned away, hoping she wouldn't say something stupid.

"It's all right. I think it's great. Leah tells me that Jacob is in love with you as well."

"She doesn't know that's true anymore," Helaina said, lifting a can of fish entrails. The foul smell was something she'd never quite gotten used to, but every time she had to deal with it, she reminded herself that she was doing it for the man she loved.

"Jacob isn't a fickle man. If he's given his heart to you, you can rest assured that he won't be changing his mind."

Helaina put down the can and straightened. Turning, she braved a glance at Adrik's face. She found only compassion there. "I know you must think me a horrible person, Mr. Ivankov."

"Call me Adrik. And, no, I don't think you a horrible person."

"I caused your family so much trouble. For that I'm sorry."

He smiled and moved toward her. "You're forgiven, even if you don't believe it."

"I believe God forgives, but I know it's hard for others. Especially when great pain was inflicted. So many suffered because of me. Lives were threatened, and . . ." She fell silent, thinking of Leah's rape.

Adrik surprised her by taking hold of her hands. "It might be hard to forget the past, especially for some. But when Jesus lives in your heart, you need to forgive and forget. The Bible says God forgets, even for His own sake. If it's good enough for God, it's good enough for me."

Helaina bit her lower lip to keep it from quivering. She felt like collapsing in Adrik's fatherly arms and crying like a baby.

"You don't have to worry about whether we can accept you as Jacob's wife," Adrik said softly. "Truth is, Jacob is a wise man, and if he loves you, that's good enough for me."

"But that's just it," Helaina said, tears spilling down her face. "*If* he loves me. He's been gone for a long time. The last time he saw me he didn't make any promises or pledges. He didn't speak wonderful words of love. How could he love me? He let me go."

"He let you go *because* he loved you. What good would it have done either of you to have him declare his love and press for your love in return, when he knew you couldn't stay here in Alaska?"

Helaina studied his face for a moment. He seemed to know everything—no doubt Leah had been open with her family about Helaina's presence in her life. It only took Adrik's letting go of her hands and opening his arms to her to finish breaking Helaina's pretense of strength. She fell into his arms and sobbed.

"I just want him back. Even if he doesn't love me. I just want him back."

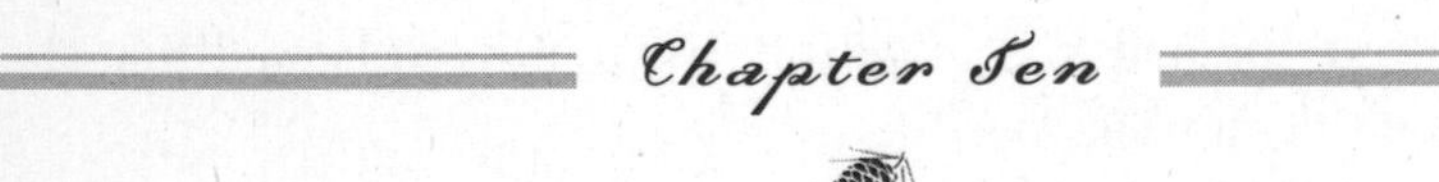

Chapter Ten

It's already August." Ben Kauffman wasn't one given to elaborate shows of emotion, but the anger was evident in his voice.

"We did as you asked, Captain," Travis added. "But we have to make plans now to leave this island and get back to civilization."

The other men quickly agreed. Jacob knew they wouldn't be satisfied to remain on the island, yet the idea of heading into the open waters was daunting. No one wanted to be home more than Jacob, but he wanted to get there alive.

The captain rubbed his bearded chin. "Look, men, I know how you feel. I, too, long to be with my family and loved ones. I would like a more palatable fare for my meals and a bed of down instead of fur. However, we have to be sensible about this matter."

"Indeed we do," Dr. Ripley said, taking a step forward. "Sir, I respect your command, but as you know, we already have two sick men. One is injured and in desperate need of more attention than I can give him here. The other has some kind of sickness that I do not even understand. I seriously doubt either one will live much longer. Not to mention we're all sick from lack of proper diet. There's not a man here who isn't suffering from scurvy."

"And well I know it, Dr. Ripley. However, would you put weakened men into boats and send them out on the water without hope of reaching their destination? Should we desert the sick men—leave them here to die?"

"Why do you speak without hope when referencing our attempt to leave by boat?" Ripley countered.

"Because I see very little hope for us if we head out wandering around the ocean. First of all, as weak as the men are, they'll be no match for the strong currents that flow in this area. Second, we won't stand a chance if a storm should come our way, which of course we can count on experiencing. These northern waters are always volatile."

"Better to take our chances and leave this accursed island before winter sets in than to suffer another year here," Ben muttered.

Jacob felt it important to back the captain's position. "We have two small umiaks, but none of you are familiar with the use of such boats. We used them to haul goods over the ice and little else. I'm very familiar with the umiaks, and yet I wouldn't begin to feel comfortable taking them out on the water with the purpose of trying to navigate the Arctic Ocean or the seas that might take us home."

"Then stay here," Travis said flatly.

"Men, we need to work together," Captain Latimore said sternly. "What we need is more driftwood for our warmth and cooking. We also need to work on sewing those skins. We need to ensure that we have proper warmth against the chilling nights. Even if we can work out a way to take the boats and leave the island, we will need to be prepared."

The men grumbled but said nothing that could really be heard. One by one they wandered away to go about their duties, but Jacob could tell it would only be a matter of time before they mutinied, and then what?

"I'm sorry about the trouble, Captain," Jacob said as the last of the men left them. "I know this is hard on the men. I wish I had a simple solution. I had hoped we would be rescued by now."

The captain picked at his well-worn jacket. "The men are right to feel a sense of desperation. They sense the change of weather. They know what's coming."

Jacob nodded. Just then Jayce came into view. He'd been off hunting and carried several ducks. They'd make a good meal to be sure.

"Captain, if you feel confident that we can navigate the ocean, I'm willing to reconsider the matter," Jacob said turning his attention back to Latimore.

"I will think on the matter and speak with the men. I see value in looking at all sides of this issue."

"As do I," Jacob replied, though he was uncertain whether he'd go along if the men decided to leave the island.

Jayce crossed the distance and held up his catch. "They're nice and fat," he said, tossing them down on the ground.

"It'll be a good change. Maybe duck has better nutritional value than seal," Jacob said with a shrug.

"When I was atop the hill I saw you had the men gathered," Jayce said, pulling the shotgun from his shoulder. "What was that all about? Nutritional values?"

"The men are restless." Jacob lowered his voice lest they be overheard by anyone other than Latimore. "I fear it will be mutiny if we can't find some way to give them hope."

"How are Bristol and Elmer?" Jayce questioned.

Bristol had been gravely ill after a wound he suffered while skinning a seal had become infected. Now the doctor was certain he would die. Elmer's ailment left the doctor with the same conclusion, although he had no real understanding of the disease that was slowly killing the man.

"Bristol isn't good. The doctor says he's gone septic. It's just a matter of time. He's been unconscious all day. Elmer isn't much better. He's in hideous pain. His abdomen is distended and feels warm to the touch. Dr. Ripley gave him a good dose of cocaine in hopes of easing the misery, but I don't see that it's helped much."

"Pity. The poor men have nothing to comfort them. They must surely realize the situation." Jayce looked toward the dwelling where the sick were being kept. Latimore readily shared the shelter with the sick, but the other men had crowded into one place to avoid having to face anyone's mortality.

"I guess I'd best get to work fixing these ducks," Jayce said, tossing the shotgun to Jacob. "There's still plenty of daylight for more hunting."

Jacob nodded. "I think some time alone would do me good. Maybe God will give me some answers."

He moved out across the land, following the shore to the east. Sometimes things just didn't make sense. He truly believed that all things happened for a reason—that God didn't just allow His children to go through situations for no reason. Of course, Jacob also believed that some things just happened because life was . . . well . . . life. There was no way to keep the natural course of living from happening. Jacob had known there was a risk when he took this expedition north. There were enough horror stories to keep any sane man from making such a choice.

"But maybe I'm not all together sane," he mused aloud. Surely a sane man wouldn't have let the woman he loved get away.

Jacob had been considering what he needed to do once he returned to Last Chance. The plans rolled through his mind once again. He would need to sell the dogs. Jacob couldn't imagine a life without the dogs; the past year had been incredibly lonely without his favorite companions. But at least he didn't have to worry about them. No doubt John would take most of them and would see that the animals were well cared for.

Jacob stopped and looked out across the island he'd called home for all these long months. It wasn't such a horrible experience. In fact, it had proven to him that he could endure most anything. And in his mind, that included leaving Alaska forever.

"If that's the price for Helaina's love," he said with a sigh, "then it will be worth the sacrifice."

They were starting to have a few hours of actual darkness, for which Jacob was grateful. He drifted into a fitful sleep that night, praying and pleading for God's intervention on their behalf.

Send us a rescue ship, Lord, he prayed. *Send someone soon to take us home.*

It seemed he'd barely closed his eyes when something caused Jacob to bolt upright. He wasn't sure what had awakened him. Nothing seemed amiss. Jayce slept not far from him, his even breathing evidence that he was alive and well.

Jacob strained his ear to hear anything else. One of the men would be on guard duty watching for ships and protecting the camp against animal attacks—especially bear, although without the vast stretches of ice for the bears to utilize, there were fewer and fewer on the island. Still, they couldn't let down their guard. A polar bear could swim over fifty miles without resting. John had told him this—had experienced it himself when a bear followed after him once. John had only had his small kayak, and the bear seemed determined to do him in. John had finally harpooned the bear and brought him home for food.

Jacob listened again for any sound that might indicate a problem. Then it dawned on him: Perhaps one of the sick men had died in the night and Latimore had found it necessary to draw the man out of the shelter. Whatever it was, something wasn't right. Jacob pulled on his boots. He needed to see what was going on in camp. Maybe it was nothing—but on the other hand, maybe it was a problem that couldn't wait until morning.

"What's wrong?" Jayce asked groggily.

"I don't know. I just have a strange feeling. It woke me from a dead sleep."

Jayce sat up, yawning. "Wait for me and I'll come with you." He threw off his fur covering and reached for his own boots. "Did you hear something?"

"I don't know. I was sound asleep, but something woke me up. I can't say that I heard anything at all, but I just feel like something is happening." He crawled to the opening of their shelter, with Jayce right behind him.

Outside, it was already getting light. Streaks of a sun on the southeast horizon showed the promise of a beautiful day. The camp was quiet. . . . Maybe too quiet. Jacob looked for the sentry but found none.

"Who was supposed to be on guard duty?"

Jayce suppressed another yawn. "I think it was Matthew."

"I don't see him anywhere." Jacob walked a few steps across the way, careful to avoid a stretched-out seal hide.

Jacob scanned the beach in both directions, but the man in question was nowhere in sight. Then it occurred to Jacob that something else was missing. "Where's the other umiak?"

"What?" Jayce looked at him oddly. "The other umiak?"

"Yeah. Look for yourself. There's the one we used to help make the shelter for Latimore and the sick men. Where's the other one?"

"Well, it was on the beach, last I knew." Jayce followed Jacob to where the boat had once been. There were clear markings to indicate it had been dragged toward the water.

"They've gone." Jacob felt a sickening sensation settle over him.

"Surely they wouldn't just load up and leave us here," Jayce said. "The captain wouldn't let them do that."

"The captain probably had nothing to say about the matter. He was on our side, remember? My guess is that he's still sleeping with the sick men." Jacob walked toward the shelter where the others would have been. One look inside confirmed his worse fears. "They're gone."

"Guess we should wake up Latimore and let him know what's happened."

Jacob straightened and shook his head. "Might as well let him sleep. There's nothing we can do at this point." Dread washed over him in waves. Dread for the men who'd gone, as well as for those left behind.

"They're completely ignorant of what they're facing," Jacob murmured as he went back to bed. "They won't make it."

"Dr. Ripley no doubt encouraged it. Those men were good about following Latimore unless Ripley got them stirred up."

"I'm sure Ripley had something to do with it, but the men were already eager to go. I'm sure it was a mutual decision. Just as I'm sure it will be a mutual disaster."

Three hours later, Latimore met Jacob and Jayce at the campfire. Jacob was working on sewing fur coverings for his well-worn boots.

"It's just as you said," Latimore confirmed. "I looked through the tent and everything of personal value is gone."

"They also took all of their furs and a good portion of the meat stores," Jayce said, looking up to meet the captain's grim expression. "They're thinking to make it back to the mainland, but I don't see that happening. They're too inexperienced."

"Indeed. For many it was their first time working on board a ship. They had little real knowledge of the sea. There's not a man among them who could navigate by the stars. Only Elmer was good at that, and he's here with us." Latimore eased onto a makeshift seat while Jayce poured him a cup of tea.

"They left us a few supplies. Probably knew it would be murder to do otherwise."

Latimore took the cup. "I'm sure they meant us no harm. I pray they make it to safety."

Jacob stretched out his feet. "I wouldn't give them much hope. It would take God's direct intervention, as far as I'm concerned. I would believe we would have a better chance walking out over the ice this winter to Siberia than trying to navigate the waters ourselves."

"I'm going to take some of the seal broth to Elmer and Bristol," Jayce announced. He lifted a tin can from the edge of the fire and got to his feet.

Once he was gone, Jacob's anger replaced his shock. "Those men considered no one but themselves. Their comrades lie sick—even dying—and they desert them."

"Jacob, everyone has their breaking point." Latimore shook his head. "Those men would not have acted as they did had they any hope of rescue or enduring the days to come. I'm also very certain Dr. Ripley influenced them. The man has given me no end of grief in trying to persuade me to change my mind about leaving. I place this event at his feet."

"Jacob, Captain, you'd better come. Bristol passed on in the night, and I don't think Elmer will be long in following."

He was right. An hour later they were faced with the task of burying two men. Jacob knew the permanently frozen ground would make burial difficult. They finally devised a place by scooping out the earth as best they could, then piling rocks atop the two dead men. It hardly seemed a fitting end.

Jacob's rage burned. He didn't know which made him angrier—the fact that the other men had deserted them or that he hadn't been able to prevent it from happening. *There should have been some way for me to stop it. Some way to persuade them from leaving. Now they'll die. They'll all die.* He shuddered at the thought of the men forever lost to the icy depths of the Arctic Ocean.

Jayce opened the Bible and began to read aloud, but Jacob hardly heard the words. *How dare they leave us to this?* The isolation of their circumstances seemed to overwhelm Jacob all at once. Somehow with nearly a dozen men on the island things hadn't seemed so bad. With just the three of them, however, Jacob felt as though they were the last men on earth.

"Jacob, would you like to pray?" Jayce asked.

The words startled Jacob. "Pray? I've been praying. I've prayed without ceasing since we were marooned on this island. Pray?" He'd had enough and walked away. If he didn't get away by himself, there was no telling what he might say. He certainly didn't want to take out his anger on Jayce or Latimore.

He stalked up the hillside as he'd done a thousand times before. Often he'd gone to the top to seek solace, other times he'd gone for information. The perch had generally afforded him a clear view for as far as he could see to the east and south, as well as a good portion of the west. Only this time he had no interest in the view.

"Wait, Jacob." Jayce followed after him.

"It would be best to just leave me to myself, Jayce. I'm not good company."

"Maybe not, but I think you need a friend. Even if it's just a silent one."

Jacob stopped. "I don't see how decent men could make the choice those men made last night. They would have to know we stood a better chance together than apart."

"They made a mistake. Dr. Ripley influenced the younger men. It's sad and may very well end tragically for them, but I don't believe they meant us harm. Just as Latimore said, we knew them to be good men overall."

Jacob let out a growl. "Being good men hasn't fixed our circumstances. I don't know what God wants from me here. I trust Him to bring us through. I believe in His power to provide, despite our failing health. I just don't know what more He wants from us."

Jayce nodded. "I know exactly what you mean. I've asked Him that very thing over and over. I don't know why I should have to spend a year away from my wife and children. Children whom I don't even know—who don't know me."

Jacob softened at this and the anger left his voice. "I know. I'm sorry."

"We've both endured a great deal, but we've known God was with us every step of the way. It's not like I understand the circumstances of our situation, but the alternative is not an option for me. I can't turn from God, even in this."

"Nor I." Jacob's voice was filled with resignation. "I've never even contemplated that, but in my anger I've known a sense of separation from God that troubles me deeply. I don't want to be filled with rage—it serves no purpose. Still, I don't understand why this situation goes on and on."

"I don't either, Jacob. But I do know that we must continue to trust the Lord."

"I know that as well. It's just hard to face the possibility of another winter here—apart from Leah and Helaina. It's hard to contemplate whether we'll be strong enough to survive."

"Jacob! Jayce!" Latimore called to them.

Jacob put his hand to his eyes and squinted against the brilliant sun. "What is it, Captain?" The concern about predatory animals caused Jacob to give a quick glance over his shoulder.

"A ship!" Latimore called again. "There's a ship on the horizon!"

Chapter Eleven

Leah slung her rifle over one shoulder and hoisted two large buckets of blueberries. The day was unseasonably warm, but the sun felt good against her skin. Lifting her face to the sky, Leah breathed in the heady aroma of sea air and spongy tundra. She loved her life here, but the longing would not leave her where Jayce was concerned.

"It's already August," she whispered. "Already August and they've still not returned." The likelihood that they'd be found yet that summer was fading quickly. Soon the ocean would start churning with ice and the temperature would drop. Ships seldom went very far north after October. Some captains refused to venture to the Bering after mid-September.

Karen and Adrik had suggested that if the men were not found, Leah and the children should come back with them to Seward. If that didn't appeal, Leah could take up residence in their cabin at Ketchikan. After all, she was familiar with the area and people. It might offer her comfort.

But nothing offered her comfort these days.

Leah was no fool. She knew the odds of finding the men before summer's end was lessening with each passing day. Winter would soon be upon them, and she had to face the facts.

She headed down the hill with the buckets in tow. At the base, a small wagon awaited her. Leo and Addy, Jacob's two favorite dogs, were at the helm. Leah put the buckets in the wagon, then went to the dogs. She took a moment to pet them. They missed Jacob as much as she did. For weeks after he'd left home, they'd done nothing but howl and whine.

Straightening, Leah sighed and released the wagon's brake. She was some three miles from home, but the dogs would make short order of the distance. The buckets had packed easily into the small wagon, leaving room for Leah if she chose. She decided against it, however, knowing the walk would do her good.

On their way, Leah made up her mind. If the men had not returned by the time Adrik and Karen felt it necessary to head back to Seward, Leah and the children would go with them. The twins would have better access to a doctor should they grow ill, and Jayce and Jacob would know to look for her there. It just made sense.

Up ahead on the trail, Leah saw Adrik hiking toward her. It seemed perfect timing to announce her decision. "What are you doing out here?" she called.

"Looking for you. Karen was worried and the twins were asking for you."

Leah laughed. "They're always asking for me." She drew up even with Adrik and slowed a bit, knowing there was no sense in delaying her announcement. "I made up my mind to return with you and Karen and the boys if the men haven't returned by the time you head out."

"I think that's for the best," Adrik replied, his voice low and gentle. "I know it isn't easy to consider them not coming home."

"I have to be realistic about the matter." Leah looked up and met his gaze. "They may never come home. I've not been willing to truly consider that matter until now. Helaina has always been so strong—so sure that they're returning, but . . ." Her voice trailed off as she remembered her father leaving for the Yukon gold fields. He had promised to return as well. Then Jacob had headed north, and had they not gone after him, Leah would probably have never seen him again.

"But the summer is fading and winter's chill is in the air," Adrik said.

He had always been a very eloquent man, despite his backwoods upbringing. Leah smiled. "Yes. I know that I have to be sensible. The twins must be safe and have the things they need. The winters are harsh here and without a man to help care for us, it will be even worse. So many times we've faced famine and death. Disease runs amuck and epidemics aren't at all unusual."

"You can face those things in Ketchikan or Seward as well," Adrik interjected. "Although I will say famine has never been an issue. That land is so plentiful with meat and other vegetation."

"And the harbors don't freeze," Leah added. "We could always get a shipment of needed goods, even in the dead of winter."

"True enough. Well, you know how we feel on the matter. We want to make you comfortable and Karen loves those babies as if they were her own grandchildren. I guess in many ways, they are exactly that."

"Yes, they are. I've always seen you and Karen as a second set of parents. God provided abundantly for me in my loss. Karen has been a mother to me in every way, and you . . ." She paused and drew a deep breath. "You've always been a father, offering security and strength. A kind of strength that I could not find in other people—with the possible exception of Jacob and now Jayce."

"I've always cared deeply for you and Jacob. You know that. I promise you, Leah, I will see you and the children amply provided for. I know Karen will enjoy your company, but even more than that, she'll be glad to know of your safety under her roof." He gave a chuckle. "You know my wife. She thinks she's the only one in the world who can care for her loved ones. It makes her positively impossible at times when she considers Ashlie living so far away."

"I'm sure it does, but Karen waited so long for a family of her own. I know how that feels. You tend to want to hold on to your children and never let go. It isn't easy. The twins are barely a year old, and yet I cringe with fear at the thought of them wandering out of sight. I can make myself ill if I dwell on all the risks at hand."

"Life is a risk, Leah. But the alternative is to die. Still, we need not fear either one. God is our strength, our help. He won't let us down. Even when it seems He's forgotten us—He's still there."

"Like now." Leah halted the dogs. "I try to have a strong faith, but honestly, I think God must find me terribly disappointing."

Adrik smiled. "I have said the same thing on many occasions. Darling, there is no easy walk on this earth. Oh, some folks seem to have a better way—a gentle existence—but they all face loss in some way. Faith wouldn't be faith if it came easy. Abraham had to stand over Isaac with a knife before his faith was fully born. Abraham learned a big lesson that day. He learned that he could trust God even when the situations around him made no sense. He learned to have faith that even when God was calling him to a frightening new place, he could rest in God's perfect faithfulness."

"I want to rest there too," Leah admitted. "I suppose that's why I decided to go back with you. I'm not doing it because I've given up hope. But rather, it seems the best choice given the circumstance."

"I agree. I want to know that you and the children will be safe. The people here are good to you, but the long winter is going to be difficult to endure."

They walked a ways in silence before Adrik posed another question. "What of Mrs. Beecham?"

"I hadn't really considered the matter much," Leah said, shaking her head. "I doubt she'll leave. But then, she doesn't have children to worry over. She can stay in my house if she chooses to remain here."

"Or she can come with us. We wouldn't deny her a place to stay. It would be a squeeze, but there's always room for one more."

Leah was deeply touched by Adrik's generosity. "I'll talk to her and let you know. I know she's been waiting for me to make up my mind. I guess now that I have . . . well . . . she'll have to make up hers as well."

With August, the long hours of summer light began to fade. Helaina wondered how she would ever bear the long dark winter if Jacob didn't return. She had prayed for his return and thought of it—dreamed it so realistically that she had to stop upon awakening in the morning to rethink what was real and what was her imagination.

Now summer was nearly over and the ships were heading south again. There'd been no word from any revenue cutter or the Coast Guard service. She longed to know the truth, even if the truth was painful and sad. Still, there was no word. Stanley wrote to tell her that no effort was being spared to locate the men, but still her heart was heavy.

Helaina heard Leah humming softly in the children's room. She was putting her babies to bed and offering them whatever comfort and peace she could. Leah had decided to go back to Seward with Karen and her family, but Helaina felt bound to Last Chance. When Jacob came home, she wanted to be here to greet him. She had to be here.

"Well, I think they're finally asleep," Leah said as she came from the children's room. She stretched and rubbed the small of her back. "I need to get outside and work on that sealskin. Seems the work is never done." She reached to pick up several toys that were on the table.

"I'll go take care of the dogs," Helaina volunteered. She got to her feet and dusted off the front of the lightweight kuspuk she wore over bibless denim overalls.

Leah paused at the door. "Do you really plan to stay?"

Helaina nodded. "I can't go. I need to feel close to him, even if it's just to care for his animals."

"It may take a long time before they come home."

"I know," Helaina said, meeting Leah's gaze. In the air hung the unspoken phrase, *If they ever come home.*

Leah shrugged, as if realizing it would do little good to try and talk Helaina out of anything once her mind was made up. "I'll be just outside if you need me."

Helaina made her way to where the dogs were staked and housed. They began to yip and howl at her appearance. They had come to accept her as their mistress and tried hard to please her. All through the winter they had performed for her as well as they had for Leah. They seemed to understand her love for them was somehow bound to their missing master.

"Hey there, Toby," she called, reaching to rub her hands over the blond-brown fur of the first dog. "How are you?" He whined in reply.

She gave attention to the first row of dogs, then gathered food from the locker and began to feed them. The other rows of dogs put up a huge fuss, believing themselves somehow slighted.

"I'm coming, fellas," she called.

She made the rounds and saw that all were fed, watered, and given due attention. There were three new batches of puppies, and Helaina checked on each of the new mothers, scandalously giving them each a nice chunk of seal liver from a new catch. Leah had told her that Jacob liked to do this for the nursing females to enrich their milk supply. Helaina could see no reason to do otherwise.

Working to clean up the grounds around the pens, Helaina was surprised when she looked up to find Leah standing not six feet away. She laughed. "I didn't hear you come up. I guess my mind was elsewhere."

Leah looked pale, almost as if she'd had bad news. A sense of dread washed over Helaina as she stopped her actions. "What is it? What have you heard?"

"Sigrid just came to the house. There's a cutter in the harbor. Word has come that it's the ship that went searching for the men of the *Regina*."

Helaina swallowed hard. "What of the men?"

"I don't know. There's a launch coming ashore. Sigrid's offered to stay with the twins. Will you come with me?"

"You know I will!" Helaina tossed down the shovel. "Let me wash my hands." She hurried to where a pail of water sat perched atop an overturned washtub. Without a word Helaina washed and then dried her hands, while shaking so hard she could hardly hold the towel.

"If they didn't find them . . ." Leah began, then halted.

"We can't worry about ifs right now. Let's go see what the truth of the matter might be. Then we can make our plans."

They hurried to the beach where a crowd of people had already gathered. Many of the villagers had returned from hunting, and there were a variety of things happening. One group had managed to bring in a whale, but without the icy shores to help slide the mammoth creature along, they were forced to pull the beast ashore by using dogs and manpower. No doubt most of the people assembled were there for the purpose of helping with the whale kill rather than to greet the cutter.

Leah pulled away from Helaina and put her hand to her forehead to shield her eyes from the setting sun. It was hard to see who the men in the launch might be, but when Helaina heard Leah gasp, she knew Leah had spotted someone.

"Who is it?" Helaina asked, but already Leah was running for the beach.

She watched from afar as Leah splashed into the water. She could hear the people shouting, but it all seemed again like one of her dreams. Moving very slowly, Helaina began to walk again toward the gathering. A man was climbing out of the launch—jumping into the knee-deep waters of the Bering Sea. He waded through until he reached Leah's outstretched arms. It was Jayce.

Helaina felt her breath catch as the couple embraced. She backed up several steps until she was hidden from view by the head of the newly caught whale. Helaina preferred to remain out of sight until she could calm her overwhelmed nerves.

Lord, what will I do if Jacob hasn't come back as well? How will I live if he's returned but no longer cares for me?

She peeked around to see that Jayce had lifted Leah and was carrying her to shore. It was the stuff of fairy tales and beautiful love stories. It was the happy ending that Leah so richly deserved. Helaina stepped out and moved toward the crowd of people. She had to know that Jacob was safe, if nothing else.

And then she saw him. The launch settled on the shore, and the men disembarked. Jacob was there, along with several other men. This was her moment of truth. This moment would determine her future.

Helaina eased her way through the crowd just as Jayce put Leah on the ground. Jacob immediately embraced his sister. Helaina fought to keep from crying, wishing he were holding her instead. *Please love me. Please still care.*

She stepped forward, inching her way toward the trio. Drawing a deep breath, she straightened her shoulders.

Just then Jacob looked up. Shock registered on his face as his gaze met hers. He immediately left his sister and crossed the distance to where Helaina now stood. For several moments neither one said a word. He looked at her so intently that Helaina felt as though he were memorizing every feature of her face.

"It took you long enough to get here," she finally managed to say. She gave him a smile as her joy threatened to bubble over.

"If I'd known you were here waiting, I would have come sooner," he said. Then without warning he pulled her hard against him and kissed her soundly on the lips.

The despair, frustration, and agony of the last year's wait faded from Helaina along with all reasonable ability to think. She felt the warmth of his hands on her face, and he deepened his kiss. When he finally pulled away, she could only look at him in wonder.

"I can't believe you're here," they murmured in unison, then laughed.

"When did you come back?" Jacob asked, his hands moving to gently touch her shoulders.

"Last year this time. I sold everything I owned and returned to Last Chance."

"Just like that?" he mused. "You traded your life there to be here?"

She shook her head. "No. I traded it all to be with you." She waited anxiously to see how he might respond. For a moment he said nothing, then he dropped his hold on her and took a step back.

"Are you sure about this?"

Helaina put her hands on her hips. "I've had a whole year to think it over." Her tone was rather indignant, but he deserved it after what he'd put her through.

Just then Bjorn and Emma joined the revelry. "Jacob!" they exclaimed before Bjorn pulled him into a hearty bear hug.

"We're so glad you've returned. Praise God for His provision!"

Emma nodded and added her own embrace. "*Ja,* Jacob, we have prayed every day for you."

"And well I know it," Jacob answered, casting a glance over their shoulders to Helaina. "Because God has just answered all of my prayers."

Chapter Twelve

The village used the men's return as a wonderful excuse to celebrate. Before long there was food and drink, as well as singing and dancing. Leah woke the twins, who, although irritable at first, adapted rather easily to the revelry. They seemed particularly interested in their papa, who happily tossed them up and down in the air and got on the floor to play. Gone was any worry that they might reject him. To Leah's amazement, they warmed to Jayce immediately.

Jacob and Helaina seemed completely engrossed with one another, although since the homecoming they had not had a moment to themselves. But Leah knew her brother. He would find a way to get Helaina alone. And if he didn't, Helaina would. It was clear that Jacob's feelings for Helaina were as strong as ever. Leah couldn't help but notice the way her brother's gaze never left Helaina, no matter where she was in the room. Leah felt the same way about her husband. She watched him so intently most of the evening, she was certain he felt her gaze boring right through him. If he minded, he never said as much.

It was so hard to believe they were really home. What had seemed like a never-ending nightmare had come to a conclusion with so little warning, that the matter seemed . . . well . . . almost common. Sailors returning home from the sea. Nothing more.

Leah longed for time alone with Jayce. She wanted to hear his stories and know what he'd gone through. She wanted to know the bad as well as the good, for it was an entire year of his life that she didn't share. She knew there would be time enough for them to be alone, but selfishly she wanted to put the children to bed and find a quiet place to curl up in Jayce's arms. She could only wonder if he felt the same. He seemed so content just to play with the children. Had he lost his passion for her? Had the experience left him with a changed heart?

"I can't believe how big they are," Jayce declared as he lifted Merry and came to sit beside his wife.

Leah watched their daughter tug at Jayce's beard, laughing and babbling all the while. Despite her shy nature, Merry seemed to take easily to her father, even though she scarcely knew him. Wills was no different. He rammed up against Jayce as though they were old buddies and shouted over and over, "Play."

"They were just little bundles when I left," he said, gently stroking Meredith's brown curls.

"It's been a long year," Leah murmured. She met Jayce's eyes and knew he understood.

"Yes. Much too long."

"If I can have everyone's attention," Bjorn announced, "I would like to offer a word of thanksgiving for the return of Jacob and Jayce and Captain Latimore. I would also like to pray for the men who struck out on their own. There's been no sign of them, and Jacob has asked that we remember them. We will pray, too, for a quick end to the war. As you know, American lives are being spent on the battlefields of Europe, and surely only God can bring a quick end to such hideous events. Let's pray."

As he began, Leah felt strangeness in the moment. It was almost as if she were dreaming the entire thing. She knew Jayce and Jacob had truly come home, but there was something that felt most awkward in their reappearance. She couldn't put her finger on it, but maybe it was something that always came with long separations. She knew when Jayce had first come back into her life years earlier that there had been an uneasiness, but she'd attributed most of that to her anger.

She wondered if the wives of soldiers felt the same way. They, too, had to wait and see if their loved ones would ever return alive. They no doubt spent endless hours of worry and anticipation without word or understanding. As the days and months drifted by, there were likely some who even faced the reality that the odds were against them. Perhaps that was the key to knowing her heart in this. There was a part of her that had accepted the possibility of her husband's and brother's death. Maybe she'd even lost hope that they would actually come back alive, and now that they had, she felt almost like a traitor for having given up. After all, she'd told Adrik earlier in the day that she would leave Last Chance and go back with him and Karen to Seward. Perhaps that was her way of declaring the matter to be a lost cause. Guilt washed over her.

Helaina never gave up hope. Why was I so easily discouraged?

Bjorn concluded his prayer and asked Captain Latimore to say a few words. The man stepped forward. Though somewhat weak and much thinner, his countenance bore a strength that reminded Leah of the first time she'd met him.

"You honor me with your kindness," he began. "I am so pleased to be here—thankful for the rescue and return to civilization. And this is a wondrous civilization compared to the place I spent the last few months."

The villagers laughed as he continued. "I never thought to be so grateful for simple things like real chairs and tables—and I'm especially looking forward to a real bed."

"So am I," Jayce said in husky whisper.

Leah felt her cheeks grow hot and knew better than to meet her husband's gaze.

"I have to say," Latimore continued, "that none of us would have survived had it not been for Jacob Barringer." The people cheered at this and Latimore motioned to Jacob. "This man, along with Jayce Kincaid, took charge and led the expedition when we were at our worst—when I was at my worst. They were able to show the rest of us how to survive the bitter Arctic cold, and for that I will be eternally grateful. Jacob, why don't you share our story with the people?"

Jacob, looking older than Leah remembered, stepped forward. "My friends, your love and training over the last twelve years saved my life out on the Arctic ice. I remembered the wisdom and traditions passed down among the Inupiat and put them into practice. Clearly the praise cannot be Jayce's or mine alone. The Real People have played their part as well. You should be proud of yourselves and the gift you gave. It is in keeping with God's direction for each of us—that we should help one another and bear one another's burdens." He paused for a moment, as if uncertain how much to say.

"We faced a difficult time. Lives were lost. Our ship was locked in ice and then destroyed. We had ample time to get our gear off the ship, but leaving its safety for nothing more than an ice floe was difficult. We were fortunate to find our way to land—a small island not far from the Russian shores. There we set up camp and began to hunt. Through it all, God was our mainstay. I can't say that I understand the time spent trapped on that island, but I do know that even in this, God had a plan. I can't say I was always strong and faithful, but I can say that God was."

Leah saw many of the people nodding. John had even managed to come for the revelry and smiled up at Jacob with pride. Oopick, too, seemed quite pleased with Jacob's words.

"I'll be happy to share further stories with you in the future, but the hour is late and I know you're tired. Thank you for the prayers and for not forgetting us."

Cheers went up as Jacob concluded and walked off the small platform. Bjorn once again took his place on the makeshift stage. "Jayce, would you like to say a few words as well?"

Jayce shook his head. "Maybe another time." He looked down at his sleeping daughter and the content expression on his face warmed Leah's heart. He loved Merry and Wills. There was no doubt about it. Fears of how he might accept or reject them faded from Leah's mind.

"He looks good," Adrik said as he and Karen came up beside Leah. "A little thin, but no doubt you women will rectify that."

Leah nodded. "I was just thinking about that." She smiled and tried to suppress a yawn. "How much longer can you stay with us?"

"Well, we figured to talk to you about that," Adrik said with a hint of mischief in his expression. "We have something to propose when we return to your home."

"I think Jacob has something to propose as well," Jayce said, grinning. He motioned to where Jacob and Helaina stood amidst well-wishers.

"If Helaina doesn't propose it first," Leah countered.

The party gradually broke up with promises to share supper together again the next night. There was great talk about working to finish the butchering of the whale, but Leah knew that wouldn't involve her. She walked alongside Jayce, carrying Wills. He slept soundly against her shoulder, having finally played himself into an exhausted state. Leah hoped they would both sleep through the night and give her some much-needed time alone with Jayce.

After putting the babies to bed, Helaina appeared at the door with suitcase in hand. "Where are you going?" Leah asked.

"I couldn't very well stay in Jacob's house." She shifted the case. "It would hardly be proper."

"You know you're welcome here," Jayce interjected. "I can't repay all you've done for my family. Leah tells me she wouldn't have made it through without you."

"Leah exaggerates," Helaina said with a grin. "She helped keep me sane. I might surely have gone mad without her company. We bore the burden together."

Jayce pulled Leah close. "I'm glad you did. We share a strange past, we three, but God has taken it and made it something quite extraordinary."

"Indeed," Helaina replied. "I just stopped by so you might tell Jacob . . ."

Just then Jacob entered the house. He took one look at Helaina and frowned. "Tell Jacob what? Where are you going?"

"Sigrid has offered to share her room with me at the Kjellmann's. They are also taking in the captain, and Emma said one more person wouldn't be a problem. I figure Leah and Jayce already have enough people, what with Karen and Adrik's family."

"Where have you been staying?" he asked.

Helaina blushed. "Well . . . if you must know, I was staying at your place. It's no longer proper for me to do so, given that you're back."

"You could always make it proper," Adrik teased as he came from the back room. Karen was right beside him and elbowed him hard. "Ow! What was that for?"

"For not minding your own business," Karen said sweetly. She smiled at Jacob and the others, then turned to Leah. "We just wanted to tell you good night. I'm hoping we'll have time to talk with you all tomorrow. Adrik has something to ask you."

"I'll be here," Jacob answered.

"Us too," Jayce threw in.

Adrik nodded. "Good. I think you'll like what I have to say. Good night, then." He turned and pulled Karen along with him to their room. Leah heard Karen giggle as Adrik whispered something in her ear. After all this time they still acted like a couple of newlyweds.

"Well, I need to be going," Helaina said, appearing uncomfortable.

"Give me that," Jacob said, reaching for the suitcase. "The least I can do is walk you over to the Kjellmanns'."

Helaina nodded, and Leah could see the hint of a smile on her lips. Things were working out. She knew from the way Jacob acted that he was still in love with Helaina. It delighted Leah in a way she hadn't expected. She was happy for both of them.

"Well, I'll expect you both for breakfast," Leah declared.

"A very late breakfast," Jayce said, yawning. "At least I hope it will be a late one."

Jacob laughed. "Me too."

When they were gone, Jayce turned to Leah. "How I've missed you. Even the smell of you." He took her in his arms and buried his face in her hair.

Leah wrapped her arms around Jayce's neck. "I despaired of ever seeing you again. I wasn't strong or brave. I hope you're not terribly disappointed in me."

He pulled back and looked at her oddly. "You aren't serious, are you?"

Leah shrugged. "Well, Helaina was so certain of your return. She kept such hope, while I felt more and more discouraged. Some days I felt confident that you would find your way back to me. Other times, however . . ." She shook her head. "There were some bleak times."

"I know—for me as well. I tried not to let on to Jacob, but I feared we would all die of some hideous and painful malady and the last thought I would have would be of regret. Regret that I ever left your side. I was a fool, Leah. Please forgive me." He stroked her jaw with his thumb, sending a shivering sensation down her spine. How she loved this man.

"You were only following a dream." She was barely able to speak. "There's nothing to forgive."

"I'm done with dreams. I want the honest truth of what my life has become. I want a future with my wife and children. I want to make a home with you." He lowered his mouth to hers. "Now and always," he whispered against her lips. "Now and always."

Jacob slowed his pace, hoping Helaina would take the hint. "I wanted to tell you something," he began, "now that we have a moment to ourselves."

Helaina looked up, but the darkness made it difficult to see her expression. "Then tell me."

He stopped and put the case on the ground. "Come here." She moved closer and he reached out to touch her face. "I still can't believe you're really here. You were all I could think about while we were gone. I knew when you left that it was a mistake, but I couldn't bring myself to beg you to stay. I knew that if you hated Alaska, you would always be miserable, even if you loved me."

Jacob buried his fingers in her carefully pinned blond hair. He knew he was making a mess of things, but he wanted this moment to last—to go on and on. There was a sense of desperation in his heart.

"I want you to know that I made a decision to leave Alaska."

"What?"

He sighed. "I can't bear to think of life without you. I'm willing to give up Alaska if it means having you at my side for the rest of our lives."

She laughed lightly. "Oh, Jacob. We are a pair. I sold everything I owned in New York and Washington, D.C. I sold the estates, the apartment, the furnishings. I even gave away and sold off most of my clothes to the secondhand stores. I kept very little because none of it mattered without you. I missed Alaska the minute I went away. I kept thinking about the beauty and the people. I realized I was no longer content in a noisy city where no one knew anyone, nor cared to."

"Then you'd make your life here—with me?"

"Of course." She reached up to place her hand against his cheek. "Jacob, I've loved you for a long time. I've loved you for so long now, I can't even really say when it began, but I suspect it was when you nearly ran me over on the streets of Nome. I came back last year so that I might be here when you came home. I wanted to see you and find out if there was a chance that you could possibly love me . . . as much . . . as I love you."

She started to cry, which took Jacob by surprise. Helaina Beecham was such a strong woman that he'd seldom ever seen her give such a display of emotion. He gently brushed away her tears with his fingers as she continued.

"When we learned that you were . . . lost . . . I thought I would die." She drew a ragged breath. "I went crazy trying to get news. It seemed the *Regina* and her whereabouts was of far less importance than other issues, like the war in Europe. Stanley tried to help me, but no one had any answers, and of course, no one would do anything until warmer weather.

"But I never gave up hope that we would see you again. Somehow I just knew you would make it—you would come home. What I didn't know . . . what I doubted in my heart . . . was whether you might love me."

Jacob pulled her against him and held her tight. "I love you, Helaina. I will always love you. Never doubt it, and never be afraid that you will lose my affection."

She held on to him as though he were her salvation. Jacob loved the feel of her in his arms; they fit each other perfectly. He'd only dared to dream of this during those long months in the north. He'd prayed and hoped against all reason that he might be able to find her again, and in answer . . . here she was.

"Marry me, Helaina," he whispered.

"Of course." She composed herself and pulled away. "When?"

"Now."

She laughed, and it filled the silence of the night like music. "Now?"

"Why not? I'm sure everyone is still awake. We've only been here for a few moments. Let's just go and get Bjorn and Emma and get married."

"What of Leah and Jayce? What of Adrik and Karen?"

"We'll get married at Leah's house. That way the babies can sleep."

She sighed. "I'm glad you've thought this all out. I'm too tired to make reasonable decisions."

Now it was his turn to laugh. He grabbed the case and reached out to pull Helaina along with him. "Are you saying that marrying me isn't a reasonable decision?"

"Well, not exactly. I think the decision is reasonable, but . . . I'm not sure the procedure is such."

Jacob knocked on his sister's door. "You stay here and tell them what we're doing. I'll go get Bjorn and Emma."

Helaina took her suitcase and nodded. Jayce opened the door as Jacob turned to go. "What's wrong?" he questioned.

"Nothing's wrong," Jacob called out. "We're just going to get married at your house—right now."

Chapter Thirteen

Leah helped Helaina get ready for her wedding by arranging her long blond hair. "I wish you'd wait and let us give you a more proper wedding."

Helaina laughed. "This is as proper a wedding as I desire. You forget—I've been married before. I had the most lavish wedding money could buy. My father bought out every white rose for two hundred miles around. There must have been hundreds of them."

"I can't imagine," Leah said, trying to mentally picture such a thing. "What about your gown?"

"That was a special creation by the finest designer of the day. I spent months going for my fittings. It had a beautiful bodice with an ivory overlay that went to my neck. The sleeves were long and fitted and the train stretched out some twenty feet. It was truly magnificent. I wore it several times in our first year of marriage, but after that it was packed away, and after Robert died, I later gave it to a distant cousin who thought she'd like to have it for her own wedding."

"You must have been a vision," Leah said, thinking back to her own simple wedding.

"I'm sure you were a vision on your wedding day too," Helaina declared, seeming to read her mind. "I will always regret not being there."

"I wish you would have been there too. Those days were so hard—so bleak. Still, after waiting all those years, I can't complain. Jayce was the prize, after all."

"Just as Jacob is all I really want. The ceremony is not nearly so important." She turned as Leah applied the final pins. "What is important is to have all of you here. Leah, I'm so glad we're friends. I never really had a friend like you. Most women were jealous of my wealth or standing. New York is a very difficult place with its hierarchies and rules. You might find peers at your own level of society, but should they somehow be lowered in status or advanced, your relationships are forever changed. It just comes with the territory."

"I can't imagine. I couldn't live like that. I mean, if I suddenly found myself elevated to a new level, I couldn't just turn my back on those I loved."

"With family, of course, you would not be expected to, but friends would be another story. Unlike in England, where having a poor but titled friend is still worthy of your attention, Americans are snobs when it comes to such matters. It was one of the reasons I refused to get too close to anyone. It was also the reason it was so very hard on me when my parents and Robert died. I had no one in whom I could confide, except Stanley, and he was far away and often too busy. Those were hard times."

"Well, you won't have to endure them again," Leah said handing her the mirror. "Now we will be sisters, as well as friends. No social standing or financial fiascos will separate us."

Helaina took the mirror, but instead of looking at her reflection, she met Leah's eyes. "I know that with confidence, and it blesses me as nothing else could. When I think of the past and all we've endured together, the things you did for me—risking your life with Chase and . . . everything else. I might not have come to believe in God had it not been for you."

Leah shook her head. "The past needs to stay in the past. I know I'm a poor one to talk, given my inability to do exactly that, but I am trying. You would have found your way to God with or without me, but the Lord knew I needed to be humbled and taught mercy. I wasn't very kind to you back then, but your forgiveness has blessed me like a warm fire after days on the icy trail. I will always be here for you."

Helaina nodded. "And I will be here for you. No matter what."

"What's this?" Jayce called from the doorway. "You two seem mighty serious about something."

"We were just having a bit of girl talk," Leah said, smiling. "Don't you think our bride is beautiful?"

"She is lovely," Jayce said, surveying Helaina as she stood.

"Thank you." Helaina looked at her reflection momentarily, then passed the mirror back to Leah. "Jayce, I hope you know that I . . . well . . . I . . ." She seemed to fail for words.

Leah knew Helaina wanted to make sure things were at peace between all of them. "I think Helaina wants to go to her wedding knowing that the past is forgiven and that we are all friends."

Jayce put his arm around Leah's shoulders. "The past is gone. Of course we are all friends. My time out in the Arctic taught me much, not the least of which was to let go of my past. The burdens I carried for years seemed unimportant in the face of that adversity. I hold nothing against you, Helaina, and I pray you hold nothing against me."

Helaina came to Jayce, tears in her eyes. "I don't deserve such mercy, but I am grateful for it. You, Leah, and Jacob have done so much to teach me about being merciful even when someone deserves otherwise. It's been hard for me, but I've finally been able to come to terms with my parents' deaths—and Robert's death as well. It hasn't happened overnight, but as I've sought God's heart in the Bible, I've realized that He offers forgiveness for all, and I must strive to do likewise. I must also learn to put guilt aside as God forgives and covers my mistakes with His love. Guilt has eaten away at my heart for so many years. Jacob was able to see that and admonished me to do something more productive with my time." She gave them a rather coy smile. "I guess Jacob will be that 'something more productive.' "

They laughed together.

"I'm back!" Jacob called from the front door.

Helaina bit her lower lip and threw a quick glance over her shoulder as if she'd forgotten something. Leah reached out to calm her. "You look perfect. Remember this moment fondly."

Helaina nodded. Jayce extended his arm to her. "Shall we? If we don't get out there soon, he'll just start bellowing again and wake up the children."

Helaina smiled and took hold of Jayce as though she needed the extra support. "I'm ready."

Leah watched them walk through the door. Jacob would finally be married. He would finally have a family of his own. She wiped a tear from her eye and drew a deep breath. Their lives were changing again, but this time it was something very good.

In the living room Jacob waited with Adrik, Karen, Sigrid, and Bjorn. "Emma stayed home with the children. She knew Sigrid would be beside herself if she missed out on seeing Helaina married," Bjorn said.

"Well, we've gotten to know each other very well this last year. As the only single, white women in the village, we had a great deal in common," Sigrid offered as an excuse.

Bjorn yawned. "Ja. They have talking in common for sure."

Leah grinned. Her husband was home, her brother was marrying the woman he'd loved for a long time, and her family was safe and sound. What more could she want?

Bjorn began the service by reading from Genesis. "God doesn't want man to be alone—He said it wasn't good." Leah always enjoyed his thick Swedish accent. "And it's not good. To be alone is a terrible thing—especially here in the north. Solomon, too, talked of two being better than one. They share warmth and a helping hand. When two people come together to marry, they share those things as well as love and hopefully a belief in God's saving grace."

Helaina looked at Jacob as though he hung the moon and the stars. Leah looked to Jayce, who was waiting to officially hand Helaina over to Jacob, already missing his absence at her side.

"Helaina, do you love the Lord and have you taken Jesus as your Savior?"

"I have."

He smiled and turned to Jacob. "And Jacob, do you love the Lord and have you taken Jesus as your Savior?"

"Yes, sir." The catch in Jacob's voice made him sound like a teenager again instead of a man in his thirties.

"Who gives this woman?"

"We do," Jayce replied. "I and her other friends."

Bjorn nodded and Jayce extended Helaina's arm to Jacob. "Take good care of her," he admonished in a fatherly way.

Jacob nodded with a grin. "You know I will. I've waited a lifetime for her."

Jayce stepped back to join Leah. He slipped his arm around her waist and pulled her close. Leah smiled up at him, sensing his happiness.

The ceremony was short and simple. They exchanged their promises of love and support, then Jacob surprised them all by producing a small gold band. Leah recognized it as having been their mother's. Jacob had tried to give it to her on one occasion, but Leah knew that their mother had wanted him to save it for his bride.

As he slipped the ring on Helaina's finger, Leah couldn't help but sniff back tears. Their mother would be so proud. Their papa too. Leah liked to believe they were watching from heaven and knew they would surely approve of this union.

"You may kiss your bride, Jacob. You are man and wife," Bjorn announced.

Jacob pulled Helaina into his arms and gave her a brief but sufficient kiss. Cheers broke out among those in the room as Leah's gaze settled on her brother. They had always been so very close. They had taken care of each other when no one else was there for them. They had endured great difficulty in just getting to Alaska, but also in living there. The land was hard and difficult, but the rewards had been so great. Leah couldn't help but wonder what the future held now. Would they all go their separate ways? Would God see fit to keep them all together?

"I want to congratulate you both," Adrik said, coming to give Jacob a bear hug. He turned to Helaina. "Do I get to kiss the bride?"

She nodded and seemed delighted to be embraced into the family in this way. Karen, too, came and offered her a kiss and a blessing. "May God richly bless your marriage. May you always remember Him first in all that you do, and may your love endure the tests of time."

"Thank you," Helaina said, embracing Karen. "I feel so very blessed."

Leah came forward and hugged Helaina. "You are truly my sister now. I've always wanted a sister."

Helaina laughed and tightened her embrace. "I have, too, and now God has answered that prayer as well."

Jayce swept Helaina into a hug as Leah turned to her brother. They just looked at each other for a moment, and in Jacob's eyes, Leah saw the passage of two decades of time. Jacob sensed it as well.

"When we first came north, I cursed it," he admitted. "I saw very little good here. You know that."

"I do. I felt the same way," Leah admitted.

"But now I see so clearly the hand of God in all the choices—good and bad. It amazes me how God could take even my rebellious choices and work them together for good."

"I know. I was thinking much the same. You were always there for me."

Jacob held her close for a moment. "I love you, Leah. No man could ask for a better sister."

Leah stepped back as he released her. "And no woman could ask for a better brother."

Helaina looked down at her finger and could scarcely believe she was finally married. Her dreams of having Jacob for a husband had come true. She thought only momentarily of Robert and of the beautiful diamond and sapphire ring he had given her on their wedding day. *He would be happy for me,* she thought. *He would tell me it was about time I stopped grieving him and moved forward with my life.*

She smiled to herself as she compared her old life to the new one. Things would never be the same—but then again, she didn't want them to be.

"Well, you can party all night if you want to," Jayce finally announced, "but Leah and I are going to take our leave. I haven't seen this woman in over a year, and . . . well . . . let's leave it at that."

Adrik laughed and pulled Karen toward their room. "We'll say good night as well. It'll be good to see you all at breakfast."

"Late breakfast," Jacob called back as he pulled Helaina close. He stunned her by lifting her in his arms. "A very, very late breakfast."

They all laughed at this, but no one protested the idea. Helaina felt rather embarrassed by Jacob's grandiose gesture, but at the same time she relished it and snuggled down in his arms. She sighed contentedly.

"I feel the same way," Jacob said as he carried her to their inne.

"I'm just amazed that it's finally happened. I'm so happy . . . so blessed," she whispered. "I love you so very much, Jacob."

"And I love you, Mrs. Barringer."

The next morning Helaina awoke with a start. For just a moment she couldn't remember where she was, and when she found Jacob sleeping beside her, it startled her even more. Then the memories of the night before flooded her mind. She moved closer to Jacob for warmth and smiled as his arms closed around her and pulled her near.

"Good morning," he said, his voice low. "How did you sleep?"

"Like a dream. In fact, I woke up thinking maybe I had dreamed it all. I'm glad to know that this is very much real."

He laughed. "I hope all of your dreams are just as sweet." He kissed her passionately and Helaina forgot about dreams and nightmares. Suddenly there was only Jacob. And Jacob was truly enough.

When they showed up an hour later for breakfast at Jayce and Leah's, they found themselves the objects of teasing.

"It's nearly lunchtime," Adrik said, looking at his pocket watch.

"It's been light for hours," Karen agreed.

"It's always light for hours during Alaskan summer," Jacob replied, not willing to let them get the better of him.

Leah brought their plates from the back of the stove. "We've been keeping this warm for you. Pay them no attention. They're old married folk who've grown quite bored with one another." She laughed as she gave Adrik and Karen a wink.

"My mama and papa aren't old," Christopher protested.

Leah gave his cheek a rub. "No, they really aren't. I was just teasing them."

Oliver had long since eaten his breakfast and was ready for adventure. "Kimik said we could hunt with him today. Can we?" he asked as Christopher nodded hopefully.

"I don't see why not," Adrik replied. "It seems like it will be a great time for you boys. Just make sure you do everything he says, and stay right with the party. This place isn't like home. You don't know the trails, and fog could come in and you'd be lost."

"We'll stay with him, I promise. I'll keep a good eye on Christopher too."

"But you're not my pa," the boy reminded his brother. "So you can't tell me what to do."

"Kimik isn't your pa either," Adrik countered, "but if you aren't willing to take instruction and correction from him, you'd best stay here with me."

Christopher grew very serious. "I promise I'll be good. I'll do what he tells me to do."

"All right, then. You boys head on over. I'm sure Kimik is more than ready to leave."

Leah put the twins on the floor to play as she began to clear away the breakfast dishes. Helaina dug into the food Leah had given her and thought nothing had ever tasted so good. She felt ravenous as she bit into the caribou sausage.

"I hope you're up for a bit of discussion," Adrik began. "There's something I've been wanting to talk to all four of you about."

"If it's one of Adrik's plans," Jacob said, leaning back with coffee cup in hand, "we'd better hold on to our seats."

Adrik exchanged a quick glance with Karen and laughed. "You're right on that count. I suppose my ideas can be a bit bold at times."

"Why don't you tell us what you have in mind?" Leah prompted.

Adrik folded his hands together and looked at each of them before he spoke. "I'd like you all to consider coming back with us."

"To Ketchikan?" Leah questioned.

"No, to Seward. Well, to Ship Creek, really—though they're starting to call it Anchorage now."

Helaina felt Jacob's interest even before he spoke. "For what purpose?"

"Well, that's what I want to talk to all of you about. Are you game to listen?"

Chapter Fourteen

"The situation is this," Adrik continued. "The railroad is going in all the way to Fairbanks, and the place is hopping with activity. I've been hired by the railroad to hunt and bring in game for the men to eat. It's a whole lot cheaper to hire me than to bring food up from the States, after all. The only problem is, I'm just one man and, frankly, the number of workers is growing every day. They estimate some four thousand workers now. I don't think the territory will stay unsettled for long."

Jacob shrugged. "We've seen people come and go with the gold strikes. Alaska requires a special kind of person to stay."

"Jacob's right. It's going to take more than a few thousand men to settle this place and make the world take notice," Jayce said.

"But it's a start. The railroad adds a sense of settlement and permanency that will draw people to come and stay."

"So you're proposing we work for the railroad?" Jacob asked.

"No, I'm proposing we work for ourselves," Adrik replied. "Look, we can team up—maybe even add another couple of men I trust and form our own corporation of sorts. You wouldn't believe the number of times I've been hired just to lead city folks out hunting wild game. Most want the thrill of bear or moose, some just want to enjoy whatever comes their way, so that's an entire different aspect to how we can make a living. Initially, we could contract with the railroad to provide a particular amount of meat per week and split the funds between us."

Jacob rubbed his chin thoughtfully. "Where would we live?"

"The Ship Creek area. That's a good place to headquarter. The railroad from Seward has just connected to that place and is headed on out to Palmer and Wasilla. If things continue this way, we might see completion in another couple of years. Of course, we have to get through those mountains up north, and that will be no easy feat."

"And do you plan to move north with the railroad?" Jacob asked Adrik.

Adrik looked to Karen and shrugged. "We're trying to be open to where the Lord would take us. We've found there's plenty of work to do in the area, but we also miss our home in Ketchikan. We'll just have to see where the Lord wants us."

"Not only that," Karen began, "Seward is a year-round harbor. We can get a steady supply of goods whenever we need them. Well, at least a decent supply," she added with a smile. "There are good doctors, plans for a hospital in Ship Creek, as well as a power plant and electricity."

"That would be incredible," Leah said, shaking her head. "I remember how wonderful it was when we were in Seattle."

"Not only that, but they're laying water pipes that will bring water right into the house," Adrik added.

"It's like we said," Karen continued. "The area offers many benefits that can't be had in the more isolated parts of Alaska. And there would be no winter isolation due to ship traffic being halting because of frozen harbors."

"That would definitely be a benefit," Leah admitted. She hated to say it, but having children gave her a much different perspective on where to live. "Still, I'm happy to live wherever Jayce wants to be. I know he'll provide for us and that we'll be well protected in his care. So long as my family is with me or close by, I'll be content."

She looked to Jayce and could see he was strongly considering the possibility. "I believe it's definitely something to think about," he said.

Jacob looked to Helaina. "What about you? What do you think of this wild scheme of Adrik's?"

"I feel the same as Leah. I had to wait all this time to get you. I don't really care where we live so long as we aren't long separated."

"That's a good point. How long are these hunting expeditions?" Jacob questioned.

Adrik shrugged. "Depends on how plentiful the game is and how far out we have to go to get to the animals. We would rotate being gone, however. A team of men would go out and hunt, while another team would stay at home and deal with the meat, the hides, and the railroad officials. There's also some good money to be made in fur trading, so seeing those hides prepared will be another big job."

"We could help with that," Leah threw in. "I've done plenty of tanning."

"I'm not sure I'd want you to help, Leah," Adrik said, shaking his head. "I suppose it would all depend on where we set up our work site. The men in the area can be a little rough—especially those from the States recruited to bring their railroad work experience to the frozen north. Don't get me wrong—it's a good place to live and most folks are perfectly well-mannered. But it's a man's world."

Leah nodded, understanding Adrik's words completely. He had no problem with a woman helping her family to exist, but he wanted to see her safe from harm.

Jayce looked to Jacob and shrugged. "What do you think, Jacob?"

"Couldn't be worse than living in the Arctic for a year." His smile broadened. "I say let's give it a try. We might find we really like the area. If nothing else, we'll have had a hand in civilizing the territory. We can someday tell our children we helped bring the railroad to Alaska."

"I agree. I think we should give it a chance."

Adrik slapped the table. "That's great news, boys."

Leah felt a strange sense of excitement mingled with regret wash over her. They were going to leave Last Chance—maybe for good. She'd miss her friends dearly, but she'd have Karen and the boys back in her life. She'd missed them all more than she could even begin to say.

Jayce turned to her and gently lifted her face to meet his. "Are you sure this is all right with you?"

She thought for a moment. "It's not without regret, but I'm happy to go wherever you lead." She threw a glance at Jacob and Adrik. "I think it will be a blessing for all of us."

"I just want you to make certain that you'll be happy."

She laughed and shook her head. "We both know there are no guarantees for that. I very much like the idea of having better things for the children, but even if you desired to stay here, I wouldn't protest. I'm just glad to have you back. I promised God if He would just send you home, I'd do my best to never be quarrelsome again."

Jayce touched her cheek. "I want you to be happy. That matters a great deal to me."

"I think it will be a good experiment," Jacob interjected. "It's not like we can't return here should things not work out. I can't really say why, but it just seems like the Lord is leading us to Anchorage. And since it's already August, we need to make up our minds and secure ship passage."

"That's true enough. We had already booked our return for the twenty-sixth," Adrik told them. "I don't know if there will be enough room for all of us, but I'd bet there will be."

Leah realized the twenty-sixth was only a few days away. It wouldn't give them much time for packing. Then again, she didn't really know what they'd need. Would they have a house or share one with Adrik and Karen? Would they need to bring all of their things, or should they wait until they had a better idea of how long they'd stay?

"We'd have to move fast to be able to head back with you," Jacob said. "We'd need to be packed by the day after tomorrow and secure Kimik and some of the others to take us to Nome."

Two days. That was all they'd have. Today and the next day. Leah shook her head. It was hard to imagine that she'd pack up their lives and leave in two days. "We could take a later ship," she said without thinking.

"You could, but I think it's better to come with us if there's room," Adrik replied. "We can help with the bulk of things you want to bring. I can get people in Seward to help us get the stuff north. Once I explain, the railroad will probably transport us for free. It would just work well for us to all go together."

"I agree," Karen added, "and I could help with the babies."

"Let's commit this to prayer. I feel good about it—very good about it—but I want to make sure it's the direction God has for us," Jacob said.

Jayce nodded thoughtfully. "I agree. God's pacing is never frantic and ill-thought. I suggest we begin our packing and make arrangements but all the while pray fervently about the matter."

Leah looked out over the landscape, turning as she stood in one place to take in the view in all directions. It would be strange to leave this place, but the adventure of a new start—a new life in Ship Creek—excited her. It seemed that all was in keeping with God's plans. John and Oopick's reaction was positive, and they promised to buy as many dogs as Jacob wanted to leave behind. They also offered to take over the inne and see to it that things remained in good repair.

Sigrid had offered to stay at Leah and Jacob's house and keep it for them until they decided if they wanted to sell it or move back. That comforted Leah greatly. It was good to know they weren't breaking all of their ties to Last Chance Creek.

"Are you all right?"

Leah turned to find her brother stalking up the hill toward her. "I was just thinking about our leaving. Jayce feels God's hand in the matter—as I know you do."

"But you don't?"

"I didn't say that." Leah looked at Jacob. He seemed so much older than he had a year ago. "I still haven't heard from you about this last year. I've not had a single moment to just sit down with you and ask about the way things went."

It was Jacob's turn to stare off into the distance. He frowned momentarily. "At first I felt we were more than capable of making it all work together for good. I didn't like the idea that God had allowed it, but I felt it wouldn't be the end of us.

"There were days, however . . ." His voice grew soft, barely audible. "I really started to despair at the end. The men were so angry. They couldn't understand why we wouldn't allow them to just set off for home. They couldn't see the dangers. They'd never been out at sea in an umiak and didn't know the risks. I fear them all dead now."

Leah put her hand firmly on Jacob's arm. "You are not in the wrong. Your admonitions to stay were sound. *They* chose to throw off the counsel of their authority."

"They didn't see our authority as valid. They felt we were just men like themselves and that our knowledge didn't give us the right to make their choices."

"People often see their authority figures in that way," Leah said. She pushed back the hood of her kuspuk. "Especially when it comes to God."

"You're right on that account. But, Leah, those were good men. I talked many nights with each one. They were homesick and longing to have their families once again at their side. Unfortunately, it caused them to make bad decisions, and I fear they'll never see civilization again, much less their families."

"If they are dead, you cannot change it by mourning what might have been," Leah said, squeezing his arm. "I've no doubt you offered sound counsel and wisdom. I believe most sincerely that you offered friendship and kindness."

He turned to her and placed his hand atop hers. "We've been through a lot in this country—you and me."

Leah saw that the sorrow had left him at least momentarily. She smiled. "Yes, we have. We've seen a great many things, good and bad."

"But the blessings have been greater than the problems."

"Yes. I wasn't honestly sure I would ever be able to say that," Leah began, "but the Lord has worked on my heart this last year. Maybe I wasn't very willing to listen to my authority either." She moved a pace away and turned to look out across the vast expanse of water.

"There were days," she said, the longing clear in her voice, "that I would stand here and stare out at the ice. I knew you were both out there. I felt you must surely be alive, because I just didn't feel like you were dead. But feeling a thing and making it so . . . well, those are two different things. I lost hope. I began to fear the worst. Helaina told me over and over that you were alive—that you'd both return. I wanted to have her faith, because mine seemed so insufficient."

"I know what you mean. I listen to her talk about how she waited here, knowing I'd come home, and it both humbles and embarrasses me. Why couldn't I have stood the test of time? I've been saved a whole lot longer than she has."

Leah laughed. Jacob always had a way of bringing a matter right down to the point. "That's the pride in both of us, I guess. We rose to the occasion and proclaimed our trust in God, then sat alone, miserable for fear that our trust had been misplaced. Then when we see that others were stronger and more inspired to believe the truth, we feel regret and frustration. And it's all because our pride is wounded. We were so confident that we would be strong. We were so confident that we could take on any trial God sent our way."

"You know the Bible talks about how we don't wrestle against flesh and blood—"

" 'But against principalities, against powers, against rulers of the darkness of this world, against wickedness in high places,' " Leah finished the verse from Ephesians 6. "I cherished that passage during your absence. I felt I was trying so hard to be all things to all people. I didn't want people to see how sad or lonely I was. I didn't even want to share that with Helaina."

"I know. I felt the same way about sharing it with Jayce." He reached out and took hold of Leah's hand. "We're so alike. I guess only having each other for so long made us that way. I hope you know you will always hold a special place in my heart. I know a lot of men have no lasting relationship with their siblings. Jayce is a good example. He hasn't heard from them in years, save Chase."

Leah frowned at the thought of Jayce's twin.

Jacob immediately recognized the mistake. "I'm sorry. I shouldn't have mentioned him."

"No, it's really all right. I'm trying hard to put him behind me. I feel bad because I can't even comfort Jayce on the loss of his brother. I never want to hear about what happened out there—not that Jayce has ever really offered me any more details than what he shared when he returned. Chase was attacked by a bear—maybe the same one I shot earlier in the day. His death was as ordained by God as a thing could be."

Jacob hugged her close. "I want things to be better for you. I felt so guilty about not being able to save you from him."

Leah pulled back. "Don't feel guilty. I've borne enough guilt for both of us."

"But you were completely innocent of everything. Even Helaina could take partial blame for what happened, but not you."

"No one is to blame but Chase." Leah forced the name from her lips. "He made bad choices. He made them all of his life. He cared more about himself and his own pleasure than anyone else. He did the things he did to gratify himself and to punish Jayce for the good life he had known."

"Still, I wish I could have saved you from it."

Leah hoped her next words would free Jacob from any further guilt. "Jacob, I never thought I could say this, but I wouldn't trade my children for anything. Not even if they are the result of what Chase did."

Jacob looked at her oddly for a moment. "Truly?"

"Truly. They are my heart. Even if they were born out of the rape, it isn't their fault. They did nothing wrong and shouldn't be punished because of someone else's sin. Not even for the sins of their father—if Chase truly played that part. I can't say I never struggle with this," she admitted, "but my struggles are not over whether or not Chase's actions caused my pregnancy, but more as to whether Jayce can accept the babies I love as his own. Or whether he will come to hate them, should we have other children that we know are his."

"I'd never considered such a matter, but I can tell you it would make no difference to me if the same had happened to Helaina. I would love any child of hers—because it was a part of her. I'm sure Jayce feels the same way. I know he regretted the separation. He talked of you and the babies often."

"I think this new start will be good for all of us. It will be a lot of work, but I think it will also benefit us greatly."

"I do too. It's rather like taking off for a whole different kind of goldfield, eh?"

Leah thought back to when their father had first dragged them to Alaska. She also remembered the trek north to find Jacob when he left Dyea and headed to the Yukon. "It is very much like those adventures, but it holds a greater promise than gold. It holds the promise of love."

Chapter Fifteen

DECEMBER 1917

The Christmas holidays were rapidly approaching, much to Leah's amazement. It seemed they had just arrived in the Ship Creek area only days before instead of months. The cabin she now shared with Jayce had only been finished a few weeks earlier. Leah felt very privileged; most folks were still living in tents, and she remembered only too well what that was like from her time in the Yukon. The cabin was much better.

To her specifications, there was one large common room with two smaller rooms off the back of this. The latter were bedrooms, one for Leah and Jayce and the other one for the twins. The twins' room held a low rope bed that could accommodate both children. A small steamer trunk served as their clothes chest, and another trunk rounded out the furnishings as a makeshift toy box. Adrik promised a much nicer one as a Christmas gift, but the twins didn't seem to mind the current arrangement.

Leah and Jayce's room wasn't much larger than the children's room. There was a more substantial bed that had been designed by Adrik. The peeled-log frame offered a sturdy foundation, while the feather-stuffed mattress provided a comfortable night's sleep. A large wooden dresser stood in one corner of the room, also compliments of Adrik. The house was a tight fit, but the snugness only added to the hominess.

Leah loved having the privacy it afforded as well. When they'd first arrived at the house Adrik had built for his wife and sons, it was clear that things would be quite crowded for a time. The land was plentiful, but the buildings were not. It took time to fell trees and put together structures. But the people were just as eager to help each other here as they had been in Last

Chance. One day a group of men from the railroad and church had gathered and cut trees and notched logs for two small houses. They accomplished an incredible amount of work in the all-day extravaganza, and only later did Leah learn that all three men in her family had offered the men pay, but they'd have none of it. Their act of kindness touched her deeply.

Another obvious difference in Leah's life was the development of the twins. They were rapidly changing in appearance and, where they had once looked very much like each other, now they were showing definite male and female qualities. Merry's face seemed more delicate, her lips fuller, and the lashes that edged her eyes were longer and thicker than her brother's. Wills developed a set to his face that reminded Leah of Jayce. He would often knit his brow together while considering some toy or other object of fascination. His nose appeared a little fuller, while his lips seemed thinner than Meredith's.

There were also changes of personality. Merry, while still shy, had taken on a personality that reflected Leah's quiet nature. Whenever Wills got into trouble, Merry was always there to smooth things over. When Leah was upset, Merry would often pat her mother's leg as if to console her while gazing sympathetically and babbling incoherent words of encouragement.

Wills' personality, on the other hand, reminded Leah so much of Jayce. His eyes were much darker blue than Merry's glacier blue. He was fiercely independent and fearless. Even now as Leah watched them play, she worried incessantly about Wills getting too close to the stove. He seemed to have no concern about whether it would cause him harm or good. Wills saw everything as an adventure. Why should the stove be any different?

A knock on her door took Leah out of her reflective thoughts. "Wills, you stay away from the stove. That's hot. It will hurt you." Wills looked up, as if trying to ascertain the validity of his mother's words.

Leah opened the door to find Karen and Helaina. Both held numerous evergreen boughs in their arms. "What a surprise. Looks like you two have been busy." She stepped back to admit them in from the cold.

"It's snowed another six inches," Karen said. She shook the branches, then handed them to Leah. "We were gathering these to decorate for Christmas and thought you might like some too. With the babies toddling around, I wasn't sure you'd have time to gather any for yourself."

"That was very thoughtful." Leah pressed her nose into the bundle. "Mmm, they smell so good."

"I can't believe Christmas is nearly here," Helaina declared. She put her branches on the nearby table and leaned down to see what Wills was playing with. "What is that, Wills?"

He held the toy up and grinned. "Doggy nice."

Helaina nodded. "It's a very nice doggy indeed."

"Baby!" Merry declared, holding out her doll from the other side of the room.

"Merry, what a pretty baby. Come show me." Helaina continued to play with the children for a moment while Leah tried to decide where would be best to store the boughs. "If I don't put them up, the children will surely destroy them."

"Oh, I wanted to tell you," Karen began, "I had three letters arrive today with the post. One was from Grace, another from Miranda, and the final one was from Ashlie."

Leah loved to hear news—especially from loved ones far away. "I wish I could hear something from Last Chance. I probably won't know how anyone is doing until spring, however. You know how impossible it is to send mail across the interior."

"Yes. There were so many times I would have loved to have sent you letters and packages during the long winter."

"Me too," Leah said, easily remembering the isolation. "So how is Grace?" Grace had once been Karen's charge when they both lived in Chicago. Karen had loved being a governess to the wealthy girl. They'd both come north to Alaska when Grace had been determined to escape an arranged marriage. Then while in Alaska, Grace and Karen had both found true love and married. Karen had stayed, but Grace had gone to San Francisco to live with her husband and his family.

"They're all very well. Grace is worried because her son talks continually about joining the army to fight in Europe. Grace is heartsick over the thought that he might sneak off in the night and do something rash."

"Hasn't Peter tried to reason with him?"

"What's a father to do?" Karen shook her head. "I'm sure Peter and Grace have both done their best to convince him to remain at home, but you know how headstrong children can be. Andrew is almost eighteen, and he's confident he knows more than his parents. At least to hear Grace tell it."

"I'm sure," Leah said with a nod. "What about the other children?"

"Well, let's see. Jeremiah is fifteen and very much in love with the sea, just like his father. Belynn is twelve, and Grace says she plans to be married with six children by the time she's twenty."

Leah laughed and tried to imagine what life would be like for the twelve-year-old Belynn. Why, there were automobiles and airplanes, not to mention all kinds of machinery that helped with the everyday chores of life. Leah's children might never know such luxury if they remained in the wilds. "And what about Miranda? Where will she and Teddy spend this Christmas?"

"Well, Teddy wanted to explore some islands off the coast of South America. They were actually in San Francisco with Peter and Grace when Miranda posted this letter, but she said they were southbound. It seems Teddy would like to write a book dealing with the flora and fauna of that area."

Leah nodded, remembering quite well that Teddy Davenport had a passion for botany that was only preceded by his love for Miranda. "And what did Miranda's brother think of that?"

"Peter was very happy to assist them. They will journey south on one of his ships, in fact. The Colton Shipping Company is quite expanded from what it used to be."

"It's too bad Peter's mother and father didn't live to see what a successful businessman Peter has become. I'm sure they would have been proud," Leah said thoughtfully. "So you've saved the best for last. What does Ashlie have to say? Oh, where are my manners? I have some hot tea. Would either of you care for a cup?"

Helaina straightened and rubbed the small of her back through the thick parka. "I'd love some. I'm still a little chilled."

"Me too. Tea sounds perfect." Karen pulled her coat off and went to hang it by the door. "I hope I haven't dripped water all over your floor."

"It needed washing anyway. It's very dirty you know," Leah said, glancing down at the hard-packed dirt with a grin.

Karen chuckled. "You'll have floors before you know it. Adrik has been very concerned that you should be living without them, you know."

"We're fine. We've certainly had to deal with worse." Leah poured her guests tea and brought the steaming mugs to the table. "You'll have to forgive the cups, my good china is otherwise engaged."

"Engaged where?" Helaina asked with a smile.

Leah shrugged and gave a girlish giggle. "I'm sure I don't know since I haven't any good china. But wherever it is, I'm sure it's otherwise engaged."

"You'll remember I had some very pretty china when I first settled in Ketchikan with Adrik. He couldn't even get his fingers around the cup handle. It was most amusing. What wasn't as humorous was his penchant for dropping them. They were just too delicate and would slip right through his fingers. Mugs turned out to be much better for us."

"I suppose that's why I've never worried about china," Leah said, shrugging. "I'm sure you must miss such things, however." She looked to Helaina, remembering the grandeur her life had once known.

"There are times," Helaina admitted, "when I miss some of the finery. But I love it here, and it's senseless to have things that serve little or no purpose. Mugs are fine by me. What I miss is the convenience of things. Hot baths, large selections of scented soaps and such. It's that kind of thing I miss."

"I can remember Seattle well enough to know exactly how pleasant it was to have a bath anytime I wanted one," Leah agreed. Seattle spurred on memories of Ashlie. "All right, tell us about your daughter."

Helaina nodded enthusiastically. "Yes, please do. Is she happy? How's school going?"

"She is happy," Karen said with a bit of regret in her tone. "It's not that I wouldn't wish her so, but there's that part of me that wouldn't mind if she were unhappy enough to return home to me. I miss her so much."

"I know you do," Leah said, putting her hand on Karen's arm. "I hope we might ease some of that longing by keeping you too preoccupied to miss her overly much."

"It has been a pleasant diversion to have you so close—both of you. The boys are poor companions at times; I'm convinced that neither of them needs me. They want to be off hunting or exploring the minute their studies are concluded. They are not exactly conversationalists." The three ladies laughed at this statement.

"Does Ashlie have plans to come home anytime soon?" Leah asked.

"No. She's busy with church activities and, of course, her studies. Cousin Myrtle has definitely enjoyed her company as well. Ashlie tells in her letter that they attend many plays and parties. Ashlie has brought new life to my cousin, and for that I'm grateful. Myrtle was never blessed with children of her own, and having Ashlie has given her a great deal of pleasure. I'd beg Ashlie to return to us, but I know it would break Myrtle's heart. Not to mention Ashlie, who would like to attend college. She's been quite smitten with school and learning."

There was a sad resignation in Karen's voice that Leah couldn't ignore. "It has been with no small amount of sacrifice on your part that Ashlie has enjoyed another kind of life. The world in Seattle is so very different from the one we know here."

"I know that's true. It was no easy feat to adjust to life in Alaska. When I came north with Grace, it was exciting to try something new, but where life in the south might allow for mere existence, Alaska demands much more. There is no mere 'getting by' up here. You will die if you don't put a definite effort into survival."

"That's true," Leah said, nodding, "but Ashlie knows about survival. She was born and raised here, and she's nobody's fool. Let her enjoy her time and see what life has to hold. She's in good hands, and obviously she's benefiting your cousin as well."

Karen nodded. "To be sure. Still, she's almost eighteen. I've already noted comments in her letters that mention young men who would like to be her suitor. So far she's kept them all at arm's length. She tells me she's not been overly impressed with any of them. But I don't try to fool myself. The day will come when that one man . . . that perfect man . . . will sweep her away."

"Just like it happened to each of us," Leah said with a smile. "Would you want anything less for her?"

Karen shook her head. "Of course not. I just . . . well . . . I worry that she'll never come back to Alaska after that."

"She'll always come to wherever you are," Leah encouraged. She gave Karen's arm a squeeze and raised her gaze to see that the twins were still happily occupied with their toys. "So did any of the letters offer news of the war in Europe?"

"Only to say that things were continuing to drag on. It's so sad. So many have died," Karen spoke more quietly. It was almost as if she didn't want the twins to overhear the bad news. "Things definitely do not look good for the Russian people. They've taken the czar and his family captive, and no one knows what will happen to them. And King George of England, who happens to be a relative—I believe a cousin perhaps to either the czar or his wife—refused to let the family come to England for asylum."

Leah shook her head. "How awful to reject your own family. What kind of man does that when he knows it will no doubt bode poorly for the czar? I read in one of the old papers that the new government is not inclined to be sympathetic toward royalty."

"I met a man who was closely affiliated with the czar and czarina," Helaina joined in. "He was here seeking to find a place to hide the family should they be able to sneak out of Russia. He believes they will face death."

"And still the King of England will not allow them refuge?" Leah questioned.

"Ashlie said in her letter that it seemed the government of England advised the king that it would be best to stay out of the situation. Apparently they feel there is little to be gained, and perhaps it would damage relationships with the new government and cause them to turn from the side of those fighting the Germans."

"That's so sad," Leah said, shaking her head. "I hate war. I can't imagine what the soldiers must have to endure. Just as bad, I can't fathom what their families must have to bear here at home. The news is so long in coming and then you can only wonder at the accuracy."

"The news is coming regularly in the States," Karen said, staring at her mug. "But it seems the news is always bad."

"Well, I for one have had enough sad talk," Helaina said, putting her mug on the table. "I have some good news that I'd like to share. I was going to wait until later, but I want you both to be the first to know." Leah and Karen both met her gaze. Helaina grinned. "I'm going to have a baby."

Leah could hardly believe the words. Her brother was finally going to be a father. "Helaina, that's wonderful!" She reached over to embrace her sister-in-law. "What did Jacob say? Oh, I can imagine he's beside himself."

"He doesn't know yet," she admitted. "I've been waiting to be certain and now I am." She gave a little shudder of excitement. "I can hardly believe it's happening."

"When is the baby due to arrive?" Karen asked.

"By my best calculations, it will be in May."

"A wedding night baby," Leah said after a quick mental calculation.

Helaina blushed. "That's the way I see it as well."

Karen laughed. "Jacob was never one for delaying things that he wanted done. That boy . . . well, hardly that . . . he's wanted a wife and family for so long, he probably figured to just accomplish it all at once."

Leah sat back in her chair. "When will you tell him?"

"Tonight, if possible. I knew they'd be busy today, and I just wanted to wait until there was plenty of time to enjoy the moment. Tonight will be soon enough."

"I won't say a word to him," Leah promised.

"Neither will I," Karen agreed.

Helaina put her hand to her stomach and shook her head. "I can hardly believe this is happening to me. I'm so happy I could cry."

"Well, don't do that, or Jacob will know that something's going on." Leah got to her feet. "I think it's time for the twins to go take their nap." She motioned to where Merry now sat groggily leaning against the log wall, while Wills yawned from where he sat on the rug.

"I need to get home to finish supper." Karen got to her feet. "Tomorrow we can make plans for our Christmas celebration. This is going to be such a merry occasion." She drew on her parka. "May will be a perfect month for a new baby."

"I was thinking the same thing," Leah said as she lifted Wills.

"Around here things will be warm and beautiful. Last year there were flowers and nice warm days where it was a pleasure to be outside in the sun. You can never tell about Alaska weather, but chances are good that it will be a very nice time to bring a new life into the world."

Helaina smiled. "It comforts me just to know you'll both be here. You will stay with me, won't you? I mean when the time comes?"

"Of course we will." Leah heard the apprehension in her voice. "You would be hard-pressed to be rid of us."

"That's right," Karen added. "I have helped with many births, as has Leah. We certainly wouldn't want to miss this most important occasion. We'll be there for you."

Jayce surprised Leah by showing up an hour later for lunch. "I hope you have something to eat. I'm starved," he said as he bounded into the house. He was covered with snow from head to foot. "I think logging is much harder than just hunting for a living."

Leah looked at him and shook her head. "Could you please leave some of winter outside?"

Jayce glanced down and shrugged. "It just seems to follow me wherever I go. I'll do what I can."

He came back in a few minutes later, parka in hand. He'd dusted himself off and had given the parka a good shake. Leah smiled over her shoulder at him. "You look better now. I'm warming up some of the stew from last night. I hope that's good enough for now. I promise to have thick moose steak for you this evening."

"Sounds good. We've been cutting logs to deliver to the railroad later this afternoon, and then Adrik says we won't go out again for quite a while. Winter weather has shut down most every aspect of the rail line. The officials are still intent on building up supplies and getting new houses up for some of their men, however."

"I don't understand why they can't continue to put in tracks during the winter. It's not that cold right now."

"The ground is frozen, though, and there's not a good way of telling how firm the ground will be come spring thaw. If we lay tracks in an area not knowing it needs to be reinforced or elevated, we could have a swamp train. It will probably save a good deal of money to just wait until May. Even if they have to rehire a new crew. I heard most of the men are heading back down to the States."

"If they're not used to Alaska winter, then I can't blame them. It's probably best they go." Leah stirred the contents of the black iron pot. "Oh, I have good news." She put the spoon down and came to where Jayce had planted himself at the table.

To her surprise, Jayce pulled her onto his lap and snuggled his bearded face against her neck. "Hmm, this is a wonderful way to warm up."

"Did you hear me? I have some wonderful news to tell you."

"Hmmm, I heard."

"I don't think you're even listening to me." She playfully pushed him away, but Jayce only tightened his hold.

He looked up at her and grinned. "What is it that's so important?"

"Well, you have to promise you won't say a word about it, until the right time, of course."

He frowned and let her ease away. "Well, I suppose I can promise that much. Now tell me."

"Helaina and Jacob are going to have a baby. But Helaina hasn't told Jacob yet."

A broad smile broke across Jayce's face. "That is good news. I know Jacob will be excited."

"It's the best news of all. I'm so happy for them."

Jayce pulled her back to him and cradled her tenderly. "Life is so different with a wife and children. Jacob will feel himself become complete. There's nothing like looking into the face of your children and knowing that a part of you will go on, even after you're dead and gone."

An image of Chase flashed through her mind. Leah pushed the thought aside, but Jayce noted the difference in her. "What's wrong?"

She covered her reaction quickly. "The stew. It's going to burn." She got up quickly and walked to the stove. *Dear Lord, how long will it be before the old thoughts stop tormenting me?* She sighed. They came fewer and farther between, so that was good. Nevertheless, Leah couldn't help but wonder what it would take to finally lay all of her demons to rest. There had to be an answer. There just had to be a way.

Chapter Sixteen

Jacob loaded the last of the peeled logs onto the wagon. "This is it."

Adrik nodded and made note in his ledger. "Not sure what they plan for all these logs, but at least they'll have a stack to work with. There are plans to expand the lumber mill, and that will prove beneficial for everyone."

"Do you think they'll start working on the railroad again before spring thaw?"

Adrik shook his head. "They'd be foolhardy to try. There are so many issues at hand. Money is always the biggest, right along with conditions. The war is another. I'm not sure how things will come out in the wash."

Jacob grinned. "You sound like Karen now. I remember her using that phrase."

Adrik leaned closer and closed the green ledger. "I have some news. I'm just about beside myself to share it with someone."

"I'm your man," Jacob said, glancing around. "You look as though it might be an issue of national security."

"Nah, just Ivankov security. I've made arrangements for Ashlie to come home for Christmas. Remember Karen's nephew Timothy?"

"Of course."

"Well, he'll accompany Ashlie. They should arrive any day."

"Karen will definitely love you for that." Jacob could only imagine her happiness.

"I've been working on it for some time. I tried to get Myrtle to come too, but she didn't feel up to making such a long trip. She'll spend the holidays with some of Karen's other family members, so she won't be alone."

"Timothy was a great help to us in Seattle," Jacob remembered. "I'll be glad to hear from him—his take on the war and such. I have to say I've had some twinges of guilt when I think of the men going off to fight. Maybe if I didn't have a wife, I'd be more inclined to give it serious consideration."

"Well, they're only requiring younger men to register—under thirty-one, I think I heard."

Jacob leaned against the cart. "I know. Still, I think about the liberty and freedom I've enjoyed all these years, and it makes me think I should do something more."

"You can always pray," Adrik suggested. "Folks need a whole lot more of that than they know."

"True enough. You about ready to head out?" Jacob asked. "Temperature's dropped so much I'm actually starting to feel it. The horses are anxious too. I'm ready to be done with this." Leo and Addy gave impatient whines. "Guess they're ready too." The two Huskies cocked their heads in unison as if knowing their master was speaking of them.

"I'll just check the area for tools," Adrik said, throwing a saw onto the wagon. "Remember to keep quiet about Ashlie," he called over his shoulder.

"You know I will. I think it's mighty thoughtful of you, Adrik. Most men wouldn't be half as considerate of their wife as you have been." Jacob climbed onto the wagon.

"Karen's a special lady. She has her ornery side, but her loving nature makes it worth living with those few times when she plays prankster."

"Like the time she kept sewing your trousers smaller and smaller?" Jacob fondly remembered the event. Adrik had refused to throw away a particularly ugly and well-worn pair of pants. To encourage her husband to part with the pants, Karen took up the seams a little every few days. At first Adrik thought he'd added a few pounds, but nothing he did helped. In fact, the pants just got tighter and tighter.

"I'd almost forgot about that," Adrik admitted with a grin. "Almost, but not quite. She's ornery. There's just no tellin' what she'll do from one minute to the next. What I do know is that she'll be as happy as she's ever been to see Ashlie come home."

Adrik took his place behind the team and picked up the reins and snapped them once. "Let's go."

Leo and Addy, longtime favorites of Jacob's, led the way. Adrik had fixed runners in place of the wheels so that the wagon could move easily over the snow, carrying the maximum amount of weight. With fewer men on the railroad's payroll, hunting had lessened to a minimum. They seldom had to go out more than once a week to keep everyone in their area well provided for. Jacob didn't mind the change of work. Trading the constant smell of death for the heady scent of spruce and earth made the hard work worthwhile. It also paid a bit better, although the railroad was not known for paying anyone very well.

Jacob thought about the days to come. He was excited to have secured a beautiful wedding ring for Helaina. He planned to give it to her Christmas morning when they were alone. Sometimes it was nice to have a lot of family around, but he also craved privacy with his wife. Helaina wouldn't be expecting his gift—of this he was confident. After all, he'd given her his mother's gold band when they'd married in Last Chance. But the simplicity of that gold band, and the fact that Jacob hadn't picked it out special for Helaina, had left him unable to think of much else. When the opportunity presented itself, Jacob had purchased the new ring with great enthusiasm. It would look perfect with the gold band and offer Helaina the best of all his love.

"You're mighty quiet over there," Adrik said as he maneuvered the wagon down the slippery roadway.

"I'm tired," Jacob said, pulling up his collar. "Tired and cold. I'm glad we'll have some time away from the railroad. The break will do us all good. It's hard to go from being your own boss to having to meet somebody else's demands."

"You talking about being married or working for the railroad?" Adrik teased.

Jacob laughed. "The railroad. I still like being married."

"Well, so do I. At least as long as I remember who's boss."

"I've been doing a lot of thinking about jobs and what I can do once the railroad moves on."

"What'd you have in mind?"

"Actually, I've been praying on that. I've thought about opening a store. I enjoyed trading with folks back in Last Chance, and it seems it would be a responsible business to start up here. Most of the places here are crude at best. I'm thinking maybe I could talk to Peter Colton and see about getting some regular shipments into Seward."

"And move down there?"

"Not necessarily. Maybe have a warehouse there if need be. Ship Creek seems to be growing enough to support more business. If the train proves successful, it would be easy enough to bring goods up from Seward. Guess I'll see just how much I like it once I've wintered here. It can't be as hard or isolated as life in Last Chance."

"Well, I'll give you that." Adrik scratched his gloved fingers against his bearded face. "A store would be a great pursuit. A lot of work, though. You sure you want that kind of work—what with having a new wife and all?"

"Helaina tells me all the time that she would love to work with me at something. Hunting isn't a good thing to drag her around doing, so I just keep thinking about the store."

"So you both plan to stay here in Alaska?" Adrik asked. He glanced at Jacob as if to read his expression. "Seriously."

"We both love it here. It's so unspoiled, and while it doesn't provide the comforts of big city life, you're also away from the burdens. You know, Helaina told me just the other night that she's never felt safer any place in the world. In New York, they worry about locking up their doors for fear of someone coming in and stealing their possessions."

"I couldn't live like that," Adrik said, shaking his head. "It's a sorry state of affairs when you have to look with suspicion at everyone who passes your way. Seems almost that you create a sort of prison for yourself and your things."

Adrik seemed to relax as the trail opened into a level snow-covered valley. He gave the horses a signal and let them move out at full speed before Jacob picked the conversation back up.

"I agree. For all the time I've been in Alaska, we never had enough to worry much about locking things up," Jacob admitted. "Folks knew they could take refuge at empty cabins on the trail—the owners would even leave enough fuel for a fire."

"That's the law of the north. Folks know not to run off without leaving some manner of provision for the next fellow."

Jacob knew that law well. "Even while running the store in Last Chance, we never worried about keeping track of things too closely. Leah kept records and such, but many was the time when people just came over and helped themselves. They always made it right later on."

Adrik nodded. "I would expect as much. Still, you have thievery up here as well. Remember how bad it was during the gold rush?"

"Oh sure," Jacob agreed. "People are always wanting something for nothing, but the weaker ones went south after they tried their hand at gold and other means of getting rich quick. It's discontentment that leads people into foolishness. I'm a content man, so I care little about chasing after things that might or might not make me happy."

The valley began to close up again, but the trail was wide and well-traveled, and Jacob knew the horses would have little trouble taking them right back to their base camp. The sounds of civilization broke through the silence. Jacob found it amazing that the little townsite was already planning for the day when electricity would ease their long winter darkness with streetlamps and well-lit homes.

"Look, I'll go ahead and drop this off at the lumberyard. Why don't you head on home?" Adrik suggested.

Before Jacob could answer, a man called to Adrik as he made his way up the trail. He waved and hailed them. "Adrik, there's word about your relatives. They've made it to Seward."

"That's great news, Morris. Thanks for coming to find me."

Morris chuckled. "Thanks for being on your way back. I feared I was in for quite a hike. Guess I got lucky. What else have you to do?"

"This is the last load of logs," Adrik replied. "I'm especially glad now that you've told me what I've been waiting to hear." He turned to Jacob. "Look, I'm gonna need some help from both of you. I want to go down to Seward and help Timothy and Ashlie make the trip here."

"I'll finish with this delivery," Jacob offered. "Just go."

"Train is taking on fuel even as we speak. I told them to wait for you," Morris offered. "They weren't too happy, but when I explained the situation, they agreed to hold off until you got back. They'll be pleased to find it'll be just minutes instead of hours."

Adrik nodded. "Sounds good. I'm indebted to both of you."

Morris grinned. "I have a packet of papers for you to deliver once you reach Seward. That way you won't have to lie to your missus. Jacob can tell your Karen that you were needed on official railroad business."

Adrik's laugh bellowed across the otherwise quiet countryside. "I see you've thought of everything."

"The light's nearly gone," Jacob said with a glance at the skies. "You go on. I'll tend to this. Morris and I will make short work of it."

Adrik nodded. "Don't forget to give Karen the ledger. She'll see to it that my figures are entered right."

"I'll do it. Just go."

Jacob watched as Adrik gathered his things from the back of the cart. He seemed happier than Jacob had seen him in ages. *I think he brought Ashlie home as much for himself as he did for Karen,* Jacob mused. Ashlie was the light of her father's life, and Adrik spoiled her terribly. Jacob supposed if God ever blessed him with a daughter of his own, he'd do likewise.

Jacob walked into his cabin well after dark. He felt an overwhelming urge to collapse at the kitchen table, but he knew he smelled pretty bad.

He pulled off his heavy parka at the door and hung the fur on a peg before bending over to pull off his muddy boots.

"I have a hot bath waiting for you," Helaina called.

Jacob noticed the tub sitting in front of the fireplace. "I don't deserve such kindness, but I'm thankful for it." He grinned up at his wife and noted the sparkle in her eyes. She seemed to be in an unusually good mood.

"I'm working on supper. I figure to have elk steaks and fresh bread. Canned vegetables too. Oh, and Karen shared part of an apple cobbler she baked."

"That sounds almost as good as the bath." He chuckled and finished pulling off his boot. "Almost."

She came toward him, but he held her off. "You don't want to get too close. I smell worse than ten men."

Helaina pinched her nose and leaned forward with a quick kiss. "Then get thee to thy bath." She headed back toward the stove. "So what did you do today?"

"Adrik and I worked on those felled trees. We cut them into manageable pieces, stripped some and loaded them. I delivered them just before coming home."

"Sounds like you'll be nursing some sore muscles. I have more of that liniment Leah made. I can rub your back later," she murmured.

Helaina busied herself at the stove while Jacob shed his filthy clothes and climbed into the tub. He eased into the hot water and sighed. Life just didn't get much better than this. A beautiful wife fixing supper in the kitchen, a hot bath to soothe his weary muscles, and a good house to hold them safe and warm. Jacob had always known God's blessings, but now he knew God's abundance.

"So what did you do today?" Jacob asked after several minutes of silence.

"Oh, I kept very busy. Karen and I gathered evergreens for Christmas wreaths and trim. We visited a little with Leah and shared news. Karen heard from her friends—the ones you knew in the Yukon. They all seem to be well."

"That's good. Peter's the one I told you about—the one who owns the shipping company. If we decided to get serious about starting a mercantile, he'd be the one I'd talk to about supplies."

"I remember," Helaina said, coming to where Jacob sat soaping himself in the tub. "You want me to get your back?"

"Sure." He handed her the washcloth and soap. "I can't tell you how nice this is. Thanks for thinking of me."

Helaina washed his back, giving special attention to his weary shoulders. "Maybe with the extra time away from the railroad work, you could check out some of the details regarding the store. Write some letters to Mr. Colton. You know we have whatever money we need. We could buy up some of the townsite lots and at least plan things out."

"You know how I feel about using your money, Helaina. It's not that I won't, but I don't want to take undue advantage. I want to make my own way."

"I thought we agreed that we would share everything. Money, possessions, good times and bad," she said, handing the cloth back to him. "You know I don't want anything like that coming between us."

Jacob rinsed off and stood to take the towel she offered. "I know that. I don't want anything coming between us either. If need be we'll use your money, but only if we both feel it's where the Lord is leading. I want this to be a good life for both of us, but I want it focused first and foremost on the Lord."

Helaina went to the chest and got clean clothes out for Jacob. He dressed quickly, then pulled her into his arms. "It's so good to be home." He kissed her passionately on the lips, then lingered to plant kisses against her cheek and neck.

"There's something I want to give you," Helaina said rather breathlessly. "An early Christmas present."

Jacob pulled back and shook his head. "No. We agreed. No presents until Christmas morning."

"But this is something really special. Something that isn't my gift to you, but rather the Lord's gift to us both." She smiled and took hold of his hand.

"I don't understand. The Lord has given us a gift?"

Helaina nodded and stepped back. As she pulled away, she drew his hand to her stomach. "He's given us a child."

For a moment the words didn't register. Jacob felt her press his hand against her as she continued. "We're going to have a baby, Jacob."

Leah was just serving dinner to Jayce when they were both startled by the sound of her brother giving out first one yell and then another.

Jayce met her eyes and it was all Leah could do to keep from laughing out loud. "I guess she told him about the baby."

Jayce chuckled. "I guess she did. Sounds like it met with his approval."

Leah laughed and spooned out peas for the twins. "I'm sure he's quite pleased with himself—and with Helaina."

Chapter Seventeen

I don't know where Adrik is," Karen confided to Leah. "Here it is Christmas morning, and he should have been back by now." She twisted her hands together and pulled back the curtain at the window for at least the tenth time.

Leah turned to her brother. "Do you know anything about this?"

Jacob shrugged. "I know he took some papers to Seward for the railroad. I don't know what else the railroad wanted of him while he was down there, but I do know they aren't working Christmas. I'm sure Adrik will be here soon. He definitely had plans to be celebrating Christmas with his family. That much I know."

Everyone had gathered at the Ivankov house to celebrate Christmas morning, but Karen's mood was far from festive. Leah decided it would be best to keep Karen's attention on something else.

"Karen, I am so impressed by the breakfast you prepared. I would have been happy to come and help."

Karen glanced at the abundant table and shook her head. "I just wanted everything perfect. I was already worried about Adrik. Do you suppose something has happened to him? Should we send Jayce or Jacob to go look for him?"

"Let's give him just a little more time. You never know. There might have been heavy snows between here and Seward. Adrik loves you and the boys more than anything. He'll be here when he can."

Karen smoothed down nonexistent wrinkles on her blue serge skirt. She had dressed with obvious care for the day. "I have a bit of a headache. Maybe I'll brew some more willow-bark tea."

"Now stop fretting. You know he'll be fine. And just look at you. You look wonderful," Leah told her. "I especially love what you've done with your hair." Karen's red hair, now marked with streaks of silver, had been fashioned in a loose bun atop her head. She had taken extra care to curl the wisps of hair that fell gracefully around her face. She looked like a proper Victorian lady, Leah thought. The only problem was, Victoria had died more than a dozen years earlier and a new age was upon them.

"Sorry I'm late!" Adrik bellowed as he pushed open the front door. "Merry Christmas!"

Karen gave a sigh. "He's safe."

Leah squeezed her arm. "Of course he is."

"I've brought my wife a special present," Adrik announced and stepped aside. All gazes turned toward the door, and even the twins were silent.

"Merry Christmas!" Timothy Rogers called to the assembly as he peered around Adrik's broad frame.

Leah couldn't hide her smile. "Timothy! How wonderful to see you. What a great surprise."

Karen shook her head. "I can't believe it. You're finally here to visit, and you pick the dead of winter to enjoy our hospitality? Whatever made you come now?"

He laughed and hugged Karen close. "I had to accompany Adrik's Christmas gift to you."

Just then Ashlie stepped into the doorway. "Merry Christmas, Mama."

Karen's eyes widened and her mouth dropped open in wordless wonder. Ashlie rushed to her mother's arms and gave her a tight embrace. "I've missed you so much."

Leah watched as Karen's shock turned to joy. She embraced her daughter, but her gaze met Adrik's. Leah saw such an exchange of love in those glances. It gave her a warm and happy feeling inside to have shared in that moment. If ever two people loved each other, it was Karen and Adrik Ivankov. How perfect that God should have put them together.

"How in the world did you arrange this?" Karen asked as Ashlie ran to greet her brothers. By now Adrik was at her side, but he only shrugged.

"Did you know about this?" Karen asked Leah.

"I did not. I doubt I could have kept such a secret."

Adrik leaned over and kissed Leah's forehead. "And that is why I did not tell you," he said, laughing.

"Just look at you," Karen said as Ashlie pulled off a long green wool coat. Ashlie was dressed in an impressive traveling suit of blue wool. Her hair was pinned up and trimmed with a smart little green hat that matched her coat.

"I've learned to be quite fashionable," Ashlie admitted. "I don't want to shame my school or Cousin Myrtle. Who, by the way, sends her regards and love. As well as a few gifts."

Leah thought Ashlie had aged considerably since they'd last seen each other. The girl was radiant and charming. Tall and slender, she had Karen's delicate features but Adrik's teasing smile and dark eyes. There was just a hint of her Tlingit ancestry in her features, and they added a rather exotic flavor to her appearance.

"Can we open our presents now?" Christopher asked impatiently. "I've waited a whole year for today to come."

Everyone laughed, but it was Adrik who started the festivities. "I believe it is time for presents. After all, I just started by giving us Ashlie and Timothy."

"That's silly, Papa. People can't be presents."

"Ah, but that's where you are wrong, Christopher. Of course they can be presents. Jesus came to earth as a present for us. Remember?"

This led quite naturally into a telling of the Christmas story. Adrik had long ago memorized the second chapter of Luke and began a recitation even as the adults found their places around the table.

Leah knew she would always remember this day as one of her very favorite Christmases. Everything seemed so perfectly right: Her menfolk were safely home from their perilous adventures; Jacob and Helaina were happily married with a new baby on the way; Jayce and the twins were all Leah could ask for or want in a family, and all were healthy and safe.

That evening as she sat beside Jayce in their home, enjoying the close of the day, Leah couldn't begin to voice her gratitude to God. *I'm so happy, Lord. You've given me far more than I could ask or imagine. Definitely more than I deserve.*

She sighed and leaned against Jayce. He put his arm around her and gently stroked her hair. Only moments before Leah had taken out the pins and brushed through the long brown curls.

"I can't believe we're really here—like this. I'm so blessed," she said, her voice barely audible.

"I was thinking the same thing. Last year I was lost at sea, waiting and watching for the ice to crush our ship and send us out across the frozen ocean. It was terrifying, but the waiting almost robbed us of our sanity."

"I can well imagine. It nearly robbed me of mine," Leah replied.

Jayce gently lifted her face. "Are you happy here?"

She pulled back and looked at him for a moment. "Haven't I just said so?"

"I know you're happy with this day, I'm just wondering, however, if you're happy here. Do you miss Last Chance?"

"Of course I miss Last Chance. I miss Emma and Sigrid and Bjorn and the children. I miss Oopick and John. I especially miss Ayoona, but I know I'll see her again someday in heaven. I loved Last Chance Creek. But it was the people who made it particularly special. I miss them most of all."

"I know. And we don't have to stay here if you find it unbearable."

Leah shook her head. "It's not unbearable. In fact, I feel blessed by God for bringing us here. What about you?"

"What about me?" He seemed genuinely surprised by her question.

"Are you happy here? Do you want to stay and call this home?"

He smiled, and it made Leah feel weak in the knees. This man always had a way of transforming her worries and concerns to feelings of comfort and security. "My home is wherever you and the twins and any other children we might have are. You are my home, Leah. I never really had a home until I married you."

"But I want you to be happy in your work. Karen has told me over and over that men must find satisfaction in their job choices. It's important to the entire family. I won't have you miserable just because you think I'm happier close to my loved ones. Please promise me you'll always be honest about such things."

Jayce laughed and pulled her close again. "I promise. And you promise me that you'll always be honest about such things as well. I find I can endure a great deal of misery when I know you are waiting for me at the end of the day."

"Leah! Leah!"

It was Ashlie calling—no, screaming—from outside the door. Leah and Jayce jumped up so quickly they nearly took a tumble. Righting each other, they hurried for the door.

"What is it?" Leah questioned, pulling Ashlie into the house as soon as Jayce had the door open.

Ashlie was crying, and it was clear that something was terribly wrong. "It's . . . it's . . . Mama."

Leah looked to Jayce and back to Ashlie. "Something's wrong with Karen?"

"Yes!" Ashlie took hold of Leah. "You have to come. She collapsed on the floor, and she won't wake up."

Chapter Eighteen

Jayce remained with the children while Leah hurried to the Ivankov house with Ashlie. The girl was so distraught, Leah couldn't imagine what had happened to Karen. She was perfectly fine when Leah had headed home with Jayce and the twins. Karen had been suffering a headache, but the day had been exhausting and Karen had worked very hard to make sure everyone had a good time.

"What happened, Ashlie?" Leah asked as they approached the house.

"I don't know. She said . . . oh, she said that her head hurt. I didn't think anything about it. I should have. I should have seen that something was wrong." She stopped and shook her head vigorously. "I should have known."

Leah halted her steps and turned. "Why?" Leah asked, hoping the matter-of-fact question would cause Ashlie to regain some composure. "You're not a doctor."

"I know. But she's my mother."

"I wasn't much younger than you when my mother died; should I have known enough to keep her alive—to prevent her death? Is it my fault that my mother is dead?"

Ashlie calmed just a bit. "Well . . . of course not."

"And neither is it yours that your mother is sick."

"She seemed fine. She really was happy." Ashlie began walking toward the house again. "She was getting ready for bed. She told me how happy she was to have me home, and then she got a funny look on her face and fell to the ground."

Leah pushed open the door to the Ivankov house without knocking. "Papa went for the doctor," Oliver announced.

Leah gently touched his shoulder. "How long ago?"

"Just after Ashlie went for you."

"What's wrong with our ma?" Christopher asked.

Leah shook her head. "I don't know. Let me check on her."

Leah went quickly to Karen's room and found that they had managed to get her into bed and her nightclothes. She touched her hand to the unconscious woman's pale brow. She didn't feel feverish or clammy. "Karen, it's Leah. I'm here. Please wake up."

Leah took hold of Karen's wrist and felt for a pulse. The beat was weak. "Karen, I don't know what's happened to you. Please wake up." Ashlie had mentioned Karen's headache, and earlier in the day Leah knew Karen had suffered enough discomfort that she had brewed some willow-bark tea to ease the pain.

"Do you know what's wrong with her?" Ashlie asked as she came into the room. Leah saw that the boys were fearfully standing guard at the door, listening for whatever answers Leah might offer.

"I don't know. Sometimes people have spells that cause them to lose consciousness. Some are very bad and others are less so. I wish I could tell you which case this was, but I can't. Your mother seems very weak, although nothing was previously wrong."

"It was her head," Oliver said quite seriously. "She told me earlier to pray for her because it hurt."

Leah let out a long breath. "She might have ruptured a vessel in her head." The thought of an aneurysm came to mind. She had once talked with a doctor about such things when she still lived in Ketchikan. The doctor explained that sometimes vessels in the brain would rupture and cause extensive bleeding, and there was very little they could do to help the patient. In some cases, he had explained, holes could be drilled into the skull to drain the blood, but the risk was great.

It seemed to take forever before Adrik returned with the doctor. The man came quickly to Karen's bedside and demanded everyone leave the room.

"I'm Leah Kincaid. I have some training in medicine," Leah offered. "I could act as your nurse."

The middle-aged man eyed her up momentarily, then nodded. "Everyone else out."

Adrik led Ashlie to the door. "Come on, boys, let's let them work. They'll tell us what's going on as soon as they know something." His gaze met Leah's, as if to confirm this.

"Of course we will. I'll come out just as soon as I can," she promised.

Once the door was closed, the doctor looked to her. "What can you tell me?"

Leah shrugged. "She's complained of a headache all day. Apparently it was bad enough to ask her son to pray about it. She also took some willow-bark tea earlier. Karen's always been a very strong woman, and when she stops to take a remedy of any kind, I know that it's because there is a strong reason. Still, she didn't really show any other signs. Do you suppose it's an aneurysm?"

"It could well be. I've seen it before and the symptoms sound quite similar."

He checked her pupils and listened to her heart. Leah watched and waited, feeling very unnecessary. She longed for Karen to open her eyes and announce to them that she felt perfectly fine, but something inside told Leah this wasn't going to be the case. For the first time since Ashlie came to the door crying for help, Leah began to fear for Karen's life.

"She's not doing well," the doctor said as he pulled the stethoscope from his ears. "Her heart is very weak and her breathing is quite shallow." He reached for his case and took out several instruments. "I'll check her reflexes, but I'm afraid there's little we can do. It may be a ruptured artery, as you suggested, or she may have had a stroke."

"A stroke?"

"Her body isn't responding as it should," he said, pointing to her left side. "The nerves show little or no reaction."

"What does it mean?" Leah bit her lip and met the man's stern expression.

"Only time will tell. . . . We have no way of knowing whether she'll recover from this or not."

"So she could . . . she might . . . die?"

"That is a strong possibility. I'm sorry. I know Mrs. Ivankov to have a reputation for kindness and generosity. Her husband too."

"What can we do?"

"Little but wait. I'll check in on her in the morning. If there's any change in the night, you can send someone for me." He put his instruments away and got to his feet. "I don't want to discourage you, but I've seen situations like this before. The outcome has never been good."

Leah nodded. She looked to Karen and then to the closed door. "I understand."

When they came out from the bedroom, Jacob and Helaina had joined Adrik and the children. The doctor looked at Adrik and shook his head.

"Mr. Ivankov, I'm sorry. It appears your wife has suffered a major trauma to her brain. There is no way of telling at this point in time whether she will recover."

"What are you saying?" Ashlie asked, her voice shrill and unnatural. "Is she going to die?"

Christopher and Oliver looked at each other in disbelief, while Ashlie began to sob. Leah went to her side. She put her arms around the girl and pulled her close. "We need to pray for your mother. We don't know what God has yet planned for her, but prayer is always the best way to help someone."

The doctor nodded and looked back to Adrik. "I'm sorry. You may send someone for me if her condition changes." He left just as quickly as he'd come, leaving the family in stunned silence.

Adrik looked to Leah as if to will the truth from her. The questioning in his eyes left her uneasy. She wanted so much to reassure him, but she had no words for it.

"This is all my fault," Ashlie said as she broke away from Leah and went to her father. "I should have been here. She's had to work too hard."

"It's not your fault," Adrik said, putting his arm around her. "Your ma would work hard whether you were here or not. We don't know why this has happened, but it has."

"Leah, do you have any idea of what can be done?" Jacob questioned. "Are there any native remedies?"

Leah shook her head. "If there are, I don't know them. I can ask around, but I don't know that it will help."

"Do whatever you can," Adrik said. Gone was the usual strength in his voice and demeanor. To Leah it appeared that Ashlie held him up as much as he supported her.

"I will," she promised. "I'm going back to tell Jayce what's happened, then I can come here and sit with her so that you can sleep."

"No. I'll take care of her. She's my mother," Ashlie stated, pulling away from her father. "I'll send for you if I need you."

Leah thought to protest but then nodded. "Please do. I'll come in the morning and relieve you and cook breakfast for everyone."

"I'll come help as well," Helaina offered.

Adrik followed Leah outside, much to her surprise. "Look, if you know something more . . ."

"I honestly don't," she said before he could continue. "The brain is a queer thing; doctors know so very little on how to treat problems related to it. It could have been a ruptured vessel, in which case she's bled into her brain. Or it could be a stroke, in which case the chances for recovery would be better." She touched his arm, feeling the warmth against the chilled night air. "Adrik, I'm so sorry. I wish I could say that things will be all right, but . . ." Her voice trailed off as tears came to her eyes.

Adrik hugged her tightly. "I didn't know she was sick. I didn't know anything was wrong. She was so happy today. So happy to have everyone here and Ashlie home. I would have been here if I'd known something was wrong. I would have let Timothy bring Ashlie here by himself if I'd thought Karen needed me."

"You didn't do anything wrong, Adrik. She was happy and healthy. What happened is no one's fault. You mustn't be hard on yourself. Of what I know, there is usually little warning. Sometimes nothing at all. Don't blame yourself."

"But I know she was worrying these past couple of days with me gone. That could have been avoided. I should have just told her the truth. I should have been here."

Leah pulled back and shook her head. "You taught me long ago that we cannot live on 'what if's' and 'should have been's.' Adrik, we need to pray and remember who is in control. God knows what His plans are, and we do not. It isn't easy, but the alternative is much worse."

Adrik nodded. "I know. But, Leah, I cannot imagine my life without her."

Leah whispered, "I can't either."

The days passed by without any sign of Karen recovering. Leah took her turn by Karen's bedside remembering both the good days and bad they'd shared. Her most frequent thoughts were of Karen's love and faithfulness. When the rest of the world had deserted her, Leah had known Karen would be her constant. She was a good second mother and a dear friend.

"And now I'm losing you," Leah whispered. "I can't bear that you won't be here to see my children grow up—to offer me advice—to comfort me in sorrow and to share my joys."

The room was dark, except for a single lantern atop the dresser Adrik had made. The light cast strange shadows on the walls of the room and bathed them in an eerie yellow glow. In a few hours everyone would wake up and welcome in a new year.

Leah yawned and dozed off and on in the hard wooden chair, then startled awake at the sound of the bedroom door opening. Adrik came in quietly and looked to Leah for information.

"She's resting easy," Leah offered. "Nothing has changed."

Adrik sat down on the bed beside Karen's still body. "I thought I'd ask the doctor about taking her to Seattle. Maybe a large hospital would know how to better help her. After all, we're always hearing about the progress made in medicine."

Leah wanted to offer him encouragement. "That's true. There are always new treatments. Perhaps Seattle would offer something good. I'm sure the doctor might have an idea about it."

Adrik took hold of Karen's hand and gently stroked it as he continued. "I'm grateful for all you've done. I know it hasn't been easy."

"Jayce has been good to stay with the children. He loves being with them and doesn't mind at all. He knows how important Karen is to me—to all of us. He loves her too."

Adrik smiled sadly. "Who could help but love her? She's done nothing but give of herself since the day she was born. She's always helping someone with something."

"No one knows that better than I do. She was such a blessing to Jacob and me. You were too, Adrik. We wouldn't have made it out of the Yukon alive had it not been for the both of you. I hate to think where we would have ended up. I probably would have been forced to marry some grizzled old prospector, and Jacob would probably be dead. You and Karen kept us safe and became the parents we no longer had."

"I don't know what I'll do without her, Leah. She's been my everything. If she dies, how will I go on without her smile? Without her touch?" He looked at her as if she honestly might offer answers. "What will the boys do? They're so young. And Ashlie. Poor girl. She blames herself for this. She's sure that if she'd stayed here, her mother would still be healthy and happy."

"I know. I've tried to talk to her. Guilt is an awful thing to try to overcome."

An hour later the doctor showed up. He was in between delivering a baby and setting the arm of a man who'd had a nasty run-in with a stack of cut wood. He quickly examined Karen, then turned to Adrik and Leah just as Ashlie joined them.

"I wondered," Adrik started before the doctor could speak, "if I should consider moving her to Seattle? I could arrange to have her on the next ship. I could even wire my friend to send a ship. Would the hospital there be able to help her?"

"I'm sorry," the doctor said, his eyes downcast. "I can't advise that." He looked up, regaining his façade of strength. "I don't expect that she'll last the day."

"No!" Ashlie cried out and rushed to her mother's side. "You can't say that. We've taken good care of her."

"The care she's received has little to do with the situation," the doctor said softly. "Just as there was little that could be done to prevent the condition, there is nothing to be done to prevent her passing. I'm so sorry. Medicine has much to offer in this modern age, but unfortunately, treatments for the brain are still limited."

Ashlie sobbed against her mother's neck while Leah shuddered at the chill that washed down her spine. Adrik stood silent as the doctor made his way to the door. "If time permits," the man said, "I'll return to check on her again."

"I should never have gone away," Ashlie sobbed. "All of this is my fault. If I'd stayed, Mama would be just fine."

"That's not true," Adrik said, coming to his daughter's side. He took hold of her and turned her to face him. "You must stop this. Your brothers will not understand. They will be frightened more than ever if they see you falling apart like this."

"I don't want Mama to die." Ashlie leaned against her father's chest. "I don't want her to go."

"Neither do I." Adrik barely managed to speak the words.

"No matter what happens, I'm staying here to take care of my family," Ashlie suddenly declared. She pushed back and wiped her eyes. "If Mama . . . if she . . . I'll be here to take care of you and the boys. You won't have to worry. I won't ever leave my family again. Never!"

Later that afternoon Leah joined her brother and Adrik and Ashlie at Karen's side. The boys had gone to be with Helaina to help pick up some things in town, and Jayce was again watching over the twins.

"Her breathing has slowed a great deal," Adrik told Leah as she took her seat.

"She's not in pain, is she?" Ashlie asked Leah.

"No, I don't see any signs of that," Leah replied. "Usually there are ways to tell. Your mother seems quite at peace."

Ashlie was stoic. "She deserves so much better than this. I don't understand how God can be so cruel."

"Sickness and death are a part of life, darling girl," Adrik said, putting his arm around her. "Your mother loves the Lord. She knows that He loves her as well. She wouldn't consider Him cruel in this and neither should you."

"Karen once told me long ago that her only fear of dying young was to leave her children without a mother. She had asked me if I would see to helping your father raise you should anything happen," Leah said as she took hold of Karen's hand. "I promised her I would."

"I remember that," Adrik said. "I asked the same of you, Jacob. Remember?"

"I do," Jacob replied. "We are here for you, Adrik. For you and the children. You are the only family we have on this earth, besides that which we are making anew."

"I can take care of my brothers," Ashlie said, her tone quite serious.

"Your mother wouldn't want you to bear this alone, Ashlie," Leah said. "No one is meant to take this on by themselves. That's what family is for."

"I can handle the job by myself." She straightened in the bedside chair and kept her gaze on Karen.

Leah decided to let the matter drop for now. She would try to talk to Ashlie when they were alone; now was not the appropriate place or time.

"I think we should sing," Leah said without thinking. "Karen loved the hymns in church. I think she'd like it if we surrounded her with music."

" 'I am Thine, O Lord, I have heard Thy voice and it told Thy love to me,' " she began, singing Karen's favorite song. The others joined, except for Ashlie.

" 'There are depths of love that I cannot know till I cross the narrow sea; there are heights of joy that I may not reach till I rest in peace with Thee.' " Leah felt an odd sensation as the words of the chorus permeated the room. " 'Draw me nearer, nearer, nearer, blessed Lord.' "

She gripped Karen's hand, feeling as best she could for a pulse but finding none. Leah knew her friend was gone. She looked across the bed to where Adrik sat. When their gaze met, Leah knew he already knew. She didn't need to say a word.

The words of the song faded just as Timothy came into the room. He looked across to where they had gathered. "The doctor has come," he announced.

Adrik put his arm around Ashlie. "Tell him . . . tell him there's no need. Tell him my beloved has gone home."

Chapter Nineteen

Two weeks passed with a series of blizzards and heavy snows. Leah felt Karen's loss deeply but tried her best to offer encouragement to Adrik and his family. Ashlie, in particular, seemed impossible to reach. As best Leah could tell, Ashlie was waging a battle within herself, divided by guilt over not having been home sooner and a fierce desire to leave again.

Ashlie was so like her mother; tall and slender, athletic in nature. Had it not been for some of her father's darker features, she might have been a strong replica of Karen in her youth. Ashlie also inherited her mother's outgoing nature and bold spirit. Very little frightened her—except the death of her mother. Losing Karen had sent Ashlie into a dark place. She refused to talk to anyone and usually kept herself hidden away working at one thing or another. A few days after Karen's death, she had requested that the others stay away from the cabin to allow the family some time alone. While Leah disagreed, she had conceded. She decided to let Ashlie have her way—at least for a short time.

To her relief, however, the situation didn't last long. Leah finally began to see hope for a return to normalcy when the girl showed up one morning asking for a lesson in making her father's favorite dried berry cobbler.

"I heard that Timothy is planning to return to Seattle."

"Yes. He's leaving at the end of the week," Ashlie said, looking away as if completely disinterested.

"What about you? Will you go back? Surely school has started again."

"I suppose it has, but I have responsibilities here with my family."

"Ashlie, have you talked to your father about this?"

"Why should I? He needs me. He's so sad over losing Mama. I have to help him."

"Ashlie, I've been very worried about you. You and I used to be close. I thought to help you share your grief."

"How do you share this?" Ashlie looked at Leah with a befuddled expression. "This is exactly why I didn't want to have you all at the house. I don't feel like talking and answering a lot of questions, and I don't want anyone trying to change my mind. I owe it to my family to be here for them."

"It's admirable, and I don't fault you for wanting to help them," Leah admitted. "I know you feel obligated to your family, but I think you should also think about what they need and want too."

"Meaning what?" Ashlie finally took a seat but still refused to look Leah in the eye.

"Meaning that they don't need you to replace your mother. No one can do that. Not you or me or Helaina. They also don't need you to stay, only to grow bitter at all the things you've had to give up. I know you don't want to be here, but you feel you have to be here."

Her head shot up. "My family is here and they need me. Of course I want to be here. How dare you say I'd grow bitter?"

Leah shook her head. "Please don't be angry with me. I'm on your side."

Ashlie's expression contorted. "I'm all they have. They need me to stay here and help. My brothers are too little to be without a mother."

"You're too young to have lost your mother as well. But you won't give yourself that much consideration." Leah leaned forward to touch Ashlie's arm. The girl stiffened, but Leah refused to pull back. "I want you to drop all the pretenses and façades related to what you think you're supposed to be right now. I want you to just talk to me honestly—openly. I'll keep your confidence, but it's important that you open up and be truthful about your feelings. You can't just keep them buried inside."

Ashlie bit her lower lip so hard Leah was certain she'd draw blood any moment. The tension in her body never eased, even when she finally spoke.

"My father needs me to take my mother's place. My brothers need me. My selfishness killed my mother. I owe it to them to be here."

Leah nodded. "All right, let's talk about this one issue at a time. First of all, your father loves you. He enjoys your company and wants only the best for you. But he does not need for you to take your mother's place. He's grieving her loss, just as you are. He isn't looking for a replacement. He needs for you to be his daughter and for your brothers to be his sons. Would you honestly thrust your father's responsibilities on the shoulders of Oliver or Chris if he'd died instead of your mother?"

"Well . . . no, but I'm older. I'm nearly grown. A lot of girls have had to take over their mother's duties. Why should I be any different?"

"Because your father has me. He has Helaina. We are here by choice to begin with, making our home in Alaska. You left because you felt called to something else. You wanted a different kind of experience, and apparently your parents saw the validity of that desire. Would you discredit them for their thinking?"

"But that was then," Ashlie began in earnest. "That was when everything was perfectly fine. I went away when things were good and everyone was happy."

"I know that, but their reasons for sending you to Seattle haven't changed." Leah had spoken with Adrik only the day before and knew that he worried about Ashlie remaining at home. He feared that she would relegate herself to being an old maid, watching over her mother's children and husband, instead of having a family of her own. He didn't want to force her to leave, but Leah knew his wish was that Ashlie should not give up her life on his behalf.

Ashlie seemed to consider Leah's words. When she looked up, Leah saw the tears that had formed. "I want to do the right thing for them, Leah. The boys are so sad. They can't believe Mama is gone. I can't either, but at least I'm old enough to know that these things happen and that they are a part of life. Christopher worries constantly that our father will die as well. Oliver too. They watch him as if he might disappear before their very eyes. I'm so glad he hasn't had to work for the railroad since Mama died, because I don't think the boys could bear it."

Leah nodded. "I know. But God has provided, Ashlie. And He's provided for you as well. It will be hard to see you go, but you need to be a young woman with the liberty to seek your own future—not just assume your mother's role. I admire your willingness to stay more than anything you could have done, but, Ashlie, I want you to have your future. Your very own future. Your father wants it too." She paused and added, "And, Ashlie, I know your mother would want it."

"I don't know what to do." The words made her sound so lost.

"Ashlie, you just need to sit down and talk with your father. He wants you to be happy, and he's worried about you giving up your dreams."

Ashlie began to cry. "But if I go . . . if I go . . . what will happen then?"

"Life will go on," Leah said softly. "It always does. People come and go in our lives; sometimes they stay for a long while and other times they are here just a brief period. The important thing is that we cherish them while we have a chance. I don't tell you to go without grave consideration to the matter—your father would say the same. It's a dangerous world; there's a war going on in Europe, and Americans are a part of the fight. But Myrtle needs you as much as anyone here. Your schooling awaits you. And who knows where it will take you and what interests you might find? Don't give it up, Ashlie. I'm afraid you'll always regret it if you do."

"But being here for my family is the right thing to do," Ashlie said, seeming to regain some composure. "I've always been taught to put my family first. That family is the one thing that lasts."

"I agree, and if there were no one else to be here for your father and brothers, I would tell you to stay. I promise you, I would." Leah smiled and gently rubbed the back of Ashlie's hand. "Your heart is full of good motives. It's full of love. That doesn't change just because you make plans to go away."

"But won't it be hard on Chris and Oliver? To see me go after losing Mama?"

Leah leaned back and crossed her arms. "It will be hard no matter what. If you stay, it will be hard because you aren't their mother. They might even resent you for trying to take her place. If you go, they will feel another sense of loss and miss you. Either way, there will be some degree of pain. But, Ashlie, life is full of pain and misery. Sorrow dogs our heels and refuses to let us be. But God has also promised that we can overcome everything in Jesus. Jesus said, 'In the world ye shall have tribulation: but be of good cheer; I have overcome the world.' "

"I don't understand that. Of course Jesus overcame. He's God. What does that have to do with me?"

"You belong to Him. He loves you and He cares what happens to you. Because you have given Him your heart, He lives in you. Therefore, you have also overcome. It doesn't mean that bad things won't happen, Ashlie, but it does mean that you have victory before they ever come to roost on your doorstep. You have Jesus. You have only to keep your eyes fixed on Him and let your faith in Him be firmly rooted.

"And, Ashlie, you aren't to blame for what happened to your mother. No one is. Something went wrong inside her head. You didn't cause it. Your brothers didn't cause it."

"But people sometimes die because they work too hard."

Leah smiled. "Your mother worked much harder when you were all at home and much younger. I remember because I was here helping for part of that time. Look, you can't continue to carry this burden, Ashlie. It isn't yours to carry for one thing, and for another, it will consume you and make you old before your time. Your mother died because it was her time to die. Nothing more. Nothing less. You don't have the power of life and death in your hands. Only God does."

For several minutes Ashlie sat in silence. Getting up, Leah decided to check on the twins and give Ashlie some time to consider what she'd said.

"I want to go back to Seattle, but I'm afraid of hurting my father."

Leah ran her hand against the smooth wood of a chair Adrik had made. "Ashlie, I think it would hurt your father more if you refuse to talk to him and share your heart. Why don't you just go to him and explain how you feel? Tell him everything you just told me. He'll understand. I promise."

"You don't think it will just make him sadder than he already is?"

"No. I don't think anything could make him as sad as losing your mother. The worst has happened, and now he's just trying to put his life back together. Talk to him."

Ashlie nodded and got to her feet. "I will. I'll go find him right now."

The snows let up and the temperature warmed just a bit the next day. The tall spruce and hemlocks were covered with a fresh frosting of white. Their heavy boughs seemed to reach to the ground, as if asking for help to free them from their bonds. Across the landscape the white coating left everything with a clean, pristine feel. It was like a world untouched.

For all of her time in Alaska, Leah had not really encountered a place like this. In Ketchikan the winters had been mild, with more rain than snow, while in Last Chance the winters had been bitterly cold, with some snow and a great deal of fog and wind. It snowed far more here in the Ship Creek area than she'd even experienced in the Yukon. There was probably two feet of snow on the ground already, and she'd been told there was bound to be a whole lot more before winter ended.

Leah looked at the canvas pieces in her hands. She was always sewing these days, it seemed. Not that she minded. Her mother used to say that the sewing basket told the family's story. Tales of adventures gone awry or of new babies born. Stories of prosperity or poverty played out in the creation of new clothes or the multiple mendings of old ones. The memory made Leah smile.

"I can't believe the way these babies are growing," Helaina, said shaking her head at the twins.

Leah looked at the new canvas trousers she had been working on for Wills. He'd grown nearly two inches taller in the past few months and all of it seemed to be in his legs. "I know. I saw it in other people's children but hadn't expected it in my own." She glanced at the clock and put her sewing aside. "I need to go make sure Ashlie is doing all right getting supper on. Could you keep an eye on the children for me?"

"Of course." Helaina raised her own sewing. "I'm just about finished with this baby gown, but it seems much too tiny."

"It won't be." Leah smiled and pulled on her parka. "You'll see. I thought the same thing when I was making clothes for the twins."

"I just want them to be perfect," she said, studying the piece.

Leah smiled. "I'll only be a minute. The twins should be asleep for at least another hour."

"I don't mind if they wake up. They're good babies. You've been a good mother to them, Leah."

"I hope so. We all come into parenting without the experience that we so desperately need. I helped Karen with her children, but it's not the same. I never remember listening through the night to make certain that Ashlie was still breathing, but I constantly fret over the twins."

Helaina gave a rather awkward laugh. "I haven't had even the experience you have."

"Nonsense. You've been a great help with Wills and Merry. I don't know how I would have survived that first year without you. You'll know what to do—of that I'm certain."

The walk to Adrik's house was a short one, but before Leah arrived there she stopped midstep. A strange noise came from behind the house. It sounded muffled, almost like sobbing. She left the path and walked through the snow to a small shed where Adrik kept tools.

Leah approached the shed slowly and saw the crumpled form of Oliver. He was nestled up against several furs, his face buried in his hands.

"Oliver?"

He looked up as if mortified to have been found. "Go away."

Leah frowned and wondered if she should. Something compelled her to stay, however. "Oliver, you don't have to be ashamed of crying."

He buried his face again. "I don't want to talk about it."

Leah went to where he sat and knelt beside him. Reaching out gently, she touched his head. "Oliver, I want to help."

"You can't help," he said, looking up at her. "My mama is dead. You can't help that."

Leah nodded. "I know. I can't change what's happened. But you need to know that I miss her too. She was like a mother to me, and it feels like there's a hole inside where her love used to be."

Oliver sobered and nodded. "There is a big empty place. It hurts a lot."

"I know, sweetie. I know." She opened her arms to him. For a minute Oliver just looked at her, then just when Leah felt he would spurn her, he dove for her, knocking them both over. Leah just held on to Oliver and fell back against the furs.

Oliver cried softly for several minutes while Leah prayed silently. *Please, God, please ease his pain. It's so hard to know what to do to help him. Please show me.*

Leah tried to imagine what Karen would want her to say to Oliver. How would she word things to help him understand about life and death? Leah drew a deep breath and let it out slowly. Was there ever a good way to talk about something so very painful and sad?

"My mama was a good person, wasn't she?" Oliver asked, easing away from Leah just a bit.

The question surprised Leah, but she tried not to show it. "Of course she was. She was helpful to everyone and she demonstrated love and kindness all of the time."

"She loved Jesus too."

Leah leaned up and smiled. "Yes. Yes, she did."

"I love Him too, but I feel bad 'cause I wish He hadn't taken my mama. I feel real bad inside, Leah. I feel mad at God for taking Mama."

Leah pulled him close and rested back in the furs. "Oh, sweetie, God understands how you feel. He knows it hurts."

"Will He get mad at me?"

"No, I don't think so. But, Oliver, He wants to offer you His comfort. He doesn't want you to be mad at Him. He knows how you feel, and He wants to help."

Oliver stayed in her arms for several minutes before pushing away. "I'm sorry I acted like a baby. I'm trying not to cry in front of Christopher or Papa. If I cry it will scare Christopher."

"You don't have to be strong for everybody else, Oliver. You miss your mother. That's going to stay with you for a long time. I know. It stayed with me a long time. Sometimes I still miss my mother."

Oliver wiped his face with the back of his coat sleeve. "I gotta go. Christopher is waiting for me to help him with the dog sled. We're going to do some errands for Papa."

Leah got up and smiled at the boy. "You know I love you, Oliver. You've always been like a little brother to me. I'll always be here for you, and you don't have to be afraid of crying around me. I won't say a word to anyone, if that helps."

Oliver nodded. "I just don't want Papa to worry about it. He's got enough to worry about right now."

Leah hugged him, then let him go. How she wished she might take away his pain. She looked to the skies overhead through the canopy of trees that surrounded Adrik's land. "Lord, this is so hard. My father used to say that life was full of death. I guess I'm seeing that more now than ever before. It's a hard lesson to learn, much less to know what to do with."

"I appreciate your writing to Grace and Miranda," Adrik said later as Leah presented him with the two letters. "I don't think I could have done it justice."

"It wasn't a problem. I know they'll be shocked and heartbroken by the news, just as we are."

"I still can't believe it's happened. I think back to how just a few short weeks ago we were laughing and making plans for Christmas." He gave a harsh laugh. "I was feeling all smug for my plans. Now I don't feel anything but a sort of numbness—a disbelief that any of this could have happened." He continued to stare at the letters. "When you lose a man on the job—like we did last week when the log chain snapped—well, you just kind of take it in stride. It's sad and it's shocking in its own way, but you know the risks are there. When your sweet wife falls over dead, never to speak another word—never to hear your words to her, well, that's just not something you think will happen."

"I know. I find myself feeling like Ashlie, wondering if I missed seeing some sign. Was there something more I could have done? But I know the dangers of trying to second-guess a situation. I've learned that much in life."

Adrik looked at the letters for a moment longer, then stuffed them in his jacket pocket. He looked up and met Leah's eyes. "Ashlie came and talked to me. I think I have you to thank for that."

Leah shrugged. "We're all here to help each other, Adrik. Did she talk to you about Seattle?"

"Yes. I'm glad she did. She said that she really would like to go back to school—maybe even college. She wondered if I could bear having her go back at least until summer."

Adrik looked to have aged about ten years since Karen's death, but today he actually looked as though a burden had been lifted.

"And what did you tell her?"

"I told her that I thought her mother would want her to finish her education. At least I didn't lie about that. Karen missed that girl something fierce, but she was so proud of what she'd accomplished in school. Her teacher wrote to say that Ashlie will probably graduate first in her class next spring."

"That is impressive," Leah admitted, then offered a smile. "So what did you lie about?"

"Huh?"

"You said you didn't lie about the fact that her mother would want her to finish her education. So what *did* you lie about?"

Adrik looked rather surprised for a moment, then came a hollow laugh. "I told her I'd be just fine—that I had plenty of help and didn't need her here to watch over us."

"And that was a lie?"

"I don't know," he said sadly. "Maybe it was about the part where I said I'd be just fine. I don't honestly know if I'll ever be fine again."

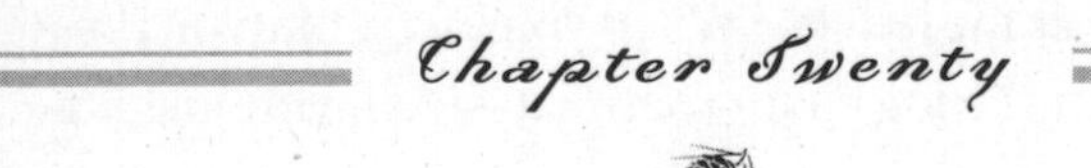

Chapter Twenty

Helaina picked her way through the mud and snow as she double-checked her list. They needed a half dozen things, most of which were for the special meal Leah had planned for Timothy and Ashlie's farewell. They would be leaving the next day for Seattle, and Leah wanted to send them off with the best of meals and plenty of warm wishes.

Helaina had to admit she was rather glad for the excuse to leave home. Everyone was still so sad over Karen's passing. Helaina mourned too, but since she hadn't known Karen as well, the others seemed not to recognize her sorrow. She paused in front of the mercantile, feeling oddly misplaced.

"Excuse me," a vaguely familiar voice said from behind her.

Helaina turned to find Cheslav Babinovich, and her eyes widened in surprise. The last time she'd seen this man had been in Nome. She started to greet him, but the man immediately turned and started to flee.

"Mr. Babinovich, whatever is wrong?"

He stopped and turned, eyeing her strangely for a moment as if to ascertain something. But what? "I . . . uh . . ." His Russian accent was thick and he seemed confused.

Helaina thought perhaps he'd again forgotten her name. "Mrs. Barringer. Although when we first met it was Mrs. Beecham. We met in Nome, remember?" It seemed so strange that every time she'd run across this man since their initial meeting, he seemed to have no recollection of who she was. Perhaps his fears and worries imposed upon his ability to remember.

"Of course. I am sorry for my poor memory. I have traveled so much over this state in my searches, meeting so many people. How might I be of service, my dear woman?"

Helaina thought his entire demeanor rather strange, but she shook off her concerns. "I have heard many troubling things about your homeland. I have thought about you, wondering if you ever managed to help your czar and his family."

Babinovich looked around him in a rather alarmed manner before hurrying back to Helaina's side. "It is best not to speak of them. Circumstances have worked against the family, I'm afraid. They are captive prisoners in the motherland. I fear the Russia that I once knew and loved is no more. The government in power now would see all of the royals killed. In fact, they will see many people killed, I fear."

"I am sorry to hear that. The newspapers have been full of negative stories to be certain. The war has left its mark all over the world."

"That is true. Should the war not have come to Europe, my czar might yet be safe in his palace. Now . . ." His voice faded off as he gazed blankly down the street. "These are desperate and sad times."

"So what will you do?" Helaina asked.

"I have no idea. I suppose I will continue to look for ways to get the royal family to safety. There might yet be a way, but God alone knows what that might be."

"And why have you come to this part of Alaska?"

"Ah, that is simple. I had heard of this growing railroad and desired to see it for myself. I thought it might be useful to my needs should the czar and his family be able to sail as far as Seward."

"But there are far more favorable areas in Alaska where Russians would feel very welcome. I am told that Sitka is still predominantly settled by the Russians. There are families there who can trace their ancestry back several generations to a time when your motherland still owned the property."

He nodded but leaned closer and whispered. "But that area could also be filled with enemies. We would have to see for ourselves if the population would be favorable toward the czar and his family. I have men checking into such matters even now."

Helaina felt her feet growing numb with cold. She felt equally sorry for Babinovich whose boots showed signs of irreparable wear. No doubt he had walked all over the territory in search of a hideaway for his beloved czar.

Just then Helaina got an idea. "I was just about to pick up a few things. We're having a grand meal tonight. A couple of family members are heading to Seattle tomorrow. Why don't you join us for supper? There will be plenty of food."

Babinovich seemed to consider this for a moment. He rubbed his mustache with the back of his index finger. "Such a meal sounds quite inviting to a weary pilgrim such as myself. I will accept with great happiness."

"Good. If you wait for me, I'll take you to my home. You can stay and visit and warm yourself by the fire. Later, my husband can bring you back by dogsled. Where are you staying?"

"I only got here this morning. I haven't really arranged for myself."

"Then you could stay with us if you like," Helaina offered. She wasn't sure what drew her to the man, but she longed to know more about him. "There isn't much to offer in the way of housing; most of the railroad men lived in tents, and now they're gone."

"It seems the area is less settled than Nome and Seward," he said, looking around the little town.

"It's almost deceptive. The area is growing, and there are far more people here now than there were just months ago—despite the railroad releasing their workers. I would expect to see this entire area boom. Especially if they were to find gold or silver."

"And do they expect to do that?" Babinovich questioned with sudden interest.

"There have been some finds—some rumors of big deposits—but nothing has been found as of yet to prove that true."

"It sounds promising."

Helaina smiled. "The thought of gold always sounds promising, but I wouldn't count on anything until you actually hold it in your hand." She turned. "I'll only be a minute, and then we can make our way home. You're welcome to join me."

She waited for him to decide. Finally he shook his head. "You go ahead, Mrs. Barringer. I'll wait here."

Helaina hurried into the store and went quickly to retrieve the items needed. She was quite pleased to learn that one of the native women had brought in a few eggs. They were frozen, but Helaina thought they would surely thaw so she could make a cake. She made certain to see the two eggs were wrapped in cotton batting before she tucked them gently into her purse. The other things went into her large canvas bag.

"I hope you are not frozen through," she told Babinovich as she emerged from the store. "I should have insisted you come in, although it was scarcely any warmer in the tent."

"I am not surprised. I do not know how people exist in such cold."

"But you have cold in your country as well, do you not?"

Babinovich took the bag from her as they turned to walk. "We have wonderful places where the cold is not so bad. Siberia, now that is different. That place is like a frozen death. Some parts are not so bad, but others are . . . well . . . I would not want to be there."

"Tell me about your home in Russia. Where did you grow up? Are your parents still there?"

Babinovich shook his head. "My parents are dead. My life there centered around my service to the czar. We are family, of course, but distantly so. I served him and serve him now. It is all I have known."

"Did you enjoy the privileges of such a life?"

He nodded but stared straight ahead. "I have known great wealth. Such parties—such foods and clothes. They were magnificent."

Helaina heard a tone of regret in his voice, but whether or not it was for the wealth of bygone days or simply missing the days that had once offered him so much, she was not sure. As they neared the place where Adrik had chosen to build their little family village, Helaina motioned to the largest of the three houses.

"That is where we'll go. The cabin to the right belongs to my sister-in-law and her husband. The one to the right of that is my home with my husband, Jacob."

"And whose home is this?" he asked as they approached the larger cabin.

"This is the home of dear friends. The man's wife just passed away, but he lives here with his two young sons. His daughter, Ashlie, is one of the people returning to Seattle. She's not yet eighteen and is returning to school."

"I see." He followed Helaina into the house but said nothing more.

"I found everything you needed and then some," Helaina announced as Leah looked up from the stove. "They had three eggs and I bought two of them." She reached into her purse and pulled out the treasures.

"Real eggs? Real eggs in January in Alaska?" Leah questioned. "That is a marvel." Just then she noticed Babinovich. "Oh, you've brought company?"

"Yes," Helaina said, handing Leah the eggs. She then turned around to take the canvas bag from the man. "This is Cheslav Babinovich. I met him in Nome some time ago. He just arrived in the area, and I—"

"Took pity on me," Babinovich interrupted. "She was quite kind to invite me to your supper and to take refuge here from the cold."

"He will stay with us a day or two," Helaina announced as Ashlie came in from the back room.

"Who is staying a day or two?" she asked.

"Mr. Babinovich. He's from Russia and has been traveling for some time. He just came to this part of the country and I encouraged him to stay with us a short time. Mr. Babinovich, this is Mrs. Kincaid, my sister-in-law, and Ashlie Ivankov."

"Ivankov?" he asked with a look that almost seemed akin to fear.

"Yes, her father is of Russian descent, like yourself," Leah explained. "However, he was born in this territory and also shares some Tlingit Indian ancestry."

"I'm sure you'll enjoy my father's company. I'm pleased to make your acquaintance and glad you could join us. I'm sure my father would love to hear your stories of Russia. He has never actually been there, but his grandfather lived there most of his life before coming to Alaska."

Babinovich rubbed at his mustache nervously. "Yes, well, the stories of our motherland are not at all pleasant these days."

Leah took the eggs to the kitchen and Helaina followed with the bag. "Just make yourself comfortable, Mr. Babinovich. Rest and warm yourself by the fire."

He nodded and moved toward the hearth, while Ashlie joined the women in the kitchen. "I'm packed," she announced. She sounded forlorn. "I hope I'm doing the right thing."

"We will miss you," Leah said as she went to work pulling things from Helaina's bag, "but I know you'll visit us in the summer."

"I've been thinking about something," she said, casting a quick glance toward the fireplace as if to make sure Babinovich wouldn't overhear. "What if Papa and the boys came with me?"

"To Seattle?" Leah asked in disbelief.

"Yes. I mean, the railroad work has stopped for the winter. I know Papa said some tasks could be done, but other things would have to wait for spring. I just think it might be nice for Papa and the boys to come back with me. I know Cousin Myrtle would love it. She owns a huge house, and there are more than enough rooms for all of us. The boys could go to school down there, and just think of what a diversion the city would be for them."

Leah looked to Helaina and then to Ashlie. "It would probably do them all a great deal of good, but it's such short notice. I don't know that your father would even consider it."

"But I could try, couldn't I?"

Helaina pulled off her coat and crossed the room to hang it by the door while Leah continued to speak on the matter with Ashlie. She felt sorry for Babinovich, who looked rather uncomfortable with his own company.

"I'm sorry we can't sit and visit properly," she said, smiling. "I'll be happy to fix you a cup of tea if you would like."

"I would like that very much," Babinovich responded. His accent sounded less thick as he relaxed.

"I'll have it ready in just a moment." She took a step toward the kitchen, then stopped abruptly as she felt something strange in her abdomen. Helaina put her hand to her belly and gasped. "I felt the baby move."

"The quickening," Leah said, coming to her side. "Isn't it marvelous!"

Helaina held her hand against her barely rounded stomach. "It's miraculous."

"I did not realize you were with child," Babinovich said. "Congratulations."

Helaina felt her cheeks grow hot. Such matters were generally not discussed with strangers—especially men. "Thank you." She knew she should go about her business, but she hated to move. Even though the moment had passed and the flutters were gone, she hated to lose the essence of what had just occurred.

"It will come again," Leah assured her with a smile.

Nearly an hour later, Adrik, Timothy, and the boys arrived. Supper was just being put on the table and Leah's cake cooled on the counter.

"Well, I see we have a visitor," Adrik announced. His boys were on either side of him, like shadows that refused to leave.

"Adrik, I hope you don't mind, but I ran into Mr. Babinovich in town. We had met in Nome. He's from Russia, and I thought you two might enjoy a chat."

"It's always good to have a brother join us," Adrik offered in their native tongue. "I'm glad you've made yourself welcome."

Babinovich shook his head—his expression one of great alarm. "Please do not speak so. I have vowed to speak only English."

"But why would you do this?" Adrik asked, again in Russian.

Helaina spoke Russian proficiently along with several other languages. She put her hand on Babinovich's arm and spoke also in his native language. "You have nothing to fear here. We want only to offer you hospitality and perhaps a bit of familiarity."

Babinovich seemed nearly panic-stricken. He looked at Helaina as if she'd suddenly sprouted horns. "I beg you both. Do not speak my mother tongue. It is not safe. There are spies everywhere. Men who would see us dead."

Adrik laughed and looked to his sons, who were wide-eyed. "He's not serious, boys. There's nothing to fear. Go wash up for supper."

Oliver looked warily at the visitor. Helaina could see there was some degree of fear in the boy's expression as he reached for his brother. "Come on, Christopher." They went to the kitchen washbasin, Oliver continuing to cast suspicious glances over his shoulders.

Adrik lowered his voice. "Mr. Babinovich, I would ask you not to say such things in my house. My boys have just lost their mother, and they aren't yet recovered from that horrific event. I don't need to have you fill their head with stories that have no foundation or basis in truth. We are quite safe here. Safe to speak Russian or not." He looked at the man oddly and added in Russian, "If you truly can speak the language."

"I cannot stay," Babinovich said, taking up his coat. "I have too much at stake. My life would mean nothing if I were to remain here." He headed for the door quickly and promptly ran into Jacob, Jayce, and the twins as they entered the cabin. Jayce turned away with the twins in his arms to avoid Babinovich crashing into either one.

"Whoa, there. What's the hurry, mister?" Jacob asked. "You'd think the house was on fire."

Helaina went to her husband's side. "This is Mr. Babinovich. I had invited him to dine with us, but he is rather upset."

Jacob eyed him in a questioning manner, but Babinovich only pushed past him. "My apologies to everyone," he called as he hurried away into the night.

"Well, that was strange," Jayce said, shaking his head. He put the twins down and laughed as they immediately ran to the door as if to see what had happened to the strange man. Jacob gently pulled them away and closed the door. Wills started to protest, but Leah quickly came to distract his attention. Merry happily followed.

"Strange, indeed," Adrik replied. "Helaina, where did you say you met him?"

"In Nome, actually. He told me a strange tale of how he was related to the royal family in Russia. He said he was here trying to find a place for them to hide, as politics were not boding well for them."

"Rumor has it the entire family is held prisoner in one of their palaces," Adrik said. "I read it some time ago in the newspaper."

Helaina nodded. "Yes, Babinovich said the same. He has always been one for secrets and queer concerns. He begged me to buy some of the royal jewels in order to help him finance his endeavors."

"And did you?"

"At first I didn't," Helaina said remembering the time only too well. "The next time we met I could not help myself. I purchased several pieces. They were quite lovely, and I figured if they helped the man, it was of little consequence to me."

"Where are those pieces now?" Adrik asked.

"In our cabin. Mr. Babinovich begged me not to show them to anyone or tell anyone about them. He said if word got back to those holding the czar and his family hostage, they might suffer more. After all, the jewels technically belong to the country, I suppose. I could show you the pieces, if you like."

"Yes, get them. I know a thing or two about jewels. You learn a lot during gold rushes when people are bartering anything and everything to get supplies. I was involved with quite a few trades in those days that included jewelry. I can tell you if the pieces are quality, but I wouldn't know what the value would be."

"I'll go get them right now."

"I'll go with you," Jacob said, taking hold of her arm. "It's snowing again. I wouldn't want you to fall."

Helaina relished the feel of his protective hold. They hurried to retrieve the pieces, with Jacob stopping only long enough to kiss her soundly as soon as they stepped inside the house. Helaina wrapped her arms around Jacob's neck and pulled his face close for another kiss as soon as the first one ended.

"I felt the baby move," she whispered against his lips. "Just a little while ago. It was the most marvelous thing. I wish you'd been there."

He pulled away and looked into her eyes with wonder. "Truly?"

Helaina giggled. "It was such a precious fluttering—almost too faint to know for sure, but it was clearly the baby."

Jacob hugged her close. "I wish we could just stay here and forget dinner."

Helaina kissed his neck and wished the same, but she pushed away, shaking her head. "This is Ashlie's and Timothy's last night here. We're expected to celebrate with them."

"I know." The disappointment was clear in his tone.

Helaina winked. "It doesn't mean we have to celebrate very long."

She went to her trunk and brought back a small bundled scarf. Arm and arm they made their way back to the Ivankov cabin, both smiling as if they knew a very special secret.

Once she uncovered the pieces and spread them atop the scarf, Adrik sat down and gave each one consideration. A ruby necklace was the largest piece. There were some twenty-five gems of reputable size. The pieces were set into heavy gold that fell in a half circle from a thick, braided chain of gold. Within a few moments he looked up with a frown. "I hope you didn't spend much to acquire these. They're fake."

"What?" Helaina shook her head. "Are you certain?"

"Definitely. These are not real—not the gems nor the gold. They are quality costume pieces—the kind you might see in the theatre or for those who want to appear to be from the upper classes of society but can't afford the price of the actual product."

"How odd. Why would Babinovich create such a story?"

"My guess from the way he acted," Adrik offered, "is that he's faking more than the jewels. I don't believe him to be Russian at all. My guess is that he's a confidence man selling these fake jewels to finance his living."

"Why would he come to Alaska?" Leah wondered aloud. "It seems so far removed and of little consequence. It's not like wealthy people linger on every corner."

"Which is probably exactly why he chose the location. The railroad officials informed me that many wanted men are venturing north. The law seems less likely to catch them up here, and information is not as easily had regarding criminals. Even our legal system is sorely lacking, as you well know. My guess is Babinovich saw a chance to play upon the pity of good-hearted people. He probably created the story about helping the czar, realizing that word of his plight could easily be had from the newspapers, but checking it out in any depth would be impossible due to the distance and the war."

"Well, I suppose that's the last of him that we'll see," Leah replied. "What a strange man."

A sense of rage washed over Helaina, and in that moment she made a silent pledge to investigate and find out the truth about Babinovich—or whoever he was. She, of course, would say nothing to Jacob or anyone else for that matter. No one would approve of a pregnant woman occupying herself with such things.

"So, Papa, what do you think about my idea?" Ashlie asked as her brothers came to join her.

Helaina tried to act natural—as if Adrik's announcement meant little to her. Jacob sensed her frustration, however, and put his arm around her in a supportive manner.

"You've only just mentioned the idea. I've hardly had time to consider it, Ashlie," Adrik said.

"Consider what?" Jacob asked.

"Ashlie suggested that the boys and I join her in Seattle—at least for a short visit. However, I had already talked a similar idea over with Timothy, and I believe it would be better for us to visit in May." He turned to Ashlie and added, "During your graduation. I hope you won't be too sad or disappointed. It just seems that for now we should probably stay here."

Ashlie smiled. "It will give me something to look forward to. How special to have you there when I graduate. I can't be sad." She went to Adrik and hugged him tight.

"I don't know about the rest of you, but I am starving," Jayce announced. "I think we need to get this party started."

Leah laughed. "I think Wills and Merry would agree with you," she said, pointing to the table. The twins had already climbed onto the bench and were reaching for whatever food was closest.

Adrik took up the pieces of jewelry and rewrapped them. He handed them to Helaina and offered a warning. "I'd be cautious of Mr. Babinovich in the future. He appears to be the kind of man who preys on gentlewomen. If he tries to approach you again, find one of us."

Helaina nodded and took the bundle. She would be cautious of Mr. Babinovich, but her kind of caution was probably different than what Adrik Ivankov had in mind.

Chapter Twenty-One

Winter passed into a muddy, wet spring. The railroad began work again, keeping the men busier than ever and leaving the women alone more than they liked. As the line moved north, the men were gone for longer and longer periods, and Leah hated the separation.

When May developed into an unseasonably warm month, Leah decided to plant a little garden despite the possibility of losing it all to late frost and even snow. They would need the vegetables, and the risk seemed worth it. She also ordered several crates of chickens from Peter Colton's shipping company. Her thought was to have fresh meat through the summer but also to keep a couple of laying hens. Perhaps she could get Jayce to build her a small attachment to the house so that they could keep them through the winter. It would be so nice to have eggs year round.

Working the land around her cabin gave Leah a sense of permanency and belonging. The twins were nearly two years old and were happy to wander at will in the forested area around them. Leah, however, was not so enthused and worked constantly to keep track of them. She tied bells to them, attached rope leashes to them, and even tried to fence them in, but nothing worked. She was forced to keep them under her surveillance at all times.

Glancing up to check the children for the fifth or sixth time, Leah was surprised to see her brother and husband walking toward her. She brushed the dirt from her hands and stood, while Wills and Merry ran for their father.

"I wasn't expecting you so soon," Leah admitted. "Although I'm quite pleased." She pressed her face between the laughing twins in order to kiss her husband.

"I know. We caught the last ride down. Adrik stayed up north again. There are big plans for lines running up through the mountains, and he's pretty interested to hear what the surveyors say about the area."

"I figured now that they were connected to the coal fields, Adrik might actually start thinking about staying home more or even heading back to Ketchikan."

Jayce put the twins down and shrugged. "I couldn't tell you. You know he's not been much of a talker since Karen's death. I try sometimes to get him to just talk about the old days, but he works himself hard, then cleans up and goes to bed."

"I know. Even when he's here he doesn't do much else. The boys aren't doing well either. Christopher has horrible nightmares. He wakes up screaming at least two or three times a week. Oliver will talk to me on occasion, but he's always filled with worry about his father and brother. He just wants to go home."

"Home? To Ketchikan?"

"Yes. But I think it's more that he just wants things to feel like they used to," Leah admitted. "I don't think it would really matter where he lived, so long as he could have his mother back and his father and brother happy. He's such a deep little guy."

"He's not that little. Adrik said he was asking about working with him."

"He's not yet fourteen. He needs an education, not a job."

"I agree," Jayce said, holding up his hands. "You don't need to convince me."

Leah watched as Wills tried to ride Champion. The dog patiently let the boy climb all over him, but when Wills climbed on Champion's back, the dog merely crumpled to the ground and let out a howl of protest. Leah smiled and shook her head. How she wished Adrik's boys could find such simple contentment.

"Well, if Adrik comes back soon," Leah began, "I'm going to insist he sit down and talk to me. I need for him to understand what's going on."

"Don't be too hard on him, Leah. I can't imagine how I'd be if I lost you." He put his arm around her. "I know I'd never be myself again."

"But those boys need him. Even though we've moved into their house to see to their needs, it's not easy on them. They resent their father's absence and my presence. I know it, although they have never said as much."

"Give them time. They all need time. It's the only thing that will help," Jayce said.

Leah knew his counsel was true; she'd said the same thing over and over herself. She also wrote letters of encouragement to Ashlie, who penned long letters about her loneliness and sorrow regarding her mother.

"When do they leave for Seattle?" Jayce asked.

"Next week. Unless Adrik has changed his plans, they'll head out on the twenty-second."

"The trip will help. It will be something fresh and different. It will see them removed from Alaska and all that is familiar, and they will be forced to come out of their cocoons and talk to each other. It's going to be all right. You'll see."

Leah hoped her husband was right. She'd watched Adrik withdraw little by little throughout the winter, and when the railroad called the men back to work, it seemed the perfect excuse for him to completely lock himself away. Leah knew that everyone had to grieve in their own way, but this had been going on now for months, and it wasn't helping anyone.

The next few days brought even more trouble, however. Newspapers reported a hideous round of influenza in the Nome and Teller areas of Alaska. They called it Spanish influenza but said little more about where it had come from or what its symptoms were. It seemed that the deadly sickness took hold in the winter months and rendered entire villages dead.

Leah was desperate for some word from her friends. She had waited patiently through the winter but now felt anxious for some good news to arrive soon. She wanted to know about Emma and the children, as well as how John and Oopick were doing. There were so many people she cared about, and she longed to hear from them.

A letter arrived from Grace with the sad announcement that her son Andrew had joined the army. Grace also wrote of her desire to come north and see Adrik and the boys. She felt a need to see them without Karen in order to make the woman's death seem real. Her letter stated, *From so many miles away, it's easy to pretend she is still with us.*

Leah didn't have that advantage. Every day she felt Karen's absence. She supposed part of it was living in Karen's house. The arrangement had just seemed easier for everyone, given that the men were gone for longer and longer periods of time. Leah and the twins took up residence in the room Adrik had intended for Ashlie. When he'd built the house, he'd made sure there was space for his daughter, just so she wouldn't feel any excuse to stay away.

At first, whenever Adrik returned, Leah and the twins would head home to their own cabin, but after a time it just seemed stressful for all concerned and Leah and Jayce moved in with Adrik and the boys. But when everyone was gone or asleep, Leah would find it particularly lonely. She could almost hear Karen's voice and envision her working in the kitchen or at the table. Due to the frozen earth and heavy snow, they had only recently been able to bury Karen. The funeral had only served to reopen the wounds of loss.

"I'm glad you'll be staying in the house," Adrik said as Leah and the others gathered for dinner a few days after his return from up north and the night before he and the boys were to head to Seattle. "I think you'll enjoy the bigger space, what with those rambunctious twins of yours." He chucked Wills under the chin and leaned over to kiss Merry. The little girl squealed with delight as Adrik's kiss trailed down her neck and then turned into a loud chopping sound. It was a game Adrik used to play with her and hadn't done in some time.

Leah was glad to see Adrik seem a little more like himself. "We'll miss you. I suppose next thing I know I'll get a letter stating that you'd decided to stay in Seattle."

Oliver looked up with a deep frown. "We won't stay there."

Adrik shrugged. "What if we like it more than we like it here?"

Oliver pushed back his chair so quickly that it clattered to the floor as he stood. "I don't even want to go to Seattle. Nobody asked me!" He ran out of the room, leaving Adrik looking rather stunned.

Christopher got up slowly and shook his head. "I don't want to go either." He followed his older brother to their loft bedroom.

"Well, I seemed to make a mess of that," Adrik said, looking rather dejected.

"They're really suffering," Leah said. She spooned some mashed up vegetables into Wills' bowl and handed him a spoon. Merry was still happily gnawing on a piece of sourdough bread with butter and had hardly touched her vegetables. Buttering bread for Wills, Leah continued, "I've been meaning to talk to you, but—"

"But I'm never home," Adrik inserted. "I know, and I'm sorry. I've allowed my work to occupy me so that I don't have to think or feel Karen's absence. I knew it was wrong, but . . . well . . . things will be different now. I've been very selfish in all of this. Jacob and Jayce helped me to see that much."

"We did?" Jayce questioned. "When did we have time to do that?"

"You did it by your actions. Every time I turned around, you were wanting to come home and be with your family. I wanted to be with the boys but wanted even more to be with Karen, and I knew she wouldn't be here.

Further, I knew the boys would have questions, and I would have to deal with their heartache on top of my own. I wasn't up to it." He shook his head. "I'm really sorry, Leah. It was selfish of me, but I intend to do better. I'm hoping this trip will give us a chance to really talk to each other and work through some of the pain."

"You owe me no apology. I was just worried about you—about them too. They haven't been doing well, Adrik. Christopher suffers from nightmares and Oliver worries incessantly about everything. They both ask me about you constantly, always wondering and worrying if you'll meet with some horrible fate."

"I didn't know." Adrik looked upward toward the loft. "I'll talk to them—help them to understand." He started to get up.

Leah touched his arm gently. "Why don't you give Oliver a little time to calm down? He'll be more inclined to listen to you once he stops being so angry."

"I doubt the anger will stop anytime soon. Not if he feels like me," Adrik said, retaking his seat. "But you're right. I'll go up after supper."

Oliver and Christopher listened to the things being said as they huddled together in their bed. Oliver shook his head and turned to Christopher. "I know what he'll say. He'll tell us that we'll have a great time in Seattle and that we won't miss Mama there as much as we do here, and before you know it he'll be buying a house and getting a job. Then we'll be stuck there. Well, I've made up my mind. I'm not going to Seattle. I'm going home."

"To Ketchikan?"

"Yes. That's where we were the happiest. That's where I want to be."

Christopher's expression turned quite serious. "I'm going home too. I want to go back to our old house. But, Oliver, how will we get there? Ketchkan's a long ways off, and we don't have any money."

"If we take the train down to Seward, we can find a boat to take us to Ketchikan. I've been asking some questions; I know all about this stuff. The fishing boats will take us so long as we work. We know how to do that kind of stuff. We'll be home in less than two weeks if we're lucky."

"You'll take me too?"

Oliver put his hand on Christopher's shoulder. "I won't leave you here. I'll take care of you, Christopher. I promise."

"And I'll take care of you," he replied.

Oliver didn't want to hurt his brother's feelings by explaining that an eleven-year-old boy could hardly take care of himself, let alone anyone else.

"We'll make it, Christopher. Together we'll do just fine. Now, come on. Let's go to bed. When Papa comes to talk to us, we'll pretend we're asleep. That way we won't have to lie about our plans."

Christopher hurriedly pulled off his heavy flannel shirt and put on his nightclothes. "When are we going to leave?"

"As soon as everyone is asleep." Oliver had everything planned out in his mind. He'd been working on this ever since his father had made the Seattle plans known. He had originally figured to part ways once they'd arrived in Seward, but maybe he'd be better off to head out now. He knew there was a freight train that would come through sometime in the night. It was the train returning to Seward for supplies needed on the rail line up north. They always stopped to take on water in Ship Creek. If he and Christopher were very careful, they could probably sneak on board and make their way south. He'd watched the train cars on many occasions. Most of the time the doors were left open. It should be easy enough to hide inside one of them for the trip south. At least he hoped it would be.

Leah hurried to get breakfast on the table while Adrik called to the boys for the third time. "Come on, guys, we'll be late for the train if you don't get your things and get down here right now."

He shook his head when there was no response and headed for the ladder. "They were so tired last night they were already asleep when I went to talk to them. No doubt they're worn out from their grief and worry. I'm really sorry I put all of that on you, Leah."

"I was glad to be here for you, Adrik. You know that. Don't blame yourself or be upset with the situation. It's just the way things go."

"I think I'll go up and talk to them before they come down. That way, maybe I can explain the way things are."

Adrik went up the steps while Leah turned to retrieve the coffeepot. The front door opened, and Jacob and Helaina entered. Leah couldn't help but smile. Helaina moved ever so slowly under the heavy burden of her child. For weeks they had discussed whether the baby was a boy or a girl, and both concluded it was a son, due to his rowdy activity in the womb.

"How are you feeling?" Leah asked as she pulled out a chair for Helaina with one hand and placed the coffeepot on the table with the other.

"I slept pretty well. As I mentioned, the baby has been less active. The doctor said that's due to his saving up his energy to be born. He doesn't think it will be long."

"Neither do I," Leah admitted. "You've really dropped since last week. I believe it will be any day now."

"Leah, have you seen anything of the boys?" Adrik asked as he came back down the ladder.

"No, not since supper. Why?"

"They're gone. They're gone and so are some of their things. They packed knapsacks to carry on the trip. Those are missing."

"Do you suppose they had a change of heart and decided to head over to the train station early—maybe to show you that they were willing to go?" Jacob questioned.

"I don't know. I guess I should head over there and see." He scratched his bearded face. "I've got a bad feeling about this."

"Why?" Leah asked. "What's wrong?"

"Is any food missing?" Adrik asked.

Leah shrugged and went to the cupboard. "I hadn't really noticed." She began to look around. "Well, several bags of jerky are gone—you know the stuff you put up last winter? And it looks like all but one loaf of sourdough bread is missing as well." She looked up fearfully. "They've run away, haven't they?"

Adrik nodded and went to the door for his coat. "That's what I'm thinking. I don't know where they think they're headed, but—"

"We'll help you look," Jayce said, as he and Jacob stood. Jacob reached over and grabbed a piece of toasted bread and a few pieces of sausage to make a sandwich. Jayce took note and did likewise.

"Let us know as soon as you find out anything," Leah declared. "Chances are they're still close by. They wouldn't have any means of getting too far."

An hour later Leah had finished cleaning the kitchen, and still there was no word from the men. She worried about the boys and had stopped to pray for the entire party over a dozen times. It was just so hard to imagine the boys out there by themselves. They were smart children, however, she kept reminding herself, and they had grown up learning to fend for themselves. Surely they would be all right.

"Leah, I think the baby is going to be born today," Helaina said rather nervously.

Leah noted that she was holding her stomach. "Are you in pain?"

Helaina looked up and nodded. "They've been coming off and on since early this morning. I thought at first it was like some of the other times, but this is different. These are getting stronger and coming more often."

Leah glanced at the clock. It was a little past nine. "Well, we should prepare. Since we don't know what's going to happen with the boys or our men, I would like to put you up here. Would that be all right?"

"I certainly don't want to be alone right now," Helaina admitted.

"Do you feel well enough to go home and get a few things, or would you rather stay here with the twins while I go?"

"I think I'll be all right." She got to her feet slowly. "What do I need?"

"Bring a clean nightgown and blankets and clothes for the baby. I have the rest." She smiled at Helaina's worried expression. "Don't fret."

"I just don't want anything to go wrong," she said. "The doctor said he lost a mother and baby last week." She fell silent.

Leah came to her side and hugged Helaina. "Don't consider such things. You'll be fine. Let's not worry until there's something to worry about."

Helaina put her hand to her abdomen and grimaced. "Seems to me that giving birth to a new individual is something to worry about."

Just then Wills ran full steam into Leah. "Mama. Mama. Look see."

Leah laughed as he held up one of his toys. "Giving birth is the easy part. Raising them up—now, that's something that causes worry."

Helaina took her leave ever so slowly, while Leah reached down to ruffle her son's hair. Her hand touched the warmth of his forehead, causing her to frown. She put her palm to his head and realized Wills was running a fever. She knew the twins were teething so she put away her concern. No doubt Merry would be feverish too. She went to her daughter and checked. Sure enough, Merry's head was also warm.

"Well, looks like I should get you two some rawhide to chew on and something to bring down that temperature." But before Leah could see to that, Helaina returned. Her face was as white as a sheet and her expression told Leah something was wrong.

"What is it?" Leah asked.

"My water just broke."

Chapter Twenty-Two

Jacob could see frustration and worry etched on Adrik's face. No one at the railroad or in town had seen Christopher or Oliver. It was as if the children had simply disappeared off the face of the earth.

"They couldn't have gotten far on foot," Jacob told Adrik.

"I tracked them here to the railroad," Adrik said, shaking his head. "If they came here in the night, they might have managed to get on the freighter headed south to pick up supplies in Seward."

"But why would they head to Seward without you?" Jacob said shaking his head. "They didn't even want to go to Seattle. Wouldn't it make more sense that they'd just hide out somewhere around here until they thought you were gone or had changed your mind about the trip?"

"I don't know. I think I'd better go back to the house and get some gear. Then I'll catch the train south just like I was going to do. That way if they have made their way to Seward, I'll be able to look around and find them there. You and Jayce could keep looking around this area."

Jacob nodded. "You know we will."

Jayce came trotting from down the road. "Nobody's seen 'em at the water," he called. The inlet wasn't all that good for ship traffic, but there were smaller vessels that could make it through the channels.

"Adrik thinks they've taken the supply train south."

Jayce looked to Adrik as he came to stop in front of the two men. "Why?"

"I tracked them here. There's no sign of their leaving the area on foot. No sign of a wagon in the area where I see the signs of their boots. Just railroad tracks. I don't know why they would do this. I just don't understand."

"Understanding can come later," Jacob said. "Let's go back to the cabin and figure out how we can help you the best."

They began walking back to the house. Jacob wished he could offer some encouragement, but he knew how awful Adrik felt about the situation. If Jacob had a son and he disappeared, he would be frantic. There would be no comforting him.

"You can get word to me by telegraph," Adrik said. "If you find them, just wire me in Seward. I'll check in periodically at the telegraph office."

"You're going to Seward?" Jayce asked.

"I don't see as I have a choice."

"We'll keep searching the area," Jacob promised. "We can hire another man to help with hunting and just devote ourselves to the search until we hear otherwise from you."

"I really appreciate your help. I don't know what I'll do if—"

"Don't borrow trouble. We'll find them," Jacob said.

They were nearly to Adrik's house when a scream tore through the air.

Adrik turned to Jacob. "What in the world was that?"

The scream came again.

"That's Helaina!" Jacob said. He made a mad dash for the house. "Helaina!"

He practically knocked the door off its hinges as he burst into the room. "Helaina!"

Leah came from the bedroom she'd been sharing with Jayce. "Calm down. You don't have to yell."

"What's happening? What's wrong?"

Leah smiled. "Nothing's wrong. You simply have a son."

Jacob stopped in midstep. "A what?"

Leah laughed. "I said you have a son. A boy, Jacob. Helaina just had the baby. It's a boy."

Leah watched as Jacob carefully took his son from Helaina. He looked at her with such love that Leah thought she might burst into tears.

"What will you call him?" she asked the couple.

"Malcolm Curtis Barringer," Jacob declared. He studied his son in apparent wonder. "Malcolm because we both like the name and Curtis for Helaina's maiden name."

"That's a good name," Adrik declared. "I wish I could stay and get to know the little guy better, but my little guys need me."

"I won't stop looking either," Jacob promised. "The baby doesn't need me right now as much as Oliver and Christopher do." He looked at Helaina, who nodded.

"You have to help them," Helaina said firmly. "I'll be fine here."

"Leah," Jayce said, coming into the bedroom, "something's wrong with the twins."

"What do mean?" She dropped the blanket she'd been holding.

"They're sick, Leah. I went to check them like you asked, but they aren't waking up. They're burning with fever."

Leah felt her stomach clench. She pushed past Jayce and went into the room where the twins shared a bed. Reaching to touch their foreheads, she pulled back in alarm. They were decidedly hotter than when she'd checked them only an hour ago. "We need the doctor. Can you find him?"

"I'll go right now. What do you think is wrong?"

Leah could only think of the newspaper accounts of influenza on the Seward Peninsula. "I don't know. I pray it's not influenza."

Leah refused to leave her babies until Jayce returned with the doctor. The man appeared quite grave as he examined each child. "It could very well be influenza," he told her. "There are several cases in the area that seem similar. I have no way of knowing for certain. At this point, their lungs are clear, and that's a very good sign."

"What can be done?" Leah asked, wringing her hands together. Jayce put his hands on her shoulders and pulled her close.

"You should work to get that fever down. I recommend tepid vinegar baths and aspirin powder. I don't have much on hand and I have none of the new tablets. I'll leave some of the powder," he said, reaching into his bag. "I'll look in on Mrs. Barringer, then check back on everyone later this afternoon."

Leah watched him leave, feeling completely helpless. In the other room Helaina was recovering from childbirth, and baby Malcolm was vulnerable to whatever sickness the twins were suffering. As soon as Helaina felt up to it, Leah would encourage her to go back to her own cabin. Maybe she would even suggest Jacob move his wife and baby there right away.

"Tell me what to do," Jayce said after seeing the doctor out.

Leah shook her head, feeling so overwhelmed. "Undress them and I'll get the vinegar bath ready."

She went into the kitchen to find the things she'd need. Tears came unbidden and before she knew it, Leah was sobbing into her hands.

"Leah, what's wrong?" It was Jacob. She looked up to see him standing only a few feet away. He reached for her, but she shook her head.

"Don't. The babies are sick and may have influenza. We don't know. They're burning up with fever, though. You should probably move Helaina and the baby to your cabin. I'm so sorry."

"The doctor is seeing her and the baby right now."

"Good. I pray they're all right. There's no telling what they've been exposed to." Her voice broke, and she began to cry again.

Jacob ignored her protests and pulled her into his arms. "Leah, please don't worry. I'll take care of Helaina and Malcolm, but is there anything I can do for you—for the children?"

"No. Nothing. This just couldn't have come at a worse time." She pushed away from him and regained her composure. She hurried to pour water into a small tub. "I didn't know they were sick. When Helaina got closer to delivering, I put them to bed. They were so tired and while they were feverish, I thought they were only teething."

"How are they now?"

"Much worse. The fever is high, but the doctor said their lungs are clear. He'll be back this afternoon to check on them."

She found the vinegar and poured a generous amount into the tepid water. "I have to go." She started to lift the tub, but Jacob took hold of the bath and motioned her to the room. "Go on. I'll bring this."

Leah saw little change in the twins' condition throughout the day. The doctor came again and left without any word of encouragement. She sat rocking and praying, never feeling more worthless in her life.

Why can't I make them well? Why did this have to happen? They're just little babies. She gently pushed back the hair on Merry's forehead. Her fever still raged. Why wouldn't it come down? Merry seemed so pale—so still. Leah lifted the baby into her arms and rocked her. Tears blurred Leah's vision. The thought of losing her daughter was more than she could bear.

"Please, God, please don't take her away from me. Don't take Wills. I love them so much." She thought back to her worries of old—of whether the children were Jayce's or Chase's. None of that would ever matter again. Never. They were hers. They were more important to her than Leah could have ever imagined.

She rocked Merry until her arms could no longer bear the weight. Carefully tucking the baby back in bed, Leah leaned down and kissed each of them on the head. Neither stirred, and her heart constricted as she realized her babies might die and there was nothing she could do to stop it.

"Oh, God, show me what to do."

She sat by their side through the night and into the day; Jayce joined the vigil from time to time. As Leah dozed she thought of life in Last Chance Creek. She still hadn't heard from Emma or Sigrid. She was desperate to know if they were well or sick, dead or alive. She wondered if Emma sat beside her babies, feeling the same hopelessness that threatened to strangle the life out of Leah.

In her dreams, Leah was taken back to working with an old Tlingit woman who had taught her much about healing. She watched the woman work, tearing the leaves of a large palmy plant.

"Use the skunk cabbage leaves, Leah. You won't cut your hands on devil's club if you do."

Leah reached for the protective skunk cabbage, then took hold of the devil's club, with its razor-sharp spiky spine. They used this plant for all kinds of ailments. Karen even called it Tlingit aspirin.

Leah awoke with a start. Her heart pounded hard, as if she'd just run miles and miles behind a dogsled team. She struggled to focus on the dream and the thoughts that had awakened her.

"Tlingit aspirin. Devil's club!" She jumped to her feet and stopped only long enough to check on Wills and Meredith. They seemed less feverish, but she thought perhaps it was her own wishful thinking.

"Jayce, are you here?" she questioned, coming into the living room. She had no idea how long she'd slept.

"What is it? Are they worse?" Jayce came from the stove, where Leah could see he was busy cooking something.

"No. They're the same. Look, I have to get some devil's club. It's a remedy for fever and pain. I dreamed about it just now and remembered it from the old days in Ketchikan. I think it's exactly what we need."

He touched her face and nodded. "Go. I'll be here."

Adrik breathed a sigh of relief as he caught sight of his sons. They were sitting on the dock, waiting . . . watching. He'd been told by local officials of two boys who were seeking work on the docks. The police officer had tried several times to speak with the boys, but they always seemed to run away before he could catch up with them. Adrik shook his head. He wasn't at all sure why they'd come here or why they wanted to get jobs on the boats. But none of that really mattered right now; they were safe. They were alive.

He didn't want to frighten them, so Adrik called to them, hoping that the distance would give them a chance to accept his presence.

"Oliver. Christopher."

They turned and looked at him momentarily before lowering their heads in complete dejection. Adrik sat beside them, wondering how he could possibly explain to them how worried he'd been—how wrong they were to leave.

"I'm sorry, Pa," Oliver offered first. "Please don't be mad. This is all my fault. Christopher just came because I told him to. Don't be mad at him."

"I'm not mad, son. I was just so scared."

Oliver looked up. "You?"

Adrik nodded. "I couldn't find you. I thought I'd lost you for good."

"Like Mama?" Christopher asked.

"I have to admit," Adrik said softly, "that I was afraid you might get killed."

"Sorry," Oliver offered again. He hung his head and refused to meet his father's gaze.

"Boys, I don't understand why you're here. I don't understand why you ran away."

"We're going home," Christopher offered.

"Home?"

"To Ketchikan. To our real house," Christopher replied.

Adrik shook his head. He didn't understand any of this. "But why?"

"It's my fault." Oliver drew a deep breath. "I don't like Ship Creek. I don't like the railroad. You're never home and we've got no friends."

"And it's where Mama died. It killed her there," Christopher added.

Adrik had known the boys had disliked Ship Creek, but he had hoped they would adapt. But he realized now, with their mother gone, they felt even more alienation toward the place.

For several minutes neither boy said a word, then Oliver looked up. There were tears streaming down his face. "I can't remember Mama's face. Sometimes I do, then it's like she disappears and there's just this cloud around her."

"There are pictures of her at home in Ketchikan," Christopher said, his lower lip quivering. "Can't we go home, Papa? I was never afraid there."

Adrik realized there was so much he didn't know about his boys and what they were thinking and feeling. He felt like a failure for not understanding their need. "Come here, boys," he said, opening his arms to them. Christopher came immediately and hugged his father tightly.

Oliver was slower to respond. He wiped his face with the back of his sleeve and coughed. "I'm too big for you to hug."

"Never," Adrik replied softly. "Even big guys need a hug now and then."

Oliver considered this for a moment, then edged over to his father. Leaning hard against Adrik, Oliver buried his face against his father's neck. Adrik felt the heat of his son's body.

"Oliver, are you sick?"

"We slept outside last night. It was cold."

Adrik put his hand to Oliver's head as the boy began to cough again. "Come on, guys. We're going to get a room at the hotel and see if we can't get you both warmed up."

"And then we'll go home?" Oliver asked.

Adrik held them both at arm's length. "I promise you this—we'll go back to Ketchikan as soon as I can get things settled in Ship Creek. We'll definitely go home before the summer is out, but for now we have to get you well and then go back to take care of business. Will that be all right?"

Oliver straightened and looked his father in the eye. "You promise we'll move back to Ketchikan?"

Adrik nodded. "I promise."

Later that night, long after the boys had fallen asleep, Adrik sat watching and listening to them breathe. Oliver would break into a spell of coughing from time to time. The deep, hacking cough worried Adrik more than he wanted to admit.

"But they're safe," he whispered. He'd been so afraid; they were too young to understand all of the dangers, but Adrik knew them only too well. He could never have forgiven himself if something had happened to them.

Tears came to his eyes as he thought of Karen and how hard it had been these last few months without her. He had never had a chance to say all the things he had wanted to say. He had never given her all of the attention he'd wanted to give. So many times he'd wanted to take her away and share some quiet moments alone, but always life got in the way and he'd put it off for another day.

"But there will never be another day," he whispered. "You're gone. You're gone and I'm here, and nothing will ever feel the same—nothing will ever be quite as good." He looked up to the ceiling, knowing he wouldn't find her there but feeling somehow comforted to just imagine Karen smiling down from heaven.

"I don't know why you had to die. You were my everything . . . and now I just feel so empty. So lost." He forced back a choking sob. "Oh, Karen, I miss you so much."

Chapter Twenty-Three

June arrived with mixed blessings. The devil's club tea seemed to do the trick in bringing down the twins' fever. They were still sleeping a great deal, but as their second birthday arrived, the doctor pronounced them out of danger. Leah had never heard words that meant more to her.

"We've had another telegram from Adrik. He said the devil's club is helping Oliver, and Christopher seems immune to whatever the sickness is.

Oliver is much better and they hope to be back here in less than a week," Jayce announced, holding up the telegram.

"I'm so glad to hear that." Leah picked up a tray of partially eaten food and glanced at her sleeping babies. "The doctor said the twins will be up and running before we know it. He's so happy with their progress that he's asked me to help him with some other patients."

"What did you tell him?" Jayce eyed her curiously.

"I told him I would make devil's club tea for him, but that I had a responsibility right here. He agreed and was happy for the tea." She smiled and went to deposit the tray in the kitchen. "Of course," she added, "he can hardly believe that such a vicious plant could prove so helpful. He told me only three weeks ago he had to treat a poor man for a leg infection after having a run-in with devil's club. Now it seems everyone will be singing its praises."

Jayce came to her and pulled her into his arms. "I feel as though the world has been quite mad for the last few weeks."

Leah nodded. "I don't honestly know what I would have done without you. I'm sorry for the trouble the railroad had without you and Adrik helping with the regular meat supplies, but I am so blessed that you were here."

"Jacob handled it well. He hired a team of dock rats down in Seward. They've managed quite well. Well enough, in fact, that Jacob is thinking of leaving the business once Adrik is back to run things. I'm thinking of leaving as well."

"And then what?" Leah asked, looking up into his eyes.

"I don't know. Jacob has asked me to consider going into the mercantile business with him, as you know. I'm definitely considering it. This seems like a good place to set up such a thing. People are moving in by the hundreds. The railroad officials told me they believe there to be some four thousand men here. Most are working in some capacity for the railroad."

"That's incredible. I knew there were more people than when we first arrived—more permanent structures too. That's always a good sign. Soon we'll have all the things any other town could offer us." Leah put her arms around Jayce's neck. "But you know it doesn't matter. I'll go with you anywhere and be happy with whatever you choose to do for a living."

A rap came at the front window. Leah and Jayce looked to find Jacob waving something at them. They'd been careful to have as little contact with the rest of the family as possible. Leah was desperate that Malcolm and Helaina, as well as Jacob, should stay well and free of the influenza.

"Mail," Jacob called. "I'll leave it at the door."

"Thanks!" Leah replied. She could hardly wait to see who had written. She prayed daily for news from Last Chance, having decided that it was far worse not to know their fate than to have to face the truth. She waited until she was certain Jacob would be well away from the door before opening it. There was probably no longer a need for quarantine, but Leah couldn't see pushing things too fast.

There were two letters, and both were addressed to Leah. One was from Grace Colton. The other was from Emma Kjellmann. Leah clutched them to her breast. "Emma has written!"

"Well, maybe now we will finally know what has happened," Jayce said, taking a seat at the table. "Why don't you come here and read it to me? We'll share whatever news together."

Leah closed the door and came to the table. "I've waited so long for this, but now I'm afraid."

"God already knows what's happened," Jayce replied. "What's happened is done—we cannot change it. If the news is bad, we'll face it together."

Leah opened the letter and drew a deep breath. " 'Dear Leah and Jayce,' " she began. " 'The news from Last Chance is bad. I'm not sure if you've heard anything of our area, so forgive me if this repeats what you already know. Around Christmas last year there were rumors of sickness in Nome and along the coast. We didn't think much of it.

" 'I was of course busy with my newest addition to the family, little Samuel. He was born in November, with Qavlunaq and Kimik's son Adam being born nearly two weeks earlier. Christmas seemed all the more special with new babies in our congregation, but soon tragedy struck.' " Leah looked up at Jayce momentarily, then continued reading.

" 'Several men returned from Teller to give us the news that the village was full of sickness. We had word come from other villages as well. It seemed no one was sure what had caused the sickness or how to treat it. It started with high fevers and labored breathing. Sometimes fierce coughing developed and sometimes the person just seemed unable to breathe at all. Most were delirious from fever and often unconscious for the duration of their illness. Leah, it was unlike anything we'd ever seen—not even the measles epidemic we'd suffered so long ago could compare. People began dying without even seeming all that sick. They would go to bed feeling poorly and be dead by morning. I nearly lost Bjorn and Sigrid, but they miraculously pulled through. Rachel and Samuel did not.' " Leah gasped. "Oh no, not the babies. Oh, poor Emma."

Tears filled her eyes as she continued. " 'Kimik died on the third of January and was soon followed by Oopick.' " Leah could hardly bear the news. Oopick was gone, and Kimik too.

" 'So many you loved are gone,' " she read from Emma's shaky handwriting. " 'The village had so few people left that we considered heading south to Nome for the remainder of the winter. However, word came that Nome was suffering and the few remaining did not wish to risk getting sick, so we remained here to wait out the winter or at least until we heard that the quarantines were lifted.

" 'But what started as an overwhelming situation became even worse.' " Leah shook her head and looked again to Jayce. "I don't see how it could be worse."

"I suppose you should read on," her husband encouraged.

Leah looked to the letter. " 'Government officials from Nome showed up here as soon as passage could be made. With them came the news that many villages had been wiped out—that there were now many orphans as well as widows and widowers. The man told the villagers that there were no orphanages for the children and that the people would have to see to adoption. To facilitate this, he further forced the remarriage of those who were now single. Leah, it was awful. People still grieving for their unburied dead were forced to agree to marriage. The men were given the choice of picking a wife from amongst the remaining women in the village. If there were no women, they were told they would have to accompany the men to another village and find a wife there.

" 'Poor John and Qavlunaq were beside themselves. Neither had any desire to marry again, but because of the officials forcing the matter, they agreed to wed each other. John said he would never treat Qavlunaq as anything other than the daughter-in-law she was, and Qavlunaq stated she would always care for John as the father of her husband. Still, they are legally married and have taken on two orphaned girls from a village near Nome to raise with Qavlunaq's two sons—both of whom I'm happy to say survived the epidemic.' "

Leah turned to the second page and continued in stunned sorrow. " 'Of course, Bjorn did not approve these forced marriages, but the officials didn't care. They had come armed with a sheaf of marriage licenses already filed and filled out with exception to the actual names of the couple and the date of their marriage. After leaving our village, the group was headed to Teller to impose the same thing on those poor unsuspecting souls. I'm so very glad you did not stay here to see this abomination. Bjorn and I will be leaving with the children and Sigrid at the end of the month and heading for a sabbatical with my family in Minnesota. I doubt seriously that we will return to Alaska. Our hearts are so completely broken at the loss of Rachel and Samuel, as well as all of our dear friends. I pray the situation has boded better for you in your part of the territory. I have not heard of sickness in your area; however, as usual we have not had much news of any kind.

" 'I will close this letter to further tell you that it has also been decided that the village will be evacuated. Most of the remaining Inupiat are heading to Teller or Wales. A few are going to Nome. Last Chance Creek will be no more.' "

Leah let the paper fall to the table. "I have no words." She shook her head and let out a heavy sigh. She felt as though her tears were dried up and there were no possible explanations that could make sense of anything she'd just read.

Jayce picked up the letter and read, " 'I will be in touch and hope to hear from you. I have written my Minnesota address at the bottom of the page. I hope you will all pray for us. Love, Emma.' " He put the letter down and reached out to take Leah's hand.

An eternity seemed to pass with Leah and Jayce doing nothing more than holding on to each other. Leah tried not to think too much of her old friends—it hurt too much. Her mind seemed to blur, and it wasn't until she felt a tug at her sleeve that she opened her eyes and met Wills' grinning face.

"I eat, Mama." He patted his stomach liked he'd seen Adrik do on occasion.

Leah lifted him in her arms and held him much tighter than she'd intended. She needed to feel his warmth—to hear his breathing. She needed just to know flesh to flesh that he was alive and well. "Oh, Wills," she said, burying her face against his neck.

Helaina read the letter sent by Stanley for the third time before tucking it into the pocket of her skirt. He had finally been able to provide her with information about Cheslav Babinovich. At least he provided information about a man who was notorious for using that alias and posing as a Russian.

Stanley had told her that the man was wanted in several states for trying to defraud a variety of people regarding the sale of faux jewelry, furs of poor quality, and even land deeds. His real name was Rutherford Mills, an actor originally from New York City. He had a list of names he used across the country and seemed to prey particularly upon wealthy women. His latest scheme of posing as Russian royalty raising money for the czar and his family had been seen up and down the coast of California, Washington, and now Alaska.

Worse than his thievery and fraud, however, Mills was considered to be a prime suspect in the disappearance of several women. Women last seen in his company had simply disappeared, leaving no trace of their whereabouts. Mills would also disappear, leaving the authorities no chance to question him. He was considered very dangerous.

Helaina began to pace the small living room space. Stanley had told her there was a good-sized reward for the man if she wanted to get back in her old line of business. Of course he knew from her letters that she was expecting a baby, but he may not yet have received her own letter telling of Malcolm's birth. Stanley's wife, Annabelle, had given birth to a son earlier in the year, and it pleased Helaina to realize that she had become both aunt and mother within a matter of months. Stanley was obviously quite proud of having a son of his own. He'd been completely captivated by his wife's daughter, Edith, a spunky four-year-old whom he'd adopted, but Helaina knew this son meant someone would carry forward the family name. Still, the matter of Babinovich or Mills captivated Helaina.

"Are you ready for a grumpy little man?" Jacob asked, bringing her a fussy Malcolm. "I've changed his diaper, but I believe there is more to the matter." He grinned. "I think he's hungry."

Helaina smiled and took her son. He cried, but there were no tears. "You are such a little duper." The words were no sooner out of her mouth than Helaina thought of Mills. Mills had duped so many. Old feelings flooded Helaina's mind and heart. Yearning for justice, to see people pay for their mistakes—of demanding retribution instead of offering forgiveness. Still, she knew there was a difference between those who sought to change their ways and those who only appeared to change when backed into a corner.

"So what did Stanley have to say?" Jacob asked as Helaina moved to the rocking chair.

"He said that the family is doing well. He's beside himself with joy, thanks to his son, and has felt even closer to Edith as she embraces her new role of sister."

"Did he have anything else to share? Word of the war?"

Helaina shook her head. "I had hoped he would tell us the war was over, but no such luck. He did, however, have some interesting news."

"News about what?"

"About Mr. Babinovich. It seems he's not Russian—just as Adrik suspected."

"If he's not Russian," Jacob began, somewhat confused, "what is he?"

"A confidence man—a trickster breaking the law for his own benefit."

Adrik smiled at the young woman making her way through the crowd at the dock. It seemed she'd matured greatly in the six months since he'd seen her.

"Father!" Ashlie fell into his open arms.

Adrik held her tight and just enjoyed the moment. He didn't even mind the more formal address of Father instead of Papa. It was just good to see her—to see the reflection of her mother and the beauty of the young woman Ashlie had become. "I was so glad you could make it home. I hated missing your graduation. I want to hear all about it—including your speech."

Ashlie laughed and pulled away. "Cousin Myrtle cried bucketfuls. It was rather embarrassing."

Adrik put his arm around her and moved her toward the hotel. "Your brothers are beside themselves waiting for you to get here."

"How's Oliver?" The concern was evident in her tone. "Your telegram was so brief."

"He's much improved. We had planned to return to Ship Creek this week. I'm glad we could arrange for you to come with us. However, I need to let you know that we won't remain long in the area. I promised the boys we'd go back to Ketchikan."

"Honestly? But why? I thought the work was good here."

Several rowdy people pushed past them, causing Adrik to pull Ashlie against him in a protective manner. "Your brothers are miserable." He began to fill her in on the turn of events.

"I can't believe they would run away. That must have been awful for you to face." Ashlie sounded so grown up to Adrik. It seemed she had been just a girl when she'd first gone away, but now a lovely young woman had returned in her place.

"It wasn't easy. Then when Oliver came down sick, I thought for sure I'd lose him. He's better though, and we can head to Ship Creek on the next train if you like."

"I don't mind at all," Ashlie replied. "I had good accommodations on the ship and slept quite well last night. I'm ready to move on." She paused and looked up at her father to add, "But there are a couple of things I'd like to talk to you about without the boys around."

Adrik heard what sounded like caution in her voice. He knew whenever Ashlie took this tone with him in the past that something was afoot. "You have my attention—and my suspicion."

Ashlie laughed. "I suppose you know me too well for me to try and fool you. I suppose, too, that it's best to just come out and tell you what's on my mind rather than to beat around the bush until I've driven everything out but what I intended to reveal."

Adrik shook his head and laughed out loud. "You sound just like your mother. She would reason around a thing rather than just deal with the matter itself."

"I just don't want to give you further cause to worry or fret." Her brow furrowed as she seemed to give the situation deep consideration.

"Stop stalling." Adrik finally said. "What do you want to talk to me about?"

Ashlie drew a deep breath and squared her shoulders. "Two things. My future education and . . . well . . . a young man named Winston Galbrith."

Chapter Twenty-Four

So this man is very dangerous," Jacob said after Helaina explained who Rutherford Mills was and what he stood accused of doing.

"Yes. Stanley says he's the prime suspect in the murders of several women," Helaina replied. "Authorities have been searching for him for over four years."

Jacob rubbed his stubbly chin. "I don't understand why a man like that would come to Alaska."

"Probably because of the isolation. He no doubt feels he can lay low here and then return south after things have calmed and the search has been given up. Stanley says there's a hefty reward for the man's capture. He wondered if I wanted to take on bounty hunting." She grinned.

Jacob shook his head. "Knowing you, you're probably already planning something."

"No." Her tone reassured him. There was no hint of desire or longing for such a task.

"I suppose I could go to the authorities and let them know what we know. We can give them your brother's information and offer descriptions and details of his approach to women—how he came to you with his sad story about the czar. Apparently he's no fool. He knows enough to keep up with world events and use them to his advantage."

"I know. I thought of that too. Most men like him are very intelligent. It's why they manage to keep at it for so long without being caught. I remember reading a case about a man in Chicago who killed dozens—maybe hundreds—of people. He was a great businessman and people liked him. He had a charm that seemed to get him into places he'd otherwise never be invited."

"It just makes that kind of person more dangerous," Jacob replied. "They aren't suspected and no one sees any need to shy away from them. They aren't perceived as dangerous."

"No, there was nothing of Babinovich that suggested danger. In fact, the man seemed quite mousy and meek."

"My ma always said the devil would come to us as a wolf in sheep's clothing. She said a lot of folks figured the devil to be a monster—ugly and scary and obviously evil—but that the Bible said otherwise. If the devil will come to us as an angel of light, why wouldn't a mere man try the same tactic to gain the trust of unsuspecting people?"

"Exactly. Most of the criminals I've dealt with are that way," Helaina replied. "Mills seemed genuinely concerned about his loved ones, and that seemed to motivate his actions."

"Well, we know now that this wasn't the case. I suppose I can go to the authorities and take your brother's letter. I can explain his work with the Pinkertons and what we experienced with Babinovich here in Ship Creek, as well as what happened in Nome. If they choose to do nothing, we'll have to take it from there." He eyed her with what he hoped was a stern expression. "Just promise me you'll have nothing further to do with this situation."

Helaina leaned forward and kissed him on the forehead. "I promise. I'm a changed woman."

"Oh, sure. You're so changed that for months you've been trying to dig up information on this man, even while carrying my unborn son. That kind of change is hardly comforting. Knowing you, you probably staked out the man's hotel and lay in wait for him."

Helaina laughed. "Not quite." She picked up an iron from the stove and tested the heat. "I did ask after him, mentioning that I wanted to buy jewelry from him, but otherwise . . ."

Jacob rolled his eyes and got to his feet. "That's enough. I don't think I want to know anymore. Please just promise me that you'll leave this in my hands now."

"Of course," Helaina replied with a sweet smile. "I'm quite happy to turn the matter over to you."

"Uh-huh. I've heard that before."

Jacob left his wife and son and headed to Jayce's cabin. Since Adrik had sent a telegram saying that he and the boys were returning home, Jayce and Leah had decided to move back into their own place. Jayce was in the back sharpening a hoe when Jacob approached.

"There's something we need to talk about," Jacob announced. "I could use some advice."

"Sure, pull up a stump," Jayce said, motioning to the thick log stumps he had yet to cut into firewood.

Jacob did as instructed, then began to tell Jayce about Mills. "I doubt he'll come here or be any real threat to our families. He knows Adrik will discover the truth regarding his Russian heritage or lack thereof, and he might fear Helaina learning the truth about the jewelry."

"But he needs to be apprehended," Jayce said, running the hoe's blade against the sharpening stone. "There's no telling what a man like that will do."

"I agree. I figure we can go to the authorities at the railroad and let them know what's going on. They are the only law in this area right now. They want people comfortable with coming to the territory and settling in around the line. They would surely want to see Mills captured."

"I think that's a good idea. Better than our trying to apprehend him ourselves. I've learned I make a poor law official."

Leah worked the dirt of her garden, feeling great pride in the appearance of new growth. The long hours of sun had worked out favorably for her garden, and she meant to take every advantage. There would surely be enough to can for the entire family.

"Did you miss me?" a female voice questioned.

Leah straightened to see Ashlie standing at the end of the carrot row.

"I didn't know you were coming home!" Leah put down her hoe and ran to where Ashlie stood. "Just look at you." Leah gave her a hug, being careful not to get dirt on Ashlie's pristine blue-and-white day dress.

"I wanted to surprise everyone."

"Well, you have certainly accomplished that. Your father was quite ornery to keep this from us."

"Don't be too hard on Father. It's my doing."

"You look so grown up. I can't believe it. At Christmas you still appeared so much a child, but now you are clearly a woman—and a beautiful one. You're doing something new with your hair, aren't you."

Ashlie smiled and reached up to touch the carefully pinned creation. "Actually, I am. But I may soon be cutting it all very short."

"Surely you're joking." Leah had seen some women cut their hair short, even in Alaska, but that was usually the result of fever having damaged it or some other such reason.

"I'm not joking. That's kind of why I came out here. I wanted to tell you what I'm thinking about."

Leah dusted off her hands. "Why don't we sit over there?" She pointed to a large bench under a collection of spruce, hemlock, and alder. "Jayce built that for me just a couple of weeks ago. It makes a nice place to sit and watch the children."

"I can hardly wait to see the twins," Ashlie declared. "Father said they were very sick. I'm glad they're better."

"They're napping now. Those times of slumber come in fewer intervals, but I still insist on an afternoon rest. For them and me." She grinned. "So what's your news?"

"I know I didn't write much, but I found myself very busy. Cousin Myrtle was of course so sad about Mama. To my amazement, however, instead of making her more reclusive, it caused her to get out more. It's almost as if seeing Mama die young was an announcement to her that she needed to cherish and use the time she had left."

"That's understandable. It definitely made me more aware of how fleeting our time on earth can be."

Ashlie nodded. "That's why I started doing some serious thinking about what I wanted out of life."

"And what did you come up with?"

Ashlie folded her hands and straightened her shoulders. "I want to be a nurse. I just kept thinking of how things might have been different for Mama if she'd been in a place where there were better-trained people who could have helped her. Of course, I do not say that to make you feel to blame; I know you and the doctor did what you could for her. I just wish there might have been a nice big hospital with the newest innovations and a well-trained staff. As I thought about this, I figured I would do well to be a part of the solution instead of the problem. Then I met someone who really helped to confirm what I was thinking."

Leah leaned back and waited for Ashlie to continue. The girl was clearly excited about her decision. No wonder she seemed more grown up. She was full of adult thoughts and feelings and now was planning a future that would take her into a job of helping people on a full-time basis.

"I'm in love."

Leah hadn't been expecting this. She looked at Ashlie, knowing her expression must have registered the shock she felt inside. "Love?"

Ashlie grinned and nodded. "He's a wonderful man. His name is Winston Galbrith. Dr. Galbrith. He's been studying to specialize in surgery. He's working now with a physician in a Seattle hospital. He's pledged four years of work with this man and hopes to be a highly qualified surgeon after completing his study. Meanwhile, I'll train to be a nurse at the same hospital."

"Whoa. Back up a little. How did you meet this young man?"

"We actually met at a church dinner. Our church has everyone bring food and share it together once a month. Myrtle decided since it was so blustery outside that this would be a good way to spend the afternoon instead of venturing across town to see one of the relatives. While at the social I met Winston. It was love at first sight for both of us. We sat and talked nearly the entire time, and when the social was over he looked at me and said, 'I feel as though I've known you all of my life. Would you permit me to call on you?' I told him I felt the same way and would very much like for him to call. We've seen each other nearly every day since. He tells me about his cases at the hospital, and he helped me to get into the training program for nurses."

"My, but this all seems so sudden," Leah said, shaking her head. "What does your father say?"

"He's concerned," Ashlie admitted. "However, I've persuaded him to come to Seattle and meet Winston for himself. I even managed to talk those ornery brothers of mine into coming as well."

"That couldn't have been easy," Leah said with a chuckle.

"Well, once I explained how important this was to me and that I couldn't move forward until I had their approval as well as Father's, I think they saw the importance. Father said we will all head down in a couple of weeks. I wish you could come too."

Leah shook her head. "I fear that would be quite impossible. I will look forward to hearing what Adrik has to say about your young man, however. He sounds very industrious."

"He is. And he loves God and wants to serve people. I want the very same thing. And here's the best part: We both plan to come to Alaska after our training is complete. We want to live here and offer the best medical care possible. We'd like to open our own hospital, in fact."

"That is very impressive," Leah replied. She was happy to hear that Ashlie planned to return to Alaska. That would have pleased Karen very much.

"I know it all seems very sudden, but if Father approves of Winston, we'd like to marry right away. Cousin Myrtle wants us to live with her, to help us get through our training without the additional cost of housing."

"I can't imagine you married," Leah said in wonder. "It seems just yesterday you were a little girl in pigtails. Now you're talking of cutting your hair short. Which, by the way, you didn't explain."

Ashlie laughed. "Well, the fashions are changing, but more important, it would be easier for me with my nursing duties. Several of the nurses at the hospital have already cut theirs, and it works quite well for them. I figured that if Winston didn't mind, I might give it a try too."

"And Winston doesn't mind?"

"Not at all. He says that whatever I choose is fine by him, as long as I'm happy." She laughed again with such girlish delight that Leah couldn't help but join in.

"I'm happy for you, Ashlie. He sounds like a wonderful man."

"He is, Leah. He's helped me so much to deal with my grief and sadness. It's like God knew exactly what I needed—before I ever knew it for myself."

"He did, Ashlie. Just as He knows what you need now. We'll pray about this young man of yours and for the future the Lord has for you. But I have a feeling that future is well on the way to being established. Come on. We'll need to start putting supper together."

"Well, the plan is to go to Seattle and then return in August or early September to Ketchikan," Adrik told them after supper that night. Oliver and Christopher nodded in unison as if they'd had great say in the matter.

"I would be happy if you would all join us there. I know I convinced you to give this area a try, but for my family, it's been anything but ideal."

"What do you have in mind, Adrik?" Jacob questioned.

"I figure to return and start making furniture again. I've already had several of the railroad officials tell me they would be happy to pay top dollar for whatever I might supply. They are working hard to put in permanent housing for some of their officials and stationmasters. Those houses will of course need furniture, and it would be much cheaper to get furnishings here in Alaska than to ship them all the way up from Seattle or San Francisco."

"You'll still have to ship it up from Ketchikan," Jacob replied.

Adrik leaned back with a nod. "I've explained all of that. They like the quality they see, however, and for now they want whatever I can provide."

"Well, it sounds like you'll have a trade," Jacob said. He appeared deep in thought.

"I mainly wanted to extend the invitation so that . . . well . . . we might remain close to each other." Adrik held up his hands before anyone else could speak. "I know, however, that we all have our own lives to live. I'm not suggesting you have to do this for me. The boys and I will be fine either way."

"Of course you will," Jacob replied. "That has never been in doubt." He reached over and tousled Christopher's hair. "With boys as ingenious as these, how could you not be fine?"

"I ask simply because I want to stay close to my family for a while," Adrik admitted. "I was foolish in spending so much time away. We need each other now more than ever."

"It wouldn't be so different opening a store in Ketchikan instead of here, would it?" Jayce asked Jacob.

"I'm sure there wouldn't be as much business—at least not if this area continues to grow as they've suggested it will. There's already talk of incorporating the town next year; with the railroad and the push for statehood, I can well imagine that this would be a more prosperous area. However, that much said, I loved growing up in Ketchikan. The area is a good place to raise a family and certainly not as given to drifters and rowdies. There's a kind of peacefulness in Ketchikan that I've not known anywhere else in Alaska."

Jayce nodded. "I agree." He looked to Leah. "What do you think?"

She smiled. "I'm happy to live wherever you choose. I simply want to make a good life with my family. I loved my home in Last Chance, but there's nothing left there except empty houses." She stopped for a moment to regain her composure. "I want to look to the future—not the past. Ketchikan would make a good home. It's true your business probably wouldn't be as prosperous, but maybe in time you could have two stores. One here and one there."

"That is a possibility," Jacob said, looking to Leah. "In fact, it just might be the answer. We could start small and work our way up." He looked to Jayce. "What do you think of that?"

"I like the idea of returning to Ketchikan. As for the stores—well, I think if the Lord is behind it we can't fail," Jayce said, grinning. "Ketchikan blessed me before—it introduced me to Leah."

"What say you, sis?" Jacob asked.

Leah smiled, excited to share her own secret. "I loved my life there. I would very much like to have my baby there," she announced. "There are good midwives who know me from my childhood."

Everyone turned in unison to look rather blankly at Leah. She laughed in delight at the expressions. "Surprise! I'm going to have another baby—this time in January. Leave it to me to pick the coldest part of winter."

"That settles it." Jayce shook his head. "Ketchikan will be less cold."

"I agree," Jacob said. "I'm for Ketchikan if that's all right with Helaina."

Helaina nodded. "I think it sounds fine."

"How soon will you be ready to leave?" Adrik asked, excitement in his voice.

"Well, there's nothing to really keep us here. I've been offered money for the cabin on several occasions," Jacob replied. "I know you and Jayce have received similar offers."

"Yes," Adrik said. "The railroad would be happy to buy all three cabins. They have people they'd like to put in them immediately."

"Then I suppose we should arrange the sale and leave as soon as that's concluded," Jacob said, looking to Jayce and Leah for approval.

"I agree," Jayce replied. "Adrik, why don't you make the arrangements. Tell them we can also leave the larger pieces of furniture and the stoves."

"I will. I'm sure they'll make it worth our while. Meantime, when you are ready to head out to Ketchikan, go ahead. You can stay at my place while you see what's available to buy. If there's nothing suitable, you can just stay with us until we can build something else. That house has plenty of room. It's twice as big as this one, and we all managed to live here without too much trouble. Your families can take the upstairs bedrooms, and my family can live downstairs."

Leah felt Jayce reach for her hand. He squeezed it and she glanced up to see the pleasure in his eyes. She had wanted to tell him about the baby when they were alone, but it seemed important to mention the matter here as they discussed their future. It seemed they had come full circle: They had met and she had fallen in love in Ketchikan. Now they would return to live and raise their family. It all seemed very right.

"And you have proof that this man is wanted by the legal authorities in the States?" a stern man asked Jayce. The gentleman had introduced himself as Zachary Hinman and declared himself to be in charge of all legal matters for the area.

"Yes, Mr. Hinman." Jacob handed him the letter from Stanley. "As you will note, my wife's brother is an agent with the Pinkertons. When my wife requested information on the man, he looked into the matter and revealed the situation that I've just told you about."

"This is indeed a find," Hinman said, sitting up a little straighter. "The man who captures this Mills fellow would make quite the name for himself." He stroked his thick black mustache. "I'm intrigued."

"I've asked around," Jacob began, "and it seems people have seen the man in town. Some even remember being approached by him."

"You can be assured, Mr. Barringer, that I'll see personally to this matter. If the man is still in the area, I will apprehend him."

Jacob got to his feet. "As you can see, the authorities warn that he is to be considered dangerous. If he comes near my family, I won't hesitate to take the matter into my own hands."

"Never fear, Mr. Barringer. We have some good men on the payroll. We'll see that this man is captured."

Chapter Twenty-Five

Ashlie Ivankov leaned against the rail of the *Spirit of Alaska* and sighed. Soon she'd be in Seattle and once again in the presence of her beloved Winston. Never had she met anyone who intrigued her or gave her reason to care as much as this soft-spoken, humorous man. She thought of his tall stature and broad shoulders and laughed to herself as she realized she'd fallen for a man who was built much like her father.

Ashlie fondly remembered her mother talking of how her father's sense of humor first attracted her—that and his honesty. Ashlie knew the same could be said of her interest in Winston. The man was good to speak his mind but also to hear her speak in return. Ashlie found him attentive to the interests and dreams she held. Not only that, but he was very supportive of her goals. Other men—boys, really—that she'd talked to for any length of time could hardly be said to have any concern for her desires at all. They were generally self-centered—more interested in war and playing soldier than anything else.

But not Winston. Winston detested the war. He wanted to heal and repair bodies, not destroy them. She felt the same way. She'd seen a few of the men who'd returned after serving in Europe. Some were missing limbs, while others were blind or suffering serious lung ailments. Winston said it was because horrible tactics were being used in this war. Men were being gassed—poisoned—as they fought under raining bullets and shrapnel. She shuddered. *It's positively hideous.*

She pushed the images away and focused on dreams of her future with Winston. If things went well, she reasoned, she and Winston could be married before her father and brothers returned to Alaska. Cousin Myrtle was all for having a summer wedding. Her gardens were a delight, and she had suggested to Ashlie on more than one occasion that such a setting would be perfect for a day wedding. Winston had liked the idea very much. His parents were deceased; after becoming parents much later in life, they had passed away in their late sixties only a year ago. First his mother had died of some stomach ailment, and within four months his father had passed peacefully in his sleep. Winston said it was from a broken heart. Given this, and the fact that Winston was an only child, neither one expected to have a large wedding. Although Ashlie had numerous friends from school and church, and Winston shared many of the same acquaintances, neither she nor Winston desired a big to-do.

Ashlie turned from the rail and began moving down the deck. She smiled at a young woman with two small children.

"Someday that shall be me," she murmured under her breath. *I shall be married to Winston and be mother to his children.* The thought of such intimacy with the man made her blush.

"Excuse me," a man dressed in a fine black suit declared. He tried to hurry away, but Ashlie was certain she recognized him. His hair was combed in a different fashion and he was clean-shaven, but she was sure she knew him. Wasn't he the Russian man who wasn't really a Russian? The one who'd come to her house only to have her father declare him a fraud? *Oh, what was his name? Bab-something. Babcock? Babinokov?* He glanced quickly over his shoulder and Ashlie suddenly remembered. "Mr. Babinovich!"

The man turned, looking rather alarmed. He hurried away without a word.

"How strange. Why would he do that?"

Ashlie thought perhaps the man had heard that his game had been found out, though she couldn't really see the harm in pretending to be someone he wasn't. These were troubled times, and perhaps the man thought that by playing a Russian nobleman, he'd avoid having to serve in the army.

She continued her stroll on the deck. Her father and brothers were enjoying an early lunch, and Ashlie was enjoying the time to herself. Her father was far too protective, watching her every move. The only reason she was able to be alone now was because her father believed her to be resting in their cabin.

Ashlie remembered protesting her father's actions once to her mother. She had argued about his need to always know where she was going. "We live on an island," she had told her mother. "Where could I possibly go?"

She smiled at the memory of her mother patiently explaining Adrik's protective nature and desire to keep his family from harm. "God has given him a family and the responsibility to provide for and protect them. Your father considers that job to be a great honor . . . but also of the utmost importance."

Ashlie took a seat on one of the deck chairs and wiped a tear from her eye. She missed her mother at times like this. She would love to talk to her about falling in love with Winston and about the wedding she had been planning since Winston first declared his love for her. How her mother would have enjoyed helping her make a gown. Instead, Ashlie had already planned to purchase a lovely gown that she'd helped a local seamstress to design. The woman was working on it in Ashlie's absence, in fact.

Oh, Mama, you would like Winston. Ashlie closed her eyes and tried to imagine her mother sitting beside her. *He's so like Papa. So gentle and sweet, yet strong and capable. He makes me laugh, and yet he cares about my tears.*

Her mother had always told her that the most important thing to have in a mate was a man who knew the Lord and loved Him. Ashlie saw that daily in Winston. He loved helping people, because he felt confident that it was what God wanted him to do. He and Ashlie had discussed this more than once. Winston had even made it clear to Ashlie that he would not impose the life of a doctor's wife on her unless she desired to serve in the medical field. Ashlie had laughed, telling him that for ages now she'd considered being a nurse.

Ashlie thought of her mother again. She couldn't help but wonder: If her mother had been closer to proper medical facilities, would she have died? *I'll become a good nurse, Mama. I'll study hard and help save lives. I just wish we could have saved you.*

"Miss Ivankov. I'm sorry that you remembered me. You've put me in a rather difficult spot."

Ashlie opened her eyes and looked up in surprise. "Mr. Babinovich?"

"Mills, actually." With a quick glance over his shoulder, the man reached out to take hold of her Ashlie's arm. "You will come with me."

"I will not." She tried to pull away, but he held her fast.

"If you do not, then I'm afraid something bad will happen to one of your brothers. Perhaps the youngest one. Little boys always have a penchant for getting into trouble."

Ashlie froze. Her heart pounded harder. "How dare you threaten my family!"

"Come, come. Your family has threatened my livelihood and you question me on my actions?"

He pulled again, and this time Ashlie, seeing there was no one nearby to help her, walked with him. "What do you want and who are you? My father says you are not Russian."

"And so he is correct, although I have fooled hundreds, maybe more, into believing I am. My name is Mills. Rutherford Mills. And your family has caused me a great deal of trouble."

"I don't understand. What kind of trouble? How problematic can it be for my father to know that you've lied about being Russian?"

He pulled her toward an inside passage and again Ashlie pulled back. "Miss Ivankov, I grow weary of your games. I am taking you to my cabin. You will either accompany me there of your own free will or I will be forced to do something rather drastic." He opened his coat just far enough to reveal a revolver.

"What? Will you shoot me here and bring everyone running? I do not easily cower, Mr. Mills, and I'm not a stupid child. Tell me now what it is you are after."

"I will tell you in my cabin. I do not wish to bring you harm." He shrugged. "Although you probably do not believe me. Still, I have something to discuss in private. I would hate to hurt you, but this is a life and death matter to me. Therefore the stakes are quite high."

"Life and death? I'm sure I do not understand you."

His grip grew stronger. "I'm losing my patience, Miss Ivankov." He narrowed his eyes and leaned close enough for Ashlie to smell the spirits on his breath. "Do not make me hurt you."

Ashlie weighed the matter briefly, allowing him to guide her down the passage as she considered her choices. She was uncertain at this point what would be best to do. There was no one in the passageway to aid her, and if she began to cause a fuss, Mills might well find a way to harm one of her brothers. Perhaps, she reasoned with herself, it was better to simply see what the man wanted and then if he wouldn't let her go, she would simply wrestle the gun away from him. He didn't know the manner of woman he was dealing with. She was, after all, an Alaskan.

"Get inside," Mills declared, giving Ashlie a push inside his cabin, then locked the door behind him. "I have watched your family closely ever since learning that the authorities were looking for me. You see, I am not inclined to be taken into custody."

"Taken into custody for what? What are you talking about?"

He looked at her oddly for a moment. "So your family didn't tell you?"

"Tell me what?" Ashlie crossed her arms and tried to look bored with the entire matter. "Why don't you just tell me why you've forced me to come here?"

Mills took a seat and motioned her to do likewise, but Ashlie refused. He acted as if it was of little consequence, but Ashlie could see in his eyes that he didn't know quite what to make of her defiance.

"Someone in your family learned of my true identity and turned that information over to the local authorities. They have dogged my heels ever since. When you recognized me, I knew I could not let you make it back to your father. You would alert him about my presence and my circumstance would be known to everyone."

"Why would my father care about your presence on this ship? Why would the local authorities care about your true identity? I know you sold fake jewels to Helaina. Is that what this is all about?"

Mills laughed. "Hardly. That is the least of my offenses as far as the criminal authorities are concerned. You need to understand, Miss Ivankov,

I am a wanted man. I had thought to seek refuge for a time in Alaska as many of my cohorts have done in the past. But alas, your friends and family made that quite impossible."

"But whatever are you wanted for?" Ashlie looked at him hard. "Not for the fake jewelry sales?"

He shrugged and looked almost proud. "I'm wanted for murdering foolish women who naïvely believed themselves capable of handling a man like me."

Ashlie raised a brow. "Are you suggesting that I am foolish or naïve with regard to you?"

"That remains to be seen. I will weigh that matter momentarily after I have told you what I mean for you to hear."

"Then please be quick about it. My father will soon be looking for me, and you will have to explain yourself to him."

Mills shook his head. "I do not think so. You see, I saw him in the dining room with your brothers. They were only beginning their meal. I had thought myself safe because no one even noticed me, but then I crossed your path on deck. I seriously doubt they will worry over your whereabouts for some time. But I am just as anxious as you to be done with this. Here's the matter as I see it: I managed to slip out of Alaska under the nose of the authorities, but if anyone believes me to have made it this far, they will no doubt have the authorities waiting for me in Seattle. That would prove to be quite uncomfortable for me. Therefore, I plan to utilize your services in two ways."

"Do tell." Ashlie tried her best not to appear afraid. She had no idea what Mills was up to, but the idea of his causing harm to either of her brothers left her feeling both angry and fearful.

"I have a friend on board who is happily assisting me. I spoke to him just moments before coming to you. He will let me know when your father and brothers are nearly done with their meal. He will also help me keep track of you and your family for the duration of our journey. Therefore, do not think that you can return to your father and declare my presence. Ridding yourself of me will not be beneficial. My assistant has his orders to slay all of you if any harm should come my way."

"That still doesn't tell me what you want," Ashlie said in what she hoped was her most severe, no-nonsense look.

"I want protection. I want help when we get to Seattle."

"Help in what way?"

"Well, I cannot trust you. You may yet manage to slip a note to someone or get word to the captain about me. This could cause the ship's crew to try something stupid in order to take me hostage. I won't tolerate that. So I have come up with a plan. A rather unsophisticated one, but one that should nevertheless be useful.

"I'm certain that your family will have little trouble passing from the ship to the dock in Seattle. If there are police officers to greet the ship, I will find it more difficult to debark, as you can well imagine. Now, my assistant will have no trouble leaving. He is not known nor expected. He will follow closely by your family and carry out my plan."

"What plan?" She wanted an end to this matter, but Mills just kept dragging it out.

"You will walk a few paces behind your father and brothers. Pretend you have a problem with your shoe or whatever. My assistant will bump into you. You will scream and declare that he is trying to rob you. He will run of course, but you will raise a ruckus that brings every officer—either in uniform or out—running. It will be up to you, Miss Ivankov, to make it appear real and to draw the attention of everyone. That way, I can slip from the ship and safely make my getaway."

"You are quite mad. I would never help you."

"You will help me, or you will be the cause of one of your brothers dying. Let me make the decision less difficult." He got to his feet and came to stand directly in front of her. "You will do this, or I will see your youngest brother dead even yet tonight. Do you understand me? You cannot protect him. I have my means . . . and my friends. It will be very easy to have the boy simply fall overboard."

Ashlie stiffened. Her father would no doubt have beat this man to a pulp for his threats, but Ashlie had no ability to fight him. At least not physically. It would not be a good idea to create a fuss at this point, she decided. "Very well. I will do as you say, but what kind of assurance do I have that no harm will come to my family?"

"You must understand, Miss Ivankov, I hold your family no personal malice. I simply want my own survival. If you do as you have promised, I will have no reason to further concern myself with your family. Otherwise, you have no guarantee—no assurances. I am what I am, and I really have nothing to offer you otherwise."

The man's dark eyes seemed lifeless—his expression void. Ashlie repressed a shiver. "Then I suppose I have no choice."

He smiled, but there was nothing of joy in his look. "Exactly. You have no choice."

A knock sounded three times on the cabin door. "They're finished," a voice called from the other side.

"Ah, we must conclude our business. It would seem your family has eaten their fill. Do you understand what is required of you? We dock in less than twenty-four hours."

"I know what I have to do," Ashlie replied.

Mills nodded and opened his cabin door. "Then you'd best return to your family, lest they believe some harm has come to you."

Ashlie moved quickly out the door and nearly ran down the passageway. She made her way back up to the deck where her father had booked their stateroom. Mills' boldness irritated her in a way she could not set aside. His threats to Christopher and Oliver were beyond all reason.

Opening the door to her cabin, Ashlie met her father's concerned expression. "Where have you been?"

"You won't believe me when I tell you," Ashlie declared. She looked at her brothers, then back to her father. "We have some trouble aboard. His name is Mr. Mills."

Adrik shook his head. "Mills?"

"He was first known to us as Mr. Babinovich. Remember him?"

"He's here? The authorities are scouring Ship Creek for him. He's a thief and a murderer."

"Yes, I know," Ashlie replied. "He told me after he forced me to accompany him to his cabin."

"What!" Adrik's booming voice caused all three of his children to jump. "I think you'd better explain everything."

Ashlie told her father in vivid detail everything that Mills had related, right down to the knock on the door from his accomplice. She could see her father was enraged, but he held his temper.

"Did you get a look at his assistant?"

Ashlie shook her head. "He merely knocked on the door, then disappeared. I would guess that Mr. Mills keeps him completely removed from his presence."

"Do you remember which cabin Mills has?" Adrik was moving to a trunk at the foot of one of the beds.

"No, I ran out of there so fast, I didn't even take note." Ashlie paused and looked at her brothers. "Father, I have an idea."

Adrik pulled a revolver from the trunk. "I have an idea too." He checked the cylinder.

Ashlie reached out, gently touching her father's arm. "Mine doesn't involve bloodshed," she said with a grin.

Her father's angry expression softened. "All right. Let's hear it."

"I think we should let Mr. Mills believe he's got the upper hand. Let him think that I'm cooperating with him. The boys and I can stay here in the cabin. After all, we have less than twenty-four hours before we arrive. If you can manage to sneak away to meet the captain, you explain the situation and have him radio the authorities. They can be prepared to meet him when we arrive."

"But obviously he has someone watching us," Adrik said, still considering the situation. "But I suppose we could pay someone to do our bidding—maybe even watch him."

"Remember the cabin steward?" Ashlie asked. "He seemed eager to earn his gratuities. Perhaps he could be persuaded to get a letter to the captain. Perhaps he would even watch Mills and his friend for us. Sooner or later Mills will have to meet with this accomplice in order to issue instructions and get information."

"That's good thinking," Adrik said with a grin. "You are your mother's daughter." He smiled and checked the revolver. "But it's always good to have an alternative plan." He pushed the open cylinder back into place. "This is my alternative plan."

Chapter Twenty-Six

But why would that man want to hurt us?" Christopher asked innocently.

Ashlie ruffled his hair and shook her head. "Because some people are just evil, Christopher. We must do exactly as Father tells us in order to be safe." She looked out her cabin window but could see nothing of the docks.

Oliver sat at the door, his father's revolver in hand. Ashlie knew the boy would do whatever was necessary to protect her. He felt a huge sense of importance and responsibility when their father had asked him to perform the task of guard.

The night before, Ashlie had managed to recall the general location of Mill's cabin. She wrote down the information in as much detail as possible, and her father managed to get word to the captain via the cabin steward. The young man was more than happy to assist for the large sum Adrik offered. The captain sent word back in return that the Ivankovs should remain in their cabin and that he would deal with the matter utilizing his crew and the authorities in Seattle. When they believed they had the right man in custody, they would send for Adrik to identify him. And that was where their father was at this moment.

Ashlie tried not to appear worried. She knew the boys were already fretting over the situation, and she didn't want to add to the problem. She almost regretted insisting they come to Seattle, given the situation.

"What if he tries to hurt Papa?" Christopher asked.

Oliver scoffed at this. "Nobody can get the best of Pa. Especially when they don't even realize Pa knows all about them."

"Oliver's right, Chris. Mr. Mills doesn't know that I've said anything to Father. He probably thinks that I would be too frightened to tell Father the truth."

"But you weren't afraid at all," Christopher said, admiration in his tone.

Ashlie smiled. "I'm not afraid, but I do believe that it's important to be obedient and cautious. We will be safe here and wait for Father's instructions. That way we won't be in harm's way, and he can focus on the things that are important for the moment."

"Are you really going to get married?" Oliver asked from his perch.

Ashlie had discussed her wedding plans off and on while sailing to Seattle. It seemed only natural that her brother might be curious about the situation. "I am," she replied. "I think you'll like Winston a lot. I'm really excited for you two to meet."

"Will I like him too?" Christopher questioned.

"Absolutely." Ashlie sat on the edge of the bed. "Winston is so much like Father. He's kind and considerate and loves Jesus. He's tall and broad at the shoulder like Papa, and when he smiles it lights up his whole face."

"And he's a doctor, right?"

"That's right, Chris. He's a doctor, and he's studying extra hard so that he can be a surgeon and operate on people who are wounded or hurting. He loves helping people."

"He's probably good, then," Oliver said. "I don't want you to marry somebody who isn't really good."

"And the best part is that we plan to move up to Alaska. I won't be very far away from you."

"Will you live in Ketchikan?" Christopher's expression looked quite hopeful.

"I don't know," Ashlie admitted. "We'll go wherever we feel God leads us."

Adrik listened as the steward explained the situation. "I've not seen him with anyone else. It's just like I told the captain. I think the gentleman is working alone."

"Well, he's no gentleman, but I'm glad to hear it. Still, my daughter said someone knocked on his door to let him know when I finished eating with my sons."

"I know about that," the steward said rather excitedly. "It wasn't an accomplice that did it at all. It was one of the dining room staff. The man was nearly fired for the event because he left his station."

Adrik shook his head. "Are you certain about this?"

"Absolutely. The man requested to be brought before the captain when his superior threatened to fire him. The man explained that he was paid a large sum of money to watch you and your boys. He was to report to Mr. Mills by knocking and declaring you were finished with the meal. I believe he's the only one who has assisted Mr. Mills."

"Then no doubt Mills is hoping that we are the type of people easily threatened—especially Ashlie." Adrik laughed. "He doesn't know my daughter. She's an Alaskan. We aren't easily intimidated."

Six armed police officers from Seattle appeared with the captain just then. Adrik knew from the information he'd been given that the captain had wired ahead and that Seattle was sending the men by launch. With them on board before the ship docked, they could have Mills in hand without involving any of the other passengers.

"Are we ready?" the captain questioned. "I mean to see this thing done."

Adrik nodded. "Let me go first." The police officers assembled on either side of the door. Adrik lowered his voice and leaned toward the steward. "If he asks to know who it is, call to him and tell him you're the cabin steward."

The young man nodded. He seemed so thrilled to be a part of the capture that Adrik nearly laughed out loud. Instead, he controlled his amusement and knocked. The sooner Mills was in custody, the better for everyone.

"Who is it?" a voice questioned from the other side of the door.

Adrik nodded at the cabin steward. The young man looked to his captain only momentarily, then answered in a loud voice, "Cabin steward, sir."

"What do you want?"

Adrik felt a momentary sense of panic, but the young man was completely under control.

"We're about to dock in Seattle. I'm here to assist with your baggage."

Adrik held his breath, wondering if this would win the day or if he'd end up having to knock down the door. He heard the latch give way and saw the knob turn slowly. As soon as the door was open a fraction of an inch, Adrik forced it back with such power that Mills landed unceremoniously on his backside.

"And I'm here to assist them with you," Adrik said, standing over the stunned Mills. The police rushed in to surround the man.

"What is this all about?" Mills declared. "You have the wrong man."

"No, I don't think so," Adrik said with a smile of satisfaction. "But you certainly messed with the wrong young woman."

The police got him on his feet and dropped their hold as Mills adjusted his coat. "I have no idea what you're talking about."

"Really doesn't matter much. You're a wanted man and you're under arrest. If I thought I could get away with it, I'd belt you just for threatening my children."

Mills' lip curled. He gave a side glance to the officer who prepared to handcuff him. Without warning, Mills pushed the man backward and rushed for the door. Adrik blocked him, however, and the officers wrestled him to the cabin floor.

"Seems he does better down on the floor," Adrik said, eyeing Mills with great contempt. "Maybe you should just leave him there—roll him off the ship like an empty whiskey barrel."

The officers laughed, but Mills was not amused. It was clear he saw his defeat and was not happy. The officer in charge quickly took down information from Adrik, then hurried to follow his associates.

"Thank you for your help in this matter," Adrik said, turning to the cabin steward as the police led Mills from the room. He looked to the captain and winked. "This young man deserves a raise. He thinks fast on his feet."

"I believe you're right," the captain replied. "Perhaps he can be moved to a better position. One that deals with our ship's security."

Adrik reached out and shook the cabin steward's hand. "Thank you, son." He turned to the captain and extended his hand. "And thank you, Captain. I'll rest easier now knowing my family doesn't have to worry about debarking in danger."

Ashlie startled as the key sounded in the lock and the door handle turned to admit their father. "The authorities have him in custody," he announced.

"Was there any trouble?" Ashlie jumped up.

"Oh, he tried to protest his innocence, and when he could see it wasn't going to do him any good, he tried to run. He was no match for the police, however. They easily overpowered him. I gave a statement and Myrtle's address in case they needed to talk to us."

"So we can leave now?" Ashlie asked. She was so anxious to see Winston. Surely he would be worried, wondering why most everyone else had left the ship but not the Ivankovs.

Her father gave her a devilish look of mischief. "I don't know. I'm not in any hurry, and the captain said we might wait here as long as we desire."

Ashlie gathered her things. "Well, you can wait here, but I don't intend to."

Oliver handed his father the revolver. "I'm tired of this ship. I want to see what everyone's been telling me about—this great city of Seattle."

"Me too," Christopher said, coming to his father. "Can we go now?"

The big man laughed out loud. "I guess we'd better. Otherwise I'll be standing here alone. Grab your things, boys. We'd best hurry or our Ashlie will leave us in the dust."

Ashlie opened the cabin door and waited impatiently for her family. The boys hurried to take up their small packs, while Adrik leisurely replaced the gun in his trunk, then hoisted it to his shoulders.

"All right. Let's go."

On the dock, Ashlie searched to find the only man she truly cared to see. "There he is!" Ashlie shouted, picking up her pace. She could see Winston standing beside Timothy Rogers. Was it possible that Winston was even more handsome than when they'd parted company earlier in the summer?

"I thought we'd never get here," she declared as she dropped her things on the dock and threw her arms around the man in a most inappropriate manner. At that point she didn't care what anyone thought. "I've missed you so much."

Winston hugged her close, then set her away from him. Ashlie could see that he'd grown rather uncomfortable in the shadow of the big man who stood watching them.

"Winston, this is my father, Adrik Ivankov."

"Sir . . . I'm . . . I'm . . . pleased to meet you." He extended his hand. Adrik balanced the trunk with one arm and took hold of Winston.

Ashlie's father eyed the younger man with great scrutiny. "Glad to finally meet you. I figure if we're to be family, we need to get right to work."

The tall dark-haired man seemed rather taken aback. "Get right to work?"

"Getting to know each other," Adrik countered. "Ashlie tells me she'd like to be married within the week. Does that set well with you?"

Winston seemed to overcome his surprise just a bit. He looked to Ashlie, then back to Adrik. "She has a way of getting what she wants," he said with a grin. "At least this time I find that it meets very well with my approval. But I would like to ask you properly for her hand and have your approval as well."

A smile broke the sternness of Adrik's expression. "She does have a way of getting what she wants, and I can tell already that I'm going to like you just fine."

Leah looked around the large open room and smiled. Earlier she and Helaina had opened every window in the house to air out the damp, stale smell. This was the home she'd grown up in with Karen and Adrik. The Ketchikan cabin had started fairly small, but over the years Adrik had added on to it with first one room and then another and finally an entire second story. It was a beautiful log home that brought back many special memories of her mother-daughter relationship with Karen.

Now after two hours of dusting and mopping, Leah felt the house was in good order. She sighed and leaned back against the front door. Adrik had told them to feel free to live with him as long as they liked. He wanted the company—no, he needed it. Leah knew that it would probably be hard for him to come back to this house and not be lonely.

"You certainly managed to accomplish a great deal," Helaina said, coming down the stairs. She and the baby, along with the twins, had been napping while Leah worked. "You really shouldn't have done so much in your condition."

"I feel fine. Besides, I can get a lot done when there aren't little ones under foot. Not to mention I enjoyed myself. I kept thinking of times when Karen and I cleaned this house together."

"I know you'll miss her," Helaina said. "I'm missing her myself. Sometimes more than I ever imagined." She frowned. "I suppose that doesn't make sense to you."

"Why wouldn't it?"

"Well, I didn't know Karen all that long, but in the time I knew her, I found she had a way of nurturing people. And she made me feel as if my mother were here again. She would come and have tea with me every day if her schedule permitted. It meant the world to me."

Leah went to Helaina and took her hand. "It doesn't matter how long you knew her. Karen had a special heart for people. I know she thought you to be a perfect mate for Jacob." Leah smiled. "We always knew it would take a strong-willed woman to be a good wife for him."

"We have definitely had our moments. Goodness, but when I think back to our first meeting and how I nearly slapped him for running into me on the street, it makes me laugh. We didn't exactly make a positive impression on each other."

"Well, you were too busy trying to hang my husband," Leah teased.

"Don't remind me. I hate those days—those times of being so hard." Helaina put her hand on Leah's shoulders. "I don't deserve the mercy I've received, but I'm so blessed to have it. I don't deserve any of the good things God has given me."

"None of us do," Leah admitted. "But then they wouldn't be so special if they were deserved."

"I never thought I'd be a part of a real family again," Helaina admitted. "I didn't want to be a part of one. I didn't want children because the pain of losing them would have been impossible to bear, and I certainly didn't want to risk having another husband. Now here I am with both husband and son, and I could not imagine my life without them. Not to mention the twins and you and Jayce." Tears came to her eyes. "Leah, the past . . . well . . . it seems like a vague dream—a nightmare, really. I never thought that would be possible. I'm so happy with my life."

Leah patted Helaina's hand. "I am too. And so many years ago I sat in this very house, crying my eyes out because Jayce rejected my love. How strange it seems to be here now—married with two beautiful children and another on the way." Leah put her hand to her stomach. "I couldn't have ever seen the possibility of this all those years ago. I never thought I could be happy, but here I am."

"Leah!" Jayce called from outside. He came bounding through the front door, Jacob right behind him.

Leah could see they were both quite excited. "What's going on?"

"We are the proud new owners of the Barringer-Kincaid Mercantile," Jayce announced.

"That's wonderful news. I'm so glad things went well." Leah went to her husband and kissed him lightly on the cheek. She had known the men were trying to put the finishing touches on their new business venture but hadn't known for sure that things would be completed that day.

"I've wired Peter Colton and will have a list of supplies delivered up here as soon as he can spare a ship to make the trip north," Jacob said. He lifted Helaina at the waist and twirled her around several times before setting her back down. "Things are finally coming together for our store."

"I knew they would," Helaina replied.

"We'll have to celebrate tonight," Leah declared. "I'll kill one of the chickens and fry it up."

"And can we have potatoes and gravy?" her husband asked.

"And biscuits and fresh rhubarb pie?" her brother added.

Leah laughed and looked to Helaina. "It would appear our work is just beginning."

September brought the grand opening of the Barringer-Kincaid Mercantile. Jacob was proud of what they'd accomplished and knew that, although there would be less traffic here than what he might have experienced in Seward or Ship Creek, Ketchikan had the feel of home to him. Only two days earlier they'd completed the renovations of the rooms above the store, and he'd moved his family into their own home. With Malcolm quite small, Jacob knew it would be some time before they would need to worry about having a bigger place with a yard. For now this was not only very adequate for their needs, it was beneficial for their business. With the store located just downstairs, Jacob wouldn't have to worry about theft in the night. With the town growing ever larger, such matters were always of concern.

Everything seemed perfect. With the store situated right at the docks, Jacob felt confident they would do very well. Jayce thought so too. He pointed out that ships might even begin allowing their passengers time to depart the ship and come to their store to purchase native-made items they could take home as souvenirs of their trip north.

"I think once we figure things up," Jayce said, looking at the ledger, "we will have made a nice profit today."

"That's to be expected," Jacob said. "It was the first day. Folks were curious about the things we had on hand. We won't have that kind of traffic in here on a daily basis. That's why I didn't want to have too big of a place."

"I've been thinking," Jayce began, "in time we might add on to this building and create rental space for additional shops. Think of it."

Jacob could imagine just such a thing. "I had been thinking perhaps we could even buy the places just up the way from us and attach them on to this building with a few places in between. It would be expensive, but just imagine what we'd have when we got done. We could rent out the other buildings and have a nice income."

Jayce laughed. "We think so much alike, it's downright scary."

The bell over the door sounded as a man looking to be in his fifties entered the store. Jacob moved down the counter. "Welcome, friend. We were just about to close up for the day."

"I'm glad I caught you, then." He moved to the counter and extended his hand. "I'm Bartholomew Turner. Bart to my friends. I've come to discuss a matter with you and your partner."

Jayce joined Jacob. "I'm Jayce Kincaid."

"And I'm Jacob Barringer. What did you want to discuss?"

"The fact of the matter is this: I own a store in Skagway. The economy in that area is quite depressed, and it is my plan to be done with the place when my lease is up at the end of October. I was here in Ketchikan to discuss with my brother the idea of leaving Alaska altogether. We are not young men anymore and a warmer climate would be to our liking."

"I don't see what that has to do with us." Jacob saw the man's expression change from serious to rather hopeful.

"I thought you might be interested in buying out my current stock. It isn't large, by any means, but no one in Skagway wishes to secure it because there are many specialty items that are of no interest. Things like musical instruments and cameras. They used to be quite sought after, I must say. I once sold a great many things. Now I do better with the odd bits of furniture, lamps, and of course food staples. We found we had to add food items just to keep our business lucrative."

"Have you had your store long?" Jayce questioned.

"I set up just after the gold rush began," Turner replied. "I had a store at the end of Main called S&T House Goods. We were in a tent for quite a while, but then one of the wealthy townsmen built several buildings, and we rented out space for our store."

"I remember that place," Jacob said. "I was up there during the rush. I was just a boy, but I do remember your place."

Turner beamed. "We had a fine store. My brother and cousin helped to make it a profitable business, but once the rush passed it became very difficult to keep things going. Not only that, but I long for home." His smile faded. "Our mother passed on while we were up here, and our father is nearly eighty. We need to return to Oregon before he dies."

"I can understand your concern," Jacob replied. "I suppose it might be possible for us to take the stock off your hands." He looked to Jayce, who was nodding.

"Maybe we could all have supper together and discuss the details?" Jayce questioned, looking to Jacob.

"I don't know why not," Turner replied. "In fact, you could join me at my brother's place."

"Nonsense. My wife would happily cook for you both," Jayce replied. "Why don't you and your brother plan to come to supper around six? Jacob and his family will be there as well."

Turner seemed quite excited. "I can't tell you how happy this makes me. I'm quite anxious to get back to Oregon before winter sets in. My brother and I will be there."

That night after supper concluded, Leah put her children to bed and returned as the men were finishing up the last of their dessert and coffee.

"Would you have any objection to my traveling to Skagway at the first of next month with Jacob?" Jayce asked. "Mr. Turner figures to have his merchandise inventoried and ready to go by then."

"I don't mind at all," Leah replied, although in her heart she knew she'd much rather neither man leave. "How long will you be gone?"

Jacob met her gaze. "I wouldn't think any longer than a couple of weeks. Maybe three at the most. I figured since Adrik and the boys plan to be home day after tomorrow, I could talk to him about keeping the store for us."

"Helaina and I could certainly tend to that," Leah replied.

"I'd rather you not have to," Jacob said sternly. "The children need you, and besides, some of the men can be quite rowdy. I wouldn't want there to be any incidents while we were gone and unable to protect you."

"Yeah, it's bad enough to leave you here," Jayce replied. "Maybe it would be better for just one of us to go." He looked at Jacob.

"We are perfectly capable," Leah said, putting her hands on her hips in a defiant pose. "You above everyone else know that."

Jacob held up his hand as Helaina opened her mouth to weigh in her opinion. "Hold on. There's no need for either one of you to get excited about this. Let me talk to Adrik, and then we'll figure it all out."

"You can stay with me while you're in Skagway," Turner said as if to change the subject and calm the ladies. "I am happy to extend the hospitality."

"That sounds great." Jacob looked at the calendar. "We'll try to leave around the first of October. If things go well, and depending on ship availability, we might be able to head home before the fifteenth of the month."

"I will do my part," Turner promised. "I'll have everything crated and ready to go. We can nail down the lids after you approve the goods. I'll even arrange to have movers standing by."

"Well, here's to our new adventure," Jacob said, holding up his coffee mug.

Leah felt a chill suddenly run down her spine as the men clicked their mugs together. She didn't know why she should feel uncomfortable, but she did.

After everyone had returned home and she sat getting ready for bed, she voiced her concern to her husband. "I have a bad feeling about this venture of yours."

"A bad feeling?" Jayce looked up from where he was reading in bed. "What are you talking about?"

Leah shrugged. "I don't know." She ran her brush through her long dark curls. "I suppose there's no reason to feel uncomfortable. Turner is obviously a legitimate businessman, otherwise there'd be no reason to go so far as to try and entice you both to come to Skagway."

"Jacob even remembered his store."

"I know. I don't know why I'm uneasy. I just am. The weather is very unpredictable this time of year. It might be rough to travel farther north." She put the brush down and went to crawl into bed. "I suppose I just worry about your safety."

"Well, stop," Jayce said, putting his book aside. He blew out the lamp. "There's no reason to be afraid. Skagway is an all-year harbor—it never freezes over like in Nome. And it's certainly not as risky as the Arctic. We won't be stuck in any ice floes. Besides, Jacob knows Skagway, and we both have decent funds so that if we need to stay in a hotel should Turner's hospitality prove to be less than desirable, we will be fully capable of doing so."

Leah snuggled into her husband's open arms. "You could get sick."

"And sled dogs could fly," he teased. "You need to stop worrying about the possibility of things that might go wrong and pay more attention to other things."

"Other things? Like what?" She tried to imagine what he might mean.

"Like this," Jayce said. He covered her mouth with his.

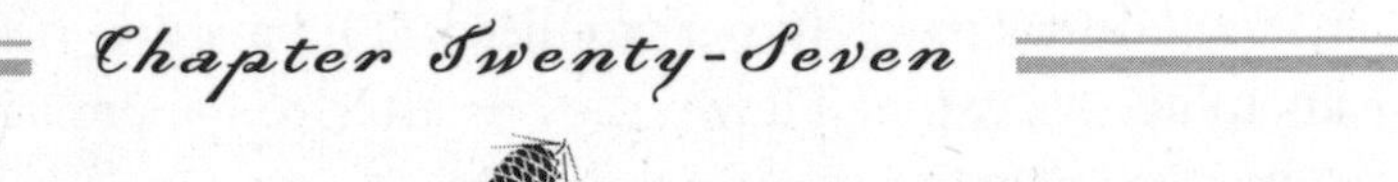

Chapter Twenty-Seven

Leah adapted easily to her new life in Ketchikan. She was amazed at how much the place had grown just since her last visit. There were now four salmon canneries, with another planned for the future, as well as mining and logging industries. The only problem with increased industry, of course, was the expansion of saloons and bordellos on Creek Street. Leah supposed it was one of those unavoidable issues, although she tried at every turn to encourage those she knew to avoid that area at all cost. In church they often talked of ways to reach out to the soiled doves who worked the houses of ill repute, but too much money was exchanging hands to keep the women away for long. This grieved Leah in a way she couldn't begin to explain. The houses had been there even when she'd been a child, but she'd never thought much about the women who worked there. Now, after becoming a wife and mother, Leah's heart went out to these poor souls. They were somebody's daughters—maybe even wives and mothers to someone. What had brought them to such a horrible fate?

Ketchikan remained scenic and beautiful despite the darker side of life. Eagles were abundant, drawn there by the presence of salmon and other good fishing. Leah loved to watch the birds on the beach. Wills and Merry loved them as well. They didn't go to watch them often, but when they did everyone seemed to have the best time.

With Adrik's house removed from the town and set a bit higher on the forested mountainside, Leah felt removed from the sorrows and dirtiness of life. Here it was quiet and lovely with a rich abundance of all they needed. The winters were mild, with more rain than snow, and the summers were warm and beneficial to growing fruits and vegetables. She'd even managed to reconnect with a couple of dear friends from her youth. The life they'd found here was far better than she could have imagined, and Leah felt they'd made the right decision in coming. It would be a good place to raise Wills and Merry and the new baby.

She put her hand to her stomach. Finding herself pregnant again stirred up some concerns as to how this would affect Jayce's love for the twins. Just as she'd overcome her fears about whether Jayce could love the children as his own, new worries came to haunt her. Would he care more about the baby he knew to be his own?

"I'm leaving now," Jayce said. He came and planted a kiss on the top of Leah's head. "I'll be home around four."

She put aside her worries and smiled. "Don't forget to take those things by the door." She pointed to a stack of ready-made shirts, two fur-lined hats, and a muff. Jacob had encouraged her to produce some items for the store since there seemed a never-ending request for such things.

"These are great, Leah. I know they'll sell quickly. We had a man in the store just the other day asking for shirts."

"I'm glad. It'll give me a bit of money to buy Christmas gifts."

He laughed. "That's still a few months away."

"So's the baby's birth," she countered, "but I'm planning for that as well."

He sobered. "It is coming up awful fast. Are you feeling all right?"

His concern touched her. "I'm just fine. Now off with you." Leah got to her feet. She was afraid if they talked much more about it that she might voice her real fears. "Having one baby is much different than having two."

"How can you be sure it's just one?" Jayce winked. "It could be twins again."

"No, when I was this far along with the twins, I was already out to here." She exaggerated, joining her hands in a circle and holding them out well away from her body. "Besides, the doctor believes it's just one."

"Well, either way, we'll take whatever the good Lord sends."

Once he'd gone, Leah refocused on her work. The house was quiet. Since Adrik had returned with the boys, Leah had enjoyed pampering and spoiling them. However, this was a school day and the boys would be gone until the afternoon. Adrik, too, was off working on getting special wood for some of the furniture he planned to build. He was already talking about expanding his workshop and teaching Oliver as well.

Putting her sewing aside, Leah picked up the newspaper Adrik had brought home last night. There were so many sad stories of problems in the world. Czar Nicholas and his family had been murdered by the people who'd taken over his country. This fact troubled Leah greatly. How could it be that royalty could just be murdered without the world rising up in protest?

There were other worrisome issues too. The influenza had once again reared its ugly head, so while the war seemed to be coming to a close, another crisis arose to claim lives. Leah didn't understand how so much death could go on without wiping the human race completely from the world. Hundreds of thousands were dead because of the war, and the influenza might claim that many and more. That seemed impossible to imagine. Leah prayed that the influenza would not come to their shores, but at the same time, she'd already gathered quite a bit of devil's club, just in case.

"I hope you'll never have to know war or sickness," she told her unborn child.

"Mama," Wills called. He came maneuvering down the stairs, as was his routine when awakening in the morning. "Let's eat!" He jumped off the last step and ran for his mother's open arms.

Hugging him close, Leah kissed his neck. "I suppose I shall feed you, my little man. Is your sister awake?"

"Merry playin'," he told her. This, too, wasn't at all unusual. Merry often woke up and played in her bed quietly until Wills started making a ruckus.

"Well, let's get both of you dressed and ready for the day. I have a feeling you're going to keep me busy."

Hours later, when the boys returned from school, Leah felt a weariness in her body that seemed to grow as the new baby grew. She had worked to reorder the pantry as well as sew on several new pieces. One piece in particular, a new quilt for Helaina and Jacob, was taking more time than she'd hoped. She had planned to have it ready to give as a Christmas present and had patterned it after the quilt Karen had given her in Last Chance. Leah had also noticed that Adrik's coat was quite worn. If she could get her hands on a good piece of fur, she could make him a new coat as a present.

"How was your day?"

"We learned more about the Silver War," Christopher told Leah as he put his books on the table.

"The Civil War, you mean," she said matter-of-factly.

He nodded. "Civil War. I always forget. Anyway, a lot of people were fighting each other, and it was like if Oliver and I decided to fight a war. It was brother against brother."

"I remember learning about that myself," Leah admitted. She put out a plate of cookies for the boys. "It wasn't a very good time for our country. There were a lot of hateful people, and a great many innocent people who were hurt."

Oliver plopped down on a chair. It seemed he had sprouted up about six inches overnight. Leah was already hard at work making him new shirts and trousers. No doubt he would be as tall as his father.

"And what of you, Oliver? What are you studying?"

"Nothing I like. We have to memorize a lot of Bible verses, and I'm no good at it." He took a cookie and popped it in his mouth.

"Memorizing is sometimes hard," Leah admitted, "but your mother taught me a little trick a long time ago. She told me if I could put the verse to music—just make up a little song to go with the words—I could memorize it much easier. I still do that today."

Oliver shrugged. "I remember her telling me that too. I never really tried it, though." He glanced up at the clock. "I have to cut wood. I promised Pa." He grabbed another cookie and headed for the door.

Once he'd gone, Leah looked to Christopher. "And what about you? Don't you have chores too?"

"I suppose so," he admitted, "but I wanted to ask you a question."

Leah could see the twins were happily occupied with their toys, so she turned her full attention on Christopher. "What did you want to ask?"

"Why did God have to take my mama away?"

She had no answers for such a question—a question she'd asked many times herself. What could she possibly tell him?

"My mama was a good woman. You said so yourself. She loved God and did good things. So why did He take her away? Why'd He do that to her?"

"You make going to heaven sound like a punishment."

"Well, dyin' sure sounds like a punishment," Christopher replied. "Dyin's no fun. You don't get to do anything anymore after you die."

"I don't know about that," Leah said, taking the seat directly across from the boy. "I think there are probably all sorts of wonderful things to do in heaven. The Bible says we'll be happy—that we won't have any more tears."

"I still don't like that God took her away. I need her."

Leah nodded. "I know you do, Christopher. I wish I could give you answers. We can't always know why God does things a certain way." She thought back over her own life. There were so many times she'd questioned God about why things were happening a certain way. Sometimes the answers became clear in time, but just as often situations remained a mystery.

"Christopher, I can tell you without any doubt, that your mama loved God and trusted Him for what was best and good for her life and for yours. She would want you to trust Him now."

"But God's scary to me."

"Why?"

Christopher looked at the cookie in his hand. "I don't know. He's just big, and He has all the power. I have to be really good all the time or He won't love me."

"Who told you that?"

Christopher shrugged. "I don't know. Just some people."

Leah smiled. "He is all-powerful and big. He has to be so that He can handle the entire world. But, Christopher, He will love you always—no matter what. He wants your love and obedience, but He loves you even when you mess up. The Bible says that even while we were still sinners, Jesus came and died for us. We weren't good—yet God still loved us and sent Jesus to die on the cross for our sins."

"He's still scary to me."

"Like your father sometimes frightens other people."

"My pa isn't scary."

"He is to some people who don't know him. He's big and very powerful. I've seen people be very afraid of him. In fact, the first few times I was around your father as a young girl, he frightened me."

Christopher looked at her in disbelief. "But my pa is good."

"So is God. Do you have any reason to believe He's not?"

"Well . . . He . . . He . . . took my mama. That wasn't a good thing to do."

Leah felt the boy's pain pierce her heart. "Christopher, I wish your mother could have stayed, but you know we all have our time to die."

"Pa told me that. It's in the Bible that we all have to die once. If we don't accept Jesus as our Savior, then we have to die twice."

"That's right. We would die once in the flesh, and then on the judgment day—if we had rejected Jesus—we would die again. That time it would be forever."

Christopher nodded. "I remember my mama saying that." He sighed and got to his feet. "I'm glad you came here, Leah. I like having you around. You remind me of Mama sometimes." He looked to where Karen's picture hung beside the fireplace. "I sure miss her, but now I can remember her face."

Leah fought back tears as Christopher left the cabin to see to his chores. *God, this is so hard. Please help those boys. Help Adrik. They need your healing touch in their lives.* She looked to where the twins were playing. She had thought she might lose them to influenza. She had worried about losing Jayce and Jacob to the Arctic Ocean when the expedition went missing. So many of her friends from Last Chance were dead. Death was just such a hard thing to bear—even the threat of it could be crippling.

Leah tried to shake off the heavy feeling. She began to hum and then to sing aloud verses she'd memorized from the latter part of Romans eight.

" 'For I am persuaded, that neither death, nor life, nor angels, nor principalities, nor powers, nor things present, nor things to come, nor height, nor depth, nor any other creature shall be able to separate us from the love of God, which is in Christ Jesus our Lord.' "

Death would always be a natural part of life, but Leah would not let it defeat her. It would not separate her from God's love. She would not allow it to.

"We have passage booked to Skagway," Jacob said, holding up the tickets for Jayce to see. "The problem will be in returning. There are only two ships coming into Skagway in October. The *Spirit of Alaska* will leave Skagway on the seventh—probably too soon for us to have concluded our business since we won't arrive in Skagway until the third. The *Princess Sophia* will be in dock on the twenty-second."

"That means we'll have to be gone an extra week." Jayce's tone made it clear he didn't like the idea at all.

"I know. I suppose we can push to get things accomplished as soon as possible. Maybe if we explain to Turner, we can work day and night to see things accounted for and loaded."

"It sure won't give us much time. Maybe we should just plan to return on the *Princess Sophia* and leave it at that. At least we can explain it to the girls and then they'll have time to get used to the idea."

"Get used to what idea?" Adrik asked as he came in from the back room. "I just left some fresh fish upstairs. Helaina is already hard at work."

Jacob smiled. "Thanks. Did you have a good catch?"

"Enough to supply us all. So what idea were you wanting the girls to get used to?"

"Well, I picked up our tickets for Skagway and learned that we probably won't have a chance to head back until the twenty-second. The only other ship that will be available will leave before we'll have time to load all the stock and equipment we're purchasing from Turner."

Adrik frowned. "And you expect me to keep track of the store in your absence? I don't know that I'm cut out to be a storekeeper for almost a month."

Jayce looked to Jacob. "I could just stay here."

Adrik laughed. "I was just joshing with you. I can handle it. The girls will handle it as well. We all do what we have to—right? This is just one of those times when everything doesn't go perfectly our way. But it will be all right. I'm confident that we can get by without you for a time. Maybe you can go visit some of the old places. I hear Dyea is nothing more than a few abandoned buildings and old-timers."

Jacob nodded. "I had thought about visiting the cemetery."

"Your father's grave?" Jayce asked.

"Yes. It's been a long time. Might do me good to visit." The thought had been on his mind ever since Turner had invited them to Skagway.

"So the extra time will serve you well," Adrik replied. "It'll probably end up being a blessing to you both."

Jayce looked to Jacob and smiled. "Probably, but I know it's going to be hard to convince Leah of such a blessing."

Chapter Twenty-Eight

Skagway proved beneficial for both parties. Jacob and Jayce were quite happy with the inventory and felt confident the supplies would serve them well. Turner even came down on the original price to compensate for the shipping prices. With the goods headed to the dock to load on the *Princess Sophia,* Jayce and Jacob finished up the paper work at the shipping office.

"You fellas want to insure the load?" the agent asked.

"I hadn't figured to," Jacob replied.

"If the cost isn't too bad, Jacob, it might be wise. There have been quite a few storms of late. Remember Peter sent you that letter about the load he lost to heavy water damage?"

Jacob considered it for a moment. "True enough. The weather's been pretty lousy of late, and with the snows and wind, I suppose it might be a good idea. Why don't you show us what you have to offer?"

The man quickly explained the details of the insurance and the prices available. Jacob and Jayce finally agreed on the coverage and concluded business with the man. In a few hours they would be on their way.

"I still can't believe the way this place has changed," Jacob said as they walked back up the main street of town. "When we lived in Dyea, this place was as busy as Seattle. Maybe not as big, but definitely as busy. People were shoulder to shoulder, and prices were outrageous. Pay was good." He grinned. "I always said the real money of the gold rush was to be had right here. People often journeyed to Dawson by way of Skagway. Packers and laborers could make great money."

The area looked rather like a ghost town now. The buildings were still there, but many were in sad disrepair. There were still people to walk the boardwalks, but the numbers were greatly reduced. If not for the railroad that had been built to take people north to the gold fields, Jacob seriously doubted Skagway would have survived.

"I wonder if it will ever revive."

Jacob shrugged. "I suppose if the politicians in this territory have their way, it will. There's a railroad already in place and a good harbor. If there proves to be a reason to bring people into the area—even if it's like last time and this is just a place to come through on the way to some other destination—then I suppose it might thrive again."

Jayce pointed to the café. "How about we grab some supper? We don't board until around five, right?"

Jacob nodded. "Yeah. We should eat. Oh, and I want to pick up a present for Helaina. She was really good-natured about our coming here for so long. She deserves something special."

"What'd you have in mind?" They went into the restaurant and took seats at the first table by the door.

"Well, Turner told me about a woman who has some great handwork for sale. She creates those nice doilies and such for tables and sofas. You know the ones."

Jayce grinned. "Never thought I'd see the day we'd be buying such things."

Jacob laughed. "Me neither, but I guess I never was quite sure I'd be happily married either."

"I know what you mean, but I'm more blessed than I can express. I love your sister more than life itself, and my children run a close second."

"I can hardly wait to get home," Jacob admitted. "It's gonna be good to get on that ship."

Unseasonable cold dropped the temperature nearly twenty degrees as October moved rapidly toward November. Snow covered the mountains and trickled down into the valley to coat everything with a dusting of white.

Jayce and Jacob had been gone for nearly a month. Malcolm had been cranky and missed his father, causing many sleepless night for Helaina, while Leah and the twins did their best to get through each day without Jayce's good-natured humor and attention. Had it not been for Adrik and the boys, neither woman would have fared well at all, as far as Leah was concerned.

Leah, now seven months pregnant, could hardly wait for the child to come. Even the twins were curious about where the baby was, insisting from time to time that Leah let them put their ears against her stomach so that they could hear their brother or sister. Their antics kept Leah from being completely lonely, but even they couldn't keep her from worrying.

A strong storm blew in on the twenty-third, causing Leah to fret about whether this would delay Jayce and Jacob's return. They were to arrive on the *Princess Sophia* by the twenty-sixth, but weather was always a factor with northern shipping routes. When things dawned calm on the twenty-fifth,

Leah breathed a sign of relief. *Just one more day,* she told herself. *One more day and they'll be home.*

"You'll never believe what I've just brought home," Adrik called from the doorway. "Come have a look."

Leah put a lid on the pot of stew she'd been working on all morning. "What in the world have you done now, Adrik?" She gave him a good-natured smile and followed him into the yard.

Adrik pulled back a tarp. "We have enough bear meat here to last the winter."

Leah looked at the mound of butchered meat. "Goodness, but I think you're right. Where did you get him?"

"Up the mountain. Never seen anything so big in all my life. Here, just look at the fur. You ought to be able to make several things out of this." He held up a portion of the bloody hide.

"Adrik, that would make a great new coat for you. I've been trying to find some decent fur for just such a project. Your own coat is nearly worn through."

Adrik sobered. "Karen was going to make me a new coat last winter. She said it was well overdue. I kept telling her not to worry with it."

Leah went to him and reached out to touch the fur. "If Karen were here now, she'd agree with me that this bear fur is perfect. I'll get to work tending the hide right away. Given the way the weather's been acting, you'll probably need its warmth."

"We're almost out of salt for treating the hide. Why don't I take care of the meat, and then we'll head into town? Helaina's been handling the store all morning, and I want to relieve her as soon as possible."

Leah considered this for a moment. The idea of getting away from the house for a little while was appealing. "We could probably get Ruth to come stay with the twins." Ruth was a young Tlingit woman who lived just a quarter mile away. "Would you mind listening for the children while I go ask?"

"Not at all. I'll be close by," Adrik assured her.

Leah returned shortly thereafter with Ruth in tow. The woman had a new baby—her first—and didn't mind at all coming to stay with Leah's children. Ruth's mother had been a good friend to Karen when Leah had been a girl.

"We shouldn't be long," Leah told Ruth. "If they wake up, just feed them some of the stew on the stove. It should be done by then. You be sure and eat as well."

The dark-eyed woman nodded as she placed her sleeping baby on a pallet by the fireplace.

"Leah, you ready?" Adrik called from the door.

"Yes. I'm coming." Leah pulled on her parka.

"We'll take the smaller cart and let the dogs help us with the load," Adrik announced. He'd fixed a team of Jacob's huskies to the wheeled cart. Adrik had taken over the animals' care since Jacob was now living in town. "These guys will be grateful for the exercise. I'm sure they miss the long trips with Jacob." He helped Leah into the cart.

"I'm sure that's true. They do love to run."

Adrik moved them out once Leah was settled, but he kept the dogs at a slow trot. Leah appreciated this, knowing that the animals would much rather move fast. The entire trip only took ten minutes. Downhill was the easy part, but coming back would be a little slower.

When they'd arrived in front of the mercantile, Leah allowed Adrik to help her down. She stretched and put a hand to the small of her back. To her surprise, Helaina came bounding out the front of the store. She looked fragile and pale, her expression suggesting something was wrong. Her eyes looked as though she'd been crying.

"Leah, there's been trouble."

Leah looked to Adrik, who'd tied off the dogs and was now coming to join the women. Leah looked back to Helaina and asked. "What is it? What's happened?"

Tears came to Helaina's already reddened eyes. "There's been word by telegraph. The *Princess Sophia* is sinking on a reef somewhere in Lynn Canal."

Leah didn't remember what had caused her to faint, but when she woke up to Adrik's worried expression and Helaina fanning her, she knew it must have been quite bad. Then little by little the memories flooded in and Helaina's words returned to haunt her.

"The Princess Sophia *is sinking. . . ."*

"Tell me everything," she said as she struggled to sit up.

"Don't you think you ought to just lie there for a little bit?" Adrik questioned.

"I want to know what's going on," Leah demanded and pushed Adrik away.

"Apparently there was a fierce storm—a blizzard," Helaina told her. "I don't know much else except that the ship began to sink after a time. They weren't too far from Juneau, and rescuers were on the scene to help, but I haven't heard anything else. I learned it this morning but had no way to come to you. I was just about to close up the shop and walk out to the cabin with Malcolm when you pulled up."

Leah sighed. "Well, we need to hear the latest and find out what's happened. Who would know?"

"We might start at the telegraph office," Adrik said. "That'd be the logical place."

Leah nodded. "Let's go there, then."

"Why don't you stay here with Helaina and I'll go," Adrik offered. "You really shouldn't risk your health. You've had a big shock."

"I need to find out for myself," Leah said. "I didn't like the idea of their going in the first place. There are always accidents and tragedies in the water. Just look at the placards in every coast town—memorials to those who've been lost at sea. I don't care if I never get on another ship."

"I'm closing the store," Helaina said. "I'll get Malcolm and come with you."

Leah looked at the woman who had become as dear as any sister. "Hurry, then."

Helaina ran upstairs, leaving Leah and Adrik to talk. "I know you don't want me to go," Leah began, "but I need to do this. Please understand. I'm not trying to be purposefully defiant."

Adrik gently put his hand on her shoulder. "I know you aren't. I'm just concerned about you and the baby. I promised Jayce and Jacob that I would look after the both of you."

Leah shook her head. "First we lose Karen and now this." She looked Adrik in the eye. "I don't think I can survive another loss. I don't think I can bear the pain."

"God knows what we can and can't bear," Adrik said softly. "I didn't think I could bear losing Karen, but my boys and Ashlie needed me. Remember how I tried to hide from it all? You were the one who stood by me—helped me to see the truth. Now I'll be there for you—no matter the outcome."

"But surely if they're close to Juneau and rescuers are on hand, the outcome shouldn't be too bad," Leah said, trying to convince herself. She still couldn't shake images of when she and Jayce had nearly lost their lives when the ship *Orion's Belt* sunk in the ocean off Sitka.

"That's my thought. We have to have hope."

"We're ready," Helaina said, adjusting a hat atop Malcolm's head.

"I wish you'd both wait here," Adrik said, giving them each a hopeful look.

"You know better." Leah headed for the door. "Come on."

There was a crowd already gathered at the telegraph office by the time Leah and the others arrived. She pushed her way through several men, using her femininity and pregnancy to gain their compassion.

"Excuse me, please." She put her hand to her expanding stomach and offered a smile she didn't feel. Her mind reeled with thoughts and images of her husband's and brother's circumstance.

Lord, she prayed silently, *I need you now more than ever. I truly cannot bear this alone. Adrik said you know what I can endure, but I know I cannot handle losing them. You brought them back to me once, please bring them back to me now.*

"If everyone will settle down," a man announced, "I have the latest word from Juneau."

Leah froze in place. She looked to the people around her and drew a deep breath before fixing her gaze on the man. She didn't know how Adrik had managed it, but he was suddenly at her side, his arm firmly wrapped around her shoulders.

"The *Princess Sophia* ran into trouble in a fierce storm," the man began. "Apparently they radioed for help and received rescue boats from Juneau. However, the storm prevented any help. Apparently the storms also kept the *Sophia* from lowering lifeboats. For quite some time the rescue was attempted, but it was to no avail. The *Princess Sophia* sank with no reported survivors."

This can't be happening. They can't be dead.

Leah and Helaina sat at the table in Adrik's home. At his insistence Helaina and Malcolm had come home with them. The shock had been so great that neither Leah nor Helaina had cried. They'd simply walked away from the crying, enraged crowd in a state of disbelief.

"I tried to telegraph Skagway for confirmation of the men boarding the ship," Adrik said as he came through the door. He and the boys had been in town trying to get more information.

"And?" Leah asked hesitantly as Christopher and Oliver moved to their bedroom. Obviously Adrik had told them to leave the adults to talk.

Adrik shook his head. "They won't send it. The lines were ordered to be kept open for the Coast Guard and those helping with the *Princess Sophia*'s situation." He took his coat off and hung it by the door. "I gave them instructions to send it at the first possible moment."

Leah heard his words but could hardly comprehend them. She tried to pray, but words failed her. Helaina had opened her Bible, but she seemed unable to read.

What will we do? Leah refused to vocalize the words, but it was the same question that had haunted her since learning about the *Princess Sophia*. She knew Adrik would offer her a home with him and the boys. He would probably offer Helaina one too, but it didn't matter. That wasn't the point of her question.

Adrik sat down between the two women. "There's always a chance that those reporting the situation don't have all the information. It's rare that a ship would sink without any survivors. Even the *Titanic* had survivors, and they were more ill prepared than the *Princess Sophia*."

"Do you really think there's a chance that passengers made it off safely?" Helaina asked. "I mean, why would the reports say no survivors if there was hope some were saved?"

"I don't know. The world is full of doomsayers. Let's give it a few days and see what happens. Either way, I want you both to listen to me."

Leah looked up and met his gaze. She saw nothing but compassion and love in his eyes. "I'm listening."

"You know you've been like a daughter to me and Jacob like a son." He turned to Helaina. "I've come to love all of you like family. I want you to know that no matter the outcome of this situation, you have a home with me. In fact, I want you to just keep the store closed until we can find out the truth."

"You're good to care so much for us," Helaina said, shaking her head. "I can't even begin to think about the store or anything but Jacob and whether he's safe."

Leah nodded. Helaina had taken the words right out of her mouth. She could barely register rational thought and care for the twins. To have to worry about anything else would be impossible.

"We're family," Adrik stated, reaching to take hold of each woman's arm. "You helped me deal with Karen's death. I want to be here for you—to see you through this. I feel confident God has put us all together for just such a time."

"I don't understand any of this," Helaina began. "I want to trust God, but I'm angry. I'm angry that after everything we've gone through—after everything that they've suffered—we should all be up against another ordeal. I hope this doesn't seem shocking, but God seems very unfair."

Adrik lowered his head and seemed to consider her words. "There are always times when God seems unfair. I wish I could give you answers—explain why this had to happen. But it wouldn't hurt any less if you knew the reasons."

"It might," Helaina interjected. "If I knew why, then maybe I could rationalize it all in my mind. Why should I have lost one husband to tragedy only to remarry and lose another? Have I not learned something God wants me to know? Am I being punished for something?"

Leah had asked the same questions and knew in her heart there were no answers. "Sometimes," she said softly, "life doesn't make sense. The war in Europe, the influenza wiping out whole villages, children losing their parents, husbands losing their wives." She looked to Adrik. "Sometimes answers don't help. Sometimes life just hurts too much to make sense."

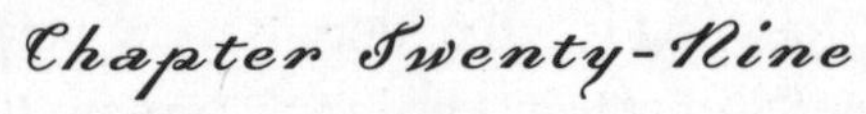

Chapter Twenty-Nine

The next few days passed ever so slowly for Leah. She often thought of the plans she had made with Jayce . . . little things and big. They had talked of building their own home in the spring. They had both looked forward to the new baby, as well as seeing the twins begin to do new things.

Walking alone in a light rain, Leah struggled to make sense of the events that had just taken place. *It seems so unreal. How in the world do I make sense of this? We were happy, Lord. Really happy. And now this. What am I supposed to do?*

She thought of Adrik's generous offer to have them all remain under his protection and care. It reminded her of the Last Chance villagers being paired off with a new spouse in order to see to the welfare of the children. Leah knew there was money to support the children and herself, however. Jayce had always been clear on the money he held in savings and stocks. Helaina was far wealthier than Leah and would have no trouble at all in seeing to Malcolm's needs. Still, there was so much more to life than money. More to surviving than material items.

"Leah?"

She looked up. "Christopher, what are you doing out here? It's cold and wet."

He shrugged. "I saw you walking and thought maybe you could use a friend."

She smiled at the boy. For such a young man his heart was always sensitive. "I can always use a friend—but especially if it's you."

He came alongside her and matched her pace as they headed up the forest path. The thick covering of spruce and fir kept much of the rain from them. "Leah, can I ask you something?"

She nodded and shoved her hands deep into her parka pockets. "What would you like to know?"

"Is God scary to you now?"

She stopped and looked at Christopher in surprise. He gazed up as if embarrassed. "I just mean . . . well . . . since Jacob and Jayce's ship sank. I wondered. . . ." He fell silent and looked back at the ground. "You don't have to answer."

Leah thought about the question for a moment. "I won't lie to you, Christopher. This is very hard. It's probably the hardest thing I've ever had to bear."

"Like me when my mother died?"

"Yes. Exactly like that." Leah started walking again, thinking that perhaps the action would help her to reason an answer. "I don't understand why it had to happen this way. So much had already happened."

"It doesn't seem fair—just like with Ma," he threw in.

"No. It definitely doesn't seem fair."

They walked a ways without speaking. The sounds of rain falling gently against the supple spruce branches and their boots against the path were the only noises.

"I guess it's hard for me to put into words," Leah finally said. It wasn't that Christopher couldn't understand; she simply wasn't sure she understood her emotions well enough to convey the matter in words.

"I've never known a time when Jacob wasn't in my life. He's my older brother, so like for you with Ashlie and Oliver, he's always been there. And with Jayce, well, I fell in love with him a long time ago. To imagine my life without them seems almost impossible for me."

"Like me with my mother," Christopher admitted. "Sometimes when I wake up in the morning . . . well . . . sometimes I think for just a minute that she'll still be there. That her dying was just a bad dream." He shrugged his shoulders. "Guess that sounds silly, huh?"

"Not at all. I felt that way many, many times when Jayce and Jacob were in the Arctic. I kept hoping I would just wake up and find that I had imagined the whole thing—that they were safe in the village and that there was nothing to fear."

"But they're in heaven with Mama," Christopher said, stopping to look at Leah. "Right?"

Leah knew Christopher needed to hear the right thing from her, but she felt completely inadequate to the task. "Yes. I would imagine they're all in heaven." She felt tears come to her eyes and turned to look upward. The canopy of trees overhead, along with the rain clouds, blocked out more and more of the light.

Turning to head back to the cabin lest they run into some kind of animal trouble, Leah tried to regroup her thoughts. "To answer your first question, I don't think God is scary. In fact, right now, He's offering me the only real comfort I can find. I know He loves me. I know He has my life in His hands, just as He had your mama and Jacob and Jayce. He's good, Christopher. Even in bad times, when we think He's stolen what we love the most. He's good, and He loves us."

"Leah, you've been real good to me and Oliver. We love you a lot."

She smiled and put her arm around Christopher's shoulder. It wouldn't be that long before he shot past her in height. "I know you do, and I love you too."

"You've been doing stuff for us like Mama would do. You've been helping us and helping Pa. I want to help you. You're being like a ma to me. I guess I want to help be like a papa to Wills and Merry. I know I'm not a real pa, but I want to play with them and keep them safe. I just want you to know that I'll do that for you."

Leah couldn't keep the tears from her eyes. She pulled Christopher close and hugged him for a long time. He didn't pull away or act embarrassed; instead, he wrapped his arms around her and held on to her as though his life depended on it.

After several moments Leah spoke as she pulled away. "That is the sweetest thing anyone has ever offered me. Thank you, Christopher. I'd be very proud to have you show the twins that kind of love."

"I just don't want them to be sad," Christopher replied. "I don't want them to miss their papa like I miss my mama. I don't want them to hurt in their heart when they grow up and wonder why he went away."

Helaina sat at the table staring at the same piece of sewing that she'd struggled with all morning. Malcolm slept soundly by the fire in a beautiful cradle Adrik had brought from the storage building, while the twins were with Leah in the kitchen. Leah had decided to give them some dough to play with, and Helaina could hear them laughing.

"This is a waste of time," she said, throwing down the material.

"What's the matter?" Leah asked, coming to the table.

"What isn't? Nothing is right. Nothing will ever be right again." She got up and shoved the chair in so hard that it hit the table and rocked backward. Teetering for just a moment, the chair finally fell forward into place.

Leah seemed surprised by Helaina's outburst, but Helaina had no desire to apologize. They were all being so very good. . . . They were all so very calm. It wasn't human. It was completely contrived.

"I don't feel content or comforted," she replied. "I know God has absolute control of this matter, but that's what grieves me most. He has control and yet this . . . this abomination has happened."

Leah nodded. "I know."

"You can't possibly or you'd feel the same way," Helaina ranted, knowing the words were unfair even as she spoke them.

"Just because I'm not throwing a temper tantrum in front of you doesn't mean I don't feel the same way. I have plenty to say to God in private. Right now I'm trying hard not to say it in front of everyone else."

"But why? Are we Christians not to feel? Can we not hurt and suffer and admit to such things? Will doing so somehow decrease or invalidate God's sovereignty and love and put our faith in doubt?" Helaina paced to the hearth and stared down at her son. "I am a widow for the second time. I vowed never to marry again in order to never again suffer this pain. I thought God understood. I thought He cared, and yet I cannot see how He could and still let this all happen to me. I'm confused, Leah. I don't understand this at all."

Leah stood and hesitantly reached out and took hold of Helaina's hands. The sticky warm dough that still clung to Leah's fingers seemed to knit them together. "I don't understand either," Leah admitted. "But, Helaina, what else can we do?"

Helaina looked away. "I'm lost and so alone, Leah. I'm awash on a sea of my own creation. A sea of tears and sorrow so deep that I will surely drown."

"You aren't lost, Helaina. He knows where you are—He's right here with us. And you aren't alone. I'm in this with you. You are my sister, remember?"

"We were sisters. We were sisters only because I married your brother."

"No," Leah said shaking her head slowly, "we are sisters first in God. And second, we are sisters in heart. My heart is bound to you—not just because of Jacob. You befriended me and helped me so much when Jacob and Jayce were in the Arctic. Will you abandon me now?"

Helaina embraced Leah tightly. "No! I will never abandon you. I'm sorry if I made it sound otherwise. Oh, Leah, I know that you care for me and for Malcolm. I know that. I'm sorry to make it sound so trivial."

Leah pulled away. "I know your heart. But more importantly, He knows our hearts. He's all we have right now. I won't turn from Him in hopes that something or someone else might offer better refuge. I know from experience that they won't."

Helaina nodded. "I know that too. I want to be strong, Leah, but it's just so hard. When the officials came and said that the recovery of bodies had begun, I wanted to die. When they said they would send Jacob and Jayce back to us once certain identification could be had, I wanted to scream. How could they sit there so calm and indifferent? There was no more emotion than if they were reading the inventory for the store."

"I know, but what would you have them do? Weep and cry out? We were already doing enough of that for everyone." Leah squared her shoulders. "We can't give up on life. We have children who need us. We have others who need us as well. We cannot grow bitter and hateful."

"Bitterness is something that seems to come quite naturally to me in times of disaster," Helaina replied. "I shall count on you to help me avoid its fetters."

"And I'll rely on you to help me avoid the shackles of hopelessness," Leah replied. "Both would see us prisoner, and neither would do a thing to keep us alive and well. Now come on. I need some help bringing in firewood. The twins are busy and Malcolm is sleeping. I don't think we'll have a better opportunity."

Helaina cast a quick glance at her son and nodded. "Let's go."

They opened the door to find Adrik on the other side. His hand was extended as though he were about to take hold of the door latch. Leah jumped back, startled, but Helaina held fast, captured by Adrik's expression. He was stunned by their appearance, but there was something in his countenance that suggested an entirely different matter.

"What are you doing here? It's only midday," Helaina said.

"I . . . I . . . that is . . . I came to share something," Adrik said, stumbling over his words.

"What is it, Adrik?" Leah asked. "We were just going out for more wood."

"I think you'd both better sit down," he said softly. Moving forward, he turned the women toward the front room.

"Why?" Leah asked. "What have you heard?" Her face grew ashen, and she put her hand to her swollen abdomen. Adrik helped her to the couch.

Helaina felt almost numb. What could Adrik possible say that could be worse than what they'd already endured? "What's happened?" she finally asked.

"Just sit." Adrik motioned her to take the place beside Leah. "I promise you won't regret this surprise."

Just then the door pushed back in full, and in walked Jacob, followed by Jayce. Helaina's hand went to her throat as she choked back a cry.

"We didn't know how else to tell you," Adrik said. "They just arrived, and we ran all the way to get here."

Leah shook her head back and forth as if seeing a ghost. Jayce came to kneel down beside her. "It's all right. I'm home. I'm here."

Helaina was on her feet. She threw herself into Jacob's arms. He smelled of sweat and fish, but she didn't care. She didn't know how this miracle had taken place.

"Papa!" Wills bounded across the room with Merry right behind him. "Papa!" He squealed and dove toward Jayce.

Helaina could see it all from where she stood. It was like something from a dream. She pulled back and stared into the face of her exhausted husband. "They said there were no survivors. No survivors."

"There were no survivors on the *Princess Sophia,*" Jacob admitted. "We weren't on the *Princess Sophia*."

"But why? You telegraphed that you would be."

Helaina turned to look at Jayce and noted he had his left arm in a sling. Leah sat beside him in stunned silence. "What happened?"

"We had just finished eating and had plans to head over to a place where I'd been told I could buy some nice handwork. I wanted to get you a gift," Jacob said, smiling. "We were just crossing the street when a team of draft horses broke away from their driver. Jayce pushed me out of the way, but he was knocked unconscious—broke his arm as well. I carried him over to the doctor's office, and by the time he regained consciousness and was well enough to travel, the *Sophia* had already sailed."

"We were upset to say the least," Jayce picked up the story. "There wasn't another ship due in for over a week. I didn't want to wait that long but figured we had no choice. By that time the telegraph office was closed for the night, so we went back to our hotel and went to bed. Come morning our efforts were again thwarted when they informed us that the telegraph wasn't working due to the bad snowstorm that came in."

Jacob continued. "So we made arrangements to book passage on the next available ship. We didn't find out about the *Princess Sophia* until a small fishing vessel came into port and announced the sinking. We knew you'd be sick with worry, but no one seemed to be able to help us. That's when Jayce hit upon an idea."

"What idea?" Helaina asked, looking to Jayce.

"We hired that same fishing vessel for an outrageous amount of money to get us as far as he could. He took us to Juneau. We had to stop several times because of the weather, but we finally made it. From there we tried again to send a telegram, but it seemed that three hundred other people were trying to do the same thing, and the only ones being allowed were related to the rescue and recovery efforts for the *Princess Sophia*. We left our money and message, and they told us they would get it out as soon as possible."

"But Adrik told us there had been no word," Jacob added. "I'm really sorry. We figured you'd at least have that much."

"I can't believe you're here," Leah said. Her gaze had never left Jayce's face. Helaina could see that the color was finally returning to her cheeks. "We thought you were dead."

Jayce shook his head. "Guess God had other plans."

"Yeah," Jacob said. "A broken arm and concussion."

"But you're both alive while everyone else perished," Leah said, looking finally to her brother. "You would have been dead if you'd made it to the ship on time."

"The way we figure it," Jayce said, "is that God must have something else for us to do."

"Or that we're too ornery to die right now," Jacob said, laughing.

Helaina felt a sense of peace settle over the house for the first time in over a month. She could scarcely believe what God had done—despite her anger and questions. Despite her fears and lack of faith.

"Well, you can't imagine how I felt when these two came walking into the store. I'd gone there to get a few items I thought we needed, and here they come. I just about passed out right there. I think we've had enough excitement to last us for a lifetime," Adrik said.

Leah suddenly moaned and clutched her stomach. "Oh no . . . the baby." She gasped for breath. "It's too early."

Helaina went immediately to Leah's side. "Jacob, help her to bed. Jayce, you go sit with her. I'll see to the children and Adrik can go for the doctor."

The doctor arrived nearly a half hour later. The pains had subsided for the most part, but Leah was scared. She didn't want to lose the baby, not when she'd just managed to get Jayce and Jacob back.

"You'll have to stay in bed until the birth," the doctor told her in a fatherly manner. "If you don't, you will most likely lose the child."

"She'll stay right here," Jayce promised. "I'll see to everything else."

"I'm glad to hear of your survival. Chances are the shock of this entire matter has just been too much for your wife. She needs to remain calm and rested."

Leah couldn't help but laugh as she heard a loud crash and Wills yelling at the top of his lungs for Merry to stop it. "Calm and rested in a house with twins. That should be easy."

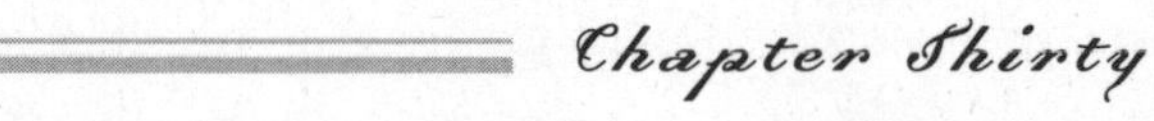

Chapter Thirty

But I'm tired of sitting in bed all the time," Leah argued. "I feel perfectly fine."

"That's because you've been sitting around in bed all the time. Just like the doctor ordered," Jayce countered. He gave her a look of utter exasperation.

"Look, I know you're bored. I've tried to get you as many books as possible, and the doctor has even allowed you your sewing. But getting up is just too risky. You would hate yourself if you insisted on it and then lost the baby because of it."

Leah sobered and fell back against the pillows. "I know." Her tone held all the dejection she felt.

"It won't be long now," Jayce reminded her. "Just a few more weeks. It's nearly Christmas, and after that the doctor said you should be out of danger. The baby can come anytime after the first of the year."

He came to sit beside her on the bed. "I know this has been hard on you."

Leah shook her head. "No harder than thinking you were dead. I have decided that you and ships do not mix. You were the common denominator in every ship problem I can think of with exception to the *Titanic,* and for all I know you may have been on that one as well."

Jayce laughed heartily. "I assure you I was not on the *Titanic*. But I agree. I think I'm land-bound for a time. I remember when we were stranded in the Arctic, I just kept thinking that if I'd just curbed the wanderlust and remained with you and the twins, I could have avoided that misery all together. Having a family makes you much more cautious."

"I think about that too. I never used to concern myself with things that others thought dangerous. I accompanied Jacob on the sleds for long trips, never thinking about the risk. Now it's all I consider."

Jayce took hold of her hand. "I love you more than life. When I sat on that fishing boat thinking of you suffering—believing me dead—well, it nearly did kill me. I kept wishing some of those old Tlingit legends about ravens or eagles flying down to swoop up folks and carry them away might be true—at least if they could fly me home to you."

"Jacob said there are people already trying to make plans for air service in Alaska, so maybe next time you can just fly and avoid the water completely."

"As long as we live in Alaska—especially Ketchikan—we'll always have to deal with the water," Jayce reminded her. "But I hope you know that I will be more cautious. For you and Wills and Merry." He let go of her hand and gently touched her swollen stomach. "And for whoever this little one might be."

"We haven't talked much about that," Leah said, covering his hand with hers. "If it's a girl, I'd like to name her Karen."

Jayce nodded, his expression quite serious. "I think that would be fine. What about if it's a boy?"

"Well, I thought you might like to pick the name. I'm partial to Michael and Paul, but I really don't mind something else."

"Like Hezekiah?" Jayce asked with a grin.

"Well, I'd rather not call my child Hezekiah," she said with a frown. "And I'm not too keen on Ezekiel or Methuselah."

"Those were my next favorites!" he teased.

"I'll try to be content no matter what name you give him—if it is a boy."

"Well, I'm proud to give him the name of Kincaid. He will be mine, just as his older brother and sister are mine."

Leah felt such a peace in her heart at those words. Jayce seemed always to know how to put her fears to rest. "I love you."

He leaned over and gave her a brief kiss on the lips. "I love you very much, Mrs. Kincaid." He got to his feet. "Can I get you anything else before I go rescue Helaina from the twins?"

Leah sighed. "No. I have my Bible and my sewing. I think I'm set."

After he'd gone, Leah tried to get comfortable. Christmas was just a few days away, and because she could do nothing out of bed, she had sewn presents for everyone. Jayce had helped her tuck most of them away, with exception to his own gift. She'd even managed to work out the pattern for Adrik's coat, and it was nearly finished. Leah knew the bearskin coat would be a real surprise for Adrik. He had known her original intentions but had also admonished her not to worry about him. He wanted her to rest, and Leah had followed orders.

"But I can't sleep all the time," she said aloud, taking up the new trousers she was making for Oliver.

She felt a twinge in her side and thought nothing of it until several minutes later when it came again, only this time it seemed to spread further toward the middle of her abdomen.

"It's the twentieth of December," she murmured. The doctor had told her it would be best for the baby not to be born until after the first of the year. At least by his and Leah's calculations.

Leah put the sewing aside and tried to relax. She closed her eyes and pictured herself in Last Chance Creek, sitting atop a small hill along the shore. She tried to imagine the warmth of the sun on her face. She tried to remember the smells and sounds.

The pain came again, however, and forced her to realize the truth. The baby was going to be born soon—maybe even today.

"Jayce?" she called. "Jayce, are you there?" She knew he had plans to retrieve the twins from Helaina. They were spending the afternoon with her and Malcolm in town. Leah also knew, however, that Jayce would not leave her by herself.

"Is anyone out there?"

No one responded. The thought of being alone and in labor filled her with a sense of apprehension. Leah sat up slowly. She drew a deep breath and waited for the contraction that she knew was sure to come. When nothing happened, she gently moved her legs over the side of the bed and got to her feet. Without warning, her water broke. There would be no waiting on the baby now.

"Did you call, Leah?" Oliver stepped in the room, looking rather surprised. "You aren't supposed to be up."

"It's the baby, Oliver." The pains came again and Leah pressed her hands to her stomach. "Jayce just left to get the twins from Helaina. Can you run after him and stop him?"

"Sure!" He turned and ran from the room, obviously happy to be free of any other obligation that might include delivering Leah's baby.

She would have laughed out loud at the situation had the circumstances not seemed so grave. "Lord, you have always held this child in your hands. I don't know why he or she wants to come so soon, but I trust you for the outcome. Please, please, keep my baby safe."

She went to retrieve a towel to wipe up the floor. There was no sense in remaining bedfast now. To her surprise, Leah was taken back in time to when Ashlie was born in this very house. Leah had been there at Karen's side along with a midwife from the Tlingit tribe. She had been honored to help in Ashlie's delivery.

"Oh, Karen. I miss you so much. I wish you could be here now to help me with this baby." She smiled to herself even as she spoke the words. In so many ways, Karen was with her in the memories and things she had taught Leah.

Pain ripped through Leah's body. This baby was not going to be slow in being born. Already she could feel the child moving lower.

"Leah!" Jayce called as the front door slammed against the wall.

She maneuvered back to the bed and sat down just as he came into the bedroom. "I'm still here," she teased.

"Oliver said that the baby was coming. I sent him for the doctor." He came to her side and saw where the floor was still wet. "Your water broke?"

"Yes. I guess there's no stopping this Kincaid." She patted her stomach. "I think she's coming fast."

"So you've decided it's a girl, eh?" He helped Leah ease back into the bed. "No doubt you're right, for all the trouble she's causing."

Leah grimaced and gripped Jayce's arm hard. "If the doctor doesn't hurry, you'll be delivering this baby yourself."

Jayce paled but squared his shoulders. "What do I need to do?"

Leah pointed to the trunk. "There are blankets and diapers, clothes for the baby in there. We'll need a couple of washbasins, some hot water, and scissors." She clutched her stomach. "Hurry . . ." She barely managed the word against the pain.

Just then Christopher came to the doorway of the room. "Where's Oliver? He was supposed to help me with the wood."

"I sent him for the doctor," Jayce said as he worked to pull a stack of things from the trunk. "Leah's going to have the baby."

Christopher looked at Leah in awe. "Truly? Right now?"

Leah nodded. She bit her lip to keep from crying out and frightening the boy. She was surprised that he didn't look in the leastwise uncomfortable with the situation, unlike Oliver, who had clearly been disturbed by the turn of events.

"Do you want to help me?" Jayce asked.

"Sure, Jayce. I'd do anything for Leah and you. What should I do?"

"Get the scissors and bring some hot water."

The boy ran without another word to do Jayce's bidding. Leah smiled and took a couple of ragged breaths. "He'll be able to help you deliver the baby."

Jayce looked at her as though she'd lost her mind. "He's just turned twelve."

Leah nodded. "But he's got two good hands and doesn't seem at all bothered by this." She felt the urge to bear down. "Jayce, I have to push. It won't be long now."

"Here, Jayce. I got the water and the scissors. What else do you need?"

Jayce frowned and looked as if he were trying to remember. "Washbasins."

"And some twine, Christopher," Leah managed to speak before the need to push once again took her focus.

Jayce came to the bed and adjusted the bedding to better facilitate the birth. Leah gritted her teeth and panted against the pain. "I see the head," Jayce told her.

Christopher came back with the basins and nearly dropped them at this declaration. "Are we really going to deliver the baby? Right now?"

Jayce pushed up his sleeves and nodded. "Right now. I need you, Christopher. Are you sure you're up to this?"

The boy nodded. "I can do it, Jayce. You can trust me."

Leah could no longer focus on the conversation. She knew these were the final moments of her baby's birth. She bore down on the pain and pushed with all her might, feeling the child slide from her body. She fell back against the pillows and gasped for breath.

"Quickly," she said, pointing toward the baby Jayce was now turning over. "Tie off the cord in two places and cut in between."

"Here's the twine," Christopher said, handing the ball to Jayce. "And the scissors." He was very efficient and matter-of-fact.

Jayce went to work doing exactly as Leah had told him. Once the cord was cut, he looked up and awaited further instruction.

"Clean the face and clear out the mouth. You need to hang her upside down and hit her bottom a couple of times to get her crying."

"She's so tiny," Jayce said, lifting the rather lifeless child. He did as instructed, hesitating only when it came to the spanking of this tiny infant.

"Hurry, Jayce. She's got to breathe."

He smacked the baby's bottom lightly at first, and then a little more firmly. This sparked life into the child, and she began to cry in an almost mewing fashion. Soon the cry built to a crescendo, and the wailing sound made Leah smile.

"Welcome to the world, Karen Kincaid," Leah murmured.

Christopher looked at her oddly. "You named her after my mama?"

Leah nodded. "I couldn't think of a better name or way to honor someone I loved so much. Is that all right with you?"

Christopher nodded. "I think Mama would like that very much."

Jayce wrapped the baby in a couple of blankets and moved the rocking chair beside the stove. "Here, Christopher, come hold her and keep her warm. I need to finish helping Leah."

The boy looked with wide eyes at Jayce and then Leah. "Me? Are you sure you want me to hold her?"

"Absolutely," Leah encouraged. "She needs to get warm, so hold her close and snug."

Christopher went to the rocker and sat. "I don't want to hurt her."

Leah smiled. He seemed so grown up sitting there waiting for Jayce to deposit the baby in her arms. "You won't hurt her if you're careful,"

Leah said. She watched the pleasure that crossed Christopher's face as Jayce handed him the baby.

The boy was immediately smitten. "She's beautiful," he murmured.

Jayce looked at Leah and smiled. The look of love in his eyes was quite evident. "Yes, she is."

"I can't believe you helped deliver a baby," Oliver told Christopher after the doctor had come and gone. Everyone had gathered in Leah's room to get their first official look at the infant.

"He was as good as any doctor," Jayce declared. "We made quite the team. Maybe we should take it up as a living. What do you say, Christopher?"

"I might want to be a doctor," he replied. "I'm thinking it would make Mama proud."

Adrik patted his son's back. "It would at that, but your mama would be proud at any profession you chose so long as you put the Lord first in all you did."

Oliver looked at the tiny baby in Leah's arms. "She's really little."

"Yes. She's a bit early, but the doctor said she's breathing well and her lungs are clear. That's a good sign."

He reached out to touch Karen's tiny fingers. "She was almost a Christmas present."

Leah laughed. "Almost. At least this way, I can be up and around with everyone on Christmas morning. What fun that will be."

"Mrs. Kincaid, I specifically remember the doctor telling you to stay in bed for a week."

Leah looked at her husband and shook her head. "No, he told me to rest for a week. I promise, I will rest on Christmas morning, but I will do it with everyone else in the front room, sharing a wonderful breakfast and opening presents."

Adrik laughed. "The women in this household have always tended to the stubborn side. I wouldn't argue with her. We can surely make provision."

"Is there room for a couple more?" Jacob called from the door.

Leah turned and saw her brother. Helaina stood directly behind him, Malcolm in her arms. "You know you're welcome. Come see your new niece."

He came to her side and leaned down to view the new baby. Oliver moved away to afford him a better view. "Well, she's mighty pretty. Going to break a few hearts, no doubt."

"If she takes anything after her namesake," Adrik said, "she'll be a handful to be sure."

"I can't believe you delivered her, Jayce. That must have been quite the experience." Jacob was in complete awe. His voice dropped a bit as he added, "Our mother died in childbirth, you know."

"I had forgotten, but I suppose Leah never did."

"Actually, I hadn't really thought of it," Leah admitted. "I was too busy."

Everyone laughed at this, but it was Adrik who spoke. "I think it's probably time for us to let you and the baby get some rest." He came to Leah's bed. Leaning down, he kissed Leah on the head. "Thank you for naming her after Karen. She'll be a special blessing to all of us." He turned and looked to his boys. "Come on, fellows, we have some cooking to do. I don't know about you, but I'm starving."

Jacob took Malcolm from Helaina. "We'll be just outside if you need anything. Adrik invited us to supper. He's making 'surprise meat' pie. At least that's what he promised. Remember the old days when he'd make those for us?"

Leah smiled. "I do indeed. Has he told you what meat he's picked out?"

Jacob shook his head and smiled. "Nope. Hasn't even hinted. Guess we'll all be surprised."

Helaina reached down and gave Leah's hand a squeeze. "I can't imagine having a baby out here without a doctor or midwife. You are very brave, Leah. I hope I can be more like you. I'll have Jacob move my things here so that I can take care of you and the twins, and of course this little one." She gently touched her finger to Karen's face.

"I'll look forward to it," Leah replied. "It will be like the days when we all lived together. Just one big happy family."

After everyone had gone, Jayce came to Leah and knelt beside the bed. "Mrs. Kincaid, you are a wonder. I think back all those years to that sweet kid who told me she thought she was falling in love with me. I can't believe I said no to that love then. I can't imagine even being able to live without it now."

"Everything in its time, Mr. Kincaid. A wise woman once told me that."

"Who? Ayoona?"

Leah shook her head. "No. Karen. Karen waited until she was considered well past a marriageable age, until true love found her as well. When

I despaired of ever finding another love to match what I felt for you, that's what she told me, 'Everything in its time.' "

Jayce took hold of her hand and kissed her fingers. "The war has ended, we're all safe and healthy, and we have each other. The blessings we know are abundant."

"Among many sorrows we have indeed been blessed." Leah shifted the sleeping baby to lean closer to her husband. "I thought after nearly losing you that I would grow afraid each time you walked out the door. I thought I would dread those moments when you had to be out of my sight—to the point where I would make us both crazy. But God has given me such a peace about life."

"How's that?" Jayce asked, his gaze never leaving hers.

"I've had weeks to lie here praying and reading the Bible. God has been good to meet me here. Perhaps it was the only way He could get me to be quiet long enough to hear Him."

Jayce grinned but appeared to know better than to speak.

Leah continued. "I heard Him speak to me, Jayce. As clearly as if you or Jacob had been here talking to me. He assured me that I would never be alone—that the future was something He had already seen—already taken care of. No matter what happens, God will walk with me—with us. I know it might sound silly; after all, we've heard it said many times that we need to put our trust in God. But somehow it's more real to me now. More understandable."

Jayce nodded. "I think I can understand it too. Seeing Karen born—feeling the breath come into her body as she took her first cry . . . well . . . it did something to me. I was praying so hard to do all the right things and in the end I knew there was nothing I could do to give her life or keep her alive. Only God can do that. And just like He'd preserved my life so many times, He faithfully brought us a new life."

Leah sighed and gave Jayce a smile. "Whether in the glory of summer or the whispers of winter, He has ordained our path. It doesn't mean there won't be uphill climbs or rocky roads, but it does mean we can count on Him—believe in Him—hope on Him. We have only to trust our hearts to Him . . . and to each other."

Jayce leaned down and kissed her ever so gently. "And we'll do just that—in good times and bad."

"For better or worse," she whispered.

"For so long as we both shall live."